ZANE GREY COMBO EDITIONS

Great way to get the books you want for a lower overall price! Excellent reading.

ZANE GREY COMBO 6

THE YOUNG PITCHER

THE REDHEADED OUTFIELD & OTHER BASEBALL STORIES

THE DAY OF THE BEAST

ZANE GREY

CreateSpace
2013

Zane Grey Combo #6

The Young Pitcher was originally published in 1911
The Redheaded Outfield and Other Baseball Stories was originally published in 1920
The Day of the Beast was originally published in 1922

The Sixth Omnibus Edition

This CreateSpace edition prepared in 2013

ISBN-13: 978-1492161295
ISBN-10: 1492161292

THE YOUNG PITCHER

The Varsity Captain

Ken Ward had not been at the big university many days before he realized the miserable lot of a freshman.

At first he was sorely puzzled. College was so different from what he had expected. At the high school of his home town, which, being the capital of the State, was no village, he had been somebody. Then his summer in Arizona, with its wild adventures, had given him a self-appreciation which made his present situation humiliating.

There were more than four thousand students at the university. Ken felt himself the youngest, the smallest, the one of least consequence. He was lost in a shuffle of superior youths. In the forestry department he was a mere boy; and he soon realized that a freshman there was the same as anywhere. The fact that he weighed nearly one hundred and sixty pounds, and was no stripling, despite his youth, made not one whit of difference.

Unfortunately, his first overture of what he considered good-fellowship had been made to an upper-classman, and had been a grievous mistake. Ken had not yet recovered from its reception. He grew careful after that, then shy, and finally began to struggle against disappointment and loneliness.

Outside of his department, on the campus and everywhere he ventured, he found things still worse. There was something wrong with him, with his fresh complexion, with his hair, with the way he wore his tie, with the cut of his clothes. In fact, there was nothing right about him. He had been so beset that he could not think of anything but himself. One day, while sauntering along a campus path, with his hands in his pockets, he met two students coming toward him. They went to right and left, and, jerking his hands from his pockets, roared in each ear, "How dare you walk with your hands in your pockets!"

Another day, on the library step, he encountered a handsome bareheaded youth with a fine, clean-cut face and keen eyes, who showed the true stamp of the great university.

"Here," he said, sharply, "aren't you a freshman?"

"Why—yes," confessed Ken.

"I see you have your trousers turned up at the bottom."

"Yes—so I have." For the life of him Ken could not understand why that simple fact seemed a crime, but so it was.

"Turn them down!" ordered the student.

Ken looked into the stern face and flashing eyes of his tormentor, and then meekly did as he had been commanded.

"Boy, I've saved your life. We murder freshmen here for that," said the student, and then passed on up the steps.

In the beginning it was such incidents as these that had bewildered Ken. He passed from surprise to anger, and vowed he would have something to say to these upper-classmen. But when the opportunity came Ken always felt so little and mean that he could not retaliate. This made him furious. He had not been in college two weeks before he could distinguish the sophomores from the seniors by the look on their faces. He hated the sneering "Sophs," and felt rising in him the desire to fight. But he both feared and admired seniors. They seemed so aloof, so far above him. He was in awe of them, and had a hopeless longing to be like them. And as for the freshmen, it took no second glance for Ken to pick them out. They were of two kinds—those who banded together in crowds and went about yelling, and running away from the Sophs, and those who sneaked about alone with timid step and furtive glance.

Ken was one of these lonesome freshmen. He was pining for companionship, but he was afraid to open his lips. Once he had dared to go into Carlton Hall, the magnificent club-house which had been given to the university by a famous graduate. The club was for all students— Ken had read that on the card sent to him, and also in the papers. But manifestly the upper-classmen had a different point of view. Ken had gotten a glimpse into the immense reading-room with its open fireplace and huge chairs, its air of quiet study and repose; he had peeped into the brilliant billiard-hall and the gymnasium; and he had been so impressed and delighted with the marble swimming-tank that he had forgotten himself and walked too near the pool. Several students accidentally bumped him into it. It appeared the students were so eager to help him out that they crowded him in again. When Ken finally got out he learned the remarkable fact that he was the sixteenth freshman who had been accidentally pushed into the tank that day.

So Ken Ward was in a state of revolt. He was homesick; he was lonely for a friend; he was constantly on the lookout for some trick; his confidence in himself had fled; his opinion of himself had suffered a damaging change; he hardly dared call his soul his own.

But that part of his time spent in study or attending lectures more than made up for the other. Ken loved his subject and was eager to learn. He had a free hour in the afternoon, and often he passed this in the library, sometimes in the different exhibition halls. He wanted to go into Carlton Club again, but his experience there made him refrain.

One afternoon at this hour Ken happened to glance into a lecture-room. It was a large amphitheatre full of noisy students. The benches were arranged in a circle running up from a small pit. Seeing safety in the number of students who were passing in, Ken went along. He thought he might hear an interesting lecture. It did not occur to him that he did not belong there. The university had many departments and he felt that any lecture-room was open to him. Still, caution had become a habit with him, and he stepped down the steep aisle looking for an empty bench.

How steep the aisle was! The benches appeared to be on the side of a hill. Ken slipped into an empty one. There was something warm and pleasant in the close contact of so many students, in the ripple of laughter and the murmur of voices. Ken looked about him with a feeling that he was glad to be there.

It struck him, suddenly, that the room had grown strangely silent. Even the shuffling steps of the incoming students had ceased. Ken gazed upward with a queer sense of foreboding. Perhaps he only imagined that all the students above were looking down at him. Hurriedly he glanced below. A sea of faces, in circular rows, was turned his way.

There was no mistake about it. He was the attraction. At the same instant when he prayed to sink through the bench out of sight a burning anger filled his breast. What on earth had he done now? He knew it was something; he felt it. That quiet moment seemed an age. Then the waiting silence burst.

"Fresh on fifth!" yelled a student in one of the lower benches.

"Fresh on fifth!" bawled another at the top of his lungs.

Ken's muddled brain could make little of the matter. He saw he was in the fifth row of benches, and that all the way around on either side of him the row was empty. The four lower rows were packed, and above him students were scattered all over. He had the fifth row of benches to himself.

"Fresh on fifth!"

Again the call rang up from below. It was repeated, now from the left of the pit and then from the right. A student yelled it from the first row and another from the fourth. It banged back and forth. Not a word came from the upper part of the room.

Ken sat up straight with a very red face. It was his intention to leave the bench, but embarrassment that was developing into resentment held him fast. What a senseless lot these students were! Why could they not leave him in peace? How foolish of him to go wandering about in strange lecture-rooms!

A hand pressed Ken's shoulder. He looked back to see a student bending down toward him.

"Hang, Freshie!" this fellow whispered.

"What's it all about?" asked Ken. "What have I done, anyway? I never was in here before."

"All Sophs down there. They don't allow freshmen to go below the sixth row. There've been several rushes this term. And the big one's coming. Hang, Freshie! We're all with you."

"Fresh on fifth!" The tenor of the cry had subtly changed. Good-humored warning had changed to challenge. It pealed up from many lusty throats, and became general all along the four packed rows.

"Hang, Freshie!" bellowed a freshman from the topmost row. It was acceptance of the challenge, the battle-cry flung down to the Sophs. A roar arose from the pit. The freshmen, outnumbering the sophomores, drowned the roar in a hoarser one. Then both sides settled back in ominous waiting.

Ken thrilled in all his being. The freshmen were with him! That roar told him of united strength. All in a moment he had found comrades, and he clenched his fingers into the bench, vowing he would hang there until hauled away.

"Fresh on fifth!" shouted a Soph in ringing voice. He stood up in the pit and stepped to the back of the second bench. "Fresh on fifth! Watch me throw him out!"

He was a sturdily built young fellow and balanced himself gracefully on the backs of the benches, stepping up from one to the other. There was a bold gleam in his eyes and a smile on his face. He showed good-natured contempt for a freshman and an assurance that was close to authority.

Ken sat glued to his seat in mingled fear and wrath. Was he to be the butt of those overbearing sophomores? He thought he could do nothing but hang on with all his might. The ascending student jumped upon the fourth bench and, reaching up, laid hold of Ken with no gentle hands. His grip was so hard that Ken had difficulty in stifling a cry of pain. This, however, served to dispel his panic and make him angry clear through.

The sophomore pulled and tugged with all his strength, yet he could not dislodge Ken. The freshmen howled gleefully for him to "Hang! hang!"

Then two more sophomores leaped up to help the leader. A blank silence followed this move, and all the freshmen leaned forward breathlessly. There was a sharp ripping of cloth. Half of Ken's coat appeared in the hands of one of his assailants.

Suddenly Ken let go his hold, pushed one fellow violently, then swung his fists. It might have been unfair, for the sophomores were beneath him and balancing themselves on the steep benches, but Ken was too angry to think of that. The fellow he pushed fell into the arms of the students below, the second slid out of sight, and the third, who had started the fray, plunged with a crash into the pit.

The freshmen greeted this with a wild yell; the sophomores answered likewise. Like climbing, tumbling apes the two classes spilled themselves up and down the benches, and those nearest Ken laid hold of him, pulling him in opposite directions.

Then began a fierce fight for possession of luckless Ken. Both sides were linked together by gripping hands. Ken was absolutely powerless. His clothes were torn to tatters in a twinkling; they were soon torn completely off, leaving only his shoes and socks. Not only was he in danger of being seriously injured, but students of both sides were handled as fiercely. A heavy trampling roar shook the amphitheatre. As they surged up and down the steep room benches were split. In the beginning the sophomores had the advantage and the tug-of-war raged near the pit and all about it. But the superior numbers of the freshmen began to tell. The web of close-locked bodies slowly mounted up the room, smashing the benches, swaying downward now and then, yet irresistibly gaining ground. The yells of the freshmen increased with the assurance of victory. There was one more prolonged, straining struggle, then Ken was pulled away from the sophomores. The wide, swinging doors of the room were knocked flat to let out the stream of wild freshmen. They howled like fiends; it was first blood for the freshman class; the first tug won that year.

Ken Ward came to his senses out in the corridor surrounded by an excited, beaming, and disreputable crowd of freshmen. Badly as he was hurt, he had to laugh. Some of them looked happy in nothing but torn underclothes. Others resembled a lot of ragamuffins. Coats were minus sleeves, vests were split, shirts were collarless. Blood and bruises were much in evidence.

Some one helped Ken into a long ulster.

"Say, it was great," said this worthy. "Do you know who that fellow was—the first one who tried to throw you out of number five?"

"I haven't any idea," replied Ken. In fact, he felt that his ideas were as scarce just then as his clothes.

"That was the president of the Sophs. He's the varsity baseball captain, too. You slugged him!... Great!"

Ken's spirit, low as it was, sank still lower. What miserable luck he had! His one great ambition, next to getting his diploma, had been to make the varsity baseball team.

A Great Arm

The shock of that battle, more than the bruising he had received, confined Ken to his room for a week. When he emerged it was to find he was a marked man; marked by the freshmen with a great and friendly distinction; by the sophomores for revenge. If it had not been for the loss of his baseball hopes, he would have welcomed the chance to become popular with his classmates. But for him it was not pleasant to be reminded that he had "slugged" the Sophs' most honored member.

It took only two or three meetings with the revengeful sophomores to teach Ken that discretion was the better part of valor. He learned that the sophomores of all departments were looking for him with deadly intent. So far luck had enabled him to escape all but a wordy bullying. Ken became an expert at dodging. He gave the corridors and campus a wide berth. He relinquished his desire to live in one of the dormitories, and rented a room out in the city. He timed his arrival at the university and his departure. His movements were governed entirely by painfully acquired knowledge of the whereabouts of his enemies.

So for weeks Ken Ward lived like a recluse. He was not one with his college mates. He felt that he was not the only freshman who had gotten a bad start in college. Sometimes when he sat near a sad-faced classmate, he knew instinctively that here was a fellow equally in need of friendship. Still these freshmen were as backward as he was, and nothing ever came of such feelings.

The days flew by and the weeks made months, and all Ken did was attend lectures and study. He read everything he could find in the library that had any bearing on forestry. He mastered his text-books before the Christmas holidays. About the vacation he had long been undecided; at length he made up his mind not to go home. It was a hard decision to reach. But his college life so far had been a disappointment; he was bitter about it, and he did not want his father to know. Judge Ward was a graduate of the university. Often and long he had talked to Ken about university life, the lasting benefit of associations and friendships. He would probably think that his son had barred himself out by some reckless or foolish act. Ken was not sure what was to blame; he knew he had fallen in his own estimation, and that the less he thought of himself the more he hated the Sophs.

On Christmas day he went to Carlton Hall. It was a chance he did not want to miss, for very few students would be there. As it turned out he spent some pleasant hours. But before he left the club his steps led him into the athletic trophy room, and there he was plunged into grief. The place was all ablaze with flags and pennants, silver cups and gold medals, pictures of teams and individuals. There were mounted sculls and oars, footballs and baseballs. The long and proud record of the university was there to be read. All her famous athletes were pictured there, and every one who had fought for his college. Ken realized that here for the first time he was in the atmosphere of college spirit for which the university was famed. What would he not have given for a permanent place in that gallery! But it was too late. He had humiliated the captain of the baseball team. Ken sought out the picture of the last season's varsity. What a stocky lot of young chaps, all consciously proud of the big letter on their shirts! Dale, the captain and pitcher, was in the centre of the group. Ken knew his record, and it was a splendid one. Ken took another look at

Dale, another at the famous trainer, Murray, and the professional coach, Arthurs—men under whom it had been his dream to play—and then he left the room, broken-hearted.

When the Christmas recess was over he went back to his lectures resigned to the thought that the athletic side of college life was not for him. He studied harder than ever, and even planned to take a course of lectures in another department. Also his adeptness in dodging was called upon more and more. The Sophs were bound to get him sooner or later. But he did not grow resigned to that; every dodge and flight increased his resentment. Presently he knew he would stop and take what they had to give, and retaliate as best he could. Only, what would they do to him when they did catch him? He remembered his watch, his money, and clothes, never recovered after that memorable tug-of-war. He minded the loss of his watch most; that gift could never be replaced. It seemed to him that he had been the greater sufferer.

One Saturday in January Ken hurried from his class-room. He was always in a hurry and particularly on Saturdays, for that being a short day for most of the departments, there were usually many students passing to and fro. A runaway team clattering down the avenue distracted him from his usual caution, and he cut across the campus. Some one stopped the horses, and a crowd collected. When Ken got there many students were turning away. Ken came face to face with a tall, bronze-haired, freckle-faced sophomore, whom he had dodged more than once. There was now no use to dodge; he had to run or stand his ground.

"Boys, here's that slugging Freshie!" yelled the Soph. "We've got him now."

He might have been an Indian chief so wild was the whoop that answered him.

"Lead us to him!"

"Oh, what we won't do to that Freshie!"

"Come on, boys!"

Ken heard these yells, saw a number of boys dash at him, then he broke and ran as if for his life. The Sophs, a dozen strong, yelling loudly, strung out after him. Ken headed across the campus. He was fleet of foot, and gained on his pursuers. But the yells brought more Sophs on the scene, and they turned Ken to the right. He spurted for Carlton Hall, and almost ran into the arms of still more sophomores. Turning tail, he fled toward the library. When he looked back it was to see the bronze-haired leader within a hundred yards, and back of him a long line of shouting students.

If there was a place to hide round that library Ken could not find it. In this circuit he lost ground. Moreover, he discovered he had not used good judgment in choosing that direction. All along the campus was a high iron fence. Ken thought desperately hard for an instant, then with renewed speed he bounded straight for College Hall.

This was the stronghold of the sophomores. As Ken sped up the gravel walk his pursuers split their throats.

"Run, you Freshie!" yelled one.

"The more you run—" yelled another.

"The more we'll skin you!" finished a third.

Ken ran into the passageway leading through College Hall.

It was full of Sophs hurrying toward the door to see where the yells came from. When Ken plunged into their midst some one recognized him and burst out with the intelligence. At the same moment Ken's pursuers banged through the swinging doors.

A yell arose then in the constricted passageway that seemed to Ken to raise College Hall from its foundation. It terrified him. Like an eel he slipped through reaching arms and darted forward. Ken was heavy and fast on his feet, and with fear lending him wings he made a run through College Hall that would have been a delight to the football coach. For Ken was not dodging any sophomores now. He had played his humiliating part of dodger long enough. He knocked them right and left, and many a surprised Soph he tumbled over. Reaching the farther door, he went through out into the open.

The path before him was clear now, and he made straight for the avenue. It was several hundred yards distant, and he got a good start toward it before the Sophs rolled like a roaring stream from the passage. Ken saw other students running, and also men and boys out on the avenue; but as they could not head him off he kept to his course. On that side of the campus a high, narrow stairway, lined by railings, led up to the sidewalk. When Ken reached it he found the steps covered with ice. He slipped and fell three times in the ascent, while his frantic pursuers gained rapidly.

Ken mounted to the sidewalk, gave vent to a gasp of relief, and, wheeling sharply, he stumbled over two boys carrying a bushel basket of potatoes. When he saw the large, round potatoes a daring inspiration flashed into his mind. Taking the basket from the boys he turned to the head of the stairway.

The bronze-haired Soph was half-way up the steps. His followers, twelve or more, were climbing after him. Then a line of others stretched all the way to College Hall.

With a grim certainty of his mastery of the situation Ken threw a huge potato at his leading pursuer. Fair and square on the bronze head it struck with a sharp crack. Like a tenpin the Soph went down. He plumped into the next two fellows, knocking them off their slippery footing. The three fell helplessly and piled up their comrades in a dense wedge half-way down the steps. If the Sophs had been yelling before, it was strange to note how they were yelling now.

Deliberately Ken fired the heavy missiles. They struck with sodden thuds against the bodies of the struggling sophomores. A poor thrower could not very well have missed that mark, and Ken Ward was remarkably accurate. He had a powerful overhand swing, and the potatoes flew like bullets. One wild-eyed Soph slipped out of the tangle to leap up the steps. Ken, throwing rather low, hit him on the shin. He buckled and dropped down with a blood-curdling yell. Another shook himself loose and faced upward. A better-aimed shot took him in the shoulder. He gave an exhibition of a high and lofty somersault. Then two more started up abreast. The first Ken hit over the eye with a very small potato, which popped like an explosive bullet and flew into bits. As far as effect was concerned a Martini could not have caused a more beautiful fall. Ken landed on the second fellow in the pit of the stomach with a very large potato. There was a sound as of a suddenly struck bass-drum. The Soph crumpled up over the railing, slid down, and fell among his comrades, effectually blocking the stairway.

For the moment Ken had stopped the advance. The sophomores had been checked by one wild freshman. There was scarcely any doubt about Ken's wildness. He had lost his hat; his dishevelled hair stood up like a mane; every time he hurled a potato he yelled. But there was nothing wild about his aim.

All at once he turned his battery on the students gathering below the crush, trying to find a way through the kicking, slipping mass on the narrow stairs. He scattered them as if they had been quail. Some ran out of range. Others dove for cover and tried to dodge. This dodging brought gleeful howls from Ken.

"Dodge, you Indian!" yelled Ken, as he threw. And seldom it was that dodging was of any use. Then, coming to the end of his ammunition, he surveyed the battle-field beneath him and, turning, ran across the avenue and down a street. At the corner of the block he looked back. There was one man coming, but he did not look like a student. So Ken slackened his pace and bent his steps toward his boarding-house.

"By George! I stole those potatoes!" he exclaimed, presently. "I wonder how I can make that good."

Several times as he turned to look over his shoulder he saw the man he had noticed at first. But that did not trouble him, for he was sure no one else was following him. Ken reached his room exhausted by exertion and excitement. He flung himself upon his bed to rest and calm his mind so that he could think. If he had been in a bad light before, what was his position now? Beyond all reasoning with, however, was the spirit that gloried in his last stand.

"By George!" he kept saying. "I wouldn't have missed that—not for anything. They made my life a nightmare. I'll have to leave college—go somewhere else—but I don't care."

Later, after dinner as he sat reading, he heard a door-bell ring, a man's voice, then footsteps in the hall. Some one tapped on his door. Ken felt a strange, cold sensation, which soon passed, and he spoke:

"Come in."

The door opened to admit a short man with little, bright eyes sharp as knives.

"Hello, Kid," he said. Then he leisurely removed his hat and overcoat and laid them on the bed.

Ken's fear of he knew not what changed to amazement. At least his visitor did not belong to the faculty. There was something familiar about the man, yet Ken could not place him.

"Well up in your studies?" he asked, cordially. Then he seated himself, put a hand on each knee, and deliberately and curiously studied Ken.

"Why, yes, pretty well up," replied Ken. He did not know how to take the man. There was a kindliness about him which relieved Ken, yet there was also a hard scrutiny that was embarrassing.

"All by your lonely here," he said.

"It is lonely," replied Ken, "but—but I don't get on very well with the students."

"Small wonder. Most of 'em are crazy."

He was unmistakably friendly. Ken kept wondering where he had seen him. Presently the man arose, and, with a wide smile on his face, reached over and grasped Ken's right arm.

"How's the whip?"

"What?" asked Ken.

"The wing—your arm, Kid, your arm."

"Oh— Why, it's all right."

"It's not sore—not after peggin' a bushel of potatoes on a cold day?"

Ken laughed and raised his arm up and down. "It's weak to-night, but not sore."

"These boys with their India-rubber arms! It's youth, Kid, it's youth. Say, how old are you?"

"Sixteen."

"What! No more than that?"

"No."

"How much do you weigh?"

"About one hundred and fifty-six."

"I thought you had some beef back of that stunt of yours to-day. Say, Kid, it was the funniest and the best thing I've seen at the university in ten years—and I've seen some fresh boys do some stunts, I have. Well... Kid, you've a grand whip—a great arm—and we're goin' to do some stunts with it."

Ken felt something keen and significant in the very air.

"A great arm! For what?... who are you?"

"Say, I thought every boy in college knew me. I'm Arthurs."

"The baseball coach! Are you the baseball coach?" exclaimed Ken, jumping up with his heart in his throat.

"That's me, my boy; and I'm lookin' you up."

Ken suddenly choked with thronging emotions and sat down as limp as a rag.

"Yes, Kid, I'm after you strong. The way you pegged 'em to-day got me. You've a great arm!"

Prisoner of the Sophs

"But if—it's really true—that I've a great arm," faltered Ken, "it won't ever do me any good. I could never get on the varsity."

"Why not?" demanded the coach. "I'll make a star of a youngster like you, if you'll take coachin'. Why not?"

"Oh, you don't know," returned Ken, with a long face.

"Say, you haven't struck me as a kid with no nerve. What's wrong with you?"

"It was I who slugged Captain Dale and caused that big rush between the freshmen and sophomores. I've lived like a hermit ever since."

"So it was you who hit Dale. Well—that's bad," replied Arthurs. He got up with sober face and began to walk the floor. "I remember the eye he had. It was a sight.... But Dale's a good fellow. He'll—"

"I'd do anything on earth to make up for that," burst out Ken.

"Good! I'll tell you what we'll do," said Arthurs, his face brightening. "We'll go right down to Dale's room now. I'll fix it up with him somehow. The sooner the better. I'm goin' to call the baseball candidates to the cage soon."

They put on coats and hats and went out. Evidently the coach was thinking hard, for he had nothing to say, but he kept a reassuring hand on Ken's arm. They crossed the campus along the very path where Ken had fled from the sophomores. The great circle of dormitories loomed up beyond with lights shining in many windows. Arthurs led Ken through a court-yard and into a wide, bright hallway. Their steps sounded with hollow click upon the tiled floor. They climbed three flights of stairs, and then Arthurs knocked at a door. Ken's heart palpitated. It was all so sudden; he did not know what he was going to say or do. He did not care what happened to him if Arthurs could only, somehow, put him right with the captain.

A merry voice bade them enter. The coach opened the door and led Ken across the threshold. Ken felt the glow of a warm, bright room, colorful with pennants and posters, and cozy in its disorder. Then he saw Dale and, behind him, several other students. There was a moment's silence in which Ken heard his heart beat.

Dale rose slowly from his seat, the look on his frank face changing from welcome to intense amazement and then wild elation.

"Whoop!" he shouted. "Lock the door! Worry Arthurs, this's your best bet ever!"

Dale dashed at the coach, hugged him frantically, then put his head out of the door to bawl: "Sophs! Sophs! Sophs! Hurry call! Number nine!... Oh, my!"

Then he faced about, holding the door partially open. He positively beamed upon the coach.

"Say, Cap, what's eatin' you?" asked Arthurs. He looked dumfounded. Ken hung to him desperately; he thought he knew what was coming. There were hurried footsteps in the corridor and excited voices.

"Worry, it's bully of you to bring this freshman here," declared the captain.

"Well, what of it?" demanded the coach. "I looked him up to-night. He's got a great arm, and will be good material for the team. He told me about the little scrap you had in the lecture-room.

He lost his temper, and no wonder. Anyway, he's sorry, Cap, and I fetched him around to see if you couldn't make it up. How about it, Kid?"

"I'm sorry—awfully sorry, Captain Dale," blurted out Ken. "I was mad and scared, too—then you fellows hurt me. So I hit right out.... But I'll take my medicine."

"So—oh!" ejaculated Dale. "Well, this beats the deuce! That's why you're here?"

The door opened wide to admit half a dozen eager-faced youths.

"Fellows, here's a surprise," said Dale. "Young Ward, the freshman! the elusive slugging freshman, fast on his feet, and, as Worry here says, a lad with a great arm!"

"Ward!" roared the Sophs in unison.

"Hold on, fellows—wait—no rough-house yet—wait," ordered Dale. "Ward's here of his own free will!"

Silence ensued after the captain spoke. While he turned to lock the door the Sophs stared open-mouthed at Ken. Arthurs had a worried look, and he kept his hand on Ken. Dale went to a table and began filling his pipe. Then he fixed sharp, thoughtful eyes upon his visitors.

"Worry, you say you brought this freshman here to talk baseball?" he asked.

"Sure I did," blustered Arthurs. It was plain now where he got the name that Dale called him. "What's in the wind, anyhow?"

Dale then gravely spoke to Ken. "So you came here to see me? Sorry you slugged me once? Want to make up for it somehow, because you think you've a chance for the team, and don't want me to be sore on you? That it?"

"Not exactly," replied Ken. "I'd want to let you get square with me even if you weren't the varsity captain."

"Well, you've more than squared yourself with me—by coming here. You'll realize that presently. But don't you know what's happened, what the freshmen have done?"

"No; I don't."

"You haven't been near the university since this afternoon when you pulled off the potato stunt?"

"I should say I haven't."

This brought a laugh from the Sophs.

"You were pretty wise," went on Dale. "The Sophs didn't love you then. But they're going to—understand?"

Ken shook his head, too bewildered and mystified to reply.

"Well, now, here's Giraffe Boswick. Look what you did to him!"

Ken's glance followed the wave of Dale's hand and took in the tall, bronze-haired sophomore who had led the chase that afternoon. Boswick wore a huge discolored bruise over his left eye. It was hideous. Ken was further sickened to recollect that Boswick was one of the varsity pitchers. But the fellow was smiling amiably at Ken, as amiably as one eye would permit. The plot thickened about Ken. He felt his legs trembling under him.

"Boswick, you forgive Ward, don't you—now?" continued Dale, with a smile.

"With all my heart!" exclaimed the pitcher. "To see him here would make me forgive anything."

Coach Arthurs was ill at ease. He evidently knew students, and he did not relish the mystery, the hidden meaning.

"Say, you wise guys make me sick," he called out, gruffly. "Here's a kid that comes right among you. He's on the level, and more'n that, he's game! Now, Cap, I fetched him here, and I won't stand for a whole lot. Get up on your toes! Get it over!"

"Sit down Worry, here's a cigar—light up," said Dale, soothingly. "It's all coming right, lovely, I say. Ward was game to hunt me up, a thousand times gamer than he knows.... See here, Ward, where are you from?"

"I live a good long day's travel from the university," answered Ken, evasively.

"I thought so. Did you ever hear of the bowl-fight, the great event of the year here at Wayne University?"

"Yes, I've heard—read a little about it. But I don't know what it is."

"I'll tell you," went on Dale. "There are a number of yearly rushes and scrapes between the freshmen and sophomores, but the bowl-fight is the one big meeting, the time-honored event. It has been celebrated here for many years. It takes place on a fixed date. Briefly, here's what comes off: The freshmen have the bowl in their keeping this year because they won it in the last fight. They are to select one of their number, always a scrappy fellow, and one honored by the class, and they call him the bowl-man. A week before the fight, on a certain date, the freshmen hide this bowl-man or protect him from the sophomores until the day of the fight, when they all march to Grant field in fighting-togs. Should the sophomores chance to find him and hold him prisoner until after the date of the bowl-fight they win the bowl. The same applies also in case the bowl is in possession of the sophomores. But for ten years neither class has captured the other's bowl-man. So they have fought it out on the field until the bowl was won."

"Well, what has all that got to do with me?" asked Ken. He felt curiously light-headed.

"It has a little to do with you—hasn't it, fellows?" said Dale, in slow, tantalizing voice.

Worry Arthurs lost his worried look and began to smile and rub his hands.

"Ward, look here," added Dale, now speaking sharply. "You've been picked for the bowl-man!"

"Me—me?" stammered Ken.

"No other. The freshmen were late in choosing a man this year. To-day, after your stunt—holding up that bunch of sophomores—they had a meeting in Carlton Club and picked you. Most of them didn't even know your name. I'll bet the whole freshman class is hunting for you right now."

"What for?" queried Ken, weakly.

"Why, I told you. The bowl-fight is only a week off—and here you are. And here you'll stay until that date's past!"

Ken drew a quick breath. He began to comprehend. The sudden huzzahs of Dale's companions gave him further enlightenment.

"But, Captain Dale," he said, breathlessly, "if it's so—if my class has picked me—I can't throw them down. I don't know a soul in my class. I haven't a friend. But I won't throw them down—not to be forever free of dodging Sophs—not even to square myself with you."

"Ward, you're all right!" shouted Dale, his eyes shining.

In the quiet moment that followed, with all the sophomores watching him intently, Ken Ward instinctively felt that his measure had been taken.

"I won't stay here," said Ken, and for the first time his voice rang.

"Oh yes, you will," replied Dale, laughing.

Quick as a cat Ken leaped for the door and got it unlocked and half open before some one clutched him. Then Dale was on him close and hard. Ken began to struggle. He was all muscle, and twice he broke from them.

"His legs! Grab his legs! He's a young bull!"

"We'll trim you now, Freshie!"

"You potato-masher!"

"Go for his wind!"

Fighting and wrestling with all his might Ken went down under a half dozen sophomores. Then Dale was astride his chest, and others were sitting on his hands and feet.

"Boys, don't hurt that arm!" yelled Worry Arthurs.

"Ward, will you be good now and stop scrapping or shall we tie you?" asked Dale. "You can't get away. The thing to do is to give your word not to try. We want to make this easy for you. Your word of honor, now?"

"Never!" cried Ken.

"I knew you wouldn't," said Dale. "We'll have to keep you under guard."

They let him get up. He was panting, and his nose was bleeding, and one of his knuckles was skinned. That short struggle had been no joke. The Sophs certainly meant to keep him prisoner. Still, he was made to feel at ease. They could not do enough for him.

"It's tough luck, Ward, that you should have fallen into our hands this way," said Dale. "But you couldn't help it. You will be kept in my rooms until after the fifteenth. Meals will be brought you, and your books; everything will be done for your comfort. Your whereabouts, of course, will be a secret, and you will be closely watched. Worry, remember you are bound to silence. And Ward, perhaps it wasn't an ill wind that blew you here. You've had your last scrap with a Soph, that's sure. As for what brought you here—it's more than square; and I'll say this: if you can play ball as well as you can scrap, old Wayne has got a star."

The Call for Candidates

There were five rooms in Dale's suite in the dormitory, and three other sophomores shared them with him. They confined Ken in the end room, where he was safely locked and guarded from any possible chance to escape.

For the first day or two it was irksome for Ken; but as he and his captors grew better acquainted the strain eased up, and Ken began to enjoy himself as he had not since coming to the university.

He could not have been better provided for. His books were at hand, and even notes of the lectures he was missing were brought to him. The college papers and magazines interested him, and finally he was much amused by an account of his mysterious disappearance. All in a day he found himself famous. Then Dale and his room-mates were so friendly and jolly that if his captivity had not meant the disgrace of the freshman class, Ken would have rejoiced in it. He began to thaw out, though he did not lose his backwardness. The life of the great university began to be real to him. Almost the whole sophomore class, in squads of twos and threes and sixes, visited Dale's rooms during that week. No Soph wanted to miss a sight of a captive bowl-man. Ken felt so callow and fresh in their presence that he scarcely responded to their jokes. Worry Arthur's nickname of "Kid" vied with another the coach conferred on Ken, and that was "Peg." It was significant slang expressing the little baseball man's baseball notion of Ken's throwing power.

The evening was the most interesting time for Ken. There was always something lively going on. He wondered when the boys studied. When some of the outside students dropped in there were banjo and guitar playing, college songs, and college gossip.

"Come on, Peg, be a good fellow," they said, and laughed at his refusal to smoke or drink beer.

"Molly!" mocked one.

"Willy-boy!" added another.

Ken was callow, young, and backward; but he had a temper, and this kind of banter roused it easily. The red flamed into his cheeks.

"I promised my mother I wouldn't smoke or drink or gamble while I was in college," he retorted, struggling with shame and anger. "And I—I won't."

Dale stopped the good-natured chaff. "Fellows, stop guying Ward; cut it out, I tell you. He's only a kid freshman, but he's liable to hand you a punch, and if he does you'll remember it. Besides, he's right.... Look here, Ward, you stick to that promise. It's a good promise to stick to, and if you're going in for athletics it's the best ever."

Worry Arthurs happened to be present on this evening, and he seconded Dale in more forceful speech. "There's too much boozin' and smokin' of them coffin nails goin' on in this college. It's none of my affair except with the boys I'm coachin', and if I ketch any one breakin' my rules after we go to the trainin'-table he'll sit on the bench. There's Murray; why, he says there are fellows in college who could break records if they'd train. Half of sprintin' or baseball or football is condition."

"Oh, Worry, you and Mac always make a long face over things. Wayne has won a few championships, hasn't she?"

"The varsity ball team will be a frost this year, that's sure," replied Arthurs, gloomily.

"How do you make that out?" demanded Dale, plainly nettled. "You've hinted it before to me. Why won't we be stronger than last season? Didn't we have a crackerjack team, the fastest that ever represented old Wayne? Didn't we smother the small college teams and beat Place twice, shut out Herne the first game, and play for a tie the second?"

"You'll see, all right, all right," replied Arthurs, gloomier than ever; and he took his hat and went out.

Dale slammed his cards down on the table.

"Fellows, is it any wonder we call him Worry? Already he's begun to fuss over the team. Ever since he's been here he has driven the baseball captains and managers crazy. It's only his way, but it's so irritating. He's a magnificent coach, and Wayne owes her great baseball teams to him. But he's hard on captains. I see my troubles. The idea of this year's team being a frost—with all the old stars back in college—with only two positions to fill! And there are half a dozen cracks in college to fight for these two positions—fellows I played against on the summer nines last year. Worry's idea is ridiculous."

This bit of baseball talk showed Ken the obstacles in the way of a freshman making the varsity team. What a small chance there would be for him! Still he got a good deal of comfort out of Arthurs' interest in him, and felt that he would be happy to play substitute this season, and make the varsity in his sophomore year.

The day of the bowl-fight passed, and Ken's captivity became history. The biggest honor of the sophomore year went to Dale and his room-mates. Ken returned to his department, where he was made much of, as he had brought fame to a new and small branch of the great university. It was a pleasure to walk the campus without fear of being pounced upon. Ken's dodging and loneliness—perhaps necessary and curbing nightmares in the life of a freshman—were things of the past. He made acquaintances, slowly lost his backwardness, and presently found college life opening to him bright and beautiful. Ken felt strongly about things. And as his self-enforced exile had been lonely and bitter, so now his feeling that he was really a part of the great university seemed almost too good to be true. He began to get a glimmering of the meaning of his father's love for the old college. Students and professors underwent some vague change in his mind. He could not tell what, he did not think much about it, but there was a warmer touch, a sense of something nearer to him.

Then suddenly a blow fell upon the whole undergraduate body. It was a thunderbolt. It affected every student, but Ken imagined it concerned his own college fortunes more intimately. The athletic faculty barred every member of the varsity baseball team! The year before the faculty had advised and requested the players not to become members of the summer baseball nines. Their wishes had not been heeded. Captain Dale and his fast players had been much in demand by the famous summer nines. Some of them went to the Orange Athletic Club, others to Richfield Springs, others to Cape May, and Dale himself had captained the Atlantic City team.

The action of the faculty was commended by the college magazine. Even the students, though chafing under it, could not but acknowledge its justice. The other universities had adopted such a rule, and Wayne must fall in line. The objections to summer ball-playing were not few, and the particular one was that it affected the amateur standing of the college player. He became open to charges of professionalism. At least, all his expenses were paid, and it was charged that usually he was paid for his services.

Ken's first feeling when he learned this news was one of blank dismay. The great varsity team wiped off the slate! How Place and Herne would humble old Wayne this year! Then the long, hard schedule, embracing thirty games, at least one with every good team in the East—how would an untried green team fare against that formidable array? Then Ken suddenly felt ashamed of a selfish glee, for he was now sure of a place on the varsity.

For several days nothing else was talked about by the students. Whenever Dale or his players appeared at Carlton Hall they were at once surrounded by a sympathetic crowd. If it was a bitter blow to the undergraduates, what was it to the members of the varsity? Their feeling showed in pale, stern faces. It was reported about the campus that Murray and Arthurs and Dale, with the whole team, went to the directors of the athletic faculty and besought them to change or modify the decision. Both the trainer and the coach, who had brought such glory to the university, threatened to resign their places. The disgrace of a pitiably weak team of freshmen being annihilated by minor colleges was eloquently put before the directors. But the decision was final.

One evening early in February Worry Arthurs called upon Ken. His face was long, and his mustache drooped.

"Kid, what do you think of 'em fat-heads on the faculty queerin' my team?" he asked. "Best team I ever developed. Say, but the way they could work the hit-and-run game! Any man on the team could hit to right field when there was a runner goin' down from first."

"Maybe things will turn out all right," suggested Ken, hopefully.

Worry regarded his youthful sympathizer with scorn.

"It takes two years to teach most college kids the rudiments of baseball. Look at this year's schedule." Worry produced a card and waved it at Ken. "The hardest schedule Wayne ever had! And I've got to play a kid team."

Ken was afraid to utter any more of his hopes, and indeed he felt them to be visionary.

"The call for candidates goes out to-morrow," went on the coach. "I'll bet there'll be a mob at the cage. Every fool kid in the university will think he's sure of a place. Now, Ward, what have you played?"

"Everywhere; but infield mostly."

"Every kid has played the whole game. What position have you played most?"

"Third base."

"Good! You've the arm for that. Well, I'm anxious to see you work, but don't exert yourself in the cage. This is a tip. See! I'll be busy weedin' out the bunch, and won't have time until we get out on the field. You can run around the track every day, get your wind and your legs right, hold in on your arm. The cage is cold. I've seen many a good wing go to the bad there. But your chance looks good. College baseball is different from any other kind. You might say it's played with the heart. I've seen youngsters go in through grit and spirit, love of playin' for their college, and beat out fellows who were their superiors physically. Well, good-night.... Say, there's one more thing. I forgot it. Are you up in your subjects?"

"I surely am," replied Ken. "I've had four months of nothing but study."

"The reason I ask is this: That faculty has made another rule, the one-year residence rule, they call it. You have to pass your exams, get your first year over, before you can represent any athletic club. So, in case I can use you on the team, you would have to go up for your exams two months or more ahead of time. That scare you?"

"Not a bit. I could pass mine right now," answered Ken, confidently.

"Kid, you and me are goin' to get along.... Well, good-night, and don't forget what I said."

Ken was too full for utterance; he could scarcely mumble good-night to the coach. He ran upstairs three steps to the jump, and when he reached his room he did a war dance and ended by standing on his head. When he had gotten rid of his exuberance he sat down at once to write to his brother Hal about it, and also his forest-ranger friend, Dick Leslie, with whom he had spent an adventurous time the last summer.

At Carlton Hall, next day, Ken saw a crowd of students before the bulletin-board and, edging in, he read the following notice:

BASEBALL!

CALL FOR CANDIDATES FOR THE VARSITY BASEBALL TEAM

The Athletic Directors of the University earnestly request every student who can play ball, or who thinks he can, to present himself to Coach Arthurs at the Cage on Feb. 3rd.

There will be no freshman team this year, and a new team entirely will be chosen for the varsity. Every student will have a chance. Applicants are requested to familiarize themselves with the new eligibility rules.

The Cage

Ken Ward dug down into his trunk for his old baseball suit and donned it with strange elation. It was dirty and torn, and the shoes that went with it were worn out, but Ken was thinking of what hard ball-playing they represented. He put his overcoat on over his sweater, took up his glove and sallied forth.

A thin coating of ice and snow covered the streets. Winter still whistled in the air. To Ken in his eagerness spring seemed a long way off. On his way across the campus he saw strings of uniformed boys making for Grant Field, and many wearing sweaters over their every-day clothes. The cage was situated at one end of the field apart from the other training-quarters. When Ken got there he found a mob of players crowding to enter the door of the big barn-like structure. Others were hurrying away. Near the door a man was taking up tickets like a doorkeeper of a circus, and he kept shouting: "Get your certificates from the doctor. Every player must pass a physical examination. Get your certificates."

Ken turned somewhat in disgust at so much red tape and he jostled into a little fellow, almost knocking him over.

"Wull! Why don't you fall all over me?" growled this amiable individual. "For two cents I'd hand you one."

The apology on Ken's lips seemed to halt of its own accord.

"Sorry I haven't any change in these clothes," returned Ken. He saw a wiry chap, older than he was, but much smaller, and of most aggressive front. He had round staring eyes, a protruding jaw, and his mouth turned down at the corners. He wore a disreputable uniform and a small green cap over one ear.

"Aw! don't get funny!" he replied.

Ken moved away muttering to himself: "That fellow's a grouch." Much to his amazement, when he got to the training-house, Ken found that he could not get inside because so many players were there ahead of him. After waiting an hour or more he decided he could not have his physical examination at that time, and he went back to the cage. The wide door was still blocked with players, but at the other end of the building Ken found an entrance. He squeezed into a crowd of students and worked forward until stopped by a railing.

Ken was all eyes and breathless with interest. The cage was a huge, open, airy room, lighted by many windows, and, with the exception of the platform where he stood, it was entirely enclosed by heavy netting. The floor was of bare ground well raked and loosened to make it soft. This immense hall was full of a motley crowd of aspiring ball-players.

Worry Arthurs, with his head sunk in the collar of his overcoat, and his shoulders hunched up as if he was about to spring upon something, paced up and down the rear end of the cage. Behind him a hundred or more players in line slowly marched toward the slab of rubber which marked the batting position. Ken remembered that the celebrated coach always tried out new players at the bat first. It was his belief that batting won games.

"Bunt one and hit one!" he yelled to the batters.

From the pitcher's box a lanky individual was trying to locate the plate. Ken did not need a second glance to see that this fellow was no pitcher.

"Stop posin', and pitch!" yelled Arthurs.

One by one the batters faced the plate, swung valiantly or wildly at balls and essayed bunts. Few hit the ball out and none made a creditable bunt. After their turn at bat they were ordered to the other end of the cage, where they fell over one another trying to stop the balls that were hit. Every few moments the coach would yell for one of them, any one, to take a turn at pitching. Ken noticed that Arthurs gave a sharp glance at each new batter, and one appeared to be sufficient. More and more ambitious players crowded into the cage, until there were so many that batted balls rarely missed hitting some one.

Presently Ken Ward awoke from his thrilling absorption in the scene to note another side of it. The students around him were making game of the players.

"What a bunch!"

"Look at that fuzzy gosling with the yellow pants!"

"Keep your shanks out of the way, Freshie!"

"Couldn't hit a balloon!"

Whenever a batter hit a ball into the crowd of dodging players down the cage these students howled with glee. Ken discovered that he was standing near Captain Dale and other members of the barred varsity.

"Say, Dale, how do the candidates shape up?" asked a student.

"This is a disgrace to Wayne," declared Dale, bitterly. "I never saw such a mob of spindle-legged kids in my life. Look at them! Scared to death! That fellow never swung at a ball before—that one never heard of a bunt—they throw like girls—Oh! this is sickening, fellows. I see where Worry goes to his grave this year and old Wayne gets humbled by one-horse colleges."

Ken took one surprised glance at the captain he had admired so much and then he slipped farther over in the crowd. Perhaps Dale had spoken truth, yet somehow it jarred upon Ken's sensitive nature. The thing that affected Ken most was the earnestness of the uniformed boys trying their best to do well before the great coach. Some were timid, uncertain; others were rash and over-zealous. Many a ball cracked off a player's knee or wrist, and more than once Ken saw a bloody finger. It was cold in the cage. Even an ordinarily hit ball must have stung the hands, and the way a hard grounder cracked was enough to excite sympathy among those scornful spectators, if nothing more. But they yelled in delight at every fumble, at everything that happened. Ken kept whispering to himself: "I can't see the fun in it. I can't!"

Arthurs dispensed with the bunting and ordered one hit each for the batters. "Step up and hit!" he ordered, hoarsely. "Don't be afraid—never mind that crowd—step into the ball and swing natural.... Next! Hurry, boys!"

Suddenly a deep-chested student yelled out with a voice that drowned every other sound.

"Hard luck, Worry! No use! You'll never find a hitter among those misfits!"

The coach actually leaped up in his anger and his face went from crimson to white. Ken thought it was likely that he recognized the voice.

"You knocker! You knocker!" he cried. "That's a fine college spirit, ain't it? You're a fine lot of students, I don't think. Now shut up, every one of you, or I'll fire you out of the cage.... And right here at the start you knockers take this from me—I'll find more than one hitter among those kids!"

A little silence fell while the coach faced that antagonistic crowd of spectators. Ken was amazed the second time, and now because of the intensity of feeling that seemed to hang in the air. Ken felt a warm rush go over him, and that moment added greatly to his already strong liking for Worry Arthurs.

Then the coach turned to his work, the batting began again, and the crack of the ball, the rush of feet, the sharp cries of the players mingled once more with the laughter and caustic wit of the unsympathetic audience.

Ken Ward went back to his room without having removed his overcoat. He was thoughtful that night and rebellious against the attitude of the student body. A morning paper announced the fact that over three hundred candidates had presented themselves to Coach Arthurs. It went on to say that the baseball material represented was not worth considering and that old Wayne's varsity team must be ranked with those of the fifth-rate colleges. This, following Ken's experience at the cage on the first day, made him angry and then depressed. The glamour of the thing seemed to fade away. Ken lost the glow, the exhilaration of his first feelings. Everybody took a hopeless view of Wayne's baseball prospects. Ken Ward, however, was not one to stay discouraged long, and when he came out of his gloom it was with his fighting spirit roused. Once and for all he made up his mind to work heart and soul for his college, to be loyal to Arthurs, to hope and believe in the future of the new varsity, whether or not he was lucky enough to win a place upon it.

Next day, going early to the training-quarters, he took his place in a squad waiting for the physical examination. It was a wearisome experience. At length Ken's turn came with two other players, one of whom he recognized as the sour-complexioned fellow of the day before.

"Wull, you're pretty fresh," he said to Ken as they went in. He had a most exasperating manner.

"Say, I don't like you a whole lot," retorted Ken.

Then a colored attendant ushered them into a large room in which were several men. The boys were stripped to the waist.

"Come here, Murray," said the doctor. "There's some use in looking these boys over, particularly this husky youngster."

A tall man in a white sweater towered over Ken. It was the famous trainer. He ran his hands over Ken's smooth skin and felt of the muscles.

"Can you run?" he asked.

"Yes," replied Ken.

"Are you fast?"

"Yes."

Further inquiries brought from Ken his name, age, weight, that he had never been ill, had never used tobacco or intoxicating drinks.

"Ward, eh? 'Peg' Ward," said Murray, smiling. "Worry Arthurs has the call on you—else, my boy, I'd whisper football in your ear. Mebbe I will, anyhow, if you keep up in your studies. That'll do for you."

Ken's companions also won praise from the trainer. They gave their names as Raymond and Weir. The former weighed only one hundred and twenty-two, but he was a knot of muscles. The other stood only five feet, but he was very broad and heavy, his remarkably compact build giving an impression of great strength. Both replied in the negative to the inquiries as to use of tobacco or spirits.

"Boys, that's what we like to hear," said the doctor. "You three ought to pull together."

Ken wondered what the doctor would have said if he had seen the way these three boys glared at each other in the dressing-room. And he wondered, too, what was the reason for such open hostility. The answer came to him in the thought that perhaps they were both trying for the position he wanted on the varsity. Most likely they had the same idea about him. That was the secret of little Raymond's pugnacious front and Weir's pompous air; and Ken realized that the same reason accounted for his own attitude toward them. He wanted very much to tell Raymond that he was a little grouch and Weir that he looked like a puffed-up toad. All the same Ken was not blind to Weir's handsome appearance. The sturdy youngster had an immense head, a great shock of bright brown hair, flashing gray eyes, and a clear bronze skin.

"They'll both make the team, I'll bet," thought Ken. "They look it. I hope I don't have to buck against them." Then as they walked toward the cage Ken forced himself to ask genially: "Raymond, what're you trying for? And you, Weir?"

"Wull, if it's any of your fresh business, I'm not trying for any place. I'm going to play infield. You can carry my bat," replied Raymond, sarcastically.

"Much obliged," retorted Ken, "I'm not going to substitute. I've a corner on that varsity infield myself."

Weir glanced at them with undisguised disdain. "You can save yourselves useless work by not trying for my position. I intend to play infield."

"Wull, puff-up, now, puff-up!" growled Raymond.

Thus the three self-appointed stars of the varsity bandied words among themselves as they crossed the field. At the cage door they became separated to mingle with the pushing crowd of excited boys in uniforms.

By dint of much squeezing and shoulder-work Ken got inside the cage. He joined the squad in the upper end and got in line for the batting. Worry Arthurs paced wildly to and fro yelling for the boys to hit. A dense crowd of students thronged the platform and laughed, jeered, and stormed at the players. The cage was in such an uproar that Arthurs could scarcely be heard. Watching from the line Ken saw Weir come to bat and stand aggressively and hit the ball hard. It scattered the flock of fielders. Then Raymond came along, and, batting left-handed, did likewise. Arthurs stepped forward and said something to both. After Ken's turn at bat the coach said to him: "Get out of here. Go run round the track. Do it every day. Don't come back until Monday."

As Ken hurried out he saw and felt the distinction with which he was regarded by the many players whom he crowded among in passing. When he reached the track he saw Weir, Raymond, and half a dozen other fellows going round at a jog-trot. Weir was in the lead, setting the pace. Ken fell in behind.

The track was the famous quarter-mile track upon which Murray trained his sprinters. When Ken felt the spring of the cinder-path in his feet, the sensation of buoyancy, the eager wildfire pride that flamed over him, he wanted to break into headlong flight. The first turn around the track was delight; the second pleasure in his easy stride; the third brought a realization of distance. When Ken had trotted a mile he was not tired, he still ran easily, but he began to appreciate that his legs were not wings. The end of the second mile found him sweating freely and panting.

Two miles were enough for the first day. Ken knew it and he began to wonder why the others, especially Weir, did not know it. But Weir jogged on, his head up, his hair flying, as if he had not yet completed his first quarter. The other players stretched out behind him. Ken saw Raymond's funny little green cap bobbing up and down, and it made him angry. Why could not the grouch get a decent cap, anyway?

At the end of the third mile Ken began to labor. His feet began to feel weighted, his legs to ache, his side to hurt. He was wringing wet; his skin burned; his breath whistled. But he kept doggedly on. It had become a contest now. Ken felt instinctively that every runner would not admit he had less staying power than the others. Ken declared to himself that he could be as bull-headed as any of them. Still to see Weir jogging on steady and strong put a kind of despair on Ken. For every lap of the fourth mile a runner dropped out, and at the half of the fifth only Weir, Raymond, and Ken kept to the track.

Ken hung on gasping at every stride. He was afraid his heart would burst. The pain in his side was as keen as a knife thrust. His feet were lead. Every rod he felt must be his last, yet spurred on desperately, and he managed to keep at the heels of the others. It might kill him, but he would not stop until he dropped. Raymond was wagging along ready to fall any moment, and Weir was trotting slowly with head down. On the last lap of the fifth mile they all stopped as by one accord. Raymond fell on the grass; Ken staggered to a bench, and Weir leaned hard against the fence. They were all blowing like porpoises and regarded each other as mortal enemies. Weir gazed grandly at the other two; Raymond glowered savagely at him and then at Ken; and Ken in turn gave them withering glances. Without a word the three contestants for a place on the varsity then went their several ways.

Out on the Field

When Ken presented himself at the cage on the following Monday it was to find that Arthurs had weeded out all but fifty of the candidates. Every afternoon for a week the coach put these players through batting and sliding practice, then ordered them out to run around the track. On the next Monday only twenty-five players were left, and as the number narrowed down the work grew more strenuous, the rivalry keener, and the tempers of the boys more irascible.

Ken discovered it was work and not by any means pleasant work. He fortified himself by the thought that the pleasure and glory, the real play, was all to come as a reward. Worry Arthurs drove them relentlessly. Nothing suited him; not a player knew how to hold a bat, to stand at the plate, to slide right, or to block a ground ball.

"Don't hit with your left hand on top—unless you're left-handed. Don't grip the end of the bat. There! Hold steady now, step out and into the ball, and swing clean and level. If you're afraid of bein' hit by the ball, get out of here!"

It was plain to Ken that not the least of Arthurs' troubles was the incessant gibing of the students on the platform. There was always a crowd watching the practice, noisy, scornful, abusive. They would never recover from the shock of having that seasoned champion varsity barred out of athletics. Every once in a while one of them would yell out: "Wait, Worry! oh! Worry, wait till the old varsity plays your yanigans!" And every time the coach's face would burn. But he had ceased to talk back to the students. Besides, the athletic directors were always present. They mingled with the candidates and talked baseball to them and talked to Arthurs. Some of them might have played ball once, but they did not talk like it. Their advice and interference served only to make the coach's task harder.

Another Monday found only twenty players in the squad. That day Arthurs tried out catchers, pitchers, and infielders. He had them all throwing, running, fielding, working like Trojans. They would jump at his yell, dive after the ball, fall over it, throw it anywhere but in the right direction, run wild, and fight among themselves. The ever-flowing ridicule from the audience was anything but a stimulus. So much of it coming from the varsity and their adherents kept continually in the minds of the candidates their lack of skill, their unworthiness to represent the great university in such a popular sport as baseball. So that even if there were latent ability in any of the candidates no one but the coach could see it. And often he could not conceal his disgust and hopelessness.

"Battin' practice!" he ordered, sharply. "Two hits and a bunt to-day. Get a start on the bunt and dig for first. Hustle now!"

He placed one player to pitch to the hitters, another to catch, and as soon as the hitters had their turn they took to fielding. Two turns for each at bat left the coach more than dissatisfied.

"You're all afraid of the ball," he yelled. "This ain't no dodgin' game. Duck your nut if the ball's goin' to hit you, but stop lookin' for it. Forget it. Another turn now. I'm goin' to umpire. Let's see if you know the difference between a ball and a strike."

He changed the catcher and, ordering Ken to the pitcher's box, he stepped over behind him. "Peg," he said, speaking low, "you're not tryin' for pitcher, I know, but you've got speed and control and I want you to peg 'em a few. Mind now, easy with your arm. By that I mean hold in, don't whip it. And you peg 'em as near where I say as you can; see?"

As the players, one after another, faced the box, the coach kept saying to Ken: "Drive that fellow away from the plate... give this one a low ball... now straight over the pan. Say, Peg, you've got a nice ball there... put a fast one under this fellow's chin."

"Another turn, now, boys!" he yelled. "I tell you—stand up to the plate!" Then he whispered to Ken. "Hit every one of 'em! Peg 'em now, any place."

"Hit them?" asked Ken, amazed.

"That's what I said."

"But—Mr. Arthurs—"

"See here, Peg. Don't talk back to me. Do as I say. We'll peg a little nerve into this bunch. Now I'll go back of the plate and make a bluff."

Arthurs went near to the catcher's position. Then he said: "Now, fellows, Ward's pretty wild and I've told him to speed up a few. Stand right up and step into 'em."

The first batter was Weir. Ken swung easily and let drive. Straight as a string the ball sped for the batter. Like a flash he dropped flat in the dust and the ball just grazed him. It was a narrow escape. Weir jumped up, his face flaring, his hair on end, and he gazed hard at Ken before picking up the bat.

"Batter up!" ordered the coach. "Do you think this's a tea-party?"

Weir managed by quick contortions to get through his time at bat without being hit. Three players following him were not so lucky.

"Didn't I say he was wild?" yelled the coach. "Batter up, now!"

The next was little Raymond. He came forward cautiously, eying Ken with disapproval. Ken could not resist putting on a little more steam, and the wind of the first ball whipped off Raymond's green cap. Raymond looked scared and edged away from the plate, and as the second ball came up he stepped wide with his left foot.

"Step into the ball," said the coach. "Don't pull away. Step in or you'll never hit."

The third ball cracked low down on Raymond's leg.

"Oh!—Oh!—Oh!" he howled, beginning to hop and hobble about the cage.

"Next batter!" called out Arthurs.

And so it went on until the most promising player in the cage came to bat. This was Graves, a light-haired fellow, tall, built like a wedge. He had more confidence than any player in the squad and showed up well in all departments of the game. Moreover, he was talky, aggressive, and more inclined to be heard and felt. He stepped up and swung his bat at Ken.

"You wild freshman! If you hit me!" he cried.

Ken Ward had not fallen in love with any of his rivals for places on the team, but he especially did not like Graves. He did not stop to consider the reason of it at the moment, still he remembered several tricks Graves had played, and he was not altogether sorry for the coach's order. Swinging a little harder, Ken threw straight at Graves.

"Wham!" The ball struck him fair on the hip. Limping away from the plate he shook his fist at Ken.

"Batter up!" yelled Arthurs. "A little more speed now, Peg. You see it ain't nothin' to get hit. Why, that's in the game. It don't hurt much. I never cared when I used to get hit. Batter up!"

Ken sent up a very fast ball, on the outside of the plate. The batter swung wide, and the ball, tipping the bat, glanced to one side and struck Arthurs in the stomach with a deep sound.

Arthurs' round face went red; he gurgled and gasped for breath; he was sinking to his knees when the yelling and crowing of the students on the platform straightened him up. He walked about a few minutes, then ordered sliding practice.

The sliding-board was brought out. It was almost four feet wide and twenty long and covered with carpet.

"Run hard, boys, and don't let up just before you slide. Keep your speed and dive. Now at it!"

A line of players formed down the cage. The first one dashed forward and plunged at the board, hitting it with a bang. The carpet was slippery and he slid off and rolled in the dust. The second player leaped forward and, sliding too soon, barely reached the board. One by one the others followed.

"Run fast now!" yelled the coach. "Don't flinch.... Go down hard and slide... light on your hands... keep your heads up... slide!"

This feature of cage-work caused merriment among the onlookers. That sliding-board was a wonderful and treacherous thing. Most players slid off it as swift as a rocket. Arthurs kept them running so fast and so close together that at times one would shoot off the board just as the next would strike it. They sprawled on the ground, rolled over, and rooted in the dust. One skinned his nose on the carpet; another slid the length of the board on his ear. All the time they kept running and sliding, the coach shouted to them, and the audience roared with laughter. But it was no fun for the sliders. Raymond made a beautiful slide, and Graves was good, but all the others were ludicrous.

It was a happy day for Ken, and for all the candidates, when the coach ordered them out on the field. This was early in March. The sun was bright, the frost all out of the ground, and a breath of spring was in the air. How different it was from the cold, gloomy cage! Then the mocking students, although more in evidence than before, were confined to the stands and bleachers, and could not so easily be heard. But the presence of the regular varsity team, practising at the far end of Grant Field, had its effect on the untried players.

The coach divided his players into two nines and had them practise batting first, then fielding, and finally started them in a game, with each candidate playing the position he hoped to make on the varsity.

It was a weird game. The majority of the twenty candidates displayed little knowledge of baseball. School-boys on the commons could have beaten them. They were hooted and hissed by the students, and before half the innings were played the bleachers and stands were empty. That was what old Wayne's students thought of Arthurs' candidates.

In sharp contrast to most of them, Weir, Raymond, and Graves showed they had played the game somewhere. Weir at short-stop covered ground well, but he could not locate first base. Raymond darted here and there quick as a flash, and pounced upon the ball like a huge frog. Nothing got past him, but he juggled the ball. Graves was a finished and beautiful fielder; he was easy, sure, yet fast, and his throw from third to first went true as a line.

Graves's fine work accounted for Ken Ward's poor showing. Both were trying for third base, and when Ken once saw his rival play out on the field he not only lost heart and became confused, but he instinctively acknowledged that Graves was far his superior. After all his hopes and the kind interest of the coach it was a most bitter blow. Ken had never played so poor a game. The ball blurred in his tear-wet eyes and looked double. He did not field a grounder. He muffed foul flies and missed thrown balls. It did not occur to him that almost all of the players around him were in the same boat. He could think of nothing but the dashing away of his hopes. What was the use of trying? But he kept trying, and the harder he tried the worse he played. At the bat he struck out, fouled out, never hit the ball square at all. Graves got two well-placed hits to right field. Then when Ken was in the field Graves would come down the coaching line and talk to him in a voice no one else could hear.

"You've got a swell chance to make this team, you have, not! Third base is my job, Freshie. Why, you tow-head, you couldn't play marbles. You butter-finger, can't you stop anything? You can't even play sub on this team. Remember, Ward, I said I'd get you for hitting me that day. You hit me with a potato once, too. I'll chase you off this team."

For once Ken's spirit was so crushed and humbled that he could not say a word to his rival. He even felt he deserved it all. When the practice ended, and he was walking off the field with hanging head, trying to bear up under the blow, he met Arthurs.

"Hello! Peg," said the coach, "I'm going your way."

Ken walked along feeling Arthurs' glance upon him, but he was ashamed to raise his head.

"Peg, you were up in the air to-day—way off—you lost your nut."

He spoke kindly and put his hand on Ken's arm. Ken looked up to see that the coach's face was pale and tired, with the characteristic worried look more marked than usual.

"Yes, I was," replied Ken, impulsively. "I can play better than I did to-day—but—Mr. Arthurs, I'm not in Graves's class as a third-baseman. I know it."

Ken said it bravely, though there was a catch in his voice. The coach looked closely at him.

"So you're sayin' a good word for Graves, pluggin' his game."

"I'd love to make the team, but old Wayne must have the best players you can get."

"Peg, I said once you and me were goin' to get along. I said also that college baseball is played with the heart. You lost your heart. So did most of the kids. Well, it ain't no wonder. This's a tryin' time. I'm playin' them against each other, and no fellow knows where he's at. Now, I've seen all along that you weren't a natural infielder. I played you at third to-day to get that idea out of your head. To-morrow I'll try you in the outfield. You ain't no quitter, Peg."

Ken hurried to his room under the stress of a complete revulsion of feeling. His liking for the coach began to grow into something more. It was strange to Ken what power a few words from Arthurs had to renew his will and hope and daring. How different Arthurs was when not on the field. There he was stern and sharp. Ken could not study that night, and he slept poorly. His revival of hope did not dispel his nervous excitement.

He went out into Grant Field next day fighting himself. When in the practice Arthurs assigned him to a right-field position, he had scarcely taken his place when he became conscious of a queer inclination to swallow often, of a numbing tight band round his chest. He could not stand still; his hands trembled; there was a mist before his eyes. His mind was fixed upon himself and upon the other five outfielders trying to make the team. He saw the players in the infield pace their positions restlessly, run without aim when the ball was hit or thrown, collide with each other, let the ball go between their hands and legs, throw wildly, and sometimes stand as if transfixed when they ought to have been in action. But all this was not significant to Ken.

He saw everything that happened, but he thought only that he must make a good showing; he must not miss any flies, or let a ball go beyond him. He absolutely must do the right thing. The air of Grant Field was charged with intensity of feeling, and Ken thought it was all his own. His baseball fortune was at stake, and he worked himself in such a frenzy that if a ball had been batted in his direction he might not have seen it at all. Fortunately none came his way.

The first time at bat he struck out ignominiously, poking weakly at the pitcher's out-curves. The second time he popped up a little fly. On the next trial the umpire called him out on strikes. At his last chance Ken was desperate. He knew the coach placed batting before any other department of the game. Almost sick with the torture of the conflicting feelings, Ken went up to the plate and swung blindly. To his amaze he cracked a hard fly to left-centre, far between the fielders. Like a startled deer Ken broke into a run. He turned first base and saw that he might stretch the hit into a three-bagger. He knew he could run, and never had he so exerted himself. Second base sailed under him, and he turned in line for the third. Watching Graves, he saw him run for the base and stand ready to catch the throw-in.

Without slacking his speed in the least Ken leaped into the air headlong for the base. He heard the crack of the ball as it hit Graves's glove. Then with swift scrape on hands and breast he was sliding in the dust. He stopped suddenly as if blocked by a stone wall. Something hard struck him on the head. A blinding light within his brain seemed to explode into glittering slivers. A piercing pain shot through him. Then from darkness and a great distance sounded a voice:

"Ward, I said I'd get you!"

Annihilation

That incident put Ken out of the practice for three days. He had a bruise over his ear as large as a small apple. Ken did not mind the pain nor the players' remarks that he had a swelled head anyway, but he remembered with slow-gathering wrath Graves's words: "I said I'd get you!"

He remembered also Graves's reply to a question put by the coach. "I was only tagging him. I didn't mean to hurt him." That rankled inside Ken. He kept his counsel, however, even evading a sharp query put by Arthurs, and as much as it was possible he avoided the third-baseman.

Hard practice was the order of every day, and most of it was batting. The coach kept at the candidates everlastingly, and always his cry was: "Toe the plate, left foot a little forward, step into the ball and swing!" At the bat Ken made favorable progress because the coach was always there behind him with encouraging words; in the field, however, he made a mess of it, and grew steadily worse.

The directors of the Athletic Association had called upon the old varsity to go out and coach the new aspirants for college fame. The varsity had refused. Even the players of preceding years, what few were in or near the city, had declined to help develop Wayne's stripling team. But some of the older graduates, among them several of the athletic directors, appeared on the field. When Arthurs saw them he threw up his hands in rage and despair. That afternoon Ken had three well-meaning but old-fashioned ball-players coach him in the outfield. He had them one at a time, which was all that saved him from utter distraction. One told him to judge a fly by the sound when the ball was hit. Another told him to play in close, and when the ball was batted to turn and run with it. The third said he must play deep and sprint in for the fly. Then each had different ideas as to how batters should be judged, about throwing to bases, about backing up the other fielders. Ken's bewilderment grew greater and greater. He had never heard of things they advocated, and he began to think he did not know anything about the game. And what made his condition of mind border on imbecility was a hurried whisper from Arthurs between innings: "Peg, don't pay the slightest attention to 'em fat-head grad. coaches."

Practice days succeeding that were worse nightmares to Ken Ward than the days he had spent in constant fear of the sophomores. It was a terribly feverish time of batting balls, chasing balls, and of having dinned into his ears thousands of orders, rules of play, talks on college spirit in athletics—all of which conflicted so that it was meaningless to him. During this dark time one ray of light was the fact that Arthurs never spoke a sharp word to him. Ken felt vaguely that he was whirling in some kind of a college athletic chaos, out of which he would presently emerge.

Toward the close of March the weather grew warm, the practice field dried up, and baseball should have been a joy to Ken. But it was not. At times he had a shameful wish to quit the field for good, but he had not the courage to tell the coach. The twenty-fifth, the day scheduled for the game with the disgraced varsity team, loomed closer and closer. Its approach was a fearful thing for Ken. Every day he cast furtive glances down the field to where the varsity held practice. Ken had nothing to say; he was as glum as most of the other candidates, but he had heard gossip in the lecture-rooms, in the halls, on the street, everywhere, and it concerned this game. What would the old varsity do to Arthurs' new team? Curiosity ran as high as the feeling toward the athletic directors. Resentment flowed from every source. Ken somehow got the impression that he was blamable for being a member of the coach's green squad. So Ken Ward fluctuated between two fears, one as bad as the other—that he would not be selected to play, and the other that he would be selected. It made no difference. He would be miserable if not chosen, and if he was—how on earth would he be able to keep his knees from wobbling? Then the awful day dawned.

Coach Arthurs met all his candidates at the cage. He came late, he explained, because he wanted to keep them off the field until time for practice. To-day he appeared more grave than worried, and where the boys expected a severe lecture, he simply said: "I'll play as many of you as I can. Do your best, that's all. Don't mind what these old players say. They were kids once, though they seem to have forgotten it. Try to learn from them."

It was the first time the candidates had been taken upon the regular diamond of Grant Field. Ken had peeped in there once to be impressed by the beautiful level playground, and especially the magnificent turreted grand-stand and the great sweeping stretches of bleachers. Then they had been empty; now, with four thousand noisy students and thousands of other spectators besides, they stunned him. He had never imagined a crowd coming to see the game.

Perhaps Arthurs had not expected it either, for Ken heard him mutter grimly to himself. He ordered practice at once, and called off the names of those he had chosen to start the game. As one in a trance Ken Ward found himself trotting out to right field.

A long-rolling murmur that was half laugh, half taunt, rose from the stands. Then it quickly subsided. From his position Ken looked for the players of the old varsity, but they had not yet come upon the field. Of the few balls batted to Ken in practice he muffed only one, and he was just beginning to feel that he might acquit himself creditably when the coach called the team in. Arthurs had hardly given his new players time enough to warm up, but likewise they had not had time to make any fumbles.

All at once a hoarse roar rose from the stands, then a thundering clatter of thousands of feet as the students greeted the appearance of the old varsity. It was applause that had in it all the feeling of the undergraduates for the championship team, many of whom they considered had been unjustly barred by the directors. Love, loyalty, sympathy, resentment—all pealed up to the skies in that acclaim. It rolled out over the heads of Arthurs' shrinking boys as they huddled together on the bench.

Ken Ward, for one, was flushing and thrilling. In that moment he lost his gloom. He watched the varsity come trotting across the field, a doughty band of baseball warriors. Each wore a sweater with the huge white "W" shining like a star. Many of those players had worn that honored varsity letter for three years. It did seem a shame to bar them from this season's team. Ken found himself thinking of the matter from their point of view, and his sympathy was theirs.

More than that, he gloried in the look of them, in the trained, springy strides, in the lithe, erect forms, in the assurance in every move. Every detail of that practice photographed itself upon Ken Ward's memory, and he knew he would never forget.

There was Dale, veteran player, captain and pitcher of the nine, hero of victories over Place and Herne. There was Hogan, catcher for three seasons, a muscular fellow, famed for his snap-throw to the bases and his fiendish chasing of foul flies. There was Hickle, the great first-baseman, whom the professional leagues were trying to get. What a reach he had; how easily he scooped in the ball; low, high, wide, it made no difference to him. There was Canton at second,

Hollis at short, Burns at third, who had been picked for the last year's All-American College Team. Then there was Dreer, brightest star of all, the fleet, hard-hitting centre-fielder. This player particularly fascinated Ken. It was a beautiful sight to see him run. The ground seemed to fly behind him. When the ball was hit high he wheeled with his back to the diamond and raced out, suddenly to turn with unerring judgment—and the ball dropped into his hands. On low line hits he showed his fleetness, for he was like a gleam of light in his forward dash; and, however the ball presented, shoulder high, low by his knees, or on a short bound, he caught it. Ken Ward saw with despairing admiration what it meant to be a great outfielder.

Then Arthurs called "Play ball!" giving the old varsity the field.

With a violent start Ken Ward came out of his rhapsody. He saw a white ball tossed on the diamond. Dale received it from one of the fielders and took his position in the pitcher's box. The uniform set off his powerful form; there was something surly and grimly determined in his face. He glanced about to his players, as if from long habit, and called out gruffly: "Get in the game, fellows! No runs for this scrub outfit!" Then, with long-practised swing, he delivered the ball. It travelled plateward swift as the flight of a white swallow. The umpire called it a strike on Weir; the same on the next pitch; the third was wide. Weir missed the fourth and was out. Raymond followed on the batting list. To-day, as he slowly stepped toward the plate, seemingly smaller and glummer than ever, it was plain he was afraid. The bleachers howled at the little green cap sticking over his ear. Raymond did not swing at the ball; he sort of reached out his bat at the first three pitches, stepping back from the plate each time. The yell that greeted his weak attempt seemed to shrivel him up. Also it had its effect on the youngsters huddling around Arthurs. Graves went up and hit a feeble grounder to Dale and was thrown out at first.

Ken knew the half-inning was over; he saw the varsity players throw aside their gloves and trot in. But either he could not rise or he was glued to the bench. Then Arthurs pulled him up, saying, "Watch sharp, Peg, these fellows are right-field hitters!" At the words all Ken's blood turned to ice. He ran out into the field fighting the coldest, most sickening sensation he ever had in his life. The ice in his veins all went to the pit of his stomach and there formed into a heavy lump. Other times when he had been frightened flitted through his mind. It had been bad when he fought with Greaser, and worse when he ran with the outlaws in pursuit, and the forest fire was appalling. But Ken felt he would gladly have changed places at that moment. He dreaded the mocking bleachers.

Of the candidates chosen to play against the varsity Ken knew McCord at first, Raymond at second, Weir at short, Graves at third. He did not know even the names of the others. All of them, except Graves, appeared too young to play in that game.

Dreer was first up for the varsity, and Ken shivered all over when the lithe centre-fielder stepped to the left side of the plate. Ken went out deeper, for he knew most hard-hitting left-handers hit to right field. But Dreer bunted the first ball teasingly down the third-base line. Fleet as a deer, he was across the bag before the infielder reached the ball. Hollis was next up. On the first pitch, as Dreer got a fast start for second, Hollis bunted down the first-base line. Pitcher and baseman ran for the bunt; Hollis was safe, and the sprinting Dreer went to third without even drawing a throw. A long pealing yell rolled over the bleachers. Dale sent coaches to the coaching lines. Hickle, big and formidable, hurried to the plate, swinging a long bat. He swung it as if he intended to knock the ball out of the field. When the pitcher lifted his arm Dreer dashed for

34

home-base, and seemed beating the ball. But Hickle deftly dumped it down the line and broke for first while Dreer scored. This bunt was not fielded at all. How the bleachers roared! Then followed bunts in rapid succession, dashes for first, and slides into the bag. The pitcher interfered with the third-baseman, and the first-baseman ran up the line, and the pitcher failed to cover the bag, and the catcher fell all over the ball. Every varsity man bunted, but in just the place where it was not expected. They raced around the bases. They made long runs from first to third. They were like flashes of light, slippery as eels. The bewildered infielders knew they were being played with. The taunting "boo-hoos" and screams of delight from the bleachers were as demoralizing as the illusively daring runners. Closer and closer the infielders edged in until they were right on top of the batters. Then Dale and his men began to bunt little infield flies over the heads of their opponents. The merry audience cheered wildly. But Graves and Raymond ran back and caught three of these little pop flies, thus retiring the side. The old varsity had made six runs on nothing but deliberate bunts and daring dashes around the bases.

Ken hurried in to the bench and heard some one call out, "Ward up!"

He had forgotten he would have to bat. Stepping to the plate was like facing a cannon. One of the players yelled: "Here he is, Dale! Here's the potato-pegger! Knock his block off!"

The cry was taken up by other players. "Peg him, Dale! Peg him, Dale!" And then the bleachers got it. Ken's dry tongue seemed pasted to the roof of his mouth. This Dale in baseball clothes with the lowering frown was not like the Dale Ken had known. Suddenly he swung his arm. Ken's quick eye caught the dark, shooting gleam of the ball. Involuntarily he ducked. "Strike," called the umpire. Then Dale had not tried to hit him. Ken stepped up again. The pitcher whirled slowly this time, turning with long, easy motion, and threw underhand. The ball sailed, floated, soared. Long before it reached Ken it had fooled him completely. He chopped at it vainly. The next ball pitched came up swifter, but just before it crossed the plate it seemed to stop, as if pulled back by a string, and then dropped down. Ken fell to his knees trying to hit it.

The next batter's attempts were not as awkward as Ken's, still they were as futile. As Ken sat wearily down upon the bench he happened to get next to coach Arthurs. He expected some sharp words from the coach, he thought he deserved anything, but they were not forthcoming. The coach put his hand on Ken's knee. When the third batter fouled to Hickle, and Ken got up to go out to the field, he summoned courage to look at Arthurs. Something in his face told Ken what an ordeal this was. He divined that it was vastly more than business with Worry Arthurs.

"Peg, watch out this time," whispered the coach. "They'll line 'em at you this inning—like bullets. Now try hard, won't you? Just try!"

Ken knew from Arthurs' look more than his words that trying was all that was left for the youngsters. The varsity had come out early in the spring, and they had practised to get into condition to annihilate this new team practically chosen by the athletic directors. And they had set out to make the game a farce. But Arthurs meant that all the victory was not in winning the game. It was left for his boys to try in the face of certain defeat, to try with all their hearts, to try with unquenchable spirit. It was the spirit that counted, not the result. The old varsity had received a bitter blow; they were aggressive and relentless. The students and supporters of old Wayne, idolizing the great team, always bearing in mind the hot rivalry with Place and Herne, were unforgiving and intolerant of an undeveloped varsity. Perhaps neither could be much blamed. But it was for the new players to show what it meant to them. The greater the prospect of defeat, the greater the indifference or hostility shown them, the more splendid their opportunity. For it was theirs to try for old Wayne, to try, to fight, and never to give up.

Ken caught fire with the flame of that spirit.

"Boys, come on!" he cried, in his piercing tenor. "They can't beat us trying!"

As he ran out into the field members of the varsity spoke to him. "You green-backed freshman! Shut up! You scrub!"

"I'm not a varsity has-been!" retorted Ken, hurrying out to his position.

The first man up, a left-hander, rapped a hard twisting liner to right field. Ken ran toward deep centre with all his might. The ball kept twisting and curving. It struck squarely in Ken's hands and bounced out and rolled far. When he recovered it the runner was on third base. Before Ken got back to his position the second batter hit hard through the infield toward right. The ball came skipping like a fiendish rabbit. Ken gritted his teeth and went down on his knees, to get the bounding ball full in his breast. But he stopped it, scrambled for it, and made the throw in. Dale likewise hit in his direction, a slow low fly, difficult to judge. Ken over-ran it, and the hit gave Dale two bases. Ken realized that the varsity was now executing Worry Arthurs' famous right-field hitting. The sudden knowledge seemed to give Ken the blind-staggers. The field was in a haze; the players blurred in his sight. He heard the crack of the ball and saw Raymond dash over and plunge down. Then the ball seemed to streak out of the grass toward him, and, as he bent over, it missed his hands and cracked on his shin. Again he fumbled wildly for it and made the throw in. The pain roused his rage. He bit his lips and called to himself: "I'll stop them if it kills me!"

Dreer lined the ball over his head for a home-run. Hollis made a bid for a three-bagger, but Ken, by another hard sprint, knocked the ball down. Hickle then batted up a tremendously high fly. It went far beyond Ken and he ran and ran. It looked like a small pin-point of black up in the sky. Then he tried to judge it, to get under it. The white sky suddenly glazed over and the ball wavered this way and that. Ken lost it in the sun, found it again, and kept on running. Would it never come down? He had not reached it, he had run beyond it. In an agony he lunged out, and the ball fell into his hands and jumped out.

Then followed a fusillade of hits, all between second base and first, and all vicious-bounding grounders. To and fro Ken ran, managing somehow to get some portion of his anatomy in front of the ball. It had become a demon to him now and he hated it. His tongue was hanging out, his breast was bursting, his hands were numb, yet he held before him the one idea to keep fiercely trying.

He lost count of the runs after eleven had been scored. He saw McCord and Raymond trying to stem the torrent of right-field hits, but those they knocked down gave him no time to recover. He blocked the grass-cutters with his knees or his body and pounced upon the ball and got it away from him as quickly as possible. Would this rapid fire of uncertain-bounding balls never stop? Ken was in a kind of frenzy. If he only had time to catch his breath!

Then Dreer was at bat again. He fouled the first two balls over the grand-stand. Some one threw out a brand-new ball. Farther and farther Ken edged into deep right. He knew what was coming. "Let him—hit it!" he panted. "I'll try to get it! This day settles me. I'm no outfielder. But I'll try!"

The tired pitcher threw the ball and Dreer seemed to swing and bound at once with the ringing crack. The hit was one of his famous drives close to the right-field foul-line.

Ken was off with all the speed left in him. He strained every nerve and was going fast when he passed the foul-flag. The bleachers loomed up indistinct in his sight. But he thought only of meeting the ball. The hit was a savage liner, curving away from him. Cinders under his flying feet were a warning that he did not heed. He was on the track. He leaped into the air, left hand outstretched, and felt the ball strike in his glove.

Then all was dark in a stunning, blinding crash—

Examinations

When Ken Ward came fully to his senses he was being half carried and half led across the diamond to the players' bench. He heard Worry Arthurs say: "He ain't hurt much—only butted into the fence."

Ken tried manfully to entertain Worry's idea about it, but he was too dazed and weak to stand alone. He imagined he had broken every bone in his body.

"Did I make the catch—hang to the ball?" he asked.

"No, Peg, you didn't," replied the coach, kindly. "But you made a grand try for it."

He felt worse over failing to hold the ball than he felt over half killing himself against the bleachers. He spent the remainder of that never-to-be-forgotten game sitting on the bench. But to watch his fellow-players try to play was almost as frightful as being back there in right field. It was no consolation for Ken to see his successor chasing long hits, misjudging flies, failing weakly on wicked grounders. Even Graves weakened toward the close and spoiled his good beginning by miserable fumbles and throws. It was complete and disgraceful rout. The varsity never let up until the last man was out. The team could not have played harder against Place or Herne. Arthurs called the game at the end of the sixth inning with the score 41 to 0.

Many beaten and despondent players had dragged themselves off Grant Field in bygone years. But none had ever been so humiliated, so crushed. No player spoke a word or looked at another. They walked off with bowed heads. Ken lagged behind the others; he was still stunned and lame. Presently Arthurs came back to help him along, and did not speak until they were clear of the campus and going down Ken's street.

"I'm glad that's over," said Worry. "I kicked against havin' the game, but 'em fat-head directors would have it. Now we'll be let alone. There won't be no students comin' out to the field, and I'm blamed glad."

Ken was sick and smarting with pain, and half crying.

"I'm sorry, Mr. Arthurs," he faltered, "we were—so—so—rotten!"

"See here, Peg," was the quick reply, "that cuts no ice with me. It was sure the rottenest exhibition I ever seen in my life. But there's excuses, and you can just gamble I'm the old boy who knows. You kids were scared to death. What hurts me, Peg, is the throw-down we got from my old team and from the students. We're not to blame for rules made by fat-head directors. I was surprised at Dale. He was mean, and so were Hollis and Hickle—all of 'em. They didn't need to disgrace us like that."

"Oh, Mr. Arthurs, what players they are!" exclaimed Ken. "I never saw such running, such hitting. You said they'd hit to right field like bullets, but it was worse than bullets. And Dreer!... When he came up my heart just stopped beating."

"Peg, listen," said Worry. "Three years ago when Dreer came out on the field he was greener than you, and hadn't half the spunk. I made him what he is, and I made all of 'em—I made that team, and I can make another."

"You are just saying that to—to encourage me," replied Ken, hopelessly. "I can't play ball. I thought I could, but I know now. I'll never go out on the field again."

"Peg, are you goin' to throw me down, too?"

"Mr. Arthurs! I—I—"

"Listen, Peg. Cut out the dumps. Get over 'em. You made the varsity to-day. Understand? You earned your big W. You needn't mention it, but I've picked you to play somewhere. You weren't a natural infielder, and you didn't make much of a showin' in the outfield. But it's the spirit I want. To-day was a bad day for a youngster. There's always lots of feelin' about college athletics, but here at Wayne this year the strain's awful. And you fought yourself and stage-fright and the ridicule of 'em quitter students. You tried, Peg! I never saw a gamer try. You didn't fail me. And after you made that desperate run and tried to smash the bleachers with your face the students shut up their guyin'. It made a difference, Peg. Even the varsity was a little ashamed. Cheer up, now!"

Ken was almost speechless; he managed to mumble something, at which the coach smiled in reply and then walked rapidly away. Ken limped to his room and took off his baseball suit. The skin had been peeled from his elbow, and his body showed several dark spots that Ken knew would soon be black-and-blue bruises. His legs from his knees down bore huge lumps so sore to the touch that Ken winced even at gentle rubbing. But he did not mind the pain. All the darkness seemed to have blown away from his mind.

"What a fine fellow Worry is!" said Ken. "How I'll work for him! I must write to brother Hal and Dick Leslie, to tell them I've made the varsity.... No, not yet; Worry said not to mention it.... And now to plug. I'll have to take my exams before the first college game, April 8th, and that's not long."

In the succeeding days Ken was very busy with attendance at college in the mornings, baseball practice in the afternoons, and study at night.

If Worry had picked any more players for the varsity, Ken could not tell who they were. Of course Graves would make the team, and Weir and Raymond were pretty sure of places. There were sixteen players for the other five positions, and picking them was only guesswork. It seemed to Ken that some of the players showed streaks of fast playing at times, and then as soon as they were opposed to one another in the practice game they became erratic. His own progress was slow. One thing he could do that brought warm praise from the coach—he could line the ball home from deep outfield with wonderful speed and accuracy.

After the varsity had annihilated Worry's "kids," as they had come to be known, the students showed no further interest. When they ceased to appear on the field the new players were able to go at their practice without being ridiculed. Already an improvement had been noticeable. But rivalry was so keen for places, and the coach's choice so deep a mystery, that the contestants played under too great a tension, and school-boys could have done better.

It was on the first of April that Arthurs took Ken up into College Hall to get permission for him to present himself to the different professors for the early examinations. While Ken sat waiting in the office he heard Arthurs talking to men he instantly took to be the heads of the Athletic Association. They were in an adjoining room with the door open, and their voices were very distinct, so that Ken could not help hearing.

"Gentlemen, I want my answer to-day," said the coach.

"Is there so great a hurry? Wait a little," was the rejoinder.

"I'm sorry, but this is April 1st, and I'll wait no longer. I'm ready to send some of my boys up for early exams, and I want to know where I stand."

"Arthurs, what is it exactly that you want? Things have been in an awful mess, we know. State your case and we'll try to give you a definite answer."

"I want full charge of the coachin'—the handlin' of the team, as I always had before. I don't want any grad coaches. The directors seem divided, one half want this, the other half that. They've cut out the trainin' quarters. I've had no help from Murray; no baths or rub-downs or trainin' for my candidates. Here's openin' day a week off and I haven't picked my team. I want to take them to the trainin'-table and have them under my eye all the time. If I can't have what I want I'll resign. If I can I'll take the whole responsibility of the team on my own shoulders."

"Very well, Arthurs, we'll let you go ahead and have full charge. There has been talk this year of abolishing a private training-house and table for this green varsity. But rather than have you resign we'll waive that. You can rest assured from now on you will not be interfered with. Give us the best team you can under the circumstances. There has been much dissension among the directors and faculty because of our new eligibility rules. It has stirred everybody up, and the students are sore. Then there has been talk of not having a professional coach this year, but we overruled that in last night's meeting. We're going to see what you can do. I may add, Arthurs, if you shape up a varsity this year that makes any kind of a showing against Place and Herne you will win the eternal gratitude of the directors who have fostered this change in athletics. Otherwise I'm afraid the balance of opinion will favor the idea of dispensing with professional coaches in the future."

Ken saw that Arthurs was white in the face when he left the room. They went out together, and Worry handed Ken a card that read for him to take his examinations at once.

"Are you up on 'em?" asked the coach, anxiously.

"I—I think so," replied Ken.

"Well, Peg, good luck to you! Go at 'em like you went at Dreer's hit."

Much to his amazement it was for Ken to discover that, now the time had come for him to face his examinations, he was not at all sanguine. He began to worry. He forgot about the text-books he had mastered in his room during the long winter when he feared to venture out because of the sophomores. It was not very long till he had worked himself into a state somewhat akin to his trepidation in the varsity ball game. Then he decided to go up at once and have it done with. His whole freshman year had been one long agony. What a relief to have it ended!

Ken passed four examinations in one morning, passed them swimmingly, smilingly, splendidly, and left College Hall in an ecstasy. Things were working out fine. But he had another examination, and it was in a subject he had voluntarily included in his course. Whatever on earth he had done it for he could not now tell. The old doctor who held the chair in that department had thirty years before earned the name of Crab. And slowly in the succeeding years he had grown crabbier, crustier, so student rumor had it. Ken had rather liked the dry old fellow, and had been much absorbed in his complex lectures, but he had never been near him, and now the prospect changed color. Foolishly Ken asked a sophomore in what light old Crab might regard a student who was ambitious to pass his exams early. The picture painted by that sophomore would have made a flaming-mouthed dragon appear tame. Nerving himself to the ordeal, Ken took his card and presented himself one evening at the doctor's house.

A maid ushered him into the presence of a venerable old man who did not look at all, even in Ken's distorted sight, like a crab or a dragon. His ponderous brow seemed as if it had all the thought in the world behind it. He looked over huge spectacles at Ken's card and then spoke in a dry, quavering voice.

"Um-m. Sit down, Mr. Ward."

Ken found his breath and strangely lost his fear and trembling. The doctor dryly asked him why he thought he knew more than the other students, who were satisfied to wait months longer before examination. Ken hastened to explain that it was no desire of his; that, although he had studied hard and had not missed many lectures, he knew he was unprepared. Then he went on to tell about the baseball situation and why he had been sent up.

"Um-m." The professor held a glass paperweight up before Ken and asked a question about it. Next he held out a ruler and asked something about that, and also a bottle of ink. Following this he put a few queries about specific gravity, atomic weight, and the like. Then he sat thrumming his desk and appeared far away in thought. After a while he turned to Ken with a smile that made his withered, parchment-like face vastly different.

"Where do you play?" he asked.

"S-sir?" stammered Ken.

"In baseball, I mean. What place do you play? Catch? Thrower? I don't know the names much."

Ken replied eagerly, and then it seemed he was telling this stern old man all about baseball. He wanted to know what fouls were, and how to steal bases, and he was nonplussed by such terms as "hit-and-run." Ken discoursed eloquently on his favorite sport, and it was like a kind of dream to be there. Strange things were always happening to him.

"I've never seen a game," said the professor. "I used to play myself long ago, when we had a yarn ball and pitched underhand. I'll have to come out to the field some day. President Halstead, why, he likes baseball, he's a—a—what do you call it?"

"A fan—a rooter?" replied Ken, smiling.

"Um-m. I guess that's it. Well, Mr. Ward, I'm glad to meet you. You may go now."

Ken got up blushing like a girl. "But, Doctor, you were to—I was to be examined."

"I've examined you," he drawled, with a dry chuckle, and he looked over his huge spectacles at Ken. "I'll give you a passing mark. But, Mr. Ward, you know a heap more about baseball than you know about physics."

As Ken went out he trod upon air. What a splendid old fellow! The sophomore had lied. For that matter, when had a sophomore ever been known to tell the truth? But, he suddenly exclaimed, he himself was no longer a freshman. He pondered happily on the rosy lining to his old cloud of gloom. How different things appeared after a little time. That old doctor's smile would linger long in Ken's memory. He felt deep remorse that he had ever misjudged him. He hurried on to Worry Arthurs' house to tell him the good news. And as he walked his mind was full with the wonder of it all—his lonely, wretched freshman days, now forever past; the slow change from hatred; the dawning of some strange feeling for the college and his teachers; and, last, the freedom, the delight, the quickening stir in the present.

President Halstead on College Spirit

Wayne's opening game was not at all what Ken had dreamed it would be. The opposing team from Hudson School was as ill-assorted an aggregation as Ken had ever seen. They brought with them a small but noisy company of cheering supporters who, to the shame of Ken and his fellows, had the bleachers all to themselves. If any Wayne students were present they either cheered for Hudson or remained silent.

Hudson won, 9 to 2. It was a game that made Arthurs sag a little lower on the bench. Graves got Wayne's two tallies. Raymond at second played about all the game from the fielding standpoint. Ken distinguished himself by trying wildly and accomplishing nothing. When he went to his room that night he had switched back to his former spirits, and was disgusted with Wayne's ball team, himself most of all.

That was on a Wednesday. The next day rain prevented practice, and on Friday the boys were out on the field again. Arthurs shifted the players around, trying resignedly to discover certain positions that might fit certain players. It seemed to Ken that all the candidates, except one or two, were good at fielding and throwing, but when they came to play a game they immediately went into a trance.

Travers College was scheduled for Saturday. They had always turned out a good minor team, but had never been known to beat Wayne. They shut Arthurs' team out without a run. A handful of Wayne students sat in the bleachers mocking their own team. Arthurs used the two pitchers he had been trying hard to develop, and when they did locate the plate they were hit hard. Ken played or essayed to play right field for a while, but he ran around like a chicken with its head off, as a Travers player expressed it, and then Arthurs told him that he had better grace the bench the rest of the game. Ashamed as Ken was to be put out, he was yet more ashamed to feel that he was glad of it. Hardest of all to bear was the arrogant air put on by the Travers College players. Wayne had indeed been relegated to the fifth rank of college baseball teams.

On Monday announcements were made in all the lecture-rooms and departments of the university, and bulletins were posted to the effect, that President Halstead wished to address the undergraduates in the Wayne auditorium on Tuesday at five o'clock.

Rumor flew about the campus and Carlton Club, everywhere, that the president's subject would be "College Spirit," and it was believed he would have something to say about the present condition of athletics. Ken Ward hurried to the hall as soon as he got through his practice. He found the immense auditorium packed from pit to dome, and he squeezed into a seat on the steps.

The students, as always, were exchanging volleys of paper-balls, matching wits, singing songs, and passing time merrily. When President Halstead entered, with two of his associates, he was greeted by a thunder of tongues, hands, and heels of the standing students. He was the best-beloved member of the university faculty, a distinguished, scholarly looking man, well-stricken in years.

He opened his address by declaring the need of college spirit in college life. He defined it as the vital thing, the heart of a great educational institution, and he went on to speak of its dangers, its fluctuations. Then he made direct reference to athletics in its relation to both college spirit and college life.

"Sport is too much with us. Of late years I have observed a great increase in the number of athletic students, and a great decrease in scholarship. The fame of the half-back and the short-stop and the stroke-oar has grown out of proportion to their real worth. The freshman is dazzled by it. The great majority of college men cannot shine in sport, which is the best thing that could be. The student's ideal, instead of being the highest scholarship, the best attainment for his career, is apt to be influenced by the honors and friendships that are heaped upon the great athlete. This is false to university life. You are here to prepare yourselves for the battle with the world, and I want to state that that battle is becoming more and more intellectual. The student who slights his studies for athletic glory may find himself, when that glory is long past, distanced in the race for success by a student who had not trained to run the hundred in ten seconds.

"But, gentlemen, to keep well up in your studies and then go in for athletics—that is entirely another question. It is not likely that any student who keeps to the front in any of the university courses will have too much time for football or baseball. I am, as you all know, heartily in favor of all branches of college sport. And that brings me to the point I want to make to-day. Baseball is my favorite game, and I have always been proud of Wayne's teams. The new eligibility rules, with which you are all familiar, were brought to me, and after thoroughly going over the situation I approved of them. Certainly it is obvious to you all that a university ball-player making himself famous here, and then playing during the summer months at a resort, is laying himself open to suspicion. I have no doubt that many players are innocent of the taint of professionalism, but unfortunately they have become members of these summer teams after being first requested, then warned, not to do so.

"Wayne's varsity players of last year have been barred by the directors. They made their choice, and so should abide by it. They have had their day, and so should welcome the opportunity of younger players. But I am constrained to acknowledge that neither they nor the great body of undergraduates welcomed the change. This, more than anything, proves to me the evil of championship teams. The football men, the baseball men, the crew men, and all the student supporters want to win all the games all the time. I would like to ask you young gentlemen if you can take a beating? If you cannot, I would like to add that you are not yet fitted to go out into life. A good beating, occasionally, is a wholesome thing.

"Well, to come to the point now: I find, after studying the situation, that the old varsity players and undergraduates of this university have been lacking in—let us be generous and say, college spirit. I do not need to go into detail; suffice it to say that I know. I will admit, however, that I attended the game between the old varsity and the new candidates. I sat unobserved in a corner, and a more unhappy time I never spent in this university. I confess that my sympathies were with the inexperienced, undeveloped boys who were trying to learn to play ball. Put yourselves in their places. Say you are mostly freshmen, and you make yourselves candidates for the team because you love the game, and because you would love to bring honor to your college. You go out and try. You meet, the first day, an implacable team of skilled veterans who show their scorn of your poor ability, their hatred of your opportunity, and ride roughshod—I should say, run with spiked shoes—over you. You hear the roar of four thousand students applauding these hero veterans. You hear your classmates, your fellow-students in Wayne, howl with ridicule at your weak attempts to compete with better, stronger players.... Gentlemen, how would you feel?

"I said before that college spirit fluctuates. If I did not know students well I would be deeply grieved at the spirit shown that day. I know that the tide will turn.... And, gentlemen, would not you and the old varsity be rather in an embarrassing position if—if these raw recruits should happen to develop into a team strong enough to cope with Place and Herne? Stranger things have happened. I am rather strong for the new players, not because of their playing, which is poor indeed, but for the way they tried under peculiarly adverse conditions.

"That young fellow Ward—what torture that inning of successive hard hits to his territory! I was near him in that end of the bleachers, and I watched him closely. Every attempt he made was a failure—that is, failure from the point of view of properly fielding the ball. But, gentlemen, that day was not a failure for young Ward. It was a grand success. Some one said his playing was the poorest exhibition ever seen on Grant Field. That may be. I want to say that to my mind it was also the most splendid effort ever made on Grant Field. For it was made against defeat, fear, ridicule. It was elimination of self. It was made for his coach, his fellow-players, his college— that is to say, for the students who shamed themselves by scorn for his trial.

"Young men of Wayne, give us a little more of such college spirit!"

New Players

When practice time rolled around for Ken next day, he went upon the field once more with his hopes renewed and bright.

"I certainly do die hard," he laughed to himself. "But I can never go down and out now—never!"

Something seemed to ring in Ken's ears like peals of bells. In spite of his awkwardness Coach Arthurs had made him a varsity man; in spite of his unpreparedness old Crab had given him a passing mark; in spite of his unworthiness President Halstead had made him famous.

"I surely am the lucky one," said Ken, for the hundredth time. "And now I'm going to force my luck." Ken had lately revolved in his mind a persistent idea that he meant to propound to the coach.

Ken arrived on the field a little later than usual, to find Arthurs for once minus his worried look. He was actually smiling, and Ken soon saw the reason for this remarkable change was the presence of a new player out in centre field.

"Hello, Peg! things are lookin' up," said the coach, beaming. "That's Homans out there in centre—Roy Homans, a senior and a crackerjack ball-player. I tried to get him to come out for the team last year, but he wouldn't spare the time. But he's goin' to play this season—said the president's little talk got him. He's a fast, heady, scientific player, just the one to steady you kids."

Before Ken could reply his attention was attracted from Homans to another new player in uniform now walking up to Arthurs. He was tall, graceful, powerful, had red hair, keen dark eyes, a clean-cut profile and square jaw.

"I've come out to try for the team," he said, quietly, to the coach.

"You're a little late, ain't you?" asked Worry, gruffly; but he ran a shrewd glance over the lithe form.

"Yes."

"Must have been stirred up by that talk of President Halstead's, wasn't you?"

"Yes." There was something quiet and easy about the stranger, and Ken liked him at once.

"Where do you play?" went on Worry.

"Left."

"Can you hit? Talk sense now, and mebbe you'll save me work. Can you hit?"

"Yes."

"Can you throw?"

"Yes." He spoke with quiet assurance.

"Can you run?" almost shouted Worry. He was nervous and irritable those days, and it annoyed him for unknown youths to speak calmly of such things.

"Run? Yes, a little. I did the hundred last year in nine and four-fifths."

"What! You can't kid me! Who are you?" cried Worry, getting red in the face. "I've seen you somewhere."

"My name's Ray."

"Say! Not Ray, the intercollegiate champion?"

45

"I'm the fellow. I talked it over with Murray. He kicked, but I didn't mind that. I promised to try to keep in shape to win the sprints at the intercollegiate meet."

"Say! Get out there in left field! Quick!" shouted Worry.... "Peg, hit him some flies. Lam 'em a mile! That fellow's a sprinter, Peg. What luck it would be if he can play ball! Hit 'em at him!"

Ken took the ball Worry tossed him, and, picking up a bat, began to knock flies out to Ray. The first few he made easy for the outfielder, and then he hit balls harder and off to the right or left. Without appearing to exert himself Ray got under them. Ken watched him, and also kept the tail of his eye on Worry. The coach appeared to be getting excited, and he ordered Ken to hit the balls high and far away. Ken complied, but he could not hit a ball over Ray's head. He tried with all his strength. He had never seen a champion sprinter, and now he marvelled at the wonderful stride.

"Oh! but his running is beautiful!" exclaimed Ken.

"That's enough! Come in here!" yelled Worry to Ray.... "Peg, he makes Dreer look slow. I never saw as fast fieldin' as that."

When Ray came trotting in without seeming to be even warmed up, Worry blurted out: "You ain't winded—after all that? Must be in shape?"

"I'm always in shape," replied Ray.

"Pick up a bat!" shouted Worry. "Here, Duncan, pitch this fellow a few. Speed 'em, curve 'em, strike him out, hit him—anything!"

Ray was left-handed, and he stood up to the plate perfectly erect, with his bat resting quietly on his shoulder. He stepped straight, swung with an even, powerful swing, and he hit the first ball clear over the right-field bleachers. It greatly distanced Dreer's hit.

"What a drive!" gasped Ken.

"Oh!" choked Worry. "That's enough! You needn't lose my balls. Bunt one, now."

Ray took the same position, and as the ball came up he appeared to drop the bat upon it and dart away at the same instant.

Worry seemed to be trying to control violent emotion. "Next batter up!" he called, hoarsely, and sat down on the bench. He was breathing hard, and beads of sweat stood out on his brow.

Ken went up to Worry, feeling that now was the time to acquaint the coach with his new idea. Eager as Ken was he had to force himself to take this step. All the hope and dread, nervousness and determination of the weeks of practice seemed to accumulate in that moment. He stammered and stuttered, grew speechless, and then as Worry looked up in kind surprise, Ken suddenly grew cool and earnest.

"Mr. Arthurs, will you try me in the box?"

"What's that, Peg?" queried the coach, sharply.

"Will you give me a trial in the box? I've wanted one all along. You put me in once when we were in the cage, but you made me hit the batters."

"Pitch? you, Peg? Why not? Why didn't I think of it? I'm sure gettin' to be like 'em fat-head directors. You've got steam, Peg, but can you curve a ball? Let's see your fingers."

"Yes, I can curve a ball round a corner. Please give me a trial, Mr. Arthurs. I failed in the infield, and I'm little good in the outfield. But I know I can pitch."

The coach gave Ken one searching glance. Then he called all the candidates in to the plate, and ordered Dean, the stocky little catcher, to don his breast-protector, mask, and mitt.

"Peg," said the coach, "Dean will sign you—one finger for a straight ball, two for a curve."

When Ken walked to the box all his muscles seemed quivering and tense, and he had a contraction in his throat. This was his opportunity. He was not unnerved as he had been when he was trying for the other positions. All Ken's life he had been accustomed to throwing. At his home he had been the only boy who could throw a stone across the river; the only one who could get a ball over the high-school tower. A favorite pastime had always been the throwing of small apples, or walnuts, or stones, and he had acquired an accuracy that made it futile for his boy comrades to compete with him. Curving a ball had come natural to him, and he would have pitched all his high-school games had it not been for the fact that no one could catch him, and, moreover, none of the boys had found any fun in batting against him.

When Ken faced the first batter a feeling came over him that he had never before had on the ball field. He was hot, trembling, hurried, but this new feeling was apart from these. His feet were on solid ground, and his arm felt as it had always in those throwing contests where he had so easily won. He seemed to decide from McCord's position at the plate what to throw him.

Ken took his swing. It was slow, easy, natural. But the ball travelled with much greater speed than the batter expected from such motion. McCord let the first two balls go by, and Arthurs called them both strikes. Then Ken pitched an out-curve which McCord fanned at helplessly. Arthurs sent Trace up next. Ken saw that the coach was sending up the weaker hitters first. Trace could not even make a foul. Raymond was third up, and Ken had to smile at the scowling second-baseman. Remembering his weakness for pulling away from the plate, Ken threw Raymond two fast curves on the outside, and then a slow wide curve, far out. Raymond could not have hit the first two with a paddle, and the third lured him irresistibly out of position and made him look ridiculous. He slammed his bat down and slouched to the bench. Duncan turned out to be the next easy victim. Four batters had not so much as fouled Ken. And Ken knew he was holding himself in—that, in fact, he had not let out half his speed. Blake, the next player, hit up a little fly that Ken caught, and Schoonover made the fifth man to strike out.

Then Weir stood over the plate, and he was a short, sturdy batter, hard to pitch to. He looked as if he might be able to hit any kind of a ball. Ken tried him first with a straight fast one over the middle of the plate. Weir hit it hard, but it went foul. And through Ken's mind flashed the thought that he would pitch no more speed to Weir or players who swung as he did. Accordingly Ken tried the slow curve that had baffled Raymond. Weir popped it up and retired in disgust.

The following batter was Graves, who strode up smiling, confident, sarcastic, as if he knew he could do more than the others. Ken imagined what the third-baseman would have said if the coach had not been present. Graves always ruffled Ken the wrong way.

"I'll strike him out if I break my arm!" muttered Ken to himself. He faced Graves deliberately and eyed his position at bat. Graves as deliberately laughed at him.

"Pitch up, pitch up!" he called out.

"Right over the pan!" retorted Ken, as quick as an echo. He went hot as fire all over. This fellow Graves had some strange power of infuriating him.

Ken took a different swing, which got more of his weight in motion, and let his arm out. Like a white bullet the ball shot plateward, rising a little so that Graves hit vainly under it. The ball surprised Dean, knocked his hands apart as if they had been paper, and resounded from his breast-protector. Ken pitched the second ball in the same place with a like result, except that

Dean held on to it. Graves had lost his smile and wore an expression of sickly surprise. The third ball travelled by him and cracked in Dean's mitt, and Arthurs called it a strike.

"Easy there—that'll do!" yelled the coach. "Come in here, Peg. Out on the field now, boys."

Homans stopped Ken as they were passing each other, and Ken felt himself under the scrutiny of clear gray eyes.

"Youngster, you look good to me," said Homans.

Ken also felt himself regarded with astonishment by many of the candidates; and Ray ran a keen, intuitive glance over him from head to foot. But it was the coach's manner that struck Ken most forcibly. Worry was utterly unlike himself.

"Why didn't you tell me about this before—you—you—" he yelled, red as a beet in the face. He grasped Ken with both hands, then he let him go, and picking up a ball and a mitt he grasped him again. Without a word he led Ken across the field and to a secluded corner behind the bleachers. Ken felt for all the world as if he was being led to execution.

Worry took off his coat and vest and collar. He arranged a block of wood for a plate and stepped off so many paces and placed another piece of wood to mark the pitcher's box. Then he donned the mitt.

"Peg, somethin's comin' off. I know it. I never make mistakes in sizin' up pitchers. But I've had such hard luck this season that I can't believe my own eyes. We've got to prove it. Now you go out there and pitch to me. Just natural like at first."

Ken pitched a dozen balls or more, some in-curves, some out-curves. Then he threw what he called his drop, which he executed by a straight overhand swing.

"Oh—a beauty!" yelled Worry. "Where, Peg, where did you learn that? Another, lower now."

Worry fell over trying to stop the glancing drop.

"Try straight ones now, Peg, right over the middle. See how many you can pitch."

One after another, with free, easy motion, Ken shot balls squarely over the plate. Worry counted them, and suddenly, after the fourteenth pitch, he stood up and glared at Ken.

"Are you goin' to keep puttin' 'em over this pan all day that way?"

"Mr. Arthurs, I couldn't miss that plate if I pitched a week," replied Ken.

"Stop callin' me Mister!" yelled Worry. "Now, put 'em where I hold my hands—inside corner... outside corner... again... inside now, low... another... a fast one over, now... high, inside. Oh, Peg, this ain't right. I ain't seein' straight. I think I'm dreamin'. Come on with 'em!"

Fast and true Ken sped the balls into Worry's mitt. Seldom did the coach have to move his hands at all.

"Peg Ward, did you know that pitchin' was all control, puttin' the ball where you wanted to?" asked Worry, stopping once more.

"No, I didn't," replied Ken.

"How did you learn to peg a ball as straight as this?"

Ken told him how he had thrown at marks all his life.

"Why didn't you tell me before?" Worry seemed not to be able to get over Ken's backwardness. "Look at the sleepless nights and the gray hairs you could have saved me." He stamped around as if furious, yet underneath the surface Ken saw that the coach was trying to hide his elation. "Here now," he shouted, suddenly, "a few more, and peg 'em! See? Cut loose and let me see what steam you've got!"

Ken whirled with all his might and delivered the ball with all his weight in the swing. The ball seemed to diminish in size, it went so swiftly. Near the plate it took an upward jump, and it knocked Worry's mitt off his hand.

Worry yelled out, then he looked carefully at Ken, but he made no effort to go after the ball or pick up the mitt.

"Did I say for you to knock my block off?... Come here, Peg. You're only a youngster. Do you think you can keep that? Are you goin' to let me teach you to pitch? Have you got any nerve? Are you up in the air at the thought of Place and Herne?"

Then he actually hugged Ken, and kept hold of him as if he might get away. He was panting and sweating. All at once he sat down on one of the braces of the bleachers and began mopping his face. He seemed to cool down, to undergo a subtle change.

"Peg," he said, quietly, "I'm as bad as some of 'em fat-head directors.... You see I didn't have no kind of a pitcher to work on this spring. I kept on hopin'. Strange why I didn't quit. And now—my boy, you're a kid, but you're a natural born pitcher."

State University Game

Arthurs returned to the diamond and called the squad around him. He might have been another coach from the change that was manifest in him.

"Boys, I've picked the varsity, and sorry I am to say you all can't be on it. Ward, Dean, McCord, Raymond, Weir, Graves, Ray, Homans, Trace, Duncan, and Schoonover—these men will report at once to Trainer Murray and obey his orders. Then pack your trunks and report to me at 36 Spring Street to-night. That's all—up on your toes now.... The rest of you boys will each get his uniform and sweater, but, of course, I can't give you the varsity letter. You've all tried hard and done your best. I'm much obliged to you, and hope you'll try again next year."

Led by Arthurs, the players trotted across the field to Murray's quarters. Ken used all his eyes as he went in. This was the sacred precinct of the chosen athletes, and it was not open to any others. He saw a small gymnasium, and adjoining it a large, bright room with painted windows that let in the light, but could not be seen through. Around the room on two sides were arranged huge box-like bins with holes in the lids and behind them along the wall were steam-pipes. On the other two sides were little zinc-lined rooms, with different kinds of pipes, which Ken concluded were used for shower baths. Murray, the trainer, was there, and two grinning negroes with towels over their shoulders, and a little dried-up Scotchman who was all one smile.

"Murray, here's my bunch. Look 'em over, and to-morrow start 'em in for keeps," said Arthurs.

"Well, Worry, they're not a bad-looking lot. Slim and trim. We won't have to take off any beef. Here's Reddy Ray. I let you have him this year, Worry, but the track team will miss him. And here's Peg Ward. I was sure you'd pick him, Worry. And this is Homans, isn't it? I remember you in the freshmen games. The rest of you boys I'll have to get acquainted with. They say I'm a pretty hard fellow, but that's on the outside. Now, hustle out of your suits, and we'll give you all a good stew and a rub-down."

What the stew was soon appeared plain to Ken. He was the first player undressed, and Murray, lifting up one of the box-lids, pushed Ken inside.

"Sit down and put your feet in that pan," he directed. "When I drop the lid let your head come out the hole. There!" Then he wrapped a huge towel around Ken's neck, being careful to tuck it close and tight. With that he reached round to the back of the box and turned on the steam.

Ken felt like a jack-in-the-box. The warm steam was pleasant. He looked about him to see the other boys being placed in like positions. Raymond had the box on one side, and Reddy Ray the one on the other.

"It's great," said Ray, smiling at Ken. "You'll like it."

Raymond looked scared. Ken wondered if the fellow ever got any enjoyment out of things. Then Ken found himself attending to his own sensations. The steam was pouring out of the pipe inside the box, and it was growing wetter, thicker, and hotter. The pleasant warmth and tickling changed to a burning sensation. Ken found himself bathed in a heavy sweat. Then he began to smart in different places, and he was hard put to it to keep rubbing them. The steam grew hotter; his body was afire; his breath labored in great heaves. Ken felt that he must cry out. He heard exclamations, then yells, from some of the other boxed-up players, and he glanced quickly around. Reddy Ray was smiling, and did not look at all uncomfortable. But Raymond was scarlet in the face, and he squirmed his head to and fro.

"Ough!" he bawled. "Let me out of here!"

One of the negro attendants lifted the lid and helped Raymond out. He danced about as if on hot bricks. His body was the color of a boiled lobster. The attendant put him under one of the showers and turned the water on. Raymond uttered one deep, low, "O-o-o-o!" Then McCord begged to be let out; Weir's big head, with its shock of hair, resembled that of an angry lion; little Trace screamed, and Duncan yelled.

"Peg, how're you?" asked Murray, walking up to Ken. "It's always pretty hot the first few times. But afterward it's fine. Look at Reddy."

"Murray, give Peg a good stewin'," put in Arthurs. "He's got a great arm, and we must take care of it."

Ken saw the other boys, except Ray, let out, and he simply could not endure the steam any longer.

"I've got—enough," he stammered.

"Scotty, turn on a little more stew," ordered Murray, cheerfully; then he rubbed his hand over Ken's face. "You're not hot yet."

Scotty turned on more steam, and Ken felt it as a wet flame. He was being flayed alive.

"Please—please—let me out!" he implored.

With a laugh Murray lifted the lid, and Ken hopped out. He was as red as anything red he had ever seen. Then Scotty shoved him under a shower, and as the icy water came down in a deluge Ken lost his breath, his chest caved in, and he gasped. Scotty led him out into the room, dried him with a towel, rubbed him down, and then, resting Ken's arm on his shoulder, began to pat and beat and massage it. In a few moments Ken thought his arm was a piece of live India rubber. He had never been in such a glow. When he had dressed he felt as light as air, strong, fresh, and keen for action.

"Hustle now, Peg," said Arthurs. "Get your things packed. Supper to-night at the trainin'-house."

It was after dark when Ken got an expressman to haul his trunk to the address on Spring Street. The house was situated about the middle of a four-storied block, and within sight of Grant Field. Worry answered his ring.

"Here you are, Peg, the last one. I was beginnin' to worry about you. Have your trunk taken right up, third floor back. Hurry down, for dinner will be ready soon."

Ken followed at the heels of the expressman up to his room. He was surprised and somewhat taken back to find Raymond sitting upon the bed.

"Hello! excuse me," said Ken. "Guess I've got the wrong place."

"The coach said you and I were to room together," returned Raymond.

"Us? Room-mates?" ejaculated Ken.

Raymond took offence at this.

"Wull, I guess I can stand it," he growled.

"I hope I can," was Ken's short reply. It was Ken's failing that he could not help retaliating. But he was also as repentant as he was quick-tempered. "Oh, I didn't mean that.... See here, Raymond, if we've got to be room-mates—"

Ken paused in embarrassment.

"Wull, we're both on the varsity," said Raymond.

"That's so," rejoined Ken, brightening. "It makes a whole lot of difference, doesn't it?"

Raymond got off the bed and looked at Ken.

"What's your first name?" queried he. "I don't like 'Peg.'"

"Kenneth. Ken, for short. What's yours?"

"Mine's Kel. Wull, Ken—"

Having gotten so far Raymond hesitated, and it was Ken who first offered his hand. Raymond eagerly grasped it. That broke the ice.

"Kel, I haven't liked your looks at all," said Ken, apologetically.

"Ken, I've been going to lick you all spring."

They went down-stairs arm in arm.

It was with great interest and curiosity that Ken looked about the cozy and comfortable rooms. The walls were adorned with pictures of varsity teams and players, and the college colors were much in evidence. College magazines and papers littered the table in the reading-room.

"Boys, we'll be pretty snug and nice here when things get to runnin' smooth. The grub will be plain, but plenty of it."

There were twelve in all at the table, with the coach seated at the head. The boys were hungry, and besides, as they had as yet had no chance to become acquainted, the conversation lagged. The newness and strangeness, however, did not hide the general air of suppressed gratification. After dinner Worry called them all together in the reading-room.

"Well, boys, here we are together like one big family, and we're shut in for two months. Now, I know you've all been fightin' for places on the team, and have had no chance to be friendly. It's always that way in the beginnin', and I dare say there'll be some scraps among you before things straighten out. We'll have more to say about that later. The thing now is you're all varsity men, and I'm puttin' you on your word of honor. Your word is good enough for me. Here's my rules, and I'm more than usually particular this year, for reasons I'll tell later.

"You're not to break trainin'. You're not to eat anything anywhere but here. You're to cut out cigarettes and drinks. You're to be in bed at ten o'clock. And I advise, although I ain't insistin', that if you have any leisure time you'll spend most of it here. That's all."

For Ken the three days following passed as so many hours. He did not in the least dread the approaching game with State University, but his mind held scarcely anything outside of Arthurs' coaching. The practice of the players had been wholly different. It was as if they had been freed from some binding spell. Worry kept them at fielding and batting for four full hours every afternoon. Ken, after pitching to Dean for a while, batted to the infield and so had opportunity to see the improvement. Graves was brilliant at third, Weir was steady and sure at short, Raymond seemed to have springs in his legs and pounced upon the ball with wonderful quickness, and McCord fielded all his chances successfully.

On the afternoon of the game Worry waited at the training-house until all the players came down-stairs in uniform.

"Boys, what's happened in the past doesn't count. We start over to-day. I'm not goin' to say much or confuse you with complex team coachin'. But I'm hopeful. I sort of think there's a nigger in the woodpile. I'll tell you to-night if I'm right. Think of how you have been roasted by the students. Play like tigers. Put out of your mind everything but tryin'. Nothin' counts for you, boys. Errors are nothin'; mistakes are nothin'. Play the game as one man. Don't think of yourselves. You all know when you ought to hit or bunt or run. I'm trustin' you. I won't say a word from the bench. And don't underrate our chances. Remember that I think it's possible we may have somethin' up our sleeves. That's all from me till after the game."

Worry walked to Grant Field with Ken. He talked as they went along, but not on baseball. The State team was already out and practising. Worry kept Ken near him on the bench and closely watched the visitors in practice. When the gong rang to call them in he sent his players out, with a remark to Ken to take his warming-up easily. Ken thought he had hardly warmed up at all before the coach called him in.

"Peg, listen!" he whispered. His gaze seemed to hypnotize Ken. "Do you have any idea what you'll do to this bunch from State?"

"Why—no—I—"

"Listen! I tell you I know they won't be able to touch you.... Size up batters in your own way. If they look as if they'd pull or chop on a curve, hand it up. If not, peg 'em a straight one over the inside corner, high. If you get in a hole with runners on bases use that fast jump ball, as hard as you can drive it, right over the pan.... Go in with perfect confidence. I wouldn't say that to you, Peg, if I didn't feel it myself, honestly. I'd say for you to do your best. But I've sized up these State fellows, and they won't be able to touch you. Remember what I say. That's all."

"I'll remember," said Ken, soberly.

When the umpire called the game there were perhaps fifty students in the bleachers and a few spectators in the grand-stand, so poor an attendance that the State players loudly voiced their derision.

"Hey! boys," yelled one, "we drew a crowd last year, and look at that!"

"It's Wayne's dub team," replied another. They ran upon the field as if the result of the game was a foregone conclusion. Their pitcher, a lanky individual, handled the ball with assurance.

Homans led off for Wayne. He stood left-handed at the plate, and held his bat almost in the middle. He did not swing, but poked at the first ball pitched and placed a short hit over third. Raymond, also left-handed, came next, and, letting two balls go, he bunted the third. Running fast, he slid into first base and beat the throw. Homans kept swiftly on toward third, drew the throw, and, sliding, was also safe. It was fast work, and the Wayne players seemed to rise off the bench with the significance of the play. Worry Arthurs looked on from under the brim of his hat, and spoke no word. Then Reddy Ray stepped up.

"They're all left-handed!" shouted a State player. The pitcher looked at Reddy, then motioned for his outfielders to play deeper. With that he delivered the ball, which the umpire called a strike. Reddy stood still and straight while two more balls sped by, then he swung on the next. A vicious low hit cut out over first base and skipped in great bounds to the fence. Homans scored. Raymond turned second, going fast. But it was Ray's speed that electrified the watching players. They jumped up cheering.

"Oh, see him run!" yelled Ken.

He was on third before Raymond reached the plate. Weir lifted a high fly to left field, and when the ball dropped into the fielder's hands Ray ran home on the throw-in. Three runs had been scored in a twinkling. It amazed the State team. They were not slow in bandying remarks among themselves. "Fast! Who's that red-head? Is this your dub team? Get in the game, boys!" They began to think more of playing ball and less of their own superiority. Graves, however, and McCord following him, went out upon plays to the infield.

As Ken walked out toward the pitcher's box Homans put a hand on his arm, and said: "Kid, put them all over. Don't waste any. Make every batter hit. Keep your nerve. We're back of you out here." Then Reddy Ray, in passing, spoke with a cool, quiet faith that thrilled Ken, "Peg, we've got enough runs now to win."

Ken faced the plate all in a white glow. He was far from calmness, but it was a restless, fiery hurry for the action of the game. He remembered the look in Worry's eyes, and every word that he had spoken rang in his ears. Receiving the ball from the umpire, he stepped upon the slab with a sudden, strange, deep tremor. It passed as quickly, and then he was eying the first batter. He drew a long breath, standing motionless, with all the significance of Worry's hope flashing before him, and then he whirled and delivered the ball. The batter struck at it after it had passed him, and it cracked in Dean's mitt.

"Speed!" called the State captain. "Quick eye, there!"

The batter growled some unintelligible reply. Then he fouled the second ball, missed the next, and was out. The succeeding State player hit an easy fly to Homans, and the next had two strikes called upon him, and swung vainly at the third.

Dean got a base on balls for Wayne, Trace went out trying to bunt, and Ken hit into short, forcing Dean at second. Homans lined to third, retiring the side. The best that the State players could do in their half was for one man to send a weak grounder to Raymond, one to fly out, and the other to fail on strikes. Wayne went to bat again, and Raymond got his base by being hit by a pitched ball. Reddy Ray bunted and was safe. Weir struck out. Graves rapped a safety through short, scoring Raymond, and sending Ray to third. Then McCord fouled out to the catcher. Again, in State's inning, they failed to get on base, being unable to hit Ken effectively.

So the game progressed, State slowly losing its aggressive playing, and Wayne gaining what its opponents had lost. In the sixth Homans reached his base on an error, stole second, went to third on Raymond's sacrifice, and scored on Reddy's drive to right. State flashed up in their half, getting two men to first on misplays of McCord and Weir, and scored a run on a slow hit to Graves.

With the bases full, Ken let his arm out and pitched the fast ball at the limit of his speed. The State batters were helpless before it, but they scored two runs on passed strikes by Dean. The little catcher had a hard time judging Ken's jump ball. That ended the run-getting for State, though they came near scoring again on more fumbling in the infield. In the eighth Ken landed a safe fly over second, and tallied on a double by Homans.

Before Ken knew the game was half over it had ended—Wayne 6, State 3. His players crowded around him and some one called for the Wayne yell. It was given with wild vehemence.

From that moment until dinner was over at the training-house Ken appeared to be the centre of a humming circle. What was said and done he never remembered. Then the coach stopped the excitement.

"Boys, now for a heart-to-heart talk," he said, with a smile both happy and grave. "We won to-day, as I predicted. State had a fairly strong team, but if Ward had received perfect support they would not have got a man beyond second. That's the only personal mention I'll make. Now, listen...."

He paused, with his eyes glinting brightly and his jaw quivering.

"I expected to win, but before the game I never dreamed of our possibilities. I got a glimpse now of what hard work and a demon spirit to play together might make this team. I've had an inspiration. We are goin' to beat Herne and play Place to a standstill."

Not a boy moved an eyelash as Arthurs made this statement, and the sound of a pin dropping could have been heard.

"To do that we must pull together as no boys ever pulled together before. We must be all one heart. We must be actuated by one spirit. Listen! If you will stick together and to me, I'll make a team that will be a wonder. Never the hittin' team as good as last year's varsity, but a faster team, a finer machine. Think of that! Think of how we have been treated this year! For that we'll win all the greater glory. It's worth all there is in you, boys. You would have the proudest record of any team that ever played for old Wayne.

"I love the old college, boys, and I've given it the best years of my life. If it's anything to you, why, understand that if I fail to build up a good team this year I shall be let go by those directors who have made the change in athletics. I could stand that, but—I've a boy of my own who's preparin' for Wayne, and my heart is set on seein' him enter—and he said he never will if they let me go. So, you youngsters and me—we've much to gain. Go to your rooms now and think, think as you never did before, until the spirit of this thing, the possibility of it, grips you as it has me."

Ken Clashes with Graves

Two weeks after the contest with State University four more games with minor colleges had been played and won by Wayne. Hour by hour the coach had drilled the players; day by day the grilling practice told in quickening grasp of team-play, in gradual correction of erratic fielding and wild throwing. Every game a few more students attended, reluctantly, in half-hearted manner.

"We're comin' with a rush," said Worry to Ken. "Say, but Dale and the old gang have a surprise in store for 'em! And the students—they're goin' to drop dead pretty soon.... Peg, Murray tells me he's puttin' weight on you."

"Why, yes, it's the funniest thing," replied Ken. "To-day I weighed one hundred and sixty-four. Worry, I'm afraid I'm getting fat."

"Fat, nothin'," snorted Worry. "It's muscle. I told Murray to put beef on you all he can. Pretty soon you'll be able to peg a ball through the back-stop. Dean's too light, Peg. He's plucky and will make a catcher, but he's too light. You're batterin' him all up."

Worry shook his head seriously.

"Oh, he's fine!" exclaimed Ken. "I'm not afraid any more. He digs my drop out of the dust, and I can't get a curve away from him. He's weak only on the jump ball, and I don't throw that often, only when I let drive."

"You'll be usin' that often enough against Herne and Place. I'm dependin' on that for those games. Peg, are you worryin' any, losin' any sleep, over those games?"

"Indeed I'm not," replied Ken, laughing.

"Say, I wish you'd have a balloon ascension, and have it quick. It ain't natural, Peg, for you not to get a case of rattles. It's comin' to you, and I don't want it in any of the big games."

"I don't want it either. But Worry, pitching is all a matter of control, you say so often. I don't believe I could get wild and lose my control if I tried."

"Peg, you sure have the best control of any pitcher I ever coached. It's your success. It'll make a great pitcher out of you. All you've got to learn is where to pitch 'em to Herne and Place."

"How am I to learn that?"

"Listen!" Worry whispered. "I'm goin' to send you to Washington next week to see Place and Herne play Georgetown. You'll pay your little money and sit in the grand-stand right behind the catcher. You'll have a pencil and a score card, and you'll be enjoyin' the game. But, Peg, you'll also be usin' your head, and when you see one of 'em players pull away on a curve, or hit weak on a drop, or miss a high fast one, or slug a low ball, you will jot it down on your card. You'll watch Place's hard hitters with hawk eyes, my boy, and a pitcher's memory. And when they come along to Grant Field you'll have 'em pretty well sized up."

"That's fine, Worry, but is it fair?" queried Ken.

"Fair? Why, of course. They all do it. We saw Place's captain in the grand-stand here last spring."

The coach made no secret of his pride and faith in Ken. It was this, perhaps, as much as anything, which kept Ken keyed up. For Ken was really pitching better ball than he knew how to pitch. He would have broken his arm for Worry; he believed absolutely in what the coach told him; he did not think of himself at all.

Worry, however, had plenty of enthusiasm for his other players. Every evening after dinner he would call them all about him and talk for an hour. Sometimes he would tell funny baseball stories; again, he told of famous Wayne-Place games, and how they had been won or lost; then at other times he dwelt on the merits and faults of his own team. In speaking of the swift development of this year's varsity he said it was as remarkable as it had been unforeseen. He claimed it would be a bewildering surprise to Wayne students and to the big college teams. He was working toward the perfection of a fast run-getting machine. In the five games already played and won a good idea could be gotten of Wayne's team, individually and collectively. Homans was a scientific short-field hitter and remarkably sure. Raymond could not bat, but he had developed into a wonder in reaching first base, by bunt or base on balls, or being hit. Reddy Ray was a hard and timely batter, and when he got on base his wonderful fleetness made him almost sure to score. Of the other players Graves batted the best; but taking the team as a whole, and comparing them with Place or Herne, it appeared that Reddy and Homans were the only great hitters, and the two of them, of course, could not make a great hitting team. In fielding, however, the coach said he had never seen the like. They were all fast, and Homans was perfect in judgment on fly balls, and Raymond was quick as lightning to knock down base hits, and as to the intercollegiate sprinter in left field, it was simply a breath-taking event to see him run after a ball. Last of all was Ken Ward with his great arm. It was a strangely assorted team, Worry said, one impossible to judge at the moment, but it was one to watch.

"Boys, we're comin' with a rush," he went on to say. "But somethin's holdin' us back a little. There's no lack of harmony, yet there's a drag. In spite of the spirit you've shown—and I want to say it's been great—the team doesn't work together as one man all the time. I advise you all to stick closer together. Stay away from the club, and everywhere except lectures. We've got to be closer 'n brothers. It'll all work out right before we go up against Herne in June. That game's comin', boys, and by that time the old college will be crazy. It'll be our turn then."

Worry's talks always sank deeply into Ken's mind and set him to thinking and revolving over and over the gist of them so that he could remember to his profit.

He knew that some of the boys had broken training, and he pondered if that was what caused the drag Worry mentioned. Ken had come to feel the life and fortunes of the varsity so keenly that he realized how the simplest deviations from honor might affect the smooth running of the team. It must be perfectly smooth. And to make it so every player must be of one mind.

Ken proved to himself how lack of the highest spirit on the part of one or two of the team tended toward the lowering of the general spirit. For he began to worry, and almost at once it influenced his playing. He found himself growing watchful of his comrades and fearful of what they might be doing. He caught himself being ashamed of his suspicions. He would as lief have cut off his hand as break his promise to the coach. Perhaps, however, he exaggerated his feeling and sense of duty. He remembered the scene in Dale's room the night he refused to smoke and drink; how Dale had commended his refusal. Nevertheless, he gathered from Dale's remark to Worry that breaking training was not unusual or particularly harmful.

"With Dale's team it might not have been so bad," thought Ken. "But it's different with us. We've got to make up in spirit what we lack in ability."

Weir and McCord occupied the room next to Ken's, and Graves and Trace, rooming together, were also on that floor. Ken had tried with all his might to feel friendly toward the third-baseman. He had caught Graves carrying cake and pie to his room and smoking cigarettes with the window open. One night Graves took cigarettes from his pocket and offered them to Kel, Trace, and Ken, who all happened to be in Ken's room at the time. Trace readily accepted; Kel demurred at first, but finally took one. Graves then tossed the pack to Ken.

"No, I don't smoke. Besides, it's breaking training," said Ken.

"You make me sick, Ward," retorted Graves. "You're a wet blanket. Do you think we're going to be as sissy as that? It's hard enough to stand the grub we get here, without giving up a little smoke."

Ken made no reply, but he found it difficult to smother a hot riot in his breast. When the other boys had gone to their rooms Ken took Kel to task about his wrong-doing.

"Do you think that's the right sort of thing? What would Worry say?"

"Ken, I don't care about it, not a bit," replied Kel, flinging his cigarette out of the window. "But Graves is always asking me to do things—I hate to refuse. It seems so—"

"Kel, if Worry finds it out you'll lose your place on the team."

"No!" exclaimed Raymond, staring.

"Mark what I say. I wish you'd stop letting Graves coax you into things."

"Ken, he's always smuggling pie and cake and candy into his room. I've had some of it. Trace said he'd brought in something to drink, too."

"It's a shame," cried Ken, in anger. "I never liked him and I've tried hard to change it. Now I'm glad I couldn't."

"He doesn't have any use for you," replied Kel. "He's always running you down to the other boys. What'd you ever do to him, Ken?"

"Oh, it was that potato stunt of mine last fall. He's a Soph, and I hit him, I guess."

"I think it's more than that," went on Raymond. "Anyway, you look out for him, because he's aching to spoil your face."

"He is, is he?" snapped Ken.

Ken was too angry to talk any more, and so the boys went to bed. The next few days Ken discovered that either out of shame or growing estrangement Raymond avoided him, and he was bitterly hurt. He had come to like the little second-baseman, and had hoped they would be good friends. It was easy to see that Graves became daily bolder, and more lax in training, and his influence upon several of the boys grew stronger. And when Dean, Schoonover, and Duncan appeared to be joining the clique, Ken decided he would have to talk to some one, so he went up to see Ray and Homans.

The sprinter was alone, sitting by his lamp, with books and notes spread before him.

"Hello, Peg! come in. You look a little glum. What's wrong?"

Reddy Ray seemed like an elder brother to Ken, and he found himself blurting out his trouble. Ray looked thoughtful, and after a moment he replied in his quiet way:

"Peg, it's new to you, but it's an old story to me. The track and crew men seldom break training, which is more than can be said of the other athletes. It seems to me baseball fellows are the most careless. They really don't have to train so conscientiously. It's only a kind of form."

"But it's different this year," burst out Ken. "You know what Worry said, and how he trusts us."

"You're right, Peg, only you mustn't take it so hard. Things will work out all right. Homans and I were talking about that to-day. You see, Worry wants the boys to elect a captain soon. But perhaps he has not confided in you youngsters. He will suggest that you elect Homans or me. Well, I won't run for the place, so it'll be Homans. He's the man to captain us, that's certain. Graves thinks, though, that he can pull the wires and be elected captain. He's way off. Besides, Peg, he's making a big mistake. Worry doesn't like him, and when he finds out about this break in training we'll have a new third-baseman. No doubt Blake will play the bag. Graves is the only drag in Worry's baseball machine now, and he'll not last.... So, Peg, don't think any more about it. Mind you, the whole team circles round you. You're the pivot, and as sure as you're born you'll be Wayne's captain next year. That's something for you to keep in mind and work for. If Graves keeps after you—hand him one! That's not against rules. Punch him! If Worry knew the truth he would pat you on the back for slugging Graves. Cheer up, Peg! Even if Graves has got all the kids on his side, which I doubt, Homans and I are with you. And you can just bet that Worry Arthurs will side with us.... Now run along, for I must study."

This conversation was most illuminating to Ken. He left Reddy's room all in a quiver of warm pleasure and friendliness at the great sprinter's quiet praise and advice. To make such a friend was worth losing a hundred friends like Graves. He dismissed the third-baseman and his scheming from mind, and believed Reddy as he had believed Arthurs. But Ken thought much of what he divined was a glimmering of the inside workings of a college baseball team. He had one wild start of rapture at the idea of becoming captain of Wayne's varsity next year, and then he dared think no more of that.

The day dawned for Ken to go to Washington, and he was so perturbed at his responsibilities that he quite forgot to worry about the game Wayne had to play in his absence. Arthurs intended to pitch Schoonover in that game, and had no doubt as to its outcome. The coach went to the station with Ken, once more repeated his instructions, and saw him upon the train. Certainly there was no more important personage on board that Washington Limited than Ken Ward. In fact, Ken was so full of importance and responsibility that he quite divided his time between foolish pride in his being chosen to "size up" the great college teams and fearful conjecture as to his ability.

At any rate, the time flew by, the trip seemed short, and soon he was on the Georgetown field. It was lucky that he arrived early and got a seat in the middle of the grand-stand, for there was a throng in attendance when the players came on the diamond. The noisy bleachers, the merry laughter, the flashing colors, and especially the bright gowns and pretty faces of the girls gave Ken pleasurable consciousness of what it would mean to play before such a crowd. At Wayne he had pitched to empty seats. Remembering Worry's prophecy, however, he was content to wait.

From that moment his duty absorbed him. He found it exceedingly fascinating to study the batters, and utterly forgot his responsibility. Not only did he jot down on his card his idea of the weakness and strength of the different hitters, but he compared what he would have pitched to them with what was actually pitched. Of course, he had no test of his comparison, but he felt intuitively that he had the better of it. Watching so closely, Ken had forced home to him Arthurs' repeated assertion that control of the ball made a pitcher. Both pitchers in this game were wild. Locating the plate with them was more a matter of luck than ability. The Herne pitcher kept wasting balls and getting himself in the hole, and then the heavy Georgetown players would know when he had to throw a strike, if he could, and accordingly they hit hard. They beat Herne badly.

The next day in the game with Place it was a different story. Ken realized he was watching a great team. They reminded him of Dale's varsity, though they did not play that fiendish right-field-hitting game. Ken had a numbness come over him at the idea of facing this Place team. It soon passed, for they had their vulnerable places. It was not so much that they hit hard on speed and curves, for they got them where they wanted them. Keene flied out on high fast balls over the inside corner; Starke bit on low drops; Martin was weak on a slow ball; MacNeff, the captain, could not touch speed under his chin, and he always struck at it. On the other hand, he killed a low ball. Prince was the only man who, in Ken's judgment, seemed to have no weakness. These men represented the batting strength of Place, and Ken, though he did not in the least underestimate them, had no fear. He would have liked to pitch against them right there.

"It's all in control of the ball," thought Ken. "Here are seventeen bases on balls in two games—four pitchers. They're wild.... But suppose I got wild, too?"

The idea made Ken shiver.

He travelled all night, sleeping on the train, and got home to the training-house about nine the next morning. Worry was out, Scotty said, and the boys had all gone over to college. Ken went up-stairs and found Raymond in bed.

"Why, Kel, what's the matter?" asked Ken.

"I'm sick," replied Kel. He was pale and appeared to be in distress.

"Oh, I'm sorry. Can't I do something? Get you some medicine? Call Murray?"

"Ken, don't call anybody, unless you want to see me disgraced. Worry got out this morning before he noticed my absence from breakfast. I was scared to death."

"Scared? Disgraced?"

"Ken, I drank a little last night. It always makes me sick. You know I've a weak stomach."

"Kel, you didn't drink, say you didn't!" implored Ken, sitting miserably down on the bed.

"Yes, I did. I believe I was half drunk. I can't stand anything. I'm sick, sick of myself, too, this morning. And I hate Graves."

Ken jumped up with kindling eyes.

"Kel, you've gone back on me—we'd started to be such friends—I tried to persuade you—"

"I know. I'm sorry, Ken. But I really liked you best. I was—you know how it is, Ken. If only Worry don't find it out!"

"Tell him," said Ken, quickly.

"What?" groaned Kel, in fright.

"Tell him. Let me tell him for you."

"No—no—no. He'd fire me off the team, and I couldn't stand that."

"I'll bet Worry wouldn't do anything of the kind. Maybe he knows more than you think."

"I'm afraid to tell him, Ken. I just can't tell him."

"But you gave your word of honor not to break training. The only thing left is to confess."

"I won't tell, Ken. It's not so much my own place on the team—there are the other fellows."

Ken saw that it was no use to argue with Raymond while he was so sick and discouraged, so he wisely left off talking and did his best to make him comfortable. Raymond dropped asleep after a little, and when he awakened just before lunch-time he appeared better.

"I won't be able to practise to-day," he said; "but I'll go down to lunch."

As he was dressing the boys began to come in from college and ran whistling up the stairs.

Graves bustled into the room with rather anxious haste.

"How're you feeling?" he asked.

"Pretty rocky. Graves—I told Ward about it," said Raymond.

Upon his hurried entrance Graves had not observed Ken.

"What did you want to do that for?" he demanded, arrogantly.

Raymond looked at him, but made no reply.

"Ward, I suppose you'll squeal," said Graves, sneeringly. "That'll about be your speed."

Ken rose and, not trusting himself to speak, remained silent.

"You sissy!" cried Graves, hotly. "Will you peach on us to Arthurs?"

"No. But if you don't get out of my room I'll hand you one," replied Ken, his voice growing thick.

Graves's face became red as fire.

"What? Why, you white-faced, white-haired freshman! I've been aching to punch you!"

"Well, why don't you commence?"

With the first retort Ken had felt a hot trembling go over him, and having yielded to his anger he did not care what happened.

"Ken—Graves," pleaded Raymond, white as a sheet. "Don't—please!" He turned from one to the other. "Don't scrap!"

"Graves, it's up to some one to call you, and I'm going to do it," said Ken, passionately. "You've been after me all season, but I wouldn't care for that. It's your rotten influence on Kel and the other boys that makes me wild. You are the drag in this baseball team. You are a crack ball-player, but you don't know what college spirit means. You're a mucker!"

"I'll lick you for that!" raved Graves, shaking his fists.

"You can't lick me!"

"Come outdoors. I dare you to come outdoors. I dare you!"

Ken strode out of the room and started down the hall. "Come on!" he called, grimly, and ran down the stairs. Graves hesitated a moment, then followed.

Raymond suddenly called after them:

"Give it to him, Ken! Slug him! Beat him all up!"

Friendship

A half-hour or less afterward Ken entered the training-house. It chanced that the boys, having come in, were at the moment passing through the hall to the dining-room, and with them was Worry Arthurs.

"Hello! you back? What's the matter with you?" demanded the coach.

Ken's lips were puffed and bleeding, and his chin was bloody. Sundry red and dark marks disfigured his usually clear complexion. His eyes were blazing, and his hair rumpled down over his brow.

"You've been in a scrap," declared Worry.

"I know it," said Ken. "Let me go up and wash."

Worry had planted himself at the foot of the stairway in front of Ken. The boys stood silent and aghast. Suddenly there came thumps upon the stairs, and Raymond appeared, jumping down three steps at a time. He dodged under Worry's arm and plunged at Ken to hold him with both hands.

"Ken! You're all bloody!" he exclaimed, in great excitement. "He didn't lick you? Say he didn't! He's got to fight me, too! You're all bunged up!"

"Wait till you see him!" muttered Ken.

"A-huh!" said Worry. "Been scrappin' with Graves! What for?"

"It's a personal matter," replied Ken.

"Come, no monkey-biz with me," said the coach, sharply. "Out with it!"

There was a moment's silence.

"Mr. Arthurs, it's my fault," burst out Raymond, flushed and eager. "Ken was fighting on my account."

"It wasn't anything of the kind," retorted Ken, vehemently.

"Yes it was," cried Raymond, "and I'm going to tell why."

The hall door opened to admit Graves. He was dishevelled, dirty, battered, and covered with blood. When he saw the group in the hall he made as if to dodge out.

"Here, come on! Take your medicine," called Worry, tersely.

Graves shuffled in, cast down and sheepish, a very different fellow from his usual vaunting self.

"Now, Raymond, what's this all about?" demanded Worry.

Raymond changed color, but he did not hesitate an instant.

"Ken came in this morning and found me sick in bed. I told him I had been half drunk last night—and that Graves had gotten me to drink. Then Graves came in. He and Ken had hard words. They went outdoors to fight."

"Would you have told me?" roared the coach in fury. "Would you have come to me with this if I hadn't caught Peg?"

Raymond faced him without flinching.

"At first I thought not—when Ken begged me to confess I just couldn't. But now I know I would."

At that Worry lost his sudden heat, and then he turned to the stricken Graves.

"Mebbe it'll surprise you, Graves, to learn that I knew a little of what you've been doin'. I told Homans to go to you in a quiet way and tip off your mistake. I hoped you'd see it. But you didn't. Then you've been knockin' Ward all season, for no reason I could discover but jealousy. Now, listen! Peg Ward has done a lot for me already this year, and he'll do more. But even if he beats Place, it won't mean any more to me than the beatin' he's given you. Now, you pack your things and get out of here. There's no position for you on this varsity."

Without a word in reply and amid intense silence Graves went slowly up-stairs. When he disappeared Worry sank into a chair, and looked as if he was about to collapse. Little Trace walked hesitatingly forward with the manner of one propelled against his will.

"Mr. Arthurs, I—I," he stammered—"I'm guilty, too. I broke training. I want to—"

The coach waved him back. "I don't want to hear it, not another word—from anybody. It's made me sick. I can't stand any more. Only I see I've got to change my rules. There won't be any rules any more. You can all do as you like. I'd rather have you all go stale than practise deceit on me. I cut out the trainin' rules."

"No!" The team rose up as one man and flung the refusal at the coach.

"Worry, we won't stand for that," spoke up Reddy Ray. His smooth, cool voice was like oil on troubled waters. "I think Homans and I can answer for the kids from now on. Graves was a disorganizer—that's the least I'll say of him. We'll elect Homans captain of the team, and then we'll cut loose like a lot of demons. It's been a long, hard drill for you, Worry, but we're in the stretch now and going to finish fast. We've been a kind of misfit team all spring. You've had a blind faith that something could be made out of us. Homans has waked up to our hidden strength. And I go further than that. I've played ball for years. I know the game. I held down left field for two seasons on the greatest college team ever developed out West. That's new to you. Well, it gives me license to talk a little. I want to tell you that I can feel what's in this team. It's like the feeling I have when I'm running against a fast man in the sprints. From now on we'll be a family of brothers with one idea. And that'll be to play Place off their feet."

Coach Arthurs sat up as if he had been given the elixir of life. Likewise the members of the team appeared to be under the spell of a powerful stimulus. The sprinter's words struck fire from all present.

Homans' clear gray eyes were like live coals. "Boys! One rousing cheer for Worry Arthurs and for Wayne!"

Lusty, strained throats let out the cheer with a deafening roar.

It was strange and significant at that moment to see Graves, white-faced and sullen, come down the stairs and pass through the hall and out of the door. It was as if discord, selfishness, and wavering passed out with him. Arthurs and Homans and Ray could not have hoped for a more striking lesson to the young players.

Dave, the colored waiter, appeared in the doorway of the dining-room. "Mr. Arthurs, I done call yo' all. Lunch is sho' gittin' cold."

That afternoon Wayne played the strong Hornell University nine.

Blake, new at third base for Wayne, was a revelation. He was all legs and arms. Weir accepted eight chances. Raymond, sick or not, was all over the infield, knocking down grounders, backing up every play. To McCord, balls in the air or at his feet were all the same. Trace caught a foul fly right off the bleachers. Homans fielded with as much speed as the old varsity's centre and with better judgment. Besides, he made four hits and four runs. Reddy Ray drove one ball into the bleachers, and on a line-drive to left field he circled the bases in time that Murray said was wonderful. Dean stood up valiantly to his battering, and for the first game had no passed balls. And Ken Ward whirled tirelessly in the box, and one after another he shot fast balls over the plate. He made the Hornell players hit; he had no need to extend himself to the use of the long swing and whip of his arm that produced the jump ball; and he shut them out without a run, and gave them only two safe hits. All through the game Worry Arthurs sat on the bench without giving an order or a sign. His worried look had vanished with the crude playing of his team.

That night the Hornell captain, a veteran player of unquestionable ability, was entertained at Carlton Club by Wayne friends, and he expressed himself forcibly: "We came over to beat Wayne's weak team. It'll be some time till we discover what happened. Young Ward has the most magnificent control and speed. He's absolutely relentless. And that frog-legged second-baseman—oh, say, can't he cover ground! Homans is an all-round star. Then, your red-headed Ray, the sprinter—he's a marvel. Ward, Homans, Ray—they're demons, and they're making demons of the kids. I can't understand why Wayne students don't support their team. It's strange."

What the Hornell captain said went from lip to lip throughout the club, and then it spread, like a flame in wind-blown grass, from club to dormitory, and thus over all the university.

"Boys, the college is wakin' up," said Worry, rubbing his hands. "Yesterday's game jarred 'em. They can't believe their own ears. Why, Hornell almost beat Dale's team last spring. Now, kids, look out. We'll stand for no fussin' over us. We don't want any jollyin'. We've waited long for encouragement. It didn't come, and now we'll play out the string alone. There'll be a rush to Grant Field. It cuts no ice with us. Let 'em come to see the boys they hissed and guyed early in the spring. We'll show 'em a few things. We'll make 'em speechless. We'll make 'em so ashamed they won't know what to do. We'll repay all their slights by beatin' Place."

Worry was as excited as on the day he discovered that Ken was a pitcher.

"One more word, boys," he went on. "Keep together now. Run back here to your rooms as quick as you get leave from college. Be civil when you are approached by students, but don't mingle, not yet. Keep to yourselves. Your reward is comin'. It'll be great. Only wait!"

And that was the last touch of fire which moulded Worry's players into a family of brothers. Close and warm and fine was the culmination of their friendship. On the field they were dominated by one impulse, almost savage in its intensity. When they were off the field the springs of youth burst forth to flood the hours with fun.

In the mornings when the mail-man came there was always a wild scramble for letters. And it developed that Weir received more than his share. He got mail every day, and his good-fortune could not escape the lynx eyes of his comrades. Nor could the size and shape of the envelope and the neat, small handwriting fail to be noticed. Weir always stole off by himself to read his daily letter, trying to escape a merry chorus of tantalizing remarks.

"Oh! Sugar!"

"Dreamy Eyes!"

"Gawge, the pink letter has come!"

Weir's reception of these sallies earned him the name of Puff.

One morning, for some unaccountable reason, Weir did not get down-stairs when the mail arrived. Duncan got the pink letter, scrutinized the writing closely, and put the letter in his coat. Presently Weir came bustling down.

"Who's got the mail?" he asked, quickly.

"No letters this morning," replied some one.

"Is this Sunday?" asked Weir, rather stupidly.

"Nope. I meant no letters for you."

Weir looked blank, then stunned, then crestfallen. Duncan handed out the pink envelope. The boys roared, and Weir strode off in high dudgeon.

That day Duncan purchased a box of pink envelopes, and being expert with a pen, he imitated the neat handwriting and addressed pink envelopes to every boy in the training-house. Next morning no one except Weir seemed in a hurry to answer the postman's ring. He came in with the letters and his jaw dropping. It so happened that his letter was the very last one, and when he got to it the truth flashed over him. Then the peculiar appropriateness of the nickname Puff was plainly manifest. One by one the boys slid off their chairs to the floor, and at last Weir had to join in the laugh on him.

Each of the boys in turn became the victim of some prank. Raymond betrayed Ken's abhorrence of any kind of perfume, and straightway there was a stealthy colloquy. Cheap perfume of a most penetrating and paralyzing odor was liberally purchased. In Ken's absence from his room all the clothing that he did not have on his back was saturated. Then the conspirators waited for him to come up the stoop, and from their hiding-place in a window of the second floor they dropped an extra quart upon him.

Ken vowed vengeance that would satisfy him thrice over, and he bided his time until he learned who had perpetrated the outrage.

One day after practice his opportunity came. Raymond, Weir, and Trace, the guilty ones, went with Ken to the training quarters to take the steam bath that Murray insisted upon at least once every week. It so turned out that the four were the only players there that afternoon. While the others were undressing, Ken bribed Scotty to go out on an errand, and he let Murray into his scheme. Now, Murray not only had acquired a strong liking for Ken, but he was exceedingly fond of a joke.

"All I want to know," whispered Ken, "is if I might stew them too much—really scald them, you know?"

"No danger," whispered Murray. "That'll be the fun of it. You can't hurt them. But they'll think they're dying."

He hustled Raymond, Weir, and Trace into the tanks and fastened the lids, and carefully tucked towels round their necks to keep in the steam.

"Lots of stew to-day," he said, turning the handles. "Hello! Where's Scotty?... Peg, will you watch these boys a minute while I step out?"

"You bet I will," called Ken to the already disappearing Murray.

The three cooped-in boys looked askance at Ken.

"Wull, I'm not much stuck—" Raymond began glibly enough, and then, becoming conscious that he might betray an opportunity to Ken, he swallowed his tongue.

"What'd you say?" asked Ken, pretending curiosity. Suddenly he began to jump up and down. "Oh, my! Hullabelee! Schoodoorady! What a chance! You gave it away!"

"Look what he's doing!" yelled Trace.

"Hyar!" added Weir.

"Keep away from those pipes!" chimed in Raymond.

"Boys, I've been laying for you, but I never thought I'd get a chance like this. If Murray only stays out three minutes—just three minutes!"

"Three minutes! You idiot, you won't keep us in here that long?" asked Weir, in alarm.

"Oh no, not at all.... Puff, I think you can stand a little more steam."

Ken turned the handle on full.

"Kel, a first-rate stewing will be good for your daily grouch."

To the accompaniment of Raymond's threats he turned the second handle.

"Trace, you little poll-parrot, you will throw perfume on me? Now roast!"

The heads of the imprisoned boys began to jerk and bob around, and their faces to take on a flush. Ken leisurely surveyed them and then did an Indian war-dance in the middle of the room.

"Here, let me out! Ken, you know how delicate I am," implored Raymond.

"I couldn't entertain the idea for a second," replied Ken.

"I'll lick you!" yelled Raymond.

"My lad, you've got a brain-storm," returned Ken, in grieved tones. "Not in the wildest flights of your nightmares have you ever said anything so impossible as that."

"Ken, dear Ken, dear old Peggie," cried Trace, "you know I've got a skinned place on my hip where I slid yesterday. Steam isn't good for that, Worry says. He'll be sore. You must let me out."

"I intend to see, Willie, that you'll be sore too, and skinned all over," replied Ken.

"Open this lid! At once!" roared Weir, in sudden anger. His big eyes rolled.

"Bah!" taunted Ken.

Then all three began to roar at Ken at once. "Brute! Devil! Help! Help! Help! We'll fix you for this!... It's hotter! it's fire! Aghh! Ouch! Oh! Ah-h-h!... O-o-o-o!... Murder! MURDER-R!"

At this juncture Murray ran in.

"What on earth! Peg, what did you do?"

"I only turned on the steam full tilt," replied Ken, innocently.

"Why, you shouldn't have done that," said Murray, in pained astonishment.

"Stop talking about it! Let me out!" shrieked Raymond.

Ken discreetly put on his coat and ran from the room.

The Herne Game

On the morning of the first of June, the day scheduled for the opening game with Herne, Worry Arthurs had Ken Ward closeted with Homans and Reddy Ray. Worry was trying his best to be soberly calculating in regard to the outcome of the game. He was always trying to impress Ken with the uncertainty of baseball. But a much younger and less observing boy than Ken could have seen through the coach. Worry was dead sure of the result, certain that the day would see a great gathering of Wayne students, and he could not hide his happiness. And the more he betrayed himself the more he growled at Ken.

"Well, we ain't goin' to have that balloon-ascension to-day, are we?" he demanded. "Here we've got down to the big games, and you haven't been up in the air yet. I tell you it ain't right."

"But, Worry, I couldn't go off my head and get rattled just to please you, could I?" implored Ken. To Ken this strain of the coach's had grown to be as serious as it was funny.

"Aw! talk sense," said Worry. "Why, you haven't pitched to a college crowd yet. Wait! Wait till you see that crowd over to Place next week! Thousands of students crazier 'n Indians, and a flock of girls that'll make you bite your tongue off. Ten thousand yellin' all at once."

"Let them yell," replied Ken; "I'm aching to pitch before a crowd. It has been pretty lonesome at Grant Field all season."

"Let 'em yell, eh?" retorted Worry. "All right, my boy, it's comin' to you. And if you lose your nut and get slammed all over the lot, don't come to me for sympathy."

"I wouldn't. I can take a licking. Why, Worry, you talk as if—as if I'd done something terrible. What's the matter with me? I've done every single thing you wanted—just as well as I could do it. What are you afraid of?"

"You're gettin' swelled on yourself," said the coach, deliberately.

The blood rushed to Ken's face until it was scarlet. He was so astounded and hurt that he could not speak. Worry looked at him once, then turning hastily away, he walked to the window.

"Peg, it ain't much wonder," he went on, smoothly, "and I'm not holdin' it against you. But I want you to forget yourself—"

"I've never had a thought of myself," retorted Ken, hotly.

"I want you to go in to-day like—like an automatic machine," went on Worry, as if Ken had not spoken. "There'll be a crowd out, the first of the season. Mebbe they'll throw a fit. Anyway, it's our first big game. As far as the university goes, this is our trial. The students are up in the air; they don't know what to think. Mebbe there won't be a cheer at first.... But, Peg, if we beat Herne to-day they'll tear down the bleachers."

"Well, all I've got to say is that you can order new lumber for the bleachers—because we're going to win," replied Ken, with a smouldering fire in his eyes.

"There you go again! If you're not stuck on yourself, it's too much confidence. You won't be so chipper about three this afternoon, mebbe. Listen! The Herne players got into town last night, and some of them talked a little. It's just as well you didn't see the morning papers. It came to me straight that Gallagher, the captain, and Stern, the first-baseman, said you were pretty good for a kid freshman, but a little too swelled to stand the gaff in a big game. They expect you to explode before the third innin'. I wasn't goin' to tell you, Peg, but you're so—"

"They said that, did they?" cried Ken. He jumped up with paling cheek and blazing eye, and the big hand he shoved under Worry's nose trembled like a shaking leaf. "What I won't do to them will be funny! Swelled! Explode! Stand the gaff! Look here, Worry, maybe it's true, but I don't believe it.... I'll beat this Herne team! Do you get that?"

"Now you're talkin'," replied Worry, with an entire change of manner. "You saw the Herne bunch play. They can field, but how about hittin'?"

"Gallagher, Stern, Hill, and Burr are the veterans of last year's varsity," went on Ken, rapidly, as one who knew his subject. "They can hit—if they get what they like."

"Now you're talkin'. How about Gallagher?"

"He hits speed. He couldn't hit a slow ball with a paddle."

"Now you're talkin'. There's Stern, how'd you size him?"

"He's weak on a low curve, in or out, or a drop."

"Peg, you're talkin' some now. How about Hill?"

"Hill is a bunter. A high ball in close, speedy, would tie him in a knot."

"Come on, hurry! There's Burr."

"Burr's the best of the lot, a good waiter and hard hitter, but he invariably hits a high curve up in the air."

"All right. So far so good. How about the rest of the team?"

"I'll hand them up a straight, easy ball and let them hit. I tell you I've got Herne beaten, and if Gallagher or any one else begins to guy me I'll laugh in his face."

"Oh, you will?... Say, you go down to your room now, and stay there till time for lunch. Study or read. Don't think another minute about this game."

Ken strode soberly out of the room.

It was well for Ken that he did not see what happened immediately after his exit. Worry and Homans fell into each other's arms.

"Say, fellows, how I hated to do it!" Worry choked with laughter and contrition. "It was the hardest task I ever had. But, Cap, you know we had to make Peg sore. He's too blamed good-natured. Oh, but didn't he take fire! He'll make some of those Herne guys play low-bridge to-day. Wouldn't it be great if he gave Gallagher the laugh?"

"Worry, don't you worry about that," said Homans. "And it would please me, too, for Gallagher is about as wordy and pompous as any captain I've seen."

"I think you were a little hard on Ken," put in Reddy. His quiet voice drew Worry and Homans from their elation. "Of course, it was necessary to rouse Ken's fighting blood, but you didn't choose the right way. You hurt his feelings. You know, Worry, that the boy is not in the least swelled."

"'Course I know it, Reddy. Why, Peg's too modest. But I want him to be dead in earnest to-day. Mind you, I'm thinkin' of Place. He'll beat Herne to a standstill. I worked on his feelin's just to get him all stirred up. You know there's always the chance of rattles in any young player, especially a pitcher. If he's mad he won't be so likely to get 'em. So I hurt his feelin's. I'll make it up to him, don't you fear for that, Reddy."

"I wish you had waited till we go over to Place next week," replied Ray. "You can't treat him that way twice. Over there's where I would look for his weakening. But it may be he won't ever weaken. If he ever does it'll be because of the crowd and not the players."

"I think so, too. A yellin' mob will be new to Peg. But, fellows, I'm only askin' one game from Herne and one, or a good close game, from Place. That'll give Wayne the best record ever made. Look at our standin' now. Why, the newspapers are havin' a fit. Since I picked the varsity we haven't lost a game. Think of that! Those early games don't count. We've had an unbroken string of victories, Peg pitchin' twelve, and Schoonover four. And if wet grounds and other things hadn't cancelled other games we'd have won more."

"Yes, we're in the stretch now, Worry, and running strong. We'll win three out of these four big games," rejoined Reddy.

"Oh, say, that'd be too much! I couldn't stand it! Oh, say, Cap, don't you think Reddy, for once, is talkin' about as swift as he sprints?"

"I'm afraid to tell you, Worry," replied Homans, earnestly. "When I look back at our work I can't realize it. But it's time to wake up. The students over at college are waking up. They will be out to-day. You are the one to judge whether we're a great team or not. We keep on making runs. It's runs that count. I think, honestly, Worry, that after to-day we'll be in the lead for championship honors. And I hold my breath when I tell you."

It was remarkably quiet about the training-house all that morning. The coach sent a light lunch to the boys in their rooms. They had orders to be dressed, and to report in the reading-room at one-thirty.

Raymond came down promptly on time.

"Where's Peg?" asked Worry.

"Why, I thought he was here, ahead of me," replied Raymond, in surprise.

A quick survey of the uniformed players proved the absence of Ken Ward and Reddy Ray. Worry appeared startled out of speech, and looked helplessly at Homans. Then Ray came downstairs, bat in one hand, shoes and glove in the other. He seated himself upon the last step and leisurely proceeded to put on his shoes.

"Reddy, did you see Peg?" asked Worry, anxiously.

"Sure, I saw him," replied the sprinter.

"Well?" growled the coach. "Where is he? Sulkin' because I called him?"

"Not so you'd notice it," answered Reddy, in his slow, careless manner. "I just woke him up."

"What!" yelled Arthurs.

"Peg came to my room after lunch and went to sleep. I woke him just now. He'll be down in a minute."

Worry evidently could not reply at the moment, but he began to beam.

"What would Gallagher say to that?" asked Captain Homans, with a smile. "Wayne's varsity pitcher asleep before a Herne game! Oh no, I guess that's not pretty good! Worry, could you ask any more?"

"Cap, I'll never open my face to him again," blurted out the coach.

Ken appeared at the head of the stairs and had started down, when the door-bell rang. Worry opened the door to admit Murray, the trainer; Dale, the old varsity captain, and the magnificently built Stevens, guard and captain of the football team.

"Hello! Worry," called out Murray, cheerily. "How're the kids? Boys, you look good to me. Trim and fit, and all cool and quiet-like. Reddy, be careful of your ankles and legs to-day. After the meet next week you can cut loose and run bases like a blue streak."

Dale stepped forward, earnest and somewhat concerned, but with a winning frankness.

"Worry, will you let Stevens and me sit on the bench with the boys to-day?"

Worry's face took on the color of a thunder-cloud. "I'm not the captain," he replied. "Ask Homans."

"How about it, Roy?" queried Dale.

Homans was visibly affected by surprise, pleasure, and something more. While he hesitated, perhaps not trusting himself to reply quickly, Stevens took a giant stride to the fore.

"Homans, we've got a hunch that Wayne's going to win," he said, in a deep-bass voice. "A few of us have been tipped off, and we got it straight. But the students don't know it yet. So Dale and I thought we'd like them to see how we feel about it—before this game. You've had a rotten deal from the students this year. But they'll more than make it up when you beat Herne. The whole college is waiting and restless."

Homans, recovering himself, faced the two captains courteously and gratefully, and with a certain cool dignity.

"Thank you, fellows! It's fine of you to offer to sit with us on the bench. I thank you on behalf of the varsity. But—not to-day. All season we've worked and fought without support, and now we're going to beat Herne without support. When we've done that you and Dale—all the college—can't come too quick to suit us."

"I think I'd say the same thing, if I were in your place," said Dale. "And I'll tell you right here that when I was captain I never plugged any harder to win than I'll plug to-day."

Then these two famous captains of championship teams turned to Homans' players and eyed them keenly, their faces working, hands clenched, their powerful frames vibrating with the feeling of the moment. That moment was silent, eloquent. It linked Homans' team to the great athletic fame of the university. It radiated the spirit to conquer, the glory of past victories, the strength of honorable defeats. Then Dale and Stevens went out, leaving behind them a charged atmosphere.

"I ain't got a word to say," announced Worry to the players.

"And I've very little," added Captain Homans. "We're all on edge, and being drawn down so fine we may be over-eager. Force that back. It doesn't matter if we make misplays. We've made many this season, but we've won all the same. At the bat, remember to keep a sharp eye on the base-runner, and when he signs he is going down, bunt or hit to advance him. That's all."

Ken Ward walked to the field between Worry Arthurs and Reddy Ray. Worry had no word to say, but he kept a tight grip on Ken's arm.

"Peg, I've won many a sprint by not underestimating my opponent," said Reddy, quietly. "Now you go at Herne for all you're worth from the start."

When they entered the field there were more spectators in the stands than had attended all the other games together. In a far corner the Herne players in dark-blue uniforms were practising batting. Upon the moment the gong called them in for their turn at field practice. The Wayne team batted and bunted a few balls, and then Homans led them to the bench.

Upon near view the grand-stand and bleachers seemed a strange sight to Ken Ward. He took one long look at the black-and-white mass of students behind the back-stop, at the straggling lines leading to the gates, at the rapidly filling rows to right and left, and then he looked no more. Already an immense crowd was present. Still it was not a typical college baseball audience. Ken realized that at once. It was quiet, orderly, expectant, and watchful. Very few girls were there. The students as a body had warmed to curiosity and interest, but not to the extent of bringing the girls. After that one glance Ken resolutely kept his eyes upon the ground. He was conscious of a feeling that he wanted to spring up and leap at something. And he brought all his will to force back his over-eagerness. He heard the crack of the ball, the shouts of the Herne players, the hum of voices in the grand-stand, and the occasional cheers of Herne rooters. There were no Wayne cheers.

"Warm up a little," said Worry, in his ear.

Ken peeled off his sweater and walked out with Dean. A long murmur ran throughout the stands. Ken heard many things said of him, curiously, wonderingly, doubtfully, and he tried not to hear more. Then he commenced to pitch to Dean. Worry stood near him and kept whispering to hold in his speed and just to use his arm easily. It was difficult, for Ken felt that his arm wanted to be cracked like a buggy-whip.

"That'll do," whispered Worry. "We're only takin' five minutes' practice.... Say, but there's a crowd! Are you all right, Peg—cool-like and determined?... Good! Say—but Peg, you'd better look these fellows over."

"I remember them all," replied Ken. "That's Gallagher on the end of the bench; Burr is third from him; Stern's fussing over the bats, and there's Hill, the light-headed fellow, looking this way. There's—"

"That'll do," said Worry. "There goes the gong. It's all off now. Homans has chosen to take the field. I guess mebbe you won't show 'em how to pitch a new white ball! Get at 'em now!" Then he called Ken back as if impelled, and whispered to him in a husky voice: "It's been tough for you and for me. Listen! Here's where it begins to be sweet."

Ken trotted out to the box, to the encouraging voices of the infield, and he even caught Reddy Ray's low, thrilling call from the far outfield.

"Play!" With the ringing order, which quieted the audience, the umpire tossed a white ball to Ken.

For a single instant Ken trembled ever so slightly in all his limbs, and the stands seemed a revolving black-and-white band. Then the emotion was as if it had never been. He stepped upon the slab, keen-sighted, cool, and with his pitching game outlined in his mind.

Burr, the curly-haired leader of Herne's batting list, took his position to the left of the plate. Ken threw him an underhand curve, sweeping high and over the inside corner. Burr hit a lofty fly to Homans. Hill, the bunter, was next. For him Ken shot one straight over the plate. Hill let it go by, and it was a strike. Ken put another in the same place, and Hill, attempting to bunt, fouled a little fly, which Dean caught. Gallagher strode third to bat. He used a heavy club, stood right-handed over the plate, and looked aggressive. Ken gave the captain a long study and then swung slowly, sending up a ball that floated like a feather. Gallagher missed it. On the second pitch he swung heavily at a slow curve far off the outside. For a third Ken tried the speedy drop, and the captain, letting it go, was out on strikes.

The sides changed. Worry threw a sweater around Ken.

"The ice's broke, Peg, and you've got your control. That settles it."

Homans went up, to a wavering ripple of applause. He drew two balls and then a strike from Murphy, and hit the next hard into short field. Frick fumbled the ball, recovered it, and threw beautifully, but too late to catch Homans. Raymond sacrificed, sending his captain to second. Murphy could not locate the plate for Reddy Ray and let him get to first on four balls. Weir came next. Homans signed he was going to run on the first pitch. Weir, hitting with the runner, sent a double into right field, and Homans and Ray scored. The bleachers cheered. Homans ran down to third base to the coaching lines, and Ray went to first base. Both began to coach the runner. Dean hit into short field, and was thrown out, while Weir reached third on the play.

"Two out, now! Hit!" yelled Homans to Blake.

Blake hit safely over second, scoring Weir. Then Trace flied out to left field.

"Three runs!" called Homans. "Boys, that's a start! Three more runs and this game's ours! Now, Peg, now!"

Ken did not need that trenchant thrilling now. The look in Worry's eyes had been enough. He threw speed to Halloway, and on the third ball retired him, Raymond to McCord. Stern came second to bat. In Ken's mind this player was recorded with a weakness on low curves. And Ken found it with two balls pitched. Stern popped up to Blake. Frick, a new player to Ken, let a strike go by, and missed a drop and a fast ball.

"They can't touch you, Ken," called Raymond, as he tossed aside his glove.

Faint cheers rose from scattered parts of the grand-stand, and here and there shouts and yells. The audience appeared to stir, to become animated, and the Herne players settled down to more sober action on the field.

McCord made a bid for a hit, but failed because of fast work by Stern. Ken went up, eager to get to first in any way. He let Murphy pitch, and at last, after fouling several good ones, he earned his base on balls. Once there, he gave Homans the sign that he would run on the first pitch, and he got a fair start. He heard the crack of the ball and saw it glinting between short and third. Running hard, he beat the throw-in to third. With two runners on bases, Raymond hit to deep short. Ken went out trying to reach home. Again Reddy Ray came up and got a base on balls, filling the bases. The crowd began to show excitement, and seemed to be stifling cheers in suspense. Weir hurried to bat, his shock of hair waving at every step. He swung hard on the first ball, and, missing it, whirled down, bothering the catcher. Homans raced home on a half-passed ball. Then Weir went out on a fly to centre.

"Peg, keep at them!" called Reddy Ray. "We've got Murphy's measure."

It cost Ken an effort to deliberate in the box, to think before he pitched. He had to fight his eagerness. But he wasted few balls, and struck Mercer out. Van Sant hit to Weir, who threw wild to first, allowing the runner to reach third. Murphy, batting next, hit one which Ken put straight over the plate, and it went safe through second, scoring Van Sant. The Herne rooters broke out in loud acclaim. Burr came up, choking his bat up short. Again Ken gave him the high, wide curve. He let it pass and the umpire called it a strike. Ken threw another, a little outside this time. Evidently Burr was trying out Ken's control.

"He can't put them over!" yelled Gallagher, from the coaching line. "Here's where he goes up! Wait him out, Burr. Good eye, old man! Here's where we explode the freshman!"

Ken glanced at Gallagher and laughed. Then he sped up another high curve, which the umpire called a strike.

"That's the place, Peg! Put another there!" floated from Reddy in the outfield.

Burr swung viciously, hitting a bounder toward second base. Raymond darted over, went down with his bird-like quickness, came up with the ball, and then he touched the bag and threw to first. It was a play in which he excelled. The umpire called both runners out, retiring the side. A short, sharp yell, like a bark, burst from the bleachers.

Worry was smilingly thoughtful as his boys trotted in to bat.

"Say, if you get a couple of runs this time we'll be It. Look at the students. Ready to fall out of the stands.... Peg, I'm glad Herne got a run. Now we won't think of a shut-out. That'll steady us up. And, boys, break loose now, for the game's ours."

Dean started off with a clean single. On the first pitch he broke for second, and had to slide to make it, as Blake missed the strike. Then Blake went out to first. Trace walked. McCord poked a little fly over the infield, scoring Dean. Ken fouled out. The unerring Homans again hit safely, sending Trace in. With two out and McCord on third and Homans on second, Raymond laid down a beautiful bunt, tallying McCord. And when the Herne catcher tried to head Homans from making third Raymond kept on toward second. It was a daring dash, and he dove to the bag with a long slide, but the decision was against him.

The coach called Homans, Ward, and Ray to him and gathered them close together.

"Boys, listen!" he said, low and tense. "MacNeff and Prince, of Place, are in the grand-stand just behind the plate. They're up there to get a line on Peg. We'll fool 'em, and make 'em sick in the bargain. Peg, you let out this innin' and show up the first three hitters. Then I'll take you out and let Schoonover finish the game. See?"

"Take me—out?" echoed Ken.

"That's it, if you make these next three hitters look like monkeys. Don't you see? We've got the Herne game cinched. We don't need to use our star twirler. See? That'll be a bone for Place to chew on. How about it, Cap? What do you think, Reddy?"

"Oh, Worry, if we dared to do it!" Homans exclaimed, under his breath. "Herne would never get over it. And it would scare Place to death.... But, Worry, Reddy, dare we risk it?"

"It's playin' into our very hands," replied Worry. His hazel eyes were afire with inspiration.

Reddy Ray's lean jaw bulged.

"Homans, it's the trick, and we can turn it."

"What's the score—7 to 1?" muttered Homans. It was a tight place for him, and he seemed tortured between ambition and doubt.

"That fellow Murphy hasn't got one in my groove yet," said Reddy. "I'm due to lace one. We're good for more runs."

That decided Homans. He patted Ken on the shoulder and led him out to the box, but he never spoke a word.

Ken felt like a wild colt just let loose. He faced Hill with a smile, and then, taking his long, overhand swing, he delivered the jump ball. Hill made no move. The umpire called strike. The crowd roared. Ken duplicated the feat. Then Hill missed the third strike. Gallagher walked up doggedly, and Ken smiled at him, too. Then using three wicked, darting drops, Ken struck Gallagher out.

"That's twice!" called Reddy's penetrating voice from the outfield. "Give him a paddle!"

Halloway drew two balls and then three strikes.

Ken ran for the bench amid an uproar most strange and startling to his untried ear. The long, tardy, and stubborn students had broken their silence.

Dale leaped out of the grand-stand to lead the cheering. The giant Stevens came piling out of the bleachers to perform a like office. And then they were followed by Bryan, captain of the crew, and Hilbrandt, captain of the track team. Four captains of Wayne teams inspiriting and directing the cheering! Ken's bewildered ears drank in one long, thundering "Ward! Ward! Ward!" and then his hearing seemed drowned. The whole mass of students and spectators rose as one, and the deafening stamp of feet only equalled the roar of voices. But now the volume of sound was regular and rhythmic. It was like the approach of a terrible army. For minutes, while the umpire held play suspended, the Wayne supporters in hoarse and stamping tumult came into their own again. It was a wild burst of applause, and as it had been long delayed, so now it was prolonged fiercely to the limit of endurance.

When those waves of sound had rolled away Ken Ward felt a difference in Grant Field, in the varsity, in himself. A different color shone from the sky.

Ken saw Reddy Ray go to bat and drive the ball against the right-field fence. Then as the sprinter got into his wonderful stride once more the whole audience rose in yelling, crashing clamor. And when on Weir's fly to the outfield Reddy raced in to the plate, making the throw-in look feeble, again the din was terrific.

As one in a glorious dream, Ken Ward crouched upon the bench and watched the remainder of that game. He grasped it all as if baseball was all that made life worth living, and as if every moment was his last. He never thought of himself. He was only a part of the team, and that team, every moment, grew sharper, faster, fiercer. He revelled in the game. Schoonover was hit hard, but fast play by Raymond and Weir kept Herne's score down. The little second-baseman was here, there, everywhere, like a glint of light. Herne made runs, but Wayne also kept adding runs. Blake caught a foul fly off the bleachers; Trace made a beautiful catch; McCord was like a tower at first base, and little Dean went through the last stages of development that made him a star.

Once in the eighth inning Ken became aware that Worry was punching him in the back and muttering:

"Look out, Peg! Listen! Murphy'll get one in Reddy's groove this time.... Oh-h!"

The crack of the ball, as well as Worry's yell, told Ken what had happened. Besides, he could see, and as the ball lined away for the fence, and the sprinter leaped into action, Ken jumped up and screamed:

"Oh, Reddy, it's over—over! No! Run! Run! Oh-h-h!"

In the shrill, piercing strife of sound Ken's scream seemed only a breath at his ears. He held to it, almost splitting his throat, while the sprinter twinkled round third base and came home like a thunderbolt.

Another inning passed, a confusion of hits, throws, runs, and plays to Ken, and then Worry was pounding him again.

"Dig for the trainin'-house!" yelled Worry, mouth on his ear. "The students are crazy! They'll eat us alive! They're tearin' the bleachers down! Run for it, Peg!"

A Matter of Principle

Ken found himself running across Grant Field, pursued by a happy, roaring mob of students. They might have been Indians, judging from the way Ken and his fellow-players fled before them. The trained athletes distanced their well-meaning but violent pursuers and gained the gate, but it was a close shave. The boys bounded up the street into the training-house and locked the door till the puffing Arthurs arrived. They let him in and locked the door again.

In another moment the street resounded with the rush of many feet and the yells of frantic students. Murray, the trainer, forced a way through the crowd and up the stoop. He closed and barred the outside door, and then pounded upon the inside door for admittance. Worry let him in.

"They'd make a bowl-fight or a football rush look tame," panted Murray. "Hey! Scotty—lock up tight down in the basement. For Heaven's sake don't let that push get in on us! Lock the windows in the front."

"Who's that poundin' on the door?" yelled Worry. He had to yell, for the swelling racket outside made ordinary conversation impossible.

"Don't open it!" shouted Murray. "What do we care for team-captains, college professors, athletic directors, or students? They're all out there, and they're crazy, I tell you. I never saw the like. It'd be more than I want to get in that jam. And it'd never do for the varsity. Somebody would get crippled sure. I'm training this baseball team."

Murray, in his zealous care of his athletes, was somewhat overshooting the mark, for not one of the boys had the slightest desire to be trusted to the mob outside. In fact, Ken looked dazed, and Raymond scared to the point of trembling; Trace was pale; and all the others, except Homans and Reddy Ray, showed perturbation. Nor were the captain and sprinter deaf to the purport of that hour; only in their faces shone a kindling glow and flush.

By-and-by the boys slipped to their rooms, removed their uniforms, dressed and crept downstairs like burglars and went in to dinner. Outside the uproar, instead of abating, gathered strength as time went by. At the dinner-table the boys had to yell in each other's ears. They had to force what they ate. No one was hungry. When Worry rose from the table they all flocked after him.

It was growing dark outside, and a red glow, brightening upon the windows, showed the students had lighted bonfires.

"They're goin' to make a night of it," yelled Worry.

"How'll my boys be able to sleep?" shouted Murray. Both coach and trainer were as excited as any of the boys.

"The street's packed solid. Listen!"

The tramp, tramp, tramp of thousands of feet keeping time was like the heavy tread of a marching multitude. Then the tramp died away in a piercing cheer, "Wayne!" nine times, clear and sustained—a long, beautiful college cheer. In the breathing spell that followed, the steady tramp of feet went on. One by one, at intervals, the university yells were given, the broken rattling rally, the floating melodious crew cheer, and the hoarse, smashing boom of football. Then again the inspiriting "Wayne!" nine times. After that came shrill calls for the varsity, for Homans, Reddy Ray, Raymond, and Peggie Ward.

"Come up-stairs to the windows, boys!" shouted Worry. "We've got to show ourselves."

Worry threw up the windows in Weir's room, and the boys gingerly poked their heads out. A roar greeted their appearance. The heads all popped in as if they had been struck.

"Homans, you'll have to make a speech," cried the coach.

"I will not!"

"You've got to say somethin'. We can't have this crazy gang out here all night."

Then Worry and Murray coaxed and led Homans to the window. The captain leaned out and said something that was unintelligible in the hubbub without. The crowd cheered him and called for Reddy, Ward, and Raymond. Worry grasped the second-baseman and shoved him half over the sill. Raymond would have fallen out but for the coach's strong hold.

"Come on, Peg!" yelled Worry.

"Not on your life!" cried Ken, in affright. He ran away from the coach, and dived under the bed. But Reddy Ray dragged him out and to the window, and held him up in the bright bonfire glare. Then he lifted a hand to silence the roaring crowd.

"Fellows, here he is—Worry's demon, Wayne's pitcher!" called Reddy, in ringing, far-reaching voice. "Listen! Peggie didn't lose his nerve when he faced Herne to-day, but he's lost it now. He's lost his voice, too. But he says for you to go away and save your cheers for this day two weeks, when we meet Place. Then, he says, you'll have something to cheer for!"

The crafty sprinter knew how to appeal to the students. All of voice and strength and enthusiasm left in them went up in a mighty bawl that rattled the windows and shook the house. They finished with nine "Waynes!" and a long, rousing "Peggie Ward!" and then they went away.

"By George! look here, Peg," said Reddy, earnestly, "they gave you Wayne's Nine! Wayne's Nine! Do you hear? I never knew a freshman varsity man to get that cheer."

"You've got to beat Place now, after tellin' 'em you'd do it," added Worry.

"But, Worry, I didn't say a word—it was Reddy," replied Ken, in distress.

"Same thing," rejoined the coach. "Now, boys, let's quiet down and talk over the game. I won't waste any time jollyin' you. I couldn't praise you enough if I spent the rest of the season tryin' to. One and all, by yourselves and in a bunch, you played Herne off their feet. I'll bet MacNeff and Prince are dizzy figurin' what'll happen Saturday week. As to the score, why, scores don't mean much to us—"

"What was the score, anyway?" asked Ken.

The boys greeted this with shouts of doubtful laughter, and Worry glanced with disapproval at his star.

"Peg, you keep me guessin' a lot. But not to know how much we beat Herne would be more 'n I could stand. On the level, now, don't you know the score?"

"Fair and square, I don't, Worry. You never would let me think of how many runs we had or needed. I can count seven—yes, and one more, that was Reddy's home-run."

"Peg, you must have been up in the air a little; 14 to 4, that's it. And we didn't take our bat in the last of the ninth."

Then followed Worry's critical account of the game, and a discussion in which the boys went over certain plays. During the evening many visitors called, but did not gain admission. The next morning, however, Worry himself brought in the newspapers, which heretofore he had forbidden the players to read, and he told them they were now free to have any callers or to go where they liked. There was a merry scramble for the papers, and presently the reading-room was as quiet as a church.

The account that held Ken Ward in rapt perusal was the Morning Times-Star's. At first the print blurred in Ken's sight. Then he read it over again. He liked the glowing praise given the team, and was shamefully conscious of the delight in his name in large letters. A third time he read it, guiltily this time, for he did not dream that his comrades were engrossed in like indulgence.

WAYNE OUTCLASSES HERNE
ARTHURS DEVELOPS ANOTHER GREAT TEAM.
PEGGIE WARD AND REDDY RAY STARS.

Wayne defeated Herne yesterday 14 to 4, and thereby leaped into the limelight. It was a surprise to every one, Herne most of all. Owing to the stringent eligibility rules now in force at Wayne, and the barring of the old varsity, nothing was expected of this season's team. Arthurs, the famous coach, has built a wonderful nine out of green material, and again establishes the advisability of professional coaches for the big universities.

With one or two exceptions Wayne's varsity is made up of players developed this year. Homans, the captain, was well known about town as an amateur player of ability. But Arthurs has made him into a great field captain and a base-getter of remarkable skill. An unofficial computing gives him the batting average of .536. No captain or any other player of any big college team in the East ever approached such percentage as that. It is so high that it must be a mistake.

Reddy Ray, the intercollegiate champion in the sprints, is the other seasoned player of the varsity, and it is safe to say that he is the star of all the college teams. A wonderful fielder, a sure and heavy hitter, and like a flash on the bases, he alone makes Homans' team formidable.

Then there is Peg Ward, Worry Arthurs' demon pitcher, of freshman bowl-fight fame. This lad has been arriving since spring, and now he has arrived. He is powerful, and has a great arm. He seems to pitch without effort, has twice the speed of Dale, and is as cool in the box as a veteran. But it is his marvellous control of the ball that puts him in a class by himself. In the fourth inning of yesterday's game he extended himself, probably on orders from Coach Arthurs, and struck out Herne's three best hitters on eleven pitched balls. Then he was taken out and Schoonover put in. This white-headed lad is no slouch of a pitcher, by-the-way. But it must have been a bitter pill for Herne to swallow. The proud Herne varsity have been used to knocking pitchers out of the box, instead of seeing them removed because they were too good. Also, MacNeff and Prince, of Place, who saw the game, must have had food for reflection. They did not get much of a line on young Ward, and what they saw will not give them pleasant dreams. We pick Ward to beat the heavy-hitting Place team.

Other youngsters of Arthurs' nine show up well, particularly Raymond and Weir, who have springs in their feet and arms like whips. Altogether Arthurs' varsity is a strangely assorted, a wonderfully chosen group of players. We might liken them to the mechanism of a fine watch, with Ward as the mainspring, and the others with big or little parts to perform, but each dependent upon the other. Wayne's greatest baseball team!

Ken read it all thirstily, wonderingly, and recorded it deep in the deepest well of his memory. It seemed a hundred times as sweet for all the misery and longing and fear and toil which it had cost to gain.

And each succeeding day grew fuller and richer with its meed of reward. All the boys of the varsity were sought by the students, Ken most of all. Everywhere he went he was greeted with a regard that made him still more bashful and ashamed. If he stepped into Carlton Club, it was to be surrounded by a frankly admiring circle of students. He could not get a moment alone in the library. Professors had a smile for him and often stopped to chat. The proudest moment of his college year was when President Halstead met him in the promenade, and before hundreds of students turned to walk a little way with him. There seemed not to be a single student of the university or any one connected with it, who did not recognize him. Bryan took him to watch the crew practise; Stevens played billiards with him at the club; Dale openly sought his society. Then the fraternities began to vie with one another for Ken. In all his life he had not imagined a fellow could be treated so well. It was an open secret that Ken Ward was extremely desired in the best fraternities. He could not have counted his friends. Through it all, by thinking of Worry and the big games coming, he managed to stay on his feet.

One morning, when he was at the height of this enjoyable popularity, he read a baseball note that set him to thinking hard. The newspaper, commenting on the splendid results following Wayne's new athletic rules, interpreted one rule in a way astounding to Ken. It was something to the effect that all players who had been on a team which paid any player or any expenses of any player were therefore ineligible. Interpretation of the rules had never been of any serious moment to Ken. He had never played on any but boy teams. But suddenly he remembered that during a visit to the mountains with his mother he had gone to a place called Eagle's Nest, a summer hotel colony. It boasted of a good ball team and had a rival in the Glenwoods, a team from an adjoining resort. Ken had been in the habit of chasing flies for the players in practice. One day Eagle's Nest journeyed over to Glenwood to play, and being short one player they took Ken to fill in. He had scarcely started in the game when the regular player appeared, thus relieving him. The incident had completely slipped Ken's mind until recalled by the newspaper note.

Whereupon Ken began to ponder. He scouted the idea of that innocent little thing endangering his eligibility at Wayne. But the rule, thus made clear, stood out in startlingly black-and-white relief. Eagle's Nest supported a team by subscription among the hotel guests. Ken had ridden ten miles in a 'bus with the team, and had worn one of the uniforms for some few minutes. Therefore, upon a technicality, perhaps, he had been on a summer nine, and had no right to play for Wayne.

Ken went to Homans and told him the circumstance. The captain looked exceedingly grave, then getting more particulars he relaxed.

"You're safe, Peg. You're perfectly innocent. But don't mention it to any one else, especially Worry. He'd have a fit. What a scare you'd throw into the varsity camp! Forget the few minutes you wore that Eagle's Nest suit."

For the time being this reassured Ken, but after a while his anxiety returned. Homans had said not to mention it, and that bothered Ken. He lay awake half of one night thinking about the thing. It angered him and pricked his conscience and roused him. He wanted to feel absolutely sure of his position, for his own sake first of all. So next morning he cornered Worry and blurted out the secret.

"Peg, what're you givin' me!" he ejaculated.

Ken repeated his story, somewhat more clearly and at greater length. Worry turned as white as a ghost.

"Good gracious, Peg, you haven't told anybody?"

"No one but Homans."

Worry gave a long sigh of relief, and his face regained some of its usual florid color.

"Well, that's all right then.... Say, didn't I tell you once that I had a weak heart? Peg, of course you're an amateur, or there never was one. But 'em fat-head directors! Why, I wouldn't have 'em find that out for a million dollars. They're idiots enough to make a shinin' example of you right before the Place games. Keep it under your hat, see!"

This last was in the nature of a command, and Ken had always religiously obeyed Worry. He went to his room feeling that the matter had been decided for him. Relief, however, did not long abide with him. He began to be torn between loyalty to Worry and duty to himself. He felt guiltless, but he was not sure of it, and until he was sure he could not be free in mind. Suddenly he thought of being actually barred from the varsity, and was miserable. That he could not bear. Strong temptation now assailed Ken and found him weak. A hundred times he reconciled himself to Worry's command, to Homan's point of view, yet every time something rose within him and rebelled. But despite the rebellion Ken almost gave in. He fought off thought of his new sweet popularity, of the glory of being Wayne's athletic star. He fought to look the thing fairly in the face. To him it loomed up a hundredfold larger than an incident of his baseball career. And so he got strength to do the thing that would ease the voice of conscience. He went straight to the coach.

"Worry, I've got to go to the directors and tell them. I—I'm sorry, but I've got to do it."

He expected a storm of rage from Worry, but never had the coach been so suave, so kindly, so magnetic. He called Homans and Raymond and Weir and others who were in the house at the moment and stated Ken's case. His speech flowed smooth and rapid. The matter under his deft argument lost serious proportions. But it seemed to Ken that Worry did not tell the boys the whole truth, or they would not have laughed at the thing and made him out over-sensitive. And Ken was now growing too discouraged and bewildered to tell them. Moreover, he was getting stubborn. The thing was far from a joke. The cunning of the coach proved that. Worry wound the boys round his little finger.

At this juncture Reddy Ray entered the training-house.

More than once Ken had gone to the great sprinter with confidences and troubles, and now he began impulsively, hurriedly, incoherently, to tell the story.

"And Reddy," concluded Ken, "I've got to tell the directors. It's something—hard for me to explain. I couldn't pitch another game with this hanging over me. I must—tell them—and take my medicine."

"Sure. It's a matter of principle," replied Reddy, in his soft, slow voice. His keen eyes left Ken's pale face and met the coach's. "Worry, I'll take Peg up to see the athletic faculty. I know Andrews, the president, and he's the one to hear Peg's story."

Worry groaned and sank into a chair crushed and beaten. Then he swore, something unusual in him. Then he began to rave at the fat-headed directors. Then he yelled that he would never coach another ball team so long as he lived.

Ken followed Reddy out of the training-house and along the street. The fact that the sprinter did not say a word showed Ken he was understood, and he felt immeasurably grateful. They crossed the campus and entered College Hall, to climb the winding stairway. To Ken that was a long, hateful climb. Andrews, and another of the directors whom Ken knew by sight, were in the office. They greeted the visitors with cordial warmth.

"Gentlemen," began Reddy, "Ward thinks he has violated one of the eligibility rules."

There was no beating about the bush with Reddy Ray, no shading of fact, no distortion of the truth. Coolly he stated the case. But, strangely to Ken, the very truth, told by Reddy in this way, somehow lost its terrors. Ken's shoulders seemed unburdened of a terrible weight.

Andrews and his colleague laughed heartily.

"You see—I—I forgot all about it," said Ken.

"Yes, and since he remembered he's been worrying himself sick," resumed Reddy. "Couldn't rest till he'd come over here."

"Ward, it's much to your credit that you should confide something there was never any chance of becoming known," said the president of the athletic faculty. "We appreciate it. You may relieve your mind of misgivings as to your eligibility. Even if we tried I doubt if we could twist a rule to affect your standing. And you may rest assured we wouldn't try in the case of so fine a young fellow and so splendid a pitcher for Wayne."

Then Andrews courteously shook hands with Ken and Reddy and bowed them out. Ken danced half-way down the stairway and slid the rest on the bannister.

"Reddy, wasn't he just fine?" cried Ken, all palpitating with joy.

"Well, Peg, Andrews is a nice old thing if you approach him right," replied Reddy, dryly. "You wouldn't believe me, would you, if I said I had my heart in my throat when we went in?"

"No, I wouldn't," replied Ken, bluntly.

"I thought not," said Reddy. Then the gravity that had suddenly perplexed Ken cleared from the sprinter's face. "Peg, let's have some fun with Worry and the boys."

"I'm in for anything now."

"We'll go back to the training-house with long faces. When we get in you run up-stairs as if you couldn't face any one, but be sure to sneak back to the head of the stairs to see and hear the fun. I'll fix Worry all right. Now, don't flunk. It's a chance."

Ken could not manage to keep a straight face as they went in, so he hid it and rushed up-stairs. He bumped into Raymond, knocking him flat.

"Running to a fire again?" growled Raymond. "Got a fire-medal, haven't you? Always falling over people."

Ken tried to simulate ungovernable rage and impotent distress at once. He waved one fist and tore his hair with the other hand.

"Get out of my way!" roared Ken. "What'll you say when I tell you I'm barred from the varsity!"

"Oh! Ken! No, no—don't say it," faltered Raymond, all sympathy in an instant.

Ken ran into his room, closed the door and then peeped out. He saw Raymond slowly sag down-stairs as if his heart was broken. Then Ken slipped out and crawled down the hall till he could see into the reading-room. All the boys were there, with anxious faces, crowded round the coach. Worry was livid. Reddy Ray seemed the only calm person in the room and he had tragedy written all over him.

"Out with it!" shouted Worry. "Don't stand there like a mournful preacher. What did 'em fat-heads say?"

Reddy threw up his hands with a significant gesture.

"I knew it!" howled Worry, jumping up and down. "I knew it! Why did you take the kid over there? Why didn't you let me and Homans handle this thing? You red-headed, iron-jawed, cold-blooded wind-chaser! You've done it now, haven't you? I—Oh—"

Worry began to flounder helplessly.

"They said a few more things," went on Reddy. "Peg is barred, Raymond is barred, I am barred. I told them about my baseball career out West. The directors said some pretty plain things about you, Worry, I'm sorry to tell. You're a rotten coach. In fact, you ought to be a coach at an undertaker's. Homans gets the credit for the work of the team. They claim you are too hard on the boys, too exacting, too brutal, in fact. Andrews recited a record of your taking sandwiches from us and aiding and abetting Murray in our slow starvation. The directors will favor your dismissal and urge the appointment of Professor Rhodes, who as coach will at least feed us properly."

Reddy stopped to catch his breath and gain time for more invention. Of all the unhappy mortals on earth Worry Arthurs looked the unhappiest. He believed every word as if it had been gospel. And that about Professor Rhodes was the last straw.

Ken could stand the deception no longer. He marvelled at Reddy's consummate lying and how he could ever stand that look on Worry's face. Bounding down-stairs four steps at a jump, Ken burst like a bomb upon the sad-faced group.

"Oh, Worry, it's all a joke!"

The First Place Game

Rain prevented the second Herne game, which was to have been played on the Herne grounds. It rained steadily all day Friday and Saturday, to the disappointment of Wayne's varsity. The coach, however, admitted that he was satisfied to see the second contest with Herne go by the board.

"I don't like big games away from home," said Worry. "It's hard on new teams. Besides, we beat Herne to death over here. Mebbe we couldn't do it over there, though I ain't doubtin'. But it's Place we're after, and if we'd had that game at Herne we couldn't have kept Place from gettin' a line on us. So I'm glad it rained."

The two Place games fell during a busy week at Wayne. Wednesday was the beginning of the commencement exercises and only a comparatively few students could make the trip to Place. But the night before the team left, the students, four thousand strong, went to the training-house and filled a half-hour with college songs and cheers.

Next morning Dale and Stevens, heading a small band of Wayne athletes and graduates, met the team at the railroad station and boarded the train with them. Worry and Homans welcomed them, and soon every Wayne player had two or more for company. Either by accident or design, Ken could not tell which, Dale and Stevens singled him out for their especial charge. The football captain filled one seat with his huge bulk and faced Ken, and Dale sat with a hand on Ken's shoulder.

"Peg, we're backing you for all we're worth," said Stevens. "But this is your first big game away from home. It's really the toughest game of the season. Place is a hard nut to crack any time. And her players on their own backyard are scrappers who can take a lot of beating and still win out. Then there's another thing that's no small factor in their strength: They are idolized by the students, and rooting at Place is a science. They have a yell that beats anything you ever heard. It'll paralyze a fellow at a critical stage. But that yell is peculiar in that it rises out of circumstances leading to almost certain victory. That is, Place has to make a strong bid for a close, hard game to work up that yell. So if it comes to-day you be ready for it. Have your ears stuffed with cotton, and don't let that yell blow you up in the air."

Dale was even more earnest than Stevens.

"Peg, Place beat me over here last year, beat me 6-3. They hit me harder than I ever was hit before, I guess. You went down to Washington, Worry said, to look them over. Tell me what you think—how you sized them up."

Dale listened attentively while Ken recited his impressions.

"You've got Prince and MacNeff figured exactly right," replied Dale. "Prince is the football captain, by-the-way. Be careful how you run into second base. If you ever slide into him head first—good-bye! He's a great player, and he can hit any kind of a ball. MacNeff now, just as you said, is weak on a high ball close in, and he kills a low ball. Kills is the word! He hits them a mile. But, Peg, I think you're a little off on Keene, Starke, and Martin, the other Place cracks. They're veterans, hard to pitch to; they make you cut the plate; they are as apt to bunt as hit, and they are fast. They keep a fellow guessing. I think Starke pulls a little on a curve, but the others have no weakness I ever discovered. But, Peg, I expect you to do more with them than I did. My control was never any too good, and you can throw almost as straight as a fellow could shoot a rifle. Then your high fast ball, that one you get with the long swing, it would beat any team. Only I'm wondering, I'm asking—can you use it right along, in the face of such coaching and yelling and hitting as you'll run against to-day? I'm asking deliberately, because I want to give you confidence."

"Why, yes, Dale, I think I can. I'm pretty sure of it. That ball comes easily, only a little longer swing and more snap, and honestly, Dale, I hardly ever think about the plate. I know where it is, and I could shut my eyes and throw strikes."

"Peg, you're a wonder," replied Dale, warmly. "If you can do that—and hang me if I doubt it—you will make Place look like a lot of dubs. We're sure to make a few runs. Homans and Ray will hit Salisbury hard. There's no fence on Place Field, and every ball Reddy hits past a fielder will be a home-run. You can gamble on that. So set a fast clip when you start in, and hang."

Some time later, when Ken had changed seats and was talking to Raymond, he heard Worry say to somebody:

"Well, if Peg don't explode to-day he never will. I almost wish he would. He'd be better for it, afterward."

This surprised Ken, annoyed him, and straightway he became thoughtful. Why this persistent harping on the chance of his getting excited from one cause or another, losing his control and thereby the game? Ken had not felt in the least nervous about the game. He would get so, presently, if his advisers did not stop hinting. Then Worry's wish that he might "explode" was puzzling. A little shade of gloom crept over the bright horizon of Ken's hopes. Almost unconsciously vague doubts of himself fastened upon him. For the first time he found himself looking forward to a baseball game with less eagerness than uncertainty. Stubbornly he fought off the mood.

Place was situated in an old college town famed for its ancient trees and quaint churches and inns. The Wayne varsity, arriving late, put on their uniforms at the St. George, a tavern that seemed never to have been in any way acquainted with a college baseball team. It was very quiet and apparently deserted. For that matter the town itself appeared deserted. The boys dressed hurriedly, in silence, with frowning brows and compressed lips. Worry Arthurs remained downstairs while they dressed. Homans looked the team over and then said:

"Boys, come on! To-day's our hardest game."

It was only a short walk along the shady street to the outskirts of the town and the athletic field. The huge stands blocked the view from the back and side. Homans led the team under the bleachers, through a narrow walled-in aisle, to the side entrance, and there gave the word for the varsity to run out upon the field. A hearty roar of applause greeted their appearance.

Ken saw a beautiful green field, level as a floor, with a great half-circle of stands and bleachers at one end. One glance was sufficient to make Ken's breathing an effort. He saw a glittering mass, a broad, moving band of color. Everywhere waved Place flags, bright gold and blue. White faces gleamed like daisies on a golden slope. In the bleachers close to the first base massed a shirt-sleeved crowd of students, row on row of them, thousands in number. Ken experienced a little chill as he attached the famous Place yell to that significant placing of rooters. A soft breeze blew across the field, and it carried low laughter and voices of girls, a merry hum, and subdued murmur, and an occasional clear shout. The whole field seemed keenly alive.

From the bench Ken turned curious, eager eyes upon the practising Place men. Never had he regarded players with as sharp an interest, curiosity being mingled with admiration, and confidence with doubt. MacNeff, the captain, at first base, veteran of three years, was a tall, powerful fellow, bold and decisive in action. Prince, Place's star on both gridiron and diamond, played at second base. He was very short, broad and heavy, and looked as if he would have made three of little Raymond. Martin, at short-stop, was of slim, muscular build. Keene and Starke, in centre and left, were big men. Salisbury looked all of six feet, and every inch a pitcher. He also played end on the football varsity. Ken had to indulge in a laugh at the contrast in height and weight of Wayne when compared to Place. The laugh was good for him, because it seemed to loosen something hard and tight within his breast. Besides, Worry saw him laugh and looked pleased, and that pleased Ken.

"Husky lot of stiffs, eh, Peg?" said Worry, reading Ken's thought. "But, say! this ain't no football game. We'll make these heavyweights look like ice-wagons. I never was much on beefy ball-players. Aha! there goes the gong. Place's takin' the field. That suits me.... Peg, listen! The game's on. I've only one word to say to you. Try to keep solid on your feet!"

A short cheer, electrifying in its force, pealed out like a blast.

Then Homans stepped to the plate amid generous hand-clapping. The Place adherents had their favorites, but they always showed a sportsmanlike appreciation of opponents. Salisbury wound up, took an enormous stride, and pitched the ball. He had speed. Homans seldom hit on the first pitch, and this was a strike. But he rapped the next like a bullet at Griffith, the third-baseman. Griffith blocked the ball, and, quickly reaching it, he used a snap underhand throw to first, catching Homans by a narrow margin. It was a fine play and the crowd let out another blast.

Raymond, coming up, began his old trick of trying to work the pitcher for a base. He was small and he crouched down until a wag in the bleachers yelled that this was no kindergarten game. Raymond was exceedingly hard to pitch to. He was always edging over the plate, trying to get hit. If anybody touched him in practice he would roar like a mad bull, but in a game he would cheerfully have stopped cannon-balls. He got in front of Salisbury's third pitch, and, dropping his bat, started for first base. The umpire called him back. Thereupon Raymond fouled balls and went through contortions at the plate till he was out on strikes.

When Reddy Ray took his position at bat audible remarks passed like a wave through the audience. Then a long, hearty cheer greeted the great sprinter. When roar once again subsided into waiting suspense a strong-lunged Wayne rooter yelled, "Watch him run!"

The outfielders edged out deeper and deeper. MacNeff called low to Salisbury: "Don't let this fellow walk! Keep them high and make him hit!" It was evident that Place had gotten a line on one Wayne player.

Salisbury delivered the ball and Reddy whirled with his level swing. There was a sharp crack.

Up started the crowd with sudden explosive: "Oh!"

Straight as a bee-line the ball sped to Keene in deep centre, and Reddy was out.

Wayne players went running out and Place players came trotting in. Ken, however, at Worry's order, walked slowly and leisurely to the pitcher's box. He received an ovation from the audience that completely surprised him and which stirred him to warm gratefulness. Then, receiving the ball, he drew one quick breath, and faced the stern issue of the day.

As always, he had his pitching plan clearly defined in mind, and no little part of it was cool deliberation, study of the batter to the point of irritating him, and then boldness of action. He had learned that he was not afraid to put the ball over the plate, and the knowledge had made him bold, and boldness increased his effectiveness.

For Keene, first batter up, Ken pitched his fast ball with all his power. Like a glancing streak it shot over. A low whistling ran through the bleachers. For the second pitch Ken took the same long motion, ending in the sudden swing, but this time he threw a slow, wide, tantalizing curve that floated and waved and circled around across the plate. It also was a strike. Keene had not offered to hit either. In those two balls, perfectly controlled, Ken deliberately showed the Place team the wide extremes of his pitching game.

"Keene, he don't waste any. Hit!" ordered MacNeff from the bench. The next ball, a high curve, Keene hit on the fly to Homans.

The flaxen-haired Prince trotted up with little, short steps. Ken did not need the wild outburst from the crowd to appreciate this sturdy hero of many gridiron and diamond battles. He was so enormously wide, almost as wide as he was long, that he would have been funny to Ken but for the reputation that went with the great shoulders and stumpy legs.

"Ward, give me a good one," said Prince, in a low, pleasant voice. He handled his heavy bat as if it had been light as a yardstick.

It was with more boldness than intention of gratifying Prince that Ken complied, using the same kind of ball he had tried first on Keene. Prince missed it. The next, a low curve, he cracked hard to the left of Raymond. The second-baseman darted over, fielded the ball cleanly, and threw Prince out.

Then the long, rangy MacNeff, home-run hitter for Place, faced Ken. His position at bat bothered Ken, for he stood almost on the plate. Remembering MacNeff's weakness, Ken lost no time putting a swift in-shoot under his chin. The Place captain lunged round at it, grunting with his swing. If he had hit the ball it would have been with the handle of his bat. So Ken, knowing his control, and sure that he could pitch high shoots all day over the incomer of the plate, had no more fear of the Place slugger. And it took only three more pitches to strike him out.

From that on the game see-sawed inning by inning, Ken outpitching Salisbury, but neither team scored. At intervals cheers marked the good plays of both teams, and time and again the work of the pitchers earned applause. The crowd seemed to be holding back, and while they waited for the unexpected the short, sharp innings slipped by.

Trace for Wayne led off in the seventh with a safe fly over short. Ken, attempting to sacrifice, rolled a little bunt down the third-base line and beat the throw. With no one out and the head of the batting list up, the Wayne players awoke to possibilities. The same fiery intensity that had characterized their play all season now manifested itself. They were all on their feet, and Weir and McCord on the coaching lines were yelling hoarsely at Salisbury, tearing up the grass with their spikes, dashing to and fro, shouting advice to the runners.

"Here's where we score! Oh! you pitcher! We're due to trim you now! Steady, boys, play it safe, play it safe!—don't let them double you!"

Up by the bench Homans was selecting a bat.

"Worry, I'd better dump one," he whispered.

"That's the trick," replied the coach. "Advance them at any cost. There's Reddy to follow."

The reliable Salisbury rolled the ball in his hands, feinted to throw to the bases, and showed his steadiness under fire. He put one square over for Homans and followed it upon the run. Homans made a perfect bunt, but instead of going along either base line, it went straight into the pitcher's hands. Salisbury whirled and threw to Prince, who covered the bag, and forced Trace. One out and still two runners on bases. The crowd uttered a yell and then quickly quieted down. Raymond bent low over the plate and watched Salisbury's slightest move. He bunted the first ball, and it went foul over the third-base line. He twisted the second toward first base, and it, too, rolled foul. And still he bent low as if to bunt again. The infield slowly edged in closer. But Raymond straightened up on Salisbury's next pitch and lined the ball out. Prince leaped into the air and caught the ball in his gloved hand. Homans dove back into first base; likewise Ken into second, just making it in the nick of time, for Martin was on the run to complete a possible double play. A shout at once hoarse and shrill went up, and heavy clattering thunder rolled along the floor of the bleachers. Two out and still two men on bases.

If there was a calm person on Place Field at that moment it was Reddy Ray, but his eyes glinted like sparks as he glanced at the coach.

"Worry, I'll lace one this time," he said, and strode for the plate.

Weir and McCord were shrieking: "Oh, look who's up! Oh-h! Oh-h! Play it safe, boys!"

"Watch him run!"

That came from the same deep-chested individual who had before hinted of the sprinter's fleetness, and this time the Wayne players recognized the voice of Murray. How hopeful and thrilling the suggestion was, coming from him!

The Place infield trotted to deep short-field; the outfielders moved out and swung around far to the right. Salisbury settled down in the box and appeared to put on extra effort as he delivered the ball. It was wide. The next also went off the outside of the plate. It looked as if Salisbury meant to pass Reddy to first. Then those on the bench saw a glance and a nod pass between Reddy Ray and Coach Arthurs. Again Salisbury pitched somewhat to the outside of the plate, but this time Reddy stepped forward and swung.

Crack!

Swift as an arrow and close to the ground the ball shot to left field. Starke leaped frantically to head it off, and as it took a wicked bound he dove forward head first, hands outstretched, and knocked it down. But the ball rolled a few yards, and Starke had to recover from his magnificent effort.

No one on the field saw Ward and Homans running for the plate. All eyes were on the gray, flitting shadow of a sprinter. One voice only, and that was Murray's, boomed out in the silence. When Reddy turned second base Starke reached the ball and threw for third. It was a beautiful race between ball and runner for the bag. As Reddy stretched into the air in a long slide the ball struck and shot off the ground with a glancing bound. They reached the base at the same time. But Griffith, trying to block the runner, went spinning down, and the ball rolled toward the bleachers. Reddy was up and racing plateward so quickly that it seemed he had not been momentarily checked. The few Wayne rooters went wild.

"Three runs!" yelled the delirious coaches. Weir was so overcome that he did not know it was his turn at bat. When called in he hurried to the plate and drove a line fly to centre that Keene caught only after a hard run.

Ken Ward rose from the bench to go out on the diamond. The voices of his comrades sounded far away, as voices in a dream.

"Three to the good now, Ward! It's yours!" said Captain Homans.

"Only nine more batters! Peg, keep your feet leaded!" called Reddy Ray.

"It's the seventh, and Place hasn't made a safe hit! Oh, Ken!" came from Raymond.

So all the boys vented their hope and trust in their pitcher.

There was a mist before Ken's eyes that he could not rub away. The field blurred at times. For five innings after the first he had fought some unaccountable thing. He had kept his speed, his control, his memory of batters, and he had pitched magnificently. But something had hovered over him, and had grown more tangible as the game progressed. There was a shadow always before his sight.

In the last of the seventh, with Keene at bat, Ken faced the plate with a strange unsteadiness and a shrinking for which he hated himself. What was wrong with him? Had he been taken suddenly ill? Anger came to his rescue, and he flung himself into his pitching with fierce ardor. He quivered with a savage hope when Keene swung ineffectually at the high in-shoot. He pitched another and another, and struck out the batter. But now it meant little to see him slam down his bat in a rage. For Ken had a foreboding that he could not do it again. When Prince came up Ken found he was having difficulty in keeping the ball where he wanted it. Prince batted a hot grounder to Blake, who fumbled. MacNeff had three balls and one strike called upon him before he hit hard over second base. But Raymond pounced upon the ball like a tiger, dashed over the bag and threw to first, getting both runners.

"Wull, Ken, make them hit to me," growled Raymond.

Ken sat down upon the bench far from the coach. He shunned Worry in that moment. The warm praise of his fellow-players was meaningless to him. Something was terribly wrong. He knew he shrank from going into the box again, yet dared not admit it to himself. He tried to think clearly, and found his mind in a whirl. When the Wayne batters went out in one, two, three order, and it was time for Ken to pitch again, he felt ice form in his veins.

"Only six more hitters!" called Reddy's warning voice. It meant cheer and praise from Reddy, but to Ken it seemed a knell.

"Am I weakening?" muttered Ken. "Am I going up in the air? What is wrong with me?"

He was nervous now and could not stand still and he felt himself trembling. The ball was wet from the sweat in his hands; his hair hung damp over his brow and he continually blew it out of his eyes. With all his spirit he crushed back the almost overwhelming desire to hurry, hurry, hurry. Once more, in a kind of passion, he fought off the dreaded unknown weakness.

With two balls pitched to Starke he realized that he had lost control of his curve. He was not frightened for the loss of his curve, but he went stiff with fear that he might lose control of his fast ball, his best and last resort. Grimly he swung and let drive. Starke lined the ball to left. The crowd lifted itself with a solid roar, and when Homans caught the hit near the foul flag, subsided with a long groan. Ken set his teeth. He knew he was not right, but did any one else know it? He was getting magnificent support and luck was still with him.

"Over the pan, Peg! Don't waste one!" floated from Reddy, warningly.

Then Ken felt sure that Reddy had seen or divined his panic. How soon would the Place players find it out? With his throat swelling and his mouth dry and his whole body in a ferment Ken pitched to Martin. The short-stop hit to Weir, who made a superb stop and throw. Two out!

From all about Ken on the diamond came the low encouraging calls of his comrades. Horton, a burly left-hander, stepped forward, swinging a wagon-tongue. Ken could no longer steady himself and he pitched hurriedly. One ball, two balls, one strike, three balls—how the big looming Horton stood waiting over the plate! Almost in despair Ken threw again, and Horton smote the ball with a solid rap. It was a low bounder. Raymond pitched forward full length toward first base and the ball struck in his glove with a crack, and stuck there. Raymond got up and tossed it to McCord. A thunder of applause greeted this star play of the game.

The relief was so great that Ken fairly tottered as he went in to the bench. Worry did not look at him. He scarcely heard what the boys said; he felt them patting him on the back. Then to his amaze, and slowly mounting certainty of disaster, the side was out, and it was again his turn to pitch.

"Only three more, Peg! The tail end of the batting list. Hang on!" said Reddy, as he trotted out.

Ken's old speed and control momentarily came back to him. Yet he felt he pitched rather by instinct than intent. He struck Griffith out.

"Only two more, Peg!" called Reddy.

The great audience sat in depressed, straining silence. Long since the few Wayne rooters had lost their vocal powers.

Conroy hit a high fly to McCord.

"Oh, Peg, only one more!" came the thrilling cry. No other Wayne player could speak a word then.

With Salisbury up, Ken had a momentary flash of his old spirit and he sent a straight ball over the plate, meaning it to be hit. Salisbury did hit it, and safely, through short. The long silent, long waiting crowd opened up with yells and stamping feet.

A horrible, cold, deadly sickness seized upon Ken as he faced the fleet, sure-hitting Keene. He lost his speed, he lost his control. Before he knew what had happened he had given Keene a base on balls. Two on bases and two out!

The Place players began to leap and fling up their arms and scream. When out of their midst Prince ran to the plate a piercing, ear-splitting sound pealed up from the stands. As in a haze Ken saw the long lines of white-sleeved students become violently agitated and move up and down to strange, crashing yells.

Then Ken Ward knew. That was the famed Place cheer for victory at the last stand. It was the trumpet-call of Ken's ordeal. His mind was as full of flashes of thought as there were streaks and blurs before his eyes. He understood Worry now. He knew now what was wrong with him, what had been coming all through that terrible game. The whole line of stands and bleachers wavered before him, and the bright colors blended in one mottled band.

Still it was in him to fight to the last gasp. The pain in his breast, and the nausea in his stomach, and the whirling fury in his mind did not make him give up, though they robbed him of strength. The balls he threw to Prince were wide of the plate and had nothing of his old speed. Prince, also, took his base on balls.

Bases full and two out!

MacNeff, the captain, fronted the plate, and shook his big bat at Ken. Of all the Place hitters Ken feared him the least. He had struck MacNeff out twice, and deep down in his heart stirred a last desperate rally. He had only to keep the ball high and in close to win this game. Oh! for the control that had been his pride!

The field and stands seemed to swim round Ken and all he saw with his half-blinded eyes was the white plate, the batter, and Dean and the umpire. Then he took his swing and delivered the ball.

It went true. MacNeff missed it.

Ken pitched again. The umpire held up one finger of each hand. One ball and one strike. Two more rapid pitches, one high and one wide. Two strikes and two balls.

Ken felt his head bursting and there were glints of red before his eyes. He bit his tongue to keep it from lolling out. He was almost done. That ceaseless, infernal din had benumbed his being. With a wrenching of his shoulder Ken flung up another ball. MacNeff leaned over it, then let it go by.

Three and two!

It was torture for Ken. He had the game in his hands, yet could not grasp it. He braced himself for the pitch and gave it all he had left in him.

"Too low!" he moaned. MacNeff killed low balls.

The big captain leaped forward with a terrific swing and hit the ball. It lined over short, then began to rise, shot over Homans, and soared far beyond, to drop and roll and roll.

Through darkening sight Ken Ward saw runner after runner score, and saw Homans pick up the ball as MacNeff crossed the plate with the winning run. In Ken's ears seemed a sound of the end of the world.

He thought himself the centre of a flying wheel. It was the boys crowding around him. He saw their lips move but caught no words. Then choking and tottering, upheld by Reddy Ray's strong arm, the young pitcher walked off the field.

Ken's Day

The slow return to the tavern, dressing and going to the station, the ride home, the arrival at the training-house, the close-pressing, silent companionship of Reddy Ray, Worry, and Raymond—these were dim details of that day of calamity. Ken Ward's mind was dead—locked on that fatal moment when he pitched a low ball to MacNeff. His friends left him in the darkness of his room, knowing instinctively that it was best for him to be alone.

Ken undressed and crawled wearily into bed and stretched out as if he knew and was glad he would never move his limbs again. The silence and the darkness seemed to hide him from himself. His mind was a whirling riot of fire, and in it was a lurid picture of that moment with MacNeff at bat. Over and over and over he lived it in helpless misery. His ears were muffled with that huge tide of sound. Again and again and again he pitched the last ball, to feel his heart stop beating, to see the big captain lunge at the ball, to watch it line and rise and soar.

But gradually exhaustion subdued his mental strife, and he wandered in mind and drifted into sleep. When he woke it was with a cold, unhappy shrinking from the day. His clock told the noon hour; he had slept long. Outside the June sunlight turned the maple leaves to gold. Was it possible, Ken wondered dully, for the sun ever to shine again? Then Scotty came bustling in.

"Mr. Wau-rd, won't ye be hovin' breakfast?" he asked, anxiously.

"Scotty, I'll never eat again," replied Ken.

There were quick steps upon the stairs and Worry burst in, rustling a newspaper.

"Hello, old man!" he called, cheerily. "Say! Look at this!"

He thrust the paper before Ken's eyes and pointed to a column:

Place Beat Wayne by a Lucky Drive.
Young Ward Pitched the Greatest Game Ever
Pitched on Place Field and Lost It in the Ninth,
with Two Men Out and Three and Two on MacNeff.

Ken's dull, gloom-steeped mind underwent a change, but he could not speak. He sat up in bed, clutching the paper, and gazing from it to the coach. Raymond came in, followed by Homans, and, last, Reddy Ray, who sat down upon the bed. They were all smiling, and that seemed horrible to Ken.

"But, Worry—Reddy—I—I lost the game—threw it away!" faltered Ken.

"Oh no, Peg. You pitched a grand game. Only in the stretch you got one ball too low," said Reddy.

"Peg, you started to go up early in the game," added Worry, with a smile, as if the fact was amusing. "You made your first balloon-ascension in the seventh. And in the ninth you exploded. I never seen a better case of up-in-the-air. But, Peg, in spite of it you pitched a wonderful game. You had me guessin'. I couldn't take you out of the box. Darn me if I didn't think you'd shut Place out in spite of your rattles!"

"Then—after all—it's not so terrible?" Ken asked, breathlessly.

"Why, boy, it's all right. We can lose a game, and to lose one like that—it's as good as winnin'. Say! I'm a liar if I didn't see 'em Place hitters turnin' gray-headed! Listen! That game over there was tough on all the kids, you most of all, of course. But you all stood the gaff. You've fought out a grillin' big game away from home. That's over. You'll never go through that again. But it was the makin' of you.... Here, look this over! Mebbe it'll cheer you up."

He took something from Raymond and tossed it upon the bed. It looked like a round, red, woolly bundle. Ken unfolded it, to disclose a beautiful sweater, with a great white "W" in the centre.

"The boys all got 'em this mornin'," added Worry.

It was then that the tragedy of the Place game lost its hold on Ken, and retreated until it stood only dimly in outline.

"I'll—I'll be down to lunch," said Ken, irrelevantly.

His smiling friends took the hint and left the room.

Ken hugged the sweater while reading the Times-Star's account of the game. Whoever the writer was, Ken loved him. Then he hid his face in the pillow, and though he denied to himself that he was crying, when he arose it was certain that the pillow was wet.

An hour later Ken presented himself at lunch, once more his old amiable self. The boys freely discussed baseball—in fact, for weeks they had breathed and dreamed baseball—but Ken noted, for the first time, where superiority was now added to the old confidence. The Wayne varsity had found itself. It outclassed Herne; it was faster than Place; it stood in line for championship honors.

"Peg, you needn't put on your uniform to-day," said the coach. "You rest up. But go over to Murray and have your arm rubbed. Is it sore or stiff?"

"Not at all. I could work again to-day," replied Ken.

That afternoon, alone in his room, he worked out his pitching plan for Saturday's game. It did not differ materially from former plans. But for a working basis he had self-acquired knowledge of the Place hitters. It had been purchased at dear cost. He feared none of them except Prince. He decided to use a high curve ball over the plate and let Prince hit, trusting to luck and the players behind him. Ken remembered how the Place men had rapped hard balls at Raymond. Most of them were right-field hitters. Ken decided to ask Homans to play Reddy Ray in right field. Also he would arrange a sign with Reddy and Raymond and McCord so they would know when he intended to pitch speed on the outside corner of the plate. For both his curve and fast ball so pitched were invariably hit toward right field. When it came to MacNeff, Ken knew from the hot rankling deep down in him that he would foil that hitter. He intended to make the others hit, pitching them always, to the best of his judgment and skill, those balls they were least likely to hit safely, yet which would cut the corners of the plate if let go. No bases on balls this game, that he vowed grimly. And if he got in a pinch he would fall back upon his last resort, the fast jump ball; and now that he had gone through his baptism of fire he knew he was not likely to lose his control. So after outlining his plan he believed beyond reasonable doubt that he could win the game.

The evening of that day he confided his plan to Reddy Ray and had the gratification of hearing it warmly commended. While Ken was with Reddy the coach sent word up to all rooms that the boys were to "cut" baseball talk. They were to occupy their minds with reading, study, or games.

"It's pretty slow," said Reddy. "Peg, let's have some fun with somebody."

"I'm in. What'll we do?"

"Can't you think? You're always leaving schemes to me. Use your brains, boy."

Ken pondered a moment and then leaped up in great glee.

"Reddy, I've got something out of sight," he cried.

"Spring it, then."

"Well, it's this: Kel Raymond is perfectly crazy about his new sweater. He moons over it and he carries it around everywhere. Now it happens that Kel is a deep sleeper. He's hard to wake up. I've always had to shake him and kick him to wake him every morning. I'm sure we could get him in that sweater without waking him. So to-morrow morning you come down early, before seven, and help me put the sweater on Kel. We'll have Worry and the boys posted and we'll call them in to see Kel, and then we'll wake him and swear he slept in his sweater."

"Peg, you've a diabolical bent of mind. That'll be great. I'll be on the job bright and early."

Ken knew he could rely on the chattering of the sparrows in the woodbine round his window. They always woke him, and this morning was no exception. It was after six and a soft, balmy breeze blew in. Ken got up noiselessly and dressed. Raymond snored in blissful ignorance of the conspiracy. Presently a gentle tapping upon the door told Ken that Reddy was in the hall. Ken let him in and they held a whispered consultation.

"Let's see," said Reddy, picking up the sweater. "It's going to be an all-fired hard job. This sweater's tight. We'll wake him."

"Not on your life!" exclaimed Ken. "Not if we're quick. Now you roll up the sweater so—and stretch it on your hands—so—and when I lift Kel up you slip it over his head. It'll be like pie."

The operation was deftly though breathlessly performed, and all it brought from Raymond was a sleepy: "Aw—lemme sleep," and then he was gone again.

Ken and Reddy called all the boys, most of whom were in their pajamas, and Worry and Scotty and Murray, and got them all up-stairs in Raymond's room. Raymond lay in bed very innocently asleep, and no one would have suspected that he had not slept in his sweater.

"Well, I'll be dog-goned!" ejaculated Worry, laughing till he cried. Murray was hugely delighted. These men were as much boys as the boys they trained.

The roar of laughter awakened Raymond, and he came out of sleep very languid and drowsy.

"Aw, Ken, lemme sleep s'more."

He opened his eyes and, seeing the room full of boys and men, he looked bewildered, then suspicious.

"Wull, what do all you guys want?"

"We only came in to see you asleep in your new varsity sweater," replied Ken, with charming candor.

At this Raymond discovered the sweater and he leaped out of bed.

"It's a lie! I never slept in it! Somebody jobbed me! I'll lick him!... It's a lie, I say!"

He began to hop up and down in a black fury. The upper half of him was swathed in the red sweater; beneath that flapped the end of his short nightgown; and out of that stuck his thin legs, all knotted and spotted with honorable bruises won in fielding hard-batted balls. He made so ludicrous a sight that his visitors roared with laughter. Raymond threw books, shoes, everything he could lay his hands upon, and drove them out in confusion.

Saturday seemed a long time in arriving, but at last it came. All morning the boys kept close under cover of the training-house. Some one sent them a package of placards. These were round, in the shape of baseballs. They were in the college colors, the background of which was a bright red, and across this had been printed in white the words: "Peg Ward's Day!"

"What do you think of that?" cried the boys, with glistening eyes. But Ken was silent.

Worry came in for lunch and reported that the whole west end of the city had been placarded.

"The students have had millions of 'em cards printed," said Worry. "They're everywhere. Murray told me there was a hundred students tackin' 'em up on the stands and bleachers. They've got 'em on sticks of wood for pennants for the girls.... 'Peg Ward's Day!' Well, I guess!"

At two-thirty o'clock the varsity ran upon the field, to the welcoming though somewhat discordant music of the university band. What the music lacked in harmony it made up in volume, and as noise appeared to be the order of the day, it was most appropriate. However, a great booming cheer from the crowded stands drowned the band.

It was a bright summer day, with the warm air swimming in the thick, golden light of June, with white clouds sailing across the blue sky. Grant Field resembled a beautiful crater with short, sloping sides of white and gold and great splashes of red and dots of black all encircling a round lake of emerald. Flashes of gray darted across the green, and these were the Place players in practice. Everywhere waved and twinkled and gleamed the red-and-white Wayne placards. And the front of the stands bore wide-reaching bands of these colored cards. The grand-stand, with its pretty girls and gowns, and waving pennants, and dark-coated students, resembled a huge mosaic of many colors, moving and flashing in the sunlight. One stand set apart for the Place supporters was a solid mass of blue and gold. And opposite to it, in vivid contrast, was a long circle of bleachers, where five thousand red-placarded, red-ribboned Wayne students sat waiting to tear the air into shreds with cheers. Dale and Stevens and Bryan, wearing their varsity sweaters, strode to and fro on the cinder-path, and each carried a megaphone. Cheers seemed to lurk in the very atmosphere. A soft, happy, subdued roar swept around the field. Fun and good-nature and fair-play and love of college pervaded that hum of many voices. Yet underneath it all lay a suppressed spirit, a hidden energy, waiting for the battle.

When Wayne had finished a brief, snappy practice, Kern, a National League umpire, called the game, with Place at bat. Ken Ward walked to the pitcher's slab amid a prolonged outburst, and ten thousand red cards bearing his name flashed like mirrors against the sunlight. Then the crashing Place yell replied in defiance.

Ken surveyed his fellow-players, from whom came low, inspiriting words; then, facing the batter, Keene, he eyed him in cool speculation, and swung into supple action.

The game started with a rush. Keene dumped the ball down the third-base line. Blake, anticipating the play, came rapidly in, and bending while in motion picked up the ball and made a perfect snap-throw to McCord, beating Keene by a foot. Prince drove a hot grass-cutter through the infield, and the Place stand let out shrill, exultant yells. MacNeff swung powerfully on the first ball, which streaked like a flitting wing close under his chin. Prince, with a good lead, had darted for second. It was wonderful how his little, short legs carried him so swiftly. And his slide was what might have been expected of a famous football player. He hit the ground and shot into the bag just as Raymond got Dean's unerring throw too late. Again the Place rooters howled. MacNeff watched his second strike go by. The third pitch, remorselessly true to that fatal place, retired him on strikes; and a roll of thunder pealed from under the Wayne bleachers. Starke struck at the first ball given him. The Place waiters were not waiting on Ken to-day; evidently the word had gone out to hit. Ken's beautiful, speedy ball, breast high, was certainly a temptation. Starke lifted a long, lofty fly far beyond Homans, who ran and ran, and turned to get it gracefully at his breast.

Worry Arthurs sat stern and intent upon the Wayne bench. "Get that hit back and go them a run better!" was his sharp order.

The big, loose-jointed Salisbury, digging his foot into the dirt, settled down and swung laboriously. Homans waited. The pitch was a strike, and so was the next. But strikes were small matters for the patient Homans. He drew three balls after that, and then on the next he hit one of his short, punky safeties through the left side of the infield. The Wayne crowd accepted it with vigor of hands and feet. Raymond trotted up, aggressive and crafty. He intended to bunt, and the Place infield knew it and drew in closer. Raymond fouled one, then another, making two strikes. But he dumped the next and raced for the base. Salisbury, big and slow as he was, got the ball and threw Raymond out. Homans over-ran second, intending to go on, but, halted by Weir's hoarse coaching, he ran back.

When Reddy Ray stepped out it was to meet a rousing cheer, and then the thousands of feet went crash! crash! crash! Reddy fouled the first ball over the grand-stand. Umpire Kern threw out a new one, gleaming white. The next two pitches were wide; the following one Reddy met with the short poke he used when hitting to left field. The ball went over Martin's head, scoring Homans with the first run of the game. That allowed the confident Wayne crowd to get up and yell long and loud. Weir fouled out upon the first ball pitched, and Blake, following him, forced Reddy out at second on an infield hit.

Place tied the score in the second inning on Weir's fumble of Martin's difficult grounder, a sacrifice by Horton, and Griffith's safe fly back of second.

With the score tied, the teams blanked inning after inning until the fifth. Wayne found Salisbury easy to bat, but a Place player was always in front of the hit. And Place found Peg Ward unsolvable when hits meant runs. Ken kept up his tireless, swift cannonading over the plate, making his opponents hit, and when they got a runner on base he extended himself with the fast raise ball. In the first of the fifth, with two out, Prince met one of Ken's straight ones hard and fair and drove the ball into the bleachers for a home-run. That solid blue-and-gold square of Place supporters suddenly became an insane tossing, screeching mêlée.

The great hit also seemed to unleash the fiery spirit which had waited its chance. The Wayne players came in for their turn like angry bees. Trace got a base on balls. Dean sacrificed. Ken also essayed to bunt and fouled himself out on strikes. Again Homans hit safely, but the crafty Keene, playing close, held Trace at third.

"We want the score!" Crash! crash! crash! went the bleachers.

With Raymond up and two out, the chance appeared slim, for he was not strong at batting. But he was great at trying, and this time, as luck would have it, he hit clean through second. Trace scored, and Homans, taking desperate risk, tried to reach home on the hit and failed. It was fast, exciting work, and the crowd waxed hotter and hotter.

For Place the lumbering Horton hit a twisting grounder to McCord, who batted it down with his mitt, jumped for it, turned and fell on the base, but too late to get his man. Griffith swung on Ken's straight ball and, quite by accident, blocked a little bunt out of reach of both Dean and Ken. It was a safe hit. Conroy stepped into Ken's fast ball, which ticked his shirt, and the umpire sent him down to first amid the vociferous objections of the Wayne rooters.

Three runners on bases and no one out. How the Place students bawled and beat their seats and kicked the floor!

Ken took a longer moment of deliberation. He showed no sign that the critical situation unnerved him. But his supple shoulders knit closer, and his long arm whipped harder as he delivered the ball.

Salisbury, a poor batter, apparently shut his eyes and swung with all his might. All present heard the ringing crack of the bat, but few saw the ball. Raymond leaped lengthwise to the left and flashed out his glove. There was another crack, of different sound. Then Raymond bounded over second base, kicking the bag, and with fiendish quickness sped the ball to first. Kern, the umpire, waved both arms wide. Then to the gasping audience the play became clear. Raymond had caught Salisbury's line hit in one hand, enabling him to make a triple play. A mighty shout shook the stands. Then strong, rhythmic, lusty cheers held the field in thrall for the moment, while the teams changed sides.

In Wayne's half of the sixth both Weir and McCord hit safely, but sharp fielding by Place held them on base.

Again the formidable head of Place's batting order was up. Keene lined to right field, a superb hit that looked good for a triple, but it had not the speed to get beyond the fleet sprinter.

Ken eyed the curly-haired Prince as if he was saying to himself: "I'm putting them over to-day. Hit if you can!"

Prince appeared to jump up and chop Ken's first pitch. The ball struck on fair ground and bounded very high, and was a safe hit. Prince took a long lead off first base, and three times slid back to the bag when Ken tried to catch him. The fast football man intended to steal; Ken saw it, Dean saw it; everybody saw it. Whereupon Ken delivered a swift ball outside of the plate. As Prince went down little Dean caught the pitch and got the ball away quick as lightning. Raymond caught it directly in the base-line, and then, from the impact of the sliding Prince, he went hurtling down. Runner, baseman, and ball disappeared in a cloud of dust. Kern ran nimbly down the field and waved Prince off.

But Raymond did not get up. The umpire called time. Worry Arthurs ran out, and he and Weir carried Raymond to the bench, where they bathed his head and wiped the blood from his face.

Presently Raymond opened his eyes.

"Wull, what struck me?" he asked.

"Oh, nothin'. There was a trolley loose in the field," replied Worry. "Can you get up? Why did you try to block that football rusher?"

Raymond shook his head.

"Did I tag the big fat devil?" he queried, earnestly. "Is he out?"

"You got him a mile," replied Worry.

After a few moments Raymond was able to stand upon his feet, but he was so shaky that Worry sent Schoonover to second.

Then the cheering leaders before the bleachers bellowed through their megaphones, and the students, rising to their feet, pealed out nine ringing "Waynes!" and added a roaring "Raymond!" to the end.

With two out, Kern called play.

Once again MacNeff was at bat. He had not made a foul in his two times up. He was at Ken's mercy, and the Wayne rooters were equally merciless.

"Ho! the slugging captain comes!"

"Get him a board!"

"Fluke hitter!"

"Mac, that was a lucky stab of yours Wednesday! Hit one now!"

No spectator of that game missed Ken's fierce impetuosity when he faced MacNeff. He was as keen strung as a wire when he stood erect in the box, and when he got into motion he whirled far around, swung back bent, like a spring, and seemed to throw his whole body with the ball. One—two—three strikes that waved up in their velocity, and MacNeff for the third time went out.

Clatter and smash came from the bleachers, long stamping of feet, whistle and bang, for voices had become weak.

A hit, an error, a double play, another hit, a steal, and a forced out—these told Wayne's dogged, unsuccessful trial for the winning run.

But Worry Arthurs had curtly said to his pitcher: "Peg, cut loose!" and man after man for Place failed to do anything with his terrific speed. It was as if Ken had reserved himself wholly for the finish.

In the last of the eighth Dean hit one that caromed off Griffith's shin, and by hard running the little catcher made second. Ken sent him to third on a fielder's choice. It was then the run seemed forthcoming. Salisbury toiled in the box to coax the wary Homans. The Wayne captain waited until he got a ball to his liking. Martin trapped the hit and shot the ball home to catch Dean. It was another close decision, as Dean slid with the ball, but the umpire decided against the runner.

"Peg, lam them over now!" called Reddy Ray.

It was the first of the ninth, with the weak end of Place's hitting strength to face Ken. Griffith, Conroy, Salisbury went down before him as grass before a scythe. To every hitter Ken seemed to bring more effort, more relentless purpose to baffle them, more wonderful speed and control of his fast ball.

Through the stands and bleachers the word went freely that the game would go to ten innings, eleven innings, twelve innings, with the chances against the tiring Salisbury.

But on the Wayne bench there was a different order of conviction. Worry sparkled like flint. Homans, for once not phlegmatic, faced the coaching line at third. Raymond leaned pale and still against the bench. Ken was radiant.

Reddy Ray bent over the row of bats and singled out his own. His strong, freckled hands clenched the bat and whipped it through the air. His eyes were on fire when he looked at the stricken Raymond.

"Kel, something may happen yet before I get up to the plate," he said. "But if it doesn't—"

Then he strode out, knocked the dirt from his spikes, and stepped into position. Something about Reddy at that moment, or something potent in the unforeseen play to come, quieted the huge crowd.

Salisbury might have sensed it. He fussed with the ball and took a long while to pitch. Reddy's lithe form whirled around and seemed to get into running motion with the crack of the ball. Martin made a beautiful pick-up of the sharply bounding ball, but he might as well have saved himself the exertion. The championship sprinter beat the throw by yards.

Suddenly the whole Wayne contingent arose in a body, a tribute to what they expected of Reddy, and rent Grant Field with one tremendous outburst.

As it ceased a hoarse voice of stentorian volume rose and swelled on the air.

"Wayne wins! Watch him run!"

It came from Murray, who loved his great sprinter.

Thrice Salisbury threw to MacNeff to hold Reddy close to first base, but he only wasted his strength. Then he turned toward the batter, and he had scarcely twitched a muscle in the beginning of his swing, when the keen sprinter was gone like a flash. His running gave the impression of something demon-like forced by the wind. He had covered the ground and was standing on the bag when Prince caught Conroy's throw.

Pandemonium broke out in the stands and bleachers, and a piercing, continuous scream. The sprinter could not be stopped. That was plain. He crouched low, watching Salisbury. Again and again the pitcher tried to keep Reddy near second base, but as soon as Martin or Prince returned the ball Reddy took his lead off the bag. He meant to run on the first pitch; he was on his toes. And the audience went wild, and the Place varsity showed a hurried, nervous strain. They yelled to Salisbury, but neither he nor any one else could have heard a thunderbolt in that moment.

Again Salisbury toed the rubber, and he hesitated, with his face turned toward second. But he had to pitch the ball, and as his elbow trembled the sprinter shot out of his tracks with the start that had made him famous. His red hair streaked in the wind like a waving flame. His beautiful stride swallowed distance. Then he sailed low and slid into the base as the ball struck Griffith's hands.

Reddy was on third now, with no one out, with two balls upon Weir and no strikes. In the fury of sound runner and batter exchanged a glance that was a sign.

The sprinter crouched low, watching Salisbury. For the third time, as the pitcher vibrated with the nervous force preceding his delivery, Reddy got his start. He was actually running before the ball left Salisbury's hand. Almost it seemed that with his marvellous fleetness he was beating the ball to the plate. But as the watchers choked in agony of suspense Weir bunted the ball, and Reddy Ray flashed across the plate with the winning run.

Then all that seemed cheering, din, and stamping roar deadened in an earth-shaking sound like an avalanche.

The students piled out of the bleachers in streams and poured on the field. An irresistible, hungry, clamoring flood, they submerged the players.

Up went Ken upon sturdy shoulders, and up went Reddy Ray and Kel and Homans and Dean—all the team, and last the red-faced Worry Arthurs. Then began the triumphant march about Grant Field and to the training-house.

It was a Wayne day, a day for the varsity, for Homans and Raymond, and for the great sprinter, but most of all it was Peg Ward's day.

Breaking Training

The Wayne varsity was a much-handled, storm-tossed team before it finally escaped the clutches of the students. Every player had a ringing in his ears and a swelling in his heart. When the baseball uniforms came off they were carefully packed in the bottoms of trunks, and twelve varsity sweaters received as tender care as if they were the flimsy finery dear to the boys' sisters.

At six the players were assembled in the big reading-room, and there was a babel of exultant conversation. Worry suddenly came in, shouting to persons without, who manifestly wanted to enter. "Nothin' doin' yet! I'll turn the boys over to you in one hour!" Then he banged the door and locked it.

Worry was a sight to behold. His collar was unbuttoned, and his necktie disarranged. He had no hat. His hair was damp and rumpled, and his red face worked spasmodically.

"Where's Peg?" he yelled, and his little bright eyes blinked at his players. It was plain that Worry could not see very well then. Some one pushed Ken out, and Worry fell on his neck. He hugged him close and hard. Then he dived at Reddy and mauled him. Next he fell all over little crippled Raymond, who sat propped up in an arm-chair. For once Raymond never murmured for being jumped on. Upon every player, and even the substitutes, Worry expressed his joy in violent manner, and then he fell down himself, perspiring, beaming, utterly exhausted. This man was not the cold, caustic coach of the cage-days, nor the stern, hard ruler from the bench, nor the smooth worker on his players' feelings. This was Worry Arthurs with his varsity at the close of a championship season. No one but the boys who had fought at his bidding for Wayne ever saw him like that.

"Oh, Peg, it was glorious! This game gives us the record and the championship. Say, Peg, this was the great game for you to win. For you made Place hit, and then when they got runners on bases you shut down on 'em. You made MacNeff look like a dub. You gave that home-run to Prince."

"I sure was after MacNeff's scalp," replied Ken. "And I put the ball over for Prince to hit. What else could I do? Why, that little chunky cuss has an eye, and he can sting the ball—he's almost as good as Reddy. But, Worry, you mustn't give me the credit. Reddy won the game, you know."

"You talk like a kid," replied Reddy, for once not cool and easy. "I cut loose and ran some; but, Peg, you and Raymond won the game."

"Wull, you make me sick," retorted Raymond, threatening to get up. "There wasn't anything to this day but Peg Ward."

Ken replied with more heat than dignity, and quick as a flash he and Reddy and Raymond were involved in a wordy war, trying to place the credit for winning the game. They dragged some of the other boys into the fierce argument.

Worry laughed and laughed; then, as this loyal bunch of players threatened to come to blows, he got angry.

"Shut up!" he roared. "I never seen such a lot of hot-headed kids. Shut up, and let me tell you who won this Place game. It'll go down on record as a famous game, so you'll do well to have it straight. Listen! The Wayne varsity won this game. Homans, your captain, won it, because he directed the team and followed orders. He hit and run some, too. Reddy Ray won this game by bein' a blue streak of chain lightnin' on the bases. Raymond won it by makin' a hit when we all expected him to fall dead. He won it twice, the second time with the greatest fieldin' play ever pulled off on Grant Field. Dean won the game by goin' up and hangin' onto Peg's jump ball. McCord won it by diggin' low throws out of the dirt. Weir was around when it happened, wasn't he—and Blake and Trace? Then there was Peg himself. He won the game a little. Say! he had Place trimmed when he stepped on the slab in the first innin'. So you all won the big Wayne-Place game."

Then Worry advanced impressively to the table, put his hand in his breast pocket and brought forth a paper.

"You've won this for me, boys," he said, spreading the paper out.

"What is it?" they asked, wonderingly.

"Nothin' of much importance to you boys as compared with winnin' the game, but some to Worry Arthurs." He paused with a little choke. "It's a five-year contract to coach Wayne's baseball teams."

A thundering cheer attested to the importance of that document to the boys.

"Oh, Worry, but I'm glad!" cried Ken. "Then your son Harry will be in college next year—will be on the team?"

"Say, he'll have to go some to make next year's varsity, with only two or three vacancies to fill. Now, fellows, I want to know things. Sit down now and listen."

They all took seats, leaving the coach standing at the table.

"Homans, is there any hope of your comin' back to college next year?"

"None, I'm sorry to say," replied the captain. "Father intends to put me in charge of his business."

"Reddy, how about a post-graduate course for you? You need that P.G."

"Worry, come to think of it, I really believe my college education would not be complete without that P.G.," replied Reddy, with the old cool speech, and a merry twinkle in his eye.

At this the boys howled like Indians, and Worry himself did a little war-dance.

"Raymond, you'll come back?" went on the coach.

The second-baseman appeared highly insulted. "Come back? Wull, what do you take me for? I'd like to see the guy who can beat me out of my place next season."

This brought another hearty cheer.

Further questioning made clear that all the varsity except Homans, Blake, and McCord would surely return to college.

"Fine! Fine! Fine!" exclaimed Worry.

Then he began to question each player as to what he intended to do through the summer months, and asked him to promise not to play ball on any summer nines.

"Peg, you're the one I'm scared about," said Worry, earnestly. "These crack teams at the seashore and in the mountains will be hot after you. They've got coin too, Peg, and they'll spend it to get you."

"All I've got to say is they'll waste their breath talking to me," replied Ken, with a short laugh.

"What are you goin' to do all summer?" asked Worry, curiously. "Where will you be?"

"I expect to go to Arizona."

"Arizona? What in the deuce are you goin' way out there for?"

Ken paused, and then when about to reply Raymond burst out.

"Worry, he says it's forestry, but he only took up that fool subject because he likes to chase around in the woods. He's nutty about trees and bears and mustangs. He was in Arizona last summer. You ought to hear some of the stories he's told me. Why, if they're true he's got Frank Nelson and Jim Hawkins skinned to a frazzle."

"For instance?" asked Worry, very much surprised and interested.

"Why stories about how he was chased and captured by outlaws, and lassoed bears, and had scraps with Mexicans, and was in wild caves and forest fires, and lots about a Texas ranger who always carried two big guns. I've had the nightmare ever since we've been in the training-house. Oh, Ken can tell stories all right. He's as much imagination as he's got speed with a ball. And say, Worry, he's got the nerve to tell me that this summer he expects to help an old hunter lasso mountain-lions out there in Arizona. What do you think of that?"

"It's straight goods!" protested Ken, solemnly facing the bright-eyed boys.

"We want to go along!" yelled everybody.

"Say, Peg, I ain't stuck on that idee, not a little bit," replied the coach, dubiously.

"Worry has begun to worry about next season. He's afraid Peg will get that arm chewed off," put in Reddy.

"Well, if I've got to choose between lettin' Peg chase mountain-lions and seein' him chased by 'em fat-head directors, I'll take my chances with the lions."

Then all in a moment Worry became serious.

"Boys, it's time to break trainin'. I ain't got much to say. You're the best team I ever developed. Let it go at that. In a few minutes you are free to go out to the banquets and receptions, to all that's waitin' for you. And it will be great. To-morrow you will be sayin' good-bye to me and to each other and scatterin' to your homes. But let's not forget each other and how we plugged this year. Sure, it was only baseball, but, after all, I think good, hard play, on the square and against long odds, will do as much for you as your studies. Let the old baseball coach assure you of that."

He paused, paced a few steps to and fro, hands behind his back, thoughtful and somewhat sad.

The members of the varsity sat pale and still, faces straight before them, eyes shining with memory of that long up-hill struggle, and glistening, too, with the thought that the time had come for parting.

"Homans, will you please see to the election of the new captain?" said Worry.

Homans stepped out briskly and placed a hat, twelve folded slips of paper, and a pencil upon the table.

"Fellows, you will follow me in our regular batting order," directed Homans. "Each man is to write his name on one side of a slip of paper and his choice for captain on the other side. Drop the paper in the hat."

Homans seated himself at the table and quickly cast his vote. Raymond hobbled up next. Reddy Ray followed him. And so, in silence, and with a certain grave dignity of manner that had yet a suggestion of pleasure, the members of the varsity voted.

When they had resumed their seats Homans turned the slips out of the hat and unfolded them.

"These votes will be given to the athletic directors and kept on record," he said. "But we will never see but one side of them. That is Wayne's rule in electing captains, so the players will not know how each voted. But this is an occasion I am happy to see when we shall all know who voted for who. It shall be a little secret of which we will never speak."

He paused while he arranged the slips neatly together.

"There are here twelve votes. Eleven have been cast for one player—one for another player! Will you all please step forward and look?"

In an intense stillness the varsity surrounded the table. There was a sudden sharp gasp from one of them.

With a frank, glad smile Homans held out his hand.

"Captain Ward!"

THE REDHEADED OUTFIELD AND OTHER BASEBALL STORIES

THE REDHEADED OUTFIELD

There was Delaney's red-haired trio—Red Gilbat, left fielder; Reddy Clammer, right fielder, and Reddie Ray, center fielder, composing the most remarkable outfield ever developed in minor league baseball. It was Delaney's pride, as it was also his trouble.

Red Gilbat was nutty—and his batting average was .371. Any student of baseball could weigh these two facts against each other and understand something of Delaney's trouble. It was not possible to camp on Red Gilbat's trail. The man was a jack-o'-lantern, a will-o'-the-wisp, a weird, long-legged, long-armed, red-haired illusive phantom. When the gong rang at the ball grounds there were ten chances to one that Red would not be present. He had been discovered with small boys peeping through knotholes at the vacant left field he was supposed to inhabit during play.

Of course what Red did off the ball grounds was not so important as what he did on. And there was absolutely no telling what under the sun he might do then except once out of every three times at bat he could be counted on to knock the cover off the ball.

Reddy Clammer was a grand-stand player—the kind all managers hated—and he was hitting .305. He made circus catches, circus stops, circus throws, circus steals—but particularly circus catches. That is to say, he made easy plays appear difficult. He was always strutting, posing, talking, arguing, quarreling—when he was not engaged in making a grand-stand play. Reddy Clammer used every possible incident and artifice to bring himself into the limelight.

Reddie Ray had been the intercollegiate champion in the sprints and a famous college ball player. After a few months of professional ball he was hitting over .400 and leading the league both at bat and on the bases. It was a beautiful and a thrilling sight to see him run. He was so quick to start, so marvelously swift, so keen of judgment, that neither

Delaney nor any player could ever tell the hit that he was not going to get. That was why Reddie Ray was a whole game in himself.

Delaney's Rochester Stars and the Providence Grays were tied for first place. Of the present series each team had won a game. Rivalry had always been keen, and as the teams were about to enter the long homestretch for the pennant there was battle in the New England air.

The September day was perfect. The stands were half full and the bleachers packed with a white-sleeved mass. And the field was beautifully level and green. The Grays were practicing and the Stars were on their bench.

"We're up against it," Delaney was saying. "This new umpire, Fuller, hasn't got it in for us. Oh, no, not at all! Believe me, he's a robber. But Scott is pitchin' well. Won his last three games. He'll bother 'em. And the three Reds have broken loose. They're on the rampage. They'll burn up this place today."

Somebody noted the absence of Gilbat.

Delaney gave a sudden start. "Why, Gil was here," he said slowly. "Lord!—he's about due for a nutty stunt."

Whereupon Delaney sent boys and players scurrying about to find Gilbat, and Delaney went himself to ask the Providence manager to hold back the gong for a few minutes.

Presently somebody brought Delaney a telephone message that Red Gilbat was playing ball with some boys in a lot four blocks down the street. When at length a couple of players marched up to the bench with Red in tow Delaney uttered an immense sigh of relief and then, after a close scrutiny of Red's face, he whispered, "Lock the gates!"

Then the gong rang. The Grays trooped in. The Stars ran out, except Gilbat, who ambled like a giraffe. The hum of conversation in the grand stand quickened for a moment with the scraping of chairs, and then grew quiet. The bleachers sent up the rollicking cry of expectancy. The umpire threw out a white ball with his stentorian "Play!" and Blake of the Grays strode to the plate.

Hitting safely, he started the game with a rush. With Dorr up, the Star infield played for a bunt. Like clockwork Dorr dumped the first ball as Blake got his flying start for second base. Morrissey tore in for the ball, got it on the run and snapped it underhand to Healy, beating the runner by an inch. The fast Blake, with a long slide, made third base. The stands stamped. The bleachers howled. White, next man up, batted a high fly to left field. This was a sun field and the hardest to play in the league. Red Gilbat was the only man who ever played it well. He judged the fly, waited under it, took a step hack, then forward, and deliberately caught the ball in his gloved hand. A throw-in to catch the runner scoring from third base would have been futile, but it was not like Red Gilbat to fail to try. He tossed the ball to O'Brien. And Blake scored amid applause.

"What do you know about that?" ejaculated Delaney, wiping his moist face. "I never before saw our nutty Redhead pull off a play like that."

Some of the players yelled at Red, "This is a two-handed league, you bat!"

The first five players on the list for the Grays were left-handed batters, and against a right-handed pitcher whose most effective ball for them was a high fast one over the outer corner they would naturally hit toward left field. It was no surprise to see Hanley bat a skyscraper out to left. Red had to run to get under it. He braced himself rather unusually for a fielder. He tried to catch the ball in his bare right hand and muffed it, Hanley got to second on the play while the audience roared. When they got through there was some roaring among the Rochester players. Scott and Captain Healy roared at Red, and Red roared back at them.

"It's all off. Red never did that before," cried Delaney in despair. "He's gone clean bughouse now."

Babcock was the next man up and he likewise hit to left. It was a low, twisting ball—half fly, half liner—and a difficult one to field. Gilbat ran with great bounds, and though he might have got two hands on the ball he did not try, but this time caught it in his right, retiring the side.

The Stars trotted in, Scott and Healy and Kane, all veterans, looking like thunderclouds. Red ambled in the last and he seemed very nonchalant.

"By Gosh, I'd 'a' ketched that one I muffed if I'd had time to change hands," he said with a grin, and he exposed a handful of peanuts. He had refused to drop the peanuts to make the catch with two hands. That explained the mystery. It was funny, yet nobody laughed. There was that run chalked up against the Stars, and this game had to be won.

"Red, I—I want to take the team home in the lead," said Delaney, and it was plain that he suppressed strong feeling. "You didn't play the game, you know."

Red appeared mightily ashamed.

"Del, I'll git that run back," he said.

Then he strode to the plate, swinging his wagon-tongue bat. For all his awkward position in the box he looked what he was—a formidable hitter. He seemed to tower over the pitcher—Red was six feet one—and he scowled and shook his bat at Wehying and called, "Put one over—you wienerwurst!" Wehying was anything but red-headed, and he wasted so many balls on Red that it looked as if he might pass him. He would have passed him, too, if Red had not stepped over on the fourth ball and swung on it. White at second base leaped high for the stinging hit, and failed to reach it. The ball struck and bounded for the fence. When Babcock fielded it in, Red was standing on third base, and the bleachers groaned.

Whereupon Chesty Reddy Clammer proceeded to draw attention to himself, and incidentally delay the game, by assorting the bats as if the audience and the game might gladly wait years to see him make a choice.

"Git in the game!" yelled Delaney.

"Aw, take my bat, Duke of the Abrubsky!" sarcastically said Dump Kane. When the grouchy Kane offered to lend his bat matters were critical in the Star camp.

Other retorts followed, which Reddy Clammer deigned not to notice. At last he got a bat that suited him—and then, importantly, dramatically, with his cap jauntily riding his red locks, he marched to the plate.

Some wag in the bleachers yelled into the silence, "Oh, Maggie, your lover has come!"

Not improbably Clammer was thinking first of his presence before the multitude, secondly of his batting average and thirdly of the run to be scored. In this instance he waited and feinted at balls and fouled strikes at length to work his base. When he got to first base suddenly he bolted for second, and in the surprise of the unlooked-for play he made it by a spread-eagle slide. It was a circus steal.

Delaney snorted. Then the look of profound disgust vanished in a flash of light. His huge face beamed.

Reddie Ray was striding to the plate.

There was something about Reddie Ray that pleased all the senses. His lithe form seemed instinct with life; any sudden movement was suggestive of stored lightning. His position at the plate was on the left side, and he stood perfectly motionless, with just a hint of tense waiting alertness. Dorr, Blake and Babcock, the outfielders for the Grays, trotted round to the right of their usual position. Delaney smiled derisively, as if he knew how futile it was to tell what field Reddie Ray might hit into. Wehying, the old fox, warily eyed the youngster, and threw him a high curve, close in. It grazed Reddie's shirt, but he never moved a hair. Then Wehying, after the manner of many veteran pitchers when trying out a new and menacing batter, drove a straight fast ball at Reddie's head. Reddie ducked, neither too slow nor too quick, just right to show what an eye he had, how hard it was to pitch to. The next was a strike. And on the next he appeared to step and swing in one action. There was a ringing rap, and the ball shot toward right, curving down, a vicious, headed hit. Mallory, at first base, snatched at it and found only the air. Babcock had only time to take a few sharp steps, and then he plunged down, blocked the hit and fought the twisting ball. Reddie turned first base, flitted on toward second, went headlong in the dust, and shot to the base before White got the throw-in from Babcock. Then, as White wheeled and lined the ball home to catch the scoring Clammer, Reddie Ray leaped up, got his sprinter's start and, like a rocket, was off for third. This time he dove behind the base, sliding in a half circle, and as Hanley caught Strickland's perfect throw and whirled with the ball, Reddie's hand slid to the bag.

Reddie got to his feet amid a rather breathless silence. Even the coachers were quiet. There was a moment of relaxation, then Wehying received the ball from Hanley and faced the batter.

This was Dump Kane. There was a sign of some kind, almost imperceptible, between Kane and Reddie. As Wehying half turned in his swing to pitch, Reddie Ray bounded homeward. It was not so much the boldness of his action as the amazing swiftness of it that held the audience spellbound. Like a thunderbolt Reddie came down the line, almost beating Wehying's pitch to the plate. But Kane's bat intercepted the ball, laying it down, and Reddie scored without sliding. Dorr, by sharp work, just managed to throw Kane out.

Three runs so quick it was hard to tell how they had come. Not in the major league could there have been faster work. And the ball had been fielded perfectly and thrown perfectly.

"There you are," said Delaney, hoarsely. "Can you beat it? If you've been wonderin' how the cripped Stars won so many games just put what you've seen in your pipe and smoke it. Red Gilbat gets on—Reddy Clammer gets on—and then Reddie Ray drives them home or chases them home."

The game went on, and though it did not exactly drag it slowed down considerably. Morrissey and Healy were retired on infield plays. And the sides changed. For the Grays, O'Brien made a scratch hit, went to second on Strickland's sacrifice, stole third and scored on Mallory's infield out. Wehying missed three strikes. In the Stars' turn the three end players on the batting list were easily disposed of. In the third inning the clever Blake, aided by a base on balls and a hit following, tied the score, and once more struck fire and brimstone from the impatient bleachers. Providence was a town that had to have its team win.

"Git at 'em, Reds!" said Delaney gruffly.

"Batter up!" called Umpire Fuller, sharply.

"Where's Red? Where's the bug? Where's the nut? Delaney, did you lock the gates? Look under the bench!" These and other remarks, not exactly elegant, attested to the mental processes of some of the Stars. Red Gilbat did not appear to be forthcoming. There was an anxious delay Capt. Healy searched for the missing player. Delaney did not say any more.

Suddenly a door under the grand stand opened and Red Gilbat appeared. He hurried for his bat and then up to the plate. And he never offered to hit one of the balls Wehying shot over. When Fuller had called the third strike Red hurried back to the door and disappeared.

"Somethin' doin'," whispered Delaney.

Lord Chesterfield Clammer paraded to the batter's box and, after gradually surveying the field, as if picking out the exact place he meant to drive the ball, he stepped to the plate. Then a roar from the bleachers surprised him.

"Well, I'll be dog-goned!" exclaimed Delaney. "Red stole that sure as shootin'."

Red Gilbat was pushing a brand-new baby carriage toward the batter's box. There was a tittering in the grand stand; another roar from the bleachers. Clammer's face turned as red as his hair. Gilbat shoved the baby carriage upon the plate, spread wide his long arms, made a short presentation speech and an elaborate bow, then backed away.

All eyes were centered on Clammer. If he had taken it right the incident might have passed without undue hilarity. But Clammer became absolutely wild with rage. It was well known that he was unmarried. Equally well was it seen that Gilbat had executed one of his famous tricks. Ball players were inclined to be dignified about the presentation of gifts upon the field, and Clammer, the dude, the swell, the lady's man, the favorite of the baseball gods—in his own estimation—so far lost control of himself that he threw his bat at his retreating tormentor. Red jumped high and the bat skipped along the ground toward the bench. The players sidestepped and leaped and, of course, the bat cracked one of Delaney's big shins. His eyes popped with pain, but he could not stop laughing. One by one the players lay down and rolled over and yelled. The superior Clammer was not overliked by his co-players.

From the grand stand floated the laughter of ladies and gentlemen. And from the bleachers—that throne of the biting, ironic, scornful fans—pealed up a howl of delight. It lasted for a full minute. Then, as quiet ensued, some boy blew a blast of one of those infernal little instruments of pipe and rubber balloon, and over the field wailed out a shrill, high-keyed cry, an excellent imitation of a baby. Whereupon the whole audience roared, and in discomfiture Reddy Clammer went in search of his bat.

To make his chagrin all the worse he ingloriously struck out. And then he strode away under the lea of the grand-stand wall toward right field.

Reddie Ray went to bat and, with the infield playing deep and the outfield swung still farther round to the right, he bunted a little teasing ball down the third-base line. Like a flash of light he had crossed first base before Hanley got his hands on the ball. Then Kane hit into second base, forcing Reddie out.

Again the game assumed less spectacular and more ordinary play. Both Scott and Wehying held the batters safely and allowed no runs. But in the fifth inning, with the Stars at bat and two out, Red Gilbat again electrified the field. He sprang up from somewhere and walked to the plate, his long shape enfolded in a full-length linen duster. The color and style of this garment might not have been especially striking, but upon Red it had a weird and wonderful effect. Evidently Red intended to bat while arrayed in his long coat, for he stepped into the box and faced the pitcher. Capt. Healy yelled for him to take the duster off. Likewise did the Grays yell.

The bleachers shrieked their disapproval. To say the least, Red Gilbat's crazy assurance was dampening to the ardor of the most blindly confident fans. At length Umpire Fuller waved his hand, enjoining silence and calling time.

"Take it off or I'll fine you."

From his lofty height Gilbat gazed down upon the little umpire, and it was plain what he thought.

"What do I care for money!" replied Red.

"That costs you twenty-five," said Fuller.

"Cigarette change!" yelled Red.

"Costs you fifty."

"Bah! Go to an eye doctor," roared Red.

"Seventy-five," added Fuller, imperturbably.

"Make it a hundred!"

"It's two hundred."

"ROB-B-BER!" bawled Red.

Fuller showed willingness to overlook Red's back talk as well as costume, and he called, "Play!"

There was a mounting sensation of prophetic certainty. Old fox Wehying appeared nervous. He wasted two balls on Red; then he put one over the plate, and then he wasted another. Three balls and one strike! That was a bad place for a pitcher, and with Red Gilbat up it was worse. Wehying swung longer and harder to get all his left behind the throw and let drive. Red lunged and cracked the ball. It went up and up and kept going up and farther out, and as the murmuring audience was slowly transfixed into late realization the ball soared to its height and dropped beyond the left-field fence. A home run!

Red Gilbat gathered up the tails of his duster, after the manner of a neat woman crossing a muddy street, and ambled down to first base and on to second, making prodigious jumps upon the bags, and round third, to come down the home-stretch wagging his red head. Then he stood on the plate, and, as if to exact revenge from the audience for the fun they made of him, he threw back his shoulders and bellowed: "HAW! HAW! HAW!"

Not a handclap greeted him, but some mindless, exceedingly adventurous fan yelled: "Redhead! Redhead! Redhead!"

That was the one thing calculated to rouse Red Gilbat. He seemed to flare, to bristle, and he paced for the bleachers.

Delaney looked as if he might have a stroke. "Grab him! Soak him with a bat! Somebody grab him!"

But none of the Stars was risking so much, and Gilbat, to the howling derision of the gleeful fans, reached the bleachers. He stretched his long arms up to the fence and prepared to vault over. "Where's the guy who called me redhead?" he yelled.

That was heaping fuel on the fire. From all over the bleachers, from everywhere, came the obnoxious word. Red heaved himself over the fence and piled into the fans. Then followed the roar of many voices, the tramping of many feet, the pressing forward of line after line of shirt-sleeved men and boys. That bleacher stand suddenly assumed the maelstrom appearance of a surging mob round an agitated center. In a moment all the players rushed down the field, and confusion reigned.

"Oh! Oh! Oh!" moaned Delaney.

However, the game had to go on. Delaney, no doubt, felt all was over. Nevertheless there were games occasionally that seemed an unending series of unprecedented events. This one had begun admirably to break a record. And the Providence fans, like all other fans, had cultivated an appetite as the game proceeded. They were wild to put the other redheads out of the field or at least out for the inning, wild to tie the score, wild to win and wilder than all for more excitement. Clammer hit safely. But when Reddie Ray lined to the second baseman, Clammer, having taken a lead, was doubled up in the play.

Of course, the sixth inning opened with the Stars playing only eight men. There was another delay. Probably everybody except Delaney and perhaps Healy had forgotten the Stars were short a man. Fuller called time. The impatient bleachers barked for action.

Capt. White came over to Delaney and courteously offered to lend a player for the remaining innings. Then a pompous individual came out of the door leading from the press boxes—he was a director Delaney disliked.

"Guess you'd better let Fuller call the game," he said brusquely.

"If you want to—as the score stands now in our favor," replied Delaney.

"Not on your life! It'll be ours or else we'll play it out and beat you to death."

He departed in high dudgeon.

"Tell Reddie to swing over a little toward left," was Delaney's order to Healy. Fire gleamed in the manager's eye.

Fuller called play then, with Reddy Clammer and Reddie Ray composing the Star outfield. And the Grays evidently prepared to do great execution through the wide lanes thus opened up. At that stage it would not have been like matured ball players to try to crop hits down into the infield.

White sent a long fly back of Clammer. Reddy had no time to loaf on this hit. It was all he could do to reach it and he made a splendid catch, for which the crowd roundly applauded him. That applause was wine to Reddy Clammer. He began to prance on his toes and sing out to Scott: "Make 'em hit to me, old man! Make 'em hit to me!" Whether Scott desired that or not was scarcely possible to say; at any rate, Hanley pounded a hit through the infield. And Clammer, prancing high in the air like a check-reined horse, ran to intercept the ball. He could have received it in his hands, but that would never have served Reddy Clammer. He timed the hit to a nicety, went down with his old grand-stand play and blocked the ball with his anatomy. Delaney swore. And the bleachers, now warm toward the gallant outfielder, lustily cheered him. Babcock hit down the right-field foul line, giving Clammer a long run. Hanley was scoring and Babcock was sprinting for third base when Reddy got the ball. He had a fine arm and he made a hard and accurate throw, catching his man in a close play.

Perhaps even Delaney could not have found any fault with that play. But the aftermath spoiled the thing. Clammer now rode the air; he soared; he was in the clouds; it was his inning and he had utterly forgotten his team mates, except inasmuch as they were performing mere little automatic movements to direct the great machinery in his direction for his sole achievement and glory.

There is fate in baseball as well as in other walks of life. O'Brien was a strapping fellow and he lifted another ball into Clammer's wide territory. The hit was of the high and far-away variety. Clammer started to run with it, not like a grim outfielder, but like one thinking of himself, his style, his opportunity, his inevitable success. Certain it was that in thinking of himself the outfielder forgot his surroundings. He ran across the foul line, head up, hair flying, unheeding the warning cry from Healy. And, reaching up to make his crowning circus play, he smashed face forward into the bleachers fence. Then, limp as a rag, he dropped. The audience sent forth a long groan of sympathy.

"That wasn't one of his stage falls," said Delaney. "I'll bet he's dead.... Poor Reddy! And I want him to bust his face!"

Clammer was carried off the field into the dressing room and a physician was summoned out of the audience.

"Cap., what'd it—do to him?" asked Delaney.

"Aw, spoiled his pretty mug, that's all," replied Healy, scornfully. "Mebee he'll listen to me now."

Delaney's change was characteristic of the man. "Well, if it didn't kill him I'm blamed glad he got it.... Cap, we can trim 'em yet. Reddie Ray'll play the whole outfield. Give Reddie a chance to run! Tell the boy to cut loose. And all of you git in the game. Win or lose, I won't forget it. I've a hunch. Once in a while I can tell what's comin' off. Some queer game this! And we're goin' to win. Gilbat lost the game; Clammer throwed it away again, and now Reddie Ray's due to win it.... I'm all in, but I wouldn't miss the finish to save my life."

Delaney's deep presaging sense of baseball events was never put to a greater test. And the seven Stars, with the score tied, exhibited the temper and timber of a championship team in the last ditch. It was so splendid that almost instantly it caught the antagonistic bleachers.

Wherever the tired Scott found renewed strength and speed was a mystery. But he struck out the hard-hitting Providence catcher and that made the third out. The Stars could not score in their half of the inning. Likewise the seventh inning passed without a run for either side; only the infield work of the Stars was something superb. When the eighth inning ended, without a tally for either team, the excitement grew tense. There was Reddy Ray playing outfield alone, and the Grays with all their desperate endeavors had not lifted the ball out of the infield.

But in the ninth, Blake, the first man up, lined low toward right center. The hit was safe and looked good for three bases. No one looking, however, had calculated on Reddie's Ray's fleetness. He covered ground and dove for the bounding ball and knocked it down. Blake did not get beyond first base. The crowd cheered the play equally with the prospect of a run. Dorr bunted and beat the throw. White hit one of the high fast balls Scott was serving and sent it close to the left-field foul line. The running Reddie Ray made on that play held White at second base. But two runs had scored with no one out.

Hanley, the fourth left-handed hitter, came up and Scott pitched to him as he had to the others—high fast balls over the inside corner of the plate. Reddy Ray's position was some fifty yards behind deep short, and a little toward center field. He stood sideways, facing two-thirds of that vacant outfield. In spite of Scott's skill, Hanley swung the ball far round into right field, but he hit it high, and almost before he actually hit it the great sprinter was speeding across the green.

The suspense grew almost unbearable as the ball soared in its parabolic flight and the red-haired runner streaked dark across the green. The ball seemed never to be coming down. And when it began to descend and reached a point perhaps fifty feet above the ground there appeared more distance between where it would alight and where Reddie was than anything human could cover. It dropped and dropped, and then dropped into Reddie Ray's outstretched hands. He had made the catch look easy. But the fact that White scored from second base on the play showed what the catch really was.

There was no movement or restlessness of the audience such as usually indicated the beginning of the exodus. Scott struck Babcock out. The game still had fire. The Grays never let up a moment on their coaching. And the hoarse voices of the Stars were grimmer than ever. Reddie Ray was the only one of the seven who kept silent. And he crouched like a tiger.

The teams changed sides with the Grays three runs in the lead. Morrissey, for the Stars, opened with a clean drive to right. Then Healy slashed a ground ball to Hanley and nearly knocked him down. When old Burns, by a hard rap to short, advanced the runners a base and made a desperate, though unsuccessful, effort to reach first the Providence crowd awoke to a strange and inspiring appreciation. They began that most rare feature in baseball audiences—a strong and trenchant call for the visiting team to win.

The play had gone fast and furious. Wehying, sweaty and disheveled, worked violently. All the Grays were on uneasy tiptoes. And the Stars were seven Indians on the warpath. Halloran fouled down the right-field line; then he fouled over the left-field fence. Wehying tried to make him too anxious, but it was in vain. Halloran was implacable. With two strikes and three balls he hit straight down to white, and was out. The ball had been so sharp that neither runner on base had a chance to advance.

Two men out, two on base, Stars wanting three runs to tie, Scott, a weak batter, at the plate! The situation was disheartening. Yet there sat Delaney, shot through and through with some vital compelling force. He saw only victory. And when the very first ball pitched to Scott hit him on the leg, giving him his base, Delaney got to his feet, unsteady and hoarse.

Bases full, Reddie Ray up, three runs to tie!

Delaney looked at Reddie. And Reddie looked at Delaney. The manager's face was pale, intent, with a little smile. The player had eyes of fire, a lean, bulging jaw and the hands he reached for his bat clutched like talons.

"Reddie, I knew it was waitin' for you," said Delaney, his voice ringing. "Break up the game!"

After all this was only a baseball game, and perhaps from the fans' viewpoint a poor game at that. But the moment when that lithe, redhaired athlete toed the plate was a beautiful one. The long crash from the bleachers, the steady cheer from the grand stand, proved that it was not so much the game that mattered.

Wehying had shot his bolt; he was tired. Yet he made ready for a final effort. It seemed that passing Reddie Ray on balls would have been a wise play at that juncture. But no pitcher, probably, would have done it with the bases crowded and chances, of course, against the batter.

Clean and swift, Reddie leaped at the first pitched ball. Ping! For a second no one saw the hit. Then it gleamed, a terrific drive, low along the ground, like a bounding bullet, straight at Babcock in right field. It struck his hands and glanced viciously away to roll toward the fence.

Thunder broke loose from the stands. Reddie Ray was turning first base. Beyond first base he got into his wonderful stride. Some runners run with a consistent speed, the best they can make for a given distance. But this trained sprinter gathered speed as he ran. He was no short-stepping runner. His strides were long. They gave an impression of strength combined with fleetness. He had the speed of a race horse, but the trimness, the raciness, the delicate legs were not characteristic of him. Like the wind he turned second, so powerful that his turn was short. All at once there came a difference in his running. It was no longer beautiful. The grace was gone. It was now fierce, violent. His momentum was running him off his legs. He whirled around third base and came hurtling down the homestretch. His face was convulsed, his eyes were wild. His arms and legs worked in a marvelous muscular velocity. He seemed a demon—a flying streak. He overtook and ran down the laboring Scott, who had almost reached the plate.

The park seemed full of shrill, piercing strife. It swelled, reached a highest pitch, sustained that for a long moment, and then declined.

"My Gawd!" exclaimed Delaney, as he fell back. "Wasn't that a finish? Didn't I tell you to watch them redheads!"

THE RUBE

It was the most critical time I had yet experienced in my career as a baseball manager. And there was more than the usual reason why I must pull the team out. A chance for a business deal depended upon the good-will of the stockholders of the Worcester club. On the outskirts of the town was a little cottage that I wanted to buy, and this depended upon the business deal. My whole future happiness depended upon the little girl I hoped to install in that cottage.

Coming to the Worcester Eastern League team, I had found a strong aggregation and an enthusiastic following. I really had a team with pennant possibilities. Providence was a strong rival, but I beat them three straight in the opening series, set a fast pace, and likewise set Worcester baseball mad. The Eastern League clubs were pretty evenly matched; still I continued to hold the lead until misfortune overtook me.

Gregg smashed an umpire and had to be laid off. Mullaney got spiked while sliding and was out of the game. Ashwell sprained his ankle and Hirsch broke a finger. Radbourne, my great pitcher, hurt his arm on a cold day and he could not get up his old speed. Stringer, who had batted three hundred and seventy-one and led the league the year before, struck a bad spell and could not hit a barn door handed up to him.

Then came the slump. The team suddenly let down; went to pieces; played ball that would have disgraced an amateur nine. It was a trying time. Here was a great team, strong everywhere. A little hard luck had dug up a slump—and now! Day by day the team dropped in the race. When we reached the second division the newspapers flayed us. Worcester would never stand for a second division team. Baseball admirers, reporters, fans—especially the fans—are fickle. The admirers quit, the reporters grilled us, and the fans, though they stuck to the games with that barnacle-like tenacity peculiar to them, made life miserable for all of us. I saw the pennant slowly fading, and the successful season, and the business deal, and the cottage, and Milly——

But when I thought of her I just could not see failure. Something must be done, but what? I was at the end of my wits. When Jersey City beat us that Saturday, eleven to two, shoving us down to fifth place with only a few percentage points above the Fall River team, I grew desperate, and locking my players in the dressing room I went after them. They had lain down on me and needed a jar. I told them so straight and flat, and being bitter, I did not pick and choose my words.

"And fellows," I concluded, "you've got to brace. A little more of this and we can't pull out. I tell you you're a championship team. We had that pennant cinched. A few cuts and sprains and hard luck—and you all quit! You lay down! I've been patient. I've plugged for you. Never a man have I fined or thrown down. But now I'm at the end of my string. I'm out to fine you now, and I'll release the first man who shows the least yellow. I play no more substitutes. Crippled or not, you guys have got to get in the game."

I waited to catch my breath and expected some such outburst as managers usually get from criticized players. But not a word! Then I addressed some of them personally.

"Gregg, your lay-off ends today. You play Monday. Mullaney, you've drawn your salary for two weeks with that spiked foot. If you can't run on it—well, all right, but I put it up to your good faith. I've played the game and I know it's hard to run on a sore foot. But you can do it. Ashwell, your ankle is lame, I know—now, can you run?"

"Sure I can. I'm not a quitter. I'm ready to go in," replied Ashwell.

"Raddy, how about you?" I said, turning to my star twirler.

"Connelly, I've seen as fast a team in as bad a rut and yet pull out," returned Radbourne. "We're about due for the brace. When it comes— look out! As for me, well, my arm isn't right, but it's acting these warm days in a way that tells me it will be soon. It's been worked too hard. Can't you get another pitcher? I'm not knocking Herne or Cairns. They're good for their turn, but we need a new man to help out. And he must be a crackerjack if we're to get back to the lead."

"Where on earth can I find such a pitcher?" I shouted, almost distracted.

"Well, that's up to you," replied Radbourne.

Up to me it certainly was, and I cudgeled my brains for inspiration. After I had given up in hopelessness it came in the shape of a notice I read in one of the papers. It was a brief mention of an amateur Worcester ball team being shut out in a game with a Rickettsville nine. Rickettsville played Sunday ball, which gave me an opportunity to look them over.

It took some train riding and then a journey by coach to get to Rickettsville. I mingled with the crowd of talking rustics. There was only one little "bleachers" and this was loaded to the danger point with the feminine adherents of the teams. Most of the crowd centered alongside and back of the catcher's box. I edged in and got a position just behind the stone that served as home plate.

Hunting up a player in this way was no new thing to me. I was too wise to make myself known before I had sized up the merits of my man. So, before the players came upon the field I amused myself watching the rustic fans and listening to them. Then a roar announced the appearance of the Rickettsville team and their opponents, who wore the name of Spatsburg on their Canton flannel shirts. The uniforms of these country amateurs would have put a Philadelphia Mummer's parade to the blush, at least for bright colors. But after one amused glance I got down to the stern business of the day, and that was to discover a pitcher, and failing that, baseball talent of any kind.

Never shall I forget my first glimpse of the Rickettsville twirler. He was far over six feet tall and as lean as a fence rail. He had a great shock of light hair, a sunburned, sharp-featured face, wide, sloping shoulders, and arms enormously long. He was about as graceful and had about as much of a baseball walk as a crippled cow.

"He's a rube!" I ejaculated, in disgust and disappointment.

But when I had seen him throw one ball to his catcher I grew as keen as a fox on a scent. What speed he had! I got round closer to him and watched him with sharp, eager eyes. He was a giant. To be sure, he was lean, rawboned as a horse, but powerful. What won me at once was his natural, easy swing. He got the ball away with scarcely any effort. I wondered what he could do when he brought the motion of his body into play.

"Bub, what might be the pitcher's name?" I asked of a boy.

"Huh, mister, his name might be Dennis, but it ain't. Huh!" replied this country youngster. Evidently my question had thrown some implication upon this particular player.

"I reckon you be a stranger in these parts," said a pleasant old fellow. "His name's Hurtle—Whitaker Hurtle. Whit fer short. He hain't lost a gol-darned game this summer. No sir-ee! Never pitched any before, nuther."

Hurtle! What a remarkably fitting name!

Rickettsville chose the field and the game began. Hurtle swung with his easy motion. The ball shot across like a white bullet. It was a strike, and so was the next, and the one succeeding. He could not throw anything but strikes, and it seemed the Spatsburg players could not make even a foul.

Outside of Hurtle's work the game meant little to me. And I was so fascinated by what I saw in him that I could hardly contain myself. After the first few innings I no longer tried to. I yelled with the Rickettsville rooters. The man was a wonder. A blind baseball manager could have seen that. He had a straight ball, shoulder high, level as a stretched string, and fast. He had a jump ball, which he evidently worked by putting on a little more steam, and it was the speediest thing I ever saw in the way of a shoot. He had a wide-sweeping outcurve, wide as the blade of a mowing scythe. And he had a drop—an unhittable drop. He did not use it often, for it made his catcher dig too hard into the dirt. But whenever he did I glowed all over. Once or twice he used an underhand motion and sent in a ball that fairly swooped up. It could not have been hit with a board. And best of all, dearest to the manager's heart, he had control. Every ball he threw went over the plate. He could not miss it. To him that plate was as big as a house.

What a find! Already I had visions of the long-looked-for brace of my team, and of the pennant, and the little cottage, and the happy light of a pair of blue eyes. What he meant to me, that country pitcher Hurtle! He shut out the Spatsburg team without a run or a hit or even a scratch. Then I went after him. I collared him and his manager, and there, surrounded by the gaping players, I bought him and signed him before any of them knew exactly what I was about. I did not haggle. I asked the manager what he wanted and produced the cash; I asked Hurtle what he wanted, doubled his ridiculously modest demand, paid him in advance, and got his name to the contract. Then I breathed a long, deep breath; the first one for weeks. Something told me that with Hurtle's signature in my pocket I had the Eastern League pennant. Then I invited all concerned down to the Rickettsville hotel.

We made connections at the railroad junction and reached Worcester at midnight in time for a good sleep. I took the silent and backward pitcher to my hotel. In the morning we had breakfast together. I showed him about Worcester and then carried him off to the ball grounds.

I had ordered morning practice, and as morning practice is not conducive to the cheerfulness of ball players, I wanted to reach the dressing room a little late. When we arrived, all the players had dressed and were out on the field. I had some difficulty in fitting Hurtle with a uniform, and when I did get him dressed he resembled a two-legged giraffe decked out in white shirt, gray trousers and maroon stockings.

Spears, my veteran first baseman and captain of the team, was the first to see us.

"Sufferin' umpires!" yelled Spears. "Here, you Micks! Look at this Con's got with him!"

What a yell burst from that sore and disgruntled bunch of ball tossers! My players were a grouchy set in practice anyway, and today they were in their meanest mood.

"Hey, beanpole!"

"Get on to the stilts!"

"Con, where did you find that?"

I cut short their chaffing with a sharp order for batting practice.

"Regular line-up, now no monkey biz," I went on. "Take two cracks and a bunt. Here, Hurtle," I said, drawing him toward the pitcher's box, "don't pay any attention to their talk. That's only the fun of ball players. Go in now and practice a little. Lam a few over."

Hurtle's big freckled hands closed nervously over the ball. I thought it best not to say more to him, for he had a rather wild look. I remembered my own stage fright upon my first appearance in fast company. Besides I knew what my amiable players would say to him. I had a secret hope and belief that presently they would yell upon the other side of the fence.

McCall, my speedy little left fielder, led off at bat. He was full of ginger, chipper as a squirrel, sarcastic as only a tried ball player can be.

"Put 'em over, Slats, put 'em over," he called, viciously swinging his ash.

Hurtle stood stiff and awkward in the box and seemed to be rolling something in his mouth. Then he moved his arm. We all saw the ball dart down straight—that is, all of us except McCall, because if he had seen it he might have jumped out of the way. Crack! The ball hit him on the shin.

McCall shrieked. We all groaned. That crack hurt all of us. Any baseball player knows how it hurts to be hit on the shinbone. McCall waved his bat madly.

"Rube! Rube! Rube!" he yelled.

Then and there Hurtle got the name that was to cling to him all his baseball days.

McCall went back to the plate, red in the face, mad as a hornet, and he sidestepped every time Rube pitched a ball. He never even ticked one and retired in disgust, limping and swearing. Ashwell was next. He did not show much alacrity. On Rube's first pitch down went Ashwell flat in the dust. The ball whipped the hair of his head. Rube was wild and I began to get worried. Ashwell hit a couple of measly punks, but when he assayed a bunt the gang yelled derisively at him.

"What's he got?" The old familiar cry of batters when facing a new pitcher!

Stringer went up, bold and formidable. That was what made him the great hitter he was. He loved to bat; he would have faced anybody; he would have faced even a cannon. New curves were a fascination to him. And speed for him, in his own words, was "apple pie." In this instance, surprise was in store for Stringer. Rube shot up the straight one, then the wide curve, then the drop. Stringer missed them all, struck out, fell down ignominiously. It was the first time he had fanned that season and he looked dazed. We had to haul him away.

I called off the practice, somewhat worried about Rube's showing, and undecided whether or not to try him in the game that day. So I went to Radbourne, who had quietly watched Rube while on the field. Raddy was an old pitcher and had seen the rise of a hundred stars. I told him about the game at Rickettsville and what I thought of Rube, and frankly asked his opinion.

"Con, you've made the find of your life," said Raddy, quietly and deliberately.

This from Radbourne was not only comforting; it was relief, hope, assurance. I avoided Spears, for it would hardly be possible for him to regard the Rube favorably, and I kept under cover until time to show up at the grounds.

Buffalo was on the ticket for that afternoon, and the Bisons were leading the race and playing in topnotch form. I went into the dressing room while the players were changing suits, because there was a little unpleasantness that I wanted to spring on them before we got on the field.

"Boys," I said, curtly, "Hurtle works today. Cut loose, now, and back him up."

I had to grab a bat and pound on the wall to stop the uproar.

"Did you mutts hear what I said? Well, it goes. Not a word, now. I'm handling this team. We're in bad, I know, but it's my judgment to pitch Hurtle, rube or no rube, and it's up to you to back us. That's the baseball of it."

Grumbling and muttering, they passed out of the dressing room. I knew ball players. If Hurtle should happen to show good form they would turn in a flash. Rube tagged reluctantly in their rear. He looked like a man in a trance. I wanted to speak encouragingly to him, but Raddy told me to keep quiet.

It was inspiring to see my team practice that afternoon. There had come a subtle change. I foresaw one of those baseball climaxes that can be felt and seen, but not explained. Whether it was a hint of the hoped-for brace, or only another flash of form before the final let-down, I had no means to tell. But I was on edge.

Carter, the umpire, called out the batteries, and I sent my team into the field. When that long, lanky, awkward rustic started for the pitcher's box, I thought the bleachers would make him drop in his tracks. The fans were sore on any one those days, and a new pitcher was bound to hear from them.

"Where! Oh, where! Oh, where!"

"Connelly's found another dead one!"

"Scarecrow!"

"Look at his pants!"

"Pad his legs!"

Then the inning began, and things happened. Rube had marvelous speed, but he could not find the plate. He threw the ball the second he got it; he hit men, walked men, and fell all over himself trying to field bunts. The crowd stormed and railed and hissed. The Bisons pranced round the bases and yelled like Indians. Finally they retired with eight runs.

Eight runs! Enough to win two games! I could not have told how it happened. I was sick and all but crushed. Still I had a blind, dogged faith in the big rustic. I believed he had not got started right. It was a trying situation. I called Spears and Raddy to my side and talked fast.

"It's all off now. Let the dinged rube take his medicine," growled Spears.

"Don't take him out," said Raddy. "He's not shown at all what's in him. The blamed hayseed is up in the air. He's crazy. He doesn't know

123

what he's doing. I tell you, Con, he may be scared to death, but he's dead in earnest."

Suddenly I recalled the advice of the pleasant old fellow at Rickettsville.

"Spears, you're the captain," I said, sharply. "Go after the rube. Wake him up. Tell him he can't pitch. Call him 'Pogie!' That's a name that stirs him up."

"Well, I'll be dinged! He looks it," replied Spears. "Here, Rube, get off the bench. Come here."

Rube lurched toward us. He seemed to be walking in his sleep. His breast was laboring and he was dripping with sweat.

"Who ever told you that you could pitch?" asked Spears genially. He was master at baseball ridicule. I had never yet seen the youngster who could stand his badinage. He said a few things, then wound up with: "Come now, you cross between a hayrack and a wagon tongue, get sore and do something. Pitch if you can. Show us! Do you hear, you tow-headed Pogie!"

Rube jumped as if he had been struck. His face flamed red and his little eyes turned black. He shoved his big fist under Capt. Spears' nose.

"Mister, I'll lick you fer thet—after the game! And I'll show you dog-goned well how I can pitch."

"Good!" exclaimed Raddy; and I echoed his word. Then I went to the bench and turned my attention to the game. Some one told me that McCall had made a couple of fouls, and after waiting for two strikes and three balls had struck out. Ashwell had beat out a bunt in his old swift style, and Stringer was walking up to the plate on the moment. It was interesting, even in a losing game, to see Stringer go to bat. We all watched him, as we had been watching him for weeks, expecting him to break his slump with one of the drives that had made him famous. Stringer stood to the left side of the plate, and I could see the bulge of his closely locked jaw. He swung on the first pitched ball. With the solid rap we all rose to watch that hit. The ball lined first, then soared and did not begin to drop till it was far beyond the right-field fence. For an instant we were all still, so were the bleachers. Stringer had broken his slump with the longest drive ever made on the grounds. The crowd cheered as he trotted around the bases behind Ashwell. Two runs.

"Con, how'd you like that drive?" he asked me, with a bright gleam in his eyes.

"O-h-!—a beaut!" I replied, incoherently. The players on the bench were all as glad as I was. Henley flew out to left. Mullaney smashed a two-bagger to right. Then Gregg hit safely, but Mullaney, in trying to score on the play, was out at the plate.

"Four hits! I tell you fellows, something's coming off," said Raddy. "Now, if only Rube——"

What a difference there was in that long rustic! He stalked into the box, unmindful of the hooting crowd and grimly faced Schultz, the first batter up for the Bisons. This time Rube was deliberate. And where he had not swung before he now got his body and arm into full motion. The ball came in like a glint of light. Schultz looked surprised. The umpire called "Strike!"

"Wow!" yelled the Buffalo coacher. Rube sped up the sidewheeler and Schultz reached wide to meet it and failed. The third was the lightning drop, straight over the plate. The batter poked weakly at it. Then Carl struck out and Manning following, did likewise. Three of the best hitters in the Eastern retired on nine strikes! That was no fluke. I knew what it meant, and I sat there hugging myself with the hum of something joyous in my ears.

Gregg had a glow on his sweaty face. "Oh, but say, boys, take a tip from me! The Rube's a world beater! Raddy knew it; he sized up that swing, and now I know it. Get wise, you its!"

When old Spears pasted a single through shortstop, the Buffalo manager took Clary out of the box and put in Vane, their best pitcher. Bogart advanced the runner to second, but was thrown out on the play. Then Rube came up. He swung a huge bat and loomed over the Bison's twirler. Rube had the look of a hitter. He seemed to be holding himself back from walking right into the ball. And he hit one high and far away. The fast Carl could not get under it, though he made a valiant effort. Spears scored and Rube's long strides carried him to third. The cold crowd in the stands came to life; even the sore bleachers opened up. McCall dumped a slow teaser down the line, a hit that would easily have scored Rube, but he ran a little way, then stopped, tried to get back, and was easily touched out. Ashwell's hard chance gave the Bison's shortstop an error, and Stringer came up with two men on bases. Stringer hit a foul over the right-field fence and the crowd howled. Then he hit a hard long drive straight into the centerfielder's hands.

"Con, I don't know what to think, but ding me if we ain't hittin' the ball," said Spears. Then to his players: "A little more of that and we're back in our old shape. All in a minute—at 'em now! Rube, you dinged old Pogie, pitch!"

Rube toed the rubber, wrapped his long brown fingers round the ball, stepped out as he swung and—zing! That inning he unloosed a few more kinks in his arm and he tried some new balls upon the Bisons. But whatever he used and wherever he put them the result was the same—they cut the plate and the Bisons were powerless.

That inning marked the change in my team. They had come hack. The hoodoo had vanished. The championship Worcester team was itself again.

The Bisons were fighting, too, but Rube had them helpless. When they did hit a ball one of my infielders snapped it up. No chances went to the outfield. I sat there listening to my men, and reveled in a moment that I had long prayed for.

"Now you're pitching some, Rube. Another strike! Get him a board!" called Ashwell.

"Ding 'em, Rube, ding 'em!" came from Capt. Spears.

"Speed? Oh-no!" yelled Bogart at third base.

"It's all off, Rube! It's all off—all off!"

So, with the wonderful pitching of an angry rube, the Worcester team came into its own again. I sat through it all without another word; without giving a signal. In a way I realized the awakening of the bleachers, and heard the pound of feet and the crash, but it was the spirit of my team that thrilled me. Next to that the work of my new find absorbed me. I gloated over his easy, deceiving swing. I rose out of my seat when he threw that straight fast ball, swift as a bullet, true as a plumb line. And when those hard-hitting, sure bunting Bisons chopped in vain at the wonderful drop, I choked back a wild yell. For Rube meant the world to me that day.

In the eighth the score was 8 to 6. The Bisons had one scratch hit to their credit, but not a runner had got beyond first base. Again Rube held them safely, one man striking out, another fouling out, and the third going out on a little fly.

Crash! Crash! Crash! Crash! The bleachers were making up for many games in which they could not express their riotous feelings.

"It's a cinch we'll win!" yelled a fan with a voice. Rube was the first man up in our half of the ninth and his big bat lammed the first ball safe over second base. The crowd, hungry for victory, got to their feet and stayed upon their feet, calling, cheering for runs. It was the moment for me to get in the game, and I leaped up, strung like a wire, and white hot with inspiration. I sent Spears to the coaching box with orders to make Rube run on the first ball. I gripped McCall with hands that made him wince.

Then I dropped back on the bench spent and panting. It was only a game, yet it meant so much! Little McCall was dark as a thunder cloud, and his fiery eyes snapped. He was the fastest man in the league, and could have bunted an arrow from a bow. The foxy Bison third baseman edged in. Mac feinted to bunt toward him then turned his bat inward and dumped a teasing curving ball down the first base line. Rube ran as if in seven-league boots. Mac's short legs twinkled; he went like the wind; he leaped into first base with his long slide, and beat the throw.

The stands and bleachers seemed to be tumbling down. For a moment the air was full of deafening sound. Then came the pause, the dying away of clatter and roar, the close waiting, suspended quiet. Spears' clear voice, as he coached Rube, in its keen note seemed inevitable of another run.

Ashwell took his stand. He was another left-hand hitter, and against a right-hand pitcher, in such circumstances as these, the most dangerous of men. Vane knew it. Ellis, the Bison captain knew it, as showed plainly in his signal to catch Rube at second. But Spears' warning held or frightened Rube on the bag.

Vane wasted a ball, then another. Ashwell could not be coaxed. Wearily Vane swung; the shortstop raced out to get in line for a possible hit through the wide space to his right, and the second baseman got on his toes as both base runners started.

Crack! The old story of the hit and run game! Ashwell's hit crossed sharply where a moment before the shortstop had been standing. With gigantic strides Rube rounded the corner and scored. McCall flitted through second, and diving into third with a cloud of dust, got the umpire's decision. When Stringer hurried up with Mac on third and Ash on first the whole field seemed racked in a deafening storm. Again it subsided quickly. The hopes of the Worcester fans had been crushed too often of late for them to be fearless.

But I had no fear. I only wanted the suspense ended. I was like a man clamped in a vise. Stringer stood motionless. Mac bent low with the sprinters' stoop; Ash watched the pitcher's arm and slowly edged off first. Stringer waited for one strike and two balls, then he hit the next. It hugged the first base line, bounced fiercely past the bag and skipped over the grass to bump hard into the fence. McCall romped home, and lame Ashwell beat any run he ever made to the plate. Rolling, swelling, crashing roar of frenzied feet could not down the high piercing sustained yell of the fans. It was great. Three weeks of submerged bottled baseball joy exploded in one mad outburst! The fans, too, had come into their own again.

We scored no more. But the Bisons were beaten. Their spirit was broken. This did not make the Rube let up in their last half inning. Grim and pale he faced them. At every long step and swing he tossed his shock of light hair. At the end he was even stronger than at the beginning. He still had the glancing, floating airy quality that baseball players call speed. And he struck out the last three batters.

In the tumult that burst over my ears I sat staring at the dots on my score card. Fourteen strike outs! one scratch hit! No base on balls since the first inning! That told the story which deadened senses doubted. There was a roar in my ears. Some one was pounding me. As I struggled to get into the dressing room the crowd mobbed me. But I did not hear what they yelled. I had a kind of misty veil before my eyes, in which I saw that lanky Rube magnified into a glorious figure. I saw the pennant waving, and the gleam of a white cottage through the trees, and a trim figure waiting at the gate. Then I rolled into the dressing room.

Somehow it seemed strange to me. Most of the players were stretched out in peculiar convulsions. Old Spears sat with drooping head. Then a wild flaming-eyed giant swooped upon me. With a voice of thunder he announced:

"I'm a-goin' to lick you, too!"

After that we never called him any name except Rube.

THE RUBE'S PENNANT

"Fellows, it's this way. You've got to win today's game. It's the last of the season and means the pennant for Worcester. One more hard scrap and we're done! Of all the up-hill fights any bunch ever made to land the flag, our has been the best. You're the best team I ever managed, the gamest gang of ball players that ever stepped in spikes. We've played in the hardest kind of luck all season, except that short trip we called the Rube's Honeymoon. We got a bad start, and sore arms and busted fingers, all kinds of injuries, every accident calculated to hurt a team's chances, came our way. But in spite of it all we got the lead and we've held it, and today we're still a few points ahead of Buffalo."

I paused to catch my breath, and looked round on the grim, tired faces of my players. They made a stern group. The close of the season found them almost played out. What a hard chance it was, after their extraordinary efforts, to bring the issue of the pennant down to this last game!

"If we lose today, Buffalo, with three games more to play at home, will pull the bunting," I went on. "But they're not going to win! I'm putting it up to you that way. I know Spears is all in; Raddy's arm is gone; Ash is playing on one leg; you're all crippled. But you've got one more game in you, I know. These last few weeks the Rube has been pitching out of turn and he's about all in, too. He's kept us in the lead. If he wins today it'll be Rube's Pennant. But that might apply to all of you. Now, shall we talk over the play today? Any tricks to pull off? Any inside work?"

"Con, you're pretty much upset an' nervous," replied Spears, soberly. "It ain't no wonder. This has been one corker of a season. I want to suggest that you let me run the team today. I've talked over the play with the fellers. We ain't goin' to lose this game, Con. Buffalo has been comin' with a rush lately, an' they're confident. But we've been holdin' in, restin' up as much as we dared an' still keep our lead. Mebbee it'll surprise you to know we've bet every dollar we could get hold of on this game. Why, Buffalo money is everywhere."

"All right, Spears, I'll turn the team over to you. We've got the banner crowd of the year out there right now, a great crowd to play before. I'm more fussed up over this game than any I remember. But I have a sort of blind faith in my team.... I guess that's all I want to say."

Spears led the silent players out of the dressing room and I followed; and while they began to toss balls to and fro, to limber up cold, dead arms, I sat on the bench.

The Bisons were prancing about the diamond, and their swaggering assurance was not conducive to hope for the Worcesters. I wondered how many of that vast, noisy audience, intent on the day's sport, even had a thought of what pain and toil it meant to my players. The Buffalo men were in good shape; they had been lucky; they were at the top of their stride, and that made all the difference.

At any rate, there were a few faithful little women in the grand stand—Milly and Nan and Rose Stringer and Kate Bogart—who sat with compressed lips and hoped and prayed for that game to begin and end.

The gong called off the practice, and Spears, taking the field, yelled gruff encouragement to his men. Umpire Carter brushed off the plate and tossed a white ball to Rube and called: "Play!" The bleachers set up an exultant, satisfied shout and sat down to wait.

Schultz toed the plate and watched the Rube pitch a couple. There seemed to be no diminution of the great pitcher's speed and both balls cut the plate. Schultz clipped the next one down the third-base Line. Bogart trapped it close to the bag, and got it away underhand, beating the speedy runner by a nose. It was a pretty play to start with, and the spectators were not close-mouthed in appreciation. The short, stocky Carl ambled up to bat, and I heard him call the Rube something. It was not a friendly contest, this deciding game between Buffalo and Worcester.

"Bing one close to his swelled nut!" growled Spears to the Rube.

Carl chopped a bouncing grounder through short and Ash was after it like a tiger, but it was a hit. The Buffalo contingent opened up. Then Manning faced the Rube, and he, too, vented sarcasm. It might not have been heard by the slow, imperturbable pitcher for all the notice he took. Carl edged off first, slid back twice, got a third start, and on the Rube's pitch was off for second base with the lead that always made him dangerous. Manning swung vainly, and Gregg snapped a throw to Mullaney. Ball and runner got to the bag apparently simultaneously; the umpire called Carl out, and the crowd uttered a quick roar of delight.

The next pitch to Manning was a strike. Rube was not wasting any balls, a point I noted with mingled fear and satisfaction. For he might have felt that he had no strength to spare that day and so could not try to work the batters. Again he swung, and Manning rapped a long line fly over McCall. As the little left fielder turned at the sound of the hit and sprinted out, his lameness was certainly not in evidence. He was the swiftest runner in the league and always when he got going the crowd rose in wild clamor to watch him. Mac took that fly right off the foul flag in deep left, and the bleachers dinned their pleasure.

The teams changed positions. "Fellers," said Spears, savagely, "we may be a bunged-up lot of stiffs, but, say! We can hit! If you love your old captain—sting the ball!"

Vane, the Bison pitcher, surely had his work cut out for him. For one sympathetic moment I saw his part through his eyes. My Worcester veterans, long used to being under fire, were relentlessly bent on taking that game. It showed in many ways, particularly in their silence, because they were seldom a silent team. McCall hesitated a moment over his bats. Then, as he picked up the lightest one, I saw his jaw set, and I knew he intended to bunt. He was lame, yet he meant to beat out an infield hit. He went up scowling.

Vane had an old head, and he had a varied assortment of balls. For Mac he used an under hand curve, rising at the plate and curving in to the left-hander. Mac stepped back and let it go.

"That's the place, Bo," cried the Buffalo infielders. "Keep 'em close on the Crab." Eager and fierce as McCall was, he let pitch after pitch go by till he had three balls and two strikes. Still the heady Vane sent up another pitch similar to the others. Mac stepped forward in the box, dropped his bat on the ball, and leaped down the line toward first base. Vane came rushing in for the bunt, got it and threw. But as the speeding ball neared the baseman, Mac stretched out into the air and shot for the bag. By a fraction of a second he beat the ball. It was one of his demon-slides. He knew that the chances favored his being crippled; we all knew that some day Mac would slide recklessly once too often. But that, too, is all in the game and in the spirit of a great player.

"We're on," said Spears; "now keep with him."

By that the captain meant that Mac would go down, and Ashwell would hit with the run.

When Vane pitched, little McCall was flitting toward second. The Bison shortstop started for the bag, and Ash hit square through his tracks. A rolling cheer burst from the bleachers, and swelled till McCall overran third base and was thrown back by the coacher. Stringer hurried forward with his big bat.

"Oh! My!" yelled a fan, and he voiced my sentiments exactly. Here we would score, and be one run closer to that dearly bought pennant.

How well my men worked together! As the pitcher let the ball go, Ash was digging for second and Mac was shooting plateward. They played on the chance of Stringer's hitting. Stringer swung, the bat cracked, we heard a thud somewhere, and then Manning, half knocked over, was fumbling for the ball. He had knocked down a terrific drive with his mitt, and he got the ball in time to put Stringer out. But Mac scored and Ash drew a throw to third base and beat it. He had a bad ankle, but no one noticed it in that daring run.

"Watch me paste one!" said Captain Spears, as he spat several yards. He batted out a fly so long and high and far that, slow as he was, he had nearly run to second base when Carl made the catch. Ash easily scored on the throw-in. Then Bogart sent one skipping over second, and Treadwell, scooping it on the run, completed a play that showed why he was considered the star of the Bison infield.

"Two runs, fellers!" said Spears. "That's some! Push 'em over, Rube."

The second inning somewhat quickened the pace. Even the Rube worked a little faster. Ellis lined to Cairns in right; Treadwell fouled two balls and had a called strike, and was out; McKnight hit a low fly over short, then Bud Wiler sent one between Spears and Mullaney. Spears went for it while the Rube with giant strides ran to cover first base. Between them they got Bud, but it was only because he was heavy and slow on his feet.

In our half of that inning Mullaney, Gregg and Cairns went out in one, two, three order.

With Pannell up, I saw that the Rube held in on his speed, or else he was tiring. Pannell hit the second slow ball for two bases. Vane sacrificed, and then the redoubtable Schultz came up. He appeared to be in no hurry to bat. Then I saw that the foxy Buffalo players were working to tire the Rube. They had the situation figured. But they were no wiser than old Spears.

"Make 'em hit, Rube. Push 'em straight over. Never mind the corners. We don't care for a few runs. We'll hit this game out."

Shultz flied to Mac, who made a beautiful throw to the plate too late to catch Pannell. Carl deliberately bunted to the right of the Rube and it cost the big pitcher strenuous effort to catch his man.

"We got the Rube waggin'!" yelled a Buffalo player.

Manning tripled down the left foul line—a hit the bleachers called a screamer. When Ellis came up, it looked like a tie score, and when the Rube pitched it was plain that he was tired. The Bisons yelled their assurance of this and the audience settled into quiet. Ellis batted a scorcher that looked good for a hit. But the fast Ashwell was moving with the ball, and he plunged lengthwise to get it square in his glove. The hit had been so sharp that he had time to get up and make the throw to beat the runner. The bleachers thundered at the play.

"You're up, Rube," called Spears. "Lam one out of the lot!"

The Rube was an uncertain batter. There was never any telling what he might do, for he had spells of good and bad hitting. But when he did get his bat on the ball it meant a chase for some fielder. He went up swinging his huge club, and he hit a fly that would have been an easy home run for a fast man. But the best Rube could do was to reach third base. This was certainly good enough, as the bleachers loudly proclaimed, and another tally for us seemed sure.

McCall bunted toward third, another of his teasers. The Rube would surely have scored had he started with the ball, but he did not try and missed a chance. Wiler, of course, held the ball, and Mac got to first without special effort. He went down on the first pitch. Then Ash lined to Carl. The Rube waited till the ball was caught and started for home. The crowd screamed, the Rube ran for all he was worth and Carl's throw to the plate shot in low and true. Ellis blocked the Rube and tagged him out.

It looked to the bleachers as if Ellis had been unnecessarily rough, and they hissed and stormed disapproval. As for me, I knew the Bisons were losing no chance to wear out my pitcher. Stringer fouled out with Mac on third, and it made him so angry that he threw his bat toward the bench, making some of the boys skip lively.

The next three innings, as far as scoring was concerned, were all for Buffalo. But the Worcester infield played magnificent ball, holding their opponents to one run each inning.

That made the score 4 to 2 in favor of Buffalo.

In the last half of the sixth, with Ash on first base and two men out, old Spears hit another of his lofty flies, and this one went over the fence and tied the score. How the bleachers roared! It was full two minutes before they quieted down. To make it all the more exciting, Bogart hit safely, ran like a deer to third on Mullaney's grounder, which Wiler knocked down, and scored on a passed ball. Gregg ended the inning by striking out.

"Get at the Rube!" boomed Ellis, the Bison captain. "We'll have him up in the air soon. Get in the game now, you stickers!"

Before I knew what had happened, the Bisons had again tied the score. They were indomitable. They grew stronger all the time. A stroke of good luck now would clinch the game for them. The Rube was beginning to labor in the box; Ashwell was limping; Spears looked as if he would drop any moment; McCall could scarcely walk. But if the ball came his way he could still run. Nevertheless, I never saw any finer fielding than these cripped players executed that inning.

"Ash—Mac—can you hold out?" I asked, when they limped in. I received glances of scorn for my question. Spears, however, was not sanguine.

"I'll stick pretty much if somethin' doesn't happen," he said; "but I'm all in. I'll need a runner if I get to first this time."

Spears lumbered down to first base on an infield hit and the heavy Manning gave him the hip. Old Spears went down, and I for one knew he was out in more ways than that signified by Carter's sharp: "Out!"

The old war-horse gathered himself up slowly and painfully, and with his arms folded and his jaw protruding, he limped toward the umpire.

"Did you call me out?" he asked, in a voice plainly audible to any one on the field.

"Yes," snapped Carter.

"What for? I beat the ball, an' Mannin' played dirty with me—gave me the hip."

"I called you out."

"But I wasn't out!"

"Shut up now! Get off the diamond!" ordered Carter, peremptorily.

"What? Me? Say, I'm captain of this team. Can't I question a decision?"

"Not mine. Spears, you're delaying the game."

"I tell you it was a rotten decision," yelled Spears. The bleachers agreed with him.

Carter grew red in the face. He and Spears had before then met in field squabbles, and he showed it.

"Fifty dollars!"

"More! You cheap-skate you piker! More!"

"It's a hundred!"

"Put me out of the game!" roared Spears.

"You bet! Hurry now—skedaddle!"

"Rob-b-ber!" bawled Spears.

Then he labored slowly toward the bench, all red, and yet with perspiration, his demeanor one of outraged dignity. The great crowd, as one man, stood up and yelled hoarsely at Carter, and hissed and railed at him. When Spears got to the bench he sat down beside me as if in pain, but he was smiling.

"Con, I was all in, an' knowin' I couldn't play any longer, thought I'd try to scare Carter. Say, he was white in the face. If we play into a close decision now, he'll give it to us."

Bogart and Mullaney batted out in short order, and once more the aggressive Bisons hurried in for their turn. Spears sent Cairns to first base and Jones to right. The Rube lobbed up his slow ball. In that tight pinch he showed his splendid nerve. Two Buffalo players, over-anxious, popped up flies. The Rube kept on pitching the slow curve until it was hit safely. Then heaving his shoulders with all his might he got all the motion possible into his swing and let drive. He had almost all of his old speed, but it hurt me to see him work with such desperate effort. He struck Wiler out.

He came stooping into the bench, apparently deaf to the stunning round of applause. Every player on the team had a word for the Rube. There was no quitting in that bunch, and if I ever saw victory on the stern faces of ball players it was in that moment.

"We haven't opened up yet. Mebbee this is the innin'. If it ain't, the next is," said Spears.

With the weak end of the batting list up, there seemed little hope of getting a run on Vane that inning. He had so much confidence that he put the ball over for Gregg, who hit out of the reach of the infield. Again Vane sent up his straight ball, no doubt expecting Cairns to hit into a double play. But Cairns surprised Vane and everybody else by poking a safety past first base. The fans began to howl and pound and whistle.

The Rube strode to bat. The infield closed in for a bunt, but the Rube had no orders for that style of play. Spears had said nothing to him. Vane lost his nonchalance and settled down. He cut loose with all his speed. Rube stepped out, suddenly whirled, then tried to dodge, but the ball hit him fair in the back. Rube sagged in his tracks, then straightened up, and walked slowly to first base. Score 5 to 5, bases full, no outs, McCall at bat. I sat dumb on the bench, thrilling and shivering. McCall! Ashwell! Stringer to bat!

"Play it safe! Hold the bags!" yelled the coacher.

McCall fairly spouted defiance as he faced Vane.

"Pitch! It's all off! An' you know it!"

If Vane knew that, he showed no evidence of it. His face was cold, unsmiling, rigid. He had to pitch to McCall, the fastest man in the league; to Ashwell, the best bunter; to Stringer, the champion batter. It was a supreme test for a great pitcher. There was only one kind of a ball that McCall was not sure to hit, and that was a high curve, in close. Vane threw it with all his power. Carter called it a strike. Again Vane swung and his arm fairly cracked. Mac fouled the ball. The third was wide. Slowly, with lifting breast, Vane got ready, whirled savagely and shot up the ball. McCall struck out.

As the Buffalo players crowed and the audience groaned it was worthy of note that little McCall showed no temper. Yet he had failed to grasp a great opportunity.

"Ash, I couldn't see 'em," he said, as he passed to the bench. "Speed, whew! look out for it. He's been savin' up. Hit quick, an' you'll get him."

Ashwell bent over the plate and glowered at Vane.

"Pitch! It's all off! An' you know it!" he hissed, using Mac's words.

Ashwell, too, was left-handed; he, too, was extremely hard to pitch to; and if he had a weakness that any of us ever discovered, it was a slow curve and change of pace. But I doubted if Vane would dare to use slow balls to Ash at that critical moment. I had yet to learn something of Vane. He gave Ash a slow, wide-sweeping sidewheeler, that curved round over the plate. Ash always took a strike, so this did not matter. Then Vane used his deceptive change of pace, sending up a curve that just missed Ash's bat as he swung.

"Oh! A-h-h! hit!" wailed the bleachers.

Vane doubled up like a contortionist, and shot up a lightning-swift drop that fooled Ash completely. Again the crowd groaned. Score tied, bases full, two out, Stringer at bat!

"It's up to you, String," called Ash, stepping aside.

Stringer did not call out to Vane. That was not his way. He stood tense and alert, bat on his shoulder, his powerful form braced, and he waited. The outfielders trotted over toward right field, and the infielders played deep, calling out warnings and encouragement to the pitcher. Stringer had no weakness, and Vane knew this. Nevertheless he did not manifest any uneasiness, and pitched the first ball without any extra motion. Carter called it a strike. I saw Stringer sink down slightly and grow tenser all over. I believe that moment was longer for me than for either the pitcher or the batter. Vane took his time, watched the base runners, feinted to throw to catch them, and then delivered the ball toward the plate with the limit of his power.

Stringer hit the ball. As long as I live, I will see that glancing low liner. Shultz, by a wonderful play in deep center, blocked the ball and thereby saved it from being a home run. But when Stringer stopped on second base, all the runners had scored.

A shrill, shrieking, high-pitched yell! The bleachers threatened to destroy the stands and also their throats in one long revel of baseball madness.

Jones, batting in place of Spears, had gone up and fouled out before the uproar had subsided.

"Fellers, I reckon I feel easier," said the Rube. It was the only time I had ever heard him speak to the players at such a stage.

"Only six batters, Rube," called out Spears. "Boys, it's a grand game, an' it's our'n!"

The Rube had enough that inning to dispose of the lower half of the Buffalo list without any alarming bids for a run. And in our half, Bogart and Mullaney hit vicious ground balls that gave Treadwell and Wiler opportunities for superb plays. Carl, likewise, made a beautiful running catch of Gregg's line fly. The Bisons were still in the game, still capable of pulling it out at the last moment.

When Shultz stalked up to the plate I shut my eyes a moment, and so still was it that the field and stands might have been empty. Yet, though I tried, I could not keep my eyes closed. I opened them to watch the Rube. I knew Spears felt the same as I, for he was blowing like a porpoise and muttering to himself: "Mebee the Rube won't last an' I've no one to put in!"

The Rube pitched with heavy, violent effort. He had still enough speed to be dangerous. But after the manner of ball players Shultz and the coachers mocked him.

"Take all you can," called Ellis to Shultz.

Every pitch lessened the Rube's strength and these wise opponents knew it. Likewise the Rube himself knew, and never had he shown better head work than in this inning. If he were to win, he must be quick. So he wasted not a ball. The first pitch and the second, delivered breast high and fairly over the plate, beautiful balls to hit, Shultz watched speed by. He swung hard on the third and the crippled Ashwell dove for it in a cloud of dust, got a hand in front of it, but uselessly, for the hit was safe. The crowd cheered that splendid effort.

Carl marched to bat, and he swung his club over the plate as if he knew what to expect. "Come on, Rube!" he shouted. Wearily, doggedly, the Rube whirled, and whipped his arm. The ball had all his old glancing speed and it was a strike. The Rube was making a tremendous effort. Again he got his body in convulsive motion—two strikes! Shultz had made no move to run, nor had Carl made any move to hit. These veterans were waiting. The Rube had pitched five strikes—could he last?

"Now, Carl!" yelled Ellis, with startling suddenness, as the Rube pitched again.

Crack! Carl placed that hit as safely through short as if he had thrown it. McCall's little legs twinkled as he dashed over the grass. He had to head off that hit and he ran like a streak. Down and forward he pitched, as if in one of his fierce slides, and he got his body in front of the ball, blocking it, and then he rolled over and over. But he jumped up and lined the ball to Bogart, almost catching Shultz at third-base. Then, as Mac tried to walk, his lame leg buckled under him, and down he went, and out.

"Call time," I called to Carter. "McCall is done.... Myers, you go to left an' for Lord's sake play ball!"

Stringer and Bogart hurried to Mac and, lifting him up and supporting him between them with his arms around their shoulders, they led him off amid cheers from the stands. Mac was white with pain.

"Naw, I won't go off the field. Leave me on the bench," he said. "Fight 'em now. It's our game. Never mind a couple of runs."

The boys ran back to their positions and Carter called play. Perhaps a little delay had been helpful to the Rube. Slowly he stepped into the box and watched Shultz at third and Carl at second. There was not much probability of his throwing to catch them off the base, but enough of a possibility to make them careful, so he held them close.

The Rube pitched a strike to Manning, then another. That made eight strikes square over the plate that inning. What magnificent control! It was equaled by the implacable patience of those veteran Bisons. Manning hit the next ball as hard as Carl had hit his. But Mullaney plunged down, came up with the ball, feinted to fool Carl, then let drive to Gregg to catch the fleeting Shultz. The throw went wide, but Gregg got it, and, leaping lengthwise, tagged Shultz out a yard from the plate.

One out. Two runners on bases. The bleachers rose and split their throats. Would the inning never end?

Spears kept telling himself: "They'll score, but we'll win. It's our game!"

I had a sickening fear that the strange confidence that obsessed the Worcester players had been blind, unreasoning vanity.

"Carl will steal," muttered Spears. "He can't be stopped."

Spears had called the play. The Rube tried to hold the little base-stealer close to second, but, after one attempt, wisely turned to his hard task of making the Bisons hit and hit quickly. Ellis let the ball pass; Gregg made a perfect throw to third; Bogart caught the ball and moved like a flash, but Carl slid under his hands to the bag. Manning ran down to second. The Rube pitched again, and this was his tenth ball over the plate. Even the Buffalo players evinced eloquent appreciation of the Rube's defence at this last stand.

Then Ellis sent a clean hit to right, scoring both Carl and Manning. I breathed easier, for it seemed with those two runners in, the Rube had a better chance. Treadwell also took those two runners in, the Rube had a way those Bisons waited. They had their reward, for the Rube's speed left him. When he pitched again the ball had control, but no shoot. Treadwell hit it with all his strength. Like a huge cat Ashwell pounced upon it, ran over second base, forcing Ellis, and his speedy snap to first almost caught Treadwell.

Score 8 to 7. Two out. Runner on first. One run to tie.

In my hazy, dimmed vision I saw the Rube's pennant waving from the flag-pole.

"It's our game!" howled Spears in my ear, for the noise from the stands was deafening. "It's our pennant!"

The formidable batting strength of the Bisons had been met, not without disaster, but without defeat. McKnight came up for Buffalo and the Rube took his weary swing. The batter made a terrific lunge and hit the ball with a solid crack It lined for center.

Suddenly electrified into action, I leaped up. That hit! It froze me with horror. It was a home-run. I saw Stringer fly toward left center. He ran like something wild. I saw the heavy Treadwell lumbering round the bases. I saw Ashwell run out into center field.

"Ah-h!" The whole audience relieved its terror in that expulsion of suspended breath. Stringer had leaped high to knock down the ball, saving a sure home-run and the game. He recovered himself, dashed back for the ball and shot it to Ash.

When Ash turned toward the plate, Treadwell was rounding third base. A tie score appeared inevitable. I saw Ash's arm whip and the ball shoot forward, leveled, glancing, beautiful in its flight. The crowd saw it, and the silence broke to a yell that rose and rose as the ball sped in. That yell swelled to a splitting shriek, and Treadwell slid in the dust, and the ball shot into Gregg's hands all at the same instant.

Carter waved both arms upwards. It was the umpire's action when his decision went against the base-runner. The audience rolled up one great stentorian cry.

"Out!"

I collapsed and sank back upon the bench. My confused senses received a dull roar of pounding feet and dinning voices as the herald of victory. I felt myself thinking how pleased Milly would be. I had a distinct picture in my mind of a white cottage on a hill, no longer a dream, but a reality, made possible for me by the Rube's winning of the pennant.

THE RUBE'S HONEYMOON

"He's got a new manager. Watch him pitch now!" That was what Nan Brown said to me about Rube Hurtle, my great pitcher, and I took it as her way of announcing her engagement.

My baseball career held some proud moments, but this one, wherein I realized the success of my matchmaking plans, was certainly the proudest one. So, entirely outside of the honest pleasure I got out of the Rube's happiness, there was reason for me to congratulate myself. He was a transformed man, so absolutely renewed, so wild with joy, that on the strength of it, I decided the pennant for Worcester was a foregone conclusion, and, sure of the money promised me by the directors, Milly and I began to make plans for the cottage upon the hill.

The Rube insisted on pitching Monday's game against the Torontos, and although poor fielding gave them a couple of runs, they never had a chance. They could not see the ball. The Rube wrapped it around their necks and between their wrists and straight over the plate with such incredible speed that they might just as well have tried to bat rifle bullets.

That night I was happy. Spears, my veteran captain, was one huge smile; Radbourne quietly assured me that all was over now but the shouting; all the boys were happy.

And the Rube was the happiest of all. At the hotel he burst out with his exceeding good fortune. He and Nan were to be married upon the Fourth of July!

After the noisy congratulations were over and the Rube had gone, Spears looked at me and I looked at him.

"Con," said he soberly, "we just can't let him get married on the Fourth."

"Why not? Sure we can. We'll help him get married. I tell you it'll save the pennant for us. Look how he pitched today! Nan Brown is our salvation!"

"See here, Con, you've got softenin' of the brain, too. Where's your baseball sense? We've got a pennant to win. By July Fourth we'll be close to the lead again, an' there's that three weeks' trip on the road, the longest an' hardest of the season. We've just got to break even on that trip. You know what that means. If the Rube marries Nan—what are we goin' to do? We can't leave him behind. If he takes Nan with us—why it'll be a honeymoon! An' half the gang is stuck on Nan Brown! An' Nan Brown would flirt in her bridal veil! ... Why Con, we're up against a worse proposition than ever."

"Good Heavens! Cap. You're right," I groaned. "I never thought of that. We've got to postpone the wedding.... How on earth can we? I've heard her tell Milly that. She'll never consent to it. Say, this'll drive me to drink."

"All I got to say is this, Con. If the Rube takes his wife on that trip it's goin' to be an all-fired hummer. Don't you forget that."

"I'm not likely to. But, Spears, the point is this—will the Rube win his games?"

"Figurin' from his work today, I'd gamble he'll never lose another game. It ain't that. I'm thinkin' of what the gang will do to him an' Nan on the cars an' at the hotels. Oh! Lord, Con, it ain't possible to stand for that honeymoon trip! Just think!"

"If the worst comes to the worst, Cap, I don't care for anything but the games. If we get in the lead and stay there I'll stand for anything.... Couldn't the gang be coaxed or bought off to let the Rube and Nan alone?"

"Not on your life! There ain't enough love or money on earth to stop them. It'll be awful. Mind, I'm not responsible. Don't you go holdin' me responsible. In all my years of baseball I never went on a trip with a bride in the game. That's new on me, an' I never heard of it. I'd be bad enough if he wasn't a rube an' if she wasn't a crazy girl-fan an' a flirt to boot, an' with half the boys in love with her, but as it is——"

Spears gave up and, gravely shaking his head, he left me. I spent a little while in sober reflection, and finally came to the conclusion that, in my desperate ambition to win the pennant, I would have taken half a dozen rube pitchers and their baseball-made brides on the trip, if by so doing I could increase the percentage of games won. Nevertheless, I wanted to postpone the Rube's wedding if it was possible, and I went out to see Milly and asked her to help us. But for once in her life Milly turned traitor.

"Connie, you don't want to postpone it. Why, how perfectly lovely! ... Mrs. Stringer will go on that trip and Mrs. Bogart.... Connie, I'm going too!"

She actually jumped up and down in glee. That was the woman in her. It takes a wedding to get a woman. I remonstrated and pleaded and commanded, all to no purpose. Milly intended to go on that trip to see the games, and the fun, and the honeymoon.

She coaxed so hard that I yielded. Thereupon she called up Mrs. Stringer on the telephone, and of course found that young woman just as eager as she was. For my part, I threw anxiety and care to the four winds, and decided to be as happy as any of them. The pennant was mine! Something kept ringing that in my ears. With the Rube working his iron arm for the edification of his proud Nancy Brown, there was extreme likelihood of divers shut-outs and humiliating defeats for some Eastern League teams.

How well I calculated became a matter of baseball history during that last week of June. We won six straight games, three of which fell to the Rube's credit. His opponents scored four runs in the three games, against the nineteen we made. Upon July 1, Radbourne beat Providence and Cairns won the second game. We now had a string of eight victories. Sunday we rested, and Monday was the Fourth, with morning and afternoon games with Buffalo.

Upon the morning of the Fourth, I looked for the Rube at the hotel, but could not find him. He did not show up at the grounds when the other boys did, and I began to worry. It was the Rube's turn to pitch and we were neck and neck with Buffalo for first place. If we won both games we would go ahead of our rivals. So I was all on edge, and kept going to the dressing-room to see if the Rube had arrived. He came, finally, when all the boys were dressed, and about to go out for practice. He had on a new suit, a tailor-made suit at that, and he looked fine. There was about him a kind of strange radiance. He stated simply that he had arrived late because he had just been married. Before congratulations were out of our mouths, he turned to me.

"Con, I want to pitch both games today," he said.

"What! Say, Whit, Buffalo is on the card today and we are only three points behind them. If we win both we'll be leading the league once more. I don't know about pitching you both games."

"I reckon we'll be in the lead tonight then," he replied, "for I'll win them both."

I was about to reply when Dave, the ground-keeper, called me to the door, saying there was a man to see me. I went out, and there stood

Morrisey, manager of the Chicago American League team. We knew each other well and exchanged greetings.

"Con, I dropped off to see you about this new pitcher of yours, the one they call the Rube. I want to see him work. I've heard he's pretty fast. How about it?"

"Wait—till you see him pitch," I replied. I could scarcely get that much out, for Morrisey's presence meant a great deal and I did not want to betray my elation.

"Any strings on him?" queried the big league manager, sharply.

"Well, Morrisey, not exactly. I can give you the first call. You'll have to bid high, though. Just wait till you see him work."

"I'm glad to hear that. My scout was over here watching him pitch and says he's a wonder."

What luck it was that Morrisey should have come upon this day! I could hardly contain myself. Almost I began to spend the money I would get for selling the Rube to the big league manager. We took seats in the grand stand, as Morrisey did not want to be seen by any players, and I stayed there with him until the gong sounded. There was a big attendance. I looked all over the stand for Nan, but she was lost in the gay crowd. But when I went down to the bench I saw her up in my private box with Milly. It took no second glance to see that Nan Brown was a bride and glorying in the fact.

Then, in the absorption of the game, I became oblivious to Milly and Nan; the noisy crowd; the giant fire-crackers and the smoke; to the presence of Morrisey; to all except the Rube and my team and their opponents. Fortunately for my hopes, the game opened with characteristic Worcester dash. Little McCall doubled, Ashwell drew his base on four wide pitches, and Stringer drove the ball over the right-field fence—three runs!

Three runs were enough to win that game. Of all the exhibitions of pitching with which the Rube had favored us, this one was the finest. It was perhaps not so much his marvelous speed and unhittable curves that made the game one memorable in the annals of pitching; it was his perfect control in the placing of balls, in the cutting of corners; in his absolute implacable mastery of the situation. Buffalo was unable to find him at all. The game was swift short, decisive, with the score 5 to 0 in our favor. But the score did not tell all of the Rube's work that morning. He shut out Buffalo without a hit, or a scratch, the first no-hit, no-run game of the year. He gave no base on balls; not a Buffalo player got to first base; only one fly went to the outfield.

For once I forgot Milly after a game, and I hurried to find Morrisey, and carried him off to have dinner with me.

"Your rube is a wonder, and that's a fact," he said to me several times. "Where on earth did you get him? Connelly, he's my meat. Do you understand? Can you let me have him right now?"

"No, Morrisey, I've got the pennant to win first. Then I'll sell him."

"How much? Do you hear? How much?" Morrisey hammered the table with his fist and his eyes gleamed.

Carried away as I was by his vehemence, I was yet able to calculate shrewdly, and I decided to name a very high price, from which I could come down and still make a splendid deal.

"How much?" demanded Morrisey.

"Five thousand dollars," I replied, and gulped when I got the words out.

Morrisey never batted an eye.

"Waiter, quick, pen and ink and paper!"

Presently my hand, none too firm, was signing my name to a contract whereby I was to sell my pitcher for five thousand dollars at the close of the current season. I never saw a man look so pleased as Morrisey when he folded that contract and put it in his pocket. He bade me good-bye and hurried off to catch a train, and he never knew the Rube had pitched the great game on his wedding day.

That afternoon before a crowd that had to be roped off the diamond, I put the Rube against the Bisons. How well he showed the baseball knowledge he had assimilated! He changed his style in that second game. He used a slow ball and wide curves and took things easy. He made Buffalo hit the ball and when runners got on bases once more let out his speed and held them down. He relied upon the players behind him and they were equal to the occasion.

It was a totally different game from that of the morning, and perhaps one more suited to the pleasure of the audience. There was plenty of hard hitting, sharp fielding and good base running, and the game was close and exciting up to the eighth, when Mullaney's triple gave us two runs, and a lead that was not headed. To the deafening roar of the bleachers the Rube walked off the field, having pitched Worcester into first place in the pennant race.

That night the boys planned their first job on the Rube. We had ordered a special Pullman for travel to Toronto, and when I got to the depot in the morning, the Pullman was a white fluttering mass of satin ribbons. Also, there was a brass band, and thousands of baseball fans, and barrels of old foot-gear. The Rube and Nan arrived in a cab and were immediately mobbed. The crowd roared, the band played, the engine whistled, the bell clanged; and the air was full of confetti and slippers, and showers of rice like hail pattered everywhere. A somewhat dishevelled bride and groom boarded the Pullman and breathlessly hid in a state room. The train started, and the crowd gave one last rousing cheer. Old Spears yelled from the back platform:

"Fellers, an' fans, you needn't worry none about leavin' the Rube an' his bride to the tender mercies of the gang. A hundred years from now people will talk about this honeymoon baseball trip. Wait till we come back—an' say, jest to put you wise, no matter what else happens, we're comin' back in first place!"

It was surely a merry party in that Pullman. The bridal couple emerged from their hiding place and held a sort of reception in which the Rube appeared shy and frightened, and Nan resembled a joyous, fluttering bird in gray. I did not see if she kissed every man on the team, but she kissed me as if she had been wanting to do it for ages. Milly kissed the Rube, and so did the other women, to his infinite embarrassment. Nan's effect upon that crowd was most singular. She was sweetness and caprice and joy personified.

We settled down presently to something approaching order, and I, for one, with very keen ears and alert eyes, because I did not want to miss anything.

"I see the lambs a-gambolin'," observed McCall, in a voice louder than was necessary to convey his meaning to Mullaney, his partner in the seat.

"Yes, it do seem as if there was joy aboundin' hereabouts," replied Mul with fervor.

"It's more spring-time than summer," said Ashwell, "an' everything in nature is runnin' in pairs. There are the sheep an' the cattle an' the birds. I see two kingfishers fishin' over here. An' there's a couple of honey-bees makin' honey. Oh, honey, an' by George, if there ain't two butterflies foldin' their wings round each other. See the dandelions kissin' in the field!"

Then the staid Captain Spears spoke up with an appearance of sincerity and a tone that was nothing short of remarkable.

"Reggie, see the sunshine asleep upon yon bank. Ain't it lovely? An' that white cloud sailin' thither amid the blue—how spontaneous! Joy is a-broad o'er all this boo-tiful land today—Oh, yes! An' love's wings hover o 'er the little lambs an' the bullfrogs in the pond an' the dicky birds in the trees. What sweetness to lie in the grass, the lap of bounteous earth, eatin' apples in the Garden of Eden, an' chasin' away the snakes an' dreamin' of Thee, Sweet-h-e-a-r-t——"

Spears was singing when he got so far and there was no telling what he might have done if Mullaney, unable to stand the agony, had not jabbed a pin in him. But that only made way for the efforts of the other boys, each of whom tried to outdo the other in poking fun at the Rube and Nan. The big pitcher was too gloriously happy to note much of what went on around him, but when it dawned upon him he grew red and white by turns.

Nan, however, was more than equal to the occasion. Presently she smiled at Spears, such a smile! The captain looked as if he had just partaken of an intoxicating wine. With a heightened color in her cheeks and a dangerous flash in her roguish eyes, Nan favored McCall with a look, which was as much as to say that she remembered him with a dear sadness. She made eyes at every fellow in the car, and then bringing back her gaze to the Rube, as if glorying in comparison, she nestled her curly black head on his shoulder. He gently tried to move her; but it was not possible. Nan knew how to meet the ridicule of half a dozen old lovers. One by one they buried themselves in newspapers, and finally McCall, for once utterly beaten, showed a white feather, and sank back out of sight behind his seat.

The boys did not recover from that shock until late in the afternoon. As it was a physical impossibility for Nan to rest her head all day upon her husband's broad shoulder, the boys toward dinner time came out of their jealous trance. I heard them plotting something. When dinner was called, about half of my party, including the bride and groom, went at once into the dining-car. Time there flew by swiftly. And later, when we were once more in our Pullman, and I had gotten interested in a game of cards with Milly and Stringer and his wife, the Rube came marching up to me with a very red face.

"Con, I reckon some of the boys have stolen my—our grips," said he.

"What?" I asked, blankly.

He explained that during his absence in the dining-car someone had entered his stateroom and stolen his grip and Nan's. I hastened at once to aid the Rube in his search. The boys swore by everything under and beyond the sun they had not seen the grips; they appeared very much grieved at the loss and pretended to help in searching the Pullman. At last, with the assistance of a porter, we discovered the missing grips in an upper berth. The Rube carried them off to his stateroom and we knew soon from his uncomplimentary remarks that the contents of the suitcases had been mixed and manhandled. But he did not hunt for the jokers.

We arrived at Toronto before daylight next morning, and remained in the Pullman until seven o'clock. When we got out, it was discovered that the Rube and Nan had stolen a march upon us. We traced them to the hotel, and found them at breakfast. After breakfast we formed a merry sight-seeing party and rode all over the city.

That afternoon, when Raddy let Toronto down with three hits and the boys played a magnificent game behind him, and we won 7 to 2, I knew at last and for certain that the Worcester team had come into its own again. Then next day Cairns won a close, exciting game, and following that, on the third day, the matchless Rube toyed with the Torontos. Eleven straight games won! I was in the clouds, and never had I seen so beautiful a light as shone in Milly's eyes.

From that day The Honeymoon Trip of the Worcester Baseball Club, as the newspapers heralded it—was a triumphant march. We won two out of three games at Montreal, broke even with the hard-fighting Bisons, took three straight from Rochester, and won one and tied one out of three with Hartford. It would have been wonderful ball playing for a team to play on home grounds and we were doing the full circuit of the league.

Spears had called the turn when he said the trip would be a hummer. Nan Hurtle had brought us wonderful luck.

But the tricks they played on Whit and his girl-fan bride!

Ashwell, who was a capital actor, disguised himself as a conductor and pretended to try to eject Whit and Nan from the train, urging that love-making was not permitted. Some of the team hired a clever young woman to hunt the Rube up at the hotel, and claim old acquaintance with him. Poor Whit almost collapsed when the young woman threw her arms about his neck just as Nan entered the parlor. Upon the instant Nan became wild as a little tigress, and it took much explanation and eloquence to reinstate Whit in her affections.

Another time Spears, the wily old fox, succeeded in detaining Nan on the way to the station, and the two missed the train. At first the Rube laughed with the others, but when Stringer remarked that he had noticed a growing attachment between Nan and Spears, my great pitcher experienced the first pangs of the green-eyed monster. We had to hold him to keep him from jumping from the train, and it took Milly and Mrs. Stringer to soothe him. I had to wire back to Rochester for a special train for Spears and Nan, and even then we had to play half a game without the services of our captain.

So far upon our trip I had been fortunate in securing comfortable rooms and the best of transportation for my party. At Hartford, however, I encountered difficulties. I could not get a special Pullman, and the sleeper we entered already had a number of occupants. After the ladies of my party had been assigned to berths, it was necessary for some of the boys to sleep double in upper berths.

It was late when we got aboard, the berths were already made up, and soon we had all retired. In the morning very early I was awakened by a disturbance. It sounded like a squeal. I heard an astonished exclamation, another squeal, the pattering of little feet, then hoarse uproar of laughter from the ball players in the upper berths. Following that came low, excited conversation between the porter and somebody, then an angry snort from the Rube and the thud of his heavy feet in the aisle. What took place after that was guess-work for me. But I gathered from the roars and bawls that the Rube was after some of the boys. I poked my head between the curtains and saw him digging into the berths.

"Where's McCall?" he yelled.

Mac was nowhere in that sleeper, judging from the vehement denials. But the Rube kept on digging and prodding in the upper berths.

"I'm a-goin' to lick you, Mac, so I reckon you'd better show up," shouted the Rube.

The big fellow was mad as a hornet. When he got to me he grasped me with his great fence-rail splitting hands and I cried out with pain.

"Say! Whit, let up! Mac's not here.... What's wrong?"

"I'll show you when I find him." And the Rube stalked on down the aisle, a tragically comic figure in his pajamas. In his search for Mac he pried into several upper berths that contained occupants who were not ball players, and these protested in affright. Then the Rube began to investigate the lower berths. A row of heads protruded in a bobbing line from between the curtains of the upper berths.

"Here, you Indian! Don't you look in there! That's my wife's berth!" yelled Stringer.

Bogart, too, evinced great excitement.

"Hurtle, keep out of lower eight or I'll kill you," he shouted.

What the Rube might have done there was no telling, but as he grasped a curtain, he was interrupted by a shriek from some woman assuredly not of our party.

"Get out! you horrid wretch! Help! Porter! Help! Conductor!"

Instantly there was a deafening tumult in the car. When it had subsided somewhat, and I considered I would be safe, I descended from my berth and made my way to the dressing room. Sprawled over the leather seat was the Rube pommelling McCall with hearty good will. I would have interfered, had it not been for Mac's demeanor. He was half frightened, half angry, and utterly unable to defend himself or even resist, because he was laughing, too.

"Dog-gone it! Whit—I didn't—do it! I swear it was Spears! Stop thumpin' me now—or I'll get sore.... You hear me! It wasn't me, I tell you. Cheese it!"

For all his protesting Mac received a good thumping, and I doubted not in the least that he deserved it. The wonder of the affair, however, was the fact that no one appeared to know what had made the Rube so furious. The porter would not tell, and Mac was strangely reticent, though his smile was one to make a fellow exceedingly sure something out of the ordinary had befallen. It was not until I was having breakfast in Providence that I learned the true cause of Rube's conduct, and Milly confided it to me, insisting on strict confidence.

"I promised not to tell," she said. "Now you promise you'll never tell."

"Well, Connie," went on Milly, when I had promised, "it was the funniest thing yet, but it was horrid of McCall. You see, the Rube had upper seven and Nan had lower seven. Early this morning, about daylight, Nan awoke very thirsty and got up to get a drink. During her absence, probably, but any way some time last night, McCall changed the number on her curtain, and when Nan came back to number seven of course she almost got in the wrong berth."

"No wonder the Rube punched him!" I declared. "I wish we were safe home. Something'll happen yet on this trip."

I was faithful to my promise to Milly, but the secret leaked out somewhere; perhaps Mac told it, and before the game that day all the players knew it. The Rube, having recovered his good humor, minded it not in the least. He could not have felt ill-will for any length of time. Everything seemed to get back into smooth running order, and the Honeymoon Trip bade fair to wind up beautifully.

But, somehow or other, and about something unknown to the rest of us, the Rube and Nan quarreled. It was their first quarrel. Milly and I tried to patch it up but failed.

We lost the first game to Providence and won the second. The next day, a Saturday, was the last game of the trip, and it was Rube's turn to pitch. Several times during the first two days the Rube and Nan about half made up their quarrel, only in the end to fall deeper into it. Then the last straw came in a foolish move on the part of wilful Nan. She happened to meet Henderson, her former admirer, and in a flash she took up her flirtation with him where she had left off.

"Don't go to the game with him, Nan," I pleaded. "It's a silly thing for you to do. Of course you don't mean anything, except to torment Whit. But cut it out. The gang will make him miserable and we'll lose the game. There's no telling what might happen."

"I'm supremely indifferent to what happens," she replied, with a rebellious toss of her black head. "I hope Whit gets beaten."

She went to the game with Henderson and sat in the grand stand, and the boys spied them out and told the Rube. He did not believe it at first, but finally saw them, looked deeply hurt and offended, and then grew angry. But the gong, sounding at that moment, drew his attention to his business of the day, to pitch.

His work that day reminded me of the first game he ever pitched for me, upon which occasion Captain Spears got the best out of him by making him angry. For several innings Providence was helpless before his delivery. Then something happened that showed me a crisis was near. A wag of a fan yelled from the bleachers.

"Honeymoon Rube!"

This cry was taken up by the delighted fans and it rolled around the field. But the Rube pitched on, harder than ever. Then the knowing bleacherite who had started the cry changed it somewhat.

"Nanny's Rube!" he yelled.

This, too, went the rounds, and still the Rube, though red in the face, preserved his temper and his pitching control. All would have been well if Bud Wiler, comedian of the Providence team, had not hit upon a way to rattle Rube.

"Nanny's Goat!" he shouted from the coaching lines. Every Providence player took it up.

The Rube was not proof against that. He yelled so fiercely at them, and glared so furiously, and towered so formidably, that they ceased for the moment. Then he let drive with his fast straight ball and hit the first Providence batter in the ribs. His comrades had to help him to the bench. The Rube hit the next batter on the leg, and judging from the crack of the ball, I fancied that player would walk lame for several days. The Rube tried to hit the next batter and sent him to first on balls. Thereafter it became a dodging contest with honors about equal between pitcher and batters. The Providence players stormed and the bleachers roared. But I would not take the Rube out and the game went on with the Rube forcing in runs.

With the score a tie, and three men on bases one of the players on the bench again yelled "Nanny's Goat!"

Straight as a string the Rube shot the ball at this fellow and bounded after it. The crowd rose in an uproar. The base runners began to score. I left my bench and ran across the space, but not in time to catch the Rube. I saw him hit two or three of the Providence men. Then the policemen got to him, and a real fight brought the big audience into the stamping melee. Before the Rube was collared I saw at least four blue-coats on the grass.

The game broke up, and the crowd spilled itself in streams over the field. Excitement ran high. I tried to force my way into the mass to get at the Rube and the officers, but this was impossible. I feared the Rube would be taken from the officers and treated with violence, so I waited with the surging crowd, endeavoring to get nearer. Soon we were in the street, and it seemed as if all the stands had emptied their yelling occupants.

A trolley car came along down the street, splitting the mass of people and driving them back. A dozen policemen summarily bundled the Rube upon the rear end of the car. Some of these officers boarded the car, and some remained in the street to beat off the vengeful fans.

I saw some one thrust forward a frantic young woman. The officers stopped her, then suddenly helped her on the car, just as I started. I recognized Nan. She gripped the Rube with both hands and turned a white, fearful face upon the angry crowd.

The Rube stood in the grasp of his wife and the policemen, and he looked like a ruffled lion. He shook his big fist and bawled in far-reaching voice:

"I can lick you all!"

To my infinite relief, the trolley gathered momentum and safely passed out of danger. The last thing I made out was Nan pressing close to the Rube's side. That moment saw their reconciliation and my joy that it was the end of the Rube's Honeymoon.

THE RUBE'S WATERLOO

It was about the sixth inning that I suspected the Rube of weakening. For that matter he had not pitched anything resembling his usual brand of baseball. But the Rube had developed into such a wonder in the box that it took time for his let-down to dawn upon me. Also it took a tip from Raddy, who sat with me on the bench.

"Con, the Rube isn't himself today," said Radbourne. "His mind's not on the game. He seems hurried and flustered, too. If he doesn't explode presently, I'm a dub at callin' the turn."

Raddy was the best judge of a pitcher's condition, physical or mental, in the Eastern League. It was a Saturday and we were on the road and finishing up a series with the Rochesters. Each team had won and lost a game, and, as I was climbing close to the leaders in the pennant race, I wanted the third and deciding game of that Rochester series. The usual big Saturday crowd was in attendance, noisy, demonstrative and exacting.

In this sixth inning the first man up for Rochester had flied to McCall. Then had come the two plays significant of Rube's weakening. He had hit one batter and walked another. This was sufficient, considering the score was three to one in our favor, to bring the audience to its feet with a howling, stamping demand for runs.

"Spears is wise all right," said Raddy.

I watched the foxy old captain walk over to the Rube and talk to him while he rested, a reassuring hand on the pitcher's shoulder. The crowd yelled its disapproval and Umpire Bates called out sharply:

"Spears, get back to the bag!"

"Now, Mister Umpire, ain't I hurrin' all I can?" queried Spears as he leisurely ambled back to first.

The Rube tossed a long, damp welt of hair back from his big brow and nervously toed the rubber. I noted that he seemed to forget the runners on bases and delivered the ball without glancing at either bag. Of course this resulted in a double steal. The ball went wild—almost a wild pitch.

"Steady up, old man," called Gregg between the yells of the bleachers. He held his mitt square over the plate for the Rube to pitch to. Again the long twirler took his swing, and again the ball went wild. Clancy had the Rube in the hole now and the situation began to grow serious. The Rube did not take half his usual deliberation, and of the next two pitches one of them was a ball and the other a strike by grace of the umpire's generosity. Clancy rapped the next one, an absurdly slow pitch for the Rube to use, and both runners scored to the shrill tune of the happy bleachers.

I saw Spears shake his head and look toward the bench. It was plain what that meant.

"Raddy, I ought to take the Rube out," I said, "but whom can I put in? You worked yesterday—Cairns' arm is sore. It's got to be nursed. And Henderson, that ladies' man I just signed, is not in uniform."

"I'll go in," replied Raddy, instantly.

"Not on your life." I had as hard a time keeping Radbourne from overworking as I had in getting enough work out of some other players. "I guess I'll let the Rube take his medicine. I hate to lose this game, but if we have to, we can stand it. I'm curious, anyway, to see what's the matter with the Rube. Maybe he'll settle down presently."

I made no sign that I had noticed Spears' appeal to the bench. And my aggressive players, no doubt seeing the situation as I saw it, sang out their various calls of cheer to the Rube and of defiance to their antagonists. Clancy stole off first base so far that the Rube, catching somebody's warning too late, made a balk and the umpire sent the runner on to second. The Rube now plainly showed painful evidences of being rattled.

He could not locate the plate without slowing up and when he did that a Rochester player walloped the ball. Pretty soon he pitched as if he did not care, and but for the fast fielding of the team behind him the Rochesters would have scored more than the eight runs it got. When the Rube came in to the bench I asked him if he was sick and at first he said he was and then that he was not. So I let him pitch the remaining innings, as the game was lost anyhow, and we walked off the field a badly beaten team.

That night we had to hurry from the hotel to catch a train for Worcester and we had dinner in the dining-car. Several of my players' wives had come over from Worcester to meet us, and were in the dining-car when I entered. I observed a pretty girl sitting at one of the tables with my new pitcher, Henderson.

"Say, Mac," I said to McCall, who was with me, "is Henderson married?"

"Naw, but he looks like he wanted to be. He was in the grand stand today with that girl."

"Who is she? Oh! a little peach!"

A second glance at Henderson's companion brought this compliment from me involuntarily.

"Con, you'll get it as bad as the rest of this mushy bunch of ball players. We're all stuck on that kid. But since Henderson came she's been a frost to all of us. An' it's put the Rube in the dumps."

"Who's the girl?"

"That's Nan Brown. She lives in Worcester an' is the craziest girl fan I ever seen. Flirt! Well, she's got them all beat. Somebody introduced the Rube to her. He has been mooney ever since."

That was enough to whet my curiosity, and I favored Miss Brown with more than one glance during dinner. When we returned to the parlor car I took advantage of the opportunity and remarked to Henderson that he might introduce his manager. He complied, but not with amiable grace.

So I chatted with Nan Brown, and studied her. She was a pretty, laughing, coquettish little minx and quite baseball mad. I had met many girl fans, but none so enthusiastic as Nan. But she was wholesome and sincere, and I liked her.

Before turning in I sat down beside the Rube. He was very quiet and his face did not encourage company. But that did not stop me.

"Hello, Whit; have a smoke before you go to bed?" I asked cheerfully.

He scarcely heard me and made no move to take the proffered cigar. All at once it struck me that the rustic simplicity which had characterized him had vanished.

"Whit, old fellow, what was wrong today?" I asked, quietly, with my hand on his arm.

"Mr. Connelly, I want my release, I want to go back to Rickettsville," he replied hurriedly.

For the space of a few seconds I did some tall thinking. The situation suddenly became grave. I saw the pennant for the Worcesters fading, dimming.

"You want to go home?" I began slowly. "Why, Whit, I can't keep you. I wouldn't try if you didn't want to stay. But I'll tell you confidentially, if you leave me at this stage I'm ruined."

"How's that?" he inquired, keenly looking at me.

"Well, I can't win the pennant without you. If I do win it there's a big bonus for me. I can buy the house I want and get married this fall if I capture the flag. You've met Milly. You can imagine what your pitching means to me this year. That's all."

He averted his face and looked out of the window. His big jaw quivered.

"If it's that—why, I'll stay, I reckon," he said huskily.

That moment bound Whit Hurtle and Frank Connelly into a far closer relation than the one between player and manager. I sat silent for a while, listening to the drowsy talk of the other players and the rush and roar of the train as it sped on into the night.

"Thank you, old chap," I replied. "It wouldn't have been like you to throw me down at this stage. Whit, you're in trouble?"

"Yes."

"Can I help you—in any way?"'

"I reckon not."

"Don't be too sure of that. I'm a pretty wise guy, if I do say it myself. I might be able to do as much for you as you're going to do for me."

The sight of his face convinced me that I had taken a wrong tack. It also showed me how deep Whit's trouble really was. I bade him good night and went to my berth, where sleep did not soon visit me. A saucy, sparkling-eyed woman barred Whit Hurtle's baseball career at its threshold.

Women are just as fatal to ball players as to men in any other walk of life. I had seen a strong athlete grow palsied just at a scornful slight. It's a great world, and the women run it. So I lay awake racking my brains to outwit a pretty disorganizer; and I plotted for her sake. Married, she would be out of mischief. For Whit's sake, for Milly's sake, for mine, all of which collectively meant for the sake of the pennant, this would be the solution of the problem.

I decided to take Milly into my confidence, and finally on the strength of that I got to sleep. In the morning I went to my hotel, had breakfast, attended to my mail, and then boarded a car to go out to Milly's house. She was waiting for me on the porch, dressed as I liked to see her, in blue and white, and she wore violets that matched the color of her eyes.

"Hello, Connie. I haven't seen a morning paper, but I know from your face that you lost the Rochester series," said Milly, with a gay laugh.

"I guess yes. The Rube blew up, and if we don't play a pretty smooth game, young lady, he'll never come down."

Then I told her.

"Why, Connie, I knew long ago. Haven't you seen the change in him before this?"

"What change?" I asked blankly.

"You are a man. Well, he was a gawky, slouchy, shy farmer boy when he came to us. Of course the city life and popularity began to influence him. Then he met Nan. She made the Rube a worshipper. I first noticed a change in his clothes. He blossomed out in a new suit, white negligee, neat tie and a stylish straw hat. Then it was evident he was making heroic struggles to overcome his awkwardness. It was plain he was studying and copying the other boys. He's wonderfully improved, but still shy. He'll always be shy. Connie, Whit's a fine fellow, too good for Nan Brown."

"But, Milly," I interrupted, "the Rube's hard hit. Why is he too good for her?"

"Nan is a natural-born flirt," Milly replied. "She can't help it. I'm afraid Whit has a slim chance. Nan may not see deep enough to learn his fine qualities. I fancy Nan tired quickly of him, though the one time I saw them together she appeared to like him very well. This new pitcher of yours, Henderson, is a handsome fellow and smooth. Whit is losing to him. Nan likes flash, flattery, excitement."

"McCall told me the Rube had been down in the mouth ever since Henderson joined the team. Milly, I don't like Henderson a whole lot. He's not in the Rube's class as a pitcher. What am I going to do? Lose the pennant and a big slice of purse money just for a pretty little flirt?"

"Oh, Connie, it's not so bad as that. Whit will come around all right."

"He won't unless we can pull some wires. I've got to help him win Nan Brown. What do you think of that for a manager's job? I guess maybe winning pennants doesn't call for diplomatic genius and cunning! But I'll hand them a few tricks before I lose. My first move will be to give Henderson his release."

I left Milly, as always, once more able to make light of discouragements and difficulties.

Monday I gave Henderson his unconditional release. He celebrated the occasion by verifying certain rumors I had heard from other managers.

He got drunk. But he did not leave town, and I heard that he was negotiating with Providence for a place on that team.

Radbourne pitched one of his gilt-edged games that afternoon against Hartford and we won. And Milly sat in the grand stand, having contrived by cleverness to get a seat next to Nan Brown. Milly and I were playing a vastly deeper game than baseball—a game with hearts. But we were playing it with honest motive, for the good of all concerned, we believed, and on the square. I sneaked a look now and then up into the grand stand. Milly and Nan appeared to be getting on famously. It was certain that Nan was flushed and excited, no doubt consciously proud of being seen with my affianced. After the game I chanced to meet them on their way out. Milly winked at me, which was her sign that all was working beautifully.

I hunted up the Rube and bundled him off to the hotel to take dinner with me. At first he was glum, but after a while he brightened up somewhat to my persistent cheer and friendliness. Then we went out on the hotel balcony to smoke, and there I made my play.

"Whit, I'm pulling a stroke for you. Now listen and don't be offended. I know what's put you off your feed, because I was the same way when Milly had me guessing. You've lost your head over Nan Brown. That's not so terrible, though I daresay you think it's a catastrophe. Because you've quit. You've shown a yellow streak. You've lain down.

"My boy, that isn't the way to win a girl. You've got to scrap. Milly told me yesterday how she had watched your love affairs with Nan, and how she thought you had given up just when things might have come your way. Nan is a little flirt, but she's all right. What's more, she was getting fond of you. Nan is meanest to the man she likes best. The way to handle her, Whit, is to master her. Play high and mighty. Get tragical. Then grab her up in your arms. I tell you, Whit, it'll all come your way if you only keep your nerve. I'm your friend and so is Milly. We're going out to her house presently—and Nan will be there."

The Rube drew a long, deep breath and held out his hand. I sensed another stage in the evolution of Whit Hurtle.

"I reckon I've taken baseball coachin'," he said presently, "an' I don't see why I can't take some other kind. I'm only a rube, an' things come hard for me, but I'm a-learnin'."

It was about dark when we arrived at the house.

"Hello, Connie. You're late. Good evening, Mr. Hurtle. Come right in. You've met Miss Nan Brown? Oh, of course; how stupid of me!"

It was a trying moment for Milly and me. A little pallor showed under the Rube's tan, but he was more composed than I had expected. Nan got up from the piano. She was all in white and deliciously pretty. She gave a quick, glad start of surprise. What a relief that was to my troubled mind! Everything had depended upon a real honest liking for Whit, and she had it.

More than once I had been proud of Milly's cleverness, but this night as hostess and an accomplice she won my everlasting admiration. She contrived to give the impression that Whit was a frequent visitor at her home and very welcome. She brought out his best points, and in her skillful hands he lost embarrassment and awkwardness. Before the evening was over Nan regarded Whit with different eyes, and she never dreamed that everything had not come about naturally. Then Milly somehow got me out on the porch, leaving Nan and Whit together.

"Milly, you're a marvel, the best and sweetest ever," I whispered. "We're going to win. It's a cinch."

"Well, Connie, not that—exactly," she whispered back demurely. "But it looks hopeful."

I could not help hearing what was said in the parlor.

"Now I can roast you," Nan was saying, archly. She had switched back to her favorite baseball vernacular. "You pitched a swell game last Saturday in Rochester, didn't you? Not! You had no steam, no control, and you couldn't have curved a saucer."

"Nan, what could you expect?" was the cool reply. "You sat up in the stand with your handsome friend. I reckon I couldn't pitch. I just gave the game away."

"Whit!—Whit!——"

Then I whispered to Milly that it might be discreet for us to move a little way from the vicinity.

It was on the second day afterward that I got a chance to talk to Nan. She reached the grounds early, before Milly arrived, and I found her in the grand stand. The Rube was down on the card to pitch and when he started to warm up Nan said confidently that he would shut out Hartford that afternoon.

"I'm sorry, Nan, but you're way off. We'd do well to win at all, let alone get a shutout."

"You're a fine manager!" she retorted, hotly. "Why won't we win?"

"Well, the Rube's not in good form. The Rube——"

"Stop calling him that horrid name."

"Whit's not in shape. He's not right. He's ill or something is wrong. I'm worried sick about him."

"Why—Mr. Connelly!" exclaimed Nan. She turned quickly toward me.

I crowded on full canvas of gloom to my already long face.

"I'm serious, Nan. The lad's off, somehow. He's in magnificent physical trim, but he can't keep his mind on the game. He has lost his head. I've talked with him, reasoned with him, all to no good. He only goes down deeper in the dumps. Something is terribly wrong with him, and if he doesn't brace, I'll have to release——"

Miss Nan Brown suddenly lost a little of her rich bloom. "Oh! you wouldn't—you couldn't release him!"

"I'll have to if he doesn't brace. It means a lot to me, Nan, for of course I can't win the pennant this year without Whit being in shape. But I believe I wouldn't mind the loss of that any more than to see him fall down. The boy is a magnificent pitcher. If he can only be brought around he'll go to the big league next year and develop into one of the greatest pitchers the game has ever produced. But somehow or other he has lost heart. He's quit. And I've done my best for him. He's beyond me now. What a shame it is! For he's the making of such a splendid man outside of baseball. Milly thinks the world of him. Well, well; there are disappointments—we can't help them. There goes the gong. I must leave you. Nan, I'll bet you a box of candy Whit loses today. Is it a go?"

"It is," replied Nan, with fire in her eyes. "You go to Whit Hurtle and tell him I said if he wins today's game I'll kiss him!"

I nearly broke my neck over benches and bats getting to Whit with that message. He gulped once.

Then he tightened his belt and shut out Hartford with two scratch singles. It was a great exhibition of pitching. I had no means to tell whether or not the Rube got his reward that night, but I was so happy that I hugged Milly within an inch of her life.

But it turned out that I had been a little premature in my elation. In two days the Rube went down into the depths again, this time clear to China, and Nan was sitting in the grand stand with Henderson. The Rube lost his next game, pitching like a schoolboy scared out of his wits. Henderson followed Nan like a shadow, so that I had no chance to talk to her. The Rube lost his next game and then another. We were pushed out of second place.

If we kept up that losing streak a little longer, our hopes for the pennant were gone. I had begun to despair of the Rube. For some occult reason he scarcely spoke to me. Nan flirted worse than ever. It seemed to me she flaunted her conquest of Henderson in poor Whit's face.

The Providence ball team came to town and promptly signed Henderson and announced him for Saturday's game. Cairns won the first of the series and Radbourne lost the second. It was Rube's turn to pitch the Saturday game and I resolved to make one more effort to put the love-sick swain in something like his old fettle. So I called upon Nan.

She was surprised to see me, but received me graciously. I fancied her face was not quite so glowing as usual. I came bluntly out with my mission. She tried to freeze me but I would not freeze. I was out to win or lose and not to be lightly laughed aside or coldly denied. I played to make her angry, knowing the real truth of her feelings would show under stress.

For once in my life I became a knocker and said some unpleasant things—albeit they were true—about Henderson. She championed Henderson royally, and when, as a last card, I compared Whit's fine record with Henderson's, not only as a ball player, but as a man, particularly in his reverence for women, she flashed at me:

"What do you know about it? Mr. Henderson asked me to marry him. Can a man do more to show his respect? Your friend never so much as hinted such honorable intentions. What's more—he insulted me!" The blaze in Nan's black eyes softened with a film of tears. She looked hurt. Her pride had encountered a fall.

"Oh, no, Nan, Whit couldn't insult a lady," I protested.

"Couldn't he? That's all you know about him. You know I—I promised to kiss him if he beat Hartford that day. So when he came I—I did. Then the big savage began to rave and he grabbed me up in his arms. He smothered me; almost crushed the life out of me. He frightened me terribly. When I got away from him—the monster stood there and coolly said I belonged to him. I ran out of the room and wouldn't see him any more. At first I might have forgiven him if he had apologized—said he was sorry, but never a word. Now I never will forgive him."

I had to make a strenuous effort to conceal my agitation. The Rube had most carefully taken my fool advice in the matter of wooing a woman.

When I had got a hold upon myself, I turned to Nan white-hot with eloquence. Now I was talking not wholly for myself or the pennant, but for this boy and girl who were at odds in that strangest game of life—love.

What I said I never knew, but Nan lost her resentment, and then her scorn and indifference. Slowly she thawed and warmed to my reason, praise, whatever it was, and when I stopped she was again the radiant bewildering Nan of old.

"Take another message to Whit for me," she said, audaciously. "Tell him I adore ball players, especially pitchers. Tell him I'm going to the game today to choose the best one. If he loses the game——"

She left the sentence unfinished. In my state of mind I doubted not in the least that she meant to marry the pitcher who won the game, and so I told the Rube. He made one wild upheaval of his arms and shoulders, like an erupting volcano, which proved to me that he believed it, too.

When I got to the bench that afternoon I was tired. There was a big crowd to see the game; the weather was perfect; Milly sat up in the box and waved her score card at me; Raddy and Spears declared we had the game; the Rube stalked to and fro like an implacable Indian chief—but I was not happy in mind. Calamity breathed in the very air.

The game began. McCall beat out a bunt; Ashwell sacrificed and Stringer laced one of his beautiful triples against the fence. Then he scored on a high fly. Two runs! Worcester trotted out into the field. The Rube was white with determination; he had the speed of a bullet and perfect control of his jump ball and drop. But Providence hit and had the luck. Ashwell fumbled, Gregg threw wild. Providence tied the score.

The game progressed, growing more and more of a nightmare to me. It was not Worcester's day. The umpire could not see straight; the boys grumbled and fought among themselves; Spears roasted the umpire and was sent to the bench; Bogart tripped, hurting his sore ankle, and had to be taken out. Henderson's slow, easy ball baffled my players, and when he used speed they lined it straight at a Providence fielder.

In the sixth, after a desperate rally, we crowded the bases with only one out. Then Mullaney's hard rap to left, seemingly good for three bases, was pulled down by Stone with one hand. It was a wonderful catch and he doubled up a runner at second. Again in the seventh we had a chance to score, only to fail on another double play, this time by the infield.

When the Providence players were at bat their luck not only held good but trebled and quadrupled. The little Texas-league hits dropped safely just out of reach of the infielders. My boys had an off day in fielding. What horror that of all days in a season this should be the one for them to make errors!

But they were game, and the Rube was the gamest of all. He did not seem to know what hard luck was, or discouragement, or poor support. He kept everlastingly hammering the ball at those lucky Providence hitters. What speed he had! The ball streaked in, and somebody would shut his eyes and make a safety. But the Rube pitched, on, tireless, irresistibly, hopeful, not forgetting to call a word of cheer to his fielders.

It was one of those strange games that could not be bettered by any labor or daring or skill. I saw it was lost from the second inning, yet so deeply was I concerned, so tantalizingly did the plays reel themselves off, that I groveled there on the bench unable to abide by my baseball sense.

The ninth inning proved beyond a shadow of doubt how baseball fate, in common with other fates, loved to balance the chances, to lift up one, then the other, to lend a deceitful hope only to dash it away.

Providence had almost three times enough to win. The team let up in that inning or grew over-confident or careless, and before we knew what had happened some scratch hits, and bases on balls, and errors, gave us three runs and left two runners on bases. The disgusted bleachers came out of their gloom and began to whistle and thump. The Rube hit safely, sending another run over the plate. McCall worked his old trick, beating out a slow bunt.

Bases full, three runs to tie! With Ashwell up and one out, the noise in the bleachers mounted to a high-pitched, shrill, continuous sound. I got up and yelled with all my might and could not hear my voice. Ashwell was a dangerous man in a pinch. The game was not lost yet. A hit, anything to get Ash to first—and then Stringer!

Ash laughed at Henderson, taunted him, shook his bat at him and dared him to put one over. Henderson did not stand under fire. The ball he pitched had no steam. Ash cracked it—square on the line into the shortstop's hands. The bleachers ceased yelling.

Then Stringer strode grimly to the plate. It was a hundred to one, in that instance, that he would lose the ball. The bleachers let out one deafening roar, then hushed. I would rather have had Stringer at the bat than any other player in the world, and I thought of the Rube and Nan and Milly—and hope would not die.

Stringer swung mightily on the first pitch and struck the ball with a sharp, solid bing! It shot toward center, low, level, exceedingly swift, and like a dark streak went straight into the fielder's hands. A rod to right or left would have made it a home run. The crowd strangled a victorious yell. I came out of my trance, for the game was over and lost. It was the Rube's Waterloo.

I hurried him into the dressing room and kept close to him. He looked like a man who had lost the one thing worth while in his life. I turned a deaf ear to my players, to everybody, and hustled the Rube out and to the hotel. I wanted to be near him that night.

To my amaze we met Milly and Nan as we entered the lobby. Milly wore a sweet, sympathetic smile. Nan shone more radiant than ever. I simply stared. It was Milly who got us all through the corridor into the parlor. I heard Nan talking.

"Whit, you pitched a bad game but—" there was the old teasing, arch, coquettishness—"but you are the best pitcher!"

"Nan!"

"Yes!"

BREAKING INTO FAST COMPANY

They may say baseball is the same in the minor leagues that it is in the big leagues, but any old ball player or manager knows better. Where the difference comes in, however, is in the greater excellence and unity of the major players, a speed, a daring, a finish that can be acquired only in competition with one another.

I thought of this when I led my party into Morrisey's private box in the grand stand of the Chicago American League grounds. We had come to see the Rube's break into fast company. My great pitcher, Whittaker Hurtle, the Rube, as we called him, had won the Eastern League Pennant for me that season, and Morrisey, the Chicago magnate, had bought him. Milly, my affianced, was with me, looking as happy as she was pretty, and she was chaperoned by her mother, Mrs. Nelson.

With me, also, were two veterans of my team, McCall and Spears, who lived in Chicago, and who would have traveled a few miles to see the Rube pitch. And the other member of my party was Mrs. Hurtle, the Rube's wife, as saucy and as sparkling-eyed as when she had been Nan Brown. Today she wore a new tailor-made gown, new bonnet, new gloves—she said she had decorated herself in a manner befitting the wife of a major league pitcher.

Morrisey's box was very comfortable, and, as I was pleased to note, so situated that we had a fine view of the field and stands, and yet were comparatively secluded. The bleachers were filling. Some of the Chicago players were on the field tossing and batting balls; the Rube, however, had not yet appeared.

A moment later a metallic sound was heard on the stairs leading up into the box. I knew it for baseball spiked shoes clanking on the wood.

The Rube, looking enormous in his uniform, stalked into the box, knocking over two chairs as he entered. He carried a fielder's glove in one huge freckled hand, and a big black bat in the other.

Nan, with much dignity and a very manifest pride, introduced him to Mrs. Nelson.

There was a little chatting, and then, upon the arrival of Manager Morrisey, we men retired to the back of the box to talk baseball.

Chicago was in fourth place in the league race, and had a fighting chance to beat Detroit out for the third position. Philadelphia was

166

scheduled for that day, and Philadelphia had a great team. It was leading the race, and almost beyond all question would land the flag. In truth, only one more victory was needed to clinch the pennant. The team had three games to play in Chicago and it was to wind up the season with three in Washington. Six games to play and only one imperatively important to win! But baseball is uncertain, and until the Philadelphians won that game they would be a band of fiends.

"Well, Whit, this is where you break in," I said. "Now, tip us straight. You've had more than a week's rest. How's that arm?"

"Grand, Con, grand!" replied the Rube with his frank smile. "I was a little anxious till I warmed up. But say! I've got more up my sleeve today than I ever had."

"That'll do for me," said Morrisey, rubbing his hands. "I'll spring something on these swelled Quakers today. Now, Connelly, give Hurtle one of your old talks—the last one—and then I'll ring the gong."

I added some words of encouragement, not forgetting my old ruse to incite the Rube by rousing his temper. And then, as the gong rang and the Rube was departing, Nan stepped forward for her say. There was a little white under the tan on her cheek, and her eyes had a darkling flash.

"Whit, it's a magnificent sight—that beautiful green field and the stands. What a crowd of fans! Why, I never saw a real baseball crowd before. There are twenty thousand here. And there's a difference in the feeling. It's sharper—new to me. It's big league baseball. Not a soul in that crowd ever heard of you, but, I believe, tomorrow the whole baseball world will have heard of you. Mr. Morrisey knows. I saw it in his face. Captain Spears knows. Connie knows. I know."

Then she lifted her face and, pulling him down within reach, she kissed him. Nan took her husband's work in dead earnest; she gloried in it, and perhaps she had as much to do with making him a great pitcher as any of us.

The Rube left the box, and I found a seat between Nan and Milly. The field was a splendid sight. Those bleachers made me glow with managerial satisfaction. On the field both teams pranced and danced and bounced around in practice.

In spite of the absolutely last degree of egotism manifested by the Philadelphia players, I could not but admire such a splendid body of men.

"So these are the champions of last season and of this season, too," commented Milly. "I don't wonder. How swiftly and cleanly they play! They appear not to exert themselves, yet they always get the ball in perfect time. It all reminds me of—of the rhythm of music. And that champion batter and runner—that Lane in center—isn't he just beautiful? He walks and runs like a blue-ribbon winner at the horse show. I tell you one thing, Connie, these Quakers are on dress parade."

"Oh, these Quakers hate themselves, I don't think!" retorted Nan. Being a rabid girl-fan it was, of course, impossible for Nan to speak baseball convictions or gossip without characteristic baseball slang. "Stuck on themselves! I never saw the like in my life. That fellow Lane is so swelled that he can't get down off his toes. But he's a wonder, I must admit that. They're a bunch of stars. Easy, fast, trained—they're machines, and I'll bet they're Indians to fight. I can see it sticking out all over them. This will certainly be some game with Whit handing up that jump ball of his to this gang of champs. But, Connie, I'll go you Whit beats them."

I laughed and refused to gamble.

The gong rang; the crowd seemed to hum and rustle softly to quiet attention; Umpire McClung called the names of the batteries; then the familiar "Play!"

There was the usual applause from the grand stand and welcome cheers from the bleachers. The Rube was the last player to go out. Morrisey was a manager who always played to the stands, and no doubt he held the Rube back for effect. If so, he ought to have been gratified. That moment reminded me of my own team and audience upon the occasion of the Rube's debut. It was the same only here it happened in the big league, before a championship team and twenty thousand fans.

The roar that went up from the bleachers might well have scared an unseasoned pitcher out of his wits. And the Quakers lined up before their bench and gazed at this newcomer who had the nerve to walk out there to the box. Cogswell stood on the coaching line, looked at the Rube and then held up both arms and turned toward the Chicago bench as if to ask Morrisey: "Where did you get that?"

Nan, quick as a flash to catch a point, leaned over the box-rail and looked at the champions with fire in her eye. "Oh, you just wait! wait!" she bit out between her teeth.

Certain it was that there was no one who knew the Rube as well as I; and I knew beyond the shadow of a doubt that the hour before me would see brightening of a great star pitcher on the big league horizon. It was bound to be a full hour for me. I had much reason to be grateful to Whit Hurtle. He had pulled my team out of a rut and won me the pennant, and the five thousand dollars I got for his release bought the little cottage on the hill for Milly and me. Then there was my pride in having developed him. And all that I needed to calm me, settle me down into assurance and keen criticism of the game, was to see the Rube pitch a few balls with his old incomparable speed and control.

Berne, first batter for the Quakers, walked up to the plate. He was another Billy Hamilton, built like a wedge. I saw him laugh at the long pitcher.

Whit swayed back, coiled and uncoiled. Something thin, white, glancing, shot at Berne. He ducked, escaping the ball by a smaller margin than appeared good for his confidence. He spoke low to the Rube, and what he said was probably not flavored with the milk of friendly sweetness.

"Wild! What'd you look for?" called out Cogswell scornfully. "He's from the woods!"

The Rube swung his enormously long arm, took an enormous stride toward third base, and pitched again. It was one of his queer deliveries. The ball cut the plate.

"Ho! Ho!" yelled the Quakers.

The Rube's next one was his out curve. It broke toward the corner of the plate and would have been a strike had not Berne popped it up.

Callopy, the second hitter, faced the Rube, and he, too, after the manner of ball players, made some remark meant only for the Rube's ears. Callopy was a famous waiter. He drove more pitchers mad with his implacable patience than any hitter in the league. The first one of the Rube's he waited on crossed the in-corner; the second crossed the out-corner and the third was Rube's wide, slow, tantalizing "stitch-ball," as we call it, for the reason that it came so slow a batter could count the stitches. I believe Callopy waited on that curve, decided to hit it, changed his mind and waited some more, and finally the ball maddened him and he had to poke at it, the result being a weak grounder.

Then the graceful, powerful Lane, champion batter, champion base runner, stepped to the plate. How a baseball crowd, any crowd, anywhere, loves the champion batter! The ovation Lane received made me wonder, with this impressive reception in a hostile camp, what could be the manner of it on his home field? Any boy ball-player from the lots seeing Lane knock the dirt out of his spikes and step into position would have known he was a 400 hitter.

I was curious to see what the Rube would pitch Lane. It must have been a new and significant moment for Hurtle. Some pitchers actually wilt when facing a hitter of Lane's reputation. But he, on his baseball side, was peculiarly unemotional. Undoubtedly he could get furious, but that only increased his effectiveness. To my amazement the Rube pitched Lane a little easy ball, not in any sense like his floater or stitch-ball, but just a little toss that any youngster might have tossed. Of all possible balls, Lane was not expecting such as that, and he let it go. If the nerve of it amazed me, what did it not do to Lane? I saw his face go fiery red. The grand stand murmured; let out one short yelp of pleasure; the Quaker players chaffed Lane.

The pitch was a strike. I was gripping my chair now, and for the next pitch I prophesied the Rube's wonderful jump ball, which he had not yet used. He swung long, and at the end of his swing seemed to jerk tensely. I scarcely saw the ball. It had marvelous speed. Lane did not offer to hit it, and it was a strike. He looked at the Rube, then at Cogswell. That veteran appeared amused. The bleachers, happy and surprised to be able to yell at Lane, yelled heartily.

Again I took it upon myself to interpret the Rube's pitching mind. He had another ball that he had not used, a drop, an unhittable drop. I thought he would use that next. He did, and though Lane reached it with the bat, the hit was a feeble one. He had been fooled and the side was out.

Poole, the best of the Quaker's pitching staff, walked out to the slab. He was a left-hander, and Chicago, having so many players who batted left-handed, always found a southpaw a hard nut to crack. Cogswell, field manager and captain of the Quakers, kicked up the dust around first base and yelled to his men: "Git in the game!"

Staats hit Poole's speed ball into deep short and was out; Mitchell flew out to Berne; Rand grounded to second.

While the teams again changed sides the fans cheered, and then indulged in the first stretch of the game. I calculated that they would be stretching their necks presently, trying to keep track of the Rube's work.

Nan leaned on the railing absorbed in her own hope and faith. Milly chattered about this and that, people in the boxes, and the chances of the game.

My own interest, while it did not wholly preclude the fortunes of the Chicago players at the bat, was mostly concerned with the Rube's fortunes in the field.

In the Rube's half inning he retired Bannister and Blandy on feeble infield grounders, and worked Cogswell into hitting a wide curve high in the air.

Poole meant to win for the Quakers if his good arm and cunning did not fail him, and his pitching was masterly. McCloskey fanned, Hutchinson fouled out, Brewster got a short safe fly just out of reach, and Hoffner hit to second, forcing Brewster.

With Dugan up for the Quakers in the third inning, Cogswell and Bannister, from the coaching lines, began to talk to the Rube. My ears, keen from long practice, caught some of the remarks in spite of the noisy bleachers.

"Say, busher, you 've lasted longer'n we expected, but you don't know it!"

"Gol darn you city ball tossers! Now you jest let me alone!"

"We're comin' through the rye!"

"My top-heavy rustic friend, you'll need an airship presently, when you go up!"

All the badinage was good-natured, which was sure proof that the Quakers had not arrived at anything like real appreciation of the Rube. They were accustomed to observe the trying out of many youngsters, of whom ninety-nine out of a hundred failed to make good.

Dugan chopped at three strikes and slammed his bat down. Hucker hit a slow fly to Hoffer. Three men out on five pitched balls! Cogswell, old war horse that he was, stood a full moment and watched the Rube as he walked in to the bench. An idea had penetrated Cogswell's brain, and I would have given something to know what it was. Cogswell was a great baseball general, and though he had a preference for matured ball-players he could, when pressed, see the quality in a youngster. He picked up his mitt and took his position at first with a gruff word to his players.

Rand for Chicago opened with a hit, and the bleachers, ready to strike fire, began to cheer and stamp. When McCloskey, in an attempt to sacrifice, beat out his bunt the crowd roared. Rand, being slow on his feet, had not attempted to make third on the play. Hutchinson sacrificed, neatly advancing the runners. Then the bleachers played the long rolling drum of clattering feet with shrill whistling accompaniment. Brewster batted a wicked ground ball to Blandy. He dove into the dust, came up with the ball, and feinting to throw home he wheeled and shot the ball to Cogswell, who in turn shot it to the plate to head Rand. Runner and ball got there apparently together, but Umpire McClung's decision went against Rand. It was fine, fast work, but how the bleachers stormed at McClung!

"Rob-b-ber!"

Again the head of the Quakers' formidable list was up. I knew from the way that Cogswell paced the coaching box that the word had gone out to look the Rube over seriously. There were possibilities even in rubes.

Berne carefully stepped into the batter's box, as if he wanted to be certain to the breadth of a hair how close he was to the plate. He was there this time to watch the Rube pitch, to work him out, to see what was what. He crouched low, and it would have been extremely hard to guess what he was up to. His great play, however, was his ability to dump the ball and beat out the throw to first. It developed presently, that this was now his intention and that the Rube knew it and pitched him the one ball which is almost impossible to bunt—a high incurve, over the inside corner. There was no mistaking the Rube's magnificent control. True as a plumb line he shot up the ball—once, twice, and Berne fouled both—two strikes. Grudgingly he waited on the next, but it, too, was over the corner, and Berne went out on strikes. The great crowd did not, of course, grasp the finesse of the play, but Berne had struck out—that was enough for them.

Callopy, the famous spiker, who had put many a player out of the game for weeks at a time, strode into the batter's place, and he, too, was not at the moment making any funny remarks. The Rube delivered a ball that all but hit Callopy fair on the head. It was the second narrow escape for him, and the roar he let out showed how he resented being threatened with a little of his own medicine. As might have been expected, and very likely as the Rube intended, Callopy hit the next ball, a sweeping curve, up over the infield.

I was trying to see all the intricate details of the motive and action on the field, and it was not easy to watch several players at once. But while Berne and Callopy were having their troubles with the Rube, I kept the tail of my eye on Cogswell. He was prowling up and down the third-base line.

He was missing no signs, no indications, no probabilities, no possibilities. But he was in doubt. Like a hawk he was watching the Rube, and, as well, the crafty batters. The inning might not tell the truth as to the Rube's luck, though it would test his control. The Rube's speed and curves, without any head work, would have made him a pitcher of no mean ability, but was this remarkable placing of balls just accident? That was the question.

When Berne walked to the bench I distinctly heard him say: "Come out of it, you dubs. I say you can't work him or wait him. He's peggin' 'em out of a gun!"

Several of the Quakers were standing out from the bench, all intent on the Rube. He had stirred them up. First it was humor; then ridicule, curiosity, suspicion, doubt. And I knew it would grow to wonder and certainty, then fierce attack from both tongues and bats, and lastly—for ball players are generous—unstinted admiration.

Somehow, not only the first climaxes of a game but the decisions, the convictions, the reputations of pitchers and fielders evolve around the great hitter. Plain it was that the vast throng of spectators, eager to believe in a new find, wild to welcome a new star, yet loath to trust to their own impulsive judgments, held themselves in check until once more the great Lane had faced the Rube.

The field grew tolerably quiet just then. The Rube did not exert himself. The critical stage had no concern for him. He pitched Lane a high curve, over the plate, but in close, a ball meant to be hit and a ball hard to hit safely. Lane knew that as well as any hitter in the world, so he let two of the curves go by—two strikes. Again the Rube relentlessly gave him the same ball; and Lane, hitting viciously, spitefully, because he did not want to hit that kind of a ball, sent up a fly that Rand easily captured.

"Oh, I don't know! Pretty fair, I guess!" yelled a tenor-voiced fan; and he struck the key-note. And the bleachers rose to their feet and gave the Rube the rousing cheer of the brotherhood of fans.

Hoffer walked to first on a base on balls. Sweeney advanced him. The Rube sent up a giant fly to Callopy. Then Staats hit safely, scoring the first run of the game. Hoffer crossed the plate amid vociferous applause. Mitchell ended the inning with a fly to Blandy.

What a change had come over the spirit of that Quaker aggregation! It was something to make a man thrill with admiration and, if he happened to favor Chicago, to fire all his fighting blood. The players poured upon the Rube a continuous stream of scathing abuse. They would have made a raging devil of a mild-mannered clergyman. Some of them were skilled in caustic wit, most of them were possessed of forked tongues; and Cogswell, he of a thousand baseball battles, had a genius for inflaming anyone he tormented. This was mostly beyond the ken of the audience, and behind the back of the umpire, but it was perfectly plain to me. The Quakers were trying to rattle the Rube, a trick of the game as fair for one side as for the other. I sat there tight in my seat, grimly glorying in the way the Rube refused to be disturbed. But the lion in him was rampant. Fortunately, it was his strange gift to pitch better the angrier he got; and the more the Quakers flayed him, the more he let himself out to their crushing humiliation.

The innings swiftly passed to the eighth with Chicago failing to score again, with Philadelphia failing to score at all. One scratch hit and a single, gifts to the weak end of the batting list, were all the lank pitcher allowed them. Long since the bleachers had crowned the Rube. He was theirs and they were his; and their voices had the peculiar strangled hoarseness due to over-exertion. The grand stand, slower to understand and approve, arrived later; but it got there about the seventh, and ladies' gloves and men's hats were sacrificed.

In the eighth the Quakers reluctantly yielded their meed of praise, showing it by a cessation of their savage wordy attacks on the Rube. It was a kind of sullen respect, wrung from the bosom of great foes.

Then the ninth inning was at hand. As the sides changed I remembered to look at the feminine group in our box. Milly was in a most beautiful glow of happiness and excitement. Nan sat rigid, leaning over the rail, her face white and drawn, and she kept saying in a low voice: "Will it never end? Will it never end?" Mrs. Nelson stared wearily.

It was the Quakers' last stand. They faced it as a team that had won many a game in the ninth with two men out. Dugan could do nothing with the Rube's unhittable drop, for a drop curve was his weakness, and he struck out. Hucker hit to Hoffer, who fumbled, making the first error of the game. Poole dumped the ball, as evidently the Rube desired, for he handed up a straight one, but the bunt rolled teasingly and the Rube, being big and tall, failed to field it in time.

Suddenly the whole field grew quiet. For the first time Cogswell's coaching was clearly heard.

"One out! Take a lead! Take a lead! Go through this time. Go through!"

Could it be possible, I wondered, that after such a wonderful exhibition of pitching the Rube would lose out in the ninth?

There were two Quakers on base, one out, and two of the best hitters in the league on deck, with a chance of Lane getting up.

"Oh! Oh! Oh!" moaned Nan.

I put my hand on hers. "Don't quit, Nan. You'll never forgive yourself if you quit. Take it from me, Whit will pull out of this hole!"

What a hole that was for the Rube on the day of his break into fast company! I measured it by his remarkable deliberation. He took a long time to get ready to pitch to Berne, and when he let drive it was as if he had been trifling all before in that game. I could think of no way to figure it except that when the ball left him there was scarcely any appreciable interval of time before it cracked in Sweeney's mitt. It was the Rube's drop, which I believed unhittable. Berne let it go by, shaking his head as McClung called it a strike. Another followed, which Berne chopped at vainly. Then with the same upheaval of his giant frame, the same flinging of long arms and lunging forward, the Rube delivered a third drop. And Berne failed to hit it.

The voiceless bleachers stamped on the benches and the grand stand likewise thundered.

Callopy showed his craft by stepping back and lining Rube's high pitch to left. Hoffer leaped across and plunged down, getting his gloved hand in front of the ball. The hit was safe, but Hoffer's valiant effort saved a tie score.

Lane up! Three men on bases! Two out!

Not improbably there were many thousand spectators of that thrilling moment who pitied the Rube for the fate which placed Lane at the bat then. But I was not one of them. Nevertheless my throat was clogged, my mouth dry, and my ears full of bells. I could have done something terrible to Hurtle for his deliberation, yet I knew he was proving himself what I had always tried to train him to be.

Then he swung, stepped out, and threw his body with the ball. This was his rarely used pitch, his last resort, his fast rise ball that jumped up a little at the plate. Lane struck under it. How significant on the instant to see old Cogswell's hands go up! Again the Rube pitched, and this time Lane watched the ball go by. Two strikes!

That whole audience leaped to its feet, whispering, yelling, screaming, roaring, bawling.

The Rube received the ball from Sweeney and quick as lightning he sped it plateward. The great Lane struck out! The game was over—Chicago, 1; Philadelphia, 0.

In that whirling moment when the crowd went mad and Milly was hugging me, and Nan pounding holes in my hat, I had a queer sort of blankness, a section of time when my sensations were deadlocked.

"Oh! Connie, look!" cried Nan. I saw Lane and Cogswell warmly shaking hands with the Rube. Then the hungry clamoring fans tumbled upon the field and swarmed about the players.

Whereupon Nan kissed me and Milly, and then kissed Mrs. Nelson. In that radiant moment Nan was all sweetness.

"It is the Rube's break into fast company," she said.

THE KNOCKER

"Yes, Carroll, I got my notice. Maybe it's no surprise to you. And there's one more thing I want to say. You're 'it' on this team. You're the topnotch catcher in the Western League and one of the best ball players in the game—but you're a knocker!"

Madge Ellston heard young Sheldon speak. She saw the flash in his gray eyes and the heat of his bronzed face as he looked intently at the big catcher.

"Fade away, sonny. Back to the bush-league for yours!" replied Carroll, derisively. "You're not fast enough for Kansas City. You look pretty good in a uniform and you're swift on your feet, but you can't hit. You've got a glass arm and you run bases like an ostrich trying to side. That notice was coming to you. Go learn the game!"

Then a crowd of players trooped noisily out of the hotel lobby and swept Sheldon and Carroll down the porch steps toward the waiting omnibus.

Madge's uncle owned the Kansas City club. She had lived most of her nineteen years in a baseball atmosphere, but accustomed as she was to baseball talk and the peculiar banterings and bickerings of the players, there were times when it seemed all Greek. If a player got his "notice" it meant he would be released in ten days. A "knocker" was a ball player who spoke ill of his fellow players. This scrap of conversation, however, had an unusual interest because Carroll had paid court to her for a year, and Sheldon, coming to the team that spring, had fallen desperately in love with her. She liked Sheldon pretty well, but Carroll fascinated her. She began to wonder if there were bad feelings between the rivals—to compare them—to get away from herself and judge them impersonally.

When Pat Donahue, the veteran manager of the team came out, Madge greeted him with a smile. She had always gotten on famously with Pat, notwithstanding her imperious desire to handle the managerial reins herself upon occasions. Pat beamed all over his round ruddy face.

"Miss Madge, you weren't to the park yesterday an' we lost without our pretty mascot. We shure needed you. Denver's playin' at a fast clip."

"I'm coming out today," replied Miss Ellston, thoughtfully. "Pat, what's a knocker?"

"Now, Miss Madge, are you askin' me that after I've been coachin' you in baseball for years?" questioned Pat, in distress.

"I know what a knocker is, as everybody else does. But I want to know the real meaning, the inside-ball of it, to use your favorite saying."

Studying her grave face with shrewd eyes Donahue slowly lost his smile.

"The inside-ball of it, eh? Come, let's sit over here a bit—the sun's shure warm today.... Miss Madge, a knocker is the strangest man known in the game, the hardest to deal with an' what every baseball manager hates most."

Donahue told her that he believed the term "knocker" came originally from baseball; that in general it typified the player who strengthened his own standing by belittling the ability of his team-mates, and by enlarging upon his own superior qualities. But there were many phases of this peculiar type. Some players were natural born knockers; others acquired the name in their later years in the game when younger men threatened to win their places. Some of the best players ever produced by baseball had the habit in its most violent form. There were players of ridiculously poor ability who held their jobs on the strength of this one trait. It was a mystery how they misled magnates and managers alike; how for months they held their places, weakening a team, often keeping a good team down in the race; all from sheer bold suggestion of their own worth and other players' worthlessness. Strangest of all was the knockers' power to disorganize; to engender a bad spirit between management and team and among the players. The team which was without one of the parasites of the game generally stood well up in the race for the pennant, though there had been championship teams noted for great knockers as well as great players.

"It's shure strange, Miss Madge," said Pat in conclusion, shaking his gray head. "I've played hundreds of knockers, an' released them, too. Knockers always get it in the end, but they go on foolin' me and workin' me just the same as if I was a youngster with my first team. They're part an' parcel of the game."

"Do you like these men off the field—outside of baseball, I mean?"

"No, I shure don't, an' I never seen one yet that wasn't the same off the field as he was on."

"Thank you, Pat. I think I understand now. And—oh, yes, there's another thing I want to ask you. What's the matter with Billie Sheldon?

Uncle George said he was falling off in his game. Then I've read the papers. Billie started out well in the spring."

"Didn't he? I was sure thinkin' I had a find in Billie. Well, he's lost his nerve. He's in a bad slump. It's worried me for days. I'm goin' to release Billie. The team needs a shake-up. That's where Billie gets the worst of it, for he's really the makin' of a star; but he's slumped, an' now knockin' has made him let down. There, Miss Madge, that's an example of what I've just been tellin' you. An' you can see that a manager has his troubles. These hulkin' athletes are a lot of spoiled babies an' I often get sick of my job."

That afternoon Miss Ellston was in a brown study all the way out to the baseball park. She arrived rather earlier than usual to find the grand-stand empty. The Denver team had just come upon the field, and the Kansas City players were practising batting at the left of the diamond. Madge walked down the aisle of the grand stand and out along the reporters' boxes. She asked one of the youngsters on the field to tell Mr. Sheldon that she would like to speak with him a moment.

Billie eagerly hurried from the players' bench with a look of surprise and expectancy on his sun-tanned face. Madge experienced for the first time a sudden sense of shyness at his coming. His lithe form and his nimble step somehow gave her a pleasure that seemed old yet was new. When he neared her, and, lifting his cap, spoke her name, the shade of gloom in his eyes and lines of trouble on his face dispelled her confusion.

"Billie, Pat tells me he's given you ten days' notice," she said.

"It's true."

"What's wrong with you, Billie?"

"Oh, I've struck a bad streak—can't hit or throw."

"Are you a quitter?"

"No, I'm not," he answered quickly, flushing a dark red.

"You started off this spring with a rush. You played brilliantly and for a while led the team in batting. Uncle George thought so well of you. Then came this spell of bad form. But, Billie, it's only a slump; you can brace."

"I don't know," he replied, despondently. "Awhile back I got my mind off the game. Then—people who don't like me have taken advantage of my slump to——"

"To knock," interrupted Miss Ellston.

"I'm not saying that," he said, looking away from her.

"But I'm saying it. See here, Billie Sheldon, my uncle owns this team and Pat Donahue is manager. I think they both like me a little. Now I don't want to see you lose your place. Perhaps——"

"Madge, that's fine of you—but I think—I guess it'd be best for me to leave Kansas City."

"Why?"

"You know," he said huskily. "I've lost my head—I'm in love—I can't think of baseball—I'm crazy about you."

Miss Ellston's sweet face grew rosy, clear to the tips of her ears.

"Billie Sheldon," she replied, spiritedly. "You're talking nonsense. Even if you were were that way, it'd be no reason to play poor ball. Don't throw the game, as Pat would say. Make a brace! Get up on your toes! Tear things! Rip the boards off the fence! Don't quit!"

She exhausted her vocabulary of baseball language if not her enthusiasm, and paused in blushing confusion.

"Madge!"

"Will you brace up?"

"Will I—will I!" he exclaimed, breathlessly.

Madge murmured a hurried good-bye and, turning away, went up the stairs. Her uncle's private box was upon the top of the grand stand and she reached it in a somewhat bewildered state of mind. She had a confused sense of having appeared to encourage Billie, and did not know whether she felt happy or guilty. The flame in his eyes had warmed all her blood. Then, as she glanced over the railing to see the powerful Burns Carroll, there rose in her breast a panic at strange variance with her other feelings.

Many times had Madge Ellston viewed the field and stands and the outlying country from this high vantage point; but never with the same mingling emotions, nor had the sunshine ever been so golden, the woods and meadows so green, the diamond so smooth and velvety, the whole scene so gaily bright.

Denver had always been a good drawing card, and having won the first game of the present series, bade fair to draw a record attendance. The long lines of bleachers, already packed with the familiar mottled crowd, sent forth a merry, rattling hum. Soon a steady stream of well-dressed men and women poured in the gates and up the grand-stand stairs. The soft murmur of many voices in light conversation and laughter filled the air. The peanut venders and score-card sellers kept up their insistent shrill cries. The baseball park was alive now and restless; the atmosphere seemed charged with freedom and pleasure. The players romped like skittish colts, the fans shrieked their witticisms—all sound and movements suggested play.

Madge Ellston was somehow relieved to see her uncle sitting in one of the lower boxes. During this game she wanted to be alone, and she believed she would be, for the President of the League and directors of the Kansas City team were with her uncle. When the bell rang to call the Denver team in from practice the stands could hold no more, and the roped-off side lines were filling up with noisy men and boys. From her seat Madge could see right down upon the players' bench, and when she caught both Sheldon and Carroll gazing upward she drew back with sharply contrasted thrills.

Then the bell rang again, the bleachers rolled out their welcoming acclaim, and play was called with Kansas City at the bat.

Right off the reel Hunt hit a short fly safely over second. The ten thousand spectators burst into a roar. A good start liberated applause and marked the feeling for the day.

Madge was surprised and glad to see Billie Sheldon start next for the plate. All season, until lately, he had been the second batter. During his slump he had been relegated to the last place on the batting list. Perhaps he had asked Pat to try him once more at the top. The bleachers voiced their unstinted appreciation of this return, showing that Billie still had a strong hold on their hearts.

As for Madge, her breast heaved and she had difficulty in breathing. This was going to be a hard game for her. The intensity of her desire to see Billie brace up to his old form amazed her. And Carroll's rude words beat thick in her ears. Never before had Billie appeared so instinct with life, so intent and strung as when he faced Keene, the Denver pitcher. That worthy tied himself up in a knot, and then, unlimbering a long arm, delivered the brand new ball.

Billie seemed to leap forward and throw his bat at it. There was a sharp ringing crack—and the ball was like a white string marvelously stretching out over the players, over the green field beyond, and then, sailing, soaring, over the right-field fence. For a moment the stands, even the bleachers, were stone quiet. No player had ever hit a ball over that fence. It had been deemed impossible, as was attested to by the many painted "ads" offering prizes for such a feat. Suddenly the far end of the bleachers exploded and the swelling roar rolled up to engulf the grand stand in thunder. Billie ran round the bases to applause never before vented on that field. But he gave no sign that it affected him; he did not even doff his cap. White-faced and stern, he hurried to the bench, where Pat fell all over him and many of the players grasped his hands.

Up in her box Madge was crushing her score-card and whispering: "Oh! Billie, I could hug you for that!"

Two runs on two pitched balls! That was an opening to stir an exacting audience to the highest pitch of enthusiasm. The Denver manager peremptorily called Keene off the diamond and sent in Steele, a south-paw, who had always bothered Pat's left-handed hitters. That move showed his astute judgment, for Steele struck out McReady and retired Curtis and Mahew on easy chances.

It was Dalgren's turn to pitch and though he had shown promise in several games he had not yet been tried out on a team of Denver's strength. The bleachers gave him a good cheering as he walked into the box, but for all that they whistled their wonder at Pat's assurance in putting him against the Cowboys in an important game.

The lad was visibly nervous and the hard-hitting and loud-coaching Denver players went after him as if they meant to drive him out of the game. Crane stung one to left center for a base, Moody was out on a liner to short, almost doubling up Crane; the fleet-footed Bluett bunted and beat the throw to first; Langly drove to left for what seemed a three-bagger, but Curtis, after a hard run, caught the ball almost off the left-field bleachers. Crane and Bluett advanced a base on the throw-in. Then Kane batted up a high foul-fly. Burns Carroll, the Kansas City catcher, had the reputation of being a fiend for chasing foul flies, and he dashed at this one with a speed that threatened a hard fall over the players' bench or a collision with the fence. Carroll caught the ball and crashed against the grand stand, but leaped back with an agility that showed that if there was any harm done it had not been to him.

Thus the sharp inning ended with a magnificent play. It electrified the spectators into a fierce energy of applause. With one accord, by baseball instinct, the stands and bleachers and roped-in-sidelines realized it was to be a game of games and they answered to the stimulus with a savage enthusiasm that inspired ballplayers to great plays.

In the first half of the second inning, Steele's will to do and his arm to execute were very like his name. Kansas City could not score. In their half the Denver team made one run by clean hitting.

Then the closely fought advantage see-sawed from one team to the other. It was not a pitchers' battle, though both men worked to the limit of skill and endurance. They were hit hard. Dazzling plays kept the score down and the innings short. Over the fields hung the portent of something to come, every player, every spectator felt the subtle baseball chance; each inning seemed to lead closer and more thrillingly up to the climax. But at the end of the seventh, with the score tied six and six, with daring steals, hard hits and splendid plays, enough to have made memorable several games, it seemed that the great portentous moment was still in abeyance.

The head of the batting list for Kansas City was up. Hunt caught the first pitched ball squarely on the end of his bat. It was a mighty drive and as the ball soared and soared over the center-field Hunt raced down the base line, and the winged-footed Crane sped outward, the bleachers split their throats. The hit looked good for a home run, but Crane leaped up and caught the ball in his gloved hand. The sudden silence and then the long groan which racked the bleachers was greater tribute to Crane's play than any applause.

Billie Sheldon then faced Steele. The fans roared hoarsely, for Billie had hit safely three times out of four. Steele used his curve ball, but he could not get the batter to go after it. When he had wasted three balls, the never-despairing bleachers howled: "Now, Billie, in your groove! Sting the next one!" But Billie waited. One strike! Two strikes! Steele cut the plate. That was a test which proved Sheldon's caliber.

With seven innings of exciting play passed, with both teams on edge, with the bleachers wild and the grand stands keyed up to the breaking point, with everything making deliberation almost impossible, Billie Sheldon had remorselessly waited for three balls and two strikes.

"Now! ... Now! ... Now!" shrieked the bleachers.

Steele had not tired nor lost his cunning. With hands before him he grimly studied Billie, then whirling hard to get more weight into his motion, he threw the ball.

Billie swung perfectly and cut a curving liner between the first baseman and the base. Like a shot it skipped over the grass out along the foul-line into right field. Amid tremendous uproar Billie stretched the hit into a triple, and when he got up out of the dust after his slide into third the noise seemed to be the crashing down of the bleachers. It died out with the choking gurgling yell of the most leather-lunged fan.

"O-o-o-o-you-Billie-e!"

McReady marched up and promptly hit a long fly to the redoubtable Crane. Billie crouched in a sprinter's position with his eye on the graceful fielder, waiting confidently for the ball to drop. As if there had not already been sufficient heart-rending moments, the chance that governed baseball meted out this play; one of the keenest, most trying known to the game. Players waited, spectators waited, and the instant of that dropping ball was interminably long. Everybody knew Crane would catch it; everybody thought of the wonderful throwing arm that had made him famous. Was it possible for Billie Sheldon to beat the throw to the plate?

Crane made the catch and got the ball away at the same instant Sheldon leaped from the base and dashed for home. Then all eyes were on the ball. It seemed incredible that a ball thrown by human strength could speed plateward so low, so straight, so swift. But it lost its force and slanted down to bound into the catcher's hands just as Billie slid over the plate.

By the time the bleachers had stopped stamping and bawling, Curtis ended the inning with a difficult grounder to the infield.

Once more the Kansas City players took the field and Burns Carroll sang out in his lusty voice: "Keep lively, boys! Play hard! Dig 'em up an' get 'em!" Indeed the big catcher was the main-stay of the home team. The bulk of the work fell upon his shoulders. Dalgren was wild and kept his catcher continually blocking low pitches and wide curves and poorly controlled high fast balls. But they were all alike to Carroll. Despite his weight, he was as nimble on his feet as a goat, and if he once got his hands on the ball he never missed it. It was his encouragement that steadied Dalgren; his judgment of hitters that carried the young pitcher through dangerous places; his lightning swift grasp of points that directed the machine-like work of his team.

In this inning Carroll exhibited another of his demon chases after a foul fly; he threw the base-stealing Crane out at second, and by a remarkable leap and stop of McReady's throw, he blocked a runner who would have tied the score.

The Cowboys blanked their opponents in the first half of the ninth, and trotted in for their turn needing one run to tie, two runs to win.

There had scarcely been a breathing spell for the onlookers in this rapid-fire game. Every inning had held them, one moment breathless, the next wildly clamorous, and another waiting in numb fear. What did these last few moments hold in store? The only answer to that was the dogged plugging optimism of the Denver players. To listen to them, to watch them, was to gather the impression that baseball fortune always favored them in the end.

"Only three more, Dal. Steady boys, it's our game," rolled out Carroll's deep bass. How virile he was! What a tower of strength to the weakening pitcher!

But valiantly as Dalgren tried to respond, he failed. The grind—the strain had been too severe. When he finally did locate the plate Bluett hit safely. Langley bunted along the base line and beat the ball.

A blank, dead quiet settled down over the bleachers and stands. Something fearful threatened. What might not come to pass, even at the last moment of this nerve-racking game? There was a runner on first and a runner on second. That was bad. Exceedingly bad was it that these runners were on base with nobody out. Worst of all was the fact that Kane was up. Kane, the best bunter, the fastest man to first, the hardest hitter in the league! That he would fail to advance those two runners was scarcely worth consideration. Once advanced, a fly to the outfield, a scratch, anything almost, would tie the score. So this was the climax presaged so many times earlier in the game. Dalgren seemed to wilt under it.

Kane swung his ash viciously and called on Dalgren to put one over. Dalgren looked in toward the bench as if he wanted and expected to be taken out. But Pat Donahue made no sign. Pat had trained many a pitcher by forcing him to take his medicine. Then Carroll, mask under his arm, rolling his big hand in his mitt, sauntered down to the pitcher's box. The sharp order of the umpire in no wise disconcerted him. He said something to Dalgren, vehemently nodding his head the while. Players and audience alike supposed he was trying to put a little heart into Dalgren, and liked him the better, notwithstanding the opposition to the umpire.

Carroll sauntered back to his position. He adjusted his breast protector, and put on his mask, deliberately taking his time. Then he stepped behind the plate, and after signing for the pitch, he slowly moved his right hand up to his mask.

Dalgren wound up, took his swing, and let drive. Even as he delivered the ball Carroll bounded away from his position, flinging off the mask as he jumped. For a single fleeting instant, the catcher's position was vacated. But that instant was long enough to make the audience gasp. Kane bunted beautifully down the third base line, and there Carroll stood, fifteen feet from the plate, agile as a huge monkey. He whipped the ball to Mahew at third. Mahew wheeled quick as thought and lined the ball to second. Sheldon came tearing for the bag, caught the ball on the run, and with a violent stop and wrench threw it like a bullet to first base. Fast as Kane was, the ball beat him ten feet. A triple play!

The players of both teams cheered, but the audience, slower to grasp the complex and intricate points, needed a long moment to realize what had happened. They needed another to divine that Carroll had anticipated Kane's intention to bunt, had left his position as the ball was pitched, had planned all, risked all, played all on Kane's sure eye; and so he had retired the side and won the game by creating and executing the rarest play in baseball.

Then the audience rose in a body to greet the great catcher. What a hoarse thundering roar shook the stands and waved in a blast over the field! Carroll stood bowing his acknowledgment, and then swaggered a little with the sun shining on his handsome heated face. Like a conqueror conscious of full blown power he stalked away to the clubhouse.

Madge Ellston came out of her trance and viewed the ragged score-card, her torn parasol, her battered gloves and flying hair, her generally disheveled state with a little start of dismay, but when she got into the thick and press of the moving crowd she found all the women more or less disheveled. And they seemed all the prettier and friendlier for that. It was a happy crowd and voices were conspicuously hoarse.

When Madge entered the hotel parlor that evening she found her uncle with guests and among them was Burns Carroll. The presence of the handsome giant affected Madge more impellingly than ever before, yet in some inexplicably different way. She found herself trembling; she sensed a crisis in her feelings for this man and it frightened her. She became conscious suddenly that she had always been afraid of him. Watching Carroll receive the congratulations of many of those present, she saw that he dominated them as he had her. His magnetism was over-powering; his great stature seemed to fill the room; his easy careless assurance emanated from superior strength. When he spoke lightly of the game, of Crane's marvelous catch, of Dalgren's pitching and of his own triple play, it seemed these looming features retreated in perspective—somehow lost their vital significance because he slighted them.

In the light of Carroll's illuminating talk, in the remembrance of Sheldon's bitter denunciation, in the knowledge of Pat Donahue's estimate of a peculiar type of ball-player, Madge Ellston found herself judging the man—bravely trying to resist his charm, to be fair to him and to herself.

Carroll soon made his way to her side and greeted her with his old familiar manner of possession. However irritating it might be to Madge when alone, now it held her bound.

Carroll possessed the elemental attributes of a conqueror. When with him Madge whimsically feared that he would snatch her up in his arms and carry her bodily off, as the warriors of old did with the women they wanted. But she began to believe that the fascination he exercised upon her was merely physical. That gave her pause. Not only was Burns Carroll on trial, but also a very foolish fluttering little moth—herself. It was time enough, however, to be stern with herself after she had tried him.

"Wasn't that a splendid catch of Crane's today?" she asked.

"A lucky stab! Crane has a habit of running round like an ostrich and sticking out a hand to catch a ball. It's a grand-stand play. Why, a good outfielder would have been waiting under that fly."

"Dalgren did fine work in the box, don't you think?"

"Oh, the kid's all right with an old head back of the plate. He's wild, though, and will never make good in fast company. I won his game today. He wouldn't have lasted an inning without me. It was dead wrong for Pat to pitch him. Dalgren simply can't pitch and he hasn't sand enough to learn."

A hot retort trembled upon Madge Ellston's lips, but she withheld it and quietly watched Carroll. How complacent he was, how utterly self-contained!

"And Billie Sheldon—wasn't it good to see him brace? What hitting! . .. That home run!"

"Sheldon flashed up today. That's the worst of such players. This talk of his slump is all rot. When he joined the team he made some lucky hits and the papers lauded him as a comer, but he soon got down to his real form. Why, to break into a game now and then, to shut his eyes and hit a couple on the nose—that's not baseball. Pat's given him ten days' notice, and his release will be a good move for the team. Sheldon's not fast enough for this league."

"I'm sorry. He seemed so promising," replied Madge. "I liked Billy—pretty well."

"Yes, that was evident," said Carroll, firing up. "I never could understand what you saw in him. Why, Sheldon's no good. He——"

Madge turned a white face that silenced Carroll. She excused herself and returned to the parlor, where she had last seen her uncle. Not finding him there, she went into the long corridor and met Sheldon, Dalgren and two more of the players. Madge congratulated the young pitcher and the other players on their brilliant work; and they, not to be outdone, gallantly attributed the day's victory to her presence at the game. Then, without knowing in the least how it came about, she presently found herself alone with Billy, and they were strolling into the music-room.

"Madge, did I brace up?"

The girl risked one quick look at him. How boyish he seemed, how eager! What an altogether different Billie! But was the difference all in him! Somehow, despite a conscious shyness in the moment she felt natural and free, without the uncertainty and restraint that had always troubled her while with him.

"Oh, Billie, that glorious home run!"

"Madge, wasn't that hit a dandy? How I made it is a mystery, but the bat felt like a feather. I thought of you. Tell me—what did you think when I hit that ball over the fence?"

"Billie, I'll never, never tell you."

"Yes—please—I want to know. Didn't you think something—nice of me?"

The pink spots in Madge's cheeks widened to crimson flames.

"Billie, are you still—crazy about me? Now, don't come so close. Can't you behave yourself? And don't break my fingers with you terrible baseball hands.... Well, when you made that hit I just collapsed and I said——"

"Say it! Say it!" implored Billie.

She lowered her face and then bravely raised it.

"I said, 'Billie, I could hug you for that!' ... Billie, let me go! Oh, you mustn't!—please!"

Quite a little while afterward Madge remembered to tell Billie that she had been seeking her uncle. They met him and Pat Donahue, coming out of the parlor.

"Where have you been all evening?" demanded Mr. Ellston.

"Shure it looks as if she's signed a new manager," said Pat, his shrewd eyes twinkling.

The soft glow in Madge's cheeks deepened into tell-tale scarlet; Billie resembled a schoolboy stricken in guilt.

"Aha! so that's it?" queried her uncle.

"Ellston," said Pat. "Billie's home-run drive today recalled his notice an' if I don't miss guess it won him another game—the best game in life."

"By George!" exclaimed Mr. Ellston. "I was afraid it was Carroll!"

He led Madge away and Pat followed with Billie.

"Shure, it was good to see you brace, Billie," said the manager, with a kindly hand on the young man's arm. "I'm tickled to death. That ten days' notice doesn't go. See? I've had to shake up the team but your job is good. I released McReady outright an' traded Carroll to Denver for a catcher and a fielder. Some of the directors hollered murder, an' I expect the fans will roar, but I'm running this team, I'll have harmony among my players. Carroll is a great catcher, but he's a knocker."

THE WINNING BALL

One day in July our Rochester club, leader in the Eastern League, had returned to the hotel after winning a double-header from the Syracuse club. For some occult reason there was to be a lay-off next day and then on the following another double-header. These double-headers we hated next to exhibition games. Still a lay-off for twenty-four hours, at that stage of the race, was a Godsend, and we received the news with exclamations of pleasure.

After dinner we were all sitting and smoking comfortably in front of the hotel when our manager, Merritt, came hurriedly out of the lobby. It struck me that he appeared a little flustered.

"Say, you fellars," he said brusquely. "Pack your suits and be ready for the bus at seven-thirty."

For a moment there was a blank, ominous silence, while we assimilated the meaning of his terse speech.

"I've got a good thing on for tomorrow," continued the manager. "Sixty per cent gate receipts if we win. That Guelph team is hot stuff, though."

"Guelph!" exclaimed some of the players suspiciously. "Where's Guelph?"

"It's in Canada. We'll take the night express an' get there tomorrow in time for the game. An' we'll hev to hustle."

Upon Merritt then rained a multiplicity of excuses. Gillinger was not well, and ought to have that day's rest. Snead's eyes would profit by a lay-off. Deerfoot Browning was leading the league in base running, and as his legs were all bruised and scraped by sliding, a manager who was not an idiot would have a care of such valuable runmakers for his team. Lake had "Charley-horse." Hathaway's arm was sore. Bane's stomach threatened gastritis. Spike Doran's finger needed a chance to heal. I was stale, and the other players, three pitchers, swore their arms should be in the hospital.

"Cut it out!" said Merritt, getting exasperated. "You'd all lay down on me—now, wouldn't you? Well, listen to this: McDougal pitched today; he doesn't go. Blake works Friday, he doesn't go. But the rest of you puffed-up, high-salaried stiffs pack your grips quick. See? It'll cost any fresh fellar fifty for missin' the train."

So that was how eleven of the Rochester team found themselves moodily boarding a Pullman en route for Buffalo and Canada. We went to bed early and arose late.

Guelph lay somewhere in the interior of Canada, and we did not expect to get there until 1 o'clock.

As it turned out, the train was late; we had to dress hurriedly in the smoking room, pack our citizen clothes in our grips and leave the train to go direct to the ball grounds without time for lunch.

It was a tired, dusty-eyed, peevish crowd of ball players that climbed into a waiting bus at the little station.

We had never heard of Guelph; we did not care anything about Rube baseball teams. Baseball was not play to us; it was the hardest kind of work, and of all things an exhibition game was an abomination.

The Guelph players, strapping lads, met us with every mark of respect and courtesy and escorted us to the field with a brass band that was loud in welcome, if not harmonious in tune.

Some 500 men and boys trotted curiously along with us, for all the world as if the bus were a circus parade cage filled with striped tigers. What a rustic, motley crowd massed about in and on that ball ground. There must have been 10,000.

The audience was strange to us. The Indians, half-breeds, French-Canadians; the huge, hulking, bearded farmers or traders, or trappers, whatever they were, were new to our baseball experience.

The players themselves, however, earned the largest share of our attention. By the time they had practiced a few moments we looked at Merritt and Merritt looked at us.

These long, powerful, big-handed lads evidently did not know the difference between lacrosse and baseball; but they were quick as cats on their feet, and they scooped up the ball in a way wonderful to see. And throw!—it made a professional's heart swell just to see them line the ball across the diamond.

"Lord! what whips these lads have!" exclaimed Merritt. "Hope we're not up against it. If this team should beat us we wouldn't draw a handful at Toronto. We can't afford to be beaten. Jump around and cinch the game quick. If we get in a bad place, I'll sneak in the 'rabbit.'"

The "rabbit" was a baseball similar in appearance to the ordinary league ball; under its horse-hide cover, however, it was remarkably different.

191

An ingenious fan, a friend of Merritt, had removed the covers from a number of league balls and sewed them on rubber balls of his own making. They could not be distinguished from the regular article, not even by an experienced professional—until they were hit. Then! The fact that after every bounce one of these rubber balls bounded swifter and higher had given it the name of the "rabbit."

Many a game had the "rabbit" won for us at critical stages. Of course it was against the rules of the league, and of course every player in the league knew about it; still, when it was judiciously and cleverly brought into a close game, the "rabbit" would be in play, and very probably over the fence, before the opposing captain could learn of it, let alone appeal to the umpire.

"Fellars, look at that guy who's goin' to pitch," suddenly spoke up one of the team.

Many as were the country players whom we seasoned and traveled professionals had run across, this twirler outclassed them for remarkable appearance. Moreover, what put an entirely different tinge to our momentary humor was the discovery that he was as wild as a March hare and could throw a ball so fast that it resembled a pea shot from a boy's air gun.

Deerfoot led our batting list, and after the first pitched ball, which he did not see, and the second, which ticked his shirt as it shot past, he turned to us with an expression that made us groan inwardly.

When Deerfoot looked that way it meant the pitcher was dangerous. Deerfoot made no effort to swing at the next ball, and was promptly called out on strikes.

I was second at bat, and went up with some reluctance. I happened to be leading the league in both long distance and safe hitting, and I doted on speed. But having stopped many mean in-shoots with various parts of my anatomy, I was rather squeamish about facing backwoods yaps who had no control.

When I had watched a couple of his pitches, which the umpire called strikes, I gave him credit for as much speed as Rusie. These balls were as straight as a string, singularly without curve, jump, or variation of any kind. I lined the next one so hard at the shortstop that it cracked like a pistol as it struck his hands and whirled him half off his feet. Still he hung to the ball and gave opportunity for the first crash of applause.

"Boys, he's a trifle wild," I said to my team-mates, "but he has the most beautiful ball to hit you ever saw. I don't believe he uses a curve, and when we once time that speed we'll kill it."

Next inning, after old man Hathaway had baffled the Canadians with his wide, tantalizing curves, my predictions began to be verified. Snead rapped one high and far to deep right field. To our infinite surprise, however, the right fielder ran with fleetness that made our own Deerfoot seem slow, and he got under the ball and caught it.

Doran sent a sizzling grasscutter down toward left. The lanky third baseman darted over, dived down, and, coming up with the ball, exhibited the power of a throwing arm that made as all green with envy.

Then, when the catcher chased a foul fly somewhere back in the crowd and caught it, we began to take notice.

"Lucky stabs!" said Merritt cheerfully. "They can't keep that up. We'll drive him to the woods next time."

But they did keep it up; moreover, they became more brilliant as the game progressed. What with Hathaway's heady pitching we soon disposed of them when at the bat; our turns, however, owing to the wonderful fielding of these backwoodsmen, were also fruitless.

Merritt, with his mind ever on the slice of gate money coming if we won, began to fidget and fume and find fault.

"You're a swell lot of champions, now, ain't you?" he observed between innings.

All baseball players like to bat, and nothing pleases them so much as base hits; on the other hand, nothing is quite so painful as to send out hard liners only to see them caught. And it seemed as if every man on our team connected with that lanky twirler's fast high ball and hit with the force that made the bat spring only to have one of these rubes get his big hands upon it.

Considering that we were in no angelic frame of mind before the game started, and in view of Merritt's persistently increasing ill humor, this failure of ours to hit a ball safely gradually worked us into a kind of frenzy. From indifference we passed to determination, and from that to sheer passionate purpose.

Luck appeared to be turning in the sixth inning. With one out, Lake hit a beauty to right. Doran beat an infield grounder and reached first. Hathaway struck out.

With Browning up and me next, the situation looked rather precarious for the Canadians.

"Say, Deerfoot," whispered Merritt, "dump one down the third-base line. He's playin' deep. It's a pipe. Then the bases will be full an' Reddy'll clean up."

In a stage like that Browning was a man absolutely to depend upon. He placed a slow bunt in the grass toward third and sprinted for first. The third baseman fielded the ball, but, being confused, did not know where to throw it.

"Stick it in your basket," yelled Merritt, in a delight that showed how hard he was pulling for the gate money, and his beaming smile as he turned to me was inspiring. "Now, Reddy, it's up to you! I'm not worrying about what's happened so far. I know, with you at bat in a pinch, it's all off!"

Merritt's compliment was pleasing, but it did not augment my purpose, for that already had reached the highest mark. Love of hitting, if no other thing, gave me the thrilling fire to arise to the opportunity. Selecting my light bat, I went up and faced the rustic twirler and softly said things to him.

He delivered the ball, and I could have yelled aloud, so fast, so straight, so true it sped toward me. Then I hit it harder than I had ever hit a ball in my life. The bat sprung, as if it were whalebone. And the ball took a bullet course between center and left. So beautiful a hit was it that I watched as I ran.

Out of the tail of my eye I saw the center fielder running. When I rounded first base I got a good look at this fielder, and though I had seen the greatest outfielders the game ever produced, I never saw one that covered ground so swiftly as he.

On the ball soared, and began to drop; on the fielder sped, and began to disappear over a little hill back of his position. Then he reached up with a long arm and marvelously caught the ball in one hand. He went out of sight as I touched second base, and the heterogeneous crowd knew about a great play to make more noise than a herd of charging buffalo.

In the next half inning our opponents, by clean drives, scored two runs and we in our turn again went out ignominiously. When the first of the eighth came we were desperate and clamored for the "rabbit."

"I've sneaked it in," said Merritt, with a low voice. "Got it to the umpire on the last passed ball. See, the pitcher's got it now. Boys, it's all off but the fireworks! Now, break loose!"

A peculiarity about the "rabbit" was the fact that though it felt as light as the regulation league ball it could not be thrown with the same speed and to curve it was an impossibility.

Bane hit the first delivery from our hoosier stumbling block. The ball struck the ground and began to bound toward short. With every bound it went swifter, longer and higher, and it bounced clear over the shortstop's head. Lake chopped one in front of the plate, and it rebounded from the ground straight up so high that both runners were safe before it came down.

Doran hit to the pitcher. The ball caromed his leg, scooted fiendishly at the second baseman, and tried to run up all over him like a tame squirrel. Bases full!

Hathaway got a safe fly over the infield and two runs tallied. The pitcher, in spite of the help of the umpire, could not locate the plate for Balknap, and gave him a base on balls. Bases full again!

Deerfoot slammed a hot liner straight at the second baseman, which, striking squarely in his hands, recoiled as sharply as if it had struck a wall. Doran scored, and still the bases were filled.

The laboring pitcher began to get rattled; he could not find his usual speed; he knew it, but evidently could not account for it.

When I came to bat, indications were not wanting that the Canadian team would soon be up in the air. The long pitcher delivered the "rabbit," and got it low down by my knees, which was an unfortunate thing for him. I swung on that one, and trotted round the bases behind the runners while the center and left fielders chased the ball.

Gillinger weighed nearly two hundred pounds, and he got all his weight under the "rabbit." It went so high that we could scarcely see it. All the infielders rushed in, and after staggering around, with heads bent back, one of them, the shortstop, managed to get under it. The "rabbit" bounded forty feet out of his hands!

When Snead's grounder nearly tore the third baseman's leg off; when Bane's hit proved as elusive as a flitting shadow; when Lake's liner knocked the pitcher flat, and Doran's fly leaped high out of the center fielder's glove—then those earnest, simple, country ballplayers realized something was wrong. But they imagined it was in themselves, and after a short spell of rattles, they steadied up and tried harder than ever. The motions they went through trying to stop that jumping jackrabbit of a ball were ludicrous in the extreme.

Finally, through a foul, a short fly, and a scratch hit to first, they retired the side and we went into the field with the score 14 to 2 in our favor.

But Merritt had not found it possible to get the "rabbit" out of play!

We spent a fatefully anxious few moments squabbling with the umpire and captain over the "rabbit." At the idea of letting those herculean railsplitters have a chance to hit the rubber ball we felt our blood run cold.

"But this ball has a rip in it," blustered Gillinger. He lied atrociously. A microscope could not have discovered as much as a scratch in that smooth leather.

"Sure it has," supplemented Merritt, in the suave tones of a stage villain. "We're used to playing with good balls."

"Why did you ring this one in on us?" asked the captain. "We never threw out this ball. We want a chance to hit it."

That was just the one thing we did not want them to have. But fate played against us.

"Get up on your toes, now an' dust," said Merritt. "Take your medicine, you lazy sit-in-front-of-the-hotel stiffs! Think of pay day!"

Not improbably we all entertained the identical thought that old man Hathaway was the last pitcher under the sun calculated to be effective with the "rabbit." He never relied on speed; in fact, Merritt often scornfully accused him of being unable to break a pane of glass; he used principally what we called floaters and a change of pace. Both styles were absolutely impractical with the "rabbit."

"It's comin' to us, all right, all right!" yelled Deerfoot to me, across the intervening grass. I was of the opinion that it did not take any genius to make Deerfoot's ominous prophecy.

Old man Hathaway gazed at Merritt on the bench as if he wished the manager could hear what he was calling him and then at his fellow-players as if both to warn and beseech them. Then he pitched the "rabbit."

Crack!

The big lumbering Canadian rapped the ball at Crab Bane. I did not see it, because it went so fast, but I gathered from Crab's actions that it must have been hit in his direction. At any rate, one of his legs flopped out sidewise as if it had been suddenly jerked, and he fell in a heap. The ball, a veritable "rabbit" in its wild jumps, headed on for Deerfoot, who contrived to stop it with his knees.

The next batter resembled the first one, and the hit likewise, only it leaped wickedly at Doran and went through his hands as if they had been paper. The third man batted up a very high fly to Gillinger. He clutched at it with his huge shovel hands, but he could not hold it. The way he pounced upon the ball, dug it out of the grass, and hurled it at Hathaway, showed his anger.

Obviously Hathaway had to stop the throw, for he could not get out of the road, and he spoke to his captain in what I knew were no complimentary terms.

Thus began retribution. Those husky lads continued to hammer the "rabbit" at the infielders and as it bounced harder at every bounce so they batted harder at every bat.

Another singular feature about the "rabbit" was the seeming impossibility for professionals to hold it. Their familiarity with it, their understanding of its vagaries and inconsistencies, their mortal dread made fielding it a much more difficult thing than for their opponents.

By way of variety, the lambasting Canadians commenced to lambast a few over the hills and far away, which chased Deerfoot and me until our tongues lolled out.

Every time a run crossed the plate the motley crowd howled, roared, danced and threw up their hats. The members of the batting team pranced up and down the side lines, giving a splendid imitation of cannibals celebrating the occasion of a feast.

Once Snead stooped down to trap the "rabbit," and it slipped through his legs, for which his comrades jeered him unmercifully. Then a brawny batter sent up a tremendously high fly between short and third.

"You take it!" yelled Gillinger to Bane.

"You take it!" replied the Crab, and actually walked backward. That ball went a mile high. The sky was hazy, gray, the most perplexing in which to judge a fly ball. An ordinary fly gave trouble enough in the gauging.

Gillinger wandered around under the ball for what seemed an age. It dropped as swiftly as a rocket shoots upward. Gillinger went forward in a circle, then sidestepped, and threw up his broad hands. He misjudged the ball, and it hit him fairly on the head and bounced almost to where Doran stood at second.

Our big captain wilted. Time was called. But Gillinger, when he came to, refused to leave the game and went back to third with a lump on his head as large as a goose egg.

Every one of his teammates was sorry, yet every one howled in glee. To be hit on the head was the unpardonable sin for a professional.

Old man Hathaway gradually lost what little speed he had, and with it his nerve. Every time he pitched the "rabbit" he dodged. That was about the funniest and strangest thing ever seen on a ball field. Yet it had an element of tragedy.

Hathaway's expert contortions saved his head and body on divers occasions, but presently a low bounder glanced off the grass and manifested an affinity for his leg.

We all knew from the crack and the way the pitcher went down that the "rabbit" had put him out of the game. The umpire called time, and Merritt came running on the diamond.

"Hard luck, old man," said the manager. "That'll make a green and yellow spot all right. Boys, we're still two runs to the good. There's one out, an' we can win yet. Deerfoot, you're as badly crippled as Hathaway. The bench for yours. Hooker will go to center, an' I'll pitch."

Merritt's idea did not strike us as a bad one. He could pitch, and he always kept his arm in prime condition. We welcomed him into the fray for two reasons—because he might win the game, and because he might be overtaken by the baseball Nemesis.

While Merritt was putting on Hathaway's baseball shoes, some of us endeavored to get the "rabbit" away from the umpire, but he was too wise.

Merritt received the innocent-looking ball with a look of mingled disgust and fear, and he summarily ordered us to our positions.

Not far had we gone, however, when we were electrified by the umpire's sharp words:

"Naw! Naw, you don't. I saw you change the ball I gave you fer one in your pocket! Naw! You don't come enny of your American dodges on us! Gimmee thet ball, an' you use the other, or I'll stop the game."

Wherewith the shrewd umpire took the ball from Merritt's hand and fished the "rabbit" from his pocket. Our thwarted manager stuttered his wrath. "Y-you be-be-wh-whiskered y-yap! I'll g-g-give——"

What dire threat he had in mind never materialized, for he became speechless. He glowered upon the cool little umpire, and then turned grandly toward the plate.

It may have been imagination, yet I made sure Merritt seemed to shrink and grow smaller before he pitched a ball. For one thing the plate was uphill from the pitcher's box, and then the fellow standing there loomed up like a hill and swung a bat that would have served as a wagon tongue. No wonder Merritt evinced nervousness. Presently he whirled and delivered the ball.

Bing!

A dark streak and a white puff of dust over second base showed how safe that hit was. By dint of manful body work, Hooker contrived to stop the "rabbit" in mid-center. Another run scored. Human nature was proof against this temptation, and Merritt's players tendered him manifold congratulations and dissertations.

"Grand, you old skinflint, grand!"

"There was a two-dollar bill stickin' on thet hit. Why didn't you stop it?"

"Say, Merritt, what little brains you've got will presently be ridin' on the 'rabbit.'"

"You will chase up these exhibition games!"

"Take your medicine now. Ha! Ha! Ha!"

After these merciless taunts, and particularly after the next slashing hit that tied the score, Merritt looked appreciably smaller and humbler.

He threw up another ball, and actually shied as it neared the plate.

The giant who was waiting to slug it evidently thought better of his eagerness as far as that pitch was concerned, for he let it go by.

Merritt got the next ball higher. With a mighty swing, the batsman hit a terrific liner right at the pitcher.

Quick as lightning, Merritt wheeled, and the ball struck him with the sound of two boards brought heavily together with a smack.

Merritt did not fall; he melted to the ground and writhed while the runners scored with more tallies than they needed to win.

What did we care! Justice had been done us, and we were unutterably happy. Crabe Bane stood on his head; Gillinger began a war dance; old man Hathaway hobbled out to the side lines and whooped like an Indian; Snead rolled over and over in the grass. All of us broke out into typical expressions of baseball frenzy, and individual ones illustrating our particular moods.

Merritt got up and made a dive for the ball. With face positively flaming he flung it far beyond the merry crowd, over into a swamp. Then he limped for the bench. Which throw ended the most memorable game ever recorded to the credit of the "rabbit."

FALSE COLORS

"Fate has decreed more bad luck for Salisbury in Saturday's game with Bellville. It has leaked out that our rivals will come over strengthened by a 'ringer,' no less than Yale's star pitcher, Wayne. We saw him shut Princeton out in June, in the last game of the college year, and we are not optimistic in our predictions as to what Salisbury can do with him. This appears a rather unfair procedure for Bellville to resort to. Why couldn't they come over with their regular team? They have won a game, and so have we; both games were close and brilliant; the deciding game has roused unusual interest. We are inclined to resent Bellville's methods as unsportsmanlike. All our players can do is to go into this game on Saturday and try the harder to win."

Wayne laid down the Salisbury Gazette, with a little laugh of amusement, yet feeling a vague, disquieting sense of something akin to regret.

"Pretty decent of that chap not to roast me," he soliloquized.

Somewhere he had heard that Salisbury maintained an unsalaried team. It was notorious among college athletes that the Bellville Club paid for the services of distinguished players. And this in itself rather inclined Wayne to sympathize with Salisbury. He knew something of the struggles of a strictly amateur club to cope with its semi-professional rivals.

As he was sitting there, idly tipped back in a comfortable chair, dreaming over some of the baseball disasters he had survived before his college career, he saw a young man enter the lobby of the hotel, speak to the clerk, and then turn and come directly toward the window where Wayne was sitting.

"Are yon Mr. Wayne, the Yale pitcher?" he asked eagerly. He was a fair-haired, clean-cut young fellow, and his voice rang pleasantly.

"Guilty," replied Wayne.

"My name's Huling. I'm captain of the Salisbury nine. Just learned you were in town and are going to pitch against us tomorrow. Won't you walk out into the grounds with me now? You might want to warm up a little."

"Thank you, yes, I will. Guess I won't need my suit. I'll just limber up, and give my arm a good rub."

It struck Wayne before they had walked far that Huling was an amiable and likable chap. As the captain of the Salisbury nine, he certainly had no reason to be agreeable to the Morristown "ringer," even though Wayne did happen to be a famous Yale pitcher.

The field was an oval, green as an emerald, level as a billiard table and had no fences or stands to obstruct the open view of the surrounding wooded country. On each side of the diamond were rows of wooden benches, and at one end of the field stood a little clubhouse.

Wayne took off his coat, and tossed a ball for a while to an ambitious youngster, and then went into the clubhouse, where Huling introduced him to several of his players. After a good rubdown, Wayne thanked Huling for his courtesy, and started out, intending to go back to town.

"Why not stay to see us practice?" asked the captain. "We're not afraid you'll size up our weaknesses. As a matter of fact, we don't look forward to any hitting stunts tomorrow, eh, Burns? Burns, here, is our leading hitter, and he's been unusually noncommittal since he heard who was going to pitch for Bellville."

"Well, I wouldn't give a whole lot for my prospects of a home run tomorrow," said Burns, with a laugh.

Wayne went outside, and found a seat in the shade. A number of urchins had trooped upon the green field, and carriages and motors were already in evidence. By the time the players came out of the dressing room, ready for practice, there was quite a little crowd in attendance.

Despite Wayne's hesitation, Huling insisted upon introducing him to friends, and finally hauled him up to a big touring car full of girls. Wayne, being a Yale pitcher, had seen several thousand pretty girls, but the group in that automobile fairly dazzled him. And the last one to whom Huling presented him—with the words: "Dorothy, this is Mr. Wayne, the Yale pitcher, who is to play with Bellville tomorrow; Mr. Wayne, my sister"—was the girl he had known he would meet some day.

"Climb up, Mr. Wayne. We can make room," invited Miss Huling.

Wayne thought the awkwardness with which he found a seat beside her was unbecoming to a Yale senior. But, considering she was the girl he had been expecting to discover for years, his clumsiness bespoke the importance of the event. The merry laughter of the girls rang in his ears. Presently, a voice detached itself from the others, and came floating softly to him.

"Mr. Wayne, so you're going to wrest our laurels from us?" asked Miss Huling.

"I don't know—I'm not infallible—I've been beaten."

"When? Not this season?" she inquired quickly, betraying a knowledge of his record that surprised and pleased him. "Mr. Wayne, I was at the Polo Grounds on June fifteenth."

Her white hand lightly touched the Princeton pin at her neck. Wayne roused suddenly out of his trance. The girl was a Princeton girl! The gleam of her golden hair, the flash of her blue eyes, became clear in sight.

"I'm very pleased to hear it," he replied.

"It was a great game, Mr. Wayne, and you may well be proud of your part in winning it. I shouldn't be surprised if you treated the Salisbury team to the same coat of whitewash. We girls are up in arms. Our boys stood a fair chance to win this game, but now there's a doubt. By the way, are you acquainted in Bellville?"

"No. I met Reed, the Bellville captain, in New York this week. He had already gotten an extra pitcher—another ringer—for this game, but he said he preferred me, if it could be arranged."

While conversing, Wayne made note of the fact that the other girls studiously left him to Miss Huling. If the avoidance had not been so marked, he would never have thought of it.

"Mr. Wayne, if your word is not involved—will you change your mind and pitch tomorrow's game for us instead of Bellville?"

Quite amazed, Wayne turned squarely to look at Miss Huling. Instead of disarming his quick suspicion, her cool, sweet voice, and brave, blue eyes confirmed it. The charms of the captain's sister were to be used to win him away from the Bellville nine. He knew the trick; it had been played upon him before.

But never had any other such occasion given him a feeling of regret. This case was different. She was the girl. And she meant to flirt with him, to use her eyes for all they were worth to encompass the Waterloo of the rival team.

No, he had made a mistake, after all—she was not the real girl. Suddenly conscious of a little shock of pain, he dismissed that dream girl from his mind, and determined to meet Miss Huling half way in her game. He could not flirt as well as he could pitch; still, he was no novice.

"Well, Miss Huling, my word certainly is not involved. But as to pitching for Salisbury—that depends."

"Upon what?"

"Upon what there is in it."

"Mr. Wayne, you mean—money? Oh, I know. My brother Rex told me how you college men are paid big sums. Our association will not give a dollar, and, besides, my brother knows nothing of this. But we girls are heart and soul on winning this game. We'll——"

"Miss Huling, I didn't mean remuneration in sordid cash," interrupted Wayne, in a tone that heightened the color in her cheeks.

Wayne eyed her keenly with mingled emotions. Was that rose-leaf flush in her cheeks natural? Some girls could blush at will. Were the wistful eyes, the earnest lips, only shamming? It cost him some bitterness to decide that they were. Her beauty fascinated, while it hardened him. Eternally, the beauty of women meant the undoing of men, whether they played the simple, inconsequential game of baseball, or the great, absorbing, mutable game of life.

The shame of the situation for him was increasingly annoying, inasmuch as this lovely girl should stoop to flirtation with a stranger, and the same time draw him, allure him, despite the apparent insincerity.

"Miss Huling, I'll pitch your game for two things," he continued.

"Name them."

"Wear Yale blue in place of that orange-and-black Princeton pin."

"I will." She said it with a shyness, a look in her eyes that made Wayne wince. What a perfect little actress! But there seemed just a chance that this was not deceit. For an instant he wavered, held back by subtle, finer intuition; then he beat down the mounting influence of truth in those dark-blue eyes, and spoke deliberately:

"The other thing is—if I win the game—a kiss."

Dorothy Huling's face flamed scarlet. But this did not affect Wayne so deeply, though it showed him his mistake, as the darkening shadow of disappointment in her eyes. If she had been a flirt, she would have been prepared for rudeness. He began casting about in his mind for some apology, some mitigation of his offense; but as he was about to speak, the sudden fading of her color, leaving her pale, and the look in her proud, dark eyes disconcerted him out of utterance.

"Certainly, Mr. Wayne. I agree to your price if you win the game."

But how immeasurable was the distance between the shy consent to wear Yale blue, and the pale, surprised agreement to his second proposal! Wayne experienced a strange sensation of personal loss.

While he endeavored to find his tongue, Miss Huling spoke to one of the boys standing near, and he started off on a run for the field. Presently Huling and the other players broke for the car, soon surrounding it in breathless anticipation.

"Wayne, is it straight? You'll pitch for us tomorrow?" demanded the captain, with shining eyes.

"Surely I will. Bellville don't need me. They've got Mackay, of Georgetown," replied Wayne.

Accustomed as he was to being mobbed by enthusiastic students and admiring friends, Wayne could not but feel extreme embarrassment at the reception accorded him now. He felt that he was sailing under false colors. The boys mauled him, the girls fluttered about him with glad laughter. He had to tear himself away; and when he finally reached his hotel, he went to his room, with his mind in a tumult.

Wayne cursed himself roundly; then he fell into deep thought. He began to hope he could retrieve the blunder. He would win the game; he would explain to her the truth; he would ask for an opportunity to prove he was worthy of her friendship; he would not mention the kiss. This last thought called up the soft curve of her red lips and that it was possible for him to kiss her made the temptation strong.

His sleep that night was not peaceful and dreamless. He awakened late, had breakfast sent to his room, and then took a long walk out into the country. After lunch he dodged the crowd in the hotel lobby, and hurried upstairs, where he put on his baseball suit. The first person he met upon going down was Reed, the Bellville man.

"What's this I hear, Wayne, about your pitching for Salisbury today? I got your telegram."

"Straight goods," replied Wayne.

"But I thought you intended to pitch for us?"

"I didn't promise, did I?"

"No. Still, it looks fishy to me."

"You've got Mackay, haven't you?"

"Yes. The truth is, I intended to use you both."

"Well, I'll try to win for Salisbury. Hope there's no hard feeling."

"Not at all. Only if I didn't have the Georgetown crack, I'd yell murder. As it is, we'll trim Salisbury anyway."

"Maybe," answered Wayne, laughing. "It's a hot day, and my arm feels good."

When Wayne reached the ball grounds, he thought he had never seen a more inspiring sight. The bright green oval was surrounded by a glittering mass of white and blue and black. Out along the foul lines were carriages, motors, and tally-hos, brilliant with waving fans and flags. Over the field murmured the low hum of many voices.

"Here you are!" cried Huling, making a grab for Wayne. "Where were you this morning? We couldn't find you. Come! We've got a minute before the practice whistle blows, and I promised to exhibit you."

He hustled Wayne down the first-base line, past the cheering crowd, out among the motors, to the same touring car that he remembered. A bevy of white-gowned girls rose like a covey of ptarmigans, and whirled flags of maroon and gray.

Dorothy Huling wore a bow of Yale blue upon her breast, and Wayne saw it and her face through a blur.

"Hurry, girls; get it over. We've got to practice," said the captain.

In the merry melee some one tied a knot of ribbon upon Wayne. Who it was he did not know; he saw only the averted face of Dorothy Huling. And as he returned to the field with a dull pang, he determined he would make her indifference disappear with the gladness of a victory for her team.

The practice was short, but long enough for Wayne to locate the glaring weakness of Salisbury at shortstop and third base. In fact, most of the players of his team showed rather poor form; they were overstrained, and plainly lacked experience necessary for steadiness in an important game.

Burns, the catcher, however, gave Wayne confidence. He was a short, sturdy youngster, with all the earmarks of a coming star. Huling, the captain, handled himself well at first base. The Bellville players were more matured, and some of them were former college cracks. Wayne saw that he had his work cut out for him.

The whistle blew. The Bellville team trotted to their position in the field; the umpire called play, and tossed a ball to Mackay, the long, lean Georgetown pitcher.

Wells, the first batter, fouled out; Stamford hit an easy bounce to the pitcher, and Clews put up a little Texas leaguer—all going out, one, two, three, on three pitched balls.

The teams changed from bat to field. Wayne faced the plate amid vociferous cheering. He felt that he could beat this team even without good support. He was in the finest condition, and his arm had been resting for ten days. He knew that if he had control of his high inshoot, these Bellville players would feel the whiz of some speed under their chins.

He struck Moore out, retired Reed on a measly fly, and made Clark hit a weak grounder to second; and he walked in to the bench assured of the outcome. On some days he had poor control; on others his drop ball refused to work properly; but, as luck would have it, he had never had greater speed or accuracy, or a more bewildering fast curve than on this day, when he meant to win a game for a girl.

"Boys, I've got everything," he said to his fellow-players, calling them around him. "A couple of runs will win for us. Now, listen, I know Mackay. He hasn't any speed, or much of a curve. All he's got is a teasing slow ball and a foxy head. Don't be too anxious to hit. Make him put 'em over."

But the Salisbury players were not proof against the tempting slow balls that Mackay delivered. They hit at wide curves far off the plate and when they did connect with the ball it was only to send an easy chance to the infielders.

The game seesawed along, inning after inning; it was a pitcher's battle that looked as if the first run scored would win the game. Mackay toyed with the Salisbury boys; it was his pleasure to toss up twisting, floating balls that could scarcely be hit out of the diamond. Wayne had the Bellville players utterly at his mercy; he mixed up his high jump and fast drop so cleverly, with his sweeping out-curve, that his opponents were unable to gauge his delivery at all.

In the first of the seventh, Barr for Bellville hit a ball which the third baseman should have fielded. But he fumbled. The second batter sent a fly to shortstop, who muffed it. The third hitter reached his base on another error by an infielder. Here the bases were crowded, and the situation had become critical all in a moment. Wayne believed the infield would go to pieces, and lose the game, then and there, if another hit went to short or third.

"Steady up, boys," called Wayne, and beckoned for his catcher.

"Burns, it's up to you and me," he said, in a low tone. "I've got to fan the rest of these hitters. You're doing splendidly. Now, watch close for my drop. Be ready to go down on your knees. When I let myself out, the ball generally hits the ground just back of the plate."

"Speed 'em over!" said Burns, his sweaty face grim and determined. "I'll get in front of 'em."

The head of the batting list was up for Bellville, and the whole Bellville contingent on the side lines rose and yelled and cheered.

Moore was a left handed hitter, who choked his bat up short, and poked at the ball. He was a good bunter, and swift on his feet. Wayne had taken his measure, as he had that of the other players, earlier in the game; and he knew it was good pitching to keep the ball in close to Moore's hands, so that if he did hit it, the chances were it would not go safe.

Summoning all his strength, Wayne took his long swing and shot the ball over the inside corner with terrific speed.

One strike!

Wayne knew it would not do to waste any balls if he wished to maintain that speed, so he put the second one in the same place. Moore struck too late.

Two strikes!

Then Burns signed for the last drop. Wayne delivered it with trepidation, for it was a hard curve to handle. Moore fell all over himself trying to hit it. Little Burns dropped to his knees to block the vicious curve. It struck the ground, and, glancing, boomed deep on the breast protector.

How the Salisbury supporters roared their approval! One man out— the bases full—with Reed, the slugging captain, at bat!

If Reed had a weakness, Wayne had not discovered it yet, although Reed had not hit safely. The captain stood somewhat back from the plate, a fact that induced Wayne to try him with the speedy outcurve. Reed lunged with a powerful swing, pulling away from the plate, and he missed the curve by a foot.

Wayne did not need to know any more. Reed had made his reputation slugging straight balls from heedless pitchers. He chopped the air twice more, and flung his bat savagely to the ground.

"Two out—play the hitter!" called Wayne to his team.

Clark, the third man up, was the surest batter on the Bellville team. He looked dangerous. He had made the only hit so far to the credit of his team. Wayne tried to work him on a high, fast ball close in. Clark swung freely and cracked a ripping liner to left. Half the crowd roared, and then groaned, for the beautiful hit went foul by several yards. Wayne wisely decided to risk all on his fast drop. Clark missed the first, fouled the second.

Two strikes!

Then he waited. He cooly let one, two, three of the fast drops go by without attempting to hit them. Burns valiantly got his body in front of them. These balls were all over the plate, but too low to be called strikes. With two strikes, and three balls, and the bases full, Clark had the advantage.

Tight as the place was, Wayne did not flinch. The game depended practically upon the next ball delivered. Wayne craftily and daringly decided to use another fast drop, for of all his assortment that would be the one least expected by Clark. But it must be started higher, so that in case Clark made no effort to swing, it would still be a strike.

Gripping the ball with a clinched hand, Wayne swung sharply, and drove it home with the limit of his power. It sped like a bullet, waist high, and just before reaching the plate darted downward, as if it had glanced on an invisible barrier.

Clark was fooled completely and struck futilely. But the ball caromed from the hard ground, hit Burns with a resounding thud, and bounced away. Clark broke for first, and Moore dashed for home. Like a tiger the little catcher pounced upon the ball, and, leaping back into line, blocked the sliding Moore three feet from the plate.

Pandemonium burst loose among the Salisbury adherents. The men bawled, the women screamed, the boys shrieked, and all waved their hats and flags, and jumped up and down, and manifested symptoms of baseball insanity.

In the first of the eighth inning, Mackay sailed up the balls like balloons, and disposed of three batters on the same old weak hits to his clever fielders. In the last of the eighth, Wayne struck out three more Bellville players.

"Burns, you're up," said Wayne, who, in his earnestness to win, kept cheering his comrades. "Do something. Get your base any way you can. Get in front of one. We must score this inning."

Faithful, battered Burns cunningly imposed his hip over the plate and received another bruise in the interests of his team. The opposing players furiously stormed at the umpire for giving him his base, but Burns' trick went through. Burnett bunted skilfully, sending Burns to second. Cole hit a fly to center. Then Huling singled between short and third.

It became necessary for the umpire to delay the game while he put the madly leaping boys back off the coaching lines. The shrill, hilarious cheering gradually died out, and the field settled into a forced quiet.

Wayne hurried up to the plate and took his position. He had always been a timely hitter, and he gritted his teeth in his resolve to settle this game. Mackay whirled his long arm, wheeled, took his long stride, and pitched a slow, tantalizing ball that seemed never to get anywhere. But Wayne waited, timed it perfectly, and met it squarely.

The ball flew safely over short, and but for a fine sprint and stop by the left fielder, would have resulted in a triple, possibly a home run. As it was, Burns and Huling scored; and Wayne, by a slide, reached second base. When he arose and saw the disorderly riot, and heard the noise of that well-dressed audience, he had a moment of exultation. Then Wells flew out to center ending the chances for more runs.

As Wayne received the ball in the pitcher's box, he paused and looked out across the field toward a white-crowned motor car, and he caught a gleam of Dorothy Huling's golden hair, and wondered if she were glad.

For nothing short of the miraculous could snatch this game from him now. Burns had withstood a severe pounding, but he would last out the inning, and Wayne did not take into account the rest of the team. He opened up with no slackening of his terrific speed, and he struck out the three remaining batters on eleven pitched balls. Then in the rising din he ran for Burns and gave him a mighty hug.

"You made the gamest stand of any catcher I ever pitched to," he said warmly.

Burns looked at his quivering, puffed, and bleeding hands, and smiled as if to say that this was praise to remember, and reward enough. Then the crowd swooped down on them, and they were swallowed up in the clamor and surge of victory. When Wayne got out of the thick and press of it, he made a bee line for his hotel, and by running a gauntlet managed to escape.

Resting, dressing, and dining were matters which he went through mechanically, with his mind ever on one thing. Later, he found a dark corner of the porch and sat there waiting, thinking. There was to be a dance given in honor of the team that evening at the hotel. He watched the boys and girls pass up the steps. When the music commenced, he arose and went into the hall. It was bright with white gowns, and gay with movement.

"There he is. Grab him, somebody," yelled Huling.

"Do something for me, quick," implored Wayne of the captain, as he saw the young people wave toward him.

"Salisbury is yours tonight," replied Huling

"Ask your sister to save me one dance."

Then he gave himself up. He took his meed of praise and flattery, and he withstood the battery of arch eyes modestly, as became the winner of many fields. But even the reception after the Princeton game paled in comparison with this impromptu dance.

She was here. Always it seemed, while he listened or talked or danced, his eyes were drawn to a slender, graceful form, and a fair face crowned with golden hair. Then he was making his way to where she stood near one of the open windows.

He never knew what he said to her, nor what reply she made, but she put her arm in his, and presently they were gliding over the polished floor. To Wayne the dance was a dream. He led her through the hall and out upon the balcony, where composure strangely came to him.

"Mr. Wayne, I have to thank you for saving the day for us. You pitched magnificently."

"I would have broken my arm to win that game," burst out Wayne. "Miss Huling, I made a blunder yesterday. I thought there was a conspiracy to persuade me to throw down Bellville. I've known of such things, and I resented it. You understand what I thought. I humbly offer my apologies, and beg that you forget the rude obligation I forced upon you."

How cold she was! How unattainable in that moment! He caught his breath, and rushed on.

"Your brother and the management of the club have asked me to pitch for Salisbury the remainder of the season. I shall be happy to—if——"

"If what?" She was all alive now, flushing warmly, dark eyes alight, the girl of his dreams.

"If you will forgive me—if you will let me be your friend—if—Miss Huling, you will again wear that bit of Yale blue."

"If, Mr. Wayne, you had very sharp eyes you would have noticed that I still wear it!"

THE MANAGER OF MADDEN'S HILL

Willie Howarth loved baseball. He loved it all the more because he was a cripple. The game was more beautiful and wonderful to him because he would never be able to play it. For Willie had been born with one leg shorter than the other; he could not run and at 11 years of age it was all he could do to walk with a crutch.

Nevertheless Willie knew more about baseball than any other boy on Madden's Hill. An uncle of his had once been a ballplayer and he had taught Willie the fine points of the game. And this uncle's ballplayer friends, who occasionally visited him, had imparted to Willie the vernacular of the game. So that Willie's knowledge of players and play, and particularly of the strange talk, the wild and whirling words on the lips of the real baseball men, made him the envy of every boy on Madden's Hill, and a mine of information. Willie never missed attending the games played on the lots, and he could tell why they were won or lost.

Willie suffered considerable pain, mostly at night, and this had given him a habit of lying awake in the dark hours, grieving over that crooked leg that forever shut him out of the heritage of youth. He had kept his secret well; he was accounted shy because he was quiet and had never been able to mingle with the boys in their activity. No one except his mother dreamed of the fire and hunger and pain within his breast. His school-mates called him "Daddy." It was a name given for his bent shoulders, his labored gait and his thoughtful face, too old for his years. And no one, not even his mother, guessed how that name hurt Willie.

It was a source of growing unhappiness with Willie that the Madden's Hill boys were always beaten by the other teams of the town. He really came to lose his sadness over his own misfortune in pondering on the wretched play of the Madden's Hill baseball club. He had all a boy's pride in the locality where he lived. And when the Bogg's Farm team administered a crushing defeat to Madden's Hill, Willie grew desperate.

Monday he met Lane Griffith, the captain of the Madden's Hill nine.

"Hello, Daddy," said Lane. He was a big, aggressive boy, and in a way had a fondness for Willie.

"Lane, you got an orful trimmin' up on the Boggs. What 'd you wanter let them country jakes beat you for?"

213

"Aw, Daddy, they was lucky. Umpire had hay-seed in his eyes! Robbed us! He couldn't see straight. We'll trim them down here Saturday."

"No, you won't—not without team work. Lane, you've got to have a manager."

"Durn it! Where 're we goin' to get one?" Lane blurted out.

"You can sign me. I can't play, but I know the game. Let me coach the boys."

The idea seemed to strike Capt. Griffith favorably. He prevailed upon all the boys living on Madden's Hill to come out for practice after school. Then he presented them to the managing coach. The boys were inclined to poke fun at Daddy Howarth and ridicule him; but the idea was a novel one and they were in such a state of subjection from many beatings that they welcomed any change. Willie sat on a bench improvised from a soap box and put them through a drill of batting and fielding. The next day in his coaching he included bunting and sliding. He played his men in different positions and for three more days he drove them unmercifully.

When Saturday came, the day for the game with Bogg's Farm, a wild protest went up from the boys. Willie experienced his first bitterness as a manager. Out of forty aspirants for the Madden's Hill team he could choose but nine to play the game. And as a conscientious manager he could use no favorites. Willie picked the best players and assigned them to positions that, in his judgment, were the best suited to them. Bob Irvine wanted to play first base and he was down for right field. Sam Wickhart thought he was the fastest fielder, and Willie had him slated to catch. Tom Lindsay's feelings were hurt because he was not to play in the infield. Eddie Curtis suffered a fall in pride when he discovered he was not down to play second base. Jake Thomas, Tay-Tay Mohler and Brick Grace all wanted to pitch. The manager had chosen Frank Price for that important position, and Frank's one ambition was to be a shortstop.

So there was a deadlock. For a while there seemed no possibility of a game. Willie sat on the bench, the center of a crowd of discontented, quarreling boys. Some were jealous, some were outraged, some tried to pacify and persuade the others. All were noisy. Lane Griffith stood by his manager and stoutly declared the players should play the positions to which they had been assigned or not at all. And he was entering into a hot argument with Tom Lindsay when the Bogg's Farm team arrogantly put in an appearance.

The way that team from the country walked out upon the field made a great difference. The spirit of Madden's Hill roused to battle. The game began swiftly and went on wildly. It ended almost before the Hill boys realized it had commenced. They did not know how they had won but they gave Daddy Howarth credit for it. They had a bonfire that night to celebrate the victory and they talked baseball until their parents became alarmed and hunted them up.

Madden's Hill practiced all that next week and on Saturday beat the Seventh Ward team. In four more weeks they had added half a dozen more victories to their record. Their reputation went abroad. They got uniforms, and baseball shoes with spikes, and bats and balls and gloves. They got a mask, but Sam Wickhart refused to catch with it.

"Sam, one of these days you'll be stoppin' a high inshoot with your eye," sagely remarked Daddy Howarth. "An' then where'll I get a catcher for the Natchez game?"

Natchez was the one name on the lips of every Madden's Hill boy. For Natchez had the great team of the town and, roused by the growing repute of the Hill club, had condescended to arrange a game. When that game was scheduled for July Fourth Daddy Howarth set to driving his men. Early and late he had them out. This manager, in keeping with all other famous managers, believed that batting was the thing which won games. He developed a hard-hitting team. He kept everlastingly at them to hit and run, hit and run.

On the Saturday before the Fourth, Madden's Hill had a game to play that did not worry Daddy and he left his team in charge of the captain.

"Fellers, I'm goin' down to the Round House to see Natchez play. I'll size up their game," said Daddy.

When he returned he was glad to find that his team had won its ninth straight victory, but he was not communicative in regard to the playing of the Natchez club. He appeared more than usually thoughtful.

The Fourth fell on Tuesday. Daddy had the boys out Monday and he let them take only a short, sharp practice. Then he sent them home. In his own mind, Daddy did not have much hope of beating Natchez. He had been greatly impressed by their playing, and one inning toward the close of the Round House game they had astonished him with the way they suddenly seemed to break loose and deluge their opponents in a flood of hits and runs. He could not understand this streak of theirs—for they did the same thing every time they played—and he was too good a baseball student to call it luck.

He had never wanted anything in his life, not even to have two good legs, as much as he wanted to beat Natchez. For the Madden's Hill boys had come to believe him infallible. He was their idol. They imagined they had only to hit and run, to fight and never give up, and Daddy would make them win. There was not a boy on the team who believed that Natchez had a chance. They had grown proud and tenacious of their dearly won reputation. First of all, Daddy thought of his team and their loyalty to him; then he thought of the glory lately come to Madden's Hill, and lastly of what it meant to him to have risen from a lonely watcher of the game—a cripple who could not even carry a bat—to manager of the famous Hill team. It might go hard with the boys to lose this game, but it would break his heart.

From time out of mind there had always been rivalry between Madden's Hill and Natchez. And there is no rivalry so bitter as that between boys. So Daddy, as he lay awake at night planning the system of play he wanted to use, left out of all account any possibility of a peaceful game. It was comforting to think that if it came to a fight Sam and Lane could hold their own with Bo Stranathan and Slugger Blandy.

In the managing of his players Daddy observed strict discipline. It was no unusual thing for him to fine them. On practice days and off the field they implicitly obeyed him. During actual play, however, they had evinced a tendency to jump over the traces. It had been his order for them not to report at the field Tuesday until 2 o'clock. He found it extremely difficult to curb his own inclination to start before the set time. And only the stern duty of a man to be an example to his players kept Daddy at home.

He lived near the ball grounds, yet on this day, as he hobbled along on his crutch, he thought the distance interminably long, and for the first time in weeks the old sickening resentment at his useless leg knocked at his heart. Manfully Daddy refused admittance to that old gloomy visitor. He found comfort and forgetfulness in the thought that no strong and swift-legged boy of his acquaintance could do what he could do.

Upon arriving at the field Daddy was amazed to see such a large crowd. It appeared that all the boys and girls in the whole town were in attendance, and, besides, there was a sprinkling of grown-up people interspersed here and there around the diamond. Applause greeted Daddy's appearance and members of his team escorted him to the soap-box bench.

Daddy cast a sharp eye over the Natchez players practicing on the field. Bo Stranathan had out his strongest team. They were not a prepossessing nine. They wore soiled uniforms that did not match in cut or color. But they pranced and swaggered and strutted! They were boastful and boisterous. It was a trial for any Madden's Hill boy just to watch them.

"Wot a swelled bunch!" exclaimed Tom Lindsay.

"Fellers, if Slugger Blandy tries to pull any stunt on me today he'll get a swelleder nut," growled Lane Griffith.

"T-t-t-t-t-te-te-tell him t-t-t-to keep out of m-m-m-my way an' not b-b-b-b-bl-block me," stuttered Tay-Tay Mohler.

"We're a-goin' to skin 'em," said Eddie Curtis.

"Cheese it, you kids, till we git in the game," ordered Daddy. "Now, Madden's Hill, hang round an' listen. I had to sign articles with Natchez—had to let them have their umpire. So we're up against it. But we'll hit this pitcher Muckle Harris. He ain't got any steam. An' he ain't got much nerve. Now every feller who goes up to bat wants to talk to Muck. Call him a big swelled stiff. Tell him he can't break a pane of glass—tell him he can't put one over the pan—tell him it he does you'll slam it down in the sand bank. Bluff the whole team. Keep scrappy all the time. See! That's my game today. This Natchez bunch needs to be gone after. Holler at the umpire. Act like you want to fight."

Then Daddy sent his men out for practice.

"Boss, enny ground rules?" inquired Bo Stranathan. He was a big, bushy-haired boy with a grin and protruding teeth. "How many bases on wild throws over first base an' hits over the sand bank?"

"All you can get," replied Daddy, with a magnanimous wave of hand.

"Huh! Lemmee see your ball?"

Daddy produced the ball that he had Lane had made for the game.

"Huh! Watcher think? We ain 't goin' to play with no mush ball like thet," protested Bo. "We play with a hard ball. Looka here! We'll trow up the ball."

Daddy remembered what he had heard about the singular generosity of the Natchez team to supply the balls for the games they played.

"We don't hev to pay nothin' fer them balls. A man down at the Round House makes them for us. They ain't no balls as good," explained Bo, with pride.

However, as Bo did not appear eager to pass over the balls for examination Daddy simply reached out and took them. They were small, perfectly round and as hard as bullets. They had no covers. The yarn had been closely and tightly wrapped and then stitched over with fine bees-waxed thread. Daddy fancied he detected a difference in the weight of the ball, but Bo took them back before Daddy could be sure of that point.

"You don't have to fan about it. I know a ball when I see one," observed Daddy. "But we're on our own grounds an' we'll use our own ball. Thanks all the same to you, Stranathan."

"Huh! All I gotta say is we'll play with my ball er there won't be no game," said Bo suddenly.

Daddy shrewdly eyed the Natchez captain. Bo did not look like a fellow wearing himself thin from generosity. It struck Daddy that Bo's habit of supplying the ball for the game might have some relation to the fact that he always carried along his own umpire. There was a strange feature about this umpire business and it was that Bo's man had earned a reputation for being particularly fair. No boy ever had any real reason to object to Umpire Gale's decisions. When Gale umpired away from the Natchez grounds his close decisions always favored the other team, rather than his own. It all made Daddy keen and thoughtful.

"Stranathan, up here on Madden's Hill we know how to treat visitors. We'll play with your ball.... Now keep your gang of rooters from crowdin' on the diamond."

"Boss, it's your grounds. Fire 'em off if they don't suit you.... Come on, let's git in the game. Watcher want—field er bat?"

"Field," replied Daddy briefly.

Billy Gale called "Play," and the game began with Slugger Blandy at bat. The formidable way in which he swung his club did not appear to have any effect on Frank Price or the player back of him. Frank's most successful pitch was a slow, tantalizing curve, and he used it. Blandy lunged at the ball, missed it and grunted.

"Frank, you got his alley," called Lane.

Slugger fouled the next one high in the air back of the plate. Sam Wickhart, the stocky bowlegged catcher, was a fiend for running after foul flies, and now he plunged into the crowd of boys, knocking them right and left, and he caught the ball. Whisner came up and hit safely over Griffith, whereupon the Natchez supporters began to howl. Kelly sent a grounder to Grace at short stop. Daddy's weak player made a poor throw to first base, so the runner was safe. Then Bo Stranathan batted a stinging ball through the infield, scoring Whisner.

"Play the batter! Play the batter!" sharply called Daddy from the bench.

Then Frank struck out Molloy and retired Dundon on an easy fly.

"Fellers, git in the game now," ordered Daddy, as his players eagerly trotted in. "Say things to that Muckle Harris! We'll walk through this game like sand through a sieve."

Bob Irvin ran to the plate waving his bat at Harris.

"Put one over, you freckleface! I 've been dyin' fer this chanst. You're on Madden's Hill now."

Muckle evidently was not the kind of pitcher to stand coolly under such bantering. Obviously he was not used to it. His face grew red and his hair waved up. Swinging hard, he threw the ball straight at Bob's head. Quick as a cat, Bob dropped flat.

"Never touched me!" he chirped, jumping up and pounding the plate with his bat. "You couldn't hit a barn door. Come on. I'll paste one a mile!"

Bob did not get an opportunity to hit, for Harris could not locate the plate and passed him to first on four balls.

"Dump the first one," whispered Daddy in Grace's ear. Then he gave Bob a signal to run on the first pitch.

Grace tried to bunt the first ball, but he missed it. His attempt, however, was so violent that he fell over in front of the catcher, who could not recover in time to throw, and Bob got to second base. At this juncture, the Madden's Hill band of loyal supporters opened up with a mingling of shrill yells and whistles and jangling of tin cans filled with pebbles. Grace hit the next ball into second base and, while he was being thrown out, Bob raced to third. With Sam Wickhart up it looked good for a score, and the crowd yelled louder. Sam was awkward yet efficient, and he batted a long fly to right field. The fielder muffed the ball. Bob scored, Sam reached second base, and the crowd yelled still louder. Then Lane struck out and Mohler hit to shortstop, retiring the side.

Natchez scored a run on a hit, a base on balls, and another error by Grace. Every time a ball went toward Grace at short Daddy groaned. In their half of the inning Madden's Hill made two runs, increasing the score 3 to 2.

The Madden's Hill boys began to show the strain of such a close contest. If Daddy had voiced aloud his fear it would have been: "They'll blow up in a minnit!" Frank Price alone was slow and cool, and he pitched in masterly style. Natchez could not beat him. On the other hand, Madden's Hill hit Muck Harris hard, but superb fielding kept runners off the bases. As Daddy's team became more tense and excited Bo Stranathan's players grew steadier and more arrogantly confident. Daddy saw it with distress, and he could not realize just where Natchez had license for such confidence. Daddy watched the game with the eyes of a hawk.

As the Natchez players trooped in for their sixth inning at bat, Daddy observed a marked change in their demeanor. Suddenly they seemed to have been let loose; they were like a band of Indians. Daddy saw everything. He did not miss seeing Umpire Gale take a ball from his pocket and toss it to Frank, and Daddy wondered if that was the ball which had been in the play. Straightway, however, he forgot that in the interest of the game.

Bo Stranathan bawled: "Wull, Injuns, hyar's were we do 'em. We've jest ben loafin' along. Git ready to tear the air, you rooters!"

Kelly hit a wonderfully swift ball through the infield. Bo batted out a single. Malloy got up in the way of one of Frank's pitches, and was passed to first base. Then, as the Natchez crowd opened up in shrill clamor, the impending disaster fell. Dundon hit a bounder down into the infield. The ball appeared to be endowed with life. It bounded low, then high and, cracking into Grace's hands, bounced out and rolled away. The runners raced around the bases.

Pickens sent up a tremendous fly, the highest ever batted on Madden's Hill. It went over Tom Lindsay in center field, and Tom ran and ran. The ball went so far up that Tom had time to cover the ground, but he could not judge it. He ran round in a little circle, with hands up in bewilderment. And when the ball dropped it hit him on the head and bounded away.

"Run, you Injun, run!" bawled Bo. "What'd I tell you? We ain't got 'em goin', oh, no! Hittin' 'em on the head!"

Bill dropped a slow, teasing ball down the third-base line. Jake Thomas ran desperately for it, and the ball appeared to strike his hands and run up his arms and caress his nose and wrap itself round his neck and then roll gently away. All the while, the Natchez runners tore wildly about the bases and the Natchez supporters screamed and whistled. Muck Harris could not bat, yet he hit the first ball and it shot like a bullet over the infield. Then Slugger Blandy came to the plate.

The ball he sent out knocked Grace's leg from under him as if it were a ten-pin. Whisner popped a fly over Tay Tay Mohler's head. Now Tay Tay was fat and slow, but he was a sure catch. He got under the ball. It struck his hands and jumped back twenty feet up into the air. It was a strangely live ball. Kelly again hit to shortstop, and the ball appeared to start slow, to gather speed with every bound and at last to dart low and shoot between Grace's legs.

"Haw! Haw!" roared Bo. "They've got a hole at short. Hit fer the hole, fellers. Watch me! Jest watch me!"

And he swung hard on the first pitch. The ball glanced like a streak straight at Grace, took a vicious jump, and seemed to flirt with the infielder's hands, only to evade them.

Malloy fouled a pitch and the ball hit Sam Wickhart square over the eye. Sam's eye popped out and assumed the proportions and color of a huge plum.

"Hey!" yelled Blandy, the rival catcher. "Air you ketchin' with yer mug?"

Sam would not delay the game nor would he don the mask.

Daddy sat hunched on his soap-box, and, as in a hateful dream, he saw his famous team go to pieces. He put his hands over his ears to shut out some of the uproar. And he watched that little yarn ball fly and shoot and bound and roll to crush his fondest hopes. Not one of his players appeared able to hold it. And Grace had holes in his hands and legs and body. The ball went right through him. He might as well have been so much water. Instead of being a shortstop he was simply a hole. After every hit Daddy saw that ball more and more as something alive. It sported with his infielders. It bounded like a huge jack-rabbit, and went swifter and higher at every bound. It was here, there, everywhere.

And it became an infernal ball. It became endowed with a fiendish propensity to run up a player's leg and all about him, as if trying to hide in his pocket. Grace's efforts to find it were heartbreaking to watch.

Every time it bounded out to center field, which was of frequent occurrence, Tom would fall on it and hug it as if he were trying to capture a fleeing squirrel. Tay Tay Mohler could stop the ball, but that was no great credit to him, for his hands took no part in the achievement. Tay Tay was fat and the ball seemed to like him. It boomed into his stomach and banged against his stout legs. When Tay saw it coming he dropped on his knees and valorously sacrificed his anatomy to the cause of the game.

Daddy tried not to notice the scoring of runs by his opponents. But he had to see them and he had to count. Ten runs were as ten blows! After that each run scored was like a stab in his heart. The play went on, a terrible fusilade of wicked ground balls that baffled any attempt to field them. Then, with nineteen runs scored, Natchez appeared to tire. Sam caught a foul fly, and Tay Tay, by obtruding his wide person to the path of infield hits, managed to stop them, and throw out the runners.

Score—Natchez, 21; Madden Hill, 3.

Daddy's boys slouched and limped wearily in.

"Wot kind of a ball's that?" panted Tom, as he showed his head with a bruise as large as a goose-egg.

"T-t-t-t-ta-ta-tay-tay-tay-tay——" began Mohler, in great excitement, but as he could not finish what he wanted to say no one caught his meaning.

Daddy's watchful eye had never left that wonderful, infernal little yarn ball. Daddy was crushed under defeat, but his baseball brains still continued to work. He saw Umpire Gale leisurely step into the pitcher's box, and leisurely pick up the ball and start to make a motion to put it in his pocket.

Suddenly fire flashed all over Daddy.

"Hyar! Don't hide that ball!" he yelled, in his piercing tenor.

He jumped up quickly, forgetting his crutch, and fell headlong. Lane and Sam got him upright and handed the crutch to him. Daddy began to hobble out to the pitcher's box.

"Don't you hide that ball. See! I've got my eye on this game. That ball was in play, an' you can't use the other."

Umpire Gale looked sheepish, and his eyes did not meet Daddy's. Then Bo came trotting up.

"What's wrong, boss?" he asked.

"Aw, nuthin'. You're tryin' to switch balls on me. That's all. You can't pull off any stunts on Madden's Hill."

"Why, boss, thet ball's all right. What you hollerin' about?"

"Sure that ball's all right," replied Daddy. "It's a fine ball. An' we want a chanst to hit it! See?"

Bo flared up and tried to bluster, but Daddy cut him short.

"Give us our innin'—let us git a whack at that ball, or I'll run you off Madden's Hill."

Bo suddenly looked a little pale and sick.

"Course youse can git a whack at it," he said, in a weak attempt to be natural and dignified.

Daddy tossed the ball to Harris, and as he hobbled off the field he heard Bo calling out low and cautiously to his players. Then Daddy was certain he had discovered a trick. He called his players around him.

"This game ain't over yet. It ain't any more'n begun. I'll tell you what. Last innin' Bo's umpire switched balls on us. That ball was lively. An' they tried to switch back on me. But nix! We're goin' to git a chanst to hit that lively ball, An' they're goin' to git a dose of their own medicine. Now, you dead ones—come back to life! Show me some hittin' an' runnin'."

"Daddy, you mean they run in a trick on us?" demanded Lane, with flashing eyes.

"Funny about Natchez's strong finishes!" replied Daddy, coolly, as he eyed his angry players.

They let out a roar, and then ran for the bats.

The crowd, quick to sense what was in the air, thronged to the diamond and manifested alarming signs of outbreak.

Sam Wickhart leaped to the plate and brandished his club.

"Sam, let him pitch a couple," called Daddy from the bench. "Mebbe we'll git wise then."

Harris had pitched only twice when the fact became plain that he could not throw this ball with the same speed as the other. The ball was heavier; besides Harris was also growing tired. The next pitch Sam hit far out over the center fielder's head for a home run. It was a longer hit than any Madden's Hill boy had ever made. The crowd shrieked its delight. Sam crossed the plate and then fell on the bench beside Daddy.

"Say! that ball nearly knocked the bat out of my hands," panted Sam. "It made the bat spring!"

"Fellers, don't wait," ordered Daddy. "Don't give the umpire a chanst to roast us now. Slam the first ball!"

The aggressive captain lined the ball at Bo Stranathan. The Natchez shortstop had a fine opportunity to make the catch, but he made an inglorious muff. Tay Tay hurried to bat. Umpire Gale called the first pitch a strike. Tay slammed down his club. "T-t-t-t-to-to-twasn't over," he cried. "T-t-t-tay——"

"Shut up," yelled Daddy. "We want to git this game over today."

Tay Tay was fat and he was also strong, so that when beef and muscle both went hard against the ball it traveled. It looked as if it were going a mile straight up. All the infielders ran to get under it. They got into a tangle, into which the ball descended. No one caught it, and thereupon the Natchez players began to rail at one another. Bo stormed at them, and they talked back to him. Then when Tom Lindsay hit a little slow grounder into the infield it seemed that a just retribution had overtaken the great Natchez team.

Ordinarily this grounder of Tom's would have been easy for a novice to field. But this peculiar grounder, after it has hit the ground once, seemed to wake up and feel lively. It lost its leisurely action and began to have celerity. When it reached Dundon it had the strange, jerky speed so characteristic of the grounders that had confused the Madden's Hill team. Dundon got his hands on the ball and it would not stay in them. When finally he trapped it Tom had crossed first base and another runner had scored. Eddie Curtis cracked another at Bo. The Natchez captain dove for it, made a good stop, bounced after the rolling ball, and then threw to Kelly at first. The ball knocked Kelly's hands apart as if they had been paper. Jake Thomas batted left handed and he swung hard on a slow pitch and sent the ball far into right field. Runners scored. Jake's hit was a three-bagger. Then Frank Price hit up an infield fly. Bo yelled for Dundon to take it and Dundon yelled for Harris. They were all afraid to try for it. It dropped safely while Jake ran home.

With the heavy batters up the excitement increased. A continuous scream and incessant rattle of tin cans made it impossible to hear what the umpire called out. But that was not important, for he seldom had a chance to call either ball or strike. Harris had lost his speed and nearly every ball he pitched was hit by the Madden's Hill boys. Irvine cracked one down between short and third. Bo and Pickens ran for it and collided while the ball jauntily skipped out to left field and, deftly evading Bell, went on and on. Bob reached third. Grace hit another at Dundon, who appeared actually to stop it four times before he could pick it up, and then he was too late. The doughty bow-legged Sam, with his huge black eye, hung over the plate and howled at Muckle. In the din no one heard what he said, but evidently Muck divined it. For he roused to the spirit of a pitcher who would die of shame if he could not fool a one-eyed batter. But Sam swooped down and upon the first ball and drove it back toward the pitcher. Muck could not get out of the way and the ball made his leg buckle under him. Then that hit glanced off to begin a marvelous exhibition of high and erratic bounding about the infield.

Daddy hunched over his soap-box bench and hugged himself. He was farsighted and he saw victory. Again he watched the queer antics of that little yarn ball, but now with different feelings. Every hit seemed to lift him to the skies. He kept silent, though every time the ball fooled a Natchez player Daddy wanted to yell. And when it started for Bo and, as if in revenge, bounded wickeder at every bounce to skip off the grass and make Bo look ridiculous, then Daddy experienced the happiest moments of his baseball career. Every time a tally crossed the plate he would chalk it down on his soap box.

But when Madden's Hill scored the nineteenth run without a player being put out, then Daddy lost count. He gave himself up to revel. He sat motionless and silent; nevertheless his whole internal being was in the state of wild tumult. It was as if he was being rewarded in joy for all the misery he had suffered because he was a cripple. He could never play baseball, but he had baseball brains. He had been too wise for the tricky Stranathan. He was the coach and manager and general of the great Madden's Hill nine. If ever he had to lie awake at night again he would not mourn over his lameness; he would have something to think about. To him would be given the glory of beating the invincible Natchez team. So Daddy felt the last bitterness leave him. And he watched that strange little yarn ball, with its wonderful skips and darts and curves. The longer the game progressed and the wearier Harris grew, the harder the Madden's Hill boys batted the ball and the crazier it bounced at Bo and his sick players. Finally, Tay Tay Mohler hit a teasing grounder down to Bo.

Then it was as if the ball, realizing a climax, made ready for a final spurt. When Bo reached for the ball it was somewhere else. Dundon could not locate it. And Kelly, rushing down to the chase, fell all over himself and his teammates trying to grasp the illusive ball, and all the time Tay Tay was running. He never stopped. But as he was heavy and fat he did not make fast time on the bases. Frantically the outfielders ran in to head off the bouncing ball, and when they had succeeded Tay Tay had performed the remarkable feat of making a home run on a ball batted into the infield.

That broke Natchez's spirit. They quit. They hurried for their bats. Only Bo remained behind a moment to try to get his yarn ball. But Sam had pounced upon it and given it safely to Daddy. Bo made one sullen demand for it.

"Funny about them fast finishes of yours!" said Daddy scornfully. "Say! the ball's our'n. The winnin' team gits the ball. Go home an' look up the rules of the game!"

Bo slouched off the field to a shrill hooting and tin canning.

"Fellers, what was the score?" asked Daddy.

Nobody knew the exact number of runs made by Madden's Hill.

"Gimme a knife, somebody," said the manager.

When it had been produced Daddy laid down the yarn ball and cut into it. The blade entered readily for a inch and then stopped. Daddy cut all around the ball, and removed the cover of tightly wrapped yarn. Inside was a solid ball of India rubber.

"Say! it ain't so funny now—how that ball bounced," remarked Daddy.

"Wot you think of that!" exclaimed Tom, feeling the lump on his head.

"T-t-t-t-t-t-ta-tr——" began Tay Tay Mohler.

"Say it! Say it!" interrupted Daddy.

"Ta-ta-ta-tr-trimmed them wa-wa-wa-wa-with their own b-b-b-b-b-ba-ba-ball," finished Tay.

OLD WELL-WELL

He bought a ticket at the 25-cent window, and edging his huge bulk through the turnstile, laboriously followed the noisy crowd toward the bleachers. I could not have been mistaken. He was Old Well-Well, famous from Boston to Baltimore as the greatest baseball fan in the East. His singular yell had pealed into the ears of five hundred thousand worshippers of the national game and would never be forgotten.

At sight of him I recalled a friend's baseball talk. "You remember Old Well-Well? He's all in—dying, poor old fellow! It seems young Burt, whom the Phillies are trying out this spring, is Old Well-Well's nephew and protege. Used to play on the Murray Hill team; a speedy youngster. When the Philadelphia team was here last, Manager Crestline announced his intention to play Burt in center field. Old Well-Well was too ill to see the lad get his tryout. He was heart-broken and said: 'If I could only see one more game!'"

The recollection of this random baseball gossip and the fact that Philadelphia was scheduled to play New York that very day, gave me a sudden desire to see the game with Old Well-Well. I did not know him, but where on earth were introductions as superfluous as on the bleachers? It was a very easy matter to catch up with him. He walked slowly, leaning hard on a cane and his wide shoulders sagged as he puffed along. I was about to make some pleasant remark concerning the prospects of a fine game, when the sight of his face shocked me and I drew back. If ever I had seen shadow of pain and shade of death they hovered darkly around Old Well-Well.

No one accompanied him; no one seemed to recognize him. The majority of that merry crowd of boys and men would have jumped up wild with pleasure to hear his well-remembered yell. Not much longer than a year before, I had seen ten thousand fans rise as one man and roar a greeting to him that shook the stands. So I was confronted by a situation strikingly calculated to rouse my curiosity and sympathy.

He found an end seat on a row at about the middle of the right-field bleachers and I chose one across the aisle and somewhat behind him. No players were yet in sight. The stands were filling up and streams of men were filing into the aisles of the bleachers and piling over the benches. Old Well-Well settled himself comfortably in his seat and gazed about him with animation. There had come a change to his massive features. The hard lines had softened; the patches of gray were no longer visible; his cheeks were ruddy; something akin to a smile shone on his face as he looked around, missing no detail of the familiar scene.

During the practice of the home team Old Well-Well sat still with his big hands on his knees; but when the gong rang for the Phillies, he grew restless, squirming in his seat and half rose several times. I divined the importuning of his old habit to greet his team with the yell that had made him famous. I expected him to get up; I waited for it. Gradually, however, he became quiet as a man governed by severe self-restraint and directed his attention to the Philadelphia center fielder.

At a glance I saw that the player was new to me and answered the newspaper description of young Burt. What a lively looking athlete! He was tall, lithe, yet sturdy. He did not need to chase more than two fly balls to win me. His graceful, fast style reminded me of the great Curt Welch. Old Well-Well's face wore a rapt expression. I discovered myself hoping Burt would make good; wishing he would rip the boards off the fence; praying he would break up the game.

It was Saturday, and by the time the gong sounded for the game to begin the grand stand and bleachers were packed. The scene was glittering, colorful, a delight to the eye. Around the circle of bright faces rippled a low, merry murmur. The umpire, grotesquely padded in front by his chest protector, announced the batteries, dusted the plate, and throwing out a white ball, sang the open sesame of the game: "Play!"

Then Old Well-Well arose as if pushed from his seat by some strong propelling force. It had been his wont always when play was ordered or in a moment of silent suspense, or a lull in the applause, or a dramatic pause when hearts heat high and lips were mute, to bawl out over the listening, waiting multitude his terrific blast: "Well-Well-Well!"

Twice he opened his mouth, gurgled and choked, and then resumed his seat with a very red, agitated face; something had deterred him from his purpose, or he had been physically incapable of yelling.

The game opened with White's sharp bounder to the infield. Wesley had three strikes called on him, and Kelly fouled out to third base. The Phillies did no better, being retired in one, two, three order. The second inning was short and no tallies were chalked up. Brain hit safely in the third and went to second on a sacrifice. The bleachers began to stamp and cheer. He reached third on an infield hit that the Philadelphia shortstop knocked down but could not cover in time to catch either runner. The cheer in the grand stand was drowned by the roar in the bleachers. Brain scored on a fly-ball to left. A double along the right foul line brought the second runner home. Following that the next batter went out on strikes.

In the Philadelphia half of the inning young Burt was the first man up. He stood left-handed at the plate and looked formidable. Duveen, the wary old pitcher for New York, to whom this new player was an unknown quantity, eyed his easy position as if reckoning on a possible weakness. Then he took his swing and threw the ball. Burt never moved a muscle and the umpire called strike. The next was a ball, the next a strike; still Burt had not moved.

"Somebody wake him up!" yelled a wag in the bleachers. "He's from Slumbertown, all right, all right!" shouted another.

Duveen sent up another ball, high and swift. Burt hit straight over the first baseman, a line drive that struck the front of the right-field bleachers.

"Peacherino!" howled a fan.

Here the promise of Burt's speed was fulfilled. Run! He was fleet as a deer. He cut through first like the wind, settled to a driving strides rounded second, and by a good, long slide beat the throw in to third. The crowd, who went to games to see long hits and daring runs, gave him a generous hand-clapping.

Old Well-Well appeared on the verge of apoplexy. His ruddy face turned purple, then black; he rose in his seat; he gave vent to smothered gasps; then he straightened up and clutched his hands into his knees.

Burt scored his run on a hit to deep short, an infielder's choice, with the chances against retiring a runner at the plate. Philadelphia could not tally again that inning. New York blanked in the first of the next. For their opponents, an error, a close decision at second favoring the runner, and a single to right tied the score. Bell of New York got a clean hit in the opening of the fifth. With no one out and chances for a run, the impatient fans let loose. Four subway trains in collision would not have equalled the yell and stamp in the bleachers. Maloney was next to bat and he essayed a bunt. This the fans derided with hoots and hisses. No team work, no inside ball for them.

"Hit it out!" yelled a hundred in unison.

"Home run!" screamed a worshipper of long hits.

As if actuated by the sentiments of his admirers Maloney lined the ball over short. It looked good for a double; it certainly would advance Bell to third; maybe home. But no one calculated on Burt. His fleetness enabled him to head the bounding ball. He picked it up cleanly, and checking his headlong run, threw toward third base. Bell was half way there. The ball shot straight and low with terrific force and beat the runner to the bag.

"What a great arm!" I exclaimed, deep in my throat. "It's the lad's day! He can't be stopped."

The keen newsboy sitting below us broke the amazed silence in the bleachers.

"Wot d'ye tink o' that?"

Old Well-Well writhed in his seat. To him if was a one-man game, as it had come to be for me. I thrilled with him; I gloried in the making good of his protege; it got to be an effort on my part to look at the old man, so keenly did his emotion communicate itself to me.

The game went on, a close, exciting, brilliantly fought battle. Both pitchers were at their best. The batters batted out long flies, low liners, and sharp grounders; the fielders fielded these difficult chances without misplay. Opportunities came for runs, but no runs were scored for several innings. Hopes were raised to the highest pitch only to be dashed astonishingly away. The crowd in the grand stand swayed to every pitched ball; the bleachers tossed like surf in a storm.

To start the eighth, Stranathan of New York tripled along the left foul line. Thunder burst from the fans and rolled swellingly around the field. Before the hoarse yelling, the shrill hooting, the hollow stamping had ceased Stranathan made home on an infield hit. Then bedlam broke loose. It calmed down quickly, for the fans sensed trouble between Binghamton, who had been thrown out in the play, and the umpire who was waving him back to the bench.

"You dizzy-eyed old woman, you can't see straight!" called Binghamton.

The umpire's reply was lost, but it was evident that the offending player had been ordered out of the grounds.

Binghamton swaggered along the bleachers while the umpire slowly returned to his post. The fans took exception to the player's objection and were not slow in expressing it. Various witty enconiums, not to be misunderstood, attested to the bleachers' love of fair play and their disgust at a player's getting himself put out of the game at a critical stage.

The game proceeded. A second batter had been thrown out. Then two hits in succession looked good for another run. White, the next batter, sent a single over second base. Burt scooped the ball on the first bounce and let drive for the plate. It was another extraordinary throw. Whether ball or runner reached home base first was most difficult to decide. The umpire made his sweeping wave of hand and the breathless crowd caught his decision.

"Out!"

In action and sound the circle of bleachers resembled a long curved beach with a mounting breaker thundering turbulently high.

"Rob—b—ber—r!" bawled the outraged fans, betraying their marvelous inconsistency.

Old Well-Well breathed hard. Again the wrestling of his body signified an inward strife. I began to feel sure that the man was in a mingled torment of joy and pain, that he fought the maddening desire to yell because he knew he had not the strength to stand it. Surely, in all the years of his long following of baseball he had never had the incentive to express himself in his peculiar way that rioted him now. Surely, before the game ended he would split the winds with his wonderful yell.

Duveen's only base on balls, with the help of a bunt, a steal, and a scratch hit, resulted in a run for Philadelphia, again tying the score. How the fans raged at Fuller for failing to field the lucky scratch.

"We had the game on ice!" one cried.

"Get him a basket!"

New York men got on bases in the ninth and made strenuous efforts to cross the plate, but it was not to be. Philadelphia opened up with two scorching hits and then a double steal. Burt came up with runners on second and third. Half the crowd cheered in fair appreciation of the way fate was starring the ambitious young outfielder; the other half, dyed-in-the-wool home-team fans, bent forward in a waiting silent gloom of fear. Burt knocked the dirt out of his spikes and faced Duveen. The second ball pitched he met fairly and it rang like a bell.

No one in the stands saw where it went. But they heard the crack, saw the New York shortstop stagger and then pounce forward to pick up the ball and speed it toward the plate. The catcher was quick to tag the incoming runner, and then snap the ball to first base, completing a double play.

When the crowd fully grasped this, which was after an instant of bewilderment, a hoarse crashing roar rolled out across the field to bellow back in loud echo from Coogan's Bluff. The grand stand resembled a colored corn field waving in a violent wind; the bleachers lost all semblance of anything. Frenzied, flinging action—wild chaos—shrieking cries—manifested sheer insanity of joy.

When the noise subsided, one fan, evidently a little longer-winded than his comrades, cried out hysterically:

"O-h! I don't care what becomes of me—now-w!"

Score tied, three to three, game must go ten innings—that was the shibboleth; that was the overmastering truth. The game did go ten innings—eleven—twelve, every one marked by masterly pitching, full of magnificent catches, stops and throws, replete with reckless base-running and slides like flashes in the dust. But they were unproductive of runs. Three to three! Thirteen innings!

"Unlucky thirteenth," wailed a superstitious fan.

I had got down to plugging, and for the first time, not for my home team. I wanted Philadelphia to win, because Burt was on the team. With Old Well-Well sitting there so rigid in his seat, so obsessed by the playing of the lad, I turned traitor to New York.

White cut a high twisting bounder inside the third base, and before the ball could be returned he stood safely on second. The fans howled with what husky voice they had left. The second hitter batted a tremendously high fly toward center field. Burt wheeled with the crack of the ball and raced for the ropes. Onward the ball soared like a sailing swallow; the fleet fielder ran with his back to the stands. What an age that ball stayed in the air! Then it lost its speed, gracefully curved and began to fall. Burt lunged forward and upwards; the ball lit in his hands and stuck there as he plunged over the ropes into the crowd. White had leisurely trotted half way to third; he saw the catch, ran back to touch second and then easily made third on the throw-in. The applause that greeted Burt proved the splendid spirit of the game. Bell placed a safe little hit over short, scoring White. Heaving, bobbing bleachers—wild, broken, roar on roar!

Score four to three—only one half inning left for Philadelphia to play—how the fans rooted for another run! A swift double-play, however, ended the inning.

Philadelphia's first hitter had three strikes called on him.

"Asleep at the switch!" yelled a delighted fan.

The next batter went out on a weak pop-up fly to second.

"Nothin' to it!"

"Oh, I hate to take this money!"

"All-l o-over!"

Two men at least of all that vast assemblage had not given up victory for Philadelphia. I had not dared to look at Old Well-Well for a long, while. I dreaded the nest portentious moment. I felt deep within me something like clairvoyant force, an intangible belief fostered by hope.

Magoon, the slugger of the Phillies, slugged one against the left field bleachers, but, being heavy and slow, he could not get beyond second base. Cless swung with all his might at the first pitched ball, and instead of hitting it a mile as he had tried, he scratched a mean, slow, teasing grounder down the third base line. It was as safe as if it had been shot out of a cannon. Magoon went to third.

The crowd suddenly awoke to ominous possibilities; sharp commands came from the players' bench. The Philadelphia team were bowling and hopping on the side lines, and had to be put down by the umpire.

An inbreathing silence fell upon stands and field, quiet, like a lull before a storm.

When I saw young Burt start for the plate and realized it was his turn at bat, I jumped as if I had been shot. Putting my hand on Old Well-Well's shoulder I whispered: "Burt's at bat: He'll break up this game! I know he's going to lose one!"

The old fellow did not feel my touch; he did not hear my voice; he was gazing toward the field with an expression on his face to which no human speech could render justice. He knew what was coming. It could not be denied him in that moment.

How confidently young Burt stood up to the plate! None except a natural hitter could have had his position. He might have been Wagner for all he showed of the tight suspense of that crisis. Yet there was a tense alert poise to his head and shoulders which proved he was alive to his opportunity.

Duveen plainly showed he was tired. Twice he shook his head to his catcher, as if he did not want to pitch a certain kind of ball. He had to use extra motion to get his old speed, and he delivered a high straight ball that Burt fouled over the grand stand. The second ball met a similar fate. All the time the crowd maintained that strange waiting silence. The umpire threw out a glistening white ball, which Duveen rubbed in the dust and spat upon. Then he wound himself up into a knot, slowly unwound, and swinging with effort, threw for the plate.

Burt's lithe shoulders swung powerfully. The meeting of ball and bat fairly cracked. The low driving hit lined over second a rising glittering streak, and went far beyond the center fielder.

Bleachers and stands uttered one short cry, almost a groan, and then stared at the speeding runners. For an instant, approaching doom could not have been more dreaded. Magoon scored. Cless was rounding second when the ball lit. If Burt was running swiftly when he turned first he had only got started, for then his long sprinter's stride lengthened and quickened. At second he was flying; beyond second he seemed to merge into a gray flitting shadow.

I gripped my seat strangling the uproar within me. Where was the applause? The fans were silent, choked as I was, but from a different cause. Cless crossed the plate with the score that defeated New York; still the tension never laxed until Burt beat the ball home in as beautiful a run as ever thrilled an audience.

In the bleak dead pause of amazed disappointment Old Well-Well lifted his hulking figure and loomed, towered over the bleachers. His wide shoulders spread, his broad chest expanded, his breath whistled as he drew it in. One fleeting instant his transfigured face shone with a glorious light. Then, as he threw back his head and opened his lips, his face turned purple, the muscles of his cheeks and jaw rippled and strung, the veins on his forehead swelled into bulging ridges. Even the back of his neck grew red.

"Well!—Well!—Well!!!"

Ear-splitting stentorian blast! For a moment I was deafened. But I heard the echo ringing from the cliff, a pealing clarion call, beautiful and wonderful, winding away in hollow reverberation, then breaking out anew from building to building in clear concatenation.

A sea of faces whirled in the direction of that long unheard yell. Burt had stopped statue-like as if stricken in his tracks; then he came running, darting among the spectators who had leaped the fence.

Old Well-Well stood a moment with slow glance lingering on the tumult of emptying bleachers, on the moving mingling colors in the grand stand, across the green field to the gray-clad players. He staggered forward and fell.

Before I could move, a noisy crowd swarmed about him, some solicitous, many facetious. Young Burt leaped the fence and forced his way into the circle. Then they were carrying the old man down to the field and toward the clubhouse. I waited until the bleachers and field were empty. When I finally went out there was a crowd at the gate surrounding an ambulance. I caught a glimpse of Old Well-Well. He lay white and still, but his eyes were open, smiling intently. Young Burt hung over him with a pale and agitated face. Then a bell clanged and the ambulance clattered away.

THE DAY OF THE BEAST

DEDICATION

Herein is embodied my tribute to the American men who gave themselves to the service in the great war, and my sleepless and eternal gratitude for what they did for me.

ZANE GREY.

CHAPTER I

His native land! Home!

The ship glided slowly up the Narrows; and from its deck Daren Lane saw the noble black outline of the Statue of Liberty limned against the clear gold of sunset. A familiar old pang in his breast—longing and homesickness and agony, together with the physical burn of gassed lungs—seemed to swell into a profound overwhelming emotion.

"My own—my native land!" he whispered, striving to wipe the dimness from his eyes. Was it only two years or twenty since he had left his country to go to war? A sense of strangeness dawned upon him. His home-coming, so ceaselessly dreamed of by night and longed for by day, was not going to be what his hopes had created. But at that moment his joy was too great to harbor strange misgivings. How impossible for any one to understand his feelings then, except perhaps the comrades who had survived the same ordeal!

The vessel glided on. A fresh cool spring breeze with a scent of land fanned Lane's hot brow. It bore tidings from home. Almost he thought he smelled the blossoms in the orchard, and the damp newly plowed earth, and the smoke from the wood fire his mother used to bake over. A hundred clamoring thoughts strove for dominance over his mind—to enter and flash by and fade. His sight, however, except for the blur that returned again and again, held fast to the entrancing and thrilling scene—the broad glimmering sun-track of gold in the rippling channel, leading his eye to the grand bulk of America's symbol of freedom, and to the stately expanse of the Hudson River, dotted by moving ferry-boats and tugs, and to the magnificent broken sky-line of New York City, with its huge dark structures looming and its thousands of windows reflecting the fire of the sun.

It was indeed a profound and stirring moment for Daren Lane, but not quite full, not all-satisfying. The great city seemed to frown. The low line of hills in the west shone dull gray and cold. Where were the screaming siren whistles, the gay streaming flags, the boats crowded with waving people, that should have welcomed disabled soldiers who had fought for their country? Lane hoped he had long passed by bitterness, but yet something rankled in the unhealed wound of his heart.

Some one put a hand in close clasp upon his arm. Then Lane heard the scrape of a crutch on the deck, and knew who stood beside him.

"Well, Dare, old boy, does it look good to you?" asked a husky voice.

"Yes, Blair, but somehow not just what I expected," replied Lane, turning to his comrade.

"Uhuh, I get you."

Blair Maynard stood erect with the aid of a crutch. There was even a hint of pride in the poise of his uncovered head. And for once Lane saw the thin white face softening and glowing. Maynard's big brown eyes were full of tears.

"Guess I left my nerve as well as my leg over there," he said.

"Blair, it's so good to get back that we're off color," returned Lane. "On the level, I could scream like a madman."

"I'd like to weep," replied the other, with a half laugh.

"Where's Red? He oughtn't miss this."

"Poor devil! He sneaked off from me somewhere," rejoined Maynard. "Red's in pretty bad shape again. The voyage has been hard on him. I hope he'll be well enough to get his discharge when we land. I'll take him home to Middleville."

"Middleville!" echoed Lane, musingly. "Home!... Blair, does it hit you—kind of queer? Do you long, yet dread to get home?"

Maynard had no reply for that query, but his look was expressive.

"I've not heard from Helen for over a year," went on Lane, more as if speaking to himself.

"My God, Dare!" exclaimed his companion, with sudden fire. "Are you still thinking of her?"

"We—we are engaged," returned Lane, slowly. "At least we *were*. But I've had no word that she——"

"Dare, your childlike faith is due for a jar," interrupted his comrade, with bitter scorn. "Come down to earth. You're a crippled soldier—coming home—and damn lucky at that."

"Blair, what do you know—that I do not know? For long I've suspected you're wise to—to things at home. You know I haven't heard much in all these long months. My mother wrote but seldom. Lorna, my kid sister, forgot me, I guess.... Helen always was a poor correspondent. Dal answered my letters, but she never *told* me anything about home. When we first got to France I heard often from Margie Henderson and Mel Iden—crazy kind of letters—love-sick over soldiers.... But nothing for a long time now."

"At first they wrote! Ha! Ha!" burst out Maynard. "Sure, they wrote love-sick letters. They sent socks and cigarettes and candy and books. And they all wanted us to hurry back to marry them.... Then—when the months had gone by and the novelty had worn off—when we went against the hell of real war—sick or worn out, sleepless and miserable, crippled or half demented with terror and dread and longing for home—then, by God, they quit!"

"Oh, no, Blair—not all of them," remonstrated Lane, unsteadily.

"Well, old man, I'm sore, and you're about the only guy I can let out on," explained Maynard, heavily. "One thing I'm glad of—we'll face it together. Daren, we were kids together—do you remember?—playing on the commons—straddling the old water-gates over the brooks—stealing cider from the country presses—barefoot boys going to school together. We played Post-Office with the girls and Indians with the boys. We made puppy love to Dal and Mel and Helen and Margie—all of them.... Then, somehow the happy thoughtless years of youth passed.... It seems strange and sudden now—but the war came. We enlisted. We had the same ideal—you and I.— We went to France—and you know what we did there together.... Now we're on this ship— getting into port of the good old U.S.—good as bad as she is!—going home together. Thank God for that. I want to be buried in Woodlawn.... Home! Home?... We feel its meaning. But, Dare, we'll have no home—no place.... We are old—we are through—we have served—we are done.... What we dreamed of as glory will be cold ashes to our lips, bitter as gall.... You always were a dreamer, an idealist, a believer in God, truth, hope and womanhood. In spite of the war these somehow survive in you.... But Dare, old friend, steel yourself now against disappointment and disillusion."

Used as Lane was to his comrade's outbursts, this one struck singularly home to Lane's heart and made him mute. The chill of his earlier misgiving returned, augmented by a strange uneasiness, a premonition of the unknown and dreadful future. But he threw it off. Faith would not die in Lane. It could not die utterly because of what he felt in himself. Yet—what was in store for him? Why was his hope so unquenchable? There could be no *resurgam* for Daren Lane. Resignation should have brought him peace—peace—when every nerve in his shell-shocked body racked him—when he could not subdue a mounting hope that all would be well at home— when he quivered at thought of mother, sister, sweetheart!

The ship glided on under the shadow of America's emblem—a bronze woman of noble proportions, holding out a light to ships that came in the night—a welcome to all the world. Daren Lane held to his maimed comrade while they stood bare-headed and erect for that moment when the, ship passed the statue. Lane knew what Blair felt. But nothing of what that feeling was could ever be spoken. The deck of the ship was now crowded with passengers, yet they were seemingly dead to anything more than a safe arrival at their destination. They were not crippled American soldiers. Except these two there were none in service uniforms. There across the windy space of water loomed the many-eyed buildings, suggestive of the great city. A low roar of traffic came on the breeze. Passengers and crew of the liner were glad to dock before dark. They took no notice of the rigid, erect soldiers. Lane, arm in arm with Blair, face to the front, stood absorbed in his sense of a nameless sublimity for them while passing the Statue of Liberty. The spirit of the first man who ever breathed of freedom for the human race burned as a white flame in the heart of Lane and his comrade. But it was not so much that spirit which held them erect, aloof, proud. It was a supreme consciousness of immeasurable sacrifice for an ideal that existed only in the breasts of men and women kindred to them—an unutterable and never-to-be-spoken glory of the duty done for others, but that they owed themselves. They had sustained immense loss of health and happiness; the future seemed like the gray, cold, gloomy expanse of the river; and there could never be any reward except this white fire of their souls. Nameless! But it was the increasing purpose that ran through the ages.

The ship docked at dark. Lane left Blair at the rail, gloomily gazing down at the confusion and bustle on the wharf, and went below to search for their comrade, Red Payson. He found him in his stateroom, half crouched on the berth, apparently oblivious to the important moment. It required a little effort to rouse Payson. He was a slight boy, not over twenty-two, sallow-faced and freckled, with hair that gave him the only name his comrades knew him by. Lane packed the boy's few possessions and talked vehemently all the time. Red braced up, ready to go, but he had little to say and that with the weary nonchalance habitual with him. Lane helped him up on deck, and the exertion, slight as it was, brought home to Lane that he needed help himself. They found Maynard waiting.

"Well, here we are—the Three Musketeers," said Lane, in a voice he tried to make cheerful.

"Where's the band?" inquired Maynard, sardonically.

"Gay old New York—and me broke!" exclaimed Red Payson, as if to himself.

Then the three stood by the rail, at the gangplank, waiting for the hurried stream of passengers to disembark. Down on the wharf under the glaring white lights, swarmed a crowd from which rose a babel of voices. A whistle blew sharply at intervals. The whirr and honk of taxicabs, and the jangle of trolley cars, sounded beyond the wide dark portal of the dock-house. The murky water below splashed between ship and pier. Deep voices rang out, and merry laughs, and shrill glad cries of welcome. The bright light shone down upon a motley, dark-garbed mass, moving slowly. The spirit of the occasion was manifest.

When the three disabled soldiers, the last passengers to disembark, slowly and laboriously descended to the wharf, no one offered to help them, no one waited with a smile and hand-clasp of welcome. No one saw them, except a burly policeman, who evidently had charge of the traffic at the door. He poked his club into the ribs of the one-legged, slowly shuffling Maynard and said with cheerful gruffness: "Step lively, Buddy, step lively!"

Lane, with his two comrades, spent three days at a barracks-hospital for soldiers in Bedford Park. It was a long flimsy structure, bare except for rows of cots along each wall, and stoves at middle, and each end. The place was overcrowded with disabled service men, all worse off than Lane and his comrades. Lane felt that he really was keeping a sicker man than himself from what attention the hospital afforded. So he was glad, at the end of the third day, to find they could be discharged from the army.

-   This enforced stay, when he knew he was on his way home, had seemed almost unbearable to Lane. He felt that he had the strength to get home, and that was about all. He began to expectorate blood—no unusual thing for him—but this time to such extent that he feared the return of hemorrhage. The nights seemed sleepless, burning, black voids; and the days were hideous with noise and distraction. He wanted to think about the fact that he was home—an astounding and unbelievable thing. Once he went down to the city and walked on Broadway and Fifth Avenue, taxing his endurance to the limit. But he had become used to pain and exhaustion. So long as he could keep up he did not mind.

That day three powerful impressions were forced upon Lane, never to be effaced. First he found that the change in him was vast and incalculable and vague. He could divine but not understand. Secondly, the men of the service, disabled or not, were old stories to New Yorkers. Lane saw soldiers begging from pedestrians. He muttered to himself: "By God, I'll starve to death before I ever do that!" He could not detect any aloofness on the part of passers-by. They were just inattentive. Lane remembered with sudden shock how differently soldiers had been regarded two or three years ago. He had read lengthy newspaper accounts of the wild and magnificent welcome accorded to the first soldiers to return to New York. How strange the contrast! But that was long ago—past history—buried under the immense and hurried and inscrutable changes of a nation. Lane divined that, as he felt the mighty resistless throb of the great city. His third and strongest impression concerned the women he met and passed on the streets. Their lips and cheeks were rouged. Their dresses were cut too low at the neck. But even this fashion was not nearly so striking as the short skirts, cut off at the knees, and in many cases above. At first this roused a strange amaze in Lane. "What's the idea, I wonder?" he mused. But in the end it disgusted him. He reflected that for two swift years he had been out of the track of events, away from centers of population. Paris itself had held no attraction for him. Dreamer and brooder, he had failed to see the material things. But this third impression troubled him more than the other two and stirred thoughts he tried to dispel. Returning to the barracks he learned that he and his friends would be free on the morrow; and long into the night he rejoiced in the knowledge. Free! The grinding, incomprehensible Juggernaut and himself were at the parting of the ways. Before he went to sleep he remembered a forgotten prayer his mother had taught him. His ordeal was over. What had happened did not matter. The Hell was past and he must bury memory. Whether or not he had a month or a year to live it must be lived without memories of his ordeal.

Next day, at the railroad station, even at the moment of departure, Lane and Blair Maynard had their problem with Red Payson. He did not want to go to Blair's home.

"But hell, Red, you haven't any home—any place to go," blurted out Maynard.

So they argued with him, and implored him, and reasoned with him. Since his discharge from the hospital in France Payson had always been cool, weary, abstracted, difficult to reach. And here at the last he grew strangely aloof and stubborn. Every word that bore relation to his own welfare seemed only to alienate him the more. Lane sensed this.

"See here, Red," he said, "hasn't it occurred to you that Blair and I need you?"

"Need me? What!" he exclaimed, with perceptible change of tone, though it was incredulous.

"Sure," interposed Blair.

"Red—listen," continued Lane, speaking low and with difficulty. "Blair and I have been through the—the whole show together.... And we've been in the hospitals with you for months.... We've all got—sort of to rely on each other.... Let's stick it out to the end. I guess—you know—we may not have a long time...."

Lane's voice trailed off. Then the stony face of the listener changed for a fleeting second.

"Boys, I'll go over with you," he said.

And then the maimed Blair, awkward with his crutch and bag, insisted on helping Lane get Red aboard the train. Red could just about walk. Sombrely they clambered up the steps into the Pullman.

Middleville was a prosperous and thriving inland town of twenty thousand inhabitants, identical with many towns of about the same size in the middle and eastern United States.

Lane had been born there and had lived there all his life, seldom having been away up to the advent of the war. So that the memories of home and town and place, which he carried away from America with him, had never had any chance, up to the time of his departure, to change from the vivid, exaggerated image of boyhood. Since he had left Middleville he had seen great cities, palaces, castles, edifices, he had crossed great rivers, he had traveled thousands of miles, he had looked down some of the famous thoroughfares of the world.

Was this then the reason that Middleville, upon his arrival, seemed so strange, sordid, shrunken, so vastly changed? He stared, even while he helped Payson off the train—stared at the little brick station at once so familiar and yet so strange, that had held a place of dignity in the picture of his memory. The moment was one of shock.

Then he was distracted from his pondering by tearful and joyful cries, and deeper voices of men. He looked up to recognize Blair's mother, father, sister; and men and women whose faces appeared familiar, but whose names he could not recall. His acute faculty of perception took quick note of a change in Blair's mother. Lane turned his gaze away. The agony of joy and sorrow—the light of her face—was more than Lane could stand. He looked at the sister Margaret—a tall, fair girl. She had paint on her cheeks. She did not see Lane. Her strained gaze held a beautiful and piercing intentness. Then her eyes opened wide, her hand went to cover her mouth, and she cried out: "Oh Blair!—poor boy! Brother!"

Only Lane heard her. The others were crying out themselves as Blair's gray-haired mother received him into her arms. She seemed a proud woman, broken and unsteady. Red Payson's grip on Lane's arm told what that scene meant to him. How pitiful the vain effort of Blair's people to hide their horror! Presently mother and sister and women relatives fell aside to let the soldier boy meet his father. This was something that rang the bells in Lane's heart. Men were different, and Blair faced his father differently. The wild boy had come home—the scapegoat of many Middleville escapades had returned—the ne'er-do-well sought his father's house. He had come home to die. It was there in Blair's white face—the dreadful truth. He wore a ribbon on his breast and he leaned on a crutch. For the instant, as father and son faced each other, there was something in Blair's poise, his look of an eagle, that carried home a poignant sense of his greatness. Lane thrilled with it and a lump constricted his throat. Then with Blair's ringing "Dad!" and the father's deep and broken: "My son! My son!" the two embraced.

In a stifling moment more it seemed, attention turned on Red Payson, who stood nearest. Blair's folk were eager, kind, soft-spoken and warm in their welcome.

Then it came Lane's turn, and what they said or did he scarcely knew, until Margaret kissed him. "Oh, Dare! I'm *so* glad to see you home." Tears were standing in her clear blue eyes. "You're changed, but—not—not so much as Blair."

Lane responded as best he could, and presently he found himself standing at the curb, watching the car move away.

"Come out to-morrow," called back Blair.

The Maynard's car was carrying his comrades away. His first feeling was one of gladness— the next of relief. He could be alone now—alone to find out what had happened to him, and to this strange Middleville. An old negro wearing a blue uniform accosted Lane, shook hands with him, asked him if he had any baggage. "Yas sir, I sho knowed you, Mistah Dare Lane. But you looks powerful bad."

Lane crossed the station platform, and the railroad yard and tracks, to make a short cut in the direction of his home. He shrank from meeting any one. He had not sent word just when he would arrive, though he had written his mother from New York that it would be soon, He was glad that no one belonging to him had been at the station. He wanted to see his mother in his home. Walking fast exhausted him, and he had to rest. How dead his legs felt! In fact he felt queer all over. The old burn and gnaw in his breast had expanded to a heavy, full, suffocating sensation. Yet his blood seemed to race. Suddenly an overwhelming emotion of rapture flooded over him. Home at last! He did not think of any one. He was walking across the railroad yards where as a boy he had been wont to steal rides on freight trains. Soon he reached the bridge. In the gathering twilight he halted to clutch at the railing and look out across where the waters met—where Sycamore Creek flowed into Middleville River. The roar of water falling over the dam came melodiously and stirringly to his ears. And as he looked again he was assailed by that strange sense of littleness, of shrunkenness, which had struck him so forcibly at the station. He listened to the murmur of running water. Then, while the sweetness of joy pervaded him, there seemed to rise from below or across the river or from somewhere the same strange misgiving, a keener dread, a chill that was not in the air, a fatal portent of the future. Why should this come to mock him at such a sacred and beautiful moment?

Passers-by stared at Lane, and some of them whispered, and one hesitated, as if impelled to speak. Wheeling away Lane crossed the bridge, turned up River Street, soon turned off again into a darker street, and reaching High School Park he sat down to rest again. He was almost spent. The park was quiet and lonely. The bare trees showed their skeleton outlines against the cold sky. It was March and the air was raw and chilly. This park that had once been a wonderful place now appeared so small. Everything he saw was familiar yet grotesque in the way it had become dwarfed. Across the street from where he sat lights shone in the windows of a house. He knew the place. Who lived there? One of the girls—he had forgotten which. From somewhere the discordance of a Victrola jarred on Lane's sensitive ears.

Lifting his bag he proceeded on his way, halting every little while to catch his breath. When he turned a corner into a side street, recognizing every tree and gate and house, there came a gathering and swelling of his emotions and he began to weaken and shake. He was afraid he could not make it half way up the street. But he kept on. The torture now was more a mingled rapture and grief than the physical protest of his racked body. At last he saw the modest little house—and then he stood at the gate, quivering. Home! A light in the window of his old room! A terrible and tremendous storm of feeling forced him to lean on the gate. How many endless hours had the pictured memory of that house haunted him? There was the beloved room where he had lived and slept and read, and cherished over his books and over his compositions a secret hope and ambition to make of himself an author. How strange to remember that! But it was true. His day labor at Manton's office, for all the years since he had graduated from High School, had been only a means to an end. No one had dreamed of his dream. Then the war had come and now his hope, if not his faith, was dead. Never before had the realization been so galling, so bitter. Endlessly and eternally he must be concerned with himself. He had driven that habit of thought away a million times, but it would return. All he had prayed for was to get home—only to reach home alive—to see his mother, and his sister Lorna—and Helen—and then.... But he was here now and all that prayer was falsehood. Just to get home was not enough.. He had been cheated of career, love, happiness.

It required extreme effort to cross the little yard, to mount the porch. In a moment more he would see his mother. He heard her within, somewhere at the back of the house. Wherefore he tip-toed round to the kitchen door. Here he paused, quaking. A cold sweat broke out all over him. Why was this return so dreadful? He pressed a shaking hand over his heart. How surely he knew he could not deceive his mother! The moment she saw him, after the first flash of joy, she would see the wreck of the boy she had let go to war. Lane choked over his emotion, but he could not spare her. Opening the door he entered.

There she stood at the stove and she looked up at the sound he made. Yes! but stranger than all other changes was the change in her. She was not the mother of his boyhood. Nor was the change alone age or grief or wasted cheek. The moment tore cruelly at Lane's heart. She did not recognize him swiftly. But when she did....

"Oh God!... Daren! My boy!" she whispered.

"Mother!"

CHAPTER II

His mother divined what he knew. And her embrace was so close, almost fierce in its tenderness, her voice so broken, that Lane could only hide his face over her, and shut his eyes, and shudder in an ecstasy. God alone had omniscience to tell what his soul needed, but something of it was embodied in home and mother.

That first acute moment past, he released her, and she clung to his hands, her face upturned, her eyes full of pain and joy, and woman's searching power, while she broke into almost incoherent speech; and he responded in feeling, though he caught little of the content of her words, and scarcely knew what he was saying.

Then he reeled a little and the kitchen dimmed in his sight. Sinking into a chair and leaning on the table he fought his weakness. He came close to fainting. But he held on to his sense, aware of his mother fluttering over him. Gradually the spell passed.

"Mother—maybe I'm starved," he said, smiling at her.

That practical speech released the strain and inspired his mother to action. She began to bustle round the kitchen, talking all the while. Lane watched her and listened, and spoke occasionally. Once he asked about his sister Lorna, but his mother either did not hear or chose not to reply. All she said was music to his ears, yet not quite what his heart longed for. He began to distrust this strange longing. There was something wrong with his mind. His faculties seemed too sensitive. Every word his mother uttered was news, surprising, unusual, as if it emanated from a home-world that had changed. And presently she dropped into complaint at the hard times and the cost of everything.

"Mother," he interrupted, "I didn't blow my money. I've saved nearly a year's pay. It's yours."

"But, Daren, you'll need money," she protested.

"Not much. And maybe—I'll be strong enough to go to work—presently," he said, hopefully. "Do you think Manton will take me back—half days at first?"

"I have my doubts, Daren," she replied, soberly. "Hattie Wilson has your old job. And I hear they're pleased with her. Few of the boys got their places back."

"Hattie Wilson!" exclaimed Lane. "Why, she was a kid in the eighth grade when I left home."

"Yes, my son. But that was nearly three years ago. And the children have sprung up like weeds. Wild weeds!"

"Well! That tousle-headed Wilson kid!" mused Lane. An uneasy conviction of having been forgotten dawned upon Lane. He remembered Blair Maynard's bitter prophecy, which he had been unable to accept.

"Anyway, Daren, are you able to work?" asked his mother.

"Sure," he replied, lying cheerfully, with a smile on his face. "Not hard work, just yet, but I can do something."

His mother did not share his enthusiasm. She went on preparing the supper.

"How do you manage to get along?" inquired Lane.

"Lord only knows," she replied, sombrely. "It has been very hard. When you left home I had only the interest on your father's life insurance. I sold the farm—"

"Oh, no!" exclaimed Lane, with a rush of boyhood memories.

"I had to," she went on. "I made that money help out for a long time. Then I—I mortgaged this place.... Things cost so terribly. And Lorna had to have so much more.... But she's just left school and gone to work. That helps."

"Lorna left school!" ejaculated Lane, incredulously. "Why, mother, she was only a child. Thirteen years old when I left! She'll miss her education. I'll send her back."

"Well, son, I doubt if you can make Lorna do anything she doesn't want to do," returned his mother. "She wanted to quit school—to earn money. Whatever she was when you left home she's grown up now. You'll not know her."

"Know Lorna! Why, mother dear, I carried Lorna's picture all through the war."

"You won't know her," returned Mrs. Lane, positively. "My boy, these years so short to you have been ages here at home. You will find your sister—different from the little girl you left. You'll find all the girls you knew changed—changed. I have given up trying to understand what's come over the world."

"How—about Helen?" inquired Lane, with strange reluctance and shyness.

"Helen who?" asked his mother.

"Helen Wrapp, of course," replied Lane, quickly in his surprise. "The girl I was engaged to when I left."

"Oh!—I had forgotten," she sighed.

"Hasn't Helen been here to see you?"

"Let me see—well, now you tax me—I think she did come once—right after you left."

"Do you—ever see her?" he asked, with slow heave of breast.

"Yes, now and then, as she rides by in an automobile. But she never sees me.... Daren, I don't know what your—your—that engagement means to you, but I must tell you—Helen Wrapp doesn't conduct herself as if she were engaged. Still, I don't know what's in the heads of girls to-day. I can only compare the present with the past."

Lane did not inquire further and his mother did not offer more comment. At the moment he heard a motor car out in front of the house, a girl's shrill voice in laughter, the slamming of a car-door—then light, quick footsteps on the porch. Lane could look from where he sat to the front door—only a few yards down the short hall. The door opened. A girl entered.

"That's Lorna," said Lane's mother. He grew aware that she bent a curious gaze upon his face.

Lane rose to his feet with his heart pounding, and a strange sense of expectancy. His little sister! Never during the endless months of drudgery, strife and conflict, and agony, had he forgotten Lorna. Not duty, nor patriotism, had forced him to enlist in the army before the draft. It had been an ideal which he imagined he shared with the millions of American boys who entered the service. Too deep ever to be spoken of! The barbarous and simian Hun, with his black record against Belgian, and French women, should never set foot on American soil.

In the lamplight Lane saw this sister throw coat and hat on the banister, come down the hall and enter the kitchen. She seemed tall, but her short skirt counteracted that effect. Her bobbed hair, curly and rebellious, of a rich brown-red color, framed a pretty face Lane surely remembered. But yet not the same! He had carried away memory of a child's face and this was a woman's. It was bright, piquant, with darkly glancing eyes, and vivid cheeks, and carmine lips.

"Oh, *hot dog*! if it isn't Dare!" she squealed, and with radiant look she ran into his arms.

The moment, or moments, of that meeting between brother and sister passed, leaving Lane conscious of hearty welcome and a sense of unreality. He could not at once adjust his mental faculties to an incomprehensible difference affecting everything.

They sat down to supper, and Lane, sick, dazed, weak, found eating his first meal at home as different as everything else from what he had expected. There had been no lack of warmth or love in Lorna's welcome, but he suffered disappointment. Again for the hundredth time he put it aside and blamed his morbid condition. Nothing must inhibit his gladness.

Lorna gave Lane no chance to question her. She was eager, voluble, curious, and most disconcertingly oblivious of a possible sensitiveness in Lane.

"Dare, you look like a dead one," she said. "Did you get shot, bayoneted, gassed, shell-shocked and all the rest? Did you go over the top? Did you kill any Germans? Gee! did you get to ride in a war-plane? Come across, now, and tell me."

"I guess about—everything happened to me—except going west," returned Lane. "But I don't want to talk about that. I'm too glad to be home."

"What's that on your breast?" she queried, suddenly, pointing at the *Croix de Guerre* he wore.

"That? Lorna, that's my medal."

"Gee! Let me see." She got up and came round to peer down closely, to finger the decoration. "French! I never saw one before.... Daren, haven't you an American medal too?"

"No."

"Why not?"

"My dear sister, that's hard to say. Because I didn't deserve it, most likely."

She leaned back to gaze more thoughtfully at him.

"What did you get this for?"

"It's a long story. Some day I'll tell you."

"Are you proud of it?"

For answer he only smiled at her.

"It's so long since the war I've forgotten so many things," she said, wonderingly. Then she smiled sweetly. "Dare, I'm proud of you."

That was a moment in which his former emotion seemed to stir for her. Evidently she had lost track of something once memorable. She was groping back for childish impressions. It was the only indication of softness he had felt in her. How impossible to believe Lorna was only fifteen! He could form no permanent conception of her. But in that moment he sensed something akin to a sister's sympathy, some vague and indefinable thought in her, too big for her to grasp. He never felt it again. The serious sweet mood vanished.

"Hot dog! I've a brother with the *Croix de Guerre*. I'll swell up over that. I'll crow over some of these Janes."

Thus she talked on while eating her supper. And Lane tried to eat while he watched her. Presently he moved his chair near to the stove. Lorna did not wait upon her mother. It was the mother who did the waiting, as silently she moved from table to stove.

Lorna's waist was cut so low that it showed the swell of her breast. The red color of her cheeks, high up near her temples, was not altogether the rosy line of health and youth. Her eyebrows were only faint, thin, curved lines, oriental in effect. She appeared to be unusually well-developed in body for so young a girl. And the air of sophistication, of experience that seemed a part of her manner completely mystified Lane. If it had not been for the slangy speech, and the false color in her face, he would have been amused at what he might have termed his little sister's posing as a woman of the world. But in the light of these he grew doubtful of his impression. Lastly, he saw that she wore her stockings rolled below her knees and that the edge of her short skirt permitted several inches of her bare legs to be seen. And at that he did not know what to think. He was stunned.

"Daren, you served a while under Captain Thesel in the war," she said.

"Yes, I guess I did," replied Lane, with sombre memory resurging.

"Do you know he lives here?"

"I knew him here in Middleville several years before the war."

"He's danced with me at the Armory. Some swell dancer! He and Dick Swann and Hardy MacLean sometimes drop in at the Armory on Saturday nights. Captain Thesel is chasing Mrs. Clemhorn now. They're always together.... Daren, did he ever have it in for you?"

"He never liked me. We never got along here in Middleville. And naturally in the service when he was a captain and I only a private—we didn't get along any better."

"Well, I've heard Captain Thesel was to blame for—for what was said about you last summer when he came home."

"And what was that, Lorna?" queried Lane, curiously puzzled at her, and darkly conscious of the ill omen that had preceded him home.

"You'll not hear it from me," declared Lorna, spiritedly. "But that *Croix de Guerre* doesn't agree with it, I'll tell the world."

A little frown puckered her smooth brow and there was a gleam in her eye.

"Seems to me I heard some of the kids talking last summer," she mused, ponderingly. "Vane Thesel was stuck on Mel Iden and Dot Dalrymple both before the war. Dot handed him a lemon. He's still trying to rush Dot, and the gossip is he'd go after Mel even now on the sly, if she'd stand for it."

"Why on the sly?" inquired Lane. "Before I left home Mel Iden was about the prettiest and most popular girl in Middleville. Her people were poor, and ordinary, perhaps, but she was the equal of any one."

"Thesel couldn't rush Mel now and get away with it, unless on the q-t," replied Lorna. "Haven't you heard about Mel?"

"No, you see the fact is, my few correspondents rather neglected to send me news," said Lane.

The significance of this was lost upon his sister. She giggled. "Hot dog! You've got some kicks coming, I'll say!"

"Is that so," returned Lane, with irritation. "A few more or less won't matter.... Lorna, do you know Helen Wrapp?"

"That red-headed dame!" burst out Lorna, with heat. "I should smile I do. She's one who doesn't shake a shimmy on tea, believe me."

Lane was somewhat at a loss to understand his sister's intimation, but as it was vulgarly inimical, and seemed to hold some subtle personal scorn or jealousy, he shrank from questioning her. This talk with his sister was the most unreal happening he had ever experienced. He could not adjust himself to its verity.

"Helen Wrapp is nutty about Dick Swann," went on Lorna. "She drives down to the office after——"

"Lorna, do you know Helen and I are engaged?" interrupted Lane.

"Hot dog!" was that young lady's exposition of utter amaze. She stared at her brother.

"We were engaged," continued Lane. "She wore my ring. When I enlisted she wanted me to marry her before I left. But I wouldn't do that."

Lorna promptly recovered from her amaze. "Well, it's a damn lucky thing you didn't take her up on that marriage stuff."

There was a glint of dark youthful passion in Lorna's face. Lane felt rise in him a desire to bid her sharply to omit slang and profanity from the conversation. But the desire faded before his bewilderment. All had suffered change. What had he come home to? There was no clear answer. But whatever it was, he felt it to be enormous and staggering. And he meant to find out. Weary as was his mind, it grasped peculiar significances and deep portents.

"Lorna, where do you work?" he began, shifting his interest.

"At Swann's," she replied.

"In the office—at the foundry?" he asked.

"No. Mr. Swann's at the head of the leather works."

"What do you do?"

"I type letters," she answered, and rose to make him a little bow that held the movement and the suggestion of a dancer.

"You've learned stenography?" he asked, in surprise.

"I'm learning shorthand," replied Lorna. "You see I had only a few weeks in business school before Dick got me the job."

"Dick Swann? Do you work for him?"

"No. For the superintendent, Mr. Fryer. But I go to Dick's office to do letters for him some of the time."

She appeared frank and nonchalant, evidently a little proud of her important position. She posed before Lane and pirouetted with fancy little steps.

"Say, Dare, won't you teach me a new dance—right from Paris?" she interposed. "Something that will put the shimmy and toddle out of biz?"

"Lorna, I don't know what the shimmy and toddle are. I've only heard of them."

"Buried alive, I'll say," she retorted.

Lane bit his tongue to keep back a hot reprimand. He looked at his mother, who was clearing off the supper table. She looked sad. The light had left her worn face. Lane did not feel sure of his ground here. So he controlled his feelings and directed his interest toward more news.

"Of course Dick Swann was in the service?" he asked.

"No. He didn't go," replied Lorna.

The information struck Lane singularly. Dick Swann had always been a prominent figure in the Middleville battery, in those seemingly long past years since before the war.

"Why didn't Dick go into the service? Why didn't the draft get him?"

"He had poor eyesight, and his father needed him at the iron works."

"Poor eyesight!" ejaculated Lane. "He was the best shot in the battery—the best hunter among the boys. Well, that's funny."

"Daren, there are people who called Dick Swann a slacker," returned Lorna, as if forced to give this information. "But I never saw that it hurt him. He's rich now. His uncle left him a million, and his father will leave him another. And I'll say it's the money people want these days."

The materialism so pregnant in Lorna's half bitter reply checked Lane's further questioning. He edged closer to the stove, feeling a little cold. A shadow drifted across the warmth and glow of his mind. At home now he was to be confronted with a monstrous and insupportable truth—the craven cowardice of the man who had been eligible to service in army or navy, and who had evaded it. In camp and trench and dug-out he had heard of the army of slackers. And of all the vile and stark profanity which the war gave birth to on the lips of miserable and maimed soldiers, that flung on the slackers was the worst.

"I've got a date to go to the movies," said Lorna, and she bounced out of the kitchen into the hall singing:

"Oh by heck You never saw a wreck Like the wreck she made of me."

She went upstairs, while Lane sat there trying to adapt himself to a new and unintelligible environment. His mother began washing the dishes. Lane felt her gaze upon his face, and he struggled against all the weaknesses that beset him.

"Mother, doesn't Lorna help you with the house work?" he asked.

"She used to. But not any more."

"Do you let her go out at night to the movies—dances, and all that?"

Mrs. Lane made a gesture of helplessness. "Lorna goes out all the time. She's never here. She stays out until midnight—one o'clock—later. She's popular with the boys. I couldn't stop her even if I wanted to. Girls can't be stopped these days. I do all I can for her—make her dresses—slave for her—hoping she'll find a good husband. But the young men are not marrying."

"Good Heavens, are you already looking for a husband for Lorna?" broke out Lane.

"You don't understand, Dare. You've been away so long. Wait till you've seen what girls—are nowadays. Then you'll not wonder that I'd like to see Lorna settled."

"Mother, you're right," he said, gravely. "I've been away so—long. But I'm back home now. I'll soon get on to things. And I'll help you. I'll take Lorna in hand. I'll relieve you of a whole lot."

"You were always a good boy, Daren, to me and Lorna," murmured Mrs. Lane, almost in tears. "It's cheered me to get you home, yet.... Oh, if you were well and strong!"

"Never mind, mother. I'll get better," he replied, rising to take up his bag. "I guess now I'd better go to bed. I'm just about all in.... Wonder how Blair and Red are."

His mother followed him up the narrow stairway, talking, trying to pretend she did not see his dragging steps, his clutch on the banisters.

"Your room's just as you left it," she said, opening the door. Then on the threshold she kissed him. "My son, I thank God you have come home alive. You give me hope in—in spite of all.... If you need me, call. Good night."

Lane was alone in the little room that had lived in waking and dreaming thought. Except to appear strangely smaller, it had not changed. His bed and desk—the old bureau—the few pictures—the bookcase he had built himself—these were identical with images in his memory.

A sweet and wonderful emotion of peace pervaded his soul—fulfilment at last of the soldier's endless longing for home, bed, quiet, rest.

"If I have to die—I can do it *now* without hate of all around me," he whispered, in the passion of his spirit.

But as he sat upon his bed, trying with shaking and clumsy hands to undress himself, that exalted mood flashed by. Some of the dearest memories of his life were associated with this little room. Here he had dreamed; here he had read and studied; here he had fought out some of the poignant battles of youth. So much of life seemed behind him. At last he got undressed, and extinguishing the light, he crawled into bed.

The darkness was welcome, and the quiet was exquisitely soothing. He lay there, staring into the blackness, feeling his body sink slowly as if weighted. How cool and soft the touch of sheets! Then, the river of throbbing fire that was his blood, seemed to move again. And the dull ache, deep in the bones, possessed his nerves. In his breast there began a vibrating, as if thousands of tiny bubbles were being pricked to bursting in his lungs. And the itch to cough came back to his throat. And all his flesh seemed in contention with a slowly ebbing force. Sleep might come perhaps after pain had lulled. His heart beat unsteadily and weakly, sometimes with a strange little flutter. How many weary interminable hours had he endured! But to-night he was too far spent, too far gone for long wakefulness. He drifted away and sank as if into black oblivion where there sounded the dreadful roll of drums, and images moved under gray clouds, and men were running like phantoms. He awoke from nightmares, wet with cold sweat, and lay staring again at the blackness, once more alive to recurrent pain. Pain that was an old, old story, yet ever acute and insistent and merciless.

The night wore on, hour by hour. The courthouse clock rang out one single deep mellow clang. One o'clock! Lane thrilled to the sound. It brought back the school days, the vacation days, the Indian summer days when the hills were golden and the purple haze hung over the land—the days that were to be no more for Daren Lane.

In the distance somewhere a motor-car hummed, and came closer, louder down the street, to slow its sound with sliding creak and jar outside in front of the house. Lane heard laughter and voices of a party of young people. Footsteps, heavy and light, came up the walk, and on to the porch. Lorna was returning rather late from the motion-picture, thought Lane, and he raised his head from the pillow, to lean toward the open window, listening.

"Come across, kiddo," said a boy's voice, husky and low.

Lane heard a kiss—then another.

"Cheese it, you boob!"

"Gee, your gettin' snippy. Say, will you ride out to Flesher's to-morrow night?"

"Nothing doing, I've got a date. Good night."

The hall door below opened and shut. Footsteps thumped off the porch and out to the street. Lane heard the giggle of girls, the snap of a car-door, the creaking of wheels, and then a low hum, dying away.

Lorna came slowly up stairs to enter her room, moving quietly. And Lane lay on his bed, wide-eyed, staring into the blackness. "My little sister," he whispered to himself. And the words that had meant so much seemed a mockery.

CHAPTER III

Lane saw the casement of his window grow gray with the glimmering light of dawn. After that he slept several hours. When he awoke it was nine o'clock. The long night with its morbid dreams and thoughts had passed, and in the sunshine of day he saw things differently.

To move, to get up was not an easy task. It took stern will, and all the strength of muscle he had left, and when he finally achieved it there was a clammy dew of pain upon his face. With slow guarded movements he began to dress himself. Any sudden or violent action might burst the delicate gassed spots in his lungs or throw out of place one of the lower vertebrae of his spine. The former meant death, and the latter bent his body like a letter S and caused such excruciating agony that it was worse than death. These were his two ever-present perils. The other aches and pains he could endure.

He shaved and put on clean things, and his best coat, and surveyed himself in the little mirror. He saw a thin face, white as marble, but he was not ashamed of it. His story was there to read, if any one had kind enough eyes to see. What would Helen think of him—and Margaret Maynard—and Dal—and Mel Iden? Bitter curiosity seemed his strongest feeling concerning his fiancee. He would hold her as engaged to him until she informed him she was not. As for the others, thought of them quickened his interest, especially in Mel. What had happened to her.

It was going to be wonderful to meet them—and to meet everybody he had once known. Wonderful because he would see what the war had done to them and they would see what it had done to him. A peculiar significance lay between his sister and Helen—all these girls, and the fact of his having gone to war.

"They may not think of it, but *I know*," he muttered to himself. And he sat down upon his bed to plan how best to meet them, and others. He did not know what he was going to encounter, but he fortified himself against calamity. Strange portent of this had crossed the sea to haunt him. As soon as he was sure of what had happened in Middleville, of the attitude people would have toward a crippled soldier, and of what he could do with the month or year that might be left him to live, then he would know his own mind. All he sensed now was that there had been some monstrous inexplicable alteration in hope, love, life. His ordeal of physical strife, loneliness, longing was now over, for he was back home. But he divined that his greater ordeal lay before him, here in this little house, and out there in Middleville. All the subtlety, intelligence, and bitter vision developed by the war sharpened here to confront him with terrible possibilities. Had his countrymen, his people, his friends, his sweetheart, all failed him? Was there justice in Blair Maynard's scorn? Lane's faith cried out in revolt. He augmented all possible catastrophe, and then could not believe that he had sacrificed himself in vain. He knew himself. In him was embodied all the potentiality for hope of the future. And it was with the front and stride of a soldier, facing the mystery, the ingratitude, the ignorance and hell of war, that he left his room and went down stairs to meet the evils in store.

His mother was not in the kitchen. The door stood open. He heard her outside talking to a neighbor woman, over the fence.

"—Daren looks dreadful," his mother was saying in low voice. "He could hardly walk... It breaks my heart. I'm glad to have him along—but to see him waste away, day by day, like Mary Dean's boy—" she broke off.

"Too bad! It's a pity," replied the neighbor. "Sad—now it comes home to us. My son Ted came in last night and said he'd talked with a boy who'd seen young Maynard and the strange soldier who was with him. They must be worse off than Daren—Blair Maynard with only one leg and—"

"Mother, where are you? I'm hungry," called Lane, interrupting that conversation.

She came hurriedly in, at once fearful he might have heard, and solicitous for his welfare.

"Daren, you look better in daylight—not so white," she said. "You sit down now, and let me get your breakfast."

Lane managed to eat a little this morning, which fact delighted his mother.

"I'm going to see Dr. Bronson," said Lane, presently. "Then I'll go to Manton's, and round town a little. And if I don't tire out I'll call on Helen. Of course Lorna has gone to work?"

"Oh yes, she leaves at half after eight."

"Mother, I was awake last night when she got home," went on Lane, seriously. "It was one o'clock. She came in a car. I heard girls tittering. And some boy came up on the porch with Lorna and kissed her. Well, that might not mean much—but something about their talk, the way it was done—makes me pretty sick. Did you know this sort of thing was going on?"

"Yes. And I've talked with mothers who have girls Lorna's age. They've all run wild the last year or so. Dances and rides! Last summer I was worried half to death. But we mothers don't think the girls are really *bad*. They're just crazy for fun, excitement, boys. Times and pleasures have changed. The girls say the mothers don't understand. Maybe we don't. I try to be patient. I trust Lorna. I can't see through it all."

"Don't worry, mother," said Lane, patting her hand. "I'll see through it for you. And if Lorna is—well, running too much—wild as you said—I'll stop her."

His mother shook her head.

"One thing we mothers all agree on. These girls, of this generation, say fourteen to sixteen, *can't* be stopped."

"Then that is a serious matter. It must be a peculiarity of the day. Maybe the war left this condition."

"The war changed all things, my son," replied his mother, sadly.

Lane walked thoughtfully down the street toward Doctor Bronson's office. As long as he walked slowly he managed not to give any hint of his weakness. The sun was shining with steely brightness and the March wind was living up to its fame. He longed for summer and hot days in quiet woods or fields where daisies bloomed. Would he live to see the Indian summer days, the smoky haze, the purple asters?

Lane was admitted at once into the office of Doctor Bronson, a little, gray, slight man with shrewd, kind eyes and a thoughtful brow. For years he had been a friend as well as physician to the Lanes, and he had always liked Daren. His surprise was great and his welcome warm. But a moment later he gazed at Lane with piercing eyes.

"Look here, boy, did you go to the bad over there?" he demanded.

"How do you mean, Doctor?"

"Did you let down—debase yourself morally?"

"No. But I went to the bad physically and spiritually."

"I see that. I don't like the color of your face.... Well, well, Daren. It was hell, wasn't it? Did you kill a couple of Huns for me?"

Questions like this latter one always alienated Lane in some unaccountable way. It must have been revealed in his face.

"Never mind, Daren. I see that you *did*.... I'm glad you're back alive. Now what can I do for you?"

"I've been discharged from three hospitals in the last two months—not because I was well, but because I was in better shape than some other poor devil. Those doctors in the service grew hard—they had to be hard—but they saw the worst, the agony of the war. I always felt sorry for them. They never seemed to eat or sleep or rest. They had no time to save a man. It was cut him up or tie him up—then on to the next.... Now, Doc, I want you to look me over and—well—tell me what to expect."

"All right," replied Doctor Bronson, gruffly.

"And I want you to promise not to tell mother or any one. Will you?"

"Yes, I promise. Now come in here and get off some of your clothes."

"Doctor, it's pretty tough on me to get in and out of my clothes."

"I'll help you. Now tell me what the Germans did to you."

Lane laughed grimly. "Doctor, do you remember I was in your Sunday School class?"

"Yes, I remember that. What's it got to do with Germans?"

"Nothing. It struck me funny, that's all.... Well, to get it over. I was injured several times at the training camp."

"Anything serious?"

"No, I guess not. Anyway I forgot about *them*. Doctor, I was shot four times, once clear through. I'll show you. Got a bad bayonet jab that doesn't seem to heal well. Then I had a dose of both gases—chlorine and mustard—and both all but killed me. Last I've a weak place in my spine. There's a vertebra that slips out of place occasionally. The least movement may do it. I *can't* guard against it. The last time it slipped out I was washing my teeth. I'm in mortal dread of this. For it twists me out of shape and hurts horribly. I'm afraid it'll give me paralysis."

"Humph! It would. But it can be fixed.... So that's all they did to you?"

Underneath the dry humor of the little doctor, Lane thought he detected something akin to anger.

"Yes, that's all they did to my body," replied Lane.

Doctor Bronson, during a careful and thorough examination of Lane's heart, lungs, blood pressure, and abdominal region, did not speak once. But when he turned him over, to see and feel the hole in Lane's back, he exclaimed: "My God, boy, what made this—a shell? I can put my fist in it."

"That's the bayonet jab."

Doctor Bronson cursed in a most undignified and unprofessional manner. Then without further comment he went on and completed the examination.

"That'll do," he said, and lent a hand while Lane put on his clothes. It was then he noticed Lane's medal.

"Ha! The *Croix de Guerre!*... Daren, I was a friend of your father's. I *know* how that medal would have made him feel. Tell me what you did to get it?"

"Nothing much," replied Lane, stirred. "It was in the Argonne, when we took to open fighting. In fact I got most of my hurts there.... I carried a badly wounded French officer back off the field. He was a heavy man. That's where I injured my spine. I had to run with him. And worse luck, he was dead when I got him back. But I didn't know that."

"So the French decorated you, hey?" asked the doctor, leaning back with hands on hips, and keenly eyeing Lane.

"Yes."

"Why did not the American Army give you equal honor?"

"Well, for one thing it was never reported. And besides, it wasn't anything any other fellow wouldn't do."

Doctor Bronson dropped his head and paced to and fro. Then the door-bell rang in the reception room.

"Daren Lane," began the doctor, suddenly stopping before Lane, "I'd hesitate to ask most men if they wanted the truth. To many men I'd lie. But I know a few words from me can't faze you."

"No, Doctor, one way or another it is all the same to me."

"Well, boy, I can fix up that vertebra so it won't slip out again.... But, if there's anything in the world to save your life, I don't know what it is."

"Thank you, Doctor. It's—something to know—what to expect," returned Lane, with a smile.

"You might live a year—and you might not.... You might improve. God only knows. Miracles *do* happen. Anyway, come back to see me."

Lane shook hands with him and went out, passing another patient in the reception room. Then as Lane opened the door and stepped out upon the porch he almost collided with a girl who evidently had been about to come in.

"I beg your——" he began, and stopped. He knew this girl, but the strained tragic shadow of her eyes was strikingly unfamiliar. The transparent white skin let the blue tracery of veins show. On the instant her lips trembled and parted.

"Oh, Daren—don't you know me?" she asked.

"Mel Iden!" he burst out. "Know you? I should smile I do. But it—it was so sudden. And you're older—different somehow. Mel, you're sweeter—why you're beautiful."

He clasped her hands and held on to them, until he felt her rather nervously trying to withdraw them.

"Oh, Daren, I'm glad to see you home—alive—whole," she said, almost in a whisper. "Are you—well?"

"No, Mel. I'm in pretty bad shape," he replied. "Lucky to get home alive—to see you all."

"I'm sorry. You're so white. You're wonderfully changed, Daren."

"So are you. But I'll say I'm happy it's not painted face and plucked eyebrows.... Mel, what's happened to you?"

She suddenly espied the decoration on his coat. The blood rose and stained her clear cheek. With a gesture of exquisite grace and sensibility that thrilled Lane she touched the medal. "Oh! The *Croix de Guerre*.... Daren, you were a hero."

"No, Mel, just a soldier."

She looked up into his face with eyes that fascinated Lane, so beautiful were they—the blue of corn-flowers—and lighted then with strange rapt glow.

"Just a soldier!" she murmured. But Lane heard in that all the sweetness and understanding possible for any woman's heart. She amazed him—held him spellbound. Here was the sympathy—and something else—a nameless need—for which he yearned. The moment was fraught with incomprehensible forces. Lane's sore heart responded to her rapt look, to the sudden strange passion of her pale face. Swiftly he divined that Mel Iden gloried in the presence of a maimed and proven soldier.

"Mel, I'll come to see you," he said, breaking the spell. "Do you still live out on the Hill road? I remember the four big white oaks."

"No, Daren, I've left home," she said, with slow change, as if his words recalled something she had forgotten. All the radiance vanished, leaving her singularly white.

"Left home! What for?" he asked, bluntly.

"Father turned me out," she replied, with face averted. The soft roundness of her throat swelled. Lane saw her full breast heave under her coat.

"What're you saying, Mel Iden?" he demanded, as quickly as he could find his voice.

Then she turned bravely to meet his gaze, and Lane had never seen as sad eyes as looked into his.

"Daren, haven't you heard—about me?" she asked, with tremulous lips.

"No. What's wrong?"

"I—I can't let you call on me."

"Why not? Are you married—jealous husband?"

"No, I'm not married—but I—I have a baby," she whispered.

"Mel!" gasped Lane. "A war baby?"

"Yes."

Lane was so shocked he could not collect his scattered wits, let alone think of the right thing to say, if there were any right thing. "Mel, this is a—a terrible surprise. Oh, I'm sorry.... How the war played hell with all of us! But for you—Mel Iden—I can't believe it."

"Daren, so terribly true," she said. "Don't I look it?"

"Mel, you look—oh—heartbroken."

"Yes, I am broken-hearted," she replied, and drooped her head.

"Forgive me, Mel. I hardly know what I'm saying.... But listen—I'm coming to see you."

"No," she said.

That trenchant word was thought-provoking. A glimmer of understanding began to dawn in Lane. Already an immense pity had flooded his soul, and a profound sense of the mystery and tragedy of Mel Iden. She had always been unusual, aloof, proud, unattainable, a girl with a heart of golden fire. And now she had a nameless child and was an outcast from her father's house. The fact, the fatality of it, stunned Lane.

"Daren, I must go in to see Dr. Bronson," she said. "I'm glad you're home. I'm proud of you. I'm happy for your mother and Lorna. You must watch Lorna—try to restrain her. She's going wrong. All the young girls are going wrong. Oh, it's a more dreadful time *now* than before or during the war. The let-down has been terrible.... Good-bye, Daren."

In other days Manton's building on Main Street had appeared a pretentious one to Lane's untraveled eyes. It was an old three-story red-brick-front edifice, squatted between higher and more modern structures. When he climbed the dirty dark stairway up to the second floor a throng of memories returned with the sensations of creaky steps, musty smell, and dim light. When he pushed open a door on which MANTON & CO. showed in black letters he caught his breath. Long—long past! Was it possible that he had been penned up for three years in this stifling place?

Manton carried on various lines of business, and for Middleville, he was held to be something of a merchant and broker. Lane was wholly familiar with the halls, the several lettered doors, the large unpartitioned office at the back of the building. Here his slow progress was intercepted by a slip of a girl who asked him what he wanted. Before answering, Lane took stock of the girl. She might have been all of fifteen—no older. She had curly bobbed hair, and a face that would have been comely but for the powder and rouge. She was chewing gum, and she ogled Lane.

"I want to see Mr. Manton," Lane said.

"What name, please."

"Daren Lane."

She tripped off toward the door leading to Manton's private offices, and Lane's gaze, curiously following her, found her costume to be startling even to his expectant eyes. Then she disappeared. Lane's gaze sought the corner and desk that once upon a time had been his. A blond young lady, also with bobbed hair, was operating a typewriter at his desk. She glanced up, and espying Lane, she suddenly stopped her work. She recognized him. But, if she were Hattie Wilson, it was certain that Lane did not recognize her. Then the office girl returned.

"Step this way, please. Mr. Smith will see you."

How singularly it struck Lane that not once in three years had he thought of Smith. But when he saw him, the intervening months were as nothing. Lean, spare, pallid, with baggy eyes, and the nose of a drinker, Smith had not changed.

"How do, Lane. So you're back? Welcome to our city," he said, extending a nerveless hand that felt to Lane like a dead fish.

"Hello, Mr. Smith. Yes, I'm back," returned Lane, taking the chair Smith indicated. And then he met the inevitable questions as best he could in order not to appear curt or uncivil.

"I'd like to see Mr. Manton to ask for my old job," interposed Lane, presently.

"He's busy now, Lane, but maybe he'll see you. I'll find out."

Smith got up and went out. Lane sat there with a vague sense of absurdity in the situation. The click of a typewriter sounded from behind him. He wanted to hurry out. He wanted to think of other things, and twice he drove away memory of the girl he had just left at Doctor Bronson's office. Presently Smith returned, slipping along in his shiny black suit, flat-footed and slightly bowed, with his set dull expression.

"Lane, Mr. Manton asks you to please excuse him. He's extremely busy," said Smith. "I told him that you wanted your old job back. And he instructed me to tell you he had been put to the trouble of breaking in a girl to take your place. She now does the work you used to have—very satisfactorily, Mr. Manton thinks, and at less pay. So, of course, a change is impossible."

"I see," returned Lane, slowly, as he rose to go. "I had an idea that might be the case. I'm finding things—a little different."

"No doubt, Lane. You fellows who went away left us to make the best of it."

"Yes, Smith, we fellows 'went away,'" replied Lane, with satire, "and I'm finding out the fact wasn't greatly appreciated. Good day."

On the way out the little office girl opened the door for him and ogled him again, and stood a moment on the threshold. Ponderingly, Lane made his way down to the street. A rush of cool spring air seemed to refresh him, and with it came a realization that he never would have been able to stay cooped up in Manton's place. Even if his services had been greatly desired he could not have given them for long. He could not have stood that place. This was a new phase of his mental condition. Work almost anywhere in Middleville would be like that in Manton's. Could he stand work at all, not only in a physical sense, but in application of mind? He began to worry about that.

Some one hailed Lane, and he turned to recognize an old acquaintance—Matt Jones. They walked along the street together, meeting other men who knew Lane, some of whom greeted him heartily. Then, during an ensuing hour, he went into familiar stores and the postoffice, the hotel and finally the Bradford Inn, meeting many people whom he had known well. The sum of all their greetings left him in cold amaze. At length Lane grasped the subtle import—that people were tired of any one or anything which reminded them of the war. He tried to drive that thought from lodgment in his mind. But it stuck. And slowly he gathered the forces of his spirit to make good the resolve with which he had faced this day—to withstand an appalling truth.

At the inn he sat before an open fire and pondered between brief conversations of men who accosted him. On the one hand it was extremely trying, and on the other a fascinating and grim study—to meet people, and find that he could read their minds. Had the war given him some magic sixth sense, some clairvoyant power, some gift of vision? He could not tell yet what had come to him, but there was something.

Business men, halting to chat with Lane a few moments, helped along his readjustment to the truth of the strange present. Almost all kinds of business were booming. Most people had money to spend. And there was a multitude, made rich by the war, who were throwing money to the four winds. Prices of every commodity were at their highest peak, and supply could not equal demand. An orgy of spending was in full swing, and all men in business, especially the profiteers, were making the most of the unprecedented opportunity.

After he had rested, Lane boarded a street car and rode out to the suburbs of Middleville where the Maynards lived. Although they had lost their money they still lived in the substantial mansion that was all which was left them of prosperous days. House and grounds now appeared sadly run down.

A maid answered Lane's ring, and let him in. Lane found himself rather nervously expecting to see Mrs. Maynard. The old house brought back to him the fact that he had never liked her. But he wanted to see Margaret. It turned out, however, that mother and daughter were out.

"Come up, old top," called Blair's voice from the hall above.

So Lane went up to Blair's room, which he remembered almost as well as his own, though now it was in disorder. Blair was in his shirt sleeves. He looked both gay and spent. Red Payson was in bed, and his face bore the hectic flush of fever.

"Aw, he's only had too much to eat," declared Blair, in answer to Lane's solicitation.

"How's that, Red?" asked Lane, sitting down on the bed beside Payson.

"It's nothing, Dare.... I'm just all in," replied Red, with a weary smile.

"I telephoned Doc Bronson to come out," said Blair, "and look us over. That made Red as sore as a pup. Isn't he the limit? By thunder, you can't do anything for some people."

Blair's tone and words of apparent vexation were at variance with the kindness of his eyes as they rested upon his sick comrade.

"I just came from Bronson's," observed Lane. "He's been our doctor for as long as I can remember."

Both Lane's comrades searched his face with questioning eyes, and while Lane returned that gaze there was a little constrained silence.

"Bronson examined me—and said I'd live to be eighty," added Lane, with dry humor.

"You're a liar!" burst out Blair.

On Red Payson's worn face a faint smile appeared. "Carry on, Dare."

Then Blair fell to questioning Lane as to all the news he had heard, and people he had met.

"So Manton turned you down cold," said Blair, ponderingly.

"I didn't get to see him," replied Lane. "He sent out word that my old job was held by a girl who did my work better and at less pay."

The blood leaped to Blair's white cheek.

"What'd you say?" he queried.

"Nothing much. I just trailed out.... But the truth is, Blair—I couldn't have stood that place—not for a day."

"I get you," rejoined Blair. "That isn't the point, though. I always wondered if we'd find our old jobs open to us. Of course, I couldn't fill mine now. It was an outside job—lots of walking."

So the conversation see-sawed back and forth, with Red Payson listening in languid interest.

"Have you seen any of the girls?" asked Blair.

"I met Mel Iden," replied Lane.

"You did? What did she—"

"Mel told me what explained some of your hints."

"Ahuh! Poor Mel! How'd she look?"

"Greatly changed," replied Lane, thoughtfully. "How do you remember Mel?"

"Well, she was pretty—soulful face—wonderful smile—that sort of thing."

"She's beautiful now, and sad."

"I shouldn't wonder. And she told you right out about the baby?"

"No. That came out when she said I couldn't call on her, and I wanted to know why."

"But you'll go anyhow?"

"Yes."

"So will I," returned Blair, with spirit. "Dare, I've known for over a year about Mel's disgrace. You used to like her, and I hated to tell you. If it had been Helen I'd have told you in a minute. But Mel ... Well, I suppose we must expect queer things. I got a jolt this morning. I was pumping my sister Margie about everybody, and, of course, Mel's name came up. You remember Margie and Mel were as thick as two peas in a pod. Looks like Mel's fall has hurt Margie. But I don't just *get* Margie yet. She might be another fellow's sister—for all the strangeness of her."

"I hardly knew *my* kid sister," responded Lane.

"Ahuh! The plot thickens.... Well, I couldn't get much out of Marg. She used to babble everything. But what little she told me made up in—in shock for what it lacked in volume."

"Tell me," said Lane, as his friend paused.

"Nothing doing." ... And turning to the sick boy on the bed, he remarked, "Red, you needn't let this—this gab of ours bother you. This is home talk between a couple of boobs who're burying their illusions in the grave. You didn't leave a sister or a lot of old schoolgirl sweethearts behind to——"

"What the hell do you know about whom I left behind?" retorted Red, with a swift blaze of strange passion.

"Oh, say, Red—I—I beg your pardon, I was only kidding," responded Blair, in surprise and contrition. "You never told me a word about yourself."

For answer Red Payson rolled over wearily and turned his back.

"Blair, I'll beat it, and let Red go to sleep," said Lane, taking up his hat. "Red, good-bye this time. I hope you'll be better soon."

"I'm—sorry, Lane," came in muffled tones from Payson.

"Cut that out, boy. You've nothing to be sorry for. Forget it and cheer up."

Blair hobbled downstairs after Lane. "Don't go just yet, Dare."

They found seats in the parlor that appeared to be the same shabby genteel place where Lane had used to call upon Blair's sister.

"What ails Red?" queried Lane, bluntly.

"Lord only knows. He's a queer duck. Once in a while he lets out a crack like that. There's a lot to Red."

"Blair, his heart is broken," said Lane, tragically.

"Well!" exclaimed Blair, with quick almost haughty uplift of head. He seemed to resent Lane's surprise and intimation. It was a rebuke that made Lane shrink.

"I never thought of Red's being hurt—you know—or as having lost.... Oh, he just seemed like so many other boys ruined in health. I——"

"All right. Cut the sentiment," interrupted Blair. "The fact is Red is more of a problem than we had any idea he'd be.... And Dare, listen to this—I'm ashamed to have to tell you. Mother raised old Harry with me this morning for fetching Red home. She couldn't see it my way. She said there were hospitals for sick soldiers who hadn't homes. I lost my temper and I said: 'The hell of it, mother, is that there's nothing of the kind.' ... She said we couldn't keep him here. I tried to coax her.... Margie helped, but nothing doing."

Blair had spoken hurriedly with again a stain of red in his white cheek, and a break in his voice.

"That's—tough," replied Lane, haltingly. He could choke back speech, but not the something in his voice he would rather not have heard. "I'll tell you what. As soon as Red is well enough we'll move him over to my house. I'm sure mother will let him share my room. There's only Lorna—and I'll pay Red's board.... You have quite a family—"

"Hell, Dare—don't apologize to me for my mother," burst out Blair, bitterly.

"Blair, I believe you realize what we are up against—and I don't," rejoined Lane, with level gaze upon his friend.

"Dare, can't you see we're up against worse than the Argonne?—worse, because back here at home—that beautiful, glorious thought—idea—spirit we had is gone. Dead!"

"No, I can't see," returned Lane, stubbornly.

"Well, I guess that's one reason we all loved you, Dare—you couldn't see.... But I'll bet you my crutch Helen makes you see. Her father made a pile out of the war. She's a war-rich snob now. And going the pace!"

"Blair, she may make me see her faithlessness—and perhaps some strange unrest—some change that's seemed to come over everything. But she can't prove to me the death of anything outside of herself. She can't prove that any more than Mel Iden's confession proved her a wanton. It didn't. Not to me. Why, when Mel put her hand on my breast—on this medal—and looked at me—I had such a thrill as I never had before in all my life. Never!... Blair, it's *not* dead. That beautiful thing you mentioned—that spirit—that fire which burned so gloriously—it is *not* dead."

"Not in you—old pard," replied Blair, unsteadily. "I'm always ashamed before your faith. And, by God, I'll say you're my only anchor."

"Blair, let's play the game out to the end," said Lane.

"I get you, Dare.... For Margie, for Lorna, for Mel—even if they have—"

"Yes," answered Lane, as Blair faltered.

CHAPTER IV

As Lane sped out Elm Street in a taxicab he remembered that his last ride in such a conveyance had been with Helen when he took her home from a party. She was then about seventeen years old. And that night she had coaxed him to marry her before he left to go to war. Had her feminine instinct been infallibly right? Would marrying her have saved her from what Blair had so forcibly suggested?

Elm Street was a newly developed part of Middleville, high on one of its hills, and manifestly a restricted section. Lane had found the number of Helen's home in the telephone book. When the chauffeur stopped before a new and imposing pile of red brick, Lane understood an acquaintance's reference to the war rich. It was a mansion, but somehow not a home. It flaunted something indefinable.

Lane instructed the driver to wait a few moments, and, if he did not come out, to go back to town and return in about an hour. The house stood rather far from the street, and as Lane mounted the terrace he observed four motor cars parked in the driveway. Also his sensitive ears caught the sound of a phonograph.

A maid answered his ring. Lane asked for both Mrs. Wrapp and Helen. They were at home, the maid informed him, and ushered Lane into a gray and silver reception room. Lane had no card, but gave his name. As he gazed around the room he tried to fit the delicate decorative scheme to Mrs. Wrapp. He smiled at the idea. But he remembered that she had always liked him in spite of the fact that she did not favor his attention to Helen. Like many mothers of girls, she wanted a rich marriage for her daughter. Manifestly now she had money. But had happiness come with prosperity?

Then Mrs. Wrapp came down. Rising, he turned to see a large woman, elaborately gowned. She had a heavy, rather good-natured face on which was a smile of greeting.

"Daren Lane!" she exclaimed, with fervor, and to his surprise, she kissed him. There was no doubt of her pleasure. Lane's thin armor melted. He had not anticipated such welcome. "Oh, I'm glad to see you, soldier boy. But you're a man now. Daren, you're white and thin. Handsomer, though!... Sit down and talk to me a little."

Her kindness made his task easy.

"I've called to pay my respects to you—and to see Helen," he said.

"Of course. But talk to me first," she returned, with a smile. "You'll find me better company than that crowd upstairs. Tell me about yourself.... Oh, I know soldiers hate to talk about themselves and the war. Never mind the war. Are you well? Did you get hurt? You look so—so frail, Daren."

There was something simple and motherly about her, that became her, and warmed Lane's cold heart. He remembered that she had always preferred boys to girls, and regretted she had not been the mother of boys. So Lane talked to her, glad to find that the most ordinary news of the service and his comrades interested her very much. The instant she espied his *Croix de Guerre* he seemed lifted higher in her estimation. Yet she had the delicacy not to question him about that. In fact, after ten minutes with her, Lane had to reproach himself for the hostility with which he had come. At length she rose with evident reluctance.

"You want to see Helen. Shall I send her down here or will you go up to her studio?"

"I think I'd like to go up," replied Lane.

"If I were you, I would," advised Mrs. Wrapp. "I'd like your opinion—of, well, what you'll see. Since you left home, Daren, we've been turned topsy-turvy. I'm old-fashioned. I can't get used to these goings-on. These young people 'get my goat,' as Helen expresses it."

"I'm hopelessly behind the times, I've seen that already," rejoined Lane.

"Daren, I respect you for it. There was a time when I objected to your courting Helen. But I couldn't see into the future. I'm sorry now she broke her engagement to you."

"I—thank you, Mrs. Wrapp," said Lane, with agitation. "But of course Helen was right. She was too young.... And even if she had been—been true to me—I would have freed her upon my return."

"Indeed. And why, Daren?"

"Because I'll never be well again," he replied sadly.

"Boy, don't say that!" she appealed, with a hand going to his shoulder.

In the poignancy of the moment Lane lost his reserve and told her the truth of his condition, even going so far as to place her hand so she felt the great bayonet hole in his back. Her silence then was more expressive than any speech. She had the look of a woman in whom conscience was a reality. And Lane divined that she felt she and her daughter, and all other women of this distraught land, owed him and his comrades a debt which could never be paid. For once she expressed dignity and sweetness and genuine sorrow.

"You shock me, Daren. But words are useless. I hope and pray you're wrong. But right or wrong—you're a real American—like our splendid forefathers. Thank God *that* spirit still survives. It is our only hope."

Lane crossed to the window and looked out, slowly conscious of resurging self-control. It was well that he had met Mrs. Wrapp first, for she gave him what he needed. His bleeding vanity, his pride trampled in the dirt, his betrayed faith, his unquenchable spirit of hope for some far-future good—these were not secrets he could hide from every one.

"Daren," said Mrs. Wrapp, as he again turned to her, "if I were in my daughter's place I'd beg you to take me back. And if you would, I'd never leave your side for an hour until you were well or—or gone. ... But girls now are possessed of some infernal frenzy.... God only knows how *far* they go, but I'm one mother who is no fool. I see little sign of real love in Helen or any of her friends.... And the men who lounge around after her! Walk upstairs—back to the end of the long hall—open the door and go in. You'll find Helen and some of her associates. You'll find the men, young, sleek, soft, well-fed—without any of the scars or ravages of war. They didn't go to war!... They *live* for their bodies. And I hate these slackers. So does Helen's father. And for three years our house has been a rendezvous for them. We've prospered, but *that* has been bitter fruit."

Strong elemental passions Lane had seen and felt in people during the short twenty-four hours since his return home. All of them had stung and astounded him, flung into his face the hard brutal facts of the materialism of the present. Surely it was an abnormal condition. And yet from the last quarter where he might have expected to find uplift, and the crystallizing of his attitude toward the world, and the sharpening of his intelligence—from the hard, grim mother of the girl who had jilted him, these had come. It was in keeping with all the other mystery.

"On second thought, I'll go up with you," continued Mrs. Wrapp, as he moved in the direction she had indicated. "Come."

The wide hall, the winding stairway with its soft carpet, the narrower hallway above—these made a long journey for Lane. But at the end, when Mrs. Wrapp stopped with hand on the farthest door, Lane felt knit like cold steel.

The discordant music and the soft shuffling of feet ceased. Laughter and murmur of voices began.

"Come, Daren," whispered Mrs. Wrapp, as if thrilled. Certainly her eyes gleamed. Then quickly she threw the door open wide and called out:

"Helen, here's Daren Lane home from the war, wearing the *Croix de Guerre*."

Mrs. Wrapp pushed Lane forward, and stood there a moment in the sudden silence, then stepping back, she went out and closed the door.

Lane saw a large well-lighted room, with colorful bizarre decorations and a bare shiny floor. The first person his glance encountered was a young girl, strikingly beautiful, facing him with red lips parted. She had violet eyes that seemed to have a startled expression as they met Lane's. Next Lane saw a slim young man standing close to this girl, in the act of withdrawing his arm from around her waist. Apparently with his free hand he had either been lowering a smoking cigarette from her lips or had been raising it there. This hand, too, dropped down. Lane did not recognize the fellow's smooth, smug face, with its tiny curled mustache and its heated swollen lines.

"Look who's here," shouted a gay, vibrant voice. "If it isn't old Dare Lane!"

That voice drew Lane's fixed gaze, and he saw a group in the far corner of the room. One man was standing, another was sitting beside a lounge, upon which lay a young woman amid a pile of pillows. She rose lazily, and as she slid off the lounge Lane saw her skirt come down and cover her bare knees. Her red hair, bobbed and curly, marked her for recognition. It was Helen. But Lane doubted if he would have at once recognized any other feature. The handsome insolence of her face was belied by a singularly eager and curious expression. Her eyes, almost green in line, swept Lane up and down, and came back to his face, while she extended her hands in greeting.

"Helen, how are you?" said Lane, with a cool intent mastery of himself, bowing over her hands. "Surprised to see me?"

"Well, I'll say so! Daren, you've changed," she replied, and the latter part of her speech flashed swiftly.

"Rather," he said, laconically. "What would you expect? So have you changed."

There came a moment's pause. Helen was not embarrassed or agitated, but something about Lane or the situation apparently made her slow or stiff.

"Daren, you—of course you remember Hardy Mackay and Dick Swann," she said.

Lane turned to greet one-time schoolmates and rivals of his. Mackay was tall, homely, with a face that lacked force, light blue eyes and thick sandy hair, brushed high. Swann was slight, elegant, faultlessly groomed and he had a dark, sallow face, heavy lips, heavy eyelids, eyes rather prominent and of a wine-dark hue. To Lane he did not have a clean, virile look.

In their greetings Lane sensed some indefinable quality of surprise or suspense. Swann rather awkwardly put out his hand, but Lane ignored it. The blood stained Swann's sallow face and he drew himself up.

"And Daren, here are other friends of mine," said Helen, and she turned him round. "Bessy, this is Daren Lane.... Miss Bessy Bell." As Lane acknowledged the introduction he felt that he was looking at the prettiest girl he had ever seen—the girl whose violet eyes had met his when he entered the room.

"Mr. Daren Lane, I'm very happy to meet some one from 'over there,'" she said, with the ease and self-possession of a woman of the world. But when she smiled a beautiful, wonderful light seemed to shine from eyes and face and lips—a smile of youth.

Helen introduced her companion as Roy Vancey. Then she led Lane to the far corner, to another couple, manifestly disturbed from their rather close and familiar position in a window seat. These also were strangers to Lane. They did not get up, and they were not interested. In fact, Lane was quick to catch an impression from all, possibly excepting Miss Bell, that the courtesy of drawing rooms, such as he had been familiar with as a young man, was wanting in this atmosphere. Lane wondered if it was antagonism toward him. Helen drew Lane back toward her other friends, to the lounge where she seated herself. If the situation had disturbed her equilibrium in the least, the moment had passed. She did not care what Lane thought of her guests or what they thought of him. But she seemed curious about him. Bessy Bell came and sat beside her, watching Lane.

"Daren, do you dance?" queried Helen. "You used to be good. But dancing is not the same. It's all fox-trot, toddle, shimmy nowadays."

"I'm afraid my dancing days are over," replied Lane.

"How so? I see you came back with two legs and arms."

"Yes. But I was shot twice through one leg—it's about all I can do to walk now."

Following his easy laugh, a little silence ensued. Helen's green eyes seemed to narrow and concentrate on Lane. Dick Swann inhaled a deep draught of his cigarette, then let the smoke curl up from his lips to enter his nostrils. Mackay rather uneasily shifted his feet. And Bessy Bell gazed with wonderful violet eyes at Lane.

"Oh! You were *shot*!" she whispered.

"Yes," replied Lane, and looked directly at her, prompted by her singular tone. A glance was enough to show Lane that this very young girl was an entirely new type to him. She seemed to vibrate with intensity. All the graceful lines of her body seemed strangely instinct with pulsing life. She was bottled lightning. In a flash Lane sensed what made her different from the fifteen-year-olds he remembered before the war. It was what made his sister Lorna different. He felt it in Helen's scrutiny of him, in the speculation of her eyes. Then Bessy Bell leaned toward Lane, and softly, reverently touched the medal upon his breast.

"The *Croix de Guerre*," she said, in awe. "That's the French badge of honor.... It means you must have done something great.... You must have—*killed* Germans!"

Bessy sank back upon the lounge, clasping her hands, and her eyes appeared to darken, to turn purple with quickening thought and emotion. Her exclamation brought the third girl of the party over to the lounge. She was all eyes. Her apathy had vanished. She did not see the sulky young fellow who had followed her.

Lane could have laughed aloud. He read the shallow souls of these older girls. They could not help their instincts and he had learned that it was instinctive with women to become emotional over soldiers. Bessy Bell was a child. Hero-worship shone from her speaking eyes. Whatever other young men might be to her, no one of them could compare with a soldier.

The situation had its pathos, its tragedy, and its gratification for Lane. He saw clearly, and felt with the acuteness of a woman. Helen had jilted him for such young men as these. So in the feeling of the moment it cost him nothing to thrill and fascinate these girls with the story of how he had been shot through the leg. It pleased him to see Helen's green eyes dilate, to see Bessy Bell shudder. Presently Lane turned to speak to the supercilious Swann.

"I didn't have the luck to run across you in France!" he queried.

"No. I didn't go," replied Swann.

"How was that? Didn't the draft get you?"

"Yes. But my eyes were bad. And my father needed me at the works. We had a big army contract in steel."

"Oh, I see," returned Lane, with a subtle alteration of manner he could not, did not want to control. But it was unmistakable in its detachment. Next his gaze on Mackay did not require the accompaniment of a query.

"I was under weight. They wouldn't accept me," he explained.

Bessy Bell looked at Mackay disdainfully. "Why didn't you drink a bucketful of water—same as Billy Means did? He got in."

Helen laughed gayly. "What! Mac drink water? He'd be ill.... Come, let's dance. Dick put on that new one. Daren, you can watch us dance."

Swann did as he was bidden, and as a loud, violent discordance blared out of the machine he threw away his cigarette, and turned to Helen. She seemed to leap at him. She had a pantherish grace. Swann drew her closely to him, with his arm all the way round her, while her arm encircled his neck. They began a fast swaying walk, in which Swann appeared to be forcing the girl over backwards. They swayed, and turned, and glided; they made strange abrupt movements in accordance with the jerky tune; they halted at the end of a walk to make little steps forward and back; then they began to bounce and sway together in a motion that Lane instantly recognized as a toddle. Lane remembered the one-step, the fox-trot and other new dances of an earlier day, when the craze for new dancing had become general, but this sort of gyration was vastly something else. It disgusted Lane. He felt the blood surge to his face. He watched Helen Wrapp in the arms of Swann, and he realized, whatever had been the state of his heart on his return home, he did not love her now. Even if the war had not disrupted his mind in an unaccountable way, even if he had loved Helen Wrapp right up to that moment, such singular abandonment to a distorted strange music, to the close and unmistakably sensual embrace of a man—that spectacle would have killed his love.

Lane turned his gaze away. The young fellow Vancey was pulling at Bessy Bell, and she shook his hand off. "No, Roy, I don't want to dance." Lane heard above the jarring, stringing notes. Mackay was smoking, and looked on as if bored. In a moment more the Victrola rasped out its last note.

Helen's face was flushed and moist. Her bosom heaved. Her gown hung closely to her lissom and rather full form. A singular expression of excitement, of titillation, almost wild, a softer expression almost dreamy, died out of her face. Lane saw Swann lead Helen up to a small table beside the Victrola. Here stood a large pitcher of lemonade, and a number of glasses. Swann filled a glass half full, from the pitcher, and then, deliberately pulling a silver flask from his hip pocket he poured some of its dark red contents into the glass. Helen took it from him, and turned to Lane with a half-mocking glance.

"Daren, I remember you never drank," she said. "Maybe the war made a man of you!... Will you have a sip of lemonade with a shot in it?"

"No, thank you," replied Lane.

"Didn't you drink over there?" she queried.

"Only when I had to," he rejoined, shortly.

All of the four dancers partook of a drink of lemonade, strengthened by something from Swann's flask. Lane was quick to observe that when it was pressed upon Bessy Bell she refused to take it: "I hate booze," she said, with a grimace. His further impression of Bessy Bell, then, was that she had just fallen in with this older crowd, and sophisticated though she was, had not yet been corrupted. The divination of this heightened his interest.

"Well, Daren, you old prune, what'd you think of the toddle?" asked Helen, as she took a cigarette offered by Swann and tipped it between her red lips.

"Is that what you danced?"

"I'll say so. And Dick and I are considered pretty spiffy."

"I don't think much of it, Helen," replied Lane, deliberately. "If you care to—to do that sort of thing I'd imagine you'd rather do it alone."

"Oh Lord, you talk like mother," she exclaimed.

"Lane, you're out of date," said Swann, with a little sneer.

Lane took a long, steady glance at Swann, but did not reply.

"Daren, everybody has been dancing jazz. It's the rage. The old dances were slow. The new ones have pep and snap."

"So I see. They have more than that," returned Lane. "But pray, never mind me. I'm out of date. Go ahead and dance.... If you'd rather, I'll leave and call on you some other time."

"No, you stay," she replied. "I'll chase this bunch pretty soon."

"Well, you won't chase me. I'll go," spoke up Swann, sullenly, with a fling of his cigarette.

"You needn't hurt yourself," returned Helen, sarcastically.

"So long, people," said Swann to the others. But it was perfectly obvious that he did not include Lane. It was also obvious, at least to Lane, that Swann showed something of intolerance and mastery in the dark, sullen glance he bestowed upon Helen. She followed him across the room and out into the hall, from whence her guarded voice sounded unintelligibly. But Lane's keen ear, despite the starting of the Victrola, caught Swann's equally low, yet clearer reply. "You can't kid me. I'm on. You'll vamp Lane if he lets you. Go to it!"

As Helen came back into the room Mackay ran for her, and locking her in the same embrace—even a tighter one than Swann's—he fell into the strange steps that had so shocked Lane. Moreover, he was manifestly a skilful dancer, and showed the thin, lithe, supple body of one trained down by this or some other violent exercise.

Lane did not watch the dancers this time. Again Bessy Bell refused to get up from the lounge. The youth was insistent. He pawed at her. And manifestly she did not like that, for her face flamed, and she snapped: "Stop it—you bonehead! Can't you see I want to sit here by Mr. Lane?"

The youth slouched away fuming to himself.

Whereupon Lane got up, and seated himself beside Bessy so that he need not shout to be heard.

"That was nice of you, Miss Bell—but rather hard on the youngster," said Lane.

"He makes me sick. All he wants to do is lolly-gag.... Besides, after what you said to Helen about the jazz I wouldn't dance in front of you on a bet."

She was forceful, frank, naive. She was impressed by his nearness; but Lane saw that it was the fact of his being a soldier with a record, not his mere physical propinquity that affected her. She seemed both bold and shy. But she did not show any modesty. Her short skirt came above her bare knees, and she did not try to hide them from Lane's sight. At fifteen, like his sister Lorna, this girl had the development of a young woman. She breathed health, and something elusive that Lane could not catch. If it had not been for her apparent lack of shame, and her rouged lips and cheeks, and her plucked eyebrows, she would have been exceedingly alluring. But no beauty, however striking, could under these circumstances, stir Lane's heart. He was fascinated, puzzled, intensely curious.

"Why wouldn't you dance jazz in front of me?" he inquired, with a smile.

"Well, for one thing I'm not stuck on it, and for another I'll say you said a mouthful."

"Is that all?" he asked, as if disappointed.

"No. I'd respect what you said—because of where you've been and what you've done."

It was a reply that surprised Lane.

"I'm out of date, you know."

She put a finger on the medal on his breast and said: "You could never be out of date."

The music and the sliding shuffle ceased.

"Now beat it," said Helen. "I want to talk to Daren." She gayly shoved the young people ahead of her in a mass, and called to Bessy: "Here, you kid vamp, lay off Daren."

Bessy leaned to whisper in his ear: "Make a date with me, quick!"

"Surely, I'll hunt you up. Good-bye."

She was the only one who made any pretension of saying good-bye to Lane. They all crowded out before Helen, with Mackay in the rear. From the hall Lane heard him say to Helen: "Dick'll sure go to the mat with you for this."

Presently Helen returned to shut the door behind her; and her walk toward Lane had a suggestion of the oriental dancer. For Lane her face was a study. This seemed a woman beyond his comprehension. She was the Helen Wrapp he had known and loved, plus an age of change, a measureless experience. With that swaying, sinuous, pantherish grace, with her green eyes narrowed and gleaming, half mocking, half serious, she glided up to him, close, closer until she pressed against him, and her face was uplifted under his. Then she waited with her eyes gazing into his. Slumberous green depths, slowly lighting, they seemed to Lane. Her presence thus, her brazen challenge, affected him powerfully, but he had no thrill.

"Aren't you going to kiss me?" she asked.

"Helen, why didn't you write me you had broken our engagement?" he counter-queried.

The question disconcerted her somewhat. Drawing back from close contact with him she took hold of his sleeves, and assumed a naive air of groping in memory. She used her eyes in a way that Lane could not associate with the past he knew. She was a flirt—not above trying her arts on the man she had jilted.

"Why, didn't I write you? Of course I did."

"Well, if you did I never got the letter. And if you were on the level you'd admit you never wrote."

"How'd you find out then?" she inquired curiously.

"I never knew for sure until your mother verified it."

"Are you curious to know why I did break it off?"

"Not in the least."

This reply shot the fire into her face, yet she still persisted in the expression of her sentimental motive. She began to finger the medal on his breast.

"So, Mr. Soldier Hero, you didn't care?"

"No—not after I had been here ten minutes," he replied, bluntly.

She whirled from him, swiftly, her body instinct with passion, her expression one of surprise and fury.

"What do you mean by that?"

"Nothing I care to explain, except I discovered my love for you was dead—perhaps had been dead for a long time."

"But you never discovered it until you *saw* me—here—with Swann—dancing, drinking, smoking?"

"No. To be honest, the shock of that enlightened me."

"Daren Lane, I'm just what *you* men have made me," she burst out, passionately.

"You are mistaken. I beg to be excluded from any complicity in the—in whatever you've been made," he said, bitterly. "I have been true to you in deed and in thought all this time."

"You must be a queer soldier!" she exclaimed, incredulously.

"I figure there were a couple of million soldiers like me, queer or not," he retorted.

She gazed at him with something akin to hate in her eyes. Then putting her hands to her full hips she began that swaying, dancing walk to and fro before the window. She was deeply hurt. Lane had meant to get under her skin with a few just words of scorn, and he had imagined his insinuation as to the change in her had hurt her feelings. Suddenly he divined it was not that at all—he had only wounded her vanity.

"Helen, let's not talk of the past," he said. "It's over. Even if you had been true to me, and I loved you still—I would have been compelled to break our engagement."

"You would! And why?"

"I am a physical wreck—and a mental one, too, I fear.... Helen, I've come home to die."

"Daren!" she cried, poignantly.

Then he told her in brief, brutal words of the wounds and ravages war had dealt him, and what Doctor Bronson's verdict had been. Lane felt shame in being so little as to want to shock and hurt her, if that were possible.

"Oh, I'm sorry," she burst out. "Your mother—your sister.... Oh, that damned horrible war! *What* has it not done to us?... Daren, you looked white and weak, but I never thought you were—going to die.... How dreadful!"

Something of her girlishness returned to her in this moment of sincerity. The past was not wholly dead. Memories lingered. She looked at Lane, wide-eyed, in distress, caught between strange long-forgotten emotions.

"Helen, it's not dreadful to have to die," replied Lane. "*That* is not the dreadful part in coming home."

"What *is* dreadful, then?" she asked, very low.

Lane felt a great heave of his breast—the irrepressible reaction of a profound and terrible emotion, always held in abeyance until now. And a fierce pang, that was physical as well as emotional, tore through him. His throat constricted and ached to a familiar sensation—the welling up of blood from his lungs. The handkerchief he put to his lips came away stained red. Helen saw it, and with dilated eyes, moved instinctively as if to touch him, hold him in her pity.

"Never mind, Helen," he said, huskily. "That's nothing.... Well, I was about to tell you what is so dreadful—for me.... It's to reach home grateful to God I was spared to get home—resigned to the ruin of my life—content to die for whom I fought—my mother, my sister, *you*, and all our women (for I fought for nothing else)—and find my mother aged and bewildered and sad, my sister a painted little hussy—and *you*—a strange creature I despise.... And all, everybody, everything changed—changed in some horrible way which proves my sacrifice in vain.... It is not death that is dreadful, but the uselessness, the hopelessness of the ideal I cherished."

Helen fell on the couch, and burying her face in the pillows she began to sob. Lane looked down at her, at her glistening auburn hair, and slender, white, ringed hand clutching the cushions, at her lissom shaking form, at the shapely legs in the rolled-down silk stockings—and he felt a melancholy happiness in the proof that he had reached her shallow heart, and in the fact that this was the moment of loss.

"Good-bye—Helen," he said.

"Daren—don't—go," she begged.

But he had to go, for other reasons beside the one that this was the end of all intimate relation between him and Helen. He had overtaxed his strength, and the burning pang in his breast was one he must heed. On the hall stairway a dizzy spell came over him. He held on to the banister until the weakness passed. Fortunately there was no one to observe him. Somehow the sumptuous spacious hall seemed drearily empty. Was this a home for that twenty-year-old girl upstairs? Lane opened the door and went out. He was relieved to find the taxi waiting. To the driver he gave the address of his home and said: "Go slow and don't give me a jar!"

But Lane reached home, and got into the house, where he sat at the table with his mother and Lorna, making a pretense of eating, and went upstairs and into his bed without any recurrence of the symptoms that had alarmed him. In the darkness of his room he gradually relaxed to rest. And rest was the only medicine for him. It had put off hour by hour and day by day the inevitable.

"If it comes—all right—I'm ready," he whispered to himself. "But in spite of all I've been through—and have come home to—I don't *want* to die."

There was no use in trying to sleep. But in this hour he did not want oblivion. He wanted endless time to think. And slowly, with infinite care and infallible memory, he went over every detail of what he had seen and heard since his arrival home. In the headlong stream of consciousness of the past hours he met with circumstances that he lingered over, and tried to understand, to no avail. Yet when all lay clearly before his mental gaze he felt a sad and tremendous fascination in the spectacle.

For many weeks he had lived on the fancy of getting home, of being honored and loved, of being given some little meed of praise and gratitude in the short while he had to live. Alas! this fancy had been a dream of his egotism. His old world was gone. There was nothing left. The day of the soldier had passed—until some future need of him stirred the emotions of a selfish people. This new world moved on unmindful, through its travail and incalculable change, to unknown ends. He, Daren Lane, had been left alone on the vast and naked shores of Lethe.

Lane made not one passionate protest at the injustice of his fate. Labor, agony, war had taught him wisdom and vision. He began to realize that no greater change could there be than this of his mind, his soul. But in the darkness there an irresistible grief assailed him. He wept as never before in all his life. And he tasted the bitter salt of his own tears. He wept for his mother, aged and bowed by trouble, bewildered, ready to give up the struggle—his little sister now forced into erotic girlhood, blind, wilful, bold, on the wrong path, doomed beyond his power or any earthly power—the men he had met, warped by the war, materialistic, lost in the maze of self-preservation and self-aggrandizement, dead to chivalry and the honor of women—Mel Iden, strangest and saddest of mysteries—a girl who had been noble, aloof, proud, with a heart of golden fire, now disgraced, ruined, the mother of a war-baby, and yet, strangest of all, not vile, not bad, not lost, but groping like he was down those vast and naked shores of life. He wept for the hard-faced Mrs. Wrapp, whose ideal had been wealth and who had found prosperity bitter ashes at her lips, yet who preserved in this modern maelstrom some sense of its falseness, its baseness. He wept for Helen, playmate of the years never to return, sweetheart of his youth, betrayer of his manhood, the young woman of the present, blase, unsexed, seeking, provocative, all perhaps, as she had said, that men had made her—a travesty on splendid girlhood. He wept for her friends, embodying in them all of their class—for little Bessy Bell, with her exquisite golden beauty, her wonderful smile that was a light of joy—a child of fifteen with character and mind, not yet sullied, not yet wholly victim to the unstable spirit of the day.

And traveling in this army that seemed to march before Lane's eyes were the slackers, like Mackay and Swann, representative of that horde of cowards who in one way or another had avoided the service—the young men who put comfort, ease, safety, pleasure before all else—who had no ideal of womanhood—who could not have protected women—who would not fight to save women from the apish Huns—who remained behind to fall in the wreck of the war's degeneration, and to dance, to drink, to smoke, to ride the women to their debasement.

And for the first and the last time Lane wept for himself, pitifully as a child lost and helpless, as a strong man facing irreparable loss, as a boy who had dreamed beautiful dreams, who had loved and given and trusted, who had suffered insupportable agonies of body and soul, who had fought like a lion for what he represented to himself, who had killed and killed—and whose reward was change, indifference, betrayal and death.

That dark hour passed. Lane lay spent in the blackness of his room. His heart had broken. But his spirit was as unquenchable as the fire of the sun. If he had a year, a month, a week, a day longer to live he could never live it untrue to himself. Life had marked him to be a sufferer, a victim. But nothing could kill his soul. And his soul was his faith—something he understood as faith in God or nature or life—in the reason for his being—in his vision of the future.

How then to spend this last remnant of his life! No one would guess what passed through his lonely soul. No one would care. But out of the suffering that now seemed to give him spirit and wisdom and charity there dawned a longing to help, to save. He would return good for evil. All had failed him, but he would fail no one.

Then he had a strange intense desire to understand the present. Only a day home—and what colossal enigma! The war had been chaos. Was this its aftermath? Had people been rocked on their foundations? What were they doing—how living—how changing? He would see, and be grateful for a little time to prove his faith. He knew he would find the same thing in others that existed in himself.

He would help his mother, and cheer her, and try to revive something of hope in her. He would bend a keen and patient eye upon Lorna, and take the place of her father, and be kind, loving, yet blunt to her, and show her the inevitable end of this dancing, dallying road. Perhaps he could influence Helen. He would see the little soldier-worshipping Bessy Bell, and if by talking hours and hours, by telling the whole of his awful experience of war, he could take up some of the time so fraught with peril for her, he would welcome the ordeal of memory. And Mel Iden—how thought of her seemed tinged with strange regret! Once she and he had been dear friends, and because of a falsehood told by Helen that friendship had not been what it might have been. Suppose Mel, instead of Helen, had loved him and been engaged to him! Would he have been jilted and would Mel have been lost? No! It was a subtle thing—that answer of his spirit. It did not agree with Mel Iden's frank confession.

It might be difficult, he reflected, to approach Mel. But he would find a way. He would rest a few days—then find where she lived and go to see her. Could he help her? And he had an infinite exaltation in his power to help any one who had suffered. Lane recalled Mel's pale sweet face, the shadowed eyes, the sad tremulous lips. And this image of her seemed the most lasting of the impressions of the day.

CHAPTER V

The arbiters of social fate in Middleville assembled at Mrs. Maynard's on a Monday afternoon, presumably to partake of tea. Seldom, however, did they meet without adding zest to the occasion by a pricking down of names.

Mrs. Wrapp was the leading spirit of this self-appointed tribunal—a circumstance of expanding, resentment to Mrs. Maynard, who had once held the reins with aristocratic hands. Mrs. Kingsley, the third member of the great triangle, claimed an ancestor on the Mayflower, which was in her estimation a guerdon of blue blood. Her elaborate and exclusive entertainments could never be rivalled by those of Mrs. Wrapp. She was a widow with one child, the daughter Elinor, a girl of nineteen.

Mrs. Maynard was tall, pale, and worldly. Traces of lost beauty flashed in her rare smiles. When Frank Maynard had failed in business she had shrouded her soul in bitterness; and she saw the slow cruel years whiten his head and bend his shoulders with the cold eye of a woman who had no forgiveness for failure. After Mr. Maynard's reverse, all that kept the pair together were the son Blair, and the sweet, fair-haired, delicate Margaret, a girl of eighteen, whom the father loved, and for whom the mother had large ambitions. They still managed, in ways mysterious to the curious, to keep their fine residence in the River Park suburb of Middleville.

On this April afternoon the tea was neglected in the cups, and there was nothing of the usual mild gossip. The discussion involved Daren Lane, and when two of those social arbiters settled back in their chairs the open sesame of Middleville's select affairs had been denied to him.

"Why did he do it?" asked Mrs. Kingsley.

"He must have been under the influence of liquor," replied Mrs. Maynard, who had her own reasons for being relieved at the disgrace of Daren Lane.

"No, Jane, you're wrong," spoke up Mrs. Wrapp, who, whatever else she might be, was blunt and fair-minded. "Lane wasn't drunk. He never drank before the war. I knew him well. He and Helen had a puppy-love affair—they were engaged before Lane went to war. Well, the day after his return he called on us. And if I never liked him before I liked him then. He's come back to die! He was ill for two weeks—and then he crawled out of bed again. I met him down town one day. He really looked better, and told me with a sad smile that he had 'his ups and downs'.... No, Lane wasn't drunk at Fanchon Smith's dance the other night. I was there, and I was with Mrs. Smith when Lane came up to us. If ever I saw a cool, smooth, handsome devil it was Lane.... Well, he said what he said. I thought Mrs. Smith would faint. It is my idea Lane had a deep motive back of his remark about Fanchon's dress and her dancing. The fact is Lane was *sick* at what he saw—sick and angry. And he wanted Fanchon's mother and me to know what he thought."

"It was an insult," declared Mrs. Maynard, vehemently.

"It made Mrs. Smith ill," added Mrs. Kingsley. "She told me Fanchon tormented the life out of her, trying to learn what Lane said. Mrs. Smith would not tell. But Fanchon came to me and *I* told her. Such a perfectly furious girl! She'll not wear *that* dress or dance *that* dance very soon again. The story is all over town."

"Friends, there are two sides to every question," interposed the forceful Mrs. Wrapp. "If Lane cared to be popular he would have used more tact. But I don't think his remark was an insult. It was pretty raw, I admit. But the dress was indecent and the dance was rotten. Helen told me Fanchon was half shot. So how could she be insulted?"

Mrs. Maynard and Mrs. Kingsley, as usual, received Mrs. Wrapp's caustic and rather crude opinions with as good grace as they could muster. Plain it was that they felt themselves a shade removed from this younger and newer member of society. But they could not show direct antagonism to her influence any more than they could understand the common sense and justice of her arguments.

"No one will ever invite him again," declared Mrs. Maynard.

"He's done in Middleville," echoed Mrs. Kingsley. And that perhaps was a gauntlet thrown.

"Rot!" exclaimed Mrs. Wrapp, with more force than elegance. "I'll invite Daren Lane to my house.... You women don't get the point. Daren Lane is a soldier come home to die. He gave himself. And he returns to find all—all this sickening—oh, what shall I call it? What does he care whether or not we invite him? Can't you see that?"

"There's a good deal in what you say," returned Mrs. Kingsley, influenced by the stronger spirit. "Maybe Lane hated the new styles. I don't blame him much. There's something wrong with our young people. The girls are crazy. The boys are wild. Few of them are marrying—or even getting engaged. They'll do *anything*. The times are different. And we mothers don't know our daughters."

"Well, I know *mine*" returned Mrs. Maynard, loftily. "What you say may be true generally, but there are exceptions. My daughter has been too well brought up."

"Yes, Margie is well-bred," retorted Mrs. Wrapp. "We'll admit she hasn't gone to extremes, as most of our girls have. But I want to observe to you that she has been a wall-flower for a year."

"It certainly *is* a problem," sighed Mrs. Kingsley. "I feel helpless—out of it. Elinor does precisely what she wants to do. She wears outlandish clothes. She smokes and—I'm afraid drinks. And dances—*dreadfully.* Just like the other girls—no better, no worse. But with all that I think she's good. I feel the same as Jane feels about that. In spite of this—this modern stuff I believe all the girls are fundamentally the same as ten years ago."

"Well, that's where you mothers get in wrong," declared Mrs. Wrapp with her vigorous bluntness. "It's your pride. Just because they're *your* daughters they are above reproach.... What have you to say about the war babies in town? Did you ever hear of *that* ten years ago? You bet you didn't. These girls are a speedy set. Some of them are just wild for the sake of wildness. Most of them *have* to stand for things, or be left out altogether."

"What in the world can we do?" queried Mrs. Maynard, divided between distress and chagrin.

"The good Lord only knows," responded Mrs. Wrapp, herein losing her assurance. "Marriage would save most of them. But Helen doesn't want to marry. She wants to paint pictures and be free."

"Perhaps marriage is a solution," rejoined Mrs. Maynard thoughtfully.

"Whom on earth can we marry them to?" asked Mrs. Kingsley. "Most of the older men, the bachelors who're eligible haven't any use for these girls except to *play* with them. True, these young boys only think of little but dances, car-rides, and sneaking off alone to spoon—they get engaged to this girl and that one. But nothing comes of it."

"You're wrong. Never in my time have I seen girls find lovers and husbands as easily as now," declared Mrs. Wrapp. "Nor get rid of them so quickly.... Jane, you can marry Margaret. She's pretty and sweet even if you have spoiled her. The years are slipping by. Margaret ought to marry. She's not strong enough to work. Marriage for her would make things so much easier for you."

With that parting dig Mrs. Wrapp rose to go. Whereupon she and Mrs. Kingsley, with gracious words of invitation and farewell, took themselves off leaving Mrs. Maynard contending with an outraged spirit. Certain terse remarks of the crude and practical Mrs. Wrapp had forced to her mind a question that of late had assumed cardinal importance, and now had been brought to an issue by a proposal for Margaret's hand. Her daughter was a great expense, really more than could longer be borne in these times of enormous prices and shrunken income. A husband had been found for Margaret, and the matter could be adjusted easily enough, if the girl did not meet it with the incomprehensible obstinacy peculiar to her of late.

Mrs. Maynard found the fair object of her hopes seated in the middle of her room with the bright contents of numerous boxes and drawers strewn in glittering heaps around her.

"Margaret, what on earth are you doing there?" she demanded.

"I'm looking for a little picture Holt Dalrymple gave me when we went to school together," responded Margaret.

"Aren't you ever going to grow up? You'll be hunting for your dolls next."

"I will if I like," said the daughter, in a tone that did not manifest a seraphic mood.

"Don't you feel well?" inquired the mother, solicitously. Margaret was frail and subject to headaches that made her violent.

"Oh, I'm well enough."

"My dear," rejoined Mrs. Maynard, changing the topic. "I'm sorry to tell you Daren Lane has lost his standing in Middleville."

The hum and the honk of a motor-car sounded in the street.

"Poor Daren! What's he done?... Any old day he'll care!"

Mrs. Maynard was looking out of the window. "Here comes a crowd of girls.... Helen Wrapp has a new suit. Well, I'll go down. And after they leave I want a serious talk with you."

"Not if I see you first!" muttered Margaret, under her breath, as her mother walked out.

Presently, following gay talk and laughter down stairs, a bevy of Margaret's friends entered her boudoir.

"Hello, old socks!" was Helen's greeting. "You look punk."

"Marg, where's the doll? Your mother tipped us off," was Elinor's greeting.

"Where's the eats?" was Flossie Dickerson's greeting. She was a bright-eyed girl, with freckles on her smiling face, and the expression of a daring, vivacious and happy spirit—and acknowledged to be the best dancer and most popular girl in Middleville. Her dress, while not to be compared with her friends' costumes in costliness, yet was extreme in the prevailing style.

"Glad to see you, old dear," was dark-eyed, dark-haired Dorothy Dalrymple's greeting. Her rich color bore no hint of the artificial. She sank down on her knees beside Margaret.

The other girls draped themselves comfortably round the room; and Flossie with a 'Yum Yum' began to dig into a box of candy on Margaret's couch. They all talked at once. "Hear the latest, Marg?"

"Look at Helen's spiffy suit!"

"Oh, money, money, what it will buy!"

"Money'll never buy *me*, I'll say."

"Marg, who's been fermentin' round lately? Girls, get wise to the flowers."

"Hot dog! See Marg blush! That comes from being so pale. What are rouge and lip-stick and powder for but to hide truth from our masculine pursuers?"

"Floss, you haven't blushed for a million years."

It was Dorothy Dalrymple who silenced the idle badinage.

"Marg, you rummaging in the past?" she cried.

"Yes, and I love it," replied Margaret. "I haven't looked over this stuff for years. Just to remember the things I did!... Here, Dal, is a picture you once drew of our old teacher, Miss Hill."

Dorothy, whom the girls nicknamed "Dal," gazed at the drawing with amaze and regret.

"She was a terror," continued Margaret. "But Dal, you never had any reason to draw such a horrible picture of her. You were her pet."

"I wasn't," declared Dorothy.

"Maybe you never knew Miss Hill adored you, Dal," interposed Elinor. "She was always holding you up as a paragon. Not in your lessons—for you were a bonehead—but for deportment you were the class!"

"Dal, you were too good for this earth *then*, let alone these days," said Margaret.

"Miss Hill," mused Elinor, gazing at the caricature. "That's not a bad drawing. I remember Miss Hill never had any use for me. Small wonder. She was an honest-to-God teacher. I think she wanted us to be good.... Wonder how she got along with the kids that came after us."

"I saw Amanda Hill the other day," spoke up Flossie. "She looked worn out. She was nice to me. I'll bet my shirt she'd like to have us back, bad as we were.... These kids of to-day! My Gawd! they're the limit. They paralyze *me*. I thought I was pretty fast. But compared to these youngsters I'm tied to a post. My kid sister Joyce—Rose Clymer—Bessy Bell!... Some kids, believe me. And take it from me, girls, these dimple-kneed chickens are vamping the older boys."

"They're all stuck on Bessy," said Helen.

Margaret squealed in delight. "Girls, look here. Valentines! Did you ever?... Look at them.... And what's this?... 'Wonders of Nature—composition by Margaret Maynard.' Heavens! Did I write that? And what's this sear and yellow document?"

A slivery peal of laughter burst from Margaret.

"Dal, here's one of your masterpieces, composed when you were thirteen, and mooney over Daren Lane."

"I? Never! I didn't write it," denied Dorothy, with color in her dark cheeks.

"Yes you did. It's signed—'Yours forever Dot Dalrymple.' ... Besides I remember now Daren gave it to me. Said he wanted to prove he could have other girls if he couldn't have me."

"How chivalrous!" exclaimed Dorothy, joining in the laugh.

"Ah! here's what I've been hunting," declared Margaret, waving aloft a small picture. "It's a photograph of Holt, taken five years ago. Only the other evening he swore I hadn't kept it—dared me to produce it. He'll want it now—for some other girl. But nix, it's mine.... Dal, isn't he a handsome boy here?"

With sisterly impartiality Dorothy declared she could not in the wildest flight of her imagination see her brother as handsome.

"Holt used to be good-looking," said she. "But he outgrew it. That South Carolina training camp and the flu changed his looks as well as his disposition."

"Holt *is* changed," mused Margaret, gazing down at the picture, and the glow faded from her face.

"Dare Lane is handsome, even if he is a wreck," said Elinor, with sudden enthusiasm. "Friday night when he beat it from Fanchon's party he sure looked splendid."

Elinor was a staunch admirer of Lane's and she was the inveterate torment of her girl friends. She gave Helen a sly glance. Helen's green eyes narrowed and gleamed.

"Yes, Dare's handsomer than ever," she said. "And to give the devil his due he's *finer* than ever. Too damn fine for this crowd!... But what's the use—" she broke off.

"Yes, poor Dare Lane!" sighed Elinor. "Dare deserves much from all of us, not to mention *you*. He has made me think. Thank Heaven, I found I hadn't forgotten how."

"El, no one would notice it," returned Helen, sarcastically.

"It's easy to see where you get off," retorted Elinor.

Then a silence ensued, strange in view of the late banter and quick sallies; a silence breathing of restraint. The color died wholly from Margaret's face, and a subtle, indefinable, almost imperceptible change came over Dorothy.

"You bet Dare is handsome," spoke up Flossie, as if to break the embarrassment. "He's so *white* since he came home. His eyes are so dark and flashing. Then the way he holds his head— the look of him.... No wonder these damned slackers seem cheap compared to him.... I'd fall for Dare Lane in a minute, even if he is half dead."

The restraint passed, and when Floss Dickerson came out with eulogy for any man his status was settled for good and all. Margaret plunged once more into her treasures of early schooldays. Floss and Elinor made merry over some verses Margaret had handed up with a blush. Helen apparently lapsed into a brooding abstraction. And presently Dorothy excused herself, and kissing Margaret good-bye, left for home.

The instant she had gone Margaret's gay and reminiscent mood underwent a change.

"Girls, I want to know what Daren Lane did or said on Friday night at Fanchon's," spoke up Margaret. "You know mother dragged me home. Said I was tired. But I wasn't. It was only because I'm a wall-flower.... So I missed what happened. But I've heard talk enough to make me crazy to know about this scandal. Kit Benson was here and she hinted things. I met Bessy Bell. She asked me if I knew. She's wild about Daren. That yellow-legged broiler! He doesn't even know her.... My brother Blair would not tell me anything. He's strong for Daren. But mother told me Daren had lost his standing in Middleville. She always hated Daren. Afraid I'd fall in love with him. The idea! I liked him, and I like him better now—poor fellow!... And last, when El mentioned Daren, did you see Dal's face? I never saw Dal look like that."

"Neither did I," replied Elinor.

"Well, I have," spoke up Helen, with all of her mother's bluntness. "Dal always was love-sick over Daren, when she was a mere kid. She never got over it and never will."

"Still water runs deep," sapiently remarked Elinor. "There's a good deal in Dal. She's fine as silk. Of course we all remember how jealous she was of other girls when Daren went with her.

But I think now it's because she's sorry for Daren. So am I. He was such a fool. Fanchon swears no nice girl in Middleville will ever dance that new camel-walk dance in public again."

"What did Daren say?" demanded Margaret, with eyes lighting.

"I was standing with Helen, and Fanchon when Daren came up. He looked—I don't know how—just wonderful. We all knew something was doing. Daren bowed to Fanchon and said to her in a perfectly clear voice that everybody heard: 'I'd like to try your camel-walk. I'm out of practice and not strong, but I can go once around, I'm sure. Will you?'"

"You're on, Dare," replied Fanchon.

"Then he asked. 'Do you like it?'"

"'I'll say so, Dare—crazy about it.'"

"Of course you know why it's danced—and how it's interpreted by men," said Daren.

"What do you mean?" asked Fanchon, growing red and flustered.

"Then Daren said: 'I'll tell your mother. If she lets you dance with that understanding—all right.' He bent over Mrs. Smith and said something. Mrs. Wrapp heard it. And so did Mrs. Mackay, who looked pretty sick. Mrs. Smith nearly *fainted*!... but she recovered enough to order Daren to leave."

"Do you know what Daren said?" demanded Margaret, in a frenzy of excitement.

"No. None of the girls know. We can only imagine. That makes it worse. If Fanchon knows she won't tell. But it is gossip all over town. We'll hear it soon. All the girls in town are imagining. It's spread like wildfire. And what *do* you think, Margie? In church—on Sunday—Doctor Wallace spoke of it. He mentioned no names. But he said that as the indecent dress and obscene dance of the young women could no longer be influenced by the home or the church it was well that one young man had the daring to fling the truth into the faces of their mothers."

"Oh, it was rotten of Daren," replied Margaret, with tears in her eyes. She was ashamed, indignant, incredulous. "For him to do a thing like that! He's always been the very prince of gentlemen. What on earth possessed him? Heaven knows the dances are vile, but that doesn't excuse Daren Lane. What do I care what Doctor Wallace said? Never in a thousand years will Mrs. Smith or mother or any one forgive him. Fanchon Smith is a little snob. I always hated her. She's spiteful and catty. She's a flirt all the way. She would dance any old thing. But that's not the point. Daren's disgraced himself. It was rotten—of him. And—I'll never—forgive—him, either."

"Don't cry, Margie," said Elinor. "It always makes your eyes red and gives you a headache. Poor Daren made a blunder. But some of us will stick to him. Don't take it so badly."

"Margie, it was rotten of Daren, one way you look at it—our way," added Flossie. "But you have to hand it to him for that stunt."

Helen Wrapp preserved her sombre mood, silent and brooding.

"Margie," went on Elinor, "there's a lot back of this. If Dare Lane could do that there must be some reason for it. Maybe we all needed a jolt. Well, we've got it. Let's stand by Daren. I will. Helen will. Floss will. You will. And surely Dal will."

"If you ask *me* I'll say Dare Lane ought to hand something to the men!" burst out Floss Dickerson, with fire in her eyes.

"You said a mouthful, kiddo," responded Helen, with her narrow contracted gaze upon Margaret. "Daren gave me the once over—and then the icepick!"

"Wonder what he gave poor Mel—when he heard about her," murmured Elinor, thoughtfully.

"Mel Iden ought to be roasted," retorted Helen. "She was always so darned superior. And all the time ..."

"Helen, don't you say a word against Mel Iden," burst out Margaret, hotly. "She was my dearest friend. She was lovely. Her ruin was a horrible shock. But it wasn't because she was bad.... Mel had some fanatical notion about soldiers giving all—going away to be slaughtered. She said to me, 'A woman's body is so little to give,'"

"Yes, I know Mel was cracked," replied Helen. "But she needn't have been a damn fool. She didn't need to have had that baby!"

"Helen, your idea of sin is to be found out," said Elinor, with satire.

Again Floss Dickerson dropped her trenchant personality into the breach.

"Aw, come off!" she ejaculated. "Let somebody roast the men once, will you? I'm the little Jane that *knows*, believe me. All this talk about the girls going to hell makes me sick. We may be going—and going in limousines—but it's the men who're stepping on the gas."

"Floss, I love to hear you elocute," drawled Helen. "Go to it! For God's sake, roast the men."

"You always have to horn in," retorted Floss. "Let me get this off my chest, will you?... We girls are getting talked about. There's no use denying it. Any but a blind girl could see it. And it's because we do what the men want. Every girl wants to go out—to be attractive—to have fellows. But the price is getting high. They say in Middleville that I'm rushed more than any other girl. Well, if I am I know what it costs.... If I didn't 'pet'—if I didn't mush, if I didn't park my corsets at dances—if I didn't drink and smoke, and wiggle like a jelly-fish, I'd be a dead one—an egg, and don't you overlook that. If any one says I *want* to do these things he's a fool. But I do love to have good times, and little by little I've been drawn on and on.... I've had my troubles staving off these fellows. Most of them get half drunk. Some of the girls do, too. I never went that far. I always kept my head. I never went the limit. But you can bet your sweet life it wasn't their fault I didn't fall for them.... I'll say I've had to walk home from more than one auto ride. There's something in the gag, 'I know she's a good girl because I met her walking home from an auto ride.' That's one thing I intend to cut out this summer—the auto rides. Nothing doing for little Flossie!"

"Oh, can't we talk of something else!" complained Margaret, wearily, with her hands pressing against her temples.

CHAPTER VI

Mrs. Maynard slowly went upstairs and along the hall to her daughter's room. Margaret sat listlessly by a window. The girls had gone.

"You were going for a long walk," said Mrs. Maynard.

"I'm tired," replied Margaret. There was a shadow in her eyes.

The mother had never understood her daughter. And of late a subtle change in Margaret had made her more of a puzzle.

"Margaret, I want to talk seriously with you," she began.

"Well?"

"Didn't I tell you I wanted you to break off your—your friendship with Holt Dalrymple?"

"Yes," replied Margaret, with a flush. "I did not—want to."

"Well, the thing which concerns you now is—he can't be regarded as a possibility for you."

"Possibility?" echoed Margaret.

"Just that, exactly. I'm not sure of your thoughts on the matter, but it's time I knew them. Holt is a ne'er-do-well. He's gone to the bad, like so many of these army boys. No nice girl will ever associate with him again."

"Then I'm not nice, for I will," declared Margaret, spiritedly.

"You will persist in your friendship for him in the face of my objection?"

"Certainly I will if I have any say about it. But I know Holt. I—I guess he has taken to drink—and carrying on. So you needn't worry much about our friendship."

Mrs. Maynard hesitated. She had become accustomed to Margaret's little bursts of fury and she expected one here. But none came; Margaret appeared unnaturally calm; she sat still with her face turned to the window. Mrs. Maynard was a little afraid of this cold, quiet girl.

"Margaret, you can't help seeing now that your mother's judgment was right. Holt Dalrymple once may have been very interesting and attractive for a friend, but as a prospective husband he was impossible. The worst I hear of him is that he drinks and gambles. I know you liked him and I don't want to be unjust. But he has kept other and better young men away from you."

Margaret's hand clenched and her face sank against the window-pane.

"We need say no more about him," went on Mrs. Maynard. "Margaret, you've been brought up in luxury. If your father happened to die now—he's far from well—we'd be left penniless. We've lived up every dollar.... We have our poor crippled Blair to care for. You know you must marry well. I've brought you up with that end in view. And it's imperative you marry soon."

"Why must a girl marry?" murmured Margaret, wistfulness in her voice. "I'd rather go to work." "Margaret, you are a Maynard," replied her mother, haughtily. "Pray spare me any of this new woman talk about liberty—equal rights—careers and all that. Life hasn't changed for the conservative families of blood.... Try to understand, Margaret, that you must marry and marry well. You're nobody without money. In society there are hundreds of girls like you, though few so attractive. That's all the more reason you should take the best chance you have, before it's lost. If you don't marry people will say you can't. They'll say you're fading, growing old, even if you grow prettier every day of your life, and in the end they'll make you a miserable old maid. Then you'll be glad to marry anybody. If you marry now you can help your father, who needs help badly enough. You can help poor Blair.... You can be a leader in society; you can have a house here, a cottage at the seashore and one in the mountains; everything a girl's heart yearns for—servants, horses, autos, gowns, diamonds——"

"Everything except love," interrupted Margaret, bitterly.

Mrs. Maynard actually flushed, but she kept her temper.

"It's desirable that you love your husband. Any sensible woman can learn to care for a man. Love, as you dream about it is merely a—a dream. If women waited for that they would never get married."

"Which would be preferable to living without love."

"But Margaret, what would become of the world? If there were fewer marriages—Heaven knows they're few enough nowadays—there would be fewer families—and in the end fewer children—less and less——"

"They'd be better children," said Margaret, calmly.

"Eventually the race would die out."

"And that'd be a good thing—if the people can't love each other."

"How silly—exasperating!" ejaculated Mrs. Maynard. "You don't mean such nonsense. What any girl wants is a home of her own, a man to fuss over. I didn't marry for love, as you dream it. My husband attended to his business and I've looked after his household. You've had every advantage. I flatter myself our marriage has been a success."

Margaret's eyes gleamed like pointed flames.

"I differ with you. Your married life hasn't been successful any more than it's been happy. You never cared for father. You haven't been kind to him since his failure."

Mrs. Maynard waved her hand imperiously in angry amaze.

"I won't stop. I'm not a baby or a doll," went on Margaret, passionately. "If I'm old enough to marry I'm old enough to talk. I can think, can't I? You never told me anything, but I could see. Ever since I can remember you and father have had one continual wrangle about money—bills—expenses. Perhaps I'd have been better off without all the advantages and luxury. It's because of these things you want to throw me at some man. I'd far rather go to work the same as Blaid did, instead of college."

"Whatever on earth has come over you?" gasped Mrs. Maynard, bewildered by the revolt of this once meek daughter.

"Maybe I'm learning a little sense. Maybe I got some of it from Daren Lane," flashed back Margaret.

"Mother, whatever I've learned lately has been learned away from home. You've no more idea what's going on in the world to-day than if you were actually dead. I never was bright like Mel Iden, but I'm no fool. I see and hear and I read. Girls aren't pieces of furniture to be handed out to some rich men. Girls are waking up. They can do things. They can be independent. And being independent doesn't mean a girl's not going to marry. For she can wait—wait for the right man—for love.... You say I dream. Well, why didn't you wake me up long ago—with the truth? I had my dreams about love and marriage. And I've learned that love and marriage are vastly different from what most mothers make them out to be, or let a girl think."

"Margaret, I'll not have you talk in this strange way. You owe me respect if not obedience," said Mrs. Maynard, her voice trembling.

"Oh, well, I won't say any more," replied Margaret, "But can't you spare me? Couldn't we live within our means?"

"After all these years—to skimp along! I couldn't endure it."

"Whom have you in mind for me to—to marry?" asked the girl, coldly curious.

"Mr. Swann has asked your hand in marriage for his son Richard. He wants Richard to settle down. Richard is wild, like all these young men. And I have—well, I encouraged the plan."

"*Mother!*" cried Margaret, springing up.

"Margaret, you will see"

"I despise Dick Swann."

"Why?" asked her mother.

"I just do. I never liked him in school. He used to do such mean things. He's selfish. He let Holt and Daren suffer for his tricks."

"Margaret, you talk like a child."

"Listen, mother." She threw her arms round Mrs. Maynard and kissed her and spoke pleadingly. "Oh, don't make me hate myself. It seems I've grown so much older in the last year or so—and lately since this marriage talk came up. I've thought of things as never before because I've—I've learned about them. I see so differently. I can't—can't love Dick Swann. I can't bear to have him touch me. He's rude. He takes liberties.... He's too free with his hands! Why, it'd be wrong to marry him. What difference can a marriage service make in a girl's feelings.... Mother, let me say no."

"Lord spare me from bringing up another girl!" exclaimed Mrs. Maynard. "Margaret, I can't make you marry Richard Swann. I'm simply trying to tell you what any sensible girl would see she had to do. You think it over—both sides of the question—before you absolutely decide."

Mrs. Maynard was glad to end the discussion and to get away. In Margaret's appeal she heard a yielding, a final obedience to her wish. And she thought she had better let well enough alone. The look in Margaret's clear blue eyes made her shrink; it would haunt her. But she felt no remorse. Any mother would have done the same. There was always the danger of that old love affair; there was new danger in these strange wild fancies of modern girls; there was never any telling what Margaret might do. But once married she would be safe and her position assured.

CHAPTER VII

Daren Lane left Riverside Park, and walked in the meadows until he came to a boulder under a huge chestnut tree. Here he sat down. He could not walk far these days. Many a time in the Indian summers long past he had gathered chestnuts there with Dal, with Mel Iden, with Helen. He would never do it again.

The April day had been warm and fresh with the opening of a late spring. The sun was now gold—rimming the low hills in the west; the sky was pale blue; the spring flowers whitened the meadow. Twilight began to deepen; the evening star twinkled out of the sky; the hush of the gloaming hour stole over the land.

"Four weeks home—and nothing done. So little time left!" he muttered.

Two weeks of that period he had been unable to leave his bed. The rest of the time he had dragged himself around, trying to live up to his resolve, to get at the meaning of the present, to turn his sister Lorna from the path of dalliance. And he had failed in all.

His sister presented the problem that most distressed Lane. She had her good qualities, and through them could be reached. But she was thoughtless, vacillating, and wilful. She had made him promises only to break them. Lane had caught her in falsehoods. And upon being called to account she had told him that if he didn't like it he could "lump" it. Of late she had grown away from what affection she had shown at first. She could not bear interference with her pleasures, and seemed uncontrollable. Lane felt baffled. This thing was a Juggernaut impossible to stop.

Lane had scraped acquaintance with Harry Hale, one of Lorna's admirers, a boy of eighteen, who lived with his widowed mother on the edge of the town. He appeared to be an industrious, intelligent, quiet fellow, not much given to the prevailing habits of the young people. In his humble worship of Lorna he was like a dog. Lorna went to the motion pictures with him occasionally, when she had no other opportunity for excitement. Lane gathered that Lorna really liked this boy, and when with him seemed more natural, more what a fifteen-year-old girl used to be. And somehow it was upon this boy that Lane placed a forlorn hope.

No more automobiles honked in front of the home to call Lorna out. She met her friends away from the house, and returning at night she walked the last few blocks. It was this fact that awoke Lane's serious suspicions.

Another problem lay upon Lane's heart; if not so distressing as Lorna's, still one that added to his sorrow and his perplexity. He had gone once to call on Mel Iden. Mel Iden was all soul. Whatever had been the facts of her downfall—and reflection on that hurt Lane so strangely he could not bear it—it had not been on her part a matter of sex. She was far above wantonness.

Through long hours in the dark of night, when Lane's pain kept him sleepless, he had pondered over the mystery of Mel Iden until it cleared. She typified the mother of the race. In all periods of the progress of the race, war had brought out this instinct in women—to give themselves for the future. It was a provision of nature, inscrutable and terrible. How immeasurable the distance between Mel Iden and those women who practised birth control! As the war had brought out hideous greed and baseness, so had it propelled forward and upward the noblest attributes of life. Mel Iden was a builder, not a destroyer. She had been sexless and selfless. Unconsciously during the fever and emotion of the training of American men for service abroad, and the poignancy of their departure, to fight, and perhaps never return, Mel Iden had answered to this mysterious instinct of nature. Then, with the emotion past, and face to face with staggering consequences, she had reacted to conscious instincts. She had proved the purity of her surrender. She was all mother. And Lane began to see her moving in a crystal, beautiful light.

For what seemed a long time Lane remained motionless there in the silence of the meadow. Then at length he arose and retraced his slow steps back to town. Darkness overtook him on the bridge that spanned Middleville River. He leaned over the railing and peered down into the shadows. A soft murmur of rushing water came up. How like strange distant voices calling him to go back or go on, or warning him, or giving mystic portent of something that would happen to him there! A cold chill crept over him and he seemed enveloped in a sombre menace of the future. But he shook it off. He had many battles to fight, not the least of which was with morbid imagination.

When he reached the center of town he entered the lobby of the Bradford Inn. He hoped to meet Blair Maynard there. A company of well-dressed youths and men filled the place, most of whom appeared to be making a merry uproar.

Lane observed two men who evidently were the focus of attention. One was a stranger, very likely a traveling man, and at the moment he presented a picture of mingled consternation and anger. He was brushing off his clothes while glaring at a little, stout, red-faced man who appeared about to be stricken by apoplexy. This latter was a Colonel Pepper, whose acquaintance Lane had recently made. He was fond of cards and sport, and appeared to be a favorite with the young men about town. Moreover he had made himself particularly agreeable to Lane, in fact to the extent of Lane's embarrassment. At this moment the stranger lost his consternation wholly in wrath, and made a threatening movement toward Pepper. Lane stepped between them just in time to save Pepper a blow.

"I know what he's done. I apologize for him," said Lane, to the stranger. "He's made a good many people victims of the same indignity. It's a weakness—a disease. He can't help himself. Pray overlook it."

The stranger appeared impressed with Lane's presence, probably with his uniform, and slowly shook himself and fell back, to glower at Pepper, and curse under his breath, still uncertain of himself.

Lane grasped Colonel Pepper and led him out of the lobby.

"Pepper, you're going to get in an awful mess with that stunt of yours," he declared, severely. "If you can't help it you ought at least pick on your friends, or the town people—not strangers."

"Have—a—drink," sputtered Pepper, with his hand at his hip.

"No, thanks."

"Have—a—cigar."

Lane laughed. He had been informed that Colonel Pepper's failing always took this form of remorse, and certainly he would have tried it upon his latest victim had not Lane interfered.

"Colonel, you're hopeless," said Lane, as they walked out. "I hope somebody will always be around to protect you. I'd carry a body guard.... Say, have you seen Blair Maynard or Holt Dalrymple to-night?"

"Not Blair, but Holt was here early with the boys," replied Pepper. "They've gone to the club rooms to have a little game. I'm going to sit in. Lately I had to put up a holler. If the boys quit cards how'm I to make a living?"

"Had Holt been drinking?"

"Not to-night. But he's been hitting the bottle pretty hard of late."

Suddenly Lane buttonholed the little man and peered down earnestly at him. "Pepper, I've been trying to straighten Holt up. He's going to the bad. But he's a good kid. It's only the company.... The fact is—this's strictly confidential, mind you—Holt's sister begged me to try to stop his drinking and gambling. I think I can do it, too, with a little help. Now, Pepper, I'm asking you to help me."

"Ahuh! Well, let's go in the writing room, where we can talk," said the other, and he took hold of Lane's arm. When they were seated in a secluded corner he lighted a cigar, and faced Lane with shrewd, kindly eyes. "Son, I like you and Blair as well as I hate these slackers Swann and Mackay, and their crowd. I could tell you a heap, and maybe help you, though I think young Holt is not a bad egg.... Is his sister the dark one who steps so straight and holds herself so well?"

"Yes, that sounds like Dorothy," replied Lane.

"She's about the only one I know who doesn't paint her face and I never saw her at—well, never mind where. But the fact I mean makes her stand out in this Middleville crowd like a light in the dark.... Lane, have you got on yet to the speed of the young people of this old burg?"

"I'm getting on, to my sorrow," said Lane.

"Ahuh! You mean you're getting wise to your kid sister?"

"Yes, I'm sorry to say. What do you know, Pepper?"

"Now, son, wait. I'm coming to that, maybe. But I want to know some things first. Is it true—what I hear about your health, bad shape, you know—all cut up in the war? Worse than young Maynard?"

Pepper's hand was close on Lane's. He had forgotten his cigar. His eyes were earnest.

"True?" laughed Lane, grimly. "Yes, it's true.... I won't last long, Pepper, according to Doctor Bronson. That's why I want to make hay while the sun shines."

"Ahuh!" Pepper cleared his throat. "Forgive this, boy.... Is it also true you were engaged to marry that Helen Wrapp—and she threw you down, while you were over there?"

"Yes, that's perfectly true," replied Lane, soberly.

"God, I guess maybe the soldier wasn't up against it!" ejaculated Pepper, with a gesture of mingled awe and wonder and scorn.

"What was the soldier up against, Pepper?" queried Lane. "Frankly, I don't know."

"Lane, the government jollied and forced the boys into the army," replied Pepper. "The country went wild with patriotism. The soldiers were heroes. The women threw themselves away on anything inside a uniform. Make the world safe for democracy—down the Hun—save France and England—ideals, freedom, God's country, and all that! Well, the first few soldiers to return from France got a grand reception, were made heroes of. They were lucky to get back while the sentiment was hot. But that didn't last.... Now, a year and more after the war, where does the soldier get off? Lane, there're over six hundred thousand of you disabled veterans, and for all I can read and find out the government has done next to nothing. New York is full of begging soldiers—on the streets. Think of it! And the poor devils are dying everywhere. My God! think of what's in the mind of one crippled soldier, let alone over half a million. I just have a dim idea of what I'd felt. You must know, or you will know, Lane, for you seem a thoughtful, lofty sort of chap. Just the kind to make a good soldier, because you had ideals and nerve!... Well, a selfish and weak administration could hardly be expected to keep extravagant promises to patriots. But that the American public, as a body, should now be sick of the sight of a crippled soldier—and that his sweetheart should turn him down!—this is the hideous blot, the ineradicable shame, the stinking truth, the damned mystery!"

When Pepper ended his speech, which grew more vehement toward the close, Lane could only stare at him in amaze.

"See here, Lane," added the other hastily, "pardon me for blowing up. I just couldn't help it. I took a shine to you—and to see you like this—brings back the resentment I've had all along. I'm blunt, but it's just as well for you to be put wise quick. You'll find friends, like me, who will stand by you, if you let them. But you'll also find that most of this rotten world has gone back on you...."

Then Pepper made a sharp, passionate gesture that broke his cigar against the arm of his chair, and he cursed low and deep. Presently he addressed Lane again. "Whatever comes of any disclosures I make—whatever you *do*—you'll not give me away?"

"Certainly not. You can trust me, Pepper," returned Lane.

"Son, I'm a wise old guy. There's not much that goes on in Middleville I don't get on to. And I'll make your hair curl. But I'll confine myself to what comes closest home to you. I *get* you, Lane. You're game. You're through. You have come back from war to find a hell of a mess. Your own sister—your sweetheart—your friend's brother and your soldier pard's sister—on the primrose path! And you with your last breath trying to turn them back! I'll say it's a damn fine stunt. I'm an old gambler, Lane. I've lived in many towns and mixed in tough crowds of crooked men and rotten women. But I'm here to confess that this after-the-war stuff of Middleville's better class has knocked out about all the faith I had left in human nature.... Then you came along to teach me a lesson."

"Well, Pepper, that's strong talk," returned Lane. "But cut it, and hurry to—to what comes home to me. What's the matter with these Middleville girls?"

"Lane, any intelligent man, who *knows* things, and who can think for himself, will tell you this—that to judge from the dress, dance, talk, conduct of these young girls—most of them have *apparently* gone wrong."

"You include our nice girls—from what we used to call Middleville's best families?"

"I don't only include them. I throw the emphasis on them. The girls you know best."

Lane straightened up, to look at his companion. Pepper certainly was not drunk.

"Do you know—anything about Lorna?"

"Nothing specifically to prove anything. She's in the thick of this thing in Middleville. Only a few nights ago I saw her at a roadhouse, out on the State Road, with a crowd of youngsters. They were having a high old time, I'll say. They danced jazz, and I saw Lorna drink lemonade into which liquor had been poured from a hip-pocket flask."

Lane put his head on his hands, as if to rest it, or still the throbbing there.

"Who took Lorna to this place?" he asked, presently, breathing heavily.

"I don't know. But it was Dick Swann who poured the drink out of the flask. Between you and me, Lane, that young millionaire is going a pace hereabouts. Listen," he went on, lowering his voice, and glancing round to see there was no one to overhear him, "there's a gambling club in Middleville. I go there. My rooms are in the same building. I've made a peep-hole through the attic floor next to my room. Do I see more things than cards and bottles? Do I! If the fathers of Middleville could see what I've seen they'd go out to the asylum.... I'm not supposed to know it's more than a place to gamble. And nobody knows I know. Dick Swann and Hardy Mackay are at the head of this club. Swann is the genius and the support of it. He's rich, and a high roller if I ever saw one.... Among themselves these young gentlemen call it the Strong Arm Club. Study over that, Lane. Do you *get* it? I know you do, and that saves me talking until I see red."

"Pepper, have you seen my sister—there?" queried Lane, tensely.

"Yes."

"With whom?"

"I'll not say, Lane. There's no need for that. I'll give you a key to my rooms, and you can go there—in the afternoons—and paste yourself to my peep-hole, and watch.... Honest to God, I believe it means bloodshed. But I can't help that. Something must be done. I'm not much good, but I can see that."

Colonel Pepper wiped his moist face. He was now quite pale and his hands shook.

"I never had a wife, or a sweetheart," he went on. "But once I had a little sister. Thank Heaven she didn't live her girlhood in times like these."

Lane again bowed his head on his hands, and wrestled with the might of reality.

"I'm going to take you to these club-rooms to-night," went on Pepper. "It'll cause a hell of a row. But once you get in, there'll be no help for them. Swann and his chums will have to stand for it."

"Did you ever take an outsider in?" asked Lane.

"Several times. Traveling men I met here. Good fellows that liked a game of cards. Swann made no kick at that. He's keen to gamble. And when he's drinking the sky's the limit."

"Wouldn't it be wiser just to show me these rooms, and let me watch from your place—until I find my sister there?" queried Lane.

"I don't know," replied Pepper, thoughtfully. "I think if I were you I'd butt in to-night with me. You can drag young Dalrymple home before he gets drunk".

"Pepper, I'll break up this—this club," declared Lane.

"I'll say you will. And I'm for you strong. If it was only the booze and cards I'd not have squealed. That's my living. But by God, I can't stand for the—the other stuff any longer!... Come on now. And I'll put you on to a slick stunt that'll take your breath away."

He led the way out of the hotel, in his excitement walking rather fast.

"Go slow, Pepper," said Lane. "We're not going over the top."

Pepper gave him a quick, comprehending look.

"Good Lord, Lane, you're not as—as bad as all that!"

Lane nodded. Then at slower pace they went out and down the bright Main Street for two blocks, and then to the right on West Street, which was quite comparable to the other thoroughfare as a business district. At the end of the street the buildings were the oldest in Middleville, and entirely familiar to Lane.

"Give White's the once over," said Pepper, indicating a brightly lighted store across the street. "That place is new to you, isn't it?"

"Yes, I don't remember White, or that there was a confectionery den along here."

"Den is right. It's some den, believe me.... White's a newcomer—a young sport, thick with Swann. For all I know Swann is backing him. Anyway he has a swell joint and a good trade. People kick about his high prices. Ice cream, candy, soda, soft drinks, and all that rot. But if he knows who you are you can get a shot. It'll strike you funny later to see he waits on the customers himself. But when you get wise it'll not be so funny. He's got a tea parlor upstairs— and they say it's some swell place, with a rest room or ladies' dressing room back. Now from this back room the girls can get into the club-rooms of the boys, and go out on the other side of the block. In one way and out the other—at night. Not necessary in the afternoon.... Come on now, well go round the block."

A short walk round the block brought them into a shaded, wide street with one of Middleville's parks on the left. A row of luxuriant elm trees helped the effect of gloom. The nearest electric light was across on the far corner, with trees obscuring it to some extent. At the corner where Pepper halted there was an outside stairway running up the old-fashioned building. The ground floor shops bore the signs of a florist and a milliner; above was a photograph gallery; and the two upper stories were apparently unoccupied. To the left of the two stores another stairway led up into the center of the building. Pepper led Lane up this stairway, a long, dark climb of three stories that taxed Lane's endurance.

"Sure is a junk heap, this old block," observed Pepper, as he fumbled in the dim light with his keys. At length he opened a door, turned on a light and led Lane into his apartment. "I have three rooms here, and the back one opens into a kind of areaway from which I get into an abandoned storeroom, or I guess it's an attic. To-morrow afternoon about three you meet me here and I'll take you in there and let you have a look through the peep-hole I made. It's no use to-night, because there'll be only boys at the club, and I'm going to take you right in."

He switched off the light, drew Lane out and locked the door. "I'm the only person who lives on this floor. There're three holes to this burrow and one of them is at the end of this hall. The exit where the girls slip out is on the floor below, through a hallway to that outside stairs. Oh, I'll say it's a Coney Island maze, this building! But just what these young rakes want.... Come on, and be careful. It'll be dark and the stairs are steep."

At the end of the short hall Pepper opened a door, and led Lane down steep steps in thick darkness, to another hall, dimly lighted by a window opening upon the street.

"You'll have to make a bluff at playing poker, unless my butting in with you causes a row," said Pepper, as he walked along. Presently he came to a door upon which he knocked several times. But before it was opened footsteps and voices sounded down the hall in the opposite direction from which Pepper had escorted Lane.

"Guess they're just coming. Hard luck," said Pepper. "'Fraid you'll not get in now."

Lane counted five dark forms against the background of dim light. He saw the red glow of a cigarette. Then the door upon which Pepper had knocked opened to let out a flare. Pepper gave Lane a shove across the threshold and followed him. Lane did not recognize the young man who had opened the door. The room was large, with old walls and high ceiling, a round table with chairs and a sideboard. It had no windows. The door on the other side was closed.

"Pepper, who's this you're ringin' in on me?" demanded the young fellow.

"A pard of mine. Now don't be peeved, Sammy," replied Pepper. "If there's any kick I'll take the blame.

Then the five young men glided swiftly into the room. The last one was Dick Swann. In the act of closing the door behind him, he saw Lane, and started violently back. His face turned white. His action, his look silenced the talk.

"Lane! What do you want?" he jerked out.

Lane eyed him without replying. He thought he read more in Swann's face and voice than any of the amazed onlookers.

"Dick, I fetched Lane up for a little game," put in Pepper, with composure.

Swann jerked as violently out of his stiffened posture as he had frozen into it. His face changed--showed comprehension--relief--then flamed with anger.

"Pepper, it's a damn high-handed imposition for you to bring strangers here," he burst out.

"Well, I'm sorry you take it that way," replied Pepper, with deprecatory spreading of his hands. He was quite cool and his little eyes held a singular gleam. "You never kicked before when I brought a stranger."

Swann fiercely threw down his cigarette.

"Hell! I told you never to bring any Middleville man in here."

"Ahuh! I forgot. You'll have to excuse me," returned Pepper, not with any particular regret.

"What's the matter with my money?" queried Lane, ironically, at last removing his steady gaze from Swann to the others. Mackay was there, and Holt Dalrymple, the boy in whom Lane had lately interested himself. Holt resembled his sister in his dark rich coloring, but his face wore a shade of sullen depression. The other two young men Lane had seen in Middleville, but they were unknown to him.

"Pepper, you beat it with your new pard," snarled Swarm. "And you'll not get in here again, take that from me."

The mandate nettled Pepper, who evidently felt more deeply over this situation than had appeared on the surface.

"Sure, I'll beat it," returned he, resentfully. "But see here, Swann. Be careful how you shoot off your dirty mouth. It's not beyond me to hand a little tip to my friend Chief of Police Bell."

"You damned squealer!" shouted Swann. "Go ahead--do your worst. You'll find I pull a stroke.... Now get out of here."

With a violent action he shoved the little man out into the hall. Then turning to Lane he pointed with shaking hand to the door.

"Lane, you couldn't be a guest of mine."

"Swann, I certainly wouldn't be," retorted Lane, in tones that rang. "Pepper didn't tell me you were the proprietor of this--this joint."

"Get out of here or I'll throw you out!" yelled Swann, now beside himself with rage. And he made a threatening move toward Lane.

"Don't lay a hand on me," replied Lane. "I don't want my uniform soiled."

With that Lane turned to Dalrymple, and said quietly: "Holt, I came here to find you, not to play cards. That was a stall. Come away with me. You were not cut out for a card sharp or a booze fighter. What's got into you that you can gamble and drink with *slackers*?"

Dalrymple jammed his hat on and stepped toward the door. "Dare, you said a lot. I'll beat it with you—and I'll never come back."

"You bet your sweet life you won't," shouted Swann.

"Hold on there, Dalrymple," interposed Mackay, stepping out. "Come across with that eighty-six bucks you owe me."

"I—I haven't got it, Mackay," rejoined the boy, flushing deeply.

Lane ripped open his coat and jerked out his pocket-book and tore bills out of it. "There, Hardy Mackay," he said, with deliberate scorn, throwing the money on the table. "There are your eighty-six dollars—*earned* in France.... I should think it'd burn your fingers."

He drew Holt out into the hall, where Pepper waited. Some one slammed the door and began to curse.

"That ends that," said Colonel Pepper, as the three moved down the dim hall.

"It ends us, Pepper, but you couldn't stop those guys with a crowbar," retorted Dalrymple.

Lane linked arms with the boy and changed the conversation while they walked back to the inn. Here Colonel Pepper left them, and Lane talked to Holt for an hour. The more he questioned Holt the better he liked him, and yet the more surprised was he at the sordid fact of the boy's inclination toward loose living. There was something perhaps that Holt would not confess. His health had been impaired in the service, but not seriously. He was getting stronger all the time. His old job was waiting for him. His mother and sister had enough to live on, but if he had been working he could have helped them in a way to afford him great satisfaction.

"Holt, listen," finally said Lane, with more earnestness. "We're friends—all boys of the service are friends. We might even become great pards, if we had time."

"What's time got to do with it?" queried the younger man. "I'm sure I'd like it—and know it'd help me."

"I'm shot to pieces, Holt.... I won't last long...."

"Aw, Lane, don't say that!"

"It's true. And if I'm to help you at all it must be now.... You haven't told me everything, boy—now have you?"

Holt dropped his head.

"I'll say—I haven't," he replied, haltingly. "Lane—the trouble is—I'm clean gone on Margie Maynard. But her mother hates the sight of me. She won't stand for me."

"Oho! So that's it?" ejaculated Lane, a light breaking in upon him. "Well, I'll be darned. It *is* serious, Holt.... Does Margie love you?"

"Sure she does. We've always cared. Don't you remember how Margie and I and Dal and you used to go to school together? And come home together? And play on Saturdays?... Ever since then!... But lately Margie and I are—we got—pretty badly mixed up."

"Yes, I remember those days," replied Lane, dreamily, and suddenly he recalled Dal's dark eyes, somehow haunting. He had to make an effort to get back to the issue at hand.

"If Margie loves you—why it's all right. Go back to work and marry her."

"Lane, it can't be all right. Mrs. Maynard has handed me the mitt," replied Holt, bitterly. "And Margie hasn't the courage to run off with me.... Her mother is throwing Margie at Swann—because he's rich."

"Oh Lord, no—Holt—you can't mean *it*!" exclaimed Lane, aghast.

"I'll say I do mean it. I *know* it," returned Holt, moodily. "So I let go—fell into the dumps—didn't care a d—— what became of me."

Lane was genuinely shocked. What a tangle he had fallen upon! Once again there seemed to confront him a colossal Juggernaut, a moving, crushing, intangible thing, beyond his power to cope with.

"Now, what can I do?" queried Holt, in sudden hope his friend might see a way out.

Despairingly, Lane racked his brain for some word of advice or assurance, if not of solution. But he found none. Then his spirit mounted, and with it passion.

"Holt, don't be a miserable coward," he began, in fierce scorn. "You're a soldier, man, and you've got your life to *live*!... The sun will rise—the days will be long and pleasant—you can work—*do* something. You can fish the streams in summer and climb the hills in autumn. You can enjoy. Bah! don't tell me one shallow girl means the world. If Margie hasn't courage enough to run off and marry you—*let her go!* But you can never tell. Maybe Margie will stick to you. I'll help you. Margie and I have always been friends and I'll try to influence her. Then think of your mother and sister. Work for *them*. Forget yourself—your little, miserable, selfish desires.... My God, boy, but it's a strange life the war's left us to face. I *hate* it. So do you hate it. Swann and Mackay giving nothing and getting all! ... So it looks.... But it's false—false. God did not intend men to live solely for their bodies. A balance *must* be struck. They have *got* to pay. Their time will come.... As for you, the harder this job is the fiercer you should be. I've got to die, Holt. But if I could live I'd show these slackers, these fickle wild girls, what they're doing.... You can do it, Holt. It's the greatest part any man could be called upon to play. It will prove the difference between you and them...."

Holt Dalrymple crushed Lane's hand in both his own. On his face was a glow—his dark eyes flashed: "Lane—that'll be about all," he burst out with a kind of breathlessness. Then his head high, he stalked out.

The next day was bad. Lane suffered from both over-exertion and intensity of emotion. He remained at home all day, in bed most of the time. At supper time he went downstairs to find Lorna pirouetting in a new dress, more abbreviated at top and bottom than any costume he had seen her wear. The effect struck him at an inopportune time. He told her flatly that she looked like a French grisette of the music halls, and ought to be ashamed to be seen in such attire.

"Daren, I don't think you're a good judge of clothes these days," she observed, complacently. "The boys will say I look spiffy in this."

So many times Lorna's trenchant remarks silenced Lane. She hit the nail on the head. Practical, logical, inevitable were some of her speeches. She knew what men wanted. That was the pith of her meaning. What else mattered?

"But Lorna, suppose you don't look nice?" he questioned.

"I *do* look nice," she retorted.

"You don't look anything of the kind."

"What's nice? It's only a word. It doesn't mean much in my young life."

"Where are you going to-night?" he asked, sitting down to the table.

"To the armory—basketball game—and dance afterward."

"With whom?"

"With Harry. I suppose that pleases you, big brother?"

"Yes, it does. I like him. I wish he'd take you out oftener."

"*Take* me! Hot dog! He'd kill himself to take me all the time. But Harry's slow. He bores me. Then he hasn't got a car."

"Lorna, you may as well know now that I'm going to stop your car rides," said Lane, losing his patience.

"You are *not*," she retorted, and in the glint of the eyes meeting his, Lane saw his defeat. His patience was exhausted, his fear almost verified. He did not mince words. With his mother standing open-mouthed and shocked, Lane gave his sister to understand what he thought of automobile rides, and that as far as she was concerned they had to be stopped. If she would not stop them out of respect to her mother and to him, then he would resort to other measures. Lorna bounced up in a fury, and in the sharp quarrel that followed, Lane realized he was dealing with flint full of fire. Lorna left without finishing her supper.

"Daren, that's not the way," said his mother, shaking her head.

"What is the way, mother?" he asked, throwing up his hands.

"I don't know, unless it's to see her way," responded the mother. "Sometimes I feel so—so old-fashioned and ignorant before Lorna. Maybe she is right. How can we tell? What makes all the young girls like that?"

What indeed, wondered Lane! The question had been hammering at his mind for over a month. He went back to bed, weary and dejected, suffering spasms of pain, like blades, through his lungs, and grateful for the darkness. Almost he wished it was all over—this ordeal. How puny his efforts! Relentlessly life marched on. At midnight he was still fighting his pangs, still unconquered. In the night his dark room was not empty. There were faces, shadows, moving images and pictures, scenes of the war limned against the blackness. At last he rested, grew as free from pain as he ever grew, and slept. In the morning it was another day, and the past was as if it were not.

May the first dawned ideally springlike, warm, fresh, fragrant, with birds singing, sky a clear blue, and trees budding green and white.

Lane yielded to an impulse that had grown stronger of late. His steps drew him to the little drab house where Mel Iden lived with her aunt. On the way, which led past a hedge, Lane gathered a bunch of violets.

"'In the spring a young man's fancy lightly turns to thoughts of love,'" he mused. "It's good, even for *me*, to be alive this morning.... These violets, the birds, the fresh smells, the bursting green! Oh, well, regrets are idle. But just to think—I had to go through all I've known—right down to this moment—to realize how stingingly sweet life is...."

Mel answered his knock, and sight of her face seemed to lift his heart with an unwonted throb. Had he unconsciously needed that? The thought made his greeting, and the tender of the violets, awkward for him.

"Violets! Oh, and spring! Daren, it was good of you to gather them for me. I remember.... But I told you not to come again."

"Yes, I know you did," he replied. "But I've disobeyed you. I wanted to see you, Mel.... I didn't know how badly until I got here."

"You should not want to see me at all. People will talk."

"So you care what people say of you?" he questioned, feigning surprise.

"Of me? No. I was thinking of you."

"You fear the poison tongues for me? Well, they cannot harm me. I'm beyond tongues or minds like those."

She regarded him earnestly, with serious gravity and slowly dawning apprehension; then, turning to arrange the violets in a tiny vase, she shook her head.

"Daren, you're beyond me, too. I feel a—a change in you. Have you had another sick spell?"

"Only for a day off and on. I'm really pretty well to-day. But I have changed. I feel that, yet I don't know how."

Lane could talk to her. She stirred him, drew him out of himself. He felt a strange desire for her sympathy, and a keen curiosity concerning her opinions.

"I thought maybe you'd been ill again or perhaps upset by the consequences of your—your action at Fanchon Smith's party."

"Who told you of that?" he asked in surprise.

"Dal. She was here yesterday. She will come in spite of me."

"So will I," interposed Lane.

She shook her head. "No, it's different for a man.... I've missed the girls. No one but Dal ever comes. I thought Margie would be true to me—no matter what had befallen.... Dal comes, and oh, Daren, she is good. She helps me so.... She told me what you did at Fanchon's party."

"She did! Well, what's your verdict?" he queried, grimly. "That break queered me in Middleville."

"I agree with what Doctor Wallace said to his congregation," returned Mel.

As Lane met the blue fire of her eyes he experienced another singularly deep and profound thrill, as if the very depths of him had been stirred. He seemed to have suddenly discovered Mel Iden.

"Doctor Wallace did back me up," said Lane, with a smile. "But no one else did."

"Don't be so sure of that. Harsh conditions require harsh measures. Dal said you killed the camel-walk dance in Middleville."

"It surely was a disgusting sight," returned Lane, with a grimace. "Mel, I just saw red that night."

"Daren," she asked wistfully, following her own train of thought, "do you know that most of the girls consider me an outcast? Fanchon rides past me with her head up in the air. Helen Wrapp cuts me. Margie looks to see if her mother is watching when she bows to me. Isn't it strange, Daren, how things turn out? Maybe my old friends are right. But I don't *feel* that I am what they think I am.... I would do what I did—over and over."

Her eyes darkened under his gaze, and a slow crimson tide stained her white face.

"I understand you, Mel," he said, swiftly. "You must forgive me that I didn't understand at once.... And I think you are infinitely better, finer, purer than these selfsame girls who scorn you."

"Daren! You—understand?" she faltered.

And just as swiftly he told her the revelation that thinking had brought to him.

When he had finished she looked at him for a long while. "Yes, Daren," she finally said, "you understand, and you have made me understand. I always felt"—and her hand went to her heart—"but my mind did not grasp.... Oh, Daren, how I thank you!" and she held her hands out to him.

Lane grasped the outstretched hands, and loosed the leaping thought her words and action created.

"Mel, let me give your boy a father—a name."

No blow could have made her shrink so palpably. It passed—that shame. Her lips parted, and other emotions claimed her.

"Daren—you would—marry me?" she gasped.

"I am asking you to be my wife for your child's sake," he replied.

Her head bowed. She sank against him, trembling. Her hands clung tightly to his. Lane divined something of her agitation from the feel of her slender form. And then again that deep and profound thrill ran over him. It was followed by an instinct to wrap her in his arms, to hold her, to share her trouble and to protect her.

Strong reserve force suddenly came to Mel. She drew away from Lane, still quivering, but composed.

"Daren, all my life I'll thank you and bless you for that offer," she said, very low. "But, of course it is impossible."

She disengaged her hands, and, turning away, looked out of the window. Lane rather weakly sat down. What had come over him? His blood seemed bursting in his veins. Then he gazed round the dingy little parlor and at this girl of twenty, whose beauty did not harmonize with her surroundings. Fair-haired, white-faced, violet-eyed, she emanated tragedy. He watched her profile, clear cut as a cameo, fine brow, straight nose, sensitive lips, strong chin. She was biting those tremulous lips. And when she turned again to him they were red. The short-bowed upper lip, full and sweet, the lower, with its sensitive droop at the corner, eloquent of sorrow—all at once Lane realized he wanted to kiss that mouth more than he had ever wanted anything. The moment was sudden and terrible, for it meant love—love such as he had never known.

"Daren," she said, turning, "tell me how you got the *Croix de Guerre*."

By the look of her and the hand that moved toward his breast, Lane felt his power over her. He began his story and it was as if he heard some one else talking. When he had finished, she asked, "The French Army honored you, why not the American?"

"It was never reported."

"How strange! Who was your officer?"

"You'll laugh when you hear," he replied, without hint of laugh himself. "Heavens, how things come about! My officer was from Middleville."

"Daren! Who?" she asked, quickly, her eyes darkening with thought.

"Captain Vane Thesel."

How singular to Lane the fact she did not laugh! She only stared. Then it seemed part of her warmth and glow, her subtle response to his emotion, slowly receded. He felt what he could not see.

"Oh! He. Vane Thesel," she said, without wonder or surprise or displeasure, or any expression Lane anticipated.

Her strange detachment stirred a hideous thought—could Thesel have been.... But Lane killed the culmination of that thought. Not, however, before dark, fiery jealousy touched him with fangs new to his endurance.

To drive it away, Lane launched into more narrative of the war. And as he talked he gradually forgot himself. It might be hateful to rake up the burning threads of memory for the curious and the soulless, but to tell Mel Iden it was a keen, strange delight. He watched the changes of her expression. He learned to bring out the horror, sadness, glory that abided in her heart. And at last he cut himself off abruptly: "But I must save something for another day."

That broke the spell.

"No, you must never come back."

He picked up his hat and his stick.

"Mel, would you shut the door in my face?"

"No, Daren—but I'll not open it," she replied resolutely.

"Why?"

"You must not come."

"For my sake—or yours?"

"Both our sakes."

He backed out on the little porch, and looked at her as she stood there. Beyond him, indeed, were his emotions then. Sad as she seemed, he wanted to make her suffer more—an inexplicable and shameful desire.

"Mel, you and I are alike," he said.

"Oh, no, Daren; you are noble and I am...."

"Mel, in my dreams I see myself standing—plodding along the dark shores of a river—that river of tears which runs down the vast naked stretch of our inner lives.... I see you now, on the opposite shore. Let us reach our hands across—for the baby's sake."

"Daren, it is a beautiful thought, but it—it can't be," she whispered.

"Then let me come to see you when I need—when I'm down," he begged.

"No."

"Mel, what harm can it do—just to let me come?"

"No—don't ask me. Daren, I am no stone."

"You'll be sorry when I'm out there in—Woodlawn.... That won't be long."

That broke her courage and her restraint.

"Come, then," she whispered, in tears.

CHAPTER VIII

Lane's intentions and his spirit were too great for his endurance. It was some time before he got downtown again. And upon entering the inn he was told some one had just called him on the telephone.

"Hello, this is Lane," he answered. "Who called me?"

"It's Blair," came the reply. "How are you, old top?"

"Not so well. I've been down and out."

"Sorry. Suppose that's why you haven't called me up for so long?"

"Well, Buddy, I can't lay it all to that.... And how're you?"

The answer did not come. So Lane repeated his query.

"Well, I'm still hobbling round on one leg," replied Blair.

"That's good. Tell me about Reddie."

Again the reply was long in coming....

"Haven't you heard—about Red?"

"No."

"Haven't seen the newspapers lately?"

"I never read the papers, Blair."

"Right-o. But I had to.... Buck up, now, Dare!"

"All right. Shoot it quick," returned Lane, feeling his breast contract and his skin tighten with a chill.

"Red Payson has gone west."

"Blair! You don't mean—dead?" exclaimed Lane.

"Yes, Reddie's gone—and I guess it's just as well, poor devil!"

"How? When?"

"Two days ago, according to papers.... He died in Washington, D.C. Fell down in the vestibule of one of the government offices—where he was waiting.... fell with another hemorrhage—and died right there—on the floor—quick."

"My—God!" gasped Lane.

"Yes, it's tough. You see, Dare, I couldn't keep Reddie here. Heaven knows I tried, but he wouldn't stay.... I'm afraid he heard my mother complaining. Say, Dare, suppose I have somebody drive me in town to see you."

"I'd like that, Blair."

"You're on. And say, I've another idea. Tonight's the Junior Prom—did you know that?"

"No, I didn't."

"Well, it is. Suppose we go up? My sister can get me cards.... I tell you, Dare, I'd like to see what's going on in that bunch. I've heard a lot and seen some things."

"Did you hear how I mussed up Fanchon Smith's party?"

"You bet I did. That's one reason I want to see some of this dancing. Will you go?"

"Yes, I can stand it if you can."

"All right, Buddy, I'll meet you at the inn—eight o'clock."

Lane slowly made his way to a secluded corner of the lobby, where he sat down. Red Payson dead! Lane felt that he should not have been surprised or shocked. But he was both. The strange, cold sensation gradually wore away and with it the slight trembling of his limbs. A mournful procession of thoughts and images returned to his mind and he sat and brooded.

At the hour of his appointment with his friend, Lane went to the front of the lobby. Blair was on time. He hobbled in, erect and martial of bearing despite the crutch, and his dark citizen's suit emphasized the whiteness of his face. Being home had softened Blair a little. Yet the pride and tragic bitterness were there. But when Blair espied Lane a warmth burned out of the havoc in his face. Lane's conscience gave him a twinge. It dawned upon him that neither his spells of illness, nor his distress over his sister Lorna, nor his obsession to see and understand what the young people were doing could hold him wholly excusable for having neglected his comrade.

Their hand-clasp was close, almost fierce, and neither spoke at once. But they looked intently into each other's faces. Emotion stormed Lane's heart. He realized that Blair loved him and that he loved Blair—and that between them was a measureless bond, a something only separation could make tangible. But little of what they felt came out in their greetings.

"Dare, why the devil don't you can that uniform," demanded Blair, cheerfully. "People might recognize you've been 'over there.'"

"Well, Blair, I expected you'd have a cork leg by this time," said Lane.

"Nothing doing," returned the other. "I want to be perpetually reminded that I was in the war. This 'forget the war' propaganda we see and hear all over acts kind of queer on a soldier.... Let's find a bench away from these people."

After they were comfortably seated Blair went on: "Do you know, Dare, I don't miss my leg so much when I'm crutching around. But when I try to sit down or get up! By heck, sometimes I forget it's gone. And sometimes I want to scratch my lost foot. Isn't that hell?"

"I'll say so, Buddy," returned Lane, with a laugh.

"Read this," said Blair, taking a paper from his pocket, and indicating a column.

Whereupon Lane read a brief Associated Press dispatch from Washington, D.C., stating that one Payson, disabled soldier of twenty-five, suffering with tuberculosis caused by gassed lungs, had come to Washington to make in person a protest and appeal that had been unanswered in letters. He wanted money from the government to enable him to travel west to a dry climate, where doctors assured him he might get well. He made his statement to several clerks and officials, and waited all day in the vestibule of the department. Suddenly he was seized with a hemorrhage, and, falling on the floor, died before aid could be summoned.

Without a word Lane handed the paper back to his friend.

"Red was a queer duck," said Blair, rather hoarsely. "You remember when I 'phoned you last over two weeks ago?... Well, just after that Red got bad on my hands. He wouldn't accept charity, he said. And he wanted to beat it. He got wise to my mother. He wouldn't give up trying to get money from the government—back money owed him, he swore—and the idea of being turned down at home seemed to obsess him. I talked and cussed myself weak. No good! Red beat it soon after that—beat it from Middleville on a freight train. And I never heard a word from him.... Not a word...."

"Blair, can't you see it Red's way?" queried Lane, sadly.

"Yes, I can," responded Blair, "but hell! he might have gotten well. Doc Bronson said Red had a chance. I could have borrowed enough money to get him out west. Red wouldn't take it."

"And he ran off—exposed himself to cold and starvation—over-exertion and anger," added Lane.

"Exactly. Brought on that hemorrhage and croaked. All for nothing!"

"No, Blair. All for a principle," observed Lane. "Red was fired out of the hospital without a dollar. There was something terribly wrong."

"Wrong?... God Almighty!" burst out Blair, with hard passion. "Let me read you something in this same paper." With shaking hands he unfolded it, searched until he found what he wanted, and began to read:

"'If the *actual* needs of disabled veterans require the expenditure of much money, then unquestionably a majority of the taxpayers of the country will favor spending it. Despite the insistent demand for economy in Washington that is arising from every part of the country, no member of House or Senate will have occasion to fear that he is running counter to popular opinion when eventually he votes to take generous care of disabled soldiers.'"

Blair's trembling voice ceased, and then twisting the newspaper into a rope, he turned to Lane. "Dare, can you understand that?... Red Payson was a bull-headed boy, not over bright. But you and I have some intelligence, I hope. We can allow for the immense confusion at Washington—the senselessness of red tape—the callosity of politicians. But when we remember the eloquent calls to us boys—the wonderfully worded appeals to our patriotism, love of country and home—the painted posters bearing the picture of a beautiful American girl—or a young mother with a baby—remembering these deep, passionate calls to the best in us, can you understand *that* sort of talk now?"

"Blair, I think I can," replied Lane. "Then—before and after the draft—the whole country was at a white heat of all that the approach of war rouses. Fear, self-preservation, love of country, hate of the Huns, inspired patriotism, and in most everybody the will to fight and to sacrifice.... The war was a long, hideous, soul-racking, nerve-destroying time. When it ended, and the wild period of joy and relief had its run, then all that pertained to the war sickened and wearied and disgusted the majority of people. It's 'forget the war.' You and Payson and I got home a year too late."

"Then—it's just—monstrous," said Blair, heavily.

"That's all, Blair. Just monstrous. But we can't beat our spirits out against this wall. No one can understand us—how alone we are. Let's forget *that*—this wall—this thing called government. Shall we spend what time we have to live always in a thunderous atmosphere of mind—hating, pondering, bitter?"

"No. I'll make a compact with you," returned Blair, with flashing eyes. "Never to speak again of *that*—so long as we live!"

"Never to a living soul," rejoined Lane, with a ring in his voice.

They shook hands much the same as when they had met half an hour earlier.

"So!" exclaimed Blair, with a deep breath. "And now, Dare, tell me how you made out with Helen. You cut me short over the 'phone."

"Blair, that day coming into New York on the ship, you didn't put it half strong enough," replied Lane. Then he told Blair about the call he had made upon Helen, and what had transpired at her studio.

Blair did not voice the scorn that his eyes expressed. And, in fact, most of his talking was confined to asking questions. Lane found it easy enough to unburden himself, though he did not mention his calls on Mel Iden, or Colonel Pepper's disclosures.

"Well, I guess it's high time we were meandering up to the hall," said Blair, consulting his watch. "I'm curious about this Prom. Think we're in for a jolt. It's four years since I went to a Prom. Now, both of us, Dare, have a sister who'll be there, besides all our old friends.... And we're not dancing! But I want to look on. They've got an out-of-town orchestra coming—a jazz orchestra. There'll probably be a hot time in the old town to-night."

"Lorna did not tell me," replied Lane, as they got up to go. "But I suppose she'd rather I didn't know. We've clashed a good deal lately."

"Dare, I hear lots of talk," said Blair. "Margaret is chummy with me, and some of her friends are always out at the house. I hear Dick Swann is rushing Lorna. Think he's doing it on the q-t."

"I know he is, Blair, but I can't catch them together," returned Lane. "Lorna is working now. Swann got her the job."

"Looks bad to me," replied Blair, soberly. "Swann is cutting a swath. I hear his old man is sore on him.... I'd take Lorna out of that office quick."

"Maybe you would," declared Lane, grimly. "For all the influence or power I have over Lorna I might as well not exist."

They walked silently along the street for a little while. Lane had to accommodate his step to the slower movement of his crippled friend. Blair's crutch tapped over the stone pavement and clicked over the curbs. They crossed the railroad tracks and turned off the main street to go down a couple of blocks.

"Shades of the past!" exclaimed Blair, as they reached a big brick building, well-lighted in front by a sizzling electric lamp. The night was rather warm and clouds of insects were wheeling round the light. "The moths and the flame!" added Blair, satirically. "Well, Dare, old bunkie, brace up and we'll go over the top. This ought to be fun for us."

"I don't see it," replied Lane. "I'll be about as welcome as a bull in a china shop."

"Oh, I didn't mean any one would throw fits over us," responded Blair. "But we ought to get some fun out of the fact."

"What fact?" queried Lane, puzzled.

"Rather far-fetched, maybe. But I'll get a kick out of looking on—watching these swell slackers with the girls *we* fought for."

"Wonder why they didn't give the dance at the armory, where they'd not have to climb stairs, and have more room?" queried Lane, as they went in under the big light.

"Dare, you're far back in the past," said Blair, sardonically. "The armory is on the ground floor—one big hall—open, you know. The Assembly Hall is a regular maze for rooms and stairways."

Blair labored up the stairway with Lane's help. At last they reached the floor from which had blared the strains of jazz. Wide doors were open, through which Lane caught the flash of many colors. Blair produced his tickets at the door. There did not appear to be any one to take them.

Lane experienced an indefinable thrill at the scene. The air seemed to reek with a mixed perfume and cigarette smoke—to resound with high-keyed youthful laughter, wild and sweet and vacant above the strange, discordant music. Then the flashing, changing, whirling colors of the dancers struck Lane as oriental, erotic, bizarre—gorgeous golds and greens and reds striped by the conventional black. Suddenly the blare ceased, and the shrill, trilling laughter had dominance. The rapid circling of forms came to a sudden stop, and the dancers streamed in all directions over the floor.

"Dare, they've called time," said Blair. "Let's get inside the ropes so we can see better."

The hall was not large, but it was long, and shaped like a letter L with pillars running down the center. Countless threads of many-colored strings of paper had been stretched from pillars to walls, hanging down almost within reach of the dancers. Flags and gay bunting helped in the riotous effect of decoration. The black-faced orchestra held forth on a raised platform at the point where the hall looked two ways. Recesses, alcoves and open doors to other rooms, which the young couples were piling over each other to reach, gave Lane some inkling of what Blair had hinted.

"Now we're out in the limelight," announced Blair, as he halted. "Let's stand here and run the gauntlet until the next dance—then we can find seats."

Almost at once a stream of gay couples enveloped them in passing. Bright, flashing, vivid faces and bare shoulders, arms and breasts appeared above the short bodices of the girls. Few of them were gowned in white. The colors seemed too garish for anything but musical comedy. But the freshness, the vividness of these girls seemed exhilarating. The murmur, the merriment touched a forgotten chord in Lane's heart. For a moment it seemed sweet to be there, once more in a gathering where pleasure was the pursuit. It breathed of what seemed long ago, in a past that was infinitely more precious to remember because he had no future of hope or of ambition or dream. Something had happened to him that now made the sensations of the moment stingingly bitter-sweet. The freshness and fragrance, the color and excitement, the beauty and gayety were not for him. Youth was dead. He could never enter the lists with these young men, many no younger than he, for the favor and smile of a girl. Resignation had not been so difficult in the spiritual moment of realization and resolve, but to be presented with one concrete and stunning actuality after another, each with its mocking might-have-been, had grown to be a terrible ordeal.

Lane looked for faces he knew. On each side of the pillar where he and Blair stood the stream of color and gayety flowed. Helen and Margaret Maynard went by on the far edge of that stream. Across the hall he caught a glimpse of the flashing golden beauty of Bessy Bell. Then near at hand he recognized Fanchon Smith, a petite, smug-faced little brunette, with naked shoulders bulging out of a piebald gown. She espied Lane and her face froze. Then there were familiar faces near and far, to which Lane could not attach names.

All at once he became aware that other of his senses besides sight were being stimulated. He had been hearing without distinguishing what he heard. And curiously he listened, still with that strange knock of memory at his heart. Everybody was talking, some low, some high, all in the spirit of the hour. And in one moment he had heard that which killed the false enchantment.

"Not a chance! ..."

"Hot dog—she's some Jane!"

"Now to the clinch—"

"What'll we do till the next spiel—"

"Have a shot?——"

"Boys, it's only the shank of the evening. Leave something peppy for the finish."

"Mame, you look like a million dollars in that rag."

"She shakes a mean shimmy, believe me...."

"That egg! Not on your life!"

"Cut the next with Ned. We'll sneak down and take a ride in my car...."

"Oh, spiffy!"

Lane's acutely strained attention was diverted by Blair's voice.

"Look who's with my sister Margie."

Lane turned to look through an open space in the dispersing stream. Blair's sister was passing with Dick Swann. Elegantly and fastidiously attired, the young millionaire appeared to be attentive to his partner. Margaret stood out rather strikingly from the other girls near her by reason of the simplicity and modesty of her dress. She did not look so much bored as discontented. Lane saw her eyes rove to and fro from the entrance of the hall. When she espied Lane she nodded and spoke with a smile and made an evident move toward him, but was restrained by Swann. He led her past Lane and Blair without so much as glancing in their direction. Lane heard Blair swear.

"Dare, if my mother throws Marg at that—slacker, I'll block the deal if it's the last thing I ever do," he declared, violently.

"And I'll help you," replied Lane, instantly.

"I know Margie hates him."

"Blair, your sister is in love with Holt Dalrymple."

"No! Not really? Thought that was only a boy-and-girl affair.... Aha! the nigger music again! Let's find a seat, Dare."

Saxophone, trombone, piccolo, snare-drum and other barbaric instruments opened with a brazen defiance of music, and a vibrant assurance of quick, raw, strong sounds. Lane himself felt the stirring effect upon his nerves. He had difficulty in keeping still. From the lines of chairs along the walls and from doors and alcoves rushed the gay-colored throng to leap, to close, to step, to rock and sway, until the floor was full of a moving mass of life.

The first half-dozen couples Lane studied all danced more or less as Helen and Swann had, that day in Helen's studio. Then, by way of a remarkable contrast, there passed two young people who danced decently. Lane descried his sister Lorna in the throng, and when she and her partner came round in the giddy circle, Lane saw that she wiggled and toddled like the others. Lane, as she passed him, caught a glance of her eyes, flashing, reproachful, furious, directed at some one across her partner's shoulder. Lane followed that glance and saw Swann. Apparently he did not notice Lorna, and was absorbed in the dance with his own partner, Helen Wrapp. This byplay further excited Lane's curiosity. On the whole, it was an ungraceful, violent mob, almost totally lacking in restraint, whirling, kicking, swaying, clasping, instinctively physical, crude, vulgar and wild. Down the line of chairs from his position, Lane saw the chaperones of the Prom, no doubt mothers of some of these girls. Lane wondered at them with sincere and persistent amaze. If they were respectable, and had even a slight degree of intelligence, how could they look on at this dance with complacence? Perhaps after all the young people were not wholly to blame for an abnormal expression of instinctive action.

That dance had its several encores and finally ended.

Margaret and Holt made their way up to Lane and Blair. The girl was now radiant. It took no second glance for Lane to see how matters stood with her at that moment.

"Say, beat it, you two," suddenly spoke up Blair. "There comes Swann. He's looking for you. Chase yourselves, now, Marg—Holt. Leave that slacker to *us*!"

Margaret gave a start, a gasp. She looked hard at her brother. Blair wore a cool smile, underneath which there was sterner hidden meaning. Then Margaret looked at Lane with slow, deep blush, making her really beautiful.

"Margie, we're for you two, strong," said Lane, with a smile. "Go hide from Swann."

"But I—I came with him," she faltered.

"Then let him find you—in other words, let him *get* you.... 'All's fair in love and war.'"

Lane had his reward in the sweet amaze and confusion of her face, as she turned away. Holt rushed her off amid the straggling couples.

"Dare, you're a wiz," declared Blair. "Margie's strong for Holt—I'm glad. If we could only put Swann out of the running."

"It's a cinch," returned Lane, with sudden heat.

"Pard, you don't know my mother. If she has picked out Swann for Margie—all I've got to say is—good night!"

"Even if we prove Swann——"

"No matter what we prove," interrupted Blair. "No matter what, so long as he's out of jail. My mother is money mad. She'd sell Margie to the devil himself for gold, position—the means to queen it over these other mothers of girls."

"Blair, you're—you're a little off your nut, aren't you?"

"Not on your life. That talk four years ago might have been irrational. But now—not on your life.... The world has come to an end.... Oh, Lord, look who's coming! Lane, did you ever in your life see such a peach as that?"

Bessy Bell had appeared, coming toward them with a callow youth near her own age. Her dress was some soft, pale blue material that was neither gaudy nor fantastical. But it was far from modest. Lane had to echo Blair's eulogy of this young specimen of the new America. She simply verified and stabilized the assertion that physically the newer generations of girls were markedly more beautiful than those of any generation before.

Bessy either forgot to introduce her escort or did not care to. She nodded a dismissal to him, spoke sweetly to Blair, and then took the empty chair next to Lane.

"You're having a rotten time," she said, leaning close to him. She seemed all fragrance and airy grace and impelling life.

Lane had to smile. "How do you know?"

"I can tell by your face. Now aren't you?"

"Well, to be honest, Miss Bessy"

"For tripe's sake, don't be so formal," she interrupted. "Call me Bessy."

"Oh, very well, Bessy. There's no use to lie to you. I'm not very happy at what I see here."

"What's the matter with it—with us?" she queried, quickly. "Everybody's doing it."

"That is no excuse. Besides, that's not so. Everybody is not—not——"

"Well, not what?"

"Not doing it, whatever you meant by that," returned Lane, with a laugh.

"Tell me straight out what *you* think of us," she shot at Lane, with a purple flash of her eyes.

She irritated Lane. Stirred him somehow, yet she seemed wholesome, full of quick response. She was daring, sophisticated, provocative. Therefore Lane retorted in brief, blunt speech what he thought of the majority of the girls present.

Bessy Bell did not look insulted. She did not blush. She did not show shame. Her eyes darkened. Her rosy mouth lost something of its soft curves.

"Daren Lane, we're not all rotten," she said.

"I did not say or imply you *all* were," he replied.

She gazed up at him thoughtfully, earnestly, with an unconscious frank interest, curiosity, and reverence.

"You strike me funny," she mused. "I never met a soldier like you."

"Bessy, how many soldiers have you met who have come back from France?"

"Not many, only Blair and you, and Captain Thesel, though I really didn't meet him. He came up to me at the armory and spoke to me. And to-night he cut in on Roy's dance. Roy was sore."

"Three. Well, that's not many," replied Lane. "Not enough to get a line on two million, is it?"

"Captain Thesel is just like all the other fellows.... But you're not a bit like them."

"Is that a compliment or otherwise?"

"I'll say it's a compliment," she replied, with arch eyes on his.

"Thank you."

"Well, you don't deserve it.... You promised to make a date with me. Why haven't you?"

"Why child, I—I don't know what to say," returned Lane, utterly disconcerted. Yet he liked this amazing girl. "I suppose I forgot. But I've been ill, for one reason."

"I'm sorry," she said, giving his arm a squeeze. "I heard you were badly hurt. Won't you tell me about your—your hurts?"

"Some day, if opportunity affords. I can't here, that's certain."

"Opportunity! What do you want? Haven't I handed myself out on a silver platter?"

Lane could find no ready retort for this query. He gazed at her, marveling at the apparently measureless distance between her exquisite physical beauty and the spiritual beauty that should have been harmonious with it. Still he felt baffled by this young girl. She seemed to resemble Lorna, yet was different in a way he could not grasp. Lorna had coarsened in fibre. This girl was fine, despite her coarse speech. She did not repel.

"Mr. Lane, will you dance with me?" she asked, almost wistfully. She liked him, and was not ashamed of it. But she seemed pondering over what to make of him—how far to go.

"Bessy, I dare not exert myself to that extent," he replied, gently. "You forget I am a disabled soldier."

"Forget that? Not a chance," she flashed. "But I hoped you might dance with me once—just a little."

"No. I might keel over."

She shivered and her eyes dilated. "You mean it as a joke. But it's no joke.... I read about your comrade—that poor Red Payson!" ... Then both devil of humor and woman of fire shone in her glance. "Daren, if you *did* keel over—you'd die in my arms—not on the floor!"

Then another partner came up to claim her. As the orchestra blurted forth and Bessy leaned to the dancer's clasp she shouted audaciously at Lane: "Don't forget that silver platter!"

Lane turned to Blair to find that worthy shaking his handsome head.

"Did you hear what she said?" asked Lane, close to Blair's ear.

"Every word," replied Blair. "Some kid!... She's like the girl in the motion-pictures. She comes along. She meets the fellow. She looks at him—she says 'good day'—then *Wham*, into his arms.... My God! ... Lane, is that kid good or bad?"

"Good!" exclaimed Lane, instantly.

"Bah!"

"Good—still," returned Lane. "But alas! She is brazen, unconscious of it. But she's no fool, that kid. Lorna is an absolute silly bull-headed fool. I wish Bessy Bell was my sister—or I mean that Lorna was like her."

"Here comes Swann without Margie. Looks sore as a pup. The——"

"Shut up, Blair. I want to listen to this jazz."

Lane shut his eyes during the next number and listened without the disconcerting spectacle in his sight. He put all the intensity of which he was capable into his attention. His knowledge of music was not extensive, but on the other hand it was enough to enable him to analyze this jazz. Neither music nor ragtime, it seemed utterly barbarian in character. It appealed only to primitive, physical, sensual instincts. It could not be danced to sanely and gracefully. When he opened his eyes again, to see once more the disorder of dancers in spirit and action, he seemed to have his analysis absolutely verified.

These dances were short, the encores very brief, and the intermissions long. Perhaps the dancers needed to get their breath and rearrange their apparel.

After this number, Lane left Blair talking to friends, and made his way across the hall to where he espied Lorna. She did not see him. She looked ashamed, hurt, almost sullen. Her young friend, Harry, was bending over talking earnestly. Lane caught the words: "Lorna dear, that Swann's only stringing you—rushing you on the sly. He won't dance with you *here*—not while he's with that swell crowd."

"It's a lie," burst out Lorna. She was almost in tears.

Lane took her arm, making her start.

"Well, kids, you're having some time, aren't you," he said, cheerfully.

"Sure—are," gulped Harry.

Lorna repressed her grief, but not her sullen resentment.

Lane pretended not to notice anything unusual, and after a few casual remarks and queries he left them. Strolling from place to place, mingling with the gay groups, in the more secluded alcoves and recesses where couples appeared, oblivious to eyes, in the check room where a sign read: "check your corsets," out in the wide landing where the stairway came up, Lane passed, missing little that might have been seen or heard. He did not mind that two of the chaperones stared at him in supercilious curiosity, as if speculating on a possible *faux pas* of his at this dance. Both boys and girls he had met since his return to Middleville, and some he had known before, encountered him face to face, and cut him dead. He heard sarcastic remarks. He was an outsider, a "dead one," a "has been" and a "lemon." But Margaret was gracious to him, and Flossie Dickerson made no bones of her regard. Dorothy, he was relieved and glad to see, was not present.

Lane had no particular object in mind. He just wanted to rub elbows with this throng of young people. This was the joy of life he had imagined he had missed while in France. How much vain longing! He had missed nothing. He had boundlessly gained.

Out on this floor a railing ran round the curve of the stairway. Girls were sitting on it, smoking cigarettes, and kicking their slipper-shod feet. Their partners were lounging close. Lane passed by, and walking to a window in the shadow he stood there. Presently one of the boys threw away his cigarette and said: "Come on, Ironsides. I gotta dance. You're a rotten dancer, but I love you."

They ran back into the hall. The young fellow who was left indolently attempted to kiss his partner, who blew smoke in his face. Then at a louder blast of jazz they bounced away. The next moment a third couple appeared, probably from another door down the hall. They did not observe Lane. The girl was slim, dainty, gorgeously arrayed, and her keen, fair face bore traces of paint wet by perspiration. Her companion was Captain Vane Thesel, in citizen's garb, well-built, ruddy-faced, with tiny curled moustache.

"Hurry, kid," he said, breathlessly, as he pulled at her. "We'll run down and take a spin."

"Spiffy! But let's wait till after the next," she replied. "It's Harold's and I came with him."

"Tell him it was up to him to find you."

"But he might get wise to a car ride."

"He'd do the same. Come on," returned Thesel, who all the time was leading her down the stairway step by step.

They disappeared. From the open window Lane saw them go down the street and get into a car and ride away. He glanced at his watch, muttering. "This is a new stunt for dances. I just wonder." He watched, broodingly and sombrely. It was not his sister, but it might just as well have been. Two dances and a long intermission ended before Lane saw the big auto return. He watched the couple get out, and hurry up, to disappear at the entrance. Then Lane changed his position, and stood directly at the head of the stairway under the light. He had no interest in Captain Vane Thesel. He just wanted to get a close look at the girl.

Presently he heard steps, heavy and light, and a man's deep voice, a girl's low thrill of laughter. They turned the curve in the stairway and did not see Lane until they had mounted to the top.

With cool steady gaze Lane studied the girl. Her clear eyes met his. If there was anything unmistakable in Lane's look at her, it was not from any deception on his part. He tried to look into her soul. Her smile—a strange indolent little smile, remnant of excitement—faded from her face. She stared, and she put an instinctive hand up to her somewhat dishevelled hair. Then she passed on with her companion.

"Of all the nerve!" she exclaimed. "Who's that soldier boob?"

Lane could not catch the low reply. He lingered there a while longer, and then returned to the hall, much surprised to find it so dark he could scarcely distinguish the dancers. The lights had been lowered. If the dance had been violent and strange before this procedure, it was now a riot.

In the semi-darkness the dancers cut loose. The paper strings had been loosened and had fallen down to become tangled with the flying feet and legs. Confetti swarmed like dark snowdrops in the hot air. Lane actually smelled the heat of bodies—a strangely stirring and yet noxious sensation. A rushing, murmuring, shrill sound—voices, laughter, cries, and the sliding of feet and brushing of gowns—filled the hall—ominous to Lane's over-sensitive faculties, swelling unnaturally, the expression of unrestrained physical abandon. Lane walked along the edge of this circling, wrestling melee, down to the corner where the orchestra held forth. They seemed actuated by the same frenzy which possessed the dancers. The piccolo player lay on his back on top of the piano, piping his shrill notes at the ceiling. And Lane made sure this player was drunk. On the moment then the jazz came to an end with a crash. The lights flashed up. The dancers clapped and stamped their pleasure.

Lane wound his way back to Blair.

"I've had enough, Blair," he said. "I'm all in. Let's go."

"Right-o," replied Blair, with evident relief. He reached a hand to Lane to raise himself, an action he rarely resorted to, and awkwardly got his crutch in place. They started out, with Lane accommodating his pace to his crippled comrade. Thus it happened that the two ran a gauntlet with watching young people on each side, out to the open part of the hall. There directly in front they encountered Captain Vane Thesel, with Helen Wrapp on his arm. Her red hair, her green eyes, and carmined lips, the white of her voluptuous neck and arms, united in a singular effect of allurement that Lane felt with scorn and melancholy.

Helen nodded to Blair and Lane, and evidently dragged at her escort's arm to hold him from passing on.

"Look who's here! Daren, old boy—and Blair," she called, and she held the officer back. The malice in her green glance did not escape Lane, as he bowed to her. She gloried in that situation. Captain Thesel had to face them.

It was Blair's hand that stiffened Lane. They halted, erect, like statues, with eyes that failed to see Thesel. He did not exist for them. With a flush of annoyance he spoke, and breaking from Helen, passed on. A sudden silence in the groups nearby gave evidence that the incident had been observed. Then whispers rose.

"Boys, aren't you dancing?" asked Helen, with a mocking sweetness. "Let me teach you the new steps."

"Thanks, Helen," replied Lane, in sudden weariness. "But I couldn't go it."

"Why did you come? To blow us up again? Lose your nerve?"

"Yes, I lost it to-night—and something more."

"Blair, you shouldn't have left one of your legs in France," she said, turning to Blair. She had always hated Blair, a fact omnipresent now in her green eyes.

Blair had left courtesy and endurance in France, as was evinced by the way he bent closer to Helen, to speak low, with terrible passion.

"If I had it to do over again—I'd see *you* and *your* kind—your dirt-cheap crowd of painted hussies where you belong—in the clutch of the Huns!"

CHAPTER IX

Miss Amanda Hill, teacher in the Middleville High School, sat wearily at her desk. She was tired, as tired as she had ever been on any day of the fifteen long years in which she had wrestled with the problems of school life. Her hair was iron gray and she bent a worn, sad, severe face over a mass of notes before her.

At that moment she was laboring under a perplexing question that was not by any means a new one. Only this time it had presented itself in a less insidious manner than usual, leaving no loophole for charitable imagination. Presently she looked up and rapped on her desk.

"These young ladies will remain after school is dismissed," she said, in her authoritative voice: "Bessy Bell—Rose Clymer—Gail Matthews—Helen Tremaine—Ruth Winthrop.... Also any other girls who are honest enough to admit knowledge of the notes found in Rose Clymer's desk."

The hush that fell over the schoolroom was broken by the gong in the main hall, sounding throughout the building. Then followed the noise of shutting books and closing desks, and the bustle and shuffling of anticipated dismissal.

In a front seat sat a girl who did not arise with the others, and as one by one several girls passed her desk with hurried step and embarrassed snicker she looked at them with purple, blazing eyes.

Miss Hill attended to her usual task with the papers of the day's lessons and the marking of the morrow's work before she glanced up at the five girls she had detained. They sat in widely separated sections of the room. Rose Clymer, pretty, fragile, curly-haired, occupied the front seat of the end row. Her face had no color and her small mouth was set in painful lines. Four seats across from her Bessy Bell leaned on her desk, with defiant calmness, and traces of scorn still in her expressive eyes. Gail Matthews looked frightened and Helen Tremaine was crying. Ruth Winthrop bent forward with her face buried in her arms.

"Girls," began Miss Hill, presently. "I know you regard me as a cross old schoolteacher."

She had spoken impulsively, a rare thing with her, and occasioned in this instance by the painful consciousness of how she was judged, when she was really so kindly disposed toward the wayward girls.

"Girls, I've tried to get into close touch with you, to sympathize, to be lenient; but somehow, I've failed," she went on. "Certainly I have failed to stop this note-writing. And lately it has become—beyond me to understand. Now won't you help me to get at the bottom of the matter? Helen, it was you who told me these notes were in Rose's desk. Have you any knowledge of more?"

"Ye—s—m," said Helen, raising her red face. "I've—I've one—I—was afraid to g—give up."

"Bring it to me."

Helen rose and came forward with an expressive little fist and opening it laid a crumpled paper upon Miss Hill's desk. As Helen returned to her seat she met Bessy Bell's fiery glance and it seemed to wither her.

The teacher smoothed out the paper and began to read. "Good Heavens!" she breathed, in amaze and pain. Then she turned to Helen. "This verse is in your handwriting."

"Yes'm—but I—I only copied it," responded the culprit.

"Who gave you the original?"

"Rose."

"Where did she get it?"

"I—I don't know—Miss Hill. Really and tru—truly I don't," faltered Helen, beginning to cry again.

Gail and Ruth also disclaimed any knowledge of the verse, except that it had been put into their hands by Rose. They had read it, copied it, written notes about it and discussed it.

"You three girls may go home now," said Miss Hill, sadly.

The girls hastily filed out and passed the scornful Bessy Bell with averted heads.

"Rose, can you explain the notes found in your possession?" asked the teacher.

"Yes, Miss Hill. They were written to me by different boys and girls," replied Rose.

"Why do you seem to have all these writings addressed to you?"

"I didn't get any more than any other girl. But I wasn't afraid to keep mine."

"Do you know where these verses came from, before Helen had them?"

"Yes, Miss Hill."

"Then you know who wrote them?"

"Yes."

"Who?"

"I won't tell," replied Rose, deliberately. She looked straight into her teacher's eyes.

"You refuse when I've assured you I'll be lenient?" demanded Miss Hill.

"I'm no tattletale." Rose's answer was sullen.

"Rose, I ask you again. A great deal depends on your answer. Will you tell me?"

The girl's lip curled. Then she laughed in a way that made Miss Hill think of her as older. But she kept silent.

"Rose, you're expelled until further notice." Miss Hill's voice trembled with disappointment and anger. "You may go now."

Rose gathered up her books and went into the cloakroom. The door in the outer hall opened and closed.

"Miss Hill, it wasn't fair!" exclaimed Bessy Bell, hotly. "It wasn't fair. Rose is no worse than the other girls. She's not as bad, for she isn't sly and deceitful. There were a dozen girls who lied when they went out. Helen lied. Ruth lied. Gail lied. But Rose told the truth so far as she went. And she wouldn't tell all because she wanted to shield me."

"Why did she want to shield you?"

"Because I wrote the verses."

"You mean you copied them?"

"I composed them," Bessy replied coolly. Her blue eyes fearlessly met Miss Hill's gaze.

"Bessy Bell!" ejaculated the teacher.

The girl stood before her desk and from the tip of her dainty boot to the crown of her golden hair breathed forth a strange, wilful and rebellious fire.

Miss Hill's lips framed to ask a certain question of Bessy, but she refrained and substituted another.

"Bessy, how old are you?"

"Fifteen last April."

"Have you any intelligent idea of—do you know—Bessy, *how* did you write those verses?" asked Miss Hill, in bewilderment.

"I know a good deal and I've imagination," replied Bessy, candidly.

"That's evident," returned the teacher. "How long has this note-and verse-writing been going on?"

"For a year, at least, among us."

"Then you caught the habit from girls gone higher up?"

"Certainly."

Bessy's trenchant brevity was not lost upon Miss Hill.

"We've always gotten along—you and I," said Miss Hill, feeling her way with this strange girl.

"It's because you're kind and square, and I like you."

Something told the teacher she had never been paid a higher compliment.

"Bessy, how much will you tell me?"

"Miss Hill, I'm in for it and I'll tell you everything, if only you won't punish Rose," replied the girl, impulsively. "Rose's my best friend. Her father's a mean, drunken brute. I'm afraid of what he'll do if he finds out. Rose has a hard time."

"You say Rose is no more guilty than the other girls?"

"Rose Clymer never had an idea of her own. She's just sweet and willing. I hate deceitful girls. Every one of them wrote notes to the boys—the same kind of notes—and some of them tried to write poetry. Most of them had a copy of the piece I wrote. They had great fun over it— getting the boys to guess what girl wrote it. I've written a dozen pieces before this and they've all had them."

"Well, that explains the verses.... Now I read in these notes about meetings with the boys?"

"That refers to mornings before school, and after school, and evenings when it's nice weather. And the literary society."

"You mean the Girl's Literary Guild, with rooms at the Atheneum?"

"Yes. But, Miss Hill, the literary part of it is bunk. We meet there to dance. The boys bring the girls cigarettes. They smoke, and sometimes the boys have something with them to drink."

"These—these girls—hardly in their teens—smoke and drink?" gasped Miss Hill.

"I'll say they do," replied Bessy Bell.

"What—does the 'Bell-garter' mean?" went on the teacher, presently.

"One of the boys stole my garter and fastened a little bell to it. Now it's going the rounds. Every girl who could has worn it."

"What's the 'Old Bench'?"

"Down in the basement here at school there's a bench under the stairway in the dark. The boys and girls have signals. One boy will get permission to go out at a certain time, and a girl from his room, or another room, will go out too. It's all arranged beforehand. They meet down on the Old Bench."

"What for?"

"They meet to spoon."

"I find the names Hardy Mackay, Captain Thesel, Dick Swann among these notes. What can these young society men be to my pupils?"

"Some of the jealous girls have been tattling to each other and mentioning names."

"Bessy! Do you imply these girls who talk have had the—the interest or attention of these young gentlemen named?"

"Yes."

"In what way?"

"I mean they've had dates to meet in the park—and other places. Then they go joy riding."

"Bessy, have you?"

"Yes—but only just lately."

"Thank you Bessy, for your—your frankness," replied Miss Hill, drawing a long breath. "I'll have another talk with you, after I see your mother. You may go now."

It was an indication of Miss Hill's mental perturbation that for once she broke her methodical routine. For many years she had carried a lunch-basket to and from school; for so many in fact that now on Saturdays when she went to town without it she carried her left hand forward in the same position that had grown habitual to her while holding it. But this afternoon, as she went out, she forgot the basket entirely.

"I'll go to Mrs. Bell," soliloquized the worried schoolteacher. "But how to explain what I can't understand! Some people would call this thing just natural depravity. But I love these girls. As I think back, every year, in the early summer, I've always had something of this sort of thing to puzzle over. But the last few years it's grown worse. The war made a difference. And since the war—how strange the girls are! They seem to feel more. They're bolder. They break out oftener. They dress so immodestly. Yet they're less deceitful. They have no shame. I can blind myself no longer to that. And this last is damning proof of—of wildness. Some of them have taken the fatal step! ... Yet—yet I seem to feel somehow Bessy Bell isn't *bad*. I wonder if my hope isn't responsible for that feeling. I'm old-fashioned. This modern girl is beyond me. How clearly she spoke! She's a wonderful, fearless, terrible girl. I never saw a girl so alive. I can't—can't understand her."

In the swift swinging from one consideration of the perplexing question to another Miss Hill's mind naturally reverted to her errand, and to her possible reception. Mrs. Bell was a proud woman. She had married against the wishes of her blue-blooded family, so rumor had it, and her husband was now Chief of Police in Middleville. Mrs. Bell had some money of her own and was slowly recovering her old position in society.

It was not without misgivings that Miss Hill presented herself at Mrs. Bell's door and gave her card to a servant. The teacher had often made thankless and misunderstood calls upon the mothers of her pupils. She was admitted and shown to a living room where a woman of fair features and noble proportions greeted her.

"Bessy's teacher, I presume?" she queried, graciously, yet with just that slight touch of hauteur which made Miss Hill feel her position.

"I am Bessy's teacher," she replied, with dignity. "Can you spare me a few minutes?"

"Assuredly. Please be seated. I've heard Bessy speak of you. By the way, the child hasn't come home yet. How late she always is!"

Miss Hill realized, with a protest at the unfairness of the situation, that to face this elegant lady, so smiling, so suave, so worldly, so graciously superior, and to tell her some unpleasant truths about her daughter, was a task by no means easy, and one almost sure to prove futile. But Miss Hill never shirked her duty, and after all, her motive was a hope to help Bessy.

"Mrs. Bell, I've come on a matter of importance," began Miss Hill. "But it is so delicate a one I don't know how to broach it. I believe plain speaking best."

Here Miss Hill went into detail, sparing not to call a spade a spade. But she held back the names of the young society gentlemen mentioned in the notes. Miss Hill was not sure of her ground there and her revelation was grave enough for any intelligent mother.

"Really, Miss Hill, you amaze me!" exclaimed Mrs. Bell. "Bessie has fallen into bad company. Oh, these public schools! I never attended one, but I've heard what they are."

"The public schools are not to blame," replied Miss Hill, bluntly.

Mrs. Bell gave her visitor a rather supercilious stare.

"May I ask you to explain?"

"I'm afraid I can't explain," replied Miss Hill, conscious of a little heat. "I've proofs of the condition. But as I can't understand it, how can I explain? I have my own peculiar ideas, only, lately, I've begun to doubt them. A year or so ago I would have said girls had their own way too much—too much time to themselves—too much freedom. But now I seem to feel life isn't like what it was a few years ago. Girls are bound to learn. And they never learn at home, that's sure. The last thing a mother will do is to tell her daughter what she *ought* to know. There's always been a shadow between most mothers and daughters. And in these days of jazz it has become a wall. Perhaps that's why girls don't confide in their mothers.... Mrs. Bell, I considered it my duty to acquaint you with the truth about these verses and notes, and what they imply. Would you care to read some of them?"

"Thank you, but they wouldn't interest me in the least," replied Mrs. Bell, coldly. "I wouldn't insult Bessy or her girl friends. I imagine it's all some risque suggestion overheard and made much of or a few verses mischievously plagiarized. I'm no prude, Miss Hill. I know enough not to be strict, which is apparently the fault of the school system. As for my own daughter I understand her perfectly and trust her implicitly. I know the blood in her. And I shall remove her from public school and place her in a private institution under a tutor, where she'll no longer be exposed to contaminating influences.... I thank you for your intention, which I'm sure is kind—and, will you please excuse me? I must dress for my bridge party. Good afternoon, Miss Hill."

The schoolteacher plodded homeward, her eyes downcast and sad. The snub given her by the mother had not hurt her as had the failure to help the daughter.

"I knew it—I knew it. I'll never try again. That woman's mind is a wilderness where her girl is concerned. How brainless these mothers are!... Yet if I'd ever had a girl—I wonder—would I have been blind? One's own blood—that must be the reason. Pride. Could I have believed of *my* girl what I admitted of hers? Perhaps not till too late. That would be so human. But, oh! the mystery—the sadness of it—the fatality!"

Rose Clymer left the High School with the settled, indifferent bitterness of one used to trouble. Every desire she followed, turn what way she would, every impulse reaching to grasp some girlish gleam of happiness, resulted in the inevitable rebuke. And this time it had been disgrace. But Rose felt she did not care if she could only deceive her father. No cheerful task was it to face him. Shivering at the thought she resolved to elude the punishment he was sure to inflict if he learned why she had been expelled.

She had no twinge of conscience. She was used to slights and unkindness, and did not now reflect upon the justice of her dismissal. What little pleasure she got came from friendships with boys, and these her father had forbidden her to have. In the bitter web of her thought ran the threads that if she had pretty clothes like Helen, and a rich mother like Bessy, and a father who was not a drunkard, her lot in life would have been happy.

Rose lived with her stepfather in three dingy rooms in the mill section of Middleville. She never left the wide avenues and lawns and stately residences, which she had to pass on her way to and from school, without contrasting them with the dirty alleys and grimy walls and squalid quarters of the working-class. She had grown up in that class, but in her mind there was always a faint vague recollection of a time when her surroundings had been bright and cheerful, where there had been a mother who had taught her to love beautiful things. To-day she climbed the rickety stairs to her home and pushed open the latchless door with a revolt brooding in her mind.

A man in his shirt sleeves sat by the little window.

"Why father—home so early?" she asked.

"Yes lass, home early," he replied wearily. "I'm losing my place again."

He had straggling gray hair, bleared eyes with an opaque, glazy look and a bluish cast of countenance. His chin was buried in the collar of his open shirt; his shoulders sagged, and he breathed heavily.

One glance assured Rose her father was not very much under the influence of drink. And fear left her. When even half-sober he was kind.

"So you've lost your place?" she asked.

"Yes. Old Swann is layin' off."

This was an untruth, Rose knew, because the mills had never been so full, and men never so in demand. Besides her father was an expert at his trade and could always have work.

"I'm sorry," she said, slowly. "I've been thinking lately that I'll give up school and go to work. In an office uptown or a department store."

"Rose, that'd be good of you," he replied. "You could help along a lot. I don't do my work so well no more. But your poor mother won't rest in her grave. She was so proud of you, always dreamin'."

The lamp Rose lighted showed comfortless rooms, with but few articles of furniture. It was with the deft fingers of long practice that the girl spread the faded table-cloth, laid the dishes, ground the coffee, peeled the potatoes, and cut the bread. Then presently she called her father to the meal. He ate in silence, having relapsed once more into the dull gloom natural to him. When he had finished he took up his hat and with slow steps left the room.

"No more study for me," mused Rose, and she felt both glad and sorry. "What will Bessy say? She won't like it. I wonder what old Hill did to her. Let her off easy. I won't get to see Bessy so much now. No more afternoons in the park. But I'll have the evenings. Best of all, some nice clothes to wear. I might some day have a lovely gown like that Miss Maynard wore the night of the Prom."

Rose washed and dried the dishes, put them away, and cleaned up the little kitchen in a way that spoke well for her. And she did it cheerfully, for in the interest of this new idea of work she forgot her trouble and discontent. Taking up the lamp she went to her room. It contained a narrow bed, a bureau, a small wardrobe and a rug. The walls held several pictures, and some touches of color in the way of ribbons, bright posters, and an orange-and-blue banner. A photograph of Bessy Bell stood on the bureau and the girl's beauty seemed like a light in the dingy room.

Rose looked in the mirror and smiled and tossed her curly head. She studied the oval face framed in its mass of curls, the steady gray-blue eyes, the soft, wistful, tenderly curved lips. "Yes, I'm pretty," she said. "And I'm going to buy nice things to wear."

Suddenly she heard a pattering on the roof.

"Rain! What do you know about that? I've got to stay in. If I spoil that relic of a hat I'll never have the nerve to go ask for a job."

She prepared for bed, and placing the lamp on the edge of the bureau, she lay down to become absorbed in a paper-backed novel. The mill-clock was striking ten when she finished. There was a dreamy light in her eyes and a glow upon her face.

"How grand to be as beautiful as she was and turn out to be an heiress with blue blood, and a lovely mother, and handsome lovers dying for her!"

Then she flung the novel against the wall.

"It's only a book. It's not true."

Rose blew out the lamp and went to sleep.

During the night she dreamed that the principal of the High School had called to see her father, and she awoke trembling.

The room was dark as pitch; the rain pattered on the roof; the wind moaned softly under the eaves. A rat somewhere in the wall made a creaking noise. Rose hated to awaken in the middle of the night. She listened for her father's breathing, and failing to hear it, knew he had not yet come home. Often she was left alone until dawn. She tried bravely to go to sleep again but found it impossible; she lay there listening, sensitive to every little sound. The silence was almost more dreadful than the stealthy unknown noises of the night. Vague shapes seemed to hover over her bed. Somehow to-night she dreaded them more. She was sixteen years old, yet there abided with her the terror of the child in the dark.

She cried out in her heart—why was she alone? It was so dark, so silent. Mother! Mother!... She would never—never say her prayers again!

The brazen-tongued mill clock clanged the hour of two, when shuffling uncertain footsteps sounded on the hollow stairs. Rose raised her head to listen. With slow, weary, dragging steps her father came in. Then she lay back on the pillow with a sigh of relief.

CHAPTER X

In the following week Rose learned that work was not to be had for the asking. Her love of pretty things and a desire to be independent of her father had occupied her mind to the exclusion of a consideration of what might be demanded of a girl seeking a position. She had no knowledge of stenography or bookkeeping; her handwriting was poor. Moreover, references from former employers were required and as she had never been employed, she was asked for recommendations from the principal of her school. These, of course, she could not supply. The stores of the better class had nothing to offer her except to put her name on the waiting-list.

Finally Rose secured a place in a second-rate establishment on Main Street. The work was hard; it necessitated long hours and continual standing on her feet. Rose was not rugged enough to accustom herself to the work all at once, and she was discharged. This disheartened her, but she kept on trying to find other employment.

One day in the shopping district, some one accosted her. She looked up to see a young man, slim, elegant, with a curl of his lips she remembered. He raised his hat.

"How do you do, Mr. Swann," she answered.

"Rose, are you on the way home?"

"Yes."

"Let's go down this side street," he said, throwing away his cigarette. "I've been looking for you."

They turned the corner. Rose felt strange to be walking alone with him, but she was not embarrassed. He had danced with her once. And she knew his friend Hardy Mackay.

"What're you crying about?" he said.

"I'm not."

"You have been then. What for?"

"Oh, nothing."

"Come, tell me."

"I—I've been disappointed."

"What about?" He was persistent, and Rose felt that he must be used to having his own way.

"It was about a job I didn't get," replied Rose, trying to laugh.

"So you're looking for a job. Heard you'd been fired by old Hill. Gail told me. I had her out last night in my new car."

"I could go back to school. Miss Hill sent for me.... Was Bessy with you and Gail?"

"No. Gail and I were alone. We had a dandy time.... Rose, will you meet me some night and take a ride? It'll be fine and cool."

"Thank you, Mr. Swann. It's very kind of you to ask me."

"Well, will you go?" he queried, impatiently.

"No," she replied, simply.

"Why not?"

"I don't want to."

"Well, that's plain enough," he said, changing his tone. "Say, Rose, you're in Clark's store, aren't you?"

"I was. But I lost the place."

"How's that?"

"I couldn't stand on my feet all day. I fainted. Then he fired me."

"So you're hunting for another job?" inquired Swann, thoughtfully.

"Yes."

"Sorry. It's too bad a sweet kid like you has to work. You're not strong, Rose.... Well, I'll turn off at this corner. You won't meet me to-night?"

"No, thanks."

Swann pulled a gold case from his pocket, and extracting a cigarette, tilted it in his lips as he struck a match. His face wore a careless smile Rose did not like. He was amiable, but he seemed so sure, so satisfied, almost as if he believed she would change her mind.

"Rose, you're turning me down cold, then?"

"Take it any way you like, Mr. Swann," she replied. "Good day."

Rose forgot him almost the instant her back was turned. He had only annoyed her. And she had her stepfather to face, with news of her discharge from the store. Her fears were verified; he treated her brutally. Next day Rose went to work in a laundry.

And then, very soon it seemed, her school days, the merry times with the boys, and Bessy— all were far back in the past. She did not meet any one who knew her, nor hear from any one. They had forgotten her. At night, after coming home from the laundry and doing the housework, she was so tired that she was glad to crawl into bed.

But one night a boy brought her a note. It was from Dick Swann. He asked her to go to Mendleson's Hall to see the moving-pictures. She could meet him uptown at the entrance. Rose told the boy to tell Swann she would not come.

This invitation made her thoughtful. If Swann had been ashamed to be seen with her he would not have invited her to go there. Mendleson's was a nice place; all the nice people of Middleville went there. Rose found herself thinking of the lights, the music, the well-dressed crowd, and then the pictures. She loved moving-pictures, especially those with swift horses and cowboys and a girl who could ride. All at once a wave of the old thrilling excitement rushed over her. Almost she regretted having sent back a refusal. But she would not go with Swann. And it was not because she knew what kind of a young man he was—what he wanted. Rose refused from dislike, not scruples.

Then came a Saturday night which seemed a climax of her troubles. She was told not to come back to work until further notice, and that was as bad as being discharged. How could she tell her stepfather? Of late he had been hard with her. She dared not tell him. The money she earned was little enough, but during his idleness it had served to keep them.

Rose had scarcely gone a block when she encountered Dick Swann. He stopped her—turned to walk with her. It was a melancholy gift of Rose's that she could tell when men were even in the slightest under the influence of drink. Swann was not careless now or indifferent. He seemed excited and gay.

"Rose, you're just the girl I'm looking for," he said. "I really was going to your home. Got that job yet?"

"No," she replied.

"I've got one for you. It's at the Telephone Exchange. They need an operator. My dad owns the telephone company. I've got a pull. I'll get you the place. You can learn it easy. Nice job—short hours—you sit down all the time—good pay. What do you say, Rose?"

"I—I don't know—what to say," she faltered. "Thanks for thinking of me."

"I've had you in mind for a month. Rose, you take this job. Take it whether you've any use for me or not. I'm not rotten enough to put this in your way just to make you under obligations to me."

"I'll think about it. I—I do need a place. My father's out of work. And he's—he's not easy to get along with."

"I tell you what, Rose. You meet me to-night. We'll take a spin in my car. It'll be fine down the river road. Then we can talk it over. Will you?"

Rose looked at him, and thought how strange it was that she did not like him any better, now when she ought to.

"Why have you tried to—to rush me?" she asked.

"I like you, Rose."

"But you don't want me to meet you—go with you, when I—I can't feel as you do?"

"Sure, I want you to, Rose. Nobody ever likes me right off. Maybe you will, after you know me. The job is yours. Don't make any date with me for that. I say here's your chance to have a ride, to win a friend. Take it or not. It's up to you. I won't say another word."

Rose's hungry, lonely heart warmed toward Swann. He seemed like a ray of light in the gloom.

"I'll meet you," she said.

They arranged the hour and then she went on her way home.

The big car sped through River Park. Rose shivered a little as she peered into the darkness of the grove. Then the car shot under the last electric light, out into the country, with the level road white in the moonlight, and the river gleaming below. There was a steady, even rush of wind. The car hummed and droned and sang. And mingled with the dry scent of dust was the sweet fragrance of new-mown hay. Far off a light twinkled or it might have been a star.

Swann put his arm around Rose. She did not shrink—she did not repulse him—she did not move. Something strange happened in her mind or heart. It was that moment she fell.

And she fell wide-eyed, knowing what she was doing, not in a fervor of excitement, without pleasure or passion, bitterly sure that it was better to be with some one she could not like than to be alone forever. The wrong to herself lay only in the fact that she could not care.

CHAPTER XI

Toward the end of June, Lane's long vigil of watchfulness from the vantage-point at Colonel Pepper's apartment resulted in a confirmation of his worst fears.

One afternoon and evening of a warm, close day in early summer he lay and crouched on the attic floor above the club-rooms from three o'clock until one the next morning. From time to time he had changed his position to rest. But at the expiration of that protracted period of spying he was so exhausted from the physical strain and mental shock that he was unable to go home. All the rest of the night he lay upon Colonel Pepper's couch, wide awake, consumed by pain and distress. About daylight he fell into a sleep, fitful and full of nightmares, to be awakened around nine o'clock by Pepper. The old gambler evinced considerable alarm until Lane explained how he happened to be there; and then his feeling changed to solicitude.

"Lane, you look awful," he said.

"If I look the way I feel it's no wonder you're shocked," returned Lane.

"Ahuh! What'd you see?" queried the other, curiously.

"When?"

"Why, you numskull, while you were peepin' all that time."

Lane sombrely shook his head. "I couldn't tell—what I saw. I want to forget.... Maybe in twenty-four hours I'll believe it was a nightmare."

"Humph! Well, I'm here to tell you what *I've* seen wasn't any nightmare," returned Pepper, with his shrewd gaze on Lane. "But we needn't discuss that. If it made an old bum like me sick what might not it do to a sensitive high-minded chap like you.... The question is are you going to bust up that club."

"I am," declared Lane, grimly.

"Good! But how—when? What's the sense in lettin' them carry on any longer?"

"I had to fight myself last night to keep from breaking in on them.... But I want to catch this fellow Swann with my sister. She wasn't there."

"Lane, don't wait for that," returned Pepper, nervously. "You might never catch him.... And if you did...."

His little plump well-cared-for hand shook as he extended it.

"I don't know what I'll do.... I don't know," said Lane, darkly, more to himself.

"Lane, this—this worry will knock you out."

"No matter. All I ask is to stand up—long enough—to do what I want to do."

"Go home and get some breakfast—and take care of yourself," replied Pepper, gruffly. "Damn me if I'm not sorry I gave Swann's secret away."

"Oh no, you're not," said Lane, quickly. "But I'd have found it out by this time."

Pepper paced up and down the faded carpet, his hands behind his back, a plodding, burdened figure.

"Have you any—doubts left?" he asked, suddenly.

"Doubts!" echoed Lane, vaguely.

"Yes—doubts. You're like most of these mothers and fathers.... You couldn't believe. You made excuses for the smoke—saying there was no fire."

"No more doubts, alas!... My God! I *saw*," burst out Lane.

"All right. Buck up now. It's something to be sure.... You've overdone your strength. You look...."

"Pepper, do me a favor," interposed Lane, as he made for the door. "Get me an axe and leave it here in your rooms. In case I want to break in on those fellows some time—quick—I'll have it ready."

"Sure, I'll get you anything. And I want to be around when you butt in on them."

"That's up to you. Good-bye now. I'll run in to-morrow if I'm up to it."

Lane went home, his mind in a tumult. His mother had just discovered that he had not slept in his bed, and was greatly relieved to see him. Breakfast was waiting, and after partaking of it Lane felt somewhat better. His mother appeared more than usually sombre. Worry was killing her.

"Lorna did not sleep at home last night," she said, presently, as if reluctantly forced to impart this information.

"Where was she?" he queried, blankly.

"She said she would stay with a friend."

"What friend?"

"Some girl. Oh, it's all right I suppose. She's stayed away before with girl friends.... But what worried me...."

"Well," queried Lane, as she paused.

"Lorna was angry again last night. And she told me if you didn't stop your nagging she'd go away from home and stay. Said she could afford to pay her board."

"She told me that, too," replied Lane, slowly. "And—I'm afraid she meant it."

"Leave her alone, Daren."

"Poor mother! I'm afraid I'm a—a worry to you as well as Lorna," he said, gently, with a hand going to her worn cheek. She said nothing, although her glance rested upon him with sad affection.

Lane clambered wearily up to his little room. It had always been a refuge. He leaned a moment against the wall, and felt in his extremity like an animal in a trap. A thousand pricking, rushing sensations seemed to be on the way to his head. That confusion, that sensation as if his blood vessels would burst, yielded to his will. He sat down on his bed. Only the physical pains and weariness, and the heartsickness abided with him. These had been nothing to daunt his spirit. But to-day was different. The dark, vivid, terrible picture in his mind unrolled like a page. Yesterday was different. To-day he seemed a changed man, confronted by imperious demands. Time was driving onward fast.

As if impelled by a dark and sinister force, he slowly leaned down to pull his bag from under the bed. He opened it, and drew out his Colt's automatic gun. Though the June day was warm this big worn metal weapon had a cold touch. He did not feel that he wanted to handle it, but he did. It seemed heavy, a thing of subtle, latent energy, with singular fascination for him. It brought up a dark flowing tide of memory. Lane shut his eyes, and saw the tide flow by with its conflict and horror. The feel of his gun, and the recall of what it had meant to him in terrible hours, drove away a wavering of will, and a still voice that tried to pierce his consciousness. It fixed his sinister intention. He threw the gun on the bed, and rising began to pace the floor.

"If I told what I saw—no jury on earth would convict me," he soliloquized. "But I'll kill him—and keep my mouth shut."

Plan after plan he had pondered in mind—and talked over with Blair—something to thwart Richard Swann—to give Margaret the chance for happiness and love her heart craved—to put out of Lorna's way the evil influence that had threatened her. Now the solution came to him. Sooner or later he would catch Swann with his sister in an automobile, or at the club rooms, or at some other questionable place. He knew Lorna was meeting Swann. He had tried to find them, all to no avail. What he might have done heretofore was no longer significant; he knew what he meant to do now.

But all at once Lane was confronted with remembrance of another thing he had resolved upon—equally as strong as his determination to save Lorna—and it was his intention to persuade Mel Iden to marry him.

He loved his sister, but not as he loved Mel Iden. Whatever had happened to Lorna or might happen, she would be equal to it. She had the boldness, the cool, calculating selfishness of the general run of modern girls. Her reactions were vastly different front Mel Iden's. Lane had lost hope of saving Lorna's soul. He meant only to remove a baneful power from her path, so that she might lean to the boy who wanted to marry her. When in his sinister intent he divined the passionate hate of the soldier for the slacker he refused to listen to his conscience. The way out in Lorna's case he had discovered. But what relation had this new factor of his dilemma to Mel Iden? He could never marry her after he had killed Swann.

Lane went to bed, and when he rested his spent body, he pondered over every phase of the case. Reason and intelligence had their say. He knew he had become morbid, sick, rancorous, base, obsessed with this iniquity and his passion to stamp on it, as if it were a venomous serpent. He would have liked to do some magnificent and awful deed, that would show this little, narrow, sordid world at home the truth, and burn forever on their memories the spirit of a soldier. He had made a sacrifice that few understood. He had no reward except a consciousness that grew more luminous and glorious in its lonely light as time went on. He had endured the uttermost agonies of hell, a thousand times worse than death, and he had come home with love, with his faith still true. To what had he returned?

No need for reason or intelligence to knock at the gates of his passion! The war had left havoc. The physical, the sensual, the violent, the simian—these instincts, engendering the Day of the Beast, had come to dominate the people he had fought for. Why not go out and deliberately kill a man, a libertine, a slacker? He would still be acting on the same principle that imbued him during the war.

His thoughts drifted to Mel Iden. Strange how he loved her! Why? Because she was a lonely soul like himself—because she was true to her womanhood—because she had fallen for the same principle for which he had sacrificed all—because she had been abandoned by family and friends—because she had become beautiful, strange, mystic, tragic. Because despite the unnamed child, the scarlet letter upon her breast, she seemed to him infinitely purer than the girl who had jilted him.

Lane now surrendered to the enchantment of emotion embodied in the very name of Mel Iden. He had long resisted a sweet, melancholy current. He had driven Mel from his mind by bitter reflection on the conduct of the people who had ostracized her. Thought of her now, of what he meant to do, of the mounting love he had so strangely come to feel for her, was his only source of happiness. She would never know his secret love; he could never tell her that. But it was something to hold to his heart, besides that unquenchable faith in himself, in some unseen genius for far-off good.

The next day Lane, having ascertained where Joshua Iden was employed, betook himself that way just at the noon hour. Iden, like so many other Middleville citizens, gained a livelihood by working for the rich Swann. In his best days he had been a master mechanic of the railroad shops; at sixty he was foreman of one of the steel mills.

As it chanced, Iden had finished his noonday meal and was resting in the shade, apart from other laborers there. Lane remembered him, in spite of the fact that the three years had aged and bowed him, and lined his face.

"Mr. Iden, do you remember me?" asked Lane. He caught the slight averting of Iden's eyes from his uniform, and divined how the father of Mel Iden hated soldiers. But nothing could daunt Lane.

"Yes, Lane, I remember you," returned Iden. He returned Lane's hand-clasp, but not cordially.

Lane had mapped out in his mind this little interview. Taking off his hat, he carefully lowered himself until his back was propped against the tree, and looked frankly at Iden.

"It's warm. And I tire so easily. The damned Huns cut me to pieces.... Not much like I was when I used to call on Mel!"

Iden lowered his shadowed face. After a moment he said: "No, you're changed, Lane.... I heard you were gassed, too."

"Oh, everything came my way, Mr. Iden.... And the finish isn't far off."

Iden shifted his legs uneasily, then sat more erect, and for the first time really looked at Lane. It was the glance of a man who had strong aversion to the class Lane represented, but who was fair-minded and just, and not without sympathy.

"That's too bad, Lane. You're a young man.... The war hit us all, I guess," he said, and at the last, sighed heavily.

"It's been a long pull—Blair Maynard and I were the first to enlist, and we left Middleville almost immediately," went on Lane.

He desired to plant in Iden's mind the fact that he had left Middleville long before the wild era of soldier-and-girl attraction which had created such havoc. Acutely sensitive as Lane was, he could not be sure of an alteration in Iden's aloofness, yet there was some slight change. Then he talked frankly about specific phases of the war. Finally, when he saw that he had won interest and sympathy from Iden he abruptly launched his purpose.

"Mr. Iden, I came to ask if you will give your consent to my marrying Mel."

The older man shrank back as if he had been struck. He stared. His lower jaw dropped. A dark flush reddened his cheek.

"What!... Lane, you must be drunk," he ejaculated, thickly.

"No. I never was more earnest in my life. I want to marry Mel Iden."

"Why?" rasped out the father, hoarsely.

"I understand Mel," replied Lane, and swiftly he told his convictions as to the meaning and cause of her sacrifice. "Mel is good. She never was bad. These rotten people who see dishonor and disgrace in her have no minds, no hearts. Mel is far above these painted, bare-kneed girls who scorn her.... And I want to show them what *I* think of her. I want to give her boy a name—so he'll have a chance in the world. I'll not live long. This is just a little thing I can do to make it easier for Mel."

"Lane, you can't be the father of her child," burst out Iden.

"No. I wish I were. I was never anything to Mel but a friend. She was only a girl—seventeen when I left home."

"So help me God!" muttered Iden, and he covered his face with his hands.

"Say yes, Mr. Iden, and I'll go to Mel this afternoon."

"No, let me think.... Lane, if you're not drunk, you're crazy."

"Not at all. Why, Mr. Iden, I'm perfectly rational. Why, I'd glory in making that splendid girl a little happier, if it's possible."

"I drove my—my girl from her mother—her home," said Iden, slowly.

"Yes, and it was a hard, cruel act," replied Lane, sharply. "You were wrong. You—"

The mill whistle cut short Lane's further speech. When its shrill clarion ended, Iden got up, and shook himself as if to reestablish himself in the present.

"Lane, you come to my house to-night," he said. "I've got to go back to work.... But I'll think—and we can talk it over. I still live where you used to come as a boy.... How strange life is!... Good day, Lane."

Lane felt more than satisfied with the result of that interview. Joshua Iden would go home and tell Mel's mother, and that would surely make the victory easier. She would be touched in her mother's heart; she would understand Mel now, and divine Lane's mission; and she would plead with her husband to consent, and to bring Mel back home. Lane was counting on that. He must never even hint such a hope, but nevertheless he had it, he believed in it. Joshua Iden would have the scales torn from his eyes. He would never have it said that a dying soldier, who owed neither him nor his daughter anything, had shown more charity than he.

Therefore, Lane went early to the Iden homestead, a picturesque cottage across the river from Riverside Park. The only change Lane noted was a larger growth of trees and a fuller foliage. It was warm twilight. The frogs had begun to trill, sweet and melodious sound to Lane, striking melancholy chords of memory. Joshua Iden was walking on his lawn, his coat off, his gray head uncovered. Mrs. Iden sat on the low-roofed porch. Lane expected to see a sad change in her, something the same as he had found in his own mother. But he was hardly prepared for the frail, white-haired woman unlike the image he carried in his mind.

"Daren Lane! You should have come to see me long ago," was her greeting, and in her voice, so like Mel's, Lane recognized her. Some fitting reply came to him, and presently the moment seemed easier for all. She asked about his mother and Lorna, and then about Blair Maynard. But she did not speak of his own health or condition. And presently Lane thought it best to come to the issue at hand.

"Mr. Iden, have you made up your mind to—to give me what I want?"

"Yes, I have, Lane," replied Iden, simply. "You've made me see what Mel's mother always believed, though she couldn't make it clear to me.... I have much to forgive that girl. Yet, if you, who owe her nothing—who have wasted your life in vain sacrifice—if you can ask her to be your wife, I can ask her to come back home."

That was a splendid, all-satisfying moment for Lane. By his own grief he measured his reward. What had counted with Joshua Iden had been his faith in Mel's innate goodness. Then Lane turned to the mother. In the dusk he could see the working of her sad face.

"God bless you, my boy!" she said. "You feel with a woman's heart. I thank you.... Joshua has already sent word for Mel to come home. She will be back to-morrow.... You must come here to see her. But, Daren, she will never marry you."

"She will," replied Lane.

"You do not know Mel. Even if you had only a day to live she would not let you wrong yourself."

"But when she learns how much it means to me? The army ruined Mel, as it ruined hundreds of thousands of other girls. She will let one soldier make it up to her. She will let me go to my death with less bitterness."

"Oh, my poor boy, I don't know—I can't tell," she replied, brokenly. "By God's goodness you have brought about one miracle. Who knows? You might change Mel. For you have brought something great back from the war."

"Mrs. Iden, I will persuade her to marry me," said Lane. "And then, Mr. Iden, we must see what is best for her and the boy—in the future."

"Aye, son. One lesson learned makes other lessons easy. I will take Mel and her mother far away from Middleville—where no one ever heard of us."

"Good! You can all touch happiness again.... And now, if you and Mrs. Iden will excuse me—I will go."

Lane bade the couple good night, and slowly, as might have a lame man, he made his way through the gloaming, out to the road, and down to the bridge, where as always he lingered to catch the mystic whispers of the river waters, meant only for his ear. Stronger to-night! He was closer to that nameless thing. The shadows of dusk, the dark murmuring river, held an account with him, sometime to be paid. How blessed to fall, to float down to that merciful oblivion.

CHAPTER XII

Several days passed before Lane felt himself equal to the momentous interview with Mel Iden. After his call upon Mel's father and mother he was overcome by one of his sick, weak spells, that happily had been infrequent of late. This one confined him to his room. He had about fought and won it out, when the old injury at the base of his spine reminded him that misfortunes did not come singly. Quite unexpectedly, as he bent over with less than his usual caution, the vertebra slipped out; and Lane found his body twisted like a letter S. And the old pain was no less terrible for its familiarity.

He got back to his bed and called his mother. She sent for Doctor Bronson. He came at once, and though solicitous and kind he lectured Lane for neglecting the osteopathic treatment he had advised. And he sent his chauffeur for an osteopath.

"Lane," said the little physician, peering severely down upon him, "I didn't think you'd last as long as this."

"I'm tough, Doctor—hard to kill," returned Lane, making a wry face. "But I couldn't stand this pain long."

"It'll be easier presently. We can fix that spine. Some good treatments to strengthen ligaments, and a brace to wear—we can fix that.... Lane, you've wonderful vitality."

"A doctor in France told me that."

"Except for your mental condition, you're in better shape now than when you came home." Doctor Bronson peered at Lane from under his shaggy brows, walked to the window, looked out, and returned, evidently deep in thought.

"Boy, what's on your mind?" he queried, suddenly.

"Oh, Lord! listen to him," sighed Lane. Then he laughed. "My dear Doctor, I have nothing on my mind—absolutely nothing.... This world is a beautiful place. Middleville is fine, clean, progressive. People are kind—thoughtful—good. What could I have on my mind?"

"You can't fool me. You think the opposite of what you say.... Lane, your heart is breaking."

"No, Doctor. It broke long ago."

"You believe so, but it didn't. You can't give up.... Lane, I want to tell you something. I'm a prohibitionist myself, and I respect the law. But there are rare cases where whiskey will effect a cure. I say that as a physician. And I am convinced now that your case is one where whiskey might give you a fighting chance."

"Doctor! What're you saying?" ejaculated Lane, wide-eyed with incredulity.

Doctor Bronson enlarged upon and emphasized his statement.

"I might *live*!" whispered Lane. "My God!... But that is ridiculous. I'm shot to pieces. I'm really tired of living. And I certainly wouldn't become a drunkard to save my life."

At this juncture the osteopath entered, putting an end to that intimate conversation. Doctor Bronson explained the case to his colleague. And fifteen minutes later Lane's body was again straight. Also he was wringing wet with cold sweat and quivering in every muscle.

"Gentlemen—your cure is—worse than—the disease," he panted.

Manifestly Doctor Branson's interest in Lane had advanced beyond the professional. His tone was one of friendship when he said, "Boy, it beats hell what you can stand. I don't know about you. Stop your worry now. Isn't there something you *care* for?"

"Yes," replied Lane.

"Think of that, or it, or *her*, then to the exclusion of all else. And give nature a chance."

"Doctor, I can't control my thoughts."

"A fellow like you can do anything," snapped Bronson. "There are such men, now and then. Human nature is strange and manifold. All great men do not have statues erected in their honor. Most of them are unknown, unsung.... Lane, you could do anything—do you hear me?—*anything*."

Lane felt surprise at the force and passion of the practical little physician. But he was not greatly impressed. And he was glad when the two men went away. He felt the insidious approach of one of his states of depression—the black mood—the hopeless despair—the hell on earth. This spell had not visited him often of late, and now manifestly meant to make up for that forbearance. Lane put forth his intelligence, his courage, his spirit—all in vain. The onslaught of gloom and anguish was irresistible. Then thought of Mel Iden sustained him—held back this madness for the moment.

Every hour he lived made her dearer, yet farther away. It was the unattainableness of her, the impossibility of a fruition of love that slowly and surely removed her. On the other hand, the image of her sweet face, of her form, of her beauty, of her movements—every recall of these physical things enhanced her charm, and his love. He had cherished a delusion that it was Mel Iden's spirit alone, the wonderful soul of her, that had stormed his heart and won it. But he found to his consternation that however he revered her soul, it was the woman also who now allured him. That moment of revelation to Lane was a catastrophe. Was there no peace on earth for him? What had he done to be so tortured? He had a secret he must hide from Mel Iden. He was human, he was alone, he needed love, but this seemed madness. And at the moment of full realization Doctor Bronson's strange words of possibility returned to haunt and flay him. He might live! A fierce thrill like a flame leaped from his heart, along his veins. And a shudder, cold as ice, followed it. Love would kill his resignation. Love would add to his despair. Mel Iden could never love him. He did not want her love. And yet, to live on and on, with such love as would swell and mount from his agony, with the barrier between them growing more terrible every day, was more than he cared to face. He would rather die.

And so, at length, Lane's black demon of despair overthrew even his thoughts of Mel, and fettered him there, in darkness and strife of soul. He was an atom under the grinding, monstrous wheels of his morbid mood.

Sometime, after endless moments or hours of lying there, with crushed breast, with locked thoughts hideous and forlorn, with slow burn of pang and beat of heart, Lane heard a heavy thump on the porch outside, on the hall inside, on the stairs. Thump—thump, slow and heavy! It roused him. It drove away the drowsy, thick and thunderous atmosphere of mind. It had a familiar sound. Blair's crutch!

Presently there was a knock on the door of his room and Blair entered. Blair, as always, bright of eye, smiling of lip, erect, proud, self-sufficient, inscrutable and sure. Lane's black demon stole away. Lane saw that Blair was whiter, thinner, frailer, a little farther on that road from which there could be no turning.

"Hello, old scout," greeted Blair, as he sat down on the bed beside Lane. "I need you more than any one—but it kills me to see you."

"Same here, Blair," replied Lane, comprehendingly.

"Gosh! we oughtn't be so finicky about each other's looks," exclaimed Blair, with a smile.

But neither Lane nor Blair made further reference to the subject.

Each from the other assimilated some force, from voice and look and presence, something wanting in their contact with others. These two had measured all emotions, spanned in little time the extremes of life, plumbed the depths, and now saw each other on the heights. In the presence of Blair, Lane felt an exaltation. The more Blair seemed to fade away from life, the more luminous and beautiful the light of his countenance. For Lane the crippled and dying Blair was a deed of valor done, a wrong expiated for the sake of others, a magnificent nobility in contrast to the baseness and greed and cowardice of the self-preservation that had doomed him. Lane had only to look at Blair to feel something elevating in himself, to know beyond all doubt that the goodness, the truth, the progress of man in nature, and of God in his soul, must grow on forever.

Mel Iden had been in her home four days when Lane first saw her there.

It was a day late in June when the rich, thick, amber light of afternoon seemed to float in the air. Warm summer lay on the land. The bees were humming in the rose vines over the porch. Mrs. Iden, who evidently heard Lane's step, appeared in the path, and nodding her gladness at sight of him, she pointed to the open door.

Lane halted on the threshold. The golden light of the day seemed to have entered the room and found Mel. It warmed the pallor of her skin and the whiteness of her dress. When he had seen her before she had worn something plain and dark. Could a white gown and the golden glow of June effect such transformation? She came slowly toward him and took his hand.

"Daren, I am home," was all she could say.

Long hours before Lane had braced himself for this ordeal. It was himself he had feared, not Mel. He played the part he had created for her imagination. Behind his composure, his grave, kind earnestness, hid the subdued and scorned and unwelcome love that had come to him. He held it down, surrounded, encompassed, clamped, so that he dared look into her eyes, listen to her voice, watch the sweet and tragic tremulousness of her lips.

"Yes, Mel, where you should be," replied Lane.

"It was you—your offer to marry me—that melted father's heart."

"Mel, all he needed was to be made think," returned Lane. "And that was how I made him do it."

"Oh, Daren, I thank you, for mother's sake, for mine—I can't tell you how much."

"Mel, please don't thank me," he answered. "You understand, and that's enough. Now say you'll marry me, Mel."

Mel did not answer, but in the look of her eyes, dark, humid, with mysterious depths below the veil, Lane saw the truth; he felt it in the clasp of her hands, he divined it in all that so subtly emanated from the womanliness of her. Mel had come to love him.

And all that he had endured seemed to rise and envelop heart and soul in a strange, cold stillness.

"Mel, will you marry me?" he repeated, almost dully.

Slowly Mel withdrew her hands. The query seemed to make her mistress of herself.

"No, Daren, I cannot," she replied, and turned away to look out of a window with unseeing eyes. "Let us talk of other things.... My father says he will move away—taking me and—and—all of us—as soon as he sells the home."

"No, Mel, if you'll forgive me, we'll not talk of something else," Lane informed her. "We can argue without quarreling. Come over here and sit down."

She came slowly, as if impelled, and she stood before him. To Lane it seemed as if she were both supplicating and inexorable.

"Do you remember the last time we sat together on this couch?" she asked.

"No, Mel, I don't."

"It was four years ago—and more. I was sixteen. You tried to kiss me and were angry because I wouldn't let you."

"Well, wasn't I rude!" he exclaimed, facetiously. Then he grew serious. "Mel, do you remember it was Helen's lying that came between you and me—as boy and girl friends?"

"I never knew. Helen Wrapp! What was it?"

"It's not worth recalling and would hurt you—now," he replied. "But it served to draw me Helen's way. We were engaged when she was seventeen.... Then came the war. And the other night she laughed in my face because I was a wreck.... Mel, it's beyond understanding how things work out. Helen has chosen the fleshpots of Egypt. You have chosen a lonelier and higher path.... And here I am in your little parlor asking you to marry me."

"No, no, no! Daren, don't, I beg of you—don't talk to me this way," she besought him.

"Mel, it's a difference of opinion that makes arguments, wars and other things," he said, with a cruelty in strange antithesis to the pity and tenderness he likewise felt. He could hurt her. He had power over her. What a pang shot through his heart! There would be an irresistible delight in playing on the emotions of this woman. He could no more help it than the shame that surged over him at consciousness of his littleness. He already loved her, she was all he had left to love, he would end in a day or a week or a month by worshipping her. Through her he was going to suffer. Peace would now never abide in his soul.

"Daren, you were never like this—as a boy," she said, in wondering distress.

"Like what?"

"You're hard. You used to be so—so gentle and nice."

"Hard! I? Yes, Mel, perhaps I am—hard as war, hard as modern life, hard as my old friends, my little sister——" he broke off.

"Daren, do not mock me," she entreated. "I should not have said hard. But you're strange to me—a something terrible flashes from you. Yet it's only in glimpses.... Forgive me, Daren, I didn't mean hard."

Lane drew her down upon the couch so that she faced him, and he did not release her hand.

"Mel, I'm softer than a jelly-fish," he said. "I've no bone, no fiber, no stamina, no substance. I'm more unstable than water. I'm so soft I'm weak. I can't stand pain. I lie awake in the dead hours of night and I cry like a baby, like a fool. I weep for myself, for my mother, for Lorna, for *you*...."

"Hush!" She put a soft hand over his lips.

"Very well, I'll not be bitter," he went on, with mounting pulse, with thrill and rush of inexplicable feeling, as if at last had come the person who would not be deaf to his voice. "Mel, I'm still the boy, your schoolmate, who used to pull the bow off your braid.... I am that boy still in heart, with all the war upon my head, with the years between then and now. I'm young and old.... I've lived the whole gamut—the fresh call of war to youth, glorious, but God! as false as stairs of sand—the change of blood, hard, long, brutal, debasing labor of hands, of body, of mind to learn to kill—to survive and kill—and go on to kill.... I've seen the marching of thousands of soldiers—the long strange tramp, tramp, tramp, the beat, beat, beat, the roll of drums, the call of bugles, the boom of cannon in the dark, the lightnings of hell flaring across the midnight skies, the thunder and chaos and torture and death and pestilence and decay—the hell of war. It is not sublime. There is no glory. The sublimity is in man's acceptance of war, not for hate or gain, but love. Love of country, home, family—love of women—I fought for women—for Helen, whom I imagined my ideal, breaking her heart over me on the battlefield. Not that Helen failed *me*, but failed the ideal for which I fought!... My little sister Lorna! I fought for her, and I fought for a dream that existed only in my heart. Lorna—Alas!... I fought for other women, all women—and *you*, Mel Iden. And in you, in your sacrifice and your strength to endure, I find something healing to my sore heart. I find my ideal embodied in you. I find hope and faith for the future embodied in you. I find—"

"Oh Daren, you shame me utterly," she protested, freeing her hands in gesture of entreaty. "I am outcast."

"To a false and rotten society, yes—you are," he returned. "But Mel, that society is a mass of maggots. It is such women as you, such men as Blair, who carry the spirit onward.... So much for that. I have spoken to try to show you where I hold you. I do not call your—your trouble a blunder, or downfall, or dishonor. I call it a misfortune because—because—"

"Because there was not love," she supplemented, as he halted at fault. "Yes, that is where I wronged myself, my soul. I obeyed nature and nature is strong, raw, inevitable. She seeks only her end, which is concerned with the species. For nature the individual perishes. Nature cannot be God. For God has created a soul in woman. And through the ages woman has advanced to hold her womanhood sacred. But ever the primitive lurks in the blood, and the primitive is nature. Soul and nature are not compatible. A woman's soul sanctions only love. That is the only progress there ever was in life. Nature and war made me traitor to my soul."

"Yes, yes, Mel, it's true—and cruel, what you say," returned Lane. "All the more reason why you should do what I ask. I am home after the war. All that was vain *is* vain. I forget it when I can. I have—not a great while left. There are a few things even I can do before that time. One of them—the biggest to me—concerns you. You are in trouble. You have a boy who can be spared much unhappiness in life. If you were married—if the boy had my name—how different the future! Perhaps there can be some measure of happiness for you. For him there is every hope. You will leave Middleville. You will go far away somewhere. You are young. You have a good education. You can teach school, or help your parents while the boy is growing up. Time is kind. You will forget.... Marry me, Mel, for his sake."

She had both hands pressed to her breast as if to stay an uncontrollable feeling. Her eyes, dilated and wide, expressed a blending of emotions.

"No, no, no!" she cried.

Lane went on just the same with other words, in other vein, reiterating the same importunity. It was a tragic game, in which he divined he must lose. But the playing of it had inexplicably bitter-sweet pain. He knew now that Mel loved him. No greater proof needed he than the perception of her reaction to one word on his lips—wife. She quivered to that like a tautly strung lyre touched by a skilful hand. It fascinated her. But the temptation to accept his offer for the sake of her boy's future was counteracted by the very strength of her feeling for Lane. She would not marry him, because she loved him.

Lane read this truth, and it wrung a deeper reverence from him. And he saw, too, the one way in which he could break her spirit, make her surrender, if he could stoop to it. If he could take her in his arms, and hold her tight, and kiss her dumb and blind, and make her understand his own love for her, his need of her, she would accede with the wondrous generosity of a woman's heart. But he could not do it.

In the end, out of sheer pity that overcame the strange delight he had in torturing her, he desisted in his appeals and demands and subtle arguments. The long strain left him spent. And with the sudden let-down of his energy, the surrender to her stronger will, he fell prey at once to the sadness that more and more was encompassing him. He felt an old and broken man.

To this sudden change in Lane Mel responded with mute anxiety and fear. The alteration of his spirit stunned her. As he bade her good-bye she clung to him.

"Daren, forgive me," she implored. "You don't understand.... Oh, it's hard."

"Never mind, Mel. I guess it was just one of my dreams. Don't cry.... Good-bye."

"But you'll come again?" she entreated, almost wildly.

Lane shook his head. He did not trust himself to look at her then.

"Daren, you can't mean that," she cried. "It's too late for me. I—I—Oh! You.... To uplift me—then to cast me down! Daren, come back."

In his heart he did not deny that cry of hers. He knew he would come back, knew it with stinging shame, but he could not tell her. It had all turned out so differently from what he had dreamed. If he had not loved her he would not have felt defeat. To have made her his wife would have been to protect her, to possess her even after he was dead.

At the last she let him go. He felt her watching him, and he carried her lingering clasp away with him, to burn and to thrill and to haunt, and yet to comfort him in lonely hours.

But the next day the old spirit resurged anew, and unreconciled to defeat, he turned to what was left him. Foolish and futile hopes! To bank on the single grain of good in his wayward sister's heart! To trust the might of his spirit—to beat down the influence of an intolerant and depraved young millionaire—verily he was mad. Yet he believed. And as a final resort he held death in his hand. Richard Swann swaggered by Lane that night in the billiard room of the Bradford Inn and stared sneeringly at him.

"I've got a date," he gayly said to his sycophantic friends, in a tone that would reach Lane's ears.

The summer night came when Lane drove a hired car out the river road, keeping ever in sight a red light in front of him. He broke the law and endangered his life by traveling with darkened lamps.

There was a crescent moon, clear and exquisitely delicate in the darkening blue sky. The gleaming river shone winding away under the dusky wooded hills. The white road stretched ahead, dimming in the distance. A night for romance and love—for a maiden at a stile and a lover who hung rapt and humble upon her whispers! But that red eye before him held no romance. It leered as the luxurious sedan swayed from side to side, a diabolical thing with speed.

Lane was driving out the state highway, mile after mile. He calculated that in less than ten minutes Swann had taken a girl from a bustling corner of Middleville out into the open country. In pleasant weather, when the roads were good, cars like Swann's swerved off into the bypaths, into the edge of woods. In bad weather they parked along the highway, darkened their lights and pulled their blinds. For this, great factories turned out automobiles. And there might have pealed out to a nation, and to God, the dolorous cry of a hundred thousand ruined girls! But who would hear? And on the lips of girls of the present there was only the wild cry for excitement, for the nameless and unknown! There was a girl in Swann's car and Lane believed it was his sister. Night after night he had watched. Once he had actually seen Lorna ride off with Swann. And to-night from a vantage point under the maples, when he had a car ready to follow, he had made sure he had seen them again.

The red eye squared off at right angles to the highway, and disappeared. Lane came to a byroad, a lane lined with trees. He stopped his car and got out. It did not appear that he would have to walk far. And he was right, for presently a black object loomed against the gray obscurity. It was an automobile, without lights, in the shadow of trees.

Lane halted. He carried a flash-light in his left hand, his gun in his right. For a moment he deliberated. This being abroad in the dark on an errand fraught with peril for some one had a familiar and deadly tang. He was at home in this atmosphere. Hell itself had yawned at his feet many and many a time. He was a different man here. He deliberated because it was wise to forestall events. He did not want to kill Swann then, unless in self-defense. He waited until that peculiarly quick and tight and cold settling of his nerves told of brain control over heart. Yet he was conscious of subdued hate, of a righteous and terrible wrath held in abeyance for the sake of his sister's name. And he regretted that he had imperiously demanded of himself this assurance of Lorna's wantonness.

Then he stole forward, closer and closer. He heard a low voice of dalliance, a titter, high-pitched and sweet—sweet and wild. That was not Lorna's laugh. The car was not Swann's.

Lane swerved to the left, and in the gloom of trees, passed by noiselessly. Soon he encountered another car—an open car with shields up—as silent as if empty. But the very silence of it was potent of life. It cried out to the night and to Lane. But it was not the car he had followed.

Again he slipped by, stealthily, yet scornful of his caution. Who cared? He might have shouted his mission to the heavens. Lane passed on. All he caught from the second car was a faint fragrance of smoke, wafted on the gentle summer breeze.

Another black object loomed up—a larger car—the sedan Lane recognized. He did not bolt or hurry. His footsteps made no sound. Crouching a little he slipped round the car to one side. At the instant he reached for the handle of the door, a pang shook him. Alas, that he should be compelled to spy on Lorna! His little sister! He saw her as a curly-headed child, adoring him. Perhaps it might not be Lorna after all. But it was for her sake that he was doing this. The softer moment passed and the soldier intervened.

With one swift turn and jerk he opened the door—then flashed his light. A scream rent the air. In the glaring circle of light Lane saw red hair—green eyes transfixed in fear—white shoulders—white arms—white ringed hands suddenly flung upward. Helen! The blood left his heart in a rush. Swann blinked in the light, bewildered and startled.

"Swann, you'll have to excuse me," said Lane, coolly. "I thought you had my sister with you. I've spotted her twice with you in this car.... It may not interest you or your—your guest, but I'll add that you're damned lucky not to have Lorna here to-night."

Then he snapped off his flash-light, and slamming the car door, he wheeled away.

CHAPTER XIII

Lane left his room and went into the shady woods, where he thought the July heat would be less unendurable, where the fever in his blood might abate. But though it was cool and pleasant there he experienced no relief. Wherever he went he carried the burden of his pangs. And his grim giant of unrest trod in his shadow.

He could not stay long in the woods. He betook himself to the hills and meadows. Action was beneficial for him, though he soon exhausted himself. He would have liked to fight out his battle that day. Should he go on spending his days and nights in a slowly increasing torment? The longer he fought the less chance he had of victory. Victory! There could be none. What victory could be won over a strange ineradicable susceptibility to the sweetness, charm, mystery of a woman? He plodded the fragrant fields with bent head, in despair. Loneliness hurt him as much as anything. And a new pang, the fiercest and most insupportable, had been added to his miseries. Jealousy! Thought of the father of Mel Iden's child haunted him, flayed him, made him feel himself ignoble and base. There was no help for that. And this fiend of jealousy added fuel to his love. Only long passionate iteration of his assurance of principle and generosity subdued that frenzy and at length gave him composure. Perhaps this had some semblance to victory.

Lane returned to town weaker in one way than when he had left, yet stronger in another. Upon the outskirts of Middleville he crossed the river road and sat down upon a stone wall. The afternoon was far spent and the sun blazing red. Lane wiped his moist face and fanned himself with his hat. Behind him the shade of a wooded garden or park looked inviting. Back in the foliage he espied the vine-covered roof of an old summer house.

A fresh young voice burst upon his meditations. "Hello, Daren Lane."

Lane turned in surprise to behold a girl in white, standing in the shade of trees beyond the wall. Somewhere he had seen that beautiful golden head, the dark blue, almost purple eyes.

"Good afternoon. You startled me," said Lane.

"I called you twice."

"Indeed? I beg pardon. I didn't hear."

"Don't you remember me?" Her tone was one of pique and doubt.

Then he remembered her. "Oh, of course. Bessy Bell! You must forgive me. I've been ill and upset lately. These bad spells of mine magnify time. It seems long since the Junior Prom."

"Oh, you're ill," she returned, compassionately. "You do look pale and—won't you come in? It's dusty and hot there. Come. I'll take you where it's nice and cool."

"Thank you. I'll be glad to."

She led him to a green, fragrant nook, where a bench with cushions stood half-hidden under heavy foliage. Lane caught a glimpse of a winding flagged path, and in the distance a cottage among the trees.

"Bessy, do you live here?" he asked. "It's pretty."

"Yes, this is my home. It's too damn far from town, I'll say. I'm buried alive," she replied, passionately.

The bald speech struck Lane forcibly. All at once he remembered Bessy Bell and his former interest. She was a type of the heretofore inexplicable modern girl. Lane looked at her, seeing her suddenly with a clearer vision. Bessy Bell had a physical perfection, a loveliness that needed neither spirit nor animation. But life had given this girl so much more than beauty. A softness of light seemed to shine round her golden head; smiles played in secret behind her red lips ready to break forth, and there was a haunting hint of a dimple in her round cheek; on her lay the sweetness of youth subtly dawning into womanhood; the flashing eyes were keen with intellect, with fire, full of promise and mystic charm; and her beautiful, supple body, so plainly visible, seemed quivering with sheer, restless joy of movement and feeling. A trace of artificial color on her face and the indelicacy of her dress but slightly counteracted Lane's first impression.

"You promised to call me up and make a date," she said, and sat down close to him.

"Yes. I meant it too. But Bessy, I was ill, and then I forgot. You didn't miss much."

"Hot dog! Hear the man. Daren, I'd throw the whole bunch down to be with you," she exclaimed.

At the end of that speech she paled slightly and her breath came quickly. She looked bold, provocative, expectant, yet sincere. Child or woman, she had to be taken seriously. Here indeed was the mystery that had baffled Lane. He realized his opportunity, like a flash all his former thought and conjecture about this girl returned to him.

"You would. Well, I'm highly flattered. Why, may I ask?"

"Because I've fallen for you," she replied, leaning close to him. "That's the main reason, I guess.... But another is, I want you to tell me all about yourself—in the war, you know."

"I'd be glad to—if we get to be real friends," he said, thoughtfully. "I don't understand you."

"And I'll say I don't just get you," she retorted. "What do you want? Have you forgotten the silver platter?"

She turned away with a restless quivering. She had shown no shyness. She was bold, intense, absolutely without fear; and however stimulating or attractive the situation evidently was, it was neither new nor novel to her. Some strange leaven worked deep in her. Lane could put no other interpretation on her words and actions than that she expected him to kiss her.

"Bessy Bell, look at me," said Lane, earnestly. "You've said a mouthful, as the slang word goes. I'm sort of surprised, you remember. Bessy, you're not a girl whose head is full of excelsior. You've got brains. You can think.... Now, if you really like me—and I believe you—try to understand this. I've been away so long. All is changed. I don't know how to take girls. I'm ill—and unhappy. But if I could be your friend and could help you a little—please you—why it'd be good for me."

"Daren, they tell me you're going to die," she returned, breathlessly. Her glance was brooding, dark, pregnant with purple fire.

"Bessy, don't believe all you hear. I'm not—not so far gone yet."

"They say you're game, too."

"I hope so, Bessy."

"Oh, you make me think. You must believe me a pill. I wanted you to—to fall for me hard.... That bunch of sapheads have spoiled me, I'll say. Daren, I'm sick of them. All they want to do is mush. I like tennis, riding, golf. I want to do things. But it's too hot, or this, or that. Yet they'll break their necks to carry a girl off to some roadhouse, and dance—dance till you're melted. Then they stop along the river to go bathing. I've been twice. You see, I have to sneak away, or lie to mother and say I've gone to Gail's or somewhere."

"Bathing, at night?" queried Lane, curiously.

"Sure thing. It's spiffy, in the dark."

"Of course you took your bathing suits?"

"Hot dog! That would be telling."

Lane dropped his head and studied the dust at his feet. His heart beat thick and heavy. Through this girl the truth was going to be revealed to him. It seemed on the moment that he could not look into her eyes. She scattered his wits. He tried to erase from his mind every impression of her, so that he might begin anew to understand her. And the very first, succeeding this erasure, was a singular idea that she was the opposite of romantic.

"Bessy, can you understand that it is hard for a soldier to talk of what has happened to him?"

"I'll say I can," she replied.

"You're sorry for me?" he went on, gently.

"Sorry!... Give me a chance to prove what I am, Daren Lane."

"Very well, then. I will. We'll make a fifty-fifty bargain. Do you regard a promise sacred?"

"I think I do. Some of the girls quarrel with me because I get sore, and swear they're not square, as I try to be. I hate a liar and a quitter."

"Come then—shake hands on our bargain."

She seemed thrilled, excited. The clasp of her little hand showed force of character. She looked wonderingly up at him. Her appeal then was one of exquisite youth and beauty. Something of the baffling suggestion of an amorous expectation and response left her. This child would give what she received.

"First, then, it's for me to know a lot about you," went on Lane. "Will you tell me?"

"Sure. I'd trust you with anything," she replied, impulsively.

"How long have you been going with boys?"

"Oh, for two years, I guess. I had a passionate love affair when I was thirteen," she replied, with the nonchalance and sophistication of experience.

It was impossible for Lane to take this latter remark for anything but the glib boldness of an erotic child. But he was not making any assurances to himself that he was right. Bessy Bell was fifteen years old, according to time. But she had the physical development of eighteen, and a mental range beyond his ken. The lawlessness unleashed by the war seemed embodied in this girl.

"With an older boy?" queried Lane.

"No. He was a kid of my own age. I guess I outgrew Ted," she replied, dreamily. "But he still tries to rush me."

"With whom do you go to the secret club-rooms—above White's ice cream parlor?" asked Lane, abruptly.

Bessy never flicked an eyelash. "Hot dog! So you're wise to that? I thought it was a secret. I told Rose Clymer those fellows weren't on the level. Who told you I was there? Your sister Lorna?"

"No. No one told me. Never mind that. Who took you there? You needn't be afraid to trust *me*. I'm going to entrust my secrets to you by and bye."

"I went with Roy Vancey, the boy who was with me at Helen's the day I met you."

"Bessy, how often have you been to those club-rooms?"

"Three times."

"Were you ever there alone without any girls?"

"No. I had my chance. Dick Swann tried his damnedest to get me to go. But I've no use for him."

"Why?"

"I just don't like him, Daren," she replied, evasively. "I love to have fun. But I haven't yet been so hard up I had to go out with some one I didn't like."

"Has Swann had my sister Lorna at the club?"

Her replies had been prompt and frank. At this sudden query she seemed checked. Lane read in Bessy Bell then more of the truth of her than he had yet divined. Falsehood was naturally abhorrent to her. To lie to her parents or teachers savored of fun, and was part of the game. She did not want to lie to Lane, but in her code she could not betray another girl, especially to that girl's brother.

"Daren, I promised I'd tell you all about myself," she said.

"I shouldn't have asked you to give away one of your friends," he returned. "Some other time I'll talk to you about Lorna. Tell you what I know, and ask you to help me save her——"

"*Save* her! What do you mean, Daren?" she interrupted, with surprise.

"Bessy, I've paid you the compliment of believing you have intelligence. Hasn't it occurred to you that Lorna—or other of her friends or yours—might be going straight to ruin?"

"Ruin! No, that hadn't occurred to me. I heard Doctor Wallace make a crack like yours. Mother hauled me to church the Sunday after you broke up Fanchon Smith's dance. Doctor Wallace didn't impress me. These old people make me sick anyhow. They don't understand.... But Daren, I think I get your drift. So snow some more."

All in a moment, it seemed to Lane, this girl passed from surprise to gravity, then to contempt, and finally to humor. She was fascinating.

"To go back to the club," resumed Lane. "Bessy, what did you do there?"

"Oh, we toddled and shimmied. Cut up! Had an immense time, I'll say."

"What do you mean by cut up?"

"Why, we just ran wild, you know. Fool stunts!... Once Roy was sore because I kicked cigarettes out of Bob's mouth. But the boob was tickled stiff when I kicked for *him*. Jealous! It's all right with any one of the boys what you do for *him*. But if you do the same for *another* boy— good night!"

Bessy had no divination of the fact that her words for Lane had a clarifying significance.

"I suppose you played what we used to call kissing games?" queried Lane.

A sweet, high trill of laughter escaped Bessy's red lips.

"Daren, you are funny. Those games are as dead as Caesar.... This bunch of boys and girls paired off by themselves to spoon.... As for myself, I don't mind spooning if I like the fellow— and he hasn't been drinking. But otherwise I hate it. All the same I got what was coming to me from some of the boys of the Strong Arm Club."

"Why do they give it that name?" asked Lane, remembering Colonel Pepper's remarks.

"Why, if a girl doesn't come across she gets the strong arm.... I had to fight like the devil that last afternoon I went there."

"*Did* you fight, Bessy?"

"I'll say I did.... Roy Vancey is sore as a pup. He hasn't been near me or called me up since."

"Bessy, will you promise to stay away from that place—and not to go joy-riding with any of those boys—day or night—if I meet you, and tell you all about my experience in the war? I'll do my best to keep the time you spend with me from being tedious."

"It's another bargain," she returned deliberately, "if you just don't spend enough time with me to make me stuck on you—then throw me down. On the level, now, Daren?"

"I'll meet you as often as you want. And I'll be your friend as long as you prove to me I can be of any help, or pleasure, or good to you."

"Hot dog, but you're taking some job, Daren. Won't it be just spiffy? We'll meet here, afternoons, and evenings when mother's out. She's nutty on bridge. She makes me promise I won't leave the yard. So I'll not have to lie to meet you.... Daren, that day at Helen's, the minute I saw you I knew you were going to have something to do with my future."

"Bessy, a little while ago I made sure you had no romance in you," replied Lane, with a smile. "Now as we've gotten serious, let's think hard about the future. What do you want most? Do you care for study, for books? Have you any gift for music? Do you ever think of fitting yourself for useful work?... Or is your mind full of this jazz stuff? Do you just want to go from day to day, like a butterfly from flower to flower? Just this boy and that one—not caring much which—all this frivolity you hinted of, and worse, living this precious time of your youth all for excitement? What is it you want most?"

She responded with a thoughtfulness that inspired Lane's hope for her. This girl could be reached. She was like Lorna in many ways, but different in mentality. Bessy watched the gyrations of her shapely little foot. She could not keep still even in abstraction.

"A girl *must* have a good time," she replied presently. "I've done things I hated because I couldn't bear to be left out of the fun.... But I like most to read and dream. Music makes me strange inside, and to want to do great things. Only there *are* no great things to do. I've never been nutty about a career, like Helen is. And I always hated work.... I guess—to tell on the level—what I want most is to be loved."

With that she raised her eyes to Lane's. He tried to read her mind, and realized that if he failed it was not because she was not baring it. Dropping his own gaze, he pondered. The girl's response to his earnestness was intensely thought-provoking. No matter how immodestly she was dressed, or what she had confessed to, or whether she had really expected and desired dalliance on his part—here was the truth as to her hidden yearning. The seething and terrible Renaissance of the modern girl seemed remarkably exemplified in Bessy Bell, yet underneath it all hid the fundamental instinct of all women of all ages. Bessy wanted most to be loved. Was that the secret of her departure from the old-fashioned canons of modesty and reserve?

"Bessy," went on Lane, presently. "I've heard my sister speak of Rose Clymer. Is she a friend of yours, too?"

"You bet. And she's the square kid."

"Lorna told me she'd been expelled from school."

"Yes. She refused to tattle."

"Tattle what?"

"I wrote some verses which one of the girls copied. Miss Hill found them and raised the roof. She kept us all in after school. She let some of the girls off. But she expelled Rose and sent me home. Then she called on mama. I don't know what she said, but mama didn't let me go back. I've had a hateful old tutor for a month. In the fall I'm going to private school."

"And Rose?"

"Rose went to work. She had a hard time. I never heard from her for weeks. But she's a telephone operator at the Exchange now. She called me up one day lately and told me. I hope to see her soon."

"About those verses, Bessy. How did Miss Hill find out who wrote them?"

"I told her. Then she sent me home."

"Have you any more verses you wrote?"

"Yes, a lot of them. If you lend me your pencil, I'll write out the verse that gave Miss Hill heart disease."

Bessy took up a book that had been lying on the seat, and tearing out the fly-leaf, she began to write. Her slim, shapely hand flew. It fascinated Lane.

"There!" she said, ending with a flourish and a smile.

But Lane, foreshadowing the import of the verse, took the page with reluctance. Then he read it. Verses of this significance were new to him. Relief came to Lane in the divination that Bessy could not have had experience of what she had written. There was worldliness in the verse, but innocence in her eyes.

"Well, Bessy, my heart isn't much stronger than Miss Hill's," he said, finally.

Her merry laughter rang out.

"Bessy, what will you do for me?"

"Anything."

"Bring me every scrap of verse you have, every note you've got from boys and girls."

"Shall I get them now?"

"Yes, if it's safe. Of course, you've hidden them."

"Mama's out. I won't be a minute."

Away she flew under the trees, out through the rose bushes, a white, graceful, flitting figure. She vanished. Presently she came bounding into sight again and handed Lane a bundle of notes.

"Did you keep back any?" he asked, as he tried to find pockets enough for the collection.

"Not one."

"I'll go home and read them all. Then I'll meet you here to-night at eight o'clock."

"But—I've a date. I'll break it, though."

"With whom?"

"Gail and a couple of boys—kids."

"Does your mother know?"

"I'd tell her about Gail, but that's all. We go for ice cream—then meet the boys and take a walk."

"Bessy, you're not going to do that sort of thing any more."

Lane bent over her, took her hands. She instinctively rebelled, then slowly yielded.

"That's part of our bargain?" she asked.

"Yes, it certainly is."

"Then I won't ever again."

"Bessy, I trust you. Do you understand me?"

"I—I think so."

"Daren, will you care for me—if I'm—if I do as you want me to?"

"I do now," he replied. "And I'll care a thousand times more when you prove you're really above these things.... Bessy, I'll care for you as a friend—as a brother—as a man who has almost lost his faith and who sees in you some hope to keep his spirit alive. I'm unhappy, Bessy. Perhaps you can help me—make me a little happier.... Anyway, I trust you. Good-bye now. To-night, at eight o'clock."

Lane went home to his room and earnestly gave himself up to the perusal of the writings Bessy Bell had given him. He experienced shocks of pain and wonder, between which he had to laugh. All the fiendish wit of youthful ingenuity flashed forth from this verse. There was a parody on Tennyson's "Break, Break, Break," featuring Colonel Pepper's famous and deplorable habit. Miss Hill came in for a great share of opprobrium. One verse, if it had ever come under the eyes of the good schoolteacher, would have broken her heart.

Lane read all Bessy's verses, and then the packet of notes written by Bessy's girl friends. The truth was unbelievable. Yet here were the proofs. Over Bessy and her friends Lane saw the dim dark shape of a ghastly phantom, reaching out, enfolding, clutching. He went downstairs to the kitchen and here he burned the writings.

"It ought to be told," he muttered. "But who's going to tell it? Who'd believe me? The truth would not be comprehended by the mothers of Middleville.... And who's to blame?"

It would not do, Lane reflected, to place the blame wholly upon blind fathers and mothers, though indeed they were culpable. And in consideration of the subject, Lane excluded all except the better class of Middleville. It was no difficult task to understand lack of moral sense in children who were poor and unfortunate, who had to work, and get what pleasures they had in the streets. But how about the best families, where there were luxurious homes, books, education, amusement, kindness, love—all the supposed stimuli needed for the proper guidance of changeful vagrant minds? These good influences had failed. There was a greater moral abandonment than would ever be known.

Before the war Bessy Bell would have presented the perfect type of the beautiful, highly sensitive, delicately organized girl so peculiarly and distinctively American. She would have ripened before her time. Perhaps she would not have been greatly different in feeling from the old-fashioned girl: only different in that she had restraint, no deceit.

But after the war—now—what was Bessy Bell? What actuated her? What was the secret spring of her abnormal tendencies? Were they abnormal? Bessy was wild to abandon herself to she knew not what. Some glint of intelligence, some force of character as exceptional in her as it was wanting in Lorna, some heritage of innate sacredness of person, had kept Bessy from the abyss. She had absorbed in mind all the impurities of the day, but had miraculously escaped them in body. If her parents could have known Bessy as Lane now realized her they would have been horrified. But Lane's horror was fading. Bessy was illuminating the darkness of his mind.

To understand more clearly what the war had done to Bessy Bell, and to the millions of American girls like her, it was necessary for Lane to understand what the war had done to soldiers, to men, and to the world.

Lane could grasp some infinitesimal truth of the sublime and horrible change war had wrought in the souls of soldiers. That change was too great for any mind but the omniscient to grasp in its entirety. War had killed in some soldiers a belief in Christ: in others it had created one. War had unleashed the old hidden primitive instincts of manhood: likewise it had fired hearts to hate of hate and love of love, to the supreme ideal consciousness could conceive. War had brought out the monstrous in men and as well the godlike. Some soldiers had become cowards; others, heroes. There were thousands of soldiers who became lions to fight, hyenas to snarl, beasts to debase, hogs to wallow. There were equally as many who were forced to fight, who could not kill, whose gentleness augmented under the brutal orders of their officers. There were those who ran toward the front, heads up, singing at the top of their lungs. There were those who slunk back. Soldiers became cold, hard, materialistic, bitter, rancorous: and qualities antithetic to these developed in their comrades.

Lane exhausted his resources of memory and searched in his notes for a clipping he had torn from a magazine. He reread it, in the light of his crystallizing knowledge:

"Had I not been afraid of the scorn of my brother officers and the scoffs of my men, I would have fled to the rear," confesses a Wisconsin officer, writing of a battle.

"I see war as a horrible, grasping octopus with hundreds of poisonous, death-dealing tentacle that squeeze out the culture and refinement of a man," writes a veteran.

A regimental sergeant-major: "I considered myself hardboiled, and acted the part with everybody, including my wife. I scoffed at religion as unworthy of a real man and a mark of the sissy and weakling." Before going over the top for the first time he tried to pray, but had even forgotten the Lord's Prayer.

"If I get out of this, I will never be unhappy again," reflected one of the contestants under shell-fire in the Argonne Forest. To-day he is "not afraid of dead men any more and is not in the least afraid to die."

"I went into the army a conscientious objector, a radical, and a recluse.... I came out of it with the knowledge of men and the philosophy of beauty," says another.

"My moral fiber has been coarsened. The war has blunted my sensitiveness to human suffering. In 1914 I wept tears of distress over a rabbit which I had shot. I could go out now at the command of my government in cold-blooded fashion and commit all the barbarisms of twentieth-century legalized murder," writes a Chicago man.

A Denver man entered the war, lost himself and God, and found manhood. "I played poker in the box-car which carried me to the front and read the Testament in the hospital train which took me to the rear," he tells us.

"To disclose it all would take the genius and the understanding of a god. I learned to talk from the side of my mouth and drink and curse with the rest of our 'noble crusaders.' Authority infuriated me and the first suspicion of an order made me sullen and dangerous.... Each man in his crudeness and lewdness nauseated me," writes a service man.

"When our boy came back," complains a mother, "we could hardly recognize for our strong, impulsive, loving son whom we had loaned to Uncle Sam this irritable, restless, nervous man with defective hearing from shells exploding all about him, and limbs aching and twitching from strain and exposure, and with that inevitable companion of all returned oversea boys, the coffin-nail, between his teeth."

"In the army I found that hard drinkers and fast livers and profane-tongued men often proved to be the kindest-hearted, squarest friends one could ever have," one mother reports.

So then the war brought to the souls of soldiers an extremity of debasement and uplift, a transformation incomprehensible to the mind of man.

Upon men outside the service the war pressed its materialism. The spiritual progress of a thousand years seemed in a day to have been destroyed. Self-preservation was the first law of nature. And all the standards of life were abased. Following the terrible fever of patriotism and sacrifice and fear came the inevitable selfishness and greed and frenzy. The primitive in man stalked forth. The world became a place of strife.

What then, reflected Lane, could have been the effect of war upon women? The mothers of the race, of men! The creatures whom emotions governed! The beings who had the sex of tigresses! "The female of the species!" What had the war done to the generation of its period—to Helen, to Mel Iden, to Lorna, to Bessy Bell? Had it made them what men wanted?

At eight o'clock that night Lane kept his tryst with Bessy. The serene, mellow light of the moon shone down upon the garden. The shade appeared spotted with patches of moonlight; the summer breeze rustled the leaves; the insects murmured their night song. Romance and beauty still lived. No war could kill them. Bessy came gliding under the trees, white and graceful like a nymph, fearless, full of her dream, ripe to be made what a man would make of her.

Lane talked to Bessy of the war. Words came like magic to his lips. He told her of the thunder and fire and blood and heroism, of fight and agony and death. He told her of himself—of his service in the hours that tried his soul. Bessy passed from fascinated intensity to rapture and terror. She clung to Lane. She kissed him. She wept.

He told her how his ideal had been to fight for Helen, for Lorna, for her, and all American girls. And then he talked about what he had come home to—of the shock—the realization—the disappointment and grief. He spoke of his sister Lorna—how he had tried so hard to make her see, and had failed. He importuned Bessy to help him as only a girl could. And lastly, he brought the conversation back to her and told her bluntly what he thought of the vile verses, how she dragged her girlhood pride in the filth and made of herself a byword for vicious boys. He told her the truth of what real men thought and felt of women. Every man had a mother. No war, no unrest, no style, no fad, no let-down of morals could change the truth. From the dark ages women had climbed on the slow realization of freedom, honor, chastity. As the future of nations depended upon women, so did their salvation. Women could never again be barbarians. All this modern license was a parody of love. It must inevitably end in the degradation and unhappiness of those of the generation who persisted on that downward path. Hard indeed it would be to encounter the ridicule of girls and the indifference of boys. But only through the intelligence and courage of one could there ever be any hope for the many.

Lane sat there under the moonlit maples and talked until he was hoarse. He could not rouse a sense of shame in Bessy, because that had been atrophied, but as he closely watched her, he realized that his victory would come through the emotion he was able to arouse in her, and the ultimate appeal to the clear logic of her mind.

When the time came for him to go she stood before him in the clear moonlight.

"I've never been so excited, so scared and sick, so miserable and thoughtful in all my life before," she said. "Daren, I know now what a soldier is. What you've seen—what you've done. Oh! it was grand! ... And you're going to be my—my friend.... Daren, I thought it was great to be bad. I thought men liked a girl to be bad. The girls nicknamed me Angel Bell, but not because I was an angel, I'll tell the world.... Now I'm going to try to be the girl you want me to be."

CHAPTER XIV

The time came when Daren had to make a painful choice. His sister Lorna grew weary of his importunities and distrustful of his espionage. One night she became violent and flatly told him she would not stay in the house another day with him in it. Then she ran out, slamming the door behind her. Lane remained awake all night, in the hope that she would return. But she did not. And then he knew he must make a choice.

He made it. Lorna must not be driven from her home. Lane divided his money with his mother and packed his few effects. Mrs. Lane was distracted over the situation. She tried to convince Lane there was some kind of a law to keep a young girl home. She pleaded and begged him to remain. She dwelt on his ill health. But Lane was obdurate; and not the least of his hurts was the last one—a divination that in spite of his mother's distress there was a feeling of relief of which she was unconscious. He assured her that he would come to see her often during the afternoons and would care as best he could for his health. Then he left, saying he would send an expressman for the things he had packed.

Broodingly Lane plodded down the street. He had feared that sooner or later he would be forced to leave home, and he had shrunk from the ordeal. But now, that it was over, he felt a kind of relief, and told himself that it was of no consequence what happened to him. All that mattered was for him to achieve the few tasks he had set himself.

Then he thought of Mel Iden. She had been driven from home and would know what it meant to him. The longing to see her increased. Every disappointment left him more in need of sympathy. And now, it seemed, he would be ashamed to go to Mel Iden or Blair Maynard. Such news could not long be kept from them. Middleville was a beehive of gossips. Lane had a moment of blank despair, a feeling of utter, sick, dazed wonder at life and human nature. Then he lifted his head and went on.

Lane's first impulse was to ask Colonel Pepper if he could share his lodgings, but upon reflection he decided otherwise. He engaged a small room in a boarding house; his meals, which did not seem of much importance, he could get anywhere.

This change of residence brought Lane downtown, and naturally increased his activities. He did not husband his strength as before, nor have the leisure for bad spells. Home had been a place of rest. He could not rest in a drab little bare room he now occupied.

He became a watcher, except during the stolen hours with Bessy Bell. Then he tried to be a teacher. But he learned more than he thought. He no longer concentrated his vigilance on his sister. Having failed to force that issue, he bided his time, sensing with melancholy portent the certainty that he would soon be confronted with the stark and hateful actuality. Thus he wore somewhat away from his grim resolve to kill Swann. That adventure on the country road, when he had discovered Swann with Helen instead of Lorna, had somehow been a boon. Nevertheless he spied upon Lorna in the summer evenings when it was possible to follow her, and he dogged Swann's winding and devious path as far as possible. Apparently Swann had checked his irregularities as far as Lorna was concerned. Still Lane trusted nothing. He became an almost impassive destiny with the iron consequences in his hands.

Days passed. Every other afternoon and night he spent hours with Bessy Bell, and found a mounting happiness in the change in her, a deep and ever deeper insight into the causes that had developed her. The balance of his waking hours, which were many, he passed on the streets, in the ice cream parlors and confectionery dens, at the motion-picture theatres. He went many and odd times to Colonel Pepper's apartment, and took a peep into the club-rooms. Some of these visits were fruitful, but he did not see whom he expected to see there. At night he haunted the parks, watching and listening. Often he hired a cheap car and drove it down the river highway, where he would note the cars he passed or met. Sometimes he would stop to get out and make one of his scouting detours, or he would follow a car to some distant roadhouse, or go to the outlying summer pavilions where popular dances were given. More than once, late at night, he was an unseen and unbidden guest at one of the gay bathing parties. Strange and startling incidents seemed to gravitate toward Lane. He might have been predestined for this accumulation of facts. How vain it seethed for wild young men and women to think they hid their tracks! Some trails could not be hidden.

Toward the end of that protracted period of surveillance, Lane knew that he had become infamous in the eyes of most of that younger set. He had been seen too often, alone, watching, with no apparent excuse for his presence. And from here and there, through Bessy and Colonel Pepper, and Blair, who faithfully hunted him up, Lane learned of the unfavorable light in which he was held. Society, in the persons of the younger matrons, took exception to Lane's queer conduct and hinted of mental unbalance. The young rakes and libertines avoided him, and there was not a slacker among them who could meet his eye across cafe or billiard room.

Yet despite the peculiar species of ignominy and disgrace that Middleville gossips heaped upon Lane's head and the slow, steady decline of his speaking acquaintance with the elite, there were some who always greeted him and spoke if he gave them a chance. Helen Wrapp never failed of a green flashing glance of mockery and enticement. She smiled, she beckoned, she once called him to her car and asked him to ride with her, to come to see her. Margaret Maynard rose above dread of her mother and greeted Lane graciously when occasion offered. Dorothy Dalrymple and Elinor always evinced such unhesitating intention of friendship that Lane grew to avoid meeting them. And twice, when he had come face to face with Mel Iden, her look, her smile had been such that he had plunged away somewhere, throbbing and thrilling, to grow blind and sick and numb. It was the failure of his hopes, and the suffering he endured, and the vain longings she inspired that heightened his love. She wrote him after the last time they had passed on the street—a note that stormed Lane's heart. He did not answer. He divined that his increasing loneliness, and the sure slow decline of his health, and the heartless intolerance of the same class that had ostracized her were added burdens to Mel Iden's faithful heart. He had seen it in her face, read it in her note. And the time would come, sooner or later, when he could go to her and make her marry him.

CHAPTER XV

To be a mystery is overpoweringly sweet to any girl and Bessy Bell was being that. Her sudden desire for solitude had worried her mother, and her distant superiority had incited the vexation of her friends. When they exerted themselves to win Bessy back to her old self she looked dreamily beyond them and became more aloof. Doctor Bronson, in reply to Mrs. Bell's appeal to him, looked the young woman over, asked her a few questions, marveled at the imperious artifice with which she evaded him, and throwing up his hands said Bessy was beyond him. The dark fever, rising from the school yards and the playgrounds and the streets, subtly poisoning the blood of Bessy Bell, slowly lost its heat and power for the time being. Bessy lived in the full secret expression of her girlish adoration. She was worshipping a hero; she was glorifying in her sacrifice; she was faithful to a man; she was being a woman. At first she grew pale, tense, quiet, and seemed to be going into a decline. Then that stage passed; and the roseleaf flush returned to her cheeks, the purple fire deepened in her eyes, the quivering life in all her supple young body. Night after night loneliness had no fears for her. If she heard a whistle on the avenue, the honk of a car—the familiar old signals of the boys and girls, she smiled her disdain, and curling comfortably in her great chair, bent her lovely head over her books.

In the beginning her dreams were all of Daren Lane, of the strangeness and glory of this soldier who spent so many secret hours with her. And when the time came that she did not see him so often her dreams were just as full. But gradually, as the days went by, other figures than Lane's were limned upon her fancy—vague figures of heroes, knights, soldiers. He still dominated her romances, though less personally. She built around him. Every day brought her new strange desires.

One evening in August when Bessy sat alone the telephone bell rang sharply. She ran to take down the receiver.

"Hello, hello, that you, Bessy?" came the hurried call in a girl's voice.

"Rose! Oh, how are you?"

"Fine. But say, Angel, I can't take time to talk. Something doing. Are you alone?"

"Yes, all alone, old girl."

"Listen, then, and get this.... I'm here, you know, telephone girl at the Exchange. Just heard your father on the wire. Some one has betrayed the secret of the club. There's a warrant out for the arrest of the boys. For gambling. You know there's a political vice drive on. Some time to-night they'll be raided.... But early. Bess, are you getting this?"

"Sure. Hurry—hurry," replied Bessy, in excitement.

"I tried to get Dick on the wire, but couldn't. Same with two more of the boys. But I did get wise to this. Gail and Lorna have a date at the club to-night.... Never mind how I found out. Dick has thrown me down for Gail. I'm sore as a pup. But I don't want your father to pinch those girls.... Now, Bess, I'm tied here. But you get a move on. Don't waste time. You can save them. You must. Do something. If you can't find somebody, go straight to the club. You know where the key for the outside entrance is kept. Hurry and it'll be safe. Good-bye."

Bessy stood statue-like for a moment, her big eyes glowing, changing, darkening with rapid thought, then she flew upstairs to her room, snatched a veil and a soft hat, and putting these on as she went, she flew out of the house without putting out the lights or locking the door.

It was a dark windy night, slightly cool for August, and a fine misty rain was blowing. Bessy's footsteps pattered softly as she ran block after block, and she did not slacken her pace till she reached the house where Daren Lane had his room. In answer to her ring a woman appeared, who told her Mr. Lane was out.

This was a severe disappointment to Bessy, and left her an alternative that required more than courage, but she did not vacillate. She sped swiftly on in the dark, for the electric lights were few and far between, until the black of the gloomy building, where the boys had their club, loomed up. On the corner Bessy saw a man standing with his back to a telegraph pole. This occasioned her much concern; perhaps he might be watching the building. But he had not seen her, of that she was certain. The possibility that he might be a spy made her task all the harder.

Bessy returned the way she come, crossed at the next corner, hurried round the block and up to the outside stairway that was her objective point.

By feeling along the brick wall she brought up, with a sudden bump, at the back of the stairway. Then she deliberated. If she went around to the front so as to get access to the steps, she might pass in range of the loiterer whom she mistrusted. That risk she would not incur. Examining the wall that enclosed the box-like stairway as best she could in the dark, she found it rickety, full of holes and cracks, and she decided she would climb it. A sheer perpendicular board wall, some twelve or fifteen feet high, shrouded in pitchy darkness and apparently within earshot of a police spy, did not daunt Bessy Bell. Slipping her strong fingers in crevices and her slim toes in cracks, she climbed up and up, till she got hold of the railing post on the first platform. Here she had great difficulty to keep from falling, but lifting and squirming her supple body, by a desperate effort she got her knees on the platform, and then pulled herself to safety. Once on the stairs she ran up the remaining few steps to the landing, where she rested panting and triumphant.

As she was about to go on she heard footsteps, which froze her. A man was crossing the street. He came from the direction of the corner where she had seen the supposed spy. Presently she saw him stop under one of the trees to scratch a match, and in the round glow of light she saw him puff at a cigar. Then he passed on with uncertain steps, as of one slightly under the influence of drink.

Bessy's heart warmed to life and began to beat again. Then she sought for the key. She had been told where it was, but did not remember. Slipping her hand under the railing, close to the wall, she felt a string, and, pulling at it suddenly, found the key in her hand. She glided into the dim hall, feeling along the wall for a door, until she found it. With trembling fingers she inserted the key in the lock, and the door swung inward silently. Bessy went in, leaving the key on the outside.

Dark as it had been without, it was light compared to the ebon blackness within. Bessy felt ice form in the marrow of her bones. The darkness was tangible; it seemed to envelop her in heavy folds. The sudden natural impulse to fly out of the thick creeping gloom, down the stairway to the light, strung her muscles for instant action, but checked by the swiftly following thought of her purpose, they relaxed, and she took not a backward step.

"Rose did her part and I'll do mine," she cogitated. "I've got to save them. But what to do—I may have to wait. I know—in the big room—the closet behind the curtain! I can find that even in this dark, and once in there I won't be afraid."

Bessy, fired by this inspiration, groped along the wall through the room to the large chamber, stumbled over chairs and a couch and at last got her hands on the drapery. She readily found the knob, turned it, opened the door and stepped in.

"I hope they won't be long," she thought. "I hope the girls come first. I don't want to burst into a room full of boys. Won't Daren be surprised when I tell him—maybe angry! But it's bound to come out all right, and father will never know."

CHAPTER XVI

Early one August evening Lane went out to find a cool misty rain blowing down from the hills. At the inn he encountered Colonel Pepper, who wore a most woebegone and ludicrous expression. He pounced at once upon Lane.

"Daren, what do you think?" he wailed, miserably.

"I don't think. I know. You've gone and done it—pulled that stunt of yours again," returned Lane.

"Yes—but oh, so much worse this time."

"Worse! How could it be worse, unless you mean some one punched your head."

"No. That would have been nothing.... Daren, this—this time I—it was a lady!" gasped Pepper.

"Oh, say now, Pepper—not really?" queried Lane, incredulously.

"It was. And a lady I—I admire very much."

"Who?"

"Miss Amanda Hill."

"The schoolteacher? Nice little woman like that! Pepper, why couldn't you pick on one of these Middleville gossips or society dames?"

"Lord—I didn't know who she was—until after—and I couldn't have helped it anyway," he replied, mopping his red face. "When—I saw her—and she recognized me—I nearly died.... It was at White's Confectionery Den. And I'm afraid some people saw me."

"Well. You old duffer! And you say you admire this lady very much?"

"Indeed I do. I call on her."

"Colonel, your name is Dennis," replied Lane, with merciless humor. "It serves you right."

The little man evidently found relief in his confession and in Lane's censure.

"I'm cured forever," he declared vehemently. "And say, Lane, I've been looking for you. Have you been at my rooms lately—you know—to take a peep?"

"I have not," replied Lane, turning sharply. A slight chill went over him. "I thought that club stuff was off."

"Off—nothing," whispered Colonel Pepper, drawing Lane aside. "Swann and his strong-arm gang just got foxy. They quit for a while. Now they're rushing the girls in there—say from four to five—and in the evenings a little while, not too late. Oh, they're the slick bunch, picking out the ice cream soda hour when everybody's downtown.... You run up to my rooms right now. And I'll gamble——"

"I'll go," interrupted Lane, grimly.

Not fifteen minutes before he had seen his sister Lorna and a chum, Gail Williams, go into White's place. Lane's pulse quickened. As he started to go he ran into Blair Maynard who grasped at him: "What's hurry, old scout?"

"Blair, I'm never in a hurry if you want me. But the fact is I've got rather urgent business. How about to-morrow?"

"Sure. Meet you here. I just wanted to unload on you, Dare. Looks as if my mother has hatched it up between Margie and our esteemed countryman, Richard Swann."

It was not often that Lane cursed, but he did so now.

"But Blair, didn't you *tell* your mother what this fellow is?" remonstrated Lane.

"Well, I'll say I did," replied Blair, sardonically. "Cut no ice whatever. She didn't believe. She didn't care for any proofs. All rich young men had their irregularities!... Good God! Doesn't it make you sick?"

"But how about Holt Dalrymple?"

"Holt's turned over a new leaf. He's working hard, and I think he has taken a tumble to himself. Listen to this. He met Margie with Dick Swann out at one of the lake dances—Watkins' Lake. And he cut her dead. I'm sorry for Margie. She sure is rank poison these days.... Well, speak of the devil!"

Holt Dalrymple collided with them at the entrance of the inn. The haggard, sullen, heated look that had characterized him was gone. He was sunburned, and his dark eyes were bright. He greeted his friends warmly. They chatted for a moment. Then Lane grew thoughtful, all the while gazing at Holt.

"What's the idea?" queried that worthy, presently. "Anything wrong with me?"

"Boy, you're just great. Seeing you has done me good.... You ask what's the idea. Holt, would you do me a favor?"

"Would I? Listen to the guy," returned young Dalrymple. "Daren, I'd do any old thing for you."

"Do you happen to know Bessy Bell?" went on Lane.

Dalrymple quickened with surprise. "Yes, I know her. Some little peach!... I almost ran into her down on West Street a few minutes ago. She wore a white veil. She didn't see me, or recognize me. But I sure knew her. She was almost running. I bet a million to myself she had a date at the club."

"You lose, Holt," replied Lane, shortly. "Bessy Bell is one Middleville kid who has come clean through this mess."

"Say Dare, I like to hear you talk," responded Blair, half in jest and half in earnest. "But aren't you getting a trifle unbalanced? That's how my mother apologizes for me."

"Cut the joshing, boys. Listen," returned Lane. "And don't ever tell this to a soul. I interested myself in Bessy Bell. I've met her more times than I can count. I wanted to see if it was possible to turn one of these girls around. I failed on my sister Lorna. But Bessy Bell is true blue. She had all this modern tommyrot. She had everything else too. Brains, sweetness, common sense, romance. All I tried to do was to make her forget the tommyrot. And I think I did."

"Well, I'll be darned!" ejaculated Blair. "Dare, that was ripping fine of you.... What'll you do next, I wonder."

"Come on with your favor," added Holt, with a keen bright smile.

"Would you be willing to see Bessy occasionally—and sort of be nice to her—you know?" asked Lane, earnestly. "I can't keep up my attention to her much longer. She might miss me. Take it from me, Holt, back of all this modern stuff—deep in Bessy, and in every girl who has not been debased—is the simple and good desire to be liked."

"Daren, I'll do that little thing, believe me," returned Holt, warmly.

Shaking hands with his friends, Lane left them, and went on his way. White's place was full as a beehive. As he passed, Lane found himself looking for Bessy Bell's golden head, though he knew he would not see it. He wondered if Holt had really met her, veiled and in a hurry. That had a strange look. But no shadow of distrust of Bessy came to Lane. In a few moments he reached the dark stairway leading to Colonel Pepper's apartment. Lane forgot he was weak. But at the top, with his breast laboring, he remembered well enough. He went into the Colonel's rooms and through them without making a light. And when he reached the place where he had spied upon the club he was wet with sweat and shaking with excitement. Carefully, so as not to make noise, he stole to the peep-hole and applied his eye.

He saw a gleam of light on shiny waxed floor, and then, moving to get the limit of his narrow vision, he descried Swann, evidently just arrived. With him was Gail Williams, a slip of a child not over fifteen—looking up at him as if excited and pleased. Next Lane espied his sister Lorna with a tall, well-built man. Although his back was toward Lane, he could not mistake the soldierly bearing of Captain Vane Thesel! Lorna looked perturbed and sulky, and once, turning her face toward Swann, she seemed resentful. Captain Thesel had his hand at her elbow and appeared to be talking earnestly.

Lane left his post, taking care to make no noise. But once back in the Colonel's rooms, he hurried. Feeling in the dark corner where he had kept the axe ready for just such an emergency as this, he grasped it and rushed out. Tiptoeing down the hall, he found the narrow door, stole down the black stairway and entered the main hall. Here he paused, suddenly checked in his hurry.

"This won't do," he thought, and shook his head. "Much as I'd like to kill those two dogs I can't—I can't.... I'll smash their faces, though—and if I ever catch...."

Breaking the thought off abruptly, he passed down the dim hallway to the door of the club-rooms. He raised the axe and was about to smash the lock when he espied a key in the keyhole. The door was not locked. Lane set down the axe and noiselessly turned the knob and peeped in. The first room was dark, but the door on the opposite side was ajar, and through it Lane saw the larger lighted room and the shiny floor. Moving figures crossed the space. Removing the key, Lane slipped inside the room and locked the door. Then he tip-toed to the opposite door.

Thesel and Lorna were now so close that Lane could hear them.

"But I thought I had a date with Dick," protested Lorna. Her face was red and she stamped her foot.

"See here, kiddo. If you're as thick as that I'll have to put you wise," answered Thesel, good-humoredly, as he tilted back his cigarette to blow smoke at the ceiling. "Dick is through with you."

"Oh, *is* he?" choked Lorna.

"Say, Cap, I heard a noise," suddenly called out Swann, rather nervously.

There was a moment's silence. Lane, too, had heard a noise, but could not be sure whether it was inside the building or not.

Swann hurried over to join Thesel. They looked blankly at each other. The air might have been charged. Both girls showed alarm.

Then Lane, with his hand on the gun in his pocket, strode out to confront them.

"Oh—h!" gasped Lorna, as if appalled at sight of her brother's face.

"Fellows, I'll have to break up your little party," said Lane, coolly.

Thesel turned ghastly white, while Swann grew livid with rage. He seemed to expand. His hand went back to his right hip.

When Lane got within six feet of them, Swann drew a small automatic pistol. But before he could raise it, Lane had leaped into startling activity. With terrific swing he brought his gun down on Swann's face. Then as swiftly he turned on Thesel. Swann had hardly hit the floor, a sodden heap, when Thesel, with bloody visage, reeled and fell like a log. Lane bent over them, ready to beat either back. But both were unconscious.

"Daren—for God's sake—don't murder them!" whispered Lorna, hoarsely.

Lane's humanity was in abeyance then, but his self-control did not desert him.

"You girls must hurry out of here," he ordered.

"Oh, Gail is fainting," cried Lorna.

The little Williams girl was indeed swaying and sinking down. Lane grasped her and shook her. "Brace up. If you keel over now, you'll be found out sure.... It's all right. You'll not be hurt. There——"

A heavy thumping on the door by which Lane had entered and a loud authoritative voice from the hall silenced him.

"Open up here! You're pinched!"

That voice Lane recognized as belonging to Chief of Police Bell. For a moment, fraught with suspense, Lane was at a loss to know what to do.

"Open up! We've got the place surrounded.... Open up, or we'll smash the door in!"

Lane whispered to the girls: "Is there a place to hide you?"

The Williams girl was beyond answering, but Lorna, despite her terror, had not lost her wits.

"Yes—there's a closet—hid by a curtain—here," she whispered, pointing.

Lane half carried Gail. Lorna brushed aside a heavy curtain and opened a door. Lane pushed both girls into the black void and closed the door after them.

"Once more—open up!" bellowed the officer in the hall, accompanying his demand with a thump on the door. Lane made sure some one had found his axe. He did not care how much smashing the policemen did. All that concerned Lane then was how to avert discovery from the girls. It looked hopeless. Then, as there came sudden splintering blows on the door, Lane espied Swann's cigarettes and matches on the music box. Lane seldom smoked. But while the officers were breaking in the door, Lane leisurely lighted a cigarette; and when two of them came in he faced them coolly.

The first was Chief Bell, a large handsome man, in blue uniform. The second one was a patrolman. Neither carried a weapon in sight. Bell swept the big room in one flashing blue glance—took in Lane and the prone figures on the floor.

"Well, I'll be damned," he ejaculated. "What am I up against?"

"Hello, Chief," replied Lane, coolly. "Don't get fussed up now. This is no murder case."

"Lane, what's this mean?" burst out Bell.

Lane was rather well acquainted with Chief Bell, and in a way there was friendship between them. Bell, for one, had always been sturdily loyal to the soldiers.

"Well, Chief, I was having a little friendly game with Mr. Swann and Captain Thesel," drawled Lane. "We got into an argument. And as both were such ferocious fighters I grew afraid they'd hurt me bad—so I had to soak them."

"Don't kid me," spoke up Bell, derisively. "Little game—hell! Where's the cards, chips, table?"

"Chief, I didn't say we played the game to-night."

"Lane, you're a liar," replied Bell, thoughtfully. "I'm sure of that. But you've got me buffaloed." He knelt on the floor beside the fallen men and examined each. Swann's shirt as well as face was bloody. "For a crippled soldier you've got some punch left. What'd you hit them with?"

"I'll tell you Chief. I fetched an axe with me to do the dirty job, but I decided I should use a dangerous weapon only on men. So I soaked them with a lollypop."

"Lane, are you really nutty?" demanded Bell, curiously.

"No more than you. I hit them with something hard, so it would leave a mark."

"You left one, I'll say. Thesel will lose that eye—it's gone now—and Swann is also disfigured for life. What a damned shame!"

"Chief, are you sure it's any kind of a shame?"

Lane's query appeared to provoke thought. Bell replaced the little automatic pistol he had picked up beside Swann, and rising he looked at Lane.

"Swann was a slacker. Thesel was your Captain in the war. Have these facts anything to do with your motive?"

"No, Chief," replied Lane, in sarcasm. "But when I got into action I think the facts you mentioned sort of rejuvenated a disabled soldier."

"Lane, you beat me," declared Bell, shaking his head. "Why, I had you figured as a pretty good chap.... But you've done some queer things in Middleville."

"Chief, if you're an honest officer you'll admit Middleville needs some queer things done."

Bell gazed doubtfully at Lane.

"Smith, search the rooms," he ordered, addressing his patrolman.

"We were alone here," spoke up Lane. "And I advise you to hurry those wounded veterans to a hospital in the rear."

Swann showed signs of recovering consciousness. Bell bent over him a moment. Lane had only one hope—that the patrolman would miss the door. But he brushed aside the curtain. Then he grunted.

"See here, Chief—a door—and somebody's holding it from the inside," he declared.

"Wait, Smith," ordered Bell, striding forward. But before he got half-way across the room the door opened. A girl stepped out and shut it back of her. Lane sustained a singular shock. That girl was Bessy Bell.

"Hello, Dad—it's Bessy," she said, clearly. She was pale, but did not seem frightened.

Chief Bell halted in the middle of a stride and staggered a little as his foot came down. A low curse of utter amaze escaped his lips. Suddenly he became tensely animated.

"How'd you come here?" he demanded, towering over her.

"I walked."

"What'd you come for?"

"To warn Daren Lane that you were going to raid these club-rooms to-night."

"Who told you?"

"I won't tell. I got it over the 'phone." I ran over here. I knew where the key was. I've been here before—afternoons—dancing.... I let myself in.... But when they—they came I got frightened and hid in the closet."

Chief Bell seemed about to give way to passion, but he controlled it. After that moment he changed subtly.

"Is Daren Lane your friend?" he demanded.

"Yes. The best and truest any girl ever had.... Dad, you know mother told you I had changed lately. I have. And it's through Daren."

"Where'd you see him?"

"He has been coming out to the house in the afternoons."

"Well, I'm damned," muttered the Chief, and wheeled away. Sight of his gaping patrolman seemed to galvanize him into further realization of the situation. "Smith, beat it out and draw the other men round in front. Give me time enough to get Bessy out. Send hurry call for ambulance.... And Smith, keep your mouth shut. I'll make it all right. If Mrs. Bell hears of this my life will be a hell on earth."

"Mum's the word, Chief. I'm a married man myself," he replied, and hurried out.

Lane was watching Bessy. What a wonderful girl! Modern tendencies might have corrupted the girls of the day, but for sheer nerve, wit and courage they were immeasurably superior to those of former generations. Bessy faced her father calmly, lied magnificently, gazed down at the ghastly, bloody faces with scarcely a shudder, and gave Lane a smile from her purple eyes, as if to cheer him, to assure him she could save the situation. It struck Lane that Chief Bell looked as if he might be following a similar line of thought.

"Bessy, put on your hat," ordered Bell. "And here ... tuck that veil around. There, now you beat it for home. Lane, go with her to the stairs. Take a good look in the street. Bessy, go home the back way. And Lane, you hurry back."

Lane followed Bessy out and caught up with her in the hall. She clasped his arm.

"Some adventure, I'll say!" she burst out, in breathless whisper. "It was great until I recognized your voice. Then all inside me went flooey."

"Bessy, you're the finest little girl in the world," returned Lane, stirred to emotion.

"Here, Daren, cut that. You didn't raise me on soft soap and mush. If you get to praising me I'll fall so far I'll never light.... Now, Dare, go back and fool Dad. You must save the girls. It doesn't matter about me. He's my Dad."

"I'll do my best," replied Lane.

They reached the landing of the outside stairway. Peering down, Lane did not see any one.

"I guess the coast is clear. Now, beat it, Bessy."

She lifted the white veil and raised her face. In the dim gray light Lane saw it as never before.

"Kiss me, Daren," she whispered.

Lane had never kissed her. For an instant he was confused.

"Why—little girl!" he exclaimed.

"Hurry!" she whispered, imperiously.

Some instinct beyond Lane's ken prompted him to do what she asked.

"Good-bye, my little Princess," he whispered. "Don't ever forget me."

"Never, Daren. Good-bye." She slipped down the stairway and in a moment more vanished in the gray gloom of the misty night.

Only then did Lane understand what she, with her woman's intuition, had divined—that they would never be together again. The realization gave him a pang. Bessy was his only victory.

Slowly Lane made his way back to the club-rooms. He had begun to weaken under the strain and felt the approach of something akin to collapse. When he reached the large room he found Swann half conscious and Thesel showing signs of coming to.

"Lane, come here," said the Chief, drawing Lane away from the writhing forms on the floor. "You're under arrest."

"Yes, sir. What's the charge?"

"Let's see. That's the puzzler," replied the Chief, scratching his head. "Suppose we say gambling and fighting."

"Fine!" granted Lane, with a smile.

"When the ambulance comes you get out of sight until we pack these fellows out. I'll leave the door open—so if there's any reason you want to come back—why—"

Chief Bell half averted his face, seemingly not embarrassed, but rather pondering in thought. "Thanks, Chief. You understand me perfectly," responded Lane. "I'll appear at police headquarters in half an hour."

The officer laughed, and returning to the injured men he knelt beside them. Swann sat up moaning. Blood had blinded his sight. He did not see Lane pass. Sounds of an ambulance bell had caught Lane's quick ear. Finding the washroom, he went in and, locking the door, leaned there to wait. In a very few moments the injured Swann and Thesel had been carried out. Lane waited five minutes after the sound of wheels had died away. Then he hurried out and opened the door of the closet.

Lorna almost fell over him in her eagerness. If she had been frightened, she had recovered. Gail staggered out, pale and sick looking.

"Oh, Daren, can you get us out?" whispered Lorna, breathlessly.

"Hurry, and don't talk," replied Lane.

He led them out into the hall and down to the stairway where he had taken Bessy. As before, all appeared quiet below.

"I guess it's safe.... Girls, let this be a lesson to you."

"Never any more for mine," whimpered Gail.

But Lorna was of more tempered metal.

"Believe me, Daren, I'm glad you knocked the lamps out of those swell boobs," she whispered, passionately. "Dick Swann used me like dirt. The next guy like him who tries to get gay with me will have some fall, I'll tell the world.... Me for Harry! There's nothing in this q-t stuff.... And say, what do you know about Bessy Bell? She came here to save us.... Hot dog, but she's a peach!"

Lane admonished the girls to hurry and watched them until they reached the street and turned the corner out of sight.

CHAPTER XVII

The reaction from that night landed Lane in the hospital, where, during long weeks when he did have a lucid interval, he saw that his life was despaired of and felt that he was glad of it.

But he did not die. As before, the weak places in his lungs healed over and he began to mend, and gradually his periods of rationality increased until he wholly gained his mental poise. It was, however, a long time before he was strong enough to leave the hospital.

During the worst of his illness his mother came often to see him; after he grew better she came but seldom. Blair and Colonel Pepper were the only others who visited Lane. And as soon as his memory returned and interest revived he learned much peculiarly significant to him.

The secret of the club-rooms, so far as girls were concerned, never became fully known to Middleville gossips. Strange and contrary rumors were rife for a long time, but the real truth never leaked out. There was never any warrant sworn for Lane's arrest. What the general public had heard and believed was the story concocted by Thesel and Swann, who claimed that Lane, over a gambling table, had been seized by one of the frenzied fits common to deranged soldiers, and had attacked them. Thesel lost his left eye and Swann carried a hideous red scar from brow to cheek. Neither the club-room scandal nor his disfigurement for life in any wise prevented Mrs. Maynard from announcing the engagement of her daughter Margaret to Richard Swann. The most amazing news was to hear that Helen Wrapp had married a rich young politician named Hartley, who was running for the office of magistrate. According to Blair, Daren Lane had divided Middleville into two dissenting factions, a large one who banned him in disgrace, and a small one who lifted their voices in his behalf. Of all the endless bits of news, little and big, the one that broke happily on Lane's ears was the word of a nurse, who told him that during his severe illness a girl had called on the telephone every day to inquire for him. She never gave her name. But Lane knew it was Mel and the mere thought of her made him quiver.

By the time Lane was strong enough to leave the hospital an early winter had set in. The hospital expenses had reduced his finances so materially that he could not afford the lodgings he had occupied before his illness. He realized fully that he should leave Middleville for a dry warm climate, if he wanted to live a while longer. But he was not greatly concerned about this. There would be time enough to consider the future after he had fulfilled the one hope and ambition he had left.

Rooms were at a premium. Lane was forced to apply in the sordid quarter of Middleville, and the place he eventually found was a small, bare hall bedroom, in a large, ramshackle old house, of questionable repute. But beggars could not be choosers. There was no heat in this room, and Lane decided that what time he spent in it must be in bed. He would not give any one his address.

Once installed here, Lane waited only a few days to assure himself that he was strong enough to carry out the plan upon which he had set his heart.

Late that afternoon he went to the town hall and had a marriage license made out for himself and Mel Iden. Upon returning, he found that snow had begun to fall heavily. Already the streets were white. Suddenly the thought of the nearness of Christmas shocked him. How time sped by!

That night he dressed himself carefully, wearing the service uniform he had so well preserved, and sallied forth to the most fashionable restaurant in Middleville, where in the glare and gayety he had his dinner. Lane recognized many of the dining, dancing throng, but showed no sign of it. He became aware that his presence had excited comment. How remote he seemed to feel himself from that eating, drinking, dancing crowd! So far removed that even the jazz music no longer affronted him. Rather surprised he was to find he really enjoyed his dinner. From the restaurant he engaged a taxi.

The bright lights, the falling snow, the mantle of white on everything, with their promise of the holiday season, pleased Lane with the memory of what great fun he used to have at Christmas-time.

When he arrived at Mel's home the snow was falling thickly in heavy flakes. Through the pall he caught a faint light, which grew brighter as he plodded toward the cottage. He stamped on the porch and flapped his arms to remove the generous covering of snow that had adhered to him. And as he was about to knock, the door opened, and Mel stood in the sudden brightness.

"Hello, Mel, how are you?—some snow, eh?" was his cheery greeting, and he went in and shut the door behind him.

"Why, Daren—you—you—"

"I—what! Aren't you glad to see me?"

Lane had not prepared himself for anything. He knew he could win now, and all he had allowed himself was gladness. But being face to face with Mel made it different. It had been long since he last saw her. That interval had been generous. To look at her now no one could have guessed her story. Warmth and richness of color had come back to her; and vividly they expressed her joy at sight of him.

"Glad?—I've been living—on my hopes—that you—"

Her faltering speech trailed off here, as Lane took one long stride toward her.

Lane put a firm hand to each of her cheeks, and tilting a suddenly rosy face, he kissed her full on the lips. Then he turned away without looking at her and stepped to the little open grate, where a small red fire glowed. Mel gasped there behind him and then became perfectly still.

"Nice fire, Mel," he spoke out, naturally, as if nothing unusual had happened. But the thin hands he extended to the warmth of the coals trembled like aspen leaves in the wind. How silent she was! It thrilled him. What strange sweet revel in the moment.

When he turned it seemed he saw her eyes, her lips, her whole face luminous. The next instant she came out of her spell; and Lane divined if he let her wholly recover, he would have a woman to deal with.

"Daren, what's wrong with you?" she inquired.

"Why, Mel!" he ejaculated, in feigned reproach.

"You don't look irrational, but you act so," she said, studying him more closely. The hand that had been pressed to her breast dropped down.

"Had my last crazy spell two weeks ago," he replied.

"Until to-night."

"You mean my kissing you? Well, I refuse to apologize. You see I was not prepared to find you so improved. Why, Mel, you're changed. You're just—just lovely."

Again the rich color stained her cheeks.

"Thank you, Daren," she said. "I have changed. *You* did it.... I've gotten well, and—almost happy.... But let's not talk of myself. You—there's so much—"

"Mel, I don't want to talk about myself, either," he declared. "When a man's got only a day or so longer—"

"Hush!—Or—Or—," she threatened, with a slight distension of nostrils and a paling of cheek.

"Or what?" demanded Lane.

"Or I'll do to you what you did to me."

"Oh, you'd kiss me to shut my lips?"

"Yes, I would."

"Fine, Mel. Come on. But you'd have to keep steadily busy all evening. For I've come to talk." Mel came closer to him, with a catch in her breathing, a loving radiance in her eyes. "Daren, you're strange—not like your old self. You're too gay—too happy. Oh, I'd be glad if you were sincere. But you have something on your mind."

Lane knew when to unmask a battery.

"No, it's in my pocket," he flashed, and with a quick motion he tore out the marriage license and thrust it upon her. As her dark eyes took in the meaning of the paper, and her expression changed, Lane gazed down upon her with a commingling of emotions.

"Oh, Daren—No—No!" she cried, in a wildness of amaze and pain.

Then Lane clasped her close, with a force too sudden to be gentle, and with his free hand he lifted her face.

"Look here. Look at me," he said sternly. "Every time you say no or shake your head—I'll do this."

And he kissed her twice, as he had upon his entrance.

Mel raised her head and gazed up at him, wide-eyed, open-mouthed, as if both appalled and enthralled.

"Daren. I—I don't understand you," she said, unsteadily. "You frighten me. Let me go—please, Daren. This is—so—so unlike you. You insult me."

"Mel, I can't see it that way," he replied. "I'm only asking you to come out and marry me to-night."

That galvanized her, and she tried to slip from his embrace.

"I told you no—no—no," she cried desperately.

"That's three," said Lane, and he took them mercilessly. "You will marry me," he said sternly.

"Oh, Daren, I can't—I dare not.... Ah!—"

"You will go right now—marry me to-night."

"Please be kind, Daren.... I don't know how you—"

"Mel, where're your coat, and hat, and overshoes?" he questioned, urgently.

"I told you—no!" she flashed, passionately.

Lane made good his threat, and this last onslaught left her spent and white.

"You must like my kisses, Mel Iden," he said.

"I implore you—Daren"

"I implore you to marry me."

"Dear friend, listen to reason," she begged. "You don't love me. You've just a chivalrous notion you can help me—and my boy—by giving us your name. It's noble, Daren, thank you. But—"

"Take care," warned Lane, bending low over her. "I can make good my word all night."

"Boy, you've gone crazy," she whispered, sadly.

"Well, now you may be talking sense," he laughed. "But that's neither here nor there.... Mel, I may die any day now!"

"Oh, my God!—don't say that," she cried, as if pierced by a blade.

"Yes. Mel, make me happy just for that little while."

"Happy?" she whispered.

"Yes. I've failed here in every way. I've lost all. And this thing would make the bitterness endurable."

"I'd die for you," she returned. "But marry you!—Daren—dearest—it will make you the laughing-stock of Middleville."

"Whatever it makes me, I shall be proud."

"Oh, I cannot, I dare not," she burst out.

"You seem to forget the penalty for these unflattering negatives of yours," he returned, coolly, bending to her lips.

This time she did not writhe or quiver or breathe. Lane felt surrender in her, and when he lifted his face from hers he was sure. Despite the fact that he had inflexibly clamped his will to one purpose, holding his emotion in abeyance, that brief instant seemed to be the fullest of his life.

"Mel, put your arm round my neck," he commanded.

Mel obeyed.

"Now the other."

Again she complied.

"Lift your face—look at me."

She essayed to do this also, but failed. Her head sank on his breast. He had won. Lane held her a moment closely. And then a great and overwhelming pity and tenderness, his first emotions, flooded his soul. He closed his eyes. Dimly, vaguely, they seemed to create vision of long future time; and he divined that good and happiness would come to Mel Iden some day through the pain he had given her.

"Where did you say your things are?" he asked. "It's a bad night."

"They're in—the hall," came in muffled tones from his shoulder. "I'll get them."

But she made no effort to remove her arms from round his neck or to lift her head from his breast. Lane had lost now that singular exaltation of will, and power to hold down his emotions. Her nearness stormed his heart. His test came then, when he denied utterance to the love that answered hers.

"No—Mel—you stay here," he said, freeing himself. "I'll get them."

Opening the hall door he saw the hat-rack where as a boy he had hung his cap. It now held garments over which Lane fumbled. Mel came into the hall.

"Daren, you'll not know which are mine," she said.

Lane watched her. How the shapely hands trembled. Her face shone white against her dark furs. Lane helped her put on the overshoes.

"Now—just a word to mother," she said.

Lane caught her hand and held it, following her to the end of the hall, where she opened a door and peeped into the sitting-room.

"Mother, is dad home?" she asked.

"No—he's out, and such a bad night! Who's with you, Mel?"

"Daren Lane."

"Oh, is he up again? I'm glad. Bring him in.... Why, Mel, you've your hat and coat on!"

"Yes, mother dear. We're going out for a while."

"On such a night! What for?"

"Daren and I are going to—to be married.... Good-bye. No more till we come back."

As one in a dream, Lane led Mel out in the whirling white pall of snow. It seemed to envelop them. It was mysterious and friendly, and silent.

They crossed the bridge, and Lane again listened for the river voices that always haunted here. Were they only murmurings of swift waters? Beyond the bridge lay the railroad station. A few dim lights shone through the white gloom. Lane found a taxi.

They were silent during the ride through the lonely streets. When the taxi stopped at the address given the driver, Lane whispered a word to Mel, jumped out and ran up the steps of a house and rang the bell.

"Is Doctor McCullen at home?" he inquired of the maid who answered the ring. He was informed the minister had just gone to his room.

"Will you ask him to come down upon a matter of importance?"

The maid invited him inside. In a few moments a tall, severe-looking man wearing a long dressing-coat entered the parlor.

"Doctor McCullen, I regret disturbing you, but my business is urgent. I want to be married at once. The lady is outside in a car. May I bring her in?"

"Ah! I seem to remember you. Isn't your name Lane?"

"Yes."

"Who is the woman you want to marry?"

"Miss Iden."

"Miss Iden! You mean Joshua Iden's daughter?"

"I do."

The minister showed a grave surprise. "Aren't you rather late in making amends? No, I will not marry you until I investigate the matter," he replied, coldly.

"You need not trouble yourself," replied Lane curtly, and went out.

The instant opposition stimulated Lane, and he asked the driver, "John, do you know where we can find a preacher?" "Yis, sor. Mr. Peters of the Methodist Church lives round the corner," answered the man.

"Drive on, then."

Lane got inside the taxi and slammed the door. "Mel, he refused to marry us."

Mel was silent, but the pressure of her hand answered him.

"Daren, the car has stopped," said Mel, presently.

Lane got out, walked up the steps, and pulled the bell. He was admitted. He had no better luck here. Lane felt that his lips shut tight, and his face set. Mel said nothing and sat by him, very quiet. The taxi rolled on and stopped again, and Lane had audience with another minister. He was repulsed here also.

"We're trying a magistrate," said Lane, when the car stopped again.

"But, Daren. This is where Gerald Hartley lives. Not him, Daren. Surely you wouldn't go to him?"

"Why not?" inquired Lane.

"It hasn't been two months since he married Helen Wrapp. Hadn't you heard?"

"I'd forgotten," said Lane.

"Besides, Daren, he—he once asked me to marry him—before the war."

Lane hesitated. Yes, he now remembered that in the days before the war the young lawyer had been Mel's persistent admirer. But a reckless mood had begun to manifest itself in Lane during the last hour, and it must have communicated its spirit to Mel, for she made no further protest. The world was against them. They were driving to the home of the man she had refused to marry, who had eventually married a girl who had jilted Lane. In an ordinary moment they would never have attempted such a thing. The mansion before which the car stopped was well lighted; music and laughter came faintly through the bright windows.

A maid opened the door to Lane and showed him into a drawing-room. In a library beyond he saw women and men playing cards, laughing and talking. Several old ladies were sitting close together, whispering and nodding their heads. A young fair-haired girl was playing the piano. Lane saw the maid advance and speak to a sharp-featured man whom he recognized as Hartley. Lane wanted to run out of the house. But he clenched his teeth and swore he would go through with it.

"Mr. Hartley," began Lane, as the magistrate came through the curtained doorway, "I hope you'll pardon my intrusion. My errand is important. I've come to ask you to marry me to a lady who is waiting outside."

When Hartley recognized his visitor he started back in astonishment. Then he laughed and looked more closely at Lane. It was a look that made Lane wince, for he understood it to relate to his mental condition.

"Lane! Well, by Jove!" he exclaimed. "Going to get married! You honor me. The regular fee, which in my official capacity I must charge, is one dollar. If you can pay that I will marry you."

"I can pay," replied Lane, quietly, and his level steady gaze disconcerted Hartley.

"Where's the woman?"

"She's outside in a taxi."

"Is she over eighteen?"

"Yes."

Lane expected the question as to who the woman was. It was singular that the magistrate neglected to ask this, the first query offered by every minister Lane has visited.

"Fetch her in," he said.

Lane went outside and hesitated at the car door, for he had an intuitive flash which made him doubtful. But what if Hartley did make a show of this marriage? The marriage itself was the vital thing. Lane helped Mel out of the car and led her up the icy steps. The maid again opened the door.

"Mr. Lane, walk right in," said Hartley. "Of course, it's natural for the lady to be a little shy, but then if she wants to be married at this hour she must not mind my family and guests. They can be witnesses."

He spoke in a voice in which Lane's ears detected insincerity. "Be seated, and wait until I get my book," he continued, and left the room.

Hartley had hardly glanced at Mel, and her veil had hidden her features. He had gone toward his study rubbing his hands in a peculiar manner which Lane remembered and which recalled the man as he had looked many a time in the Bradford billiard room when a good joke was going the rounds. Lane saw him hurry from his study with pleasant words of invitation to his guests, a mysterious air about him, a light upon his face. The ladies and gentlemen rose from their tables and advanced from the library to the door of the drawing-room. A girl of striking figure seized Hartley's arm and gesticulated almost wildly. It was Helen Wrapp. Her husband laughed at her and waved a hand toward the drawing-room and his guests. Turning swiftly with tigerish grace, she bent upon Lane great green eyes whose strange expression he could not fathom. What passionately curious eyes did she now fasten on his prospective bride!

Lane gripped Mel's hand. He felt the horror of what might be coming. What a blunder he had made!

"Will the lady kindly remove her veil?" Hartley's voice sounded queer. His smile had vanished.

As Mel untied and thrust back the veil her fingers trembled. The action disclosed a lovely face as white as snow.

"*Mel Iden!*" burst from the magistrate. For a moment there was an intense silence. Then, "I'll not marry you," cried Hartley vindictively.

"Why not? You said you would," demanded Lane.

"Not to save your worthless lives," Hartley returned, facing them with a dark meaning in his eyes.

Lane turned to Mel and led her from the house and down to the curb without speaking once.

Once more they went out into the blinding snow-storm. Lane threw back his head and breathed the cold air. What a relief to get out of that stifling room!

"Mel, I'm afraid it's no use," he said, finally.

"We are finding what the world thinks of us," replied Mel. "Tell the man to drive to 204 Locust Street."

Once more the driver headed his humming car into the white storm.

Once more Lane sat silent, with his heart raging. Once more Mel peered out into the white turmoil of gloom.

"Daren, we're going to Dr. Wallace, my old minister. He'll marry us," she said, presently.

"Why didn't I think of him?"

"I did," answered Mel, in a low voice. "I know he would marry us. He baptized me; he has known and loved me all my life. I used to sing in his choir and taught his Sunday School for years."

"Yet you let me go to those others. Why?"

"Because I shrank from going to him."

Once more the car lurched into the gutter, and this time they both got out and mounted the high steps. Lane knocked. They waited what appeared a long time before they heard some one fumbling with the lock. Just then the bell in the church tower nearby began chiming the midnight hour. The door opened, and Doctor Wallace himself admitted them.

"Well! Who's this?... Why, if it's not Mel Iden! What a night to be out in!" he exclaimed. He led them into a room, evidently his study, where a cheerful wood fire blazed. There he took both her hands and looked from her to Lane. "You look so white and distressed. This late hour—this young man whom I know. What has happened? Why do you come to me—the first time in so many months?"

"To ask you to marry us," answered Mel.

"To *marry* you?... Is this the soldier who wronged you?"

"No. This is Daren Lane.... He wants to marry me to give my boy a name.... Somehow he finally made me consent."

"Well, well, here is a story. Come, take off this snowy cloak and get nearer the fire. Your hands are like ice." His voice was very calm and kind. It soothed Lane's strained nerves. With what eagerness did he scrutinize the old minister's face. He knew the penetrating eye, the lofty brow and white hair, the serious lined face, sad in a noble austerity. But the lips were kind with that softness and sweetness which comes from gentle words and frequent smiles. Lane's aroused antagonism vanished in the old man's presence.

"Doctor Wallace," went on Mel. "We have been to several ministers, and to Mr. Hartley, the magistrate. All refused to marry us. So I came to my old friend. You've known me all my life. Daren has at last convinced me—broke down my resistance. So—I ask—will you marry us?"

Doctor Wallace was silent for many moments while he gazed into the fire and stroked her hand. Suddenly a smile broke over his fine face.

"You say you asked Hartley to marry you?"

"Yes, we went to him. It was a reckless thing to do. I'm sorry."

"To say the least, it was original." The old minister seemed to have difficulty in restraining a laugh. Then for a moment he pondered.

"My friends, I am very old," he said at length, "but you have taught me something. I will marry you."

It was a strange marriage. Behind Mel and Daren stood the red-faced, grinning driver, his coarse long coat covered with snow, and the simpering housemaid, respectful, yet glorifying in her share in this midnight romance. The old minister with his striking face and white hair, gravely turned the leaves of his book. No bridegroom ever wore such a stern, haggard countenance. The bride's face might have been a happier one, but it could not have been more beautiful.

Doctor Wallace's voice was low and grave; it quavered here and there in passages. Lane's was hardly audible. Mel's rang deep and full.

The witnesses signed their names; husband and wife wrote theirs; the minister filled out the license, and the ceremony was over.

Then Doctor Wallace took a hand of each.

"Mel and Daren," he said. "No human can read the secret ways of God. But it seems there is divinity in you both. You have been sacrificed to the war. You are builders, not destroyers. You are Christians, not pagans. You have a vision limned against the mystery of the future. Mammon seems now to rule. Civilization rocks on its foundations. But the world will go on growing better. Peace on earth, good will to men! That is the ultimate. It was Christ's teaching.... You two give me greater faith.... Go now and face the world with heads erect—whatever you do, Mel— and however long you live, Daren. Who can tell what will happen? But time proves all things, and the blindness of people does not last forever.... You both belong to the Kingdom of God."

But few words were spoken by Lane or Mel on the ride home. Mel seemed lost in a trance. She had one hand slipped under Lane's arm, the other clasped over it. As for Lane, he had overestimated his strength. A deadly numbness attacked his nerves, and he had almost lost the sense of touch. When they arrived at Mel's home the snow-storm had abated somewhat, and the lighted windows of the cottage shone brightly.

Lane helped Mel wade through the deep snow, or he pretended to help her, for in reality he needed her support more than she needed his. They entered the warm little parlor. Some one had replenished the fire. The clock pointed to the hour of one. Lane laid the marriage certificate on the open book Mel had been reading. Mel threw off hat, coat, overshoes and gloves. Her hair was wet with melted snow.

"Now, Daren Lane," she said softly. "Now that you have made me your wife—!"

Up until then Lane had been master of the situation. He had thought no farther than this moment. And now he weakened. Was this beautiful woman, with head uplifted and eyes full of fire, the Mel Iden of his school days? Now that he had made her his wife—.

"Mel, there's no *now* for me," he replied, with a sad finality. "From this moment, I'll live in the past. I have no future.... Thank God, you let me do what I could. I'll try to come again soon. But I must go now. I'm afraid—I overtaxed my strength."

"Oh, you look so—so," she faltered. "Stay, Daren—and let me nurse you.... We have a little spare room, warm, cozy. I'll wait on you, Daren. Oh, it would mean so much to me—now I am your wife."

The look of her, the tones of her voice, made him weak. Then he thought of his cold, sordid lodgings, and he realized that one more moment here alone with Mel Iden would make him a coward in his own eyes. He thanked her, and told her how impossible it was for him to stay, and bidding her good night he reeled out into the white gloom. At the gate he was already tired; at the bridge he needed rest. Once more, then, he heard the imagined voices of the waters calling to him.

CHAPTER XVIII

Seldom did Blair Maynard ever trust himself any more in the presence of his mother's guests. Since Mrs. Maynard had announced the engagement of his sister Margaret to Richard Swann, she had changed remarkably. Blair did not love her any the better for the change. All his life, as long as he could remember, he and Margaret had hated pretension, and the littleness of living beyond their means. But now, with this one *coup d'etat,* his mother had regained her position as the leader of Middleville society. Haughty, proud, forever absorbed in the material side of everything, she moved in a self-created atmosphere Blair could not abide. He went hungry many a time rather than sit at table with guests such as Mrs. Maynard delighted to honor.

Blair and Margaret had become estranged, and Blair spent most of his time alone, reading or dreaming, but mostly sleeping. He knew he grew weaker every day and his weakness appeared to induce slumber.

On New Year's day, after dinner, he fell asleep in a big chair, across the hall from the drawing-room. And when he awoke the drawing-room was full of people making New Year's calls. If there was anything Blair hated it was to thump on his crutch past curious, cold-eyed persons. So he remained where he was, hoping not to be seen. But unfortunately for him, he had exceedingly keen ears and exceedingly sensitive feelings.

Some of the guests he knew very well without having to see them. The Swanns, and Fanchon Smith, with her brother and mother, Gerald Hartley and his bride, Helen Wrapp, and a number of others prominent as Middleville's elect were recognizable by their voices. While he was sitting there, trying not to hear what he could not help hearing, a number more arrived.

They talked. It gradually dawned on Blair that some gossip was rife anent a midnight marriage between his friend Daren Lane and Mel Iden. Blair was deeply shocked. Then his emotions, never calm, grew poignant. He listened. What he heard spoken of Daren and Mel made his blood boil. Sweet voices, low-pitched, well-modulated, with the intonation of culture, made witty and scarcely veiled remarks of a suggestiveness that gave rise to laughter. Voices of men, bland, blase, deriding Daren Lane! Blair listened, and slowly his passion mounted to a white heat. And then it seemed, fate fully, in a lull of the conversation, some one remarked graciously to Mrs. Maynard that it was a pity that Blair had lost a leg in the war.

Blair thumped up on his crutch, and thumped across the hall to confront this assembly.

"Ladies and gentlemen, pray pardon me," he said, in his high-pitched tenor, cold now, and under perfect control. "I could not help hearing your conversation. And I cannot help illuminating your minds. It seems exceedingly strange to me that people of intelligence should make the blunders they do. So strange that in the future I intend to take such as you have made as nothing but the plain cold fact of perversion of human nature! Daren Lane is so far above your comprehension that it seems useless to defend him. I have never done it before. He would not thank me. But this once I will speak.... In our group of service men—so few of whom came home—he was a hero. We all loved him. And for soldiers at war that tribute is the greatest. If there was a dirty job to be done, Daren Lane volunteered for it. If there was a comrade to be helped, Daren Lane was the first to see it. He never thought of himself. The dregs of war did not engulf him as they did so many of us. He was true to his ideal. He would have been advanced for honors many a time but for the enmity of our captain. He won the *Croix de Guerre* by as splendid a feat as I saw during the war.... Thank God, we had some officers who treated us like men—who were men themselves. But for the majority we common soldiers were merely beasts of burden, dogs to drive. This captain of whom I speak was a padded shape—shirker from the front line—a parader of his uniform before women. And he is that to-day—a chaser of women—girls—*girls* of fifteen.... Yet he has the adulation of Middleville while Daren Lane is an outcast.... My God, is there no justice? At home here Daren Lane has not done one thing that was not right. Some of the gossip about him is as false as hell. He has tried to do noble things. If he married Mel Iden, as you say, it was in some exalted mood to help her, or to give his name to her poor little nameless boy."

Blair paused a moment in a deliberate speech that toward the end had grown breathless. The faces before him seemed swaying in a mist.

"As for myself," he continued in passionate hurry, "I did not *lose* my leg!... I *sacrificed* it. I *gave* my career, my youth, my health, my body—and I will soon have given my life—for my country and my people. I was proud to do it. Never for a moment have I regretted it.... What I lost—Ah! what I *lost* was respect for"—Blair choked—"for the institution that had deluded me. What I *lost* was not my leg but my faith in God, in my country, in the gratitude of men left at home, in the honor of women."

Friday, the tenth of January, dawned cold, dark, dreary, and all day a dull clouded sky promised rain or snow. From a bride's point of view it was not a propitious day for a wedding. A half hour before five o'clock a stream of carriages began to flow toward St. Marks and promptly at five the door of the church shut upon a large and fashionable assembly.

The swelling music of the wedding march pealed out. The bridal party filed into the church. The organ peals hushed. The resonant voice of a minister, with sing-song solemnity, began the marriage service.

Margaret Maynard knew she stood there in the flesh, yet the shimmering white satin, the flowing veil, covered some one who was a stranger to her.

And this other, this strange being who dominated her movements, stood passively and willingly by, while her despairing and truer self saw the shame and truth. She was a lie. The guests, friends, attendants, bridesmaids, the minister, the father, mother, groom—all were lies. They expressed nothing of their true feelings.

The unwelcomed curious, who had crowded into the back of the church, were the sincerest, for in their eyes, covetousness was openly unveiled. The guests and friends wore the conventional shallow smiles of guests and friends. They whispered to one another—a beautiful wedding—a gorgeous gown—a perfect bride—a handsome groom; and exclaimed in their hearts: How sad the father! How lofty, proud, exultant the mother! How like her to move heaven and earth to make this marriage! The attendants posed awkwardly, a personification of the uselessness of their situation, and they pitied the bride while they envied him for whose friendship they stood. The bridesmaids graced their position and gloried in it, and serenely smiled, and thought that to be launched in life in such dazzling manner might be compensation for the loss of much. He of the flowing robe, of the saintly expression, of the trained earnestness, the minister who had power to unite these lives, saw nothing behind that white veil, saw only his fashionable audience, while his resonant voice rolled down the aisles of the church: "Who gives this woman to be wedded to this man?" The father answered and straightway the years rolled back to his youth, to hope, to himself as he stood at the altar with love and trust, and then again to the present, to the failure of health and love and life, to the unalterable destiny accorded him, to the one shame of an honest if unsuccessful life—the countenancing of this marriage. The worldly mother had, for once, a full and swelling heart. For her this was the crowning moment. In one sense this fashionable crowd had been pitted against her and she had won. What to her had been the pleading of a daughter, the importunity of a father, the reasoning of a few old-fashioned friends? The groom, who represented so much and so little in this ceremony, had entered the church with head held high, had faced his bride with gratified smile and the altar with serene unconsciousness.

Margaret Maynard saw all this; saw even the bride, with her splendidly regular loveliness; and then, out of heaven, it seemed there thundered an awful command, rolling the dream away, striking terror to her heart.

"If any man can show just cause why they may not lawfully be joined together, let him now speak, or else hereafter for ever hold his peace!"

One long, silent, terrible moment! Would not an angel appear, with flaming sword, to smite her dead? But the sing-song voice went on, like flowing silk.

The last guest at Mrs. Maynard's reception had gone, reluctantly, out into the snow, and the hostess sat in her drawing-room, amid the ruins of flowers and palms. She was alone with her triumph. Mr. Maynard and Mr. Swann were smoking in the library. Owing to the storm and delicate health of the bride the wedding journey had been postponed.

Margaret was left alone, at length, in the little blue-and-white room which had known her as a child and maiden, where she now sat as wife. For weeks past she had been emotionless. To-night, with that trenchant command, unanswered except in her heart, a spasm of pain had broken the serenity of her calm, and had left her quivering.

"It is done," she whispered.

The endless stream of congratulations, meaningless and abhorrent to her, the elaborate refreshments, the warm embraces of old friends had greatly fatigued her. But she could not rest. She paced the little room; she passed the beautiful white bridal finery, so neatly folded by the bridesmaids, and she averted her eyes. She seemed not to hate her mother, nor love her father; she had no interest in her husband. She was slipping back again into that creature apart from her real self.

The house became very quiet; the snow brushed softly against the windows.

A step in the hall made Margaret pause like a listening deer; a tap sounded lightly on her door; a voice awoke her at last to life and to torture.

"Margaret, may I come in?"

It was Swann's voice, a little softer than usual, with a subtle eagerness.

"No" answered Margaret, involuntarily.

"I beg your pardon. I'll wait." Swann's footsteps died away in the direction of the library.

The spring of a panther was in Margaret's action as she began to repace the room. All her blood quickened to the thought suggested by her husband's soft voice. In the mirror she saw a crimsoned face and shamed eyes from which she turned away.

All the pain and repression, the fight and bitter resignation and trained indifference of the past months were as if they had never been. This was her hour of real agony; now was the time to pay the price. Pride, honor, love never smothered, reserve rooted in the very core of a sensitive woman's heart, availed nothing. Once again catching sight of her reflection in the mirror she stopped before it, and crossing her hands on her heaving breast, she regarded herself with scorn. She was false to her love, she was false to herself, false to the man to whom she had sold herself. "Oh! Why did I yield!" she cried. She was a coward; she belonged to the luxurious class that would suffer anything rather than lose position. Fallen had she as low as any of them; gold had been the price of her soul. To keep her position she must marry one man when she loved another. She cried out in her wretchedness; she felt in her whole being a bitter humiliation; she felt stir in her a terrible tumult.

Margaret wondered how many thousands of girls had been similarly placed, and pitied them. She thought of the atmosphere in which she lived, where it seemed to her every mother was possessed singularly and entirely of one aim, to marry her daughter as soon as possible to a man as rich as possible. Marrying well simply meant marrying money. Only a few days before her mother had come to her and said: "Mrs. Fisher called and she was telling me about her daughter Alice. It seems Alice is growing very pretty and very popular. She said she was afraid Alice had taken, a liking to that Brandeth fellow, who's only a clerk. So Mrs. Fisher intends taking Alice to the seashore this summer, to an exclusive resort, of course, but one where there will be excitement and plenty of young gentlemen."

At the remembrance Margaret gave a little contemptuous laugh. A year ago she would not have divined the real purport of her mother's words. How easy that was now! Mrs. Fisher had decided that as Alice was eighteen it was time a suitable husband was found for her. Poor Alice! Balls, parties, receptions there would be, and trips to the seashore and all the other society manoeuvers, made ostensibly to introduce Alice to the world; but if the truth were told in cold blood all this was simply a parading of the girl before a number of rich and marriageable men. Poor Harry Brandeth!

She recalled many marriages of friends and acquaintances. With strange intensity of purpose she brought each one to mind, and thought separately and earnestly over her. What melancholy facts this exercise revealed! She could not recall one girl who was happy, perfectly happy, unless it was Jane Silvey who ran off with and married a telegraph operator. Jane was still bright-eyed and fresh, happy no doubt in her little house with her work and her baby, even though her people passed her by as if she were a stranger. Then Margaret remembered with a little shock there was another friend, a bride who had been found on her wedding night wandering in the fields. There had been some talk, quickly hushed, of a drunken husband, but it had never definitely transpired what had made her run out into the dark night. Margaret recollected the time she had seen this girl's husband, when he was drunk, beat his dog brutally. Then Margaret reflected on the gossip she never wanted to hear, yet could not avoid hearing, over her mother's tea-table; on the intimations and implications. Many things she would not otherwise have thought of again, but they now recurred and added their significance to her awakening mind. She was not keen nor analytical; she possessed only an ordinary intelligence; she could not trace her way through a labyrinth of perplexing problems; still, suffering had opened her eyes and she saw something terribly wrong in her mother's world.

Once more she stopped pacing her room, for a step in the hall arrested her, and made her stand quivering, as if under the lash.

"I won't!" she breathed intensely. Swiftly and lightly she sped across her room, opened a door leading to the balcony and went out, closing the door behind her softly.

Mr. Maynard sat before the library fire with a neglected cigar between his fingers. The events of the day had stirred him deeply. The cold shock he had felt when he touched his daughter's cheek in the accustomed good-night kiss remained with him, still chilled his lips. For an hour he sat there motionless, with his eyes fixed on the dying fire, and in his mind hope, doubt and remorse strangely mingled. Hope persuaded him that Margaret was only a girl, still sentimental and unpoised. Unquestionably she had made a good marriage. Her girlish notions about romance and love must give way to sane acceptance of real human life. After all money meant a great deal. She would come around to a sensible view, and get that strange look out of her eyes, that strained blighted look which hurt him. Then he writhed in his self-contempt; doubt routed all his hope, and remorse made him miserable.

A hurried step on the stairs aroused Mr. Maynard. Swann came running into the library. He was white; his sharp featured face wore a combination of expressions; alarm, incredulity, wonder were all visible there, but the most striking was mortification.

"Mr. Maynard, Margaret has left her room. I can't find her anywhere."

The father stared blankly at his son-in-law.

Swann repeated his statement.

"What!" All at once Mr. Maynard sank helplessly into his chair. In that moment certainty made him an old broken man.

"She's gone!" said Swann, in a shaken voice. "She has run off from me. I knew she would; I knew she'd do something. I've never been able to kiss her—only last night we quarreled about it. I tell you it's—"

"Pray do not get excited," interrupted Mr. Maynard, bracing up. "I'm sure you exaggerate. Tell me what you know."

"I went to her room an hour, two hours ago, and knocked. She was there but refused me admittance. She spoke sharply—as if—as if she was afraid. I went and knocked again long after. She didn't answer. I knocked again and again. Then I tried her door. It was not locked. I opened it. She was not in the room. I waited, but she didn't come. I—I am afraid something is—wrong."

"She might be with her mother," faltered Mr. Maynard.

"No, I'm sure not," asserted Swann. "Not to-night of all nights. Margaret has grown—somewhat cold toward her mother. Besides Mrs. Maynard retired hours ago."

The father and the husband stole noiselessly up the stairs and entered Margaret's room. The light was turned on full. The room was somewhat disordered; bridal finery lay littered about; a rug was crumpled; a wicker basket overturned. The father's instinct was true. His first move was to open the door leading out upon the balcony. In the thin snow drifted upon this porch were the imprints of little feet.

Something gleamed pale blue in the light of the open door. Mr. Maynard picked it up, and with a sigh that was a groan held it out to Swann. It was a blue satin slipper.

"Heavens!" exclaimed Swann. "She's run out in the snow—she might as well be barefooted."

"S-sh-h!" warned Mr. Maynard. Unhappy and excited as he was he did not forget Mrs. Maynard. "Let us not alarm any one."

"There! See, her footsteps down the stairs," whispered Swann. "I can see them clear to the ground."

"You stay here, Swann, so in case Mrs. Maynard or the servants awake you can prevent alarm. We must think of that. I'll bring her back."

Mr. Maynard descended the narrow stairway to the lower porch and went out into the yard. The storm had ceased. A few inches of snow had fallen and in places was deeper in drifts. The moon was out and shone down on a white world. It was cold and quiet. When Mr. Maynard had trailed the footsteps across his wide lawn and saw them lead out into the street toward the park, he fell against a tree, unable, for a moment, to command himself. Hope he had none left, nor a doubt. On the other side of the park, hardly a quarter of a mile away, was the river. Margaret had gone straight toward it.

Outside in the middle of the street he found her other slipper. She had not even stockings on now; he could tell by the impressions of her feet in the snow. He remembered quite mournfully how small Margaret's feet were, how perfectly shaped. He hurried into the park, but was careful to obliterate every vestige of her trail by walking in the soft snow directly over her footprints. A hope that she might have fainted before she could carry out her determination arose in him and gave him strength. He kept on. Her trail led straight across the park, in the short cut she had learned and run over hundreds of times when a little girl. It was hastening her now to her death.

At first her footsteps were clear-cut, distinct and wide apart. Soon they began to show evidences of weariness; the stride shortened; the imprints dragged. Here a great crushing in a snow drift showed where she had fallen.

Mr. Maynard's hope revived; he redoubled his efforts. She could not be far. How she dragged along! Then with a leap of his heart, and a sob of thankfulness he found her, with disheveled hair, and face white as the snow where it rested, sad and still in the moonlight.

CHAPTER XIX

Middleville was noted for its severe winters, but this year the zero weather held off until late in January. Lane was peculiarly susceptible to the cold and he found himself facing a discomfort he knew he could not long endure. Every day he felt more and more that he should go to a warm and dry climate; and yet he could not determine to leave Middleville. Something held him.

The warmth of bright hotel lobbies and theatres and restaurants uptown was no longer available for Lane. His money had dwindled beyond the possibility of luxury, and besides he shrank now from meeting any one who knew him. His life was empty, dreary and comfortless.

One wintry afternoon Lane did not wander round as long as usual, for the reason that his endurance was lessening. He returned early to his new quarters, and in the dim hallway he passed a slight pale girl who looked at him. She seemed familiar, but Lane could not place her. Evidently she had a room in the building. Lane hated the big barn-like house, and especially the bare cold room where he had to seek rest. Of late he had not eaten any dinner. He usually remained in bed as long as he could, and made a midday meal answer all requirements. Appetite, like many other things, was failing him. This day he sat upon his bed, in the abstraction of the lonely and unhappy, until the cold forced him to get under the covers.

His weary eyelids had just closed when he was awakened. The confused sense of being torn from slumber gave way to a perception of a voice in the room next to his. It was a man's voice, rough with the huskiness Lane recognized as peculiar to drunkards. And the reply to it seemed to be a low-toned appeal from a woman.

"Playin' off sick, eh? You don't want to work. But you'll get me some money, girl, d'ye hear?"

A door slammed, rattling the thin partition between the two rooms, and heavy footsteps dragged in the hall and on the stairway.

Sleep refused to come back to Lane. As he lay there he was surprised at the many sounds he heard. The ramshackle old structure, which he had supposed almost vacant, was busy with life. Stealthy footfalls in the hallways passed and repassed; a piano drummed somewhere; a man's loud voice rang out, and a woman's laugh faint, hollow and far away, like the ghost of laughter, returned in echo. The musical clinking of glasses, the ring of a cash register, the rattling click of pool balls, came up from below.

Presently Lane remembered the nature of the place. It was a house of night. In daylight it was silent; its inmates were asleep. But as the darkness unfolded a cloak over it, all the hidden springs of its obscure humanity began to flow. Lying there with the woman's appeal haunting him and all those sounds in his ears he thought of their meaning. The drunkard with his lust for money; his moaning victim; the discordant piano; the man with the vacant laugh; the lost hope and youth in the woman's that echoed it; the stealing, slipping feet of those who must tread softly—all conveyed to Lane that he had awakened in another world, a world which shunned sunlight.

Toward morning he dozed off into a fitful sleep which lasted until ten o'clock when he arose and dressed. As he was about to go out a knock on the door of the room next to his recalled the incident of the night. He listened. Another knock followed, somewhat louder, but no response came from within.

"Say, you in there," cried a voice Lane recognized as the landlady's. She rattled the door-knob.

A girl's voice answered weakly: "Come in."

Lane heard the door open.

"I wants my room rent. I can't get a dollar out of your drunken father. Will you pay? It's four weeks overdue."

"I have no money."

"Then get out an' leave me the room." The landlady spoke angrily.

"I'm ill. I can't get up." The answer was faint.

Lane opened his door quickly, and confronted the broad person of the landlady.

"How much does the woman owe?" he asked, quietly.

"Ah-huh!" the exclamation was trenchant with meaning. "Twenty dollars, if it's anything to you."

"I'll pay it. I think I heard the woman say she was ill."

"She says she is."

"May I be of any assistance?"

"Ask her."

Lane glanced into the little room, a counterpart of his. But it was so dark he could see nothing distinctly.

"May I come in? Let me raise the blind. There, the sun is fine this morning. Now, may I not—"

He looked down at a curly head and a sweet pretty face that he knew.

"I know you," he said, groping among past associations.

"I am Rose Clymer," she whispered, and a momentary color came into her wan cheeks.

"Rose Clymer! Bessy Bell's friend!"

"Yes, Mr. Lane. I'm not so surprised as you. I recognized you last night."

"Then it was you who passed me in the hall?"

"Yes."

"Well! And you're ill? What is the matter? Ah! Last night—it was your—your father—I heard?"

"Yes," she answered. "I've not been well since—for a long time, and I gave out last night."

"Here I am talking when I might be of some use," said Lane, and he hurried out of the room. The landlady had discreetly retired to the other end of the hall. He thrust some money into her hands.

"She seems pretty sick. Do all you can for her, be kind to her. I'll pay. I'm going for a doctor."

He telephoned for Doctor Bronson.

An hour later Lane, coming upstairs from his meal, met the physician at Rose's door. He looked strangely at Lane and shook his head.

"Daren, how is it I find you here in this place?"

"Beggars can't be choosers," answered Lane, with his old frank smile.

"Humph!" exclaimed the doctor, gruffly.

"How about the girl?" asked Lane.

"She's in bad shape," replied Bronson.... "Lane, are you aware of her condition?"

"Why, she's ill—that's all I know," replied Lane, slowly. "Rose didn't tell me what ailed her. I just found out she was here."

Doctor Bronson looked at Lane. "Too bad you didn't find out sooner. I'll call again to-day and see her.... And say, Daren, you look all in yourself."

"Never mind me, Doctor. It's mighty good of you to look after Rose. I know you've more patients than you can take care of. Rose has nothing and her father's a poor devil. But I'll pay you."

"Never mind about money," rejoined Bronson, turning to go.

Lane could learn little from Rose. Questions seemed to make her shrink, so Lane refrained from them and tried to cheer her. The landlady had taken a sudden liking to Lane which evinced itself in her change of attitude toward Rose, and she was communicative. She informed Lane that the girl had been there about two months; that her father had made her work till she dropped. Old Clymer had often brought men to the hotel to drink and gamble, and to the girl's credit she had avoided them.

For several days Doctor Bronson came twice daily to see Rose. He made little comment upon her condition, except to state that she had developed peritonitis, and he was not hopeful. Soon Rose took a turn for the worse. The doctor came to Lane's room and told him the girl would not have the strength to go through with her ordeal. Lane was so shocked he could not speak. Dr. Bronson's shoulders sagged a little, an unusual thing for him. "I'm sorry, Daren," he said. "I know you wanted to help the poor girl out of this. But too late. I can ease her pain, and that's all."

Strangely shaken and frightened Lane lay down in the dark. The partition between his room and Rose's might as well have been paper for all the sound it deadened. He could have escaped that, but he wanted to be near her.... And he listened to Rose's moans in the darkness. Lane shuddered there, helpless, suffering, realizing. Then the foreboding silence became more dreadful than any sound.... It was terrible for Lane. That strange cold knot in his breast, that coil of panic, seemed to spring and tear, quivering through all his body. What had he known of torture, of sacrifice, of divine selflessness? He understood now how the loved and guarded woman went down into the Valley of the Shadow for the sake of a man. Likewise, he knew the infinite tragedy of a ruined girl who lay in agony, gripped by relentless nature.

Lane was called into the hall by Mrs. O'Brien. She was weeping. Bronson met him at the door.

"She's dying," he whispered. "You'd better come in. I've 'phoned to Doctor Wallace."

Lane went in, almost blinded. The light seemed dim. Yet he saw Rose with a luminous glow radiating from her white face.

"I feel—so light," she said, with a wan smile.

Lane sat by the bed, but he could not speak. The moments dragged. He had a feeling of their slow but remorseless certainty.

Then there were soft steps outside—Mrs. O'Brien opened the door—and Doctor Wallace entered the room.

"My child," he gravely began, bending over her.

Rose's big eyes with their strained questioning gaze sought his face and Doctor Bronson's and Lane's.

"Rose—are you—in pain?"

"The burning's gone," she said.

"My child," began Doctor Wallace, again. "Your pain is almost over. Will you not pray with me?"

"No. I never was two-faced," replied Rose, with a weary shake of the tangled curls. "I won't show yellow now."

Lane turned away blindly. It was terrible to think of her dying bitter, unrepentant.

"Oh! if I could hope!" murmured Rose. "To see my mother!"

Then there were shuffling steps outside and voices. The door was opened by Mrs. O'Brien. Old Clymer crossed the threshold. He was sober, haggard, grieved. He had been told. No one spoke as he approached Rose's bedside.

"Lass—lass—" he began, brokenly.

Then he sought from the men confirmation of a fear borne by a glance into Rose's white still face. And silence answered him.

"Lass, if you're goin'—tell me—who was to blame?"

"No one—but myself—father," she replied.

"Tell me, who was to blame?" demanded Clymer, harshly.

Her pale lips curled a little bitterly, and suddenly, as a change seemed to come over her, they set that way. She looked up at Lane with a different light in her eyes. Then she turned her face to the wall.

Lane left the room, to pace up and down the hall outside. His thoughts seemed deadlocked. By and bye, Doctor Bronson came out with Doctor Wallace, who was evidently leaving.

"She is unconscious and dying," said Doctor Bronson to Lane, and then bade the minister good-bye and returned to the room.

"How strangely bitter she was!" exclaimed Doctor Wallace to Lane. "Yet she seemed such a frank honest girl. Her attitude was an acknowledgment of sin. But she did not believe it herself. She seemed to have a terrible resentment. Not against one man, or many persons, but perhaps life itself! She was beyond me. A modern girl—a pagan! But such a brave, loyal, generous little soul. What a pity! I find my religion at fault because it can accomplish nothing these days."

CHAPTER XX

Lane took Rose's death to heart as if she had been his sister or sweetheart. The exhaustion and exposure he was subjected to during these days dragged him farther down.

One bitter February day he took refuge in the railroad station. The old negro porter who had known Lane since he was a boy evidently read the truth of Lane's condition, for he contrived to lead him back into a corner of the irregular room. It was an obscure corner, rather hidden by a supporting pillar and the projecting end of a news counter. This seat was directly over the furnace in the cellar. Several pipes, too hot to touch, came up through the floor. It was the warmest place Lane had found, and he sat there for hours. He could see the people passing to and fro through the station, arriving and leaving on trains, without himself being seen. That afternoon was good for him, and he went back next day.

But before he could get to the coveted seat he was accosted by Blair Maynard. Lane winced under Blair's piercing gaze; and the haggard face of his friend renewed Lane's deadened pangs. Lane led Blair to the warm corner, and they sat down. It had been many weeks since they had seen each other. Blair talked in one uninterrupted flow for an hour, and so the life of the people Lane had given up was once again open to him. It was like the scoring of an old wound. Then Lane told what little there was to tell about himself. And the things he omitted Blair divined. After that they sat silent for a while.

"Of course you knew Mel's boy died," said Blair, presently.

"Oh—No!" exclaimed Lane.

"Hadn't you heard? I thought—of course you—.... Yes, he died some time ago. Croup or flu, I forget."

"Dead!" whispered Lane, and he leaned forward to cover his face with his hands. He had seemed so numb to feeling. But now a storm shook him.

"Dare, it's better for him—and Mel too," said Blair, with a hand going to his friend's shoulder. "That idea never occurred to me until day before yesterday when I ran into Mel. She looked— Oh, I can't tell you how. But I got that strange impression."

"Did—did she ask about me?" queried Lane, hoarsely, as he uncovered his face, and sat back.

"She certainly did," replied Blair, warmly. "And I lied like a trooper. I didn't know where you were or how you were, but I pretended you were O.K."

"And then—" asked Lane, breathlessly.

"She said, 'Tell Daren I must see him.' I promised and set out to find you. I was pretty lucky to run into you.... And now, old sport, let me get personal, will you?"

"Go as far as you like," replied Lane, in muffled voice.

"Well, I think Mel loves you," went on Blair, in hurried softness. "I always thought so—even when we were kids. And now I know it.... And Lord! Dare you just ought to see her now. She's lovely. And she's your wife."

"What if she is—both lovely—and my wife?" queried Lane, bitterly.

"If I were you I'd go to her. I'd sure let her take care of me.... Dare, the way you're living is horrible. I have a home, such as it is. My room is warm and clean, and I can stay in it. But you— Dare, it hurts me to see you—as you are——"

"No!" interrupted Lane, passionately. The temptation Blair suggested was not to be borne.

Lane met Blair the next afternoon at the station, and again on the next. That established a habit in which both found much comfort and some happiness. Thereafter they met every day at the same hour. Often for long they sat silent, each occupied with his own thoughts. Occasionally Blair would bring a package which contained food he had ransacked from the larder at home. Together they would fall upon it like two schoolboys. But what Lane was most grateful for was just Blair's presence.

It was distressing then, after these meetings had extended over a period of two weeks, to be confronted one afternoon by a new station agent who called Blair and Lane bums and ordered them out of the place.

Blair raised his crutch to knock the man down. But Lane intercepted it, and got his friend out of the station. It was late afternoon with the sun going down over the hill across the railroad yards. Blair stood a moment bare-headed, with the light on his handsome haggard face. How frail he seemed—too frail of body for the magnificent spirit so flashing in his eyes, so scathing on his bitter lips. Lane bade him good-bye and turned away, with a strange intimation that this was the last time he would ever see Blair alive.

Wretched and desperate, Lane bought drink and took it to his room with him. On that dark winter night he sat by the window of his room. Insensible now to the cold, to the wind moaning outside, to the snow whirling against the pane, he lived with phantoms. To and fro, to and fro glided the wraith-forms, vanishing and appearing. The soft rustling sound of the snow was the rustle of their movements. Across the gleam of light, streaking coldly through the pane, flickering fitfully on the wall, floated shadows and faces.

He did not know when he succumbed to drowsy weakness. But he awoke at daylight, lying on the floor, stiff with cold. Drink helped him to drag through that day. Then something happened to him, and time meant nothing. Night and day were the same. He did not eat. When he lay back upon his bed he became irrational, yet seemed to be conscious of it. When he sat up his senses slowly righted. But he preferred the spells of aberration. Sometimes he was possessed by hideous nightmares, out of which he awoke with the terror of a child. Then he would have to sit up in the dark, in a cold sweat, and wait, and wait, until he dared to lie back again.

In the daytime delusions grew upon him. One was that he was always hearing the strange voices of the river, and another that he was being pursued by an old woman clad in a flowing black mantle, with a hood on her head and a crooked staff in her hand. The voices and apparition came to him, now in his waking hours; they came suddenly without any prelude or warning. He explained them as odd fancies resulting from strong drink; they grew on him until his harsh laugh could not shake them off. He managed occasionally to drag himself out of the house. In the streets he felt this old black hag following him; but later she came to him in the lonely silence of his room. He never noticed her unless he glanced behind him, and he was powerless to resist that impulse. At length the dreary old woman, who seemed to grow more gaunt and ghostly every day, took the form in Lane's disordered fancy of the misfortune that war had put upon him.

Lane dreamed once that it was a gray winter afternoon; dark lowering clouds hung over the drab-colored hills, and a chill north wind scurried over the bare meadows, sending the dead leaves rustling over the heath and moaning through the leafless oaks. What a sad day it was, he thought, as he faced the biting wind: sad as was his life and a fitting one for the deed on which he had determined! Long since he had left the city and was on the country road. He ascended a steep hill. From its highest point he looked back toward the city he was leaving forever. Faint it lay in the distance, only a few of its white spires shining out dimly from the purple haze.

What was that dark shadow? Far down the winding road he discerned an object moving slowly up the hill. Closer he looked, and trembled. An old woman with flowing black robes was laboriously climbing the hill. Whirling, he placed his hand on his breast, firmly grasped something there, and then strode onward. Soon he glanced over his shoulder. Yes, there she came, hobbling over the crest, her bent form and long crooked staff clearly silhouetted against the gray background. She raised the long staff and pointed it at him.

Now it seemed the day was waning; deep shadows lay in the valleys, and night already enveloped the forest. Through rents in the broken clouds a few pale stars twinkled fitfully. Soon dark cloud curtains scurried across these spaces shutting out the light.

He plunged into the forest. His footsteps made no sound on the soft moss as he glided through wooded aisles and under giant trees. Once well into the deep woods, he turned to look behind him. He saw a shadow, blacker than the forest-gloom, stealthily slipping from tree to tree. He looked no more. For hours he traveled on and on, never stopping, never looking backward, never listening, intent only on placing a great distance between him and his pursuer.

He came upon a swamp where his feet sank in the soft earth, and through all the night, with tireless strength and fateful resolve, he toiled into this dreamy waste of woods and waters, until at length a huge black rock loomed up in his way. He ascended to its summit and looked beyond.

It seemed now that he had reached his destination. Wood spirits and phantoms of night would mourn over him, but they would keep his secret. He peered across a shining lake, and tried to pierce the gloom. No living thing moved before his vision. Silver rippling waves shimmered under that starlit sky; tall weird pines waved gently in the night breeze; slender cedars, resembling spectres, reared their heads toward the blue-black vault of heaven. He listened intently. There was a faint rustling of the few leaves left upon the oaks. The strange voices that had always haunted him, the murmuring of river waters, or whispering of maidens, or muttering of women were now clear.

Suddenly two white forms came gliding across the waters. The face of one was that of a young girl. Golden hair clustered round the face and over the fair brow. The lips smiled with mournful sweetness. The other form seemed instinct with life. The face was that of a living, breathing girl, soulful, passionate, her arms outstretched, her eyes shining with a strange hopeful light.

Down, down, down he fell and sank through chill depths, falling slowly, falling softly. The cool waters passed; he floated through misty, shadowy space. An infinitude of silence enclosed him. Then a dim and sullen roar of waters came to his ears, borne faintly, then stronger, on a breeze that was not of earth. Anguish and despair tinged that sodden wind. Weird and terrible came a cry. Steaming, boiling, burning, rumbling chaos—a fearful rushing sullen water! Then a flash of light like a falling star sped out of the dark clouds.

Lane found himself sitting up in bed, wet and shaking. The room was dark. Some one was pounding on the door.

"Hello, Lane, are you there?" called a man's deep voice.

"Yes. What's wanted?" answered Lane.

The door opened wide, impelled by a powerful arm. Light from the hallway streamed in over the burly form of a man in a heavy coat. He stood in the doorway evidently trying to see.

"Sick in bed, hey?" he queried, with gruff kind voice.

"I guess I am. Who're you?"

"I'm Joshua Iden and I've come to pack you out of here," he said.

"No!" protested Lane, faintly.

"Your wife is downstairs in a taxi waiting," went on his strange visitor.

"My wife!" whispered Lane.

"Yes. Mel Iden, my daughter. You've forgotten maybe, but she hasn't. She learned to-day from Doctor Bronson how ill you were. And so she's come to take you home."

Mel Iden! The name seemed a part of the past. This was only another dream, thought Lane, and slowly fell back upon his bed.

"Say, aren't you able to sit up?" queried this visitor Lane took for the spectre of a dream. He advanced into the room. He grasped Lane with firm hand. And then Lane realized this was no nightmare. He began to shake.

"Sit up?" he echoed, vaguely. "Sure I can.... You're Mel's father?"

"Yes," replied the other. "Come, get out of this.... Well, you haven't much dressing to do. And that's good.... Steady there."

As he rose, Lane would have fallen but for a quick move of Iden's.

"Only shoes and coat," said Lane, fumbling around. "They're somewhere."

"Here you are.... Let me help.... There. Have you an overcoat?"

"No," replied Lane.

"Well, there's a robe in the taxi. Come on now. I'll come back and pack your belongings."

He put an arm under Lane's and led him out into the hall and down the dim stairway to the street. Under the yellow light Lane saw a cab, toward which Iden urged him. Lane knew that he moved, but he seemed not to have any feeling in his legs. The cabman put a hand back to open the door.

"Mel, here he is," called out Iden, cheerfully.

Lane felt himself being pushed into the cab. His knees failed and he sank forward, even as he saw Mel's face.

"Daren!" she cried, and caught him.

Then all went black.

CHAPTER XXI

Lane's return to consciousness was an awakening into what seemed as unreal and unbelievable as any of his morbid dreams.

But he knew that his mind was clear. It did not take him a moment to realize from the feel of his body and the fact that he could not lift his hand that he had been prostrate a long time.

The room he lay in was strange to him. It had a neatness and cleanliness that spoke of a woman's care. It had two small windows, one of which was open. Sunshine flooded in, and the twitter of swallows and hum of bees filled the air outside. Lane could scarcely believe his senses. A warm fragrance floated in. Spring! What struck Lane then most singularly was the fact of the silence. There were no city sounds. This was not the Iden home. Presently he heard soft footfalls downstairs, and a low voice, as of some one humming a tune. What then had happened?

As if in answer to his query there came from below a sound of heavy footfalls on a porch, the opening and closing of a door, a man's cheery voice, and then steps on the stairs. The door opened and Doctor Bronson entered.

"Hello, Doc," said Lane, in a very faint voice.

"Well, you son of a gun!" ejaculated the doctor, in delight. Then he called down the stairs. "Mel, come up here quick."

Then came a low cry and a flying patter of light feet. Mel ran past the doctor into the room. To Lane she seemed to have grown along with the enchantments his old memories had invoked. With parted lips, eager-eyed, she flashed a look from Lane to Doctor Bronson and back again. Then she fell upon her knees by the bed.

"Do you know me?" she asked, her voice tremulous.

"Sure. You're the wife—of a poor sick soldier—Daren Lane."

"Oh, Doctor, he has come to," cried Mel, in rapture.

"Fine. I've been expecting it every day," said Doctor Bronson, rubbing his hands. "Now, Daren, you can listen all you want. But don't try to talk. You've really been improving ever since we got you out here to the country. For a while I was worried about your mind. Lately, though, you showed signs of rationality. And now all's O.K. In a few days we'll have you sitting up."

Doctor Bronson's prophecy was more than fulfilled. From the hour of Lane's return to consciousness, he made rapid improvement. Most of the time he slept and, upon awakening, he seemed to feel stronger. Lane had been ill often during the last eighteen months, but after this illness there was a difference, inasmuch as he began to make surprising strides toward recovery. Doctor Bronson was nonplussed, and elated. Mel seemed mute in her gratitude. Lane could have told them the reason for his improvement, but it was a secret he hid in his heart.

In less than a week he was up, walking round his little room, peering out of the windows.

Mel had told Lane the circumstances attending his illness. It had been late in February when she and her father had called for him at his lodgings. He had collapsed in the cab. They took him to the Iden home where he was severely ill during March. In April he began to improve, although he did not come to his senses. One day Mr. Iden brought Jacob Lane, an uncle of Lane's, to see him. Lane's uncle had been at odds with the family for many years. There had been a time when he had cared much for his nephew Daren. The visit had evidently revived the old man's affection, for the result was that Jacob Lane offered Daren the use of a cottage and several acres of land on Sycamore River, just out of town. Joshua Iden had seen to the overhauling of the cottage; and as soon as the weather got warm, Doctor Bronson had consented to Lane's removal to the country. And in a few days after his arrival at the cottage, Lane recovered consciousness.

"Well, this beats me," said Lane, for the hundredth time. "Uncle Jake letting us have this farm. I thought he hated us all."

"Daren, it was your going to war—and coming back—that you were ill and fell to so sad a plight. I think if your uncle had known, he'd have helped you."

"Mel, I couldn't ask anybody for help," said Lane. "Don't you understand that?"

"You were a stubborn fellow," mused Mel.

"Me? Never. I'm the meekest of mortals.... Mel, I know every rock along the river here. This is just above where at flood time the Sycamore cuts across that rocky flat below, and makes a bad rapid. There's a creek above and a big woods. I used to fish and hunt there a good deal."

Two weeks passed by and Daren felt himself slowly but surely getting stronger. Every morning when he came down to breakfast he felt a little better, had a little more color in his pale cheeks. At first he could not eat, but as the days went by he regained an appetite which, to Mel's delight, manifestly grew stronger. No woman could have been brighter and merrier. She laughed at the expression on his face when he saw her hands red from hot dish-water, and she would not allow him to help her. The boast she had made to him of her housekeeping abilities had not been an idle one. She prepared the meals and kept the cottage tidy, and went about other duties in a manner that showed she was thoroughly conversant with them.

The way in which she had absolutely put aside the past, her witty sallies and her innocent humor, her habit of singing while at work, the depth of her earnest conversation; in all, the sweet wholesome strength and beauty of her nature had a remarkable effect on Lane. He began to live again. It was simply impossible to be morbid in her presence. While he was with her he escaped from himself.

The day came when he felt strong enough to take a walk. He labored up the hillside toward a wood. Thereafter he went every day and walked farther every time.

With his returning strength there crept into his mind the dawning of a hope that he might get well. At first he denied it, denied even the conviction that he wished to live. But not long. The hope grew, and soon he found himself deliberately trying to build up his health. Every day he put a greater test upon himself, and as summer drew on he felt his strength gradually increasing. Against Doctor Bronson's advice, he got an axe and set to work on the wood pile, very cautiously at first.

Every day he wielded the axe until from sheer exhaustion he could not lift it. Then he would sit on a log and pant and scorn his weakness. What a poor man it was who could not chop wood for ten minutes without getting out of breath! This pile of logs became to him a serious and meaning obstacle. Every morning he went at it doggedly. His back grew lame, his arms sore, his hands raw and blistered. But he did not give up.

Mel seemed happy to see him so occupied, and was loath to call him even when it was necessary. After lunch it was his habit to walk in the woods. Unmindful of weather, every day he climbed the hill, plunged into the woods, and tramped until late in the afternoon. Returning, he usually slept until Mel called him to dinner. Afterward they spent the evening in the little library. The past seemed buried. Lane's curiosity as to family and friends had not reawakened.

Mel possessed a rich contralto voice which had been carefully cultivated. Every evening in the twilight, with only the flickering of the wood fire in the room, she would sit at the piano and sing. Lane would close his eyes and let the mellow voice charm his every sense. It called up his highest feelings; it lingered in his soul, thrilled along his heart and played on the chords of love and hope. It dispelled the heavy gloom that so often pressed down upon him; it vanquished the depression that was the forerunner of his old terrible black mood.

It came about that Lane spent most of his time outdoors, in the fields, along the river, on the wooded hills. The morbid brooding lost its hold on his mind, and in its place came memories, dreams, imaginations. He walked those hills with phantoms of the past and phantoms of his fancy.

The birds sang, the leaves fluttered, the wind rustled through the branches. White clouds sailed across the blue sky, a crow cawed from a hilltop, a hawk screeched from above, the roar of the river rapids came faintly upward. And Lane saw eyes gazing dreamily downward, thoughtful at a word, looking into life, trying to pierce the veil. It was all so beautiful—so terrible.

The peeping of frogs roused in Lane sensations thrilling and strange. The quick sharp notes were suggestive of cool nights, of flooded streams and marshy places. How often Lane wandered in the dusk along the shore to listen to this chorus!

At that hour twilight stole down; the dark hills rose to the pale blue sky; there was a fair star and a wisp of purple cloud; and the shadowy waters gleamed. Breaking into the trill of the frogs came the song of a lonely whippoorwill.

Lane felt a better spirit resurging. He felt the silence, the beauty, the mystery, the eternal that was there. All that was small and frail was passing from him. There came a regurgitation of physical strength—a change of blood.

The following morning while Lane was laboring over his wood pile, he thought he heard voices in the front yard, and presently Mel came around the walk accompanied by Doctor Wallace and Doctor Bronson.

"Well, Lane, glad to see you," said Doctor Bronson, in his hearty tones. "Doctor Wallace and I are on our way to the Grange and thought we'd stop off a minute."

"How are you, Mr. Lane? I see you're taking work seriously," put in Doctor Wallace, in his kindly way.

"Oh, I'm coming round all right," replied Lane.

He stood there with his shirt sleeves rolled up, his face bronzed a little and now warm and moist from the exercise, with something proven about him, with a suggestion of a new force which made him different.

There was an unmistakable kindliness in the regard of both men and a scarcely veiled fear Lane was quick to read. Both men were afraid they would not find him as they had hoped to.

"Mel, you've chosen a charming location for a home," observed Doctor Wallace.

When Mel was showing her old teacher and friend the garden and flowerbeds the practical Doctor Bronson asked Lane: "Did you chop all that wood?"

The doctor pointed to three long piles of wood, composed of short pieces regularly stacked one upon another.

"I did."

"How long did it take you?"

"I've been weeks at it. That's a long time, but you know, Doctor, I was in pretty poor condition. I had to go slow."

"Well, you've done wonders. I want to tell you that. I hardly knew you. You're still thin, but you're gaining. I won't say now what I think. Be careful of sudden or violent exertion. That's all. You've done more than doctors can do."

CHAPTER XXII

"Mel, come here," called Lane from the back porch, "who the deuce are those people coming down the hill?"

Mel shaded her eyes from the glare of the bright morning sun. "The lady is Miss Hill, my old schoolteacher. I'd know her as far as I could see her. Look how she carries her left arm. This is Saturday, for she has neither a lunch basket nor a prayer book in that outstretched hand. If you see Miss Hill without either you can be certain it's Saturday. As to the gentleman—Daren, can it possibly be Colonel Pepper?"

"That's the Colonel, sure as you're alive," declared Lane, with alacrity. "They must be coming here. Where else could they be making for? But Mel, for them to be together! Why, the Colonel's an old sport, and she—Mel—you know Miss Hill!"

Whereupon Mel acquainted Daren with the circumstances of a romance between Miss Hill and the gallant Colonel.

"Well—of all things!" gasped Lane, and straightway became speechless.

"You're right, Daren; they are coming in. Isn't that nice of them? Now, don't you dare show I told you anything. Miss Hill is so easily embarrassed. She's the most sensitive woman I ever knew."

Lane recovered in time to go through the cottage to the front porch and to hear Miss Hill greet Mel affectionately, and announce with the tone of a society woman that she had encountered Colonel Pepper on the way and had brought him along. Lane had met the little schoolteacher, but did not remember her as she appeared now, for she was no longer plain, and there was life and color in her face. And as for embarrassment, not a trace of it was evident in her bearing. According to Mel, the mere sight of man, much less of one of such repute as Colonel Pepper, would once have been sufficient to reduce Miss Hill to a trembling shadow.

But the Colonel! None of his courage manifested an appearance now. To Lane's hearty welcome he mumbled some incoherent reply and mopped his moist red face. He was wonderfully and gorgeously arrayed in a new suit of light check, patent leather shoes, a tie almost as bright as his complexion, and he had a carnation in his buttonhole. This last proof of the Colonel's mental condition was such an overwhelming shock to Lane that all he could do for a moment was stare. The Colonel saw the stare and it rendered him helpless.

Miss Hill came to the rescue with pleasant chat and most interesting news to the exiles. She had intended coming out to the cottage for ever so long, but the weather and one thing or another falling on a Saturday, had prevented until to-day. How pretty the little home! Did not the Colonel agree with her that it was so sweet, so cosy, and picturesquely situated? Did they have chickens? What pleasure to have chickens, and flowers, too! Of course they had heard about Mr. Harry White and the widow, about the dissension in Doctor Wallace's church. And Margaret Maynard was far from well, and Helen Wrapp had gone back home to her mother, and Bessy Bell had grown into a tall ravishingly beautiful girl and had distracted her mother by refusing a millionaire, and seemed very much in love with young Dalrymple.

"And I've the worst class of girls I ever had," went on Miss Hill. "The one I had last year was a class of angels compared to what I have now. I reproved one girl whose mother wrote me that as long as Middleville had preachers like Doctor Wallace and teachers like myself there wasn't much chance of a girl being good. So I'm going to give up teaching."

The little schoolmistress straightened up in her chair and looked severe. Colonel Pepper shifted uneasily, bent his glance for the hundredth time on his shiny shoes and once more had recourse to his huge handkerchief and heated brow.

"Well, Colonel, it seems good to see you once more," put in Lane. "Tell me about yourself. How do you pass the time?"

"Same old story, Daren, same old way, a game of billiards now and then, and a little game of cards. But I'm more lonely than I used to be."

"Why, you never were lonely!" exclaimed Lane.

"Oh, yes indeed I was, always," protested the Colonel.

"A little game of cards," mused Lane. "How well I remember! You used to have some pretty big games, too."

"Er—yes—you see—once in a while, very seldom, just for fun," he replied.

"How about your old weakness? Hope you've conquered that," went on Lane, mercilessly.

The Colonel was thrown into utter confusion. And when Miss Hill turned terrible eyes upon him, poor Pepper looked as if he wanted to sink through the porch.

Lane took pity on him and carried him off to the garden and the river bank, where he became himself again.

They talked for a while, but neither mentioned the subject that had once drawn them together. For both of them a different life had begun.

A little while afterward Mel and Lane watched the bright figure and the slight dark one go up the hillside cityward.

"What do you know about that!" ejaculated Lane for the tenth time.

"Hush!" said Mel, and she touched his lips with a soft exquisite gesture.

At three o'clock one June afternoon Mel and Daren were lounging on a mossy bank that lined the shady side of a clear rapid-running brook. A canoe was pulled up on the grass below them. With an expression of utter content, Lane was leaning over the brook absorbed in the contemplation of a piece of thread which was tied to a crooked stick he held in his hand. He had gone back to his boyhood days. Just then the greatest happiness on earth was the outwitting of bright-sided minnows and golden flecked sunfish. Mel sat nearby with her lap full of flowers which she had gathered in the long grass and was now arranging. She was dressed in blue; a sunbonnet slipped back from her head; her glossy hair waved in the breeze. She looked as fresh as a violet.

"Well, Daren, we have spent four delightful, happy hours. How time flies! But it's growing late and we must go," said Mel.

"Wait a minute or two," replied Lane. "I'll catch this fellow. See him bite! He's cunning. He's taken my bait time and again, but I'll get him. There! See him run with the line. It's a big sunfish!"

"How do you know? You haven't seen him."

"I can tell by the way he bites. Ha! I've got him now," cried Lane, giving a quick jerk. There was a splash and he pulled out a squirming eel.

"Ugh! The nasty thing!" cried Mel, jumping up. Lane had flung the eel back on the bank and it just missed falling into Mel's lap. She screamed, and then when safely out of the way she laughed at the disgust in his face.

"So it was a big sunfish? My! What a disillusion! So much for a man's boastful knowledge."

"Well, if it isn't a slimy old eel. There! be off with you; go back into the water," said Lane, as he shook the eel free from the hook.

"Come, we must be starting."

He pushed the canoe into the brook, helped Mel to a seat in the bow and shoved off. In some places the stream was only a few feet wide, but there was enough room and water for the light craft and it went skimming along. The brook turned through the woods and twisted through the meadows, sometimes lying cool and dark in the shade and again shining in the sunlight. Often Lane would have to duck his head to get under the alders and willows. Here in an overshadowed bend of the stream a heron rose lumbering from his weedy retreat and winged his slow flight away out of sight; a water wagtail, that cunning sentinel of the brooks, gave a startled *tweet! tweet!* and went flitting like a gray streak of light round the bend.

"Daren, please don't be so energetic," said Mel, nervously.

"I'm strong as a horse now. I'm—hello! What's that?"

"I didn't hear anything."

"I imagined I heard a laugh or shout."

The stream was widening now as it neared its mouth. Lane was sending the canoe along swiftly with vigorous strokes. It passed under a water-gate, round a quick turn in the stream, where a bridge spanned it, and before Lane had a suspicion of anything unusual he was right upon a merry picnic party. There were young men and girls resting on the banks and several sitting on the bridge. Automobiles were parked back on the bank.

Lane swore under his breath. He recognized Margaret, Dick Swann and several other old-time acquaintances and friends of Mel's.

"Who is it?" asked Mel. Her back was turned. She did not look round, though she heard voices.

"It doesn't matter," said Lane, calmly.

He would have given the world to spare Mel the ordeal before her, but that was impossible. He put more power into his stroke and the canoe shot ahead.

It passed under the bridge, not twenty feet from Margaret Swann. There was a strange, eager, wondering look in Margaret's clear eyes as she recognized Mel. Then she seemed to be swallowed up by the green willows.

"That was damned annoying," muttered Lane to himself. He could have met them all face to face without being affected, but he realized how painful this meeting must be to Mel. These were Mel's old friends. He had caught Margaret's glance. Old memories came surging back. His gaze returned to Mel. Her face was grave and sad; her eyes had darkened, and there was a shadow in them. His glance sought the green-lined channel ahead. The canoe cut the placid water, turned the last bend, and glided into the swift river. Soon Lane saw the little cottage shining white in the light of the setting sun.

One afternoon, as Lane was returning from the woods, he met a car coming out of the grassy road that led down to his cottage. As he was about to step aside, a gay voice hailed him. He waited. The car came on. It contained Holt Dalrymple and Bessy Bell.

"Say, don't you dodge us," called Holt.

"Daren Lane!" screamed Bessy.

Then the car halted, and with two strides Lane found himself face to face with the young friends he had not seen for months. Holt appeared a man now. And Bessy—no longer with bobbed hair—older, taller, changed incalculably, struck him as having fulfilled her girlish promise of character and beauty. "Well, it's good to see you youngsters", said Lane, as he shook hands with them.

Holt seemed trying to hide emotion. But Bessy, after that first scream, sat staring at Lane with a growing comprehending light in her purple eyes.

Suddenly she burst out. "Daren—you're *well!*.... Oh, how glad I am! Holt, just look at him."

"I'm looking, Bess. And if he's really Daren Lane, I'll eat him," responded Holt.

"This is all I needed to make to-day the happiest day of my life," said Bessy, with serious sweetness.

"This? Do you mean meeting me? I'm greatly flattered, Bessy," said Lane, with a smile.

Then both a blush and a glow made her radiant.

"Daren, I'm sixteen to-day. Holt and I are—we're engaged I told mother, and expected a row. She was really pleased.... And then seeing you well again. Why, Daren, you've actually got color. Then Holt has been given a splendid business opportunity.... And—Oh! it's all too good to be true."

"Well, of all things!" cried Lane, when he had a chance to speak. "You two engaged! I—I could never tell you how glad I am." Lane felt that he could have hugged them both. "I congratulate you with all my heart. Now Holt—Bessy, make a go of it. You're the luckiest kids in the world."

"Daren, we've both had our fling and we've both been hurt," said Bessy, seriously. "And you bet *we* know how lucky we are—and what we owe Daren Lane for our happiness to-day."

"Bessy, that means a great deal to me," replied Lane, earnestly. "I know you'll be happy. You have everything to live for. Just be true to yourself."

So the moment of feeling passed.

"We went down to your place," said Holt, "and stayed a while waiting for you."

"Daren, I think Mel is lovely. May I not come often to see you both?" added Bessy.

"You know how pleased we'll be.... Bessy, do you ever see my sister Lorna?" asked Lane, hesitantly.

"Yes, I see her now and then. Only the other day I met her in a store. Daren, she's getting some sense. She has a better position now. And she said she was not going with any fellow but Harry."

"And my mother?" Lane went on.

"She is quite well, Lorna said. And they are getting along well now. Lorna hinted that a relative—an uncle, I think, was helping them."

Lane was silent a moment, too stirred to trust his voice. Presently he said: "Bessy, your birthday has brought happiness to some one besides yourself."

He bade them good-bye and strode on down the hill toward the cottage. How strangely meetings changed the future! Holt's pride of possession in Bessy brought poignantly back to Lane his own hidden love for Mel. And Bessy's rapture of amaze at his improvement in health put Lane face to face with a possibility he had dreamed of but had never believed in—that he might live.

That night was for Lane a sleepless one. He seemed to have traveled in a dreamy circle, and was now returning to memories and pangs from which he had long been free.

Next morning, without any hint to Mel of his intentions, he left the cottage and made his way into town. Almost he felt as he had upon his return from France. He dropped in to see his mother and was happy to find her condition of mind and health improved. She was overjoyed to see Lane. Her surprise was pitiful. She told him she was sure that he had recovered.

It was this matter of his physical condition that had brought Lane into Middleville. For many months he had resigned himself to death. And now he could not deny even his morbid fancy that he felt stronger than at any time since he left France. He had worked hard to try to get well, but he had never, in his heart, believed that possible.

Lane called upon Doctor Bronson and asked to be thoroughly examined. The doctor manifestly found the examination a task of mounting gratification. At length he concluded.

"Daren, I told you over a year ago I didn't know of anything that could save your life," he said. "I didn't. But something *has* saved your life. You are thirty pounds heavier and gaining fast. That hole in your back is healed. Your lungs are nearly normal. You have only to be careful of a very violent physical strain. That weak place in your back seems gone.... You're going to *live*, my boy.... There has been some magic at work. I'm very happy about it. How little doctors know!"

Dazed and stunned by this intelligence, Lane left the doctor's residence and turned through town on his way homeward. As he plodded on, he began to realize the marvelous truth. What would Blair say? He hurried to a telephone exchange to acquaint his friend with the strange thing that had happened. But Blair had been taken to a sanitarium in the mountains. Lane hurried out of town into the country, down the river road, to the cottage, there to burst in upon Mel.

"Daren!" she cried, in alarm. "What's happened?"

She rose unsteadily, her eyes dilating.

"Doctor Bronson said—I was—well," panted Lane.

"Oh!... Daren, is *that* it?" she replied, with a wonderful light coming to her face. "I've known that for weeks."

"After all—I'm not going—to die!... My God!"

Lane rushed out and strode along the river, and followed the creek into the woods. Once hidden in the leafy recesses he abandoned himself to a frenzy of rapture. What he had given up had come back to him. Life! And he lay on his back with his senses magnified to an intense degree.

The day was late in June, and a rich, thick amber light floated through the glades of the forest. Majestic white clouds sailed in the deep blue sky. The sun shone hot down into the glades. Under the pines and maples there was a cool sweet shade. Wild flowers bloomed. A fragrance of the woods came on the gentle breeze. The leaves rustled. The melancholy song of a hermit thrush pierced the stillness. A crow cawed from a high oak. The murmur of shallow water running over rocks came faintly to Lane's ears.

Lane surrendered utterly to the sheer primitive exultation of life. The supreme ecstasy of that hour could never have been experienced but for the long hopeless months which had preceded it. For a long time he lay there in a transport of the senses, without thinking. As soon as thought regained dominance over his feelings there came a subtle change in his reaction to this situation.

He had forgotten much. He had lived in a dream. He had unconsciously grown well. He had been strangely, unbelievably happy. Why? Mel Iden had nursed him, loved him, inspired him back to health. Her very presence near him, even unseen, had been a profound happiness. He made the astonishing discovery that for months he had thought of little else besides his wife. He had lived a lonely life, in his room, and in the open, but all of it had been dominated by his dreams and fancies and emotions about her. He had roused from his last illness with the past apparently dead. There was no future. So he lived in the moment, the hour. While he lay awake in the silence of night, or toiled over his wood pile, or wandered by the brook under the trees, his dreamy thoughts centered about her. And now the truth burst upon him. His love for her had been stronger than his ruined health and blasted life, stronger than misfortune, stronger than death. It had made him well. He had not now to face death, but life. And the revelation brought on shuddering dread.

Lane lingered in the woods until late afternoon. Then he felt forced to return to the cottage. The look of the whole world seemed changed. All was actual, vivid, striking. Mel's loveliness burst upon him as new and strange and terrible as the fact of his recovery. He had hidden his secret from her. He had been like a brother, kind, thoughtful, gay at times, always helpful. But he had remained aloof. He had basked in the sunshine of her presence, dreamily reveling in the consciousness of what she was to him. That hour had passed forever.

He saw her now as his wife, a girl still, one who had been cruelly wronged by life, who had turned her back upon the past and who lived for him alone. She had beauty and brains, a wonderful voice, and personality that might have fitted her for any career or station in life. She thought only of him. She had found content in ministering to him. She was noble and good.

In the light of these truths coming to him, Lane took stock of his love for Mel. It had come to be too mighty a thing to understand in a moment. He lived with it in the darkness of midnight and in the loneliness of the hills. He had never loved Helen. Always he had loved Mel Iden—all his life. Clear as a crystal he saw the truth. The war with its ruin for both of them had only augmented the powers to love. Lane's year of agony in Middleville had been the mere cradling of a mounting and passionate love. He must face it now, no longer in dreamy lulled unconsciousness, but in all its insidious and complex meaning. The spiritual side of it had not changed. This girl with the bloom of woman's loveliness upon her, with her grace and sweetness and fire, with the love that comes only once in life, belonged to him, was his wife. She did not try to hide anything. She was unconscious of appeal. Her wistfulness came from her lonely soul.

The longer Lane dwelt on this matter of his love for Mel the deeper he found it, the more inexplicable and alluring. And when at last it stood out appallingly, master of him, so beautiful and strange and bitter, he realized that between him and Mel was an insurmountable and indestructible barrier.

Then came storm and strife of soul. Night and day the conflict went on. Outwardly he did not show much sign of his trouble, though he often caught Mel's dark eyes upon him, sadly conjecturing. He worked in the garden; he fished the creek, and rowed miles on the river; he wandered in the woods. And the only change that seemed to rise out of his tumult was increasing love for this girl with whom his fate had been linked.

So once more Lane became a sufferer, burdened by pangs, a wanderer along the naked and lonely shore of grief. His passion and his ideal were at odds. Unless he changed his nature, his reverence for womanhood, he could never realize the happiness that might become his. All that he had sacrificed had indeed been in vain. But he had been true to himself. His pity for Mel was supreme. It was only by the most desperate self-control that he could resist taking her in his arms, confessing his love, swearing with lying lips he had forgotten the wrong done her and asking her to face the future as his loving wife. The thought was maddening. It needed no pity for Mel to strengthen it. He needed love. He needed to fulfill his life.

But Lane did not yield, though he knew that if he continued to live with Mel, in time the sweetness and enchantment of her would be too great for him. This he confessed.

More and more he had to fight his jealousy and the treacherous imagination that would create for him scenes of torment. He cursed himself as base and ignoble. Yet the truth was always there. If Mel had only loved the father of her child—if she had only loved blindly and passionately as a woman—it would have been different. But her sacrifice had not been one of love. It had been one of war. It had the nobility of woman's sacrifice to the race. But as an individual she had perished.

CHAPTER XXIII

Summer waned. The long hot days dragged by. The fading rushes along the river drooped wearily over their dry beds. The yellowing leaves of the trees hung dejected; they were mute petitioners for cool breezes and rain. The grasshoppers chirped monotonously, the locusts screeched shrilly, both being products of the long hot summer, and survivors of the heat, inclined to voice their exultation far into the fall season.

September yielded them full sway, and burned away day by day, week by week, dusty and scorching, without even a promise of rain. October, however, dawned, misty and dark; the clouds crept up reluctantly at first and then, as if to make amends for neglect, trooped black and threatening toward the zenith. Storm followed storm, and at evening, after the violent crashing thunder and vivid lightning and driving torrents of rain had ceased, a soft, steady downpour persisted all night and all the next day.

The drought was broken. A rainy fall season was prophesied. The old danger of the river rising in flood was feared.

After the sear and lifeless color of the fields and forests, what a welcome relief to Daren Lane were the freshened green, the dawning red, the tinging gold! The forest on the hill was soft and warm, and but for the gleams of autumn, would have showed some of the tenderness of spring. Down in the lowlands a sea of color waved under a blue, smoky, melancholy haze.

Lane climbed high that Sunday afternoon and penetrated deep into the woods.

There was rest here. The forest was rich, warm with the scent of pine, of arbor vitae. There was the haunting promise of more brilliant hues. Thoughts swept through Lane's mind. The great striving world was out of sight. Here in the gold-flecked shade, under the murmuring pines and pattering poplars, there was a world full of joy, wise in its teaching, significant of the glory that was fading but which would come again.

Lane loved the low hills, the deep, colorful woods in autumn. There he lost himself. He learned. Silence and solitude taught him. From there he had vision of the horde of men righting down the false impossible trails of the world. He felt the sweetness, the frailty, the dependence, the glory and the doom of women battling with life. He realized the hopeless traits of human nature. Like dead scales his egotism dropped from him. He divined the weaving of chances, the unknown and unnamed, the pondering fates in store. The dominance of pain over all—the wraith of the past—the importunity of a future never to be gained—the insistence of nature, ever-pressing closer its ruthless claims—all these which became intelligible to Lane, could not keep life from looming sweet, hopeful, wonderful, worthy man's best fight.

And sometimes the old haunting voices whispered to him out of the river shadows—deeper, different, strangely more unintelligible than ever before, calling more to his soul.

Next morning Lane got up at the usual hour and went outdoors, but returned almost immediately.

"The river is rising fast. Listen. Hear that roar. There's a regular old Niagara just below."

"I imagined that roar was the wind."

"The water has come up three feet since daylight. I guess I'll go down now and pull in some driftwood."

"Oh, Daren! Don't be so adventurous. When the river is high there's a dangerous rapid below."

"You're right about that. But I won't take any risks. I can easily manage the boat, and I'll be careful."

The following three days it rained incessantly. Outside, on the gravel walks, there was a ceaseless drip, drip, drip.

Friday evening the rain ceased, the murky clouds cleared away and for a few moments a rainbow mingled its changing hues with the ruddy glow of the setting sun. The next day dawned bright and dear.

Lane was indeed grateful for a change. Mel had been unaccountably depressed during those gloomy days. And it worried him that this morning she did not appear her usual self.

"Mel, are you well?" he asked.

"Yes, I am perfectly well," she replied. "I couldn't sleep much last night on account of that roar."

"Don't wonder. This flood will be the greatest ever known in Middleville."

"Yes, and that makes more suffering for the poor."

"There are already many homeless. It's fortunate our cottage is situated on this high bank. Just look! I declare, jostling logs and whirling drifts! There's a pen of some kind with an object upon it."

"It's a pig. Oh! poor piggy!" said Mel, compassionately.

A hundred yards out in the rushing yellow current a small house or shed drifted swiftly down stream. Upon it stood a pig. The animal seemed to be stolidly contemplating the turbid flood as if unaware of its danger.

Here the river was half a mile wide, and full of trees, stumps, fences, bridges, sheds—all kinds of drifts. Just below the cottage the river narrowed between two rocky cliffs and roared madly over reefs and rocks which at a low stage of water furnished a playground for children. But now that space was terrible to look upon and the dull roar, with a hollow boom at intervals, was dreadful to hear.

"Daren—I—I've kept something from you," said Mel, nervously. "I should have told you yesterday."

"What?" interrupted Lane, sharply.

"It's this. It's about poor Blair.... He—he's dead!"

Lane stared at her white face as if it were that of a ghost.

"Blair! You should have told me. I must go to see him."

It was not a long ride from the terminus of the car line to where the Maynards lived, yet measured by Lane's growing distress of mind it seemed a never-ending journey.

He breathed a deep breath of relief when he got off the car, and when the Maynard homestead loomed up dark and silent, he hung back slightly. A maid admitted Lane, and informed him that Mr. Maynard was ill and Mrs. Maynard would not see any one. Margaret was not at home. The maid led Lane across the hall into the drawing-room and left him alone.

In the middle of the room stood a long black cloth-covered box. Lane stepped forward. Upon the dark background, in striking contrast, lay a white, stern face, marble-like in its stone-cold rigidity. Blair, his comrade!

The moment Lane saw the face, his strange fear and old gloomy bitterness returned. Something shot through him which trembled in his soul. To him the story of Blair's sacrifice was there to read in his quiet face, and with it was an expression he had never seen, a faint wonder of relief, which suggested peace.

How strange to look upon Blair and find him no longer responsive! Something splendid, loyal, generous, loving had passed away. Gone was the vital spark that had quickened and glowed to noble thoughts; gone was the strength that had been weakness; gone the quick, nervous, high-strung spirit; gone the love that had no recompense. The drawn face told of physical suffering. Hard Blair had found the world, bitter the reward of the soldier, wretched the unholy worship of money and luxury, vain and hollow mockery the home of his boyhood.

Lane went down the path and out of the gate. He had faint perceptions of the dark trees along the road. He came to a little pine grove. It was very quiet. There was a hum of insects, and the familiar, sad, ever-present swishing of the wind through the trees. He listened to its soft moan, and it eased the intensity of his feelings. This emotion was new to him. Death, however, had touched him more than once. Well he remembered his stunned faculties, the unintelligible mystery, the awe and the grief consequent on the death of his first soldier comrade in France. But this was different; it was a strange disturbance of his heart. Oppression began to weight him down, and a nameless fear.

He had to cross the river on his way home to the cottage. In the middle of the bridge he halted to watch the sliding flood go over the dam, to see the yellow turgid threshing of waves below. The mystic voices that had always assailed his ears were now roaring. They had a message for him. It was death. Had he not just looked upon the tragic face of his comrade? Out over the tumbling waters Lane's strained gaze swept, up and down, to and fro, while the agony in his heart reached its height. The tumult of the flood resembled his soul. He spent an hour there, then turned slowly homeward.

He stopped at the cottage gate. It was now almost dark. The evening star, lonely and radiant, peeped over the black hill. With some strange working at his heart, with some strange presence felt, Lane gazed at the brilliant star. How often had he watched it! Out there in the gloom somewhere, perhaps near at hand, had lurked the grim enemy waiting for Blair, that now might be waiting for him. He trembled. The old morbidness knocked at his heart. He shivered again and fought against something intangible. The old conviction thrust itself upon him. He had been marked by fate, life, war, death! He knew it; he had only forgotten.

"Daren! Daren!"

Mel's voice broke the spell. Lane made a savage gesture, as if he were in the act of striking. Thought of Mel recalled the stingingly sweet and bitter fact of his love, and of life that called so imperiously.

CHAPTER XXIV

"If Amanda would only marry me!" sighed Colonel A Pepper, as he stacked the few dishes on the cupboard shelf and surveyed his untidy little kitchen with disparaging eyes.

The once-contented Colonel was being consumed by two great fires—remorse and love. For more years than he could remember he had been a victim of a deplorable habit. Then two soft eyes shone into his life, and in their light he saw things differently, and he tried to redeem himself.

Even good fortune, in the shape of some half-forgotten meadow property suddenly becoming valuable, had not revived his once genial spirits. Remorse was with him because Miss Hill refused to marry him till he overcame the habit which had earned him undesirable fame.

So day by day poor Colonel Pepper grew sicker of his lonely rooms, his lonely life, and of himself.

"If Amanda only would," he murmured for the thousandth time, and taking his hat he went out. The sunshine was bright, but did not give him the old pleasure. He walked and walked, taking no interest in anything. Presently he found himself on the outskirts of Middleville within sound of the muffled roar of the flooded river, and he wandered in its direction. At sight of the old wooden bridge he remembered he had read that it was expected to give way to the pressure of the rushing water. On the levee, which protected the low-lying country above the city, were crowds of people watching the river.

"Ye've no rivers loike thot in Garminy," observed a half-drunken Irishman. He and several more of his kind evidently were teasing a little German.

Colonel Pepper had not stood there long before he heard a number of witticisms from these red-faced men.

After the manner of his kind the German had stolidly swallowed the remarks about his big head, and its shock of stubby hair, and his checked buff trousers; but at reference to his native country his little blue eyes snapped, and he made a remark that this river was extremely like one in Germany.

At this the characteristic contrary spirit of the Irishman burst forth.

"Dutchy, I'd loike ye to know ye're exaggeratin'," he said. "Garminy ain't big enough for a river the loike o' this. An' I'll leave it to me intilligint-lookin' fri'nd here."

Colonel Pepper, thus appealed to, blushed, looked embarrassed, coughed, and then replied that he thought Germany was quite large enough for such a river.

"Did ye study gographie?" questioned the Irishman with fine scorn.

Colonel Pepper retired within himself.

The unsteady and excitable fellow had been crowded to the rear by his comrades, who evidently wished to lessen, in some degree, the possibilities of a fight.

"Phwat's in thim rivers ye're spoutin' about?" asked one.

"Vater, ov course."

"Me wooden-shoed fri'nd, ye mane beer—beer."

"You insolt me, you red-headed——"

"Was that Dutchman addressin' of me?" demanded the half-drunken Irishman, trying to push by his friends.

"It'd be a foiner river if it wasn't yaller," said a peacemaker, holding his comrade.

In the slight scuffle which ensued one of the men unintentionally jostled the German. His pipe fell to the ground. He bent to recover it.

Through Colonel Pepper's whole being shot the lightning of his strange impulse, a tingling tremor ran over him; a thousand giants lifted and swung his arm. He fought to check it, but in vain. With his blood bursting, with his strength expending itself in one irresistible effort, with his soul expanding in fiendish, unholy glee he brought his powerful hand down upon the bending German.

There was a great shout of laughter.

The German fell forward at length and knocked a man off the levee wall. Then the laughter changed to excited shouts.

The wall was steep but not perfectly perpendicular. Several men made frantic grabs at the sliding figure; they failed, however, to catch it. Then the man turned over and rolled into the river with a great splash. Cries of horror followed his disappearance in the muddy water, and when, an instant later, his head bobbed up yells filled the air.

No one had time to help him. He tried ineffectually to reach the levee; then the current whirled him away. The crowd caught a glimpse of a white despairing face, which rose on the crest of a muddy wave, and then was lost.

In the excitement of the moment the Colonel hurried from the spot. Horror possessed him; he felt no less than a murderer. Again he walked and walked. Retribution had overtaken him. The accursed habit that had disgraced him for twenty years had wrought its punishment. Plunged into despair he plodded along the streets, till at length, out of his stupefaction, came the question—what would Amanda say?

With that an overwhelming truth awakened him. He was free. He might have killed a man, but he certainly had killed his habit. He felt the thing dead within him. Wildly he gazed around to see where he was, and thought it a deed of fate that he had unconsciously traveled toward the home of his love. For there before his eyes was Amanda's cottage with the red geranium in her window. He ran to the window and tapped mysteriously and peered within. Then he ran to the door and knocked. It opened with a vigorous swing.

"Mr. Pepper, what do you mean—tapping on my window in such clandestine manner, and in broad daylight, too?" demanded Miss Hill with a stern voice none of her scholars had ever heard.

"Amanda, dear, I am a murderer!" cried Pepper, in tones of unmistakable joy. "I am a murderer, but I'll never do *it* again."

"Laws!" exclaimed Miss Hill

He pushed her aside and closed the door, and got possession of her hands, all the time pouring out incoherent speech, in which only *it* was distinguishable.

"Man alive! Are you crazy?" asked Miss Hill, getting away from him into a corner. But it happened to be a corner with a couch, and when her trembling legs touched it she sat down.

"Never, never again will I do it!" cried the Colonel, with a grand gesture.

"Can you talk sense?" faltered the schoolmistress.

Colonel Pepper flung himself down beside her, and with many breathless stops and repetitions and eloquent glances and applications of his bandana to his heated face, he finally got his tragic story told.

"Is that all?" inquired Miss Hill, with a touch of sarcasm. "Why, you're not a murderer, even if the man drowns, which isn't at all likely. You've only fallen again."

"Fallen. But I never fell so terribly. This was the worst."

"Stuff! Where's the chivalry you tried to make me think you were full of? Didn't you humiliate me, a poor helpless woman? Wasn't that worse? Didn't you humiliate me before a crowd of people in a candy-store? Could anything be more monstrous? You did *it*, you remember?"

"Amanda! Never! Never!" gasped the Colonel.

"You did, and I let you think I believed your lies."

"Amanda! I'll never do it again, never to any one, so long as I live. It's dead, same as the card tricks. Forgive me, Amanda, and marry me. I'm so fond of you, and I'm so lonely, and those meadow lots of mine, they'll make me rich. Amanda, would you marry me? Would you love an old duffer like me? Would you like a nice little home, and an occasional silk dress, and no more teaching, and some one to love you—always? Would you, Amanda, would you?"

"Yes, I would," replied Amanda.

CHAPTER XXV

Lane was returning from a restless wandering in the woods. As he neared the flooded river he thought he heard a shout for help. He hurried down to the bank, and looked around him, but saw no living thing. Then he was brought up sharply by a cry, the unmistakable scream of a human being in distress. It seemed to come from behind a boathouse. Running as far round the building as the water would permit he peered up and down the river in both directions.

At first he saw only the half-submerged float, the sunken hull of a launch, the fast-running river, and across the wide expanse of muddy water the outline of the levee. Suddenly he spied out in the river a piece of driftwood to which a man was clinging.

"Help! Help!" came faintly over the water.

Lane glanced quickly about him. Several boats were pulled up on the shore, one of which evidently had been used by a boatman collecting driftwood that morning, for it contained oars and a long pike-pole. The boat was long, wide of beam, and flat of bottom, with a sharp bow and a blunt stern, a craft such as experienced rivermen used for heavy work. Without a moment's hesitation Lane shoved it into the water and sprang aboard.

Meanwhile, short though the time had been, the log with its human freight had disappeared beyond the open space in the willows.

Although Lane pulled a powerful stroke, when he got out of the slack water into the current, so swift was it that the boat sheered abruptly and went down stream with a sweep. Marking the piece of driftwood and aided by the swiftly running stream Lane soon overhauled it.

The log which the man appeared to be clutching was a square piece of timber, probably a beam of a bridge, for it was long and full of spikes. When near enough Lane saw that the fellow was not holding on but was helpless and fast on the spikes. His head and arms were above water.

Lane steered the boat alongside and shouted to the man. As he made no outcry or movement, Lane, after shipping the oars, reached over and grasped his collar. Steadying himself, so as not to overturn the boat, Lane pulled him half-way over the gunwale, and then with a second effort, he dragged him into the boat.

The man evidently had fainted after his last outcry. His body slipped off the seat and flopped to the bottom of the boat where it lay with the white face fully exposed to the glare of the sun. A broad scar, now doubly sinister in the pallid face, disfigured the brow.

Lane recoiled from the well-remembered features of Richard Swann.

"God Almighty!" he cried. And his caustic laughter rolled out over the whirling waters. The boat, now disengaged from the driftwood, floated swiftly down the river.

Lane stared in bewilderment at Swann's pale features. His amazement at being brought so strangely face to face with this man made him deaf to the increasing roar of the waters and blind to the greater momentum of the boat.

A heavy thump, a grating sound and splintering of wood, followed by a lurch of the boat and a splashing of cold water in his face brought Lane back to a realization of the situation.

He looked up from the white face of the unconscious man. The boat had turned round. He saw a huge stone that poked its ugly nose above the water. He turned his face down stream. A sea of irregular waves, twisting currents, dark, dangerous rocks and patches of swirling foam met his gaze.

When Lane stood up, with a boatman's instinct, to see the water far ahead, the spectacle thrilled him. A yellow flood, in changeful yet consistent action, rolled and whirled down the wide incline between the stony banks, and lost itself a mile below in a smoky veil of mist. Visions of past scenes whipped in and out his mind, and he saw an ocean careening and frothing under a golden moon; a tide sweeping down, curdled with sand, a grim stream of silt, rushing on with the sullen sweep of doom and the wildfire of the prairie, leaping, cavorting, reaching out, turning and shooting, irresistibly borne under the lash of the wind. He saw in the current a live thing freeing itself in terror.

A roar, like the blending of a thousand storms among the pines, filled his ears and muffled his sense of hearing and appalled him. He sat down with his cheeks blanching, his skin tightening, his heart sinking, for in that roar he heard death. Escape was impossible. The end he had always expected was now at hand. But he was not to meet it alone. The man who had ruined his sister and so many others must go to render his accounting, and in this justice of fate Lane felt a wretched gratification.

The boat glanced with a hard grind on a rock and shot down a long yellow incline; a great curling wave whirled back on Lane; a heavy shock sent him flying from his seat; a gurgling demoniacal roar deafened his ears and a cold eager flood engulfed him. He was drawn under, as the whirlpool sucks a feather; he was tossed up, as the wind throws a straw. The boat bobbed upright near him. He grasped the gunwale and held on.

It bounced on the buffeting waves and rode the long swells like a cork; it careened on the brink of falls and glided over them; it thumped on hidden stones and floating logs; it sped by black-nosed rocks; it drifted through fogs of yellow mist; it ran on piles of driftwood; it trembled with the shock of beating waves and twisted with the swirling current.

Still Lane held on with a vise-like clutch.

Suddenly he seemed to feel some mighty propelling force under him; he rose high with the stern of the boat. Then the bow pitched down into a yawning hole. A long instant he and the boat slid down a glancing fall—then thunderous roar—furious contending wrestle—cold, yellow, flying spray—icy, immersing, enveloping blackness!

A giant tore his hands from the boat. He whirled round and round as he sank. A languid softness stole over him. He saw the smile of his mother, the schoolmate of his boyhood, the old attic where he played on rainy days, and the spotted cows in the pasture and the running brook. He saw himself a tall young man, favorite of all, winning his way in life that was bright.

Then terrible blows of his heart hammered at his ribs, throbs of mighty pain burst his brain; great constrictions of his throat choked him. He began fighting the encompassing waters with frenzied strength. Up and up he fought his way to see at last the light, to gasp at the air. But the flood sucked at him, a weight pulled at his feet. As he went down again something hard struck him. With the last instinctive desperate love of life in his action he flung out his hand and grasped the saving thing. It was the boat. He hooked his elbow over the gunwale. Then darkness filmed over his eyes and he seemed to feel himself whirling round and round, round and round. A long time, seemingly, he whirled, while the darkness before his eyes gave way to smoky light, his dead ears awoke to confused blur of sound. But the weight on his numb legs did not lessen.

All at once the boat grated on a rock, and his knees struck. He lay there holding on while life and sense seemed to return. Something black and awful retreated. Then the rush and roar of the rapids was again about him. He saw that he had drifted into a back eddy behind the ledge of rock, and had whirled slowly round and round with a miscellaneous collection of driftwood.

Lane steadied himself on the slippery ledge and got to his feet. The boat was half full of water, out of which Swarm's ghastly face protruded. By dint of great effort Lane pulled it sideways on the ledge, and turned most of the water out.

Swann lay limp and sodden. But for his eyes he would have appeared dead, and they shone with a conscious light of terror, of passionate appeal and hope, the look with which a man prayed for his life. Presently his lips moved imperceptibly. "Save me! for God's sake, save me!"

Shuddering emotion that had the shock of electricity shook Lane. In his ears again rang the sullen, hollow, reverberating boom of the flood. Here was the man who had done most to harm him, begging to be saved. Swann, poor wretch, was afraid to die; he feared the unknown; he had a terror of that seething turmoil of waters; he could not face the end of that cold ride. Why?

"Fool!" Lane cried, glaring wildly about him. Was it another dream? Unreality swayed him again. He heard the roar, he saw the splitting white-crested waves, the clouds of yellow vapor. He beat his numb legs and shook himself like a savage dog. Then he made a discovery—in some way he could not account for, the oars had remained in the boat. They had been loose in their oar-locks.

Questions formed in Lane's mind, questions that seemed put by a dawning significance. Why had he heard the cry for help? Why had he found the boat? Why had the drowning man proved to be one of two men on earth he hated, one of the two men whom he wanted to kill? Why had he drifted into the rapids? Why had he come safely through a vortex of death? Why had Swann's lips formed that prayer? Why had the oars remained in the boat?

Far below over the choppy sea of waves he saw a bridge. It was his old familiar resting place. Through the white enveloping glow he seemed to see himself standing on that bridge. Then came to him a strange revelation. Yesterday he had stood on that bridge, after seeing Blair for the last time. He had stood there while he lived through an hour of the keenest anguish that had come to him; and in that agony he had watched the plunging river. He had watched it with eyes that could never forget. His mind, exquisitely alive, with the sensibility of a plexus of racked and broken nerves, had taken up every line, every channel and stone and rapid of that flood, and had engraved them in ineffaceable characters. With the unintelligible vagary of thought, while his breast seemed crushed, his heart broken, he had imagined himself adrift on that surging river, and he had planned his escape through the rapids.

As Lane stood on the ledge, knee-deep in the water, with the certainty that he had a perfect photograph of the field of tumbling waters below in his mind's eye, a strange voice seemed to whisper in his ear.

"This is your great trial!"

Without further hesitation he shoved the boat off the ledge.

Round and round the back eddy he floated. At the outlet on the down-stream side, where the gleaming line of foam marked the escape of water into the on-rushing current, he whirled his boat, stern ahead. Down he shot with a plunge and then up with a rise. Racing on over the uneven swells he felt the hissing spray, and the malignant tips of the waves that broke their fury on the boat and expended it in a shower of stinging drops. The wind cut his face. He rode a sea of foam, then turgid rolling mounds of water that heaved him up and up, and down long planes that laughed with hollow boom, then into channels of smooth current, where the torrent wreathed the black stones in yellowish white.

Lane saw the golden sun, the blue sky, the fleecy clouds, the red and purple of the colored hills; and felt his chest expand with the mounting glory of great effort. The muscles of his back and arms, strengthened by the long toil with his heavy axe, rippled and swelled and burned, and stretched like rubber cords, and strung tight like steel bands. The boat was a toy.

He rodes the waves, and threaded a labyrinth of ugly stones, and shot an unobstructed channel, and evaded a menacing drift. The current carried him irresistibly onward. When his keen eye caught danger ahead he sunk the oars deep and pulled back. A powerful stroke made the boat pause, another turned her bow to the right or left, then the swift water hitting her obliquely sheered her in the safe direction. So Lane kept afloat through the spray that smelled fresh and dank, through the crash and surge and roar and boom, through the boiling caldron.

The descent quickened. On! On! he was borne with increasing velocity. The yellow demons rose in fury. Boo—oom! Boo—oom! The old river god voiced his remorseless roar. The shrill screaming shriek of splitting water on sharp stones cut into the boom. On! On! Into the yellow mist that might have been smoke from hell streaked the boat, out upon a curving billow, then down! down! upon an upheaving curl of frothy water. The river, like a huge yellow mound, hurled its mass at Lane. All was fog and steam and whistling spray and rumble.

At length the boat swept out into the open with a long plunge over the last bit of roughened water. Here the current set in a curve to the left, running off the rocky embankment into the natural channel of the river. The dam was now only a couple of hundred yards distant. The water was smooth and the drift had settled to a slow, ponderous, sliding movement.

Lane pulled powerfully against the current and toward the right-hand shore. That was closest. Besides, he remembered a long sluice at the end of the dam where the water ran down as on a mill-race. If he could row into that!

In front of Lane, extending some distance, was a broad unbroken expanse of water leading to the dam. A tremendous roar issued from that fall. The muddy spray and mist rose high. To drift over there would be fatal. Logs and pieces of debris were kept rolling there for hours before some vagary of current caught them and released them.

Lane calculated the distance with cunning eye. He had been an expert boatman all his boyhood days. By the expenditure of his last bit of reserve strength he could make the sluice. And he redoubled his efforts to such an extent that the boat scarcely went down stream at all, yet edged closer to the right hand shore. Lane saw a crowd of people on the bridge below the dam. They were waving encouragement. He saw men run down the steep river bank below the mill; and he knew they were going to be ready to assist him if he were fortunate enough to ride down the sluice into the shallow backwater on that side.

Rowing now with the most powerful of strokes, Lane kept the bow of the boat upstream and a little to the right. Thus he gained more toward the shore. But he must time the moment when it would be necessary to turn sharply.

"I can—make—it," muttered Lane. He felt no excitement. The thing had been given him to do. His strokes were swift, but there was no hurry.

Suddenly he felt a strange catching of breath in his lungs. He coughed. Blood, warm and salt, welled up from his throat. Then his bitter, strangled cry went out over the waters. At last he understood the voices of the river.

Lane quickened his strokes. He swung the bow in. He pointed it shoreward. Straight for the opening of the sluice! His last strokes were prodigious. The boat swung the right way and shot into the channel. Lane dropped his oars. He saw men below wading knee-deep in the water. The boat rode the incline, down to the long swell and curled yellow billows below, where it was checked with violent shock. Lane felt himself propelled as if into darkness.

When Lane opened his eyes he recognized as through a veil the little parlor of the Idens. All about him seemed dim and far away. Faces and voices were there, indistinguishable. A dark cloud settled over his eyes. He dreamed but could not understand the dreams. The black veil came and went.

What was the meaning of the numbness of his body? The immense weight upon his breast! Then it seemed he saw better, though he could not move. Sunlight streamed in at the window. Outside were maple leaves, gold and red and purple, swaying gently. Then a great roaring sound seemed to engulf him. The rapids? The voice of the river.

Then Mel was there kneeling beside him. All save her face grew vague.

"Swann?" he whispered.

"You saved his life," said Mel.

"Ah!" And straightway he forgot. "Mel—what's—wrong—with me?"

Mel's face was like white marble and her hands on his trembled violently. She could not answer. But he knew. There seemed to be a growing shadow in the room. Her eyes held a terrible darkness.

"Mel, I—never told—you," he whispered. "I married you—because I loved you.... But I was—jealous.... I hated.... I couldn't forgive. I couldn't understand.... Now I know. There's a law no woman—can transgress. Soul and love are the same—in a woman. They must be inviolable.... If I could have lived—I'd have surrendered to you. For I loved you—beyond words to tell. It was love that made me well.... But we could not have been happy. Never, with that spectre between us.... And, so—it must be—always.... In spite of war—and wealth—in spite of men—women must rise...."

His voice failed, and again the strange rush and roar enveloped him. But it seemed internal, dimmer and farther away. Mel's face was fading. She spoke. And her words were sweet, without meaning. Then the fading grayness merged into night.

THE END

Made in United States
Troutdale, OR
07/02/2023

10925619R00221